Nacogdoches

Trinity River

Angelina River

Sabine River

Louisiana

...lement Washington-
on-the-
...ttlement Brazos

San Jacinto River

Liberty

Groce's Landing Lynchburg

Buffalo Bayou Anahuac

San Felipe

Harrisburg

Columbia Galveston
Island

Brazoria

Velasco

Matagorda

Matagorda Peninsula

Paso Caballo

Matagorda Island

...ano Bay

Joseph Island

...us

...isti

...y

N

Gulf of Mexico

PROMISED LANDS

F
CRO   Crook, Elizabeth

              Promised lands

$22.50

DATE			
5-24	2-2		
6-9	3-25		
6-30	5-9		
7-20	5-17		
9-6	1-15		
10-6	5-6		
11-23	5-14		
12-20	2-18		
2-6	3-21-11		
4-21	2-18-63		
11-17			
11-19			

ALSO BY ELIZABETH CROOK

The Raven's Bride

Elizabeth Crook

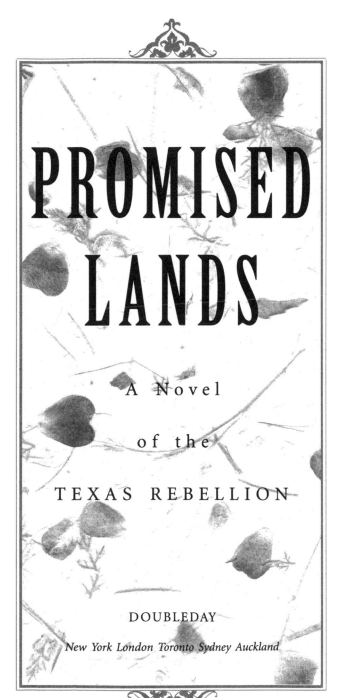

PROMISED LANDS

A Novel

of the

TEXAS REBELLION

DOUBLEDAY

New York London Toronto Sydney Auckland

PUBLISHED BY DOUBLEDAY
a division of Bantam Doubleday Dell Publishing Group, Inc.
1540 Broadway, New York, New York 10036

DOUBLEDAY and the portrayal of an anchor with a
dolphin are trademarks of Doubleday, a division of Bantam Doubleday
Dell Publishing Group, Inc.

Map by Ben Livingston

Book design by Patrice Fodero

Library of Congress Cataloging-in-Publication Data

Crook, Elizabeth, 1959–
   Promised lands : a novel of the Texas Rebellion / Elizabeth Crook.
— 1st ed.
      p.   cm.
   1. Texas—History—Revolution, 1835–1836—Fiction.   2. Mexican
Americans—Texas—Fiction.   3. Family—Texas—Fiction.   I. Title.
PS3553.R545P76   1994
813'.54—dc20   93-24144
                                                                      CIP

ISBN 0-385-41858-2

FOR MY BROTHER AND MY SISTER—
BILL AND NOEL

CONTENTS

PROMISED LANDS

BOOK ONE

AN
ABIDING
PLACE

A   PITTED   STONE

JULY 1835, DEWITT COLONY, TEXAS, MEXICO

September was the common month for raiding expeditions to the southern regions, but Ysambanbi had his own timing and started out in midsummer while heat glistened on the plains like water. He came from the Yamparika band of Comanches, and crossed the canyons and escarpments of the Llano Estacado leading his party of twenty-three Comanche men and two women and a young female Apache whom he had taken captive the previous winter. The Apache woman was his, not to be shared, not even with his brother.

With them, also, was a guide intimate with trails to the most profitable ranches in Mexico. They knew him as Louie Métis, "Louie" being his given name and "Métis" the French word for a person of mixed Indian and European blood. He called himself simply Métis, though his Comanche comrades used the full name combined to a single word, Loo-e-may-tee, lingering on the final sound of *e*. He communicated with them in Spanish, with some phrases in Comanche or Caddoan, his own native language, the speech as oddly blended as his features—a wide, hairless face with a delicate nose. The skin around his eyes was as thick and rough as tree bark and a scar above one eyebrow was encircled by a blue tattoo. He was a guide by profession, the son of a French trader

1

from Louisiana and a Caddoan woman, born at the old Caddo village and French trading post called Grappe's in the east Texas woodlands. The place had been abandoned for forty years, but Métis, in spite of his discordant origins and a birthplace obscured now by the wilderness, was by nature a man of place, possessing at any moment the ground on which he stood, by no other right than his presence.

At the moment he was standing on a patch of earth lit by a moon two days' past full, the shadow of a tree limb scraping across his beaded moccasins when the breeze gusted. This ground was sacred ground to his companions, on a narrow tributary where Yamparikas had long before discovered a pitted black stone they believed to have fallen from the sky. It sat placidly as a sleeping newborn bison at the roots of a tree in a crevice made of its own weight, an object of mystery and power, as hard as the steel and iron trade points they used for war and hunting. Callous to heat and weather, it did not rust; it sang like a bird when they struck it with their flint or metal points. They would rub their bodies on it, and present it with beads and tobacco, and receive in return its medicine that made their southern raids successful. On this night they had come after a full day's ride with the moon already high, expecting to see the stone's reflective surface like water shining in the light through the leafy branches.

And it was gone. Ysambanbi, after squatting in silence for a while beside the hollow where the stone had been, sent out scouts who returned directly. They had seen the stone. A short distance downstream was a log dwelling on cleared land with the sacred stone placed like a shiny trinket beside the entry door.

Ysambanbi was uneasy in the woods, with the moon's pale shadows moving on his body, over his bare chest, across the strings of conch shells from the Concho River and turquoise beads around his neck. In the woods the trees had power over the moon, to block its light or move it about, and the wind had power over the trees, to wag them as it would. There was a capriciousness in all this movement that one did not encounter on the plains. Here, nothing was solid, nothing certain; even what was sacred had been uprooted—debased in such a manner—the white creatures' hairy hands maneuvering it to take it where they pleased. There must have been more than one white-skinned man, to move such weight. They must have dragged it like a butchered fat cow on a white man's travois. He thought: the power has been spoiled.

He thought also: my southern raid will fail.

And he would suffer for that failure. If they did not return with horses, he could not win his Comanche lover from her father. His people could not hunt bison. Without bison, they had neither food nor shelter.

But more awesome was the intruding suspicion that the singing stone had always been an object of impotence, without medicine, to have allowed itself to be moved. Or—more galling still—perhaps it had betrayed the Comanches, the Real People, and been carted willingly to guard the white beast's door.

Either way, the stone must be returned to that place where the gods had put it, and there must be retribution. Ysambanbi spread his people through the trees surrounding the clearing. They were mounted on mules and horses that had Spanish brands and ears notched with Comanche markings. The Apache woman straddled her gray mule on a wooden saddle made in the Spanish mode of double-trees nailed together front and back and tacked over with buffalo hide. The mule's back was raw with draining saddle sores and smelled of rotting meat, the same smell the woman herself had suffered at her husband's death when she cut her arms and breasts in mourning and for weeks prevented the lacerations from healing by prying them open and clawing off the scabs. She was badly marked, and wore her scars like clothing. She wore nothing else besides a deerskin skirt split up the sides for riding. Her hair had not yet grown long enough to braid or to fall loose down over her breasts; she had sliced it off in a frenzy the day of her husband's death, while she was cutting her skin, and now it hung in coarse, uneven patches without adornment.

Ysambanbi's men were armed with bows and knives. One man carried a saber, one an old Spanish *escopeta* which was useful only at close range. Another had a carbine with the stock covered by the neck skin of a horse, the black mane still attached. All of them had bullhide shields decorated in individual fashion with paint and feathers, displaying each warrior's personal medicine, and Ysambanbi wore a headdress of bison horns. Ysambanbi and six chosen men went in on foot, silent amid the night sounds and the sudden call of a wolf howling in the trees near the water.

Had it not been for the stone, they would have wanted only horses and mules, and left with those prizes and the same silence they carried in. But now, they also needed revenge.

Sarah Mackay was awakened by a long, trailing howl from the timber near Buckner's Creek and sat up in bed. It was the wolves again. Callum was already at the window with his rifle, the shutters pushed open, his lean, naked form against the blue light of a moon just past full. A warm breeze lifted the shock of red hair from his forehead as he leaned out.

"Is Bet in the yard?" Sarah whispered, throwing the covers back, rising and tossing a shawl over her shoulders; she had witnessed once before the wolves bringing down a milch cow, and Bet was her last. These wolves were huge shaggy beasts that hunted in packs. The wilder cattle could fend them off, forming a ring around the calves and goring the wolves if they sprang to break it, but domestic cows would scramble for the yard, and were often overtaken.

Callum did not answer, and Sarah went to the window, her dark braid catching the moonlight like a beaded necklace. Together they stood peering out into the blue night, the moon high over a gentle slope of cleared land before them, the lean-to shed, the corn standing tall in the field to the right, rustling slightly in the night air, and to the left, the dark belt of timber. Again the long howl split the stillness. Bet was not in sight.

Sarah saw them first, two shapes crouched low to the ground and moving from the cornfield, then another from behind the shed. She did not speak or move.

Her husband saw them too. "Hide the children under the bed," Callum said in his hoarse Scots brogue, already kneeling to take aim.

Sarah moved out of the light. "For the love of God, Callum, latch the shutters closed."

"I were not born to shirk," he said.

From behind, a child's voice queried, "Mummy?"

Sarah turned; a shaft of moonlight from a narrow crack in the mud

chinking of the logs lit her daughter's sleepy face. She was sitting up in bed, her nightshirt slipping from one shoulder. "Matty," Sarah whispered, "take Samuel and get under the bed."

"Aye," Callum said, and then to Sarah, "Stay clear o' the window."

A wild bellowing sounded from the pens around back, and the braying of a mule. In a tortured, listing gait old Bet struggled into the yard, her large head lifted toward the moon, a dozen shafts piercing her body. She floundered, her bellows fading to a grotesque rasp, a sound like suckling pigs, then rose and made as if to rush the door. But another arrow came from the side of the house and pierced her eye, and she fell.

Instantly the child, Matty, was at the window clutching at the sill to lift herself and see out. Callum saw her tiny hands pulling at the sill, and reached for her. As his hand passed before her face to brush her aside there came from the opposite side of the room, through a small gap in the chinking, an arrow shaft the length of the girl's body. It entered her back and passed through, pinning her to the wall. He leaned to support her, saw her child's eyes lifted to his and her hands grabbing at the shaft that bound her to the wall, blood coming from her mouth, and then no life at all. Sarah fell to her knees, groping toward her daughter. Behind them, baby Samuel began to cry. Pulling the shaft from the wall, Callum knelt and folded the girl in his arms. Twice he said her name. Another arrow struck and lodged in the wall beside him. Sarah whimpered and reached for Matty as Callum rose; with a crash of shattering dishes he pulled the corner cabinet across the room and shoved it against the far wall, blocking the gap through which the arrow had come. Again he took aim at the window; Sarah was near him on the floor, her body folded over Matty's. An Indian wearing a military coat of Spanish style above his naked legs was almost to the door when Callum shot him in the face and he fell. By then, they were coming from the trees, riding in at full speed, shouting in a guttural language. He heard them chopping at the side wall. He heard them on the roof. And then he knew their methods; they were famous for such stunts; they would toss lighted branches down the chimney shaft and cover the opening; they would smoke them out.

But he was wrong. They were not so patient now. They were tearing away the flimsy chimney shaft of mud and twigs, pulling it in one piece

from the cabin's side. He reloaded and tried for another shot from the window, but as they came within range the Indians slid down against their mounts; it seemed a band of riderless, crazed horses was stampeding toward him of their own accord.

He was crawling for his broadsword in the corner when an arrow cut across his temple. For a moment he held steady, squatting on his heels, then fell against his wife.

Sarah, bewildered, caressed his bleeding temple and went on cradling her daughter's head in her lap, watching blood drip from the childish mouth onto her own cotton gown. She fixed her eyes on the feathered tip protruding from one side of the girl's back, just catching the moonlight, red feathers, a cardinal's feathers. She felt the warmth of summer with sunlight and the cardinals. But it was night: a patch of moonlight shone on the blood in the folds of her gown. Her breasts were dripping milk. And her baby was crying from the bed in the corner. Gently she laid her daughter aside, and as she had done a thousand times, went to comfort the baby. She was crouching in the corner by the bed, holding him, when they entered the house.

Métis was the first to enter, breaking open the door, his medicine bag of a bull's testicles tied to the inside of his breechclout and dangling close against his groin. It was filled with his woodlands medicine—pollen, bits of red earth, and a carved bone figure of a gar, a fish that lies quietly in the shallows of a sluggish stream and in a flurry of sudden motion attacks its prey. He came for loot. He wanted metal, cloth, paper to draw on, pelts and skins. He wanted silver more than gold, for most tribes preferred it in trade, finding silver ornaments more lovely than gold. He cared little for scalping or taking coup, he wanted no credit for the kill, and glanced at the white man only long enough to see that he was dead. The chimney gave way and fell back from the wall in a single piece; through the opening came an onslaught of Comanches. Two of them took coup, piercing with their lances the naked white-skinned man who lay prone with light from the window shining on his red hair. His body hair also was red, and they marveled at it. One sliced the center of his scalp in a square, placed a foot on his shoulder to anchor him, and

ripped the scalp from the bone. They studied the color of the hair, turning the scalp in the light. One warrior spat on it and tried to rub the color off. Another cut the girl's scalp; her hair was short and not so prizeworthy but for the fine texture.

Sarah began to scream.

The baby also was wailing.

Métis demanded in English, "Silver; do you have silver?" When the white woman continued to crouch and scream and did not answer he showed his blade and took one step toward her. She stood, as if to try some escape, and the half-breed saw the blood across her gown and whispered *"Elle saigne."* The smear of blood was down across her thighs. Two Comanches were advancing on her. Métis shouted a warning to them: *"Déjala! Déjala! Esa mujer está sangrando por la vagina! Véte!"* The presence of a woman in her menstrual time would contaminate them all, and spoil their medicine and power. They left in an instant, Métis and all of them, without chaos, without noise and without plunder.

Sarah was quiet. She looked at the mutilated bodies of her husband and her daughter near the window. Her baby's cries fell to a whimper. She stood with both arms locked around him, his head pressed under her chin, and turned to face the wall so not to see anymore.

In a moment, Ysambanbi, wearing his headdress of bison horns, stepped near to the cabin doorway and stopped at the threshold. Beside him was his Apache woman. He gave her his bow; she entered without a sound and drew the bowstring and shot the white woman in the back.

Sarah did not hear when the woman entered, did not know she was there until the arrow pierced her back, or know when she left, and did not understand as she slumped in the corner with the life bleeding out of her, holding her baby Samuel, petting his downy head and feeling his baby mouth probing for her breast, that Matty's blood had saved the boy.

Without any movement and without opening his eyes, Callum wrestled his mind into consciousness. The back of his head lay hard against the floor and he could smell the blood. Nearby was a noise, a shuffling like a dog scratching at the door, or near it, near the stone, and voices in a language that meant nothing to him but for one word: Matty. The voices came from outside. He heard the ring of metal on the stone. He heard the word again, mangled with a long *a* sound, a long and lingering *e;* it was his daughter's name: May-tee. How did they know her name? He tried to lift his head and could not. For a moment he stayed conscious, listening for her name.

THE CLEARING

SEPTEMBER 1835, SOUTH TEXAS

Adelaido Pacheco cherished the drama of life, with all its ambiguities. He was young. His eyes did not reflect the firelight or the gray day or the sunlight glittering on the water, but shone coal black like the onyx buttons on his fine linen shirts and the ebony beads of his rosary, and he could tell stories. With touches of light like fingertips grappling with the shadows, he merged the somber and the vivid hues. Friends of Adelaido Pacheco all knew the posture he would take when he was telling stories, how he would sit cross-legged with his elbows resting on his knees and his hands clasped. His skin was beautiful, golden without a flaw, and he was composed even in the midst of trauma, his lovely face with the long mustache and the deep, onyx eyes showing great emotion when he told his stories in his perfect Spanish or his perfect, practiced English, passing his fingers through his heavy hair, which fell straight to his shoulders.

He loved his life. He loved to tell about it. And even while he lived each day—an episode in a grand adventure—he thought how to recount it later, endowing it with dramatic proportions even at the moment of happening.

Adelaido was running illegal tobacco from Louisiana south through thorny mesquite plains to the interior of Mexico. He had three men and twelve mules, each mule carrying over three hundred pounds of cheap tobacco leaf from Louisiana, worth as much as two dollars a pound in the interior. On the return trip he would have specie, as well as furs to trade. He would have to bribe his way down and back to avoid paying tariffs, and would need to pay his men, but even so he would make a fat profit on both ends of the journey.

They were traveling a minor road which Adelaido had chosen for its privacy, and had located a small clearing south of Escondida Creek in a grove of live oaks just off the road, where they could rest the burdened mules and cook tortillas over a fire. It was a bright, warm afternoon. Leaves were not yet turning this early in the autumn and this far south. The mules were oppressed by heat and flies as well as by the huge bundles strapped on their backs, and the men's shirts stuck to their bodies in sweaty patches.

Toribio piled up scrappy sticks and twigs and lit the fire while Ramón mixed cornmeal with water from his gourd and patted out tortillas. Daniel, the only Anglo, searched the mule packs for the frying pan; he was fat and very short and had a saintly patience. There was not time enough to unload the mules of their packs but he went from one to the next and loosened the cinch ropes to give them some relief, meanwhile feeling the outside of the canvas bags for the shape of a frying pan. Ramón had wanted to keep all the camp equipment together on one mule, but Daniel had a unique sense of fair order and distribution, and had quietly, without argument, loaded the mules his own way, two heavy bags of tobacco and one slight bag of supplies to each.

Adelaido tethered his horse in the trees apart from the other mounts and the mules because it often picked fights and was abusive to the mules. He understood his gelding's sentiment: they were both elitist. The other horses were a dingy lot in comparison to the *bayo-cabos-negros,* a powerful dun marked with black feet, mane, and tail, a black stripe down the center of his back, and a streak of silver in his tail. And the mules, though they inspired Adelaido's pity with their raw, infested backs, mothy fur, and stoic faces, did not inspire his respect. As Daniel loosened the ropes and the beasts groaned long and mournfully, Adelaido whispered to his horse, "We have never cared for mules, have we,

Donde—" and then went to the fire and said aloud to his companions, in a thoughtful tone, "I have never cared for mules."

Daniel found the frying pan and brought it to the fire, a single plume of flame.

"They are more smart than horses," Ramón said.

Adelaido had asked Ramón and Toribio to speak in English for Daniel's sake and because they should know the language better. They resented the request, and had grumbled to each other that Daniel should learn to speak Spanish if he was to travel with *Tejanos*. But Adelaido Pacheco was their employer on this trip—younger than they were—a mere twenty-two—yet adamant about his wishes. And he insisted on English.

Toribio leaned over the fire and lit a cigarillo. He was tall and muscular with eyes that slanted upward toward the temples, a high forehead, and a penchant for hard work. "It's truth," he remarked, inhaling deeply from the cigarillo. "The mules are better than the horses to find water."

"Maybe," Adelaido answered, settling onto his side with his legs stretched out, his elbow cocked against the prickly grass and his palm supporting his head. "But that only means they have a better sense of smell."

"No," Toribio said, *"Ellas son más intelligentes que los caballos. Por ejemplo—"*

"Speak English," Adelaido interrupted. He knew how he annoyed Toribio, and took pleasure in it. "Daniel cannot understand you."

Toribio complied with hostility. "Like, when one of the mule smell one of the panther close to her, she fall down and roll down and start to kicking and farting and make a lot of noise until the panther, she get scared and run away. The reason she do this is she know the panther is fight only by jump to the neck, and while the mule do all these funny tricks even the most fast cat they cannot take the neck."

Adelaido laughed, his golden face in the sunlight, his black hair falling down against the soil and stubbled grass. "Fear," he said. "The mules fall down and kick their legs in fear. It is not intelligence, but cowardice." To goad his friends, he added, "I would not subject Donde to the close company of mules."

As if they didn't know. Donde was a spoiled and arrogant animal. Adelaido never hobbled him, claiming that hobbling precipitated a ridic-

ulous, hopping gait that could demean the most dignified of beasts. He
said he had seen hobbled horses that after being liberated had continued
to jump like rabbits for two days before they regained their dignity and
their proper gait. Donde was never subjected to such disrespect—he was
secured with a tether, usually under tree cover. His earthy coloring was a
perfect camouflage, and Adelaido called him "Donde," meaning
"Where," because he could never locate him in the woods at first glance.
"Donde," he would whisper, "Donde," and the gelding would blow a
soft snort through his nose and stamp his feet in eagerness for Adelaido's attention.

"But it is intelligent to feel scared of the panther," Toribio said,
reaching into the skillet for a tortilla. Ramón whacked his hand away,
saying the tortilla was not cooked yet: the fire was not even hot.

Daniel was hungry, and wished he would get one of the first tortillas.
He wished Ramón and Toribio liked him better. They considered him
hardly worth the food he ate, and it seemed there was nothing he could
do to impress them. He tried at least not to aggravate them, but Adelaido's insistence that they speak English for his sake made that impossible. Often he made pathetic attempts at Spanish, which they seemed
only to disdain. Still, that was better than listening to them struggle
bitterly with English. He said, by way of compliment, "Ramón, *esos
tortillas oler muy bueno.*"

Ramón only grunted and did not lift his round face to look at him.

Adelaido returned to his topic. "Horses show affection," he said.
"They have loyalties."

He spoke with authority. Adelaido Pacheco was famous for his
horsemanship; he was known as the best *domador*—horse-breaker—in
south Texas. He would not resort to clogging or starving the horses into
submission, nor would he blindfold them and run them to exhaustion,
goading with spurs. He wore no spurs and trained horses to trust him,
breathing into the animals' nostrils so they could know his smell and
running his hands around the back and belly and down the quivering
legs and finally to the soft ears that twitched with wariness. He rubbed a
blanket over every inch of fur, and repeated this for days before he lifted
a saddle to the back, and then nurtured the *potro* through his panic
when the weight of the saddle settled in and the girth was cinched. Later
he introduced the bit, never making the mouth bleed and seldom using

enough force to make the soft mouth open in resistance. Before he finished, he would pull five hairs from the horse's tail and splice the leather reins with them, and with only the strength of the hairs he would control the horse perfectly. He rode Donde without a saddle, using a surcingle of tanned rawhide and a hide *jáquima* with reins woven from the manes and tails of various colored horses. Spanish stirrups weighed up to forty pounds apiece and encumbered the strongest of mounts, so Adelaido used loops of rawhide instead. He insisted that a *domador* was a *domador* in spirit, not in dress or in equipment. He had his own flamboyant style: a silk handkerchief around his neck, elaborate embroidery on his pristine linen shirts, and a rosary that was a work of art inside his pocket, with ebony beads and a silver cross. But his style had nothing to do with his horsemanship. It had to do with his pride, and with the money he had made. His friends tolerated his vanity because they liked him. The more devout did not always understand his odd notions of honor, but they trusted him.

He reflected and said, "Instinctive fears show less intelligence than acquired fears. Horses can learn what to be afraid of, and mules can't. I have taught Donde to fear Indians. He can smell them, the same as Comanche horses smell white men. I paid two Indians to frighten and abuse him, and now if any Indian comes close, he goes wild. He can break a tether. I've seen him uproot stakes. Once he dragged a fat log for a distance the length of this clearing before I calmed him." He paused to accept a hot tortilla, and ate it in silence, being too fastidious to talk with food in his mouth. The others doubted his tale, as he was known to overdramatize, but they did not say so. Crickets hopped in the grass and a buzzard circled overhead in an open sky. The horseflies were tormenting the mules, which stood at the edge of the clearing in the bright sun with their floppy ears and their hides twitching. Adelaido's bladder was full and he needed to empty it, but he was comfortable, lying on his side with the insects droning, and did not get up. When he swallowed the last bite of his tortilla, and was waiting for another, he said, "I swear it on the Virgin. Afterward I had to pay those Indians who trained him, to keep away, and take another road through town if they saw Donde at a hitching rail."

"Liar," Toribio said. "I have *poco* blood of Comanche. Why Donde don't run away from me?"

"Because you wear spurs and a vaquero's hat," Adelaido answered, brushing a fly away from the bowl of soggy cornmeal. "My horse is not a fool."

From the trees, Donde snorted and paced around his tether. "He smell you now, Toribio," Ramón said, flipping a tortilla with his fingers.

The Anglo Daniel laughed at that, but cut the laughter short when Toribio shot him a look with his slanted eyes.

Again Donde snorted, scraping the ground twice with his foreleg and pulling against his rope, and Ramón taunted, "Toribio, Toribio, he smell your Comanche blood."

But Adelaido did not laugh. He stood and went to his horse and was reaching one hand to take the tether and the other to stroke the arched neck when Donde threw his head back with a noise like a human scream and lifted onto his hindquarters in such sudden and absolute panic that Adelaido knew at once, with certainty, even before the Comanches launched themselves into the clearing, that his men were doomed. He turned and witnessed it, the arrows flying like fierce and hellish birds, and then the Indians—five or six of them on horseback exploding into the clearing where the flies were droning and the little fire licked at the bottom of the frying pan and the wad of pasty cornmeal was pressed between Ramón's palms.

One rode directly for Adelaido, who continued in his motion, laying the one hand on the tether and the other on the horse's neck to calm him and mounting with the tip of his boot in the slender loop of rawhide. When the Indian was almost on him, and the lance was bearing down, Pacheco drew a pistol, shot the man, and fled. The other Comanches did not follow. He traveled north beside the road through the chaparral on his *bayo-cabos-negros* at a speed that would have killed another horse, his bladder full and aching, and then emptying like a baby's onto Donde's hide, his mind haunted with imagined horrors that he had not seen, but had known, from twenty yards' distance while firing his pistol into the tattooed body of an old man: the scalping of Daniel—the Anglo —who was fat and had soft eyes and a birthmark on his forehead, the scalping of Ramón, who had a wife in Goliad, the butchering of Toribio, who had Comanche blood himself.

He had hired these men, he had led them into it, and he alone had escaped. It did not slow his speed or corrupt his sense of direction as he retreated north toward Rancho de la Rosa through a warm day with the sunlight fanning down over the scrubby brush, but it pounded on his conscience like a beating. He had never lost a man before on a tobacco run. With all the responsibilities he had assumed in his life and the dangers he had faced, he had not yet carried the burden of a friend's death. And now three men lay mutilated beside a withering fire near the deserted road that he had chosen to take. "Holy Mary, Mother of God, pray for us sinners . . ."

At Escondida Creek he drank and allowed Donde to suck the cool water, but not too much. The urine on his pants made a patch across his groin like a token of his depravity, so he sat in the rocky shallows to wash it off. He needed to scream and purge his lungs of horror, but had to keep his stealth and silence. Directly he resumed his pace to Rancho de la Rosa where he rode to the front door with his black hair flapping and his legs in wet trousers clinging close around Donde's heaving sides. Within fifteen minutes six vaqueros were mounted and on their way with Adelaido northwest to La Mora Rancho, the ranch of Erasmo Seguín. Four others headed east to Los Corralitos. When the sun dropped over the horizon and the gray landscape stretched coarse and wiry with cactus and mesquite and mottes of oak trees scattered on the plains, the men gathered on Escondida Creek and rode together to the clearing: Adelaido, five Anglos from a corp of rangers who had been stopping at Seguín's and twenty-six vaqueros from the nearby ranches.

They found the bodies, naked and scalped, lying beside the meager pile of ashes. The Indians had taken everything: twelve mules, three horses, camp utensils, and almost four thousand pounds of Louisiana tobacco bundled in twenty-four canvas bags. The weary mules had plodded off with the tribesmen like errant disciples led by a new savior.

Adelaido stood in the twilight in the center of the clearing, still tainted with the faint smell of his urine, holding the horsehair reins and fingering the smooth, braided hairs. The rangers watched him, but said nothing. The vaqueros did not look at him and did not comfort him: they knew he had been smuggling; it was a common business and not an honored one. Some of them had known his savaged comrades. They allowed Adelaido his shame. He deserved it. He might even need it if he were ever to regain his soul. Because Adelaido Pacheco, they knew, had long ago grown careless with his soul—had tossed it to the winds for money and risk and for the fun of teasing with the devil. He rode like a madman and courted married women and seduced horses as you would seduce a virgin. And now he had led three men to their deaths by way of a deserted trace, in the name of profit. He would not be favored by God.

They could not help him gain forgiveness, but they could help him take revenge. Leaving one man to defend the bodies from scavenging animals, the others followed the route of the Indians. They found them after dark, a band of almost twenty camped six miles away on a narrow tributary with two hundred exhausted, stolen horses grazing on the plain under the watch of several boys. The mules stood in a dismal group beside the water; Adelaido saw them beneath the new moon from a low rise in the landscape, some of them with bags of tobacco leaf still bloating out from their sides. He lay on his belly beside a shy Anglo ranger, and saw them.

Planning the attack from a motte of oaks, the men spoke in voices so soft they had to crowd in close to hear. They knew their success depended on surprise: they would follow the hill around below the creek and come up through the trees. They knew some among them would be killed. It would be a bitter death, they knew. But they executed their plan without reticence.

It was a massacre. The *caballada* stampeded and fled; some of those that had been hobbled broke their legs in the attempt and were trampled. The Comanches were quick and agile, but the vaqueros and rangers were mounted and outnumbered them. Several Indian women were killed. Later it was said that two of them were not squaws, but Mexican captives from a ranch across the Rio Grande.

One woman, who wore almost nothing and whose breasts were laced with scars, fought with a blade until her throat was slit.

A few warriors and small boys escaped into the trees along the water, above the place where the horsemen rode in with their blazing firearms. Several lost their lives trying to drag the dead with them. One of these was wearing a headdress of bison horns; at the moment of attack he reached with a steady hand for his warrior's attire and placed the headdress on his head before taking up his bow, and then fought until there was no hope, and pulled the wounded and the dead alike into the dark trees, and died there.

Only one man was taken captive. He was a half-breed named Louie

Métis. With the first gunfire, he stood up from his pallet, flung his arms up, and shouted in English and in Spanish that he was not Comanche. He was wearing only a breechclout. His strident voice was heard above the noise of battle, and no one wasted a shot on him. He stood there in the fray beneath the silver moon with his lean arms lifted to heaven and his eyes fixed on nothing at all, shouting over and over, "I am Louie Métis. I am not Comanche. Do not shoot me. *No me maten. Mi nombre es Louis Métis. No me disparen.*" He was hit in the forearm by a stray ball and his knee was grazed with an arrow, but in the end he was still standing, saying, "I am Louie Métis," his arms lifted and the blood streaming down his side and the dead scattered all around him.

Later, they let him go. He told them while they bound his wrists and made him sit and shoved his head between his knees, that he'd been taken captive by the Comanche band one week before, on their horse-stealing mission south of the Rio Grande. He was not Comanche: they could know that by his features. He spoke Caddoan, French, Spanish, and some English. When one of the rangers began scalping the dead Indians, Métis did not appear to care. And when a vaquero with a hare lip and a cut across his chin found a string of dried scalps on one of the dead, and showed it to the rangers, and a ranger said, "This one is not Mexican, it is Callum Mackay's, I would bet my life on it," Métis denied any knowledge of the origins of that pathetic remnant, and asked if they would loosen the thongs around his wrists enough to let the blood flow.

And Adelaido knew he was lying. He knew, because he knew Métis, and Métis always lied. But when the half-breed sat there in the moonlight with his wrists tied behind him and his ankles bound together and his balding head between his knees, and then lifted his wide face with the pouches of fatty skin beneath his bloodshot eyes, and stared directly into Adelaido's eyes, and lied, Adelaido did not say he should be killed, or that he was a liar. It was a mystery to Adelaido why he did not. Some day when he became an old man, he would understand. His reasoning would find its way into the story, and he would say it was his own shame in the day's work that stopped him from condemning the half-breed. But for now the day's events were too unsettling to mold into a parable. He looked at the stony ground, the grass prickling up around his bloodstained boots, and thought of Daniel's Anglo face with the birthmark and the scalp hacked away and the naked bodies, all three, lying in a heap like puppies.

And so the rangers and vaqueros gave the half-breed a water gourd, and nothing else, and let him go. Adelaido watched him turn and lift his bloody arm in a slight wave, or a salute, as he vanished into the brush, the gourd slung over his shoulder and the scant moonlight painting his bare skin like chalk.

A VISIT FROM AN
ENGLISHMAN

O CTOBER 1835, THE SAN MARCOS RIVER

Toby Kenner held his breath and floated face-down on the surface of the water, his arms spread wide open, his eyes staring downward through the green water at the dreamy movement of underwater grasses and a catfish foraging in bottom weeds. He was at that point in the counting— one thousand sixty-two, one thousand sixty-three—when his insides began to gulp for air, his abdomen heaving and sucking. But he did not yet lift his face and breathe. He could feel the sunlight and autumn breezes on his bare buttocks, and if he jackknifed slightly he could see his penis nestled pale and flaccid in the water between his legs. The water was very cold; it made his nipples hard. A small, darting fish appeared from nowhere and showed some interest in his nipples, and Toby tried to keep still so not to scare him off. But he ached for breath. One thousand eighty-one, one thousand eighty-two, and in a sudden splash of triumph at one thousand eighty-three he spun his face up and his feet down and gulped in sweet autumn air.

His shaggy hair flung water droplets everywhere. Without his spectacles and with water in his eyes the outside world seemed less certain than the underwater world. Branches still holding their summer green were rustling in the breeze, and the bay mare tethered in the spotty sunlight on the bank a stone's throw downstream dipped her head and lifted it again. Toby's red shirt, dangling from a limb above the mare, billowed suddenly with air. The movement out here was less tranquil than the underwater movement, and the light more disconcerting.

When Toby saw the corner of the raft obscured in the shadows underneath the foliage where the stream and river joined, he had to squint to make out what it was. He had not seen it there before. How could there be a ferry flat which he had never seen, here so close to home, not two miles upriver from the house?

Swimming with the current to the edge of the raft where the water was shallow and bottom grasses brushed around his ankles, Toby pulled himself out of the water onto the solid planks. There, in the speckled light, he saw the notches that held the planks together. They were his brother's notches, perfect notches: nobody made notches like Miles.

The autumn wind was rising and darkness setting in when Toby rode up from the river. The sound of his brother chopping wood carried to him on the wind, steady and cadenced; he rode from the timber into the field of high grass, reined in the old bay mare and sat listening, squinting through his spectacles at his older brother's silhouette in the barnyard, the ax rising and falling in a fluid movement. Miles made an art of chopping wood. The ax became a powerful extension of his body; he could wield an ax or a gun, a lasso, a tool of any kind, with the precision of an artist, exacting obedience from it as if by some uncanny orchestration in his mind.

The ax rose and fell with the throbbing croak of frogs and the humming of cicadas in pecan and cypress trees that lined the river. Nearby a sow rooted for mast, and from the western hill the lowing of cattle drifted on the gusting wind. Miles rested from his work, dropped the ax, lifted both his arms to stretch, and looked down toward the river. Seeing Toby there, he spread one hand to greet him, and Toby lifted a hand too and held it there a moment with the fingers spread, before urging the bay mare forward to a gallop. He slowed on approach and dismounted, knowing Miles was noting the horse's bare rump, no deer or antelope tied on, not even a rabbit dangling from the saddle.

"I missed a buck with a huge rack," Toby said.

Miles started piling the firewood onto a sled. "I'll go hunting tomorrow," he answered.

Leading his mount to the barn, Toby called over his shoulder, "I went upriver two miles, where the stream butts in." He loosened the saddle girth, hoisted the saddle and blanket and carried them into the barn, then came back out with an armful of hay and a bucket of corn for the mare. After he fed the mare he brought out hay for the two mustangs in the paddock and for his father's fat gelding in the pen. The gelding still had sweat marks from the recent ride to town. "You seen Father since he got back?"

"Nope," Miles answered.

In the twilight Toby could just make out Miles's figure stretching the hide strap of the sled over his shoulder, and behind him, on the northern rise, the log house. He stepped beside his brother and took the second strap, and together they threw their weight forward toward the house.

"I saw a ferry raft on our land," Toby said suddenly, unable to keep it any longer, "hid in the brush where the stream butts in." He glanced at Miles's profile against the darkening sky, at his blond hair fallen over his forehead. "Think it's a smuggler's?"

"Could be," Miles said.

Toby looked at his brother. "Those notches were your notches," he said. "You been ferrying smugglers?"

"Yeah."

"They smuggling niggers?"

"Hell no," Miles said impatiently. "It's nothing but coffee and tobacco. Look, I just built the raft and they paid me for it. I ain't doing the running myself."

"It's the same thing," Toby said. "Law'll get you just the same."

"Law ain't gonna get nobody," Miles answered.

As they neared the house they heard the frantic barking of a dog. They could see him, tied to a stump near the house and lunging on his rope. Miles said, "Coon Dog took out after you straightaway. I tried letting him loose but he took out every time."

The house was built of split pecan logs, two rooms under a single roof with a sleeping loft in the second room. It had no porch. While the Kenners built it in the winter of 1829 they had lived under a hasty lean-to with a prairie sod roof, all sick and cold with raw throats. But Miles was at his best then, cutting shakes and pegging them like shingles to purlins, which he set parallel to the ridgepole and pegged to the end framework of the house. He'd done the same for the barn the following year, and the smokehouse the next, and in the end the Kenners had a solid homestead here on the outer reaches of the DeWitt Colony.

When Miles and Toby walked into the house, each carrying an arm-load of wood, their grandmother looked over her shoulder at them from the rocking chair beside the fire, and she was not rocking, and she said, "Mr. Mackay's scalp has been returned to him."

Toby clutched his load of logs close to his chest and looked to his mother. She was a sweet-faced woman with Irish heritage and the name of Rose, and she stood at the table serving a loaf of corn bread. A cat was rubbing against her legs.

"Callum showed the scalp to your father," Rose said. "Callum has gone mad."

The grandmother, Grand Irma, asked Rose to repeat what she had said. She had not heard her. But Rose didn't answer. Even Katie declined to repeat the awful words for Grand's sake. Katie was the only girl in the family and a middle child, a savior at heart with her dark braid falling over one shoulder and her eyes resting on this loved one and that loved one like a blessing, but there were things she could not say. She had loved Callum Mackay and his sweet baby Samuel, and had nursed them through the worst of it after the happening.

Hugh Kenner's scant hair was in disarray and his face looked sunken. "I saw Callum in Gonzales," he said. "He told me that some rangers and Mexican ranchers killed some Indians who had scalps with them. One of the scalps was Callum's. A ranger brought it to him."

Katie placed the last of the tin plates on the table and said to Miles and Toby, "Callum has gone looking for a half-breed that was with the Indians. His name's Maytee, and he told the rangers that the Indians had captured him down south just a week or two before, which wasn't true. He was with them in July when they raided the Mackays. Callum recognized Maytee's name when the rangers told him; he remembered the name from that night. He heard the Indians say it that night when he came to."

Hugh stepped out for a load of wood and came back in with his chin resting on the top log to steady it.

"Has Callum gone alone?" Miles asked, still holding the wood, a brown beetle crawling on one log.

Hugh took his time in answering. He stacked the logs he'd carried in carefully beside the hearth. His shirttail was hanging out in back. He piled the wood on the side of the fireplace that was not near his book-shelves, which was his custom to prevent the worms and beetles and the ants from getting in his books. In the darkening room, with the same firelight that illumined his mother's old face casting shadows on his, he seemed an odd derivative of her but without the flaccid skin; they both had deep eyes that moved in a steady, curious way and their full lips were expressive even in repose. "Yes, I saw him ride out alone, he wanted to go alone," he said, arranging kindling splinters in a separate pile.

"What about the baby?" Miles asked.

"Callum left him in Gonzales with a midwife."

Toby and Miles stacked their wood on top of Hugh's, and Toby worked at the fire with a poker.

"Any word on Santa Anna's march?" Miles asked his father.

"No."

"What about his troops?"

"General Cós is finally here," Hugh answered, brushing his palms on his trousers. "He landed at Cópano with four or five hundred troops and they're marching toward San Antonio de Béxar, through Goliad."

Miles flung himself into a chair at the table. "Ain't anybody planning to try and stop him?"

"Who's going to stop four hundred trained soldiers?" Hugh responded quietly.

"If there's a call to arms I'll go," Miles said. "You ain't gonna keep me from it."

Rose went to the fire and leaned to turn the pork sizzling in a pot. Katie took the poker from Toby and knelt beside her mother, jabbing the flames out from under the Dutch oven in the corner of the fireplace, leaving only coals to keep it warm. She piled the fried pork on a platter, put it on the table, and Rose began serving the plates. Grand stood up from her rocking chair beside the fire and took up her cane, and Toby sidled in to give her his elbow. She was no larger than he, and she leaned her slight weight into him while he paced his steps to hers and seated her. She had just begun to arrange her napkin in her lap when Coon Dog started barking from around the back of the house. Toby started for the door.

Grand said softly, "Toby, come back and sit down. Your food will get cold."

"Coon's barking," he said.

"I know Coon is barking. Sit down."

"He never barks unless there's a reason."

"Sit down. He's a silly dog."

Toby felt the injustice of it. Coon was a fine watchdog and a good cow dog too: he could sniff out a wormy calf in the brush from fifty yards away.

Katie said, "I have to go out for water. I'll check on Coon." She went out before Grand could stop her.

The evening was blanketed with stars, a sliver of moon just rising above the timber lining the river. Scattered clouds gusted on the wind. Katie set her bucket down and stretched her arms high, breathing the autumn air. She was glad to be out of the house. Taking up her bucket, she went around back to see why the dog was barking. She was a tall, large-boned girl, nineteen years old. Her braid swung behind her, as heavy as hemp rope. As she rounded the side of the house she saw a figure walking on the path that topped the ridge line of the western slope, above the cornfield. "Hush, Coon," she said, but the dog kept on yapping, straining at his tether, his whiskered mouth opening and shut- ting like a pair of scissors. His face was exactly like a coon's, masked with a turned-up nose. Poor dog, he thought he was big. "You hush," Katie said again, watching the man turn from the ridge line onto the path which led down to the house. He was carrying a large satchel. She pulled her braid over her shoulder and fingered the tip of it.

———

William Mullins was feeling edgy. Five miles out of town his clumsy mount had stumbled and then limped so badly that William had left him in the road. He'd been planning to reach his sister's home sometime that night, but now, on foot, toting his satchel along, that would be impossible. From the crude map she'd drawn and sent him last winter he estimated twenty miles to go.

William had landed on the coast three days before, made a sorry deal on the sorry horse, and started inland. He'd been delayed in a primitive town called Gonzales by an annoying circumstance: there was a commotion over a scrappy six-pound cannon that Mexican officials were demanding from the colonists. It was a worthless tool, having been "spiked," to make it useless, many years back. Later the spike had been pried out, leaving the touchhole too enlarged for the cannon to launch a ball more than a few yards, but the cannon could still make enough noise to scare off Indians. It had been lent to the colonists by Mexican officials for that purpose several years before. Now Mexico was in the grip of a man who was centralizing the government and acting as dictator, and he wanted the cannon back. His name was El Presidente Antonio López de Santa Anna Pérez de Lebrón. From what William had heard, El Presidente Santa Anna had good reasons to disarm the colonists. They felt taxes were an unfair imposition and resisted paying, they thought the ban on slavery discriminated against their economy, which was largely based on cotton, and they'd harassed a number of federal troops and sent them packing south into the interior of the country. Mostly, these white settlers, who called themselves "Anglos," weren't keen on Mexican leadership, which was unpredictable and given to reverses. And they were not fond of Mexicans. But they loved Texas and it seemed to William that their affection for the place exceeded commitment and became a sort of devotion and reverence. He did not understand their fervency; this was, after all, only their adopted home—a howling wilderness—and most had not been here long. But they had wed themselves to it and seemed to think it owed them something. (He himself was not at all seduced by the place. It was an enormous, chaotic country where peoples of various races and religions mingled in belligerent attempts—full of folly, sometimes abortive, more often savage—to claim the land.)

Santa Anna, it was said, had turned into a despot, and intended to

disarm the colonists and garrison their towns. To this end, he was sending more troops and supposedly coming himself, and he'd made a point
of demanding the six-pounder. He had taken similar measures in other
Mexican states, disarming militias: when the state of Zacatecas had
revolted, it had been brutally put down. Texas, it appeared, would be
next.

The cannon was merely a token of a greater significance, William
understood, but it seemed such a pathetic remnant that he couldn't help
but feel disdainful of it. The colonists had buried it and dug it up again,
saying they would fire it at any troops who came to take it, and someone
had cut a flag from a wedding dress and painted on it a crude likeness of
the cannon, which was crude enough in the original, and written underneath it: "COME AND TAKE IT."

Now the Mexicans had come to take it, and that very evening were
positioned in the woods across the river from Gonzales. William had
had to pick his way around them and had lost the road, and was an
hour finding it again. Then his horse had started limping. He wasn't in a
mood to have adventure foisted on him. His own personal journey—
graduation from university and a hasty departure from England for the
unknown, with the cursings of a bitter father—was worrisome enough,
even if he had not sailed off into a choppy sea on a leaky ship captained
by a sot, and then landed in the midst of political turmoil. And now
here he was at a solitary farmhouse with a dog barking its bloody head
off at him. He studied the place, and saw in the meager light of the
rising moon a woman standing in the yard with a bucket dangling from
her hand and the wind tugging at her skirt. When he lifted his hand in a
cursory wave, she responded likewise. The wind molded her homespun
skirt against her body; a heavy braid of hair hung over her shoulder and
past her waist. "Hello!" he called.

She answered with another wave, and watched him. A few early
fallen leaves skittered across the yard. When he came up to her he saw
that she was very young; younger than he. He introduced himself and
touched his hat. She told him her name and scolded the dog until it
quieted.

"My horse went lame," he said, and told her that his destination was
twenty miles on up the road. "I wondered if I might sleep in your barn."

She answered that of course he could, and while she filled her bucket from the water catch under the roof ease, she invited him in for food. He left his satchel in the yard and offered to carry the bucket, and they walked together with the water sloshing in the bucket between them.

"Where are you from?" she asked.

"Manchester," he answered. "England."

"I like your hat," she said. It was a narrow-brimmed beaver hat. And then she said, "My great-great-grandfather came from England."

The door of the house was open, and when they came around the corner he could see the firelight inside and several people around a long table. The girl led him in, and while she introduced him he took in the room at a glance. There was a handmade cabinet in one corner, a shelf clock of fine wood, a spinning wheel. There were shelves of books, and several cats. An oval mirror on the far wall reflected the light, tossing it back into the room and onto the faces at the table. A man stood up from the table, extending his hand, and William set the bucket down, removed his hat, and shook hands in the custom he had learned from American men.

"This is my wife, Rose Kenner," the man was saying, "my mother, and my sons, Miles and Toby."

The man's wife got up and took the hat from William, then pulled a rocking chair from the hearth to the table, and invited him to sit. The girl got a plate from the corner cabinet and by the time William was seated she had it before him, heaped with pork and corn bread. It was a china plate, he noticed, fine English bone china.

The oldest of the two boys, Miles, whom William judged to be about his age, tossed him a small bundle of dried meat bound with a rawhide thong. William managed to chew some of it down.

"Do you like it?" Miles asked him.

He nodded.

"It's mustang jerky," Miles said, digging a finger in his ear. "Horse, wild horse."

What a rude bastard. William scraped sweet potatoes onto his fork with the blade and addressed the father, who had an easy manner and a good, expressive face with the sideburns of an Englishman. "I'm sorry to be an imposition, but my horse gave out. I wonder if you might have a mount I could purchase or rent for a few days."

The man answered that they didn't have a decent one to spare. "What brings you to Texas from England?"

"Family, sir. I have a sister living here. I also thought to make some profit on a number of pipes I brought along to sell, but the bowls and stems were somehow lost in transit. Only the mouthpieces came intact. They're worthless without the bowls and stems of course, so I abandoned them." He took a bite of pork, which tasted gamey. "Could I leave my satchel here and come back for it later, when I have a horse?"

Hugh Kenner said he could leave whatever he liked; they would look after it.

Miles said, "I've got a half-broke mustang mare I could loan you, if that would help," but his father answered quickly, "That would be no favor, Miles."

"How ridable is she?" William asked.

"Depends on who's ridin' her." Miles shrugged. "I ride her fine."

"Would you consider selling her?"

Miles hesitated, then said, "I'll tell you what. If you can ride her, you can have her. For free."

"You're betting I can't ride her."

"Yep."

Hugh Kenner said, "I advise against it. She's intractable."

The girl stayed busy at the fire, her face blushed with heat. Her mother got up to join her. The youngest son, whom William guessed to be about ten years of age, cast his squint toward William and ventured in a soft voice, "Her name's Loco. It means Crazy in Mexican. She's wall-eyed and she's cat-marked."

"Cat-marked?"

"That means a panther rode her once when she was wild, and she pitched it. We know because she's got a bunch of claw marks on her sides. Most the times if a panther gets on top and gets ahold it'll rip a mustang's belly out with its hind claws. But Loco pitched it."

The kettle put out a sudden wail and the girl lifted it from the fire.

"Well, I need a horse," William said. "I suppose I'll try her."

Hugh Kenner answered, "It's your choice. It wouldn't be mine."

"Why not loan him the gelded mustang?" the girl asked Miles, leaning over the table to drop tea leaves into tin cups and pour the boiling water over. "You were fixing to sell him anyway."

"Gelding's mine," Miles answered as he bit off another chunk of pork. "If the Meskins come, I'll need him." He looked at William. "Which way did you come from? Seen any Meskin troops?"

"Meskin?"

"Mexican. We say Meskin."

"*You* say it, Miles," the old woman injected, and added, to William, "It's used insultingly."

William was uncomfortable. He'd left England to escape this sort of family tension. He said, "The boat I arrived on was scheduled to land at Cópano, but we spied the Mexican army there and changed course to Velasco. The closest I came to troops was in Gonzales this morning."

Miles stopped chewing. "Gonzales?"

"They've come after the cannon there."

Miles looked at his father. "You were there today. You knew and came home and didn't tell."

"It isn't our fight, Miles," Hugh Kenner said.

"Like hell it ain't," Miles answered, and turned to William, saying with plain hostility, "My father here's a tory; you've sure heard of those I guess. He says the Meskins gave us free land, and pardoned us from taxes, and asked for nothing in return. Which is a goddamn lie. They've had us fighting off savages and plowing land and settling towns just so they can come in and take it after we've done all the work. Well, over my dead body. How many men we got in town? Our men."

"I have no idea."

"Guess."

"One hundred and fifty, perhaps."

"And how many Meskins?"

"I don't know."

"Guess."

"No."

Miles leaned back in his chair and passed a hand down over his face. "God," he said, looking at his father, who sat at the head of the table with his food untouched. "You were gonna let me stay here chopping wood and feeding sows while other folks were out fighting for our rights. You're a coward. Or a traitor. I'm cuttin' out."

"Then go," his father said.

Miles stood and went to the door. He lifted a shot pouch from a hook beside the door. His mother got up from the table and silently began packing a canvas bag of foodstuffs, a tin cup and plate, a fork.

"You could give this gentleman some instruction on riding that horse, before you go," Hugh Kenner said.

Miles said, "I guess he can figure it out." Then he turned to William and said impatiently, "All right. If you're game to try, I'll show ya. But she's very green. Fair warning. All right?"

"All right."

The moon was well above the trees. The wind was pushing from the north. Katie pulled her shawl around her. Miles roped the mare and began to saddle her. She was spooky in the wind, pacing and pulling against the reins. Toby tried to quiet her. William said, "She's the ugliest horse I've ever seen." She was a mottled brown color, with lumps and warts on her nose. Her ears drooped like a dog's, and Toby explained it was because wood ticks had chewed on the cartilage. The contour of her face had a hint of Arabian delicacy with prominent eyes and flared nostrils, but she had not one graceful curve to her body, and her flanks were scarred with claw marks. When Miles tossed the saddle on, she reared and threw it off. Then Miles yanked down on the reins with all his strength, dragging the mare's front end nearly to the ground. "She's got her sides bloated, you see there," he said. "If you cinch her up like that she'll unbloat soon as you get on her, and throw you and roll the saddle down under her belly, then go wild. Now, you toss the saddle on and watch. Toby, come hold these," and he gave him the reins, "put your weight in it." William lifted the saddle on and Miles jolted the mare's ribs with his knee. She grunted and exhaled her air; as she did so Miles pulled the girth tight and secured it. Toby let up on his hold. "She's yours," Miles said to William. "Only half broke. I've ridden her, but I don't hanker after it."

"You've rode her once is all," Toby said.

"When a mustang bucks," Miles explained, "it leaves the ground on all fours and lands that way. She'll arch up like a cat and come down hard. The best thing is to stay loose, but watch your neck doesn't jolt back when she pitches forward or comes down. She'll twist side to side;

you move with that motion. But when she comes down, brace against it. Got it?"

Rose Kenner held the lantern. The older Mrs. Kenner had stayed inside the house. Hugh leaned against the top fence rail; beside him the dog crouched peering through the bottom slats. Katie stood in the shadows behind the others; now and then the wind caught the whale-oil flame of the lantern and threw light in her direction.

"Sir," Toby ventured, "me, and Miles too, we've been thrown plenty of times. You got to count on being thrown. On your first go, the trick ain't staying on, it's trying again after you get thrown. That mare busted my specs one time, and I got back on her."

William lifted his boot to the stirrup and swung himself up. Miles tossed him the reins and stepped out of the way as Loco arched, sprang forward, and set off pitching from side to side. William pulled back, every muscle going tight, but the impact of the mare's weight against the ground on the third twist jarred him out of the saddle and he was thrown down.

Miles helped him up. "Try again?" he asked.

William caught his breath and said he would. Toby retrieved the mare, who had gone off kicking, her hind legs five feet off the ground and the stirrups cracking together over her back. Again William took the reins and swung into the saddle. It proved a repeat performance. His head slammed down into the dirt and he was dragged a few feet, managing to twist his boot from the stirrup just as he glimpsed a hind hoof coming down toward his head. He rolled, and saw the hoof plant itself two inches from his face. Dirt was gritty in his mouth.

Hugh Kenner climbed over the fence and went to him. "It's enough, don't you think?" he said.

Miles was standing over him. "You had enough?" he asked. William could taste blood. The wind blew dirt around him. Toby was leaning down to help him up, his spectacles catching the lantern light. When William got to his feet, a forceful pain shot up from his ankle through his leg. Miles brought the mare back up, and William pulled himself into the saddle, holding on to her ruddy mane and wrestling to get a leg over. She was off again but he was ready this time and pulled back so hard that she squatted on her haunches. When he let up, she took him by surprise, rearing back and then lunging onto her forelegs, throwing him over her head several yards where he landed with a grunt. A cloud driven by the north wind passed over the moon. William crawled to his knees, then stood up and walked in a stooped fashion to where Miles was waiting with the hellish mare. He felt his ankle was sprained, if not worse. He was blacking out. He reached the mare and groped for the stirrup, found it, clung to it, managed to get his foot in, then grappled with the saddle horn, straining to pull himself up.

"You don't have to do this," Miles said.

But the thing had come down to principle.

Miles hoisted him into the saddle and pushed one leg over. William sat hunched over, holding on. No wonder American stirrups were so long; a rider here had to grip with his legs. The mare planted herself in the scuffed earth, her head lowered and her feet asprawl, the wide nostrils flared and puffing. William gave her a nudge in the ribs. She took a step forward. "Don't let her fool you," Toby called.

William gave the mare another nudge. She went rigid then let out a snort and again started thrashing and rearing side to side, her hooves pounding holes into the dirt. He caught glimpses of the tree line on the horizon, the quarter moon, the faces at the rail lit by the lantern. The world and the mare were spinning in opposite directions so that William no longer had any bearings at all; he dimly recalled a scene played out in a shabby theater house, an actor in seaman's rags holding to the rearing masthead of a sinking ship in a make-believe, formidable sea. Just so, one hand clutched the saddle horn, the other pulled at the reins, and his knees locked around her. When he fell he was dizzy and barely conscious.

"Looks like you got yourself a horse," he heard Miles say. "You rode her long enough I guess. Congratulations." He was calling it quits. He was anxious to leave.

William pulled his knees to his chest and hung his face and vomited.

Inside, Rose Kenner centered the lantern on the table as Toby helped William into a chair. Then Rose retreated to the window and stood looking toward the ridge line where Miles was disappearing in the dark on the road to Gonzales. Toby went to the doorway, also watching him go.

Katie helped her grandmother to bed in the adjoining room, then came back in.

Taking a satchel from the corner cabinet, Hugh turned and saw Toby step out of the door. "Whoa, son!" he called.

Toby came back in. "I just want to see him off," he said.

His father looked at him a moment, then nodded, and Toby was out in an instant, leaving the door open behind him.

With his head resting on the table, William watched Hugh Kenner standing over him taking cloth and scissors from the bag. "I used to be a doctor," Hugh said directly, dipping the cloth into a bowl of water and stroking a cut above William's eye. "You might have a scar here, it's fairly deep."

When his head was cleaned and bound and the ankle wrapped, Hugh unbuttoned William's shirt and made him stand. He examined his sore ribs and said that none were broken.

Toby came back in. "Gone, Mother," he said to her in such a gentle way that he seemed older than his years.

"I saw him go," she answered. Her daughter made a gesture toward her, but she turned away and went into the sleeping room. William saw Toby's eyes meet his sister's with some sort of understanding; it was a sweet and intimate exchange, strangely touching, and William was embarrassed to be privy to it.

Turning to the stack of dishes, Katie began piling up the scraps. The fire had burned low. Hugh sent Toby to bed and went to fetch a clean shirt for William. Katie said to William as she moved to put a log on the fire, "Mother would break her heart over it, if Miles was to go for good. She likes Miles best."

When Hugh returned he helped William with the shirt and told him he was welcome to sleep beside the fire or in the barn.

"I apologize for the trouble," William answered. "I only wish I could have reached Sarah's tonight."

Hugh asked tentatively, "Your sister's name is Sarah?"

"Sarah Mackay. She isn't expecting me, and I'm afraid that with the troops advancing she'll leave home. Do you know her?"

Hugh nodded, but said nothing.

"She's married to a Scotsman, Callum Mackay. They live just over on the Guadalupe, and I guess I should have traveled the road up that river from Gonzales, but with the troops around Gonzales I was told it would be easier to follow this road here along this river and then cut over there."

A rush of wind pressed down the chimney, playing with the flames, and then the room was quiet. Hugh Kenner stared directly into William's eyes. His lips parted, and William thought he was so near he could have smelled the man's breath, except that he seemed not to be breathing.

The girl did not turn from the fire.

William felt a shiver in his body, and asked uneasily, "You said you know her, sir? Sarah?"

Hugh Kenner spoke slowly, deliberately. "Comanche Indians raided the Mackay place several months ago. Your sister was killed."

A silence followed, broken only by a whine of gasses from the logs and the wind pushing down the chimney.

"Her husband, too?" He was hardly aware he was speaking.

"No, Callum wasn't killed. He was wounded and left for dead, but he lived. The little girl, the daughter, she was killed. The baby survived. I tended Callum and the baby myself, afterward." The doctor shoved both hands through his thinning hair in a useless gesture. "Callum's horse was away from the house when the Comanches came, but returned in the morning. Callum managed to ride here with the child. Miles found them a mile from here, and brought them in."

"Where is Callum now?" William whispered. He felt utterly alone.

The man's voice seemed to come from a long way off. "He stayed here for a month, then took the baby to Gonzales, to a woman. Apparently now he has gone after one of the Indians. A half-breed. He left the child in Gonzales."

A charred log fell into embers, shooting sparks onto the hearth and startling the yellow cat that was sleeping in the rocking chair. William looked away from Hugh, to the corner cabinet with the china dishes stacked in rows, his long arms hanging idle in the borrowed shirt. He said in a voice so quiet that he doubted he was heard, "I didn't know she had another baby."

It was the girl who answered, almost as softly, only just now turning from the fire to look at him. "His name is Samuel. William Samuel, but Callum calls him Samuel."

Without a word, William left the house and groped his way under the rushing clouds and over the stubbled ground to the barn.

Katie made herself ready for bed, and tried to sleep, but the thought of him out there in the cold barn kept her awake. At last she got up, careful not to wake Grand, who slept beside her, and wrapping a heavy shawl around her shoulders went out with the lantern and a blanket. The wind was laying and a damp fog was creeping in.

William was seated on a hewn bench beside a mound of hay, his head in his hands. He lifted his face when she came in. "I brought you a blanket," she said quietly, and laid it down, then turned to go.

"Kate?" he said.

She turned back to him. The lantern cast his shadow huge against the hay piled high behind him.

"I—" He lifted one hand in a futile gesture and spoke in a whisper. "I didn't know she had a son." He paused, then his voice broke. "I thought she was only just on down the road. I thought to see her tomorrow."

She wanted to comfort him somehow, but she did not try, for there was an air of resistance or composure about him that stopped her.

She waited a moment more. He thanked her for the blanket, and she put the lantern down and left it there for him, and returned to the house.

In the sleeping loft he shared with Rose, Hugh sat on the floorboards near the foot of their spindle bed with his bare feet perched on the top rung of the ladder that led down to the sleeping room below. Staring down at the rungs fading into darkness, he listened to the sounds of his mother's breathing and Toby muttering in his sleep. He heard Katie rise and get a blanket from the chest and knew where she was going with it. He was still sitting there when she returned, and he listened to her crawl back in the bed beside her grandmother, rustling the corn shucks of the mattress. Grand must have wakened briefly or turned over in her sleep, for her deep breathing quieted.

Rose, behind him, was a silent sleeper. Sometimes he thought while listening to her quiet breath that she was only feigning sleep. He wanted now to talk with her and tell her of the Englishman's sad story and purge himself that way. But he knew that any conversation they had now would lead to Miles, and that Rose would blame him for Miles's leaving. She would never say it, but she would believe that he had driven Miles away. With her green eyes she accused him of so much. He was deserving of some accusations: he had brought his family here to this wilderness against her wishes, selfishly perhaps. But he had been a good father and a faithful husband, true to himself and to his family, if not to his past. In many ways he'd been a better parent to the youngest two than Rose had been. It was Rose who drew the battle lines, defending Miles against all others from the time he was a child until long past the time he needed a defender.

Rose was so different from them all, so strange to Hugh with her belief in God and superstitions, mystifying, the way she planted radishes downward at the decrease of the moon because they tapered downward, and prohibited hog-killing while the moon was waning for fear the pork would wither in the barrel. Rose needed rhythm for security; she needed rules to follow. She needed order and a place for things and had somehow managed to create that order out on this frontier. She had carved it out.

But now Miles had ridden off, and everything was splintered.

Hugh should get in bed beside his wife; if he reached out to her she would receive him. She never did turn him away. But he needed more than that, just now. He needed her to see life as he saw it: with shadows creeping in around the edges. Rose always missed the subtleties he saw, and he missed everything else, and when a day was over they had seen two different days and lived those days apart and there was nothing much to say.

Both of them were lonely.

And so Hugh Kenner sat there with the arches of his bare feet pressing down onto the ladder rung and growing cold. He thought of Miles riding in the dark along the road to war, and the Englishman in the cold barn with his grief, and Callum Mackay wandering the landscape like a living shade in search of revenge, carrying the shriveled remnant of his scalp.

Chapter 4

EL CORAZÓN

GOLIAD, TEXAS, ON THE SAN ANTONIO RIVER

Crucita could see that the great ranchero, Domingo de la Rosa, was not interested in the fighting cocks. It was not his custom to attend the fights. He had come instead to see the Mexican general Martín Perfecto de Cós, a handsome man in uniform whose eyes were fixed on the cocks, his table near the pit, his head dipped slightly toward De la Rosa, who spoke quietly, without animation. There seemed to be no urgency in the conversation; De la Rosa leaned forward with his elbows on his knees, his fingers laced casually together in the posture of a man telling stories to a sleepy child. Occasionally Cós responded with a nod or a single word, but he did not look at the ranchero.

Crucita, however, did. She watched them both. She watched them as she delivered mescal to a table in the corner and as she pressed her way through the crowd and the smoke of reeking sheep-oil lanterns. She tossed her hair over her shoulder and watched them without their noticing, for they were accustomed to being observed and paid no attention.

The cocks did not divert Cós, though he appeared preoccupied with them. He did not like this town. The citizens of Refugio, farther south, mostly Mexican Texans—called *Tejanos*—and Catholics from Ireland, had received him so warmly that he had declined to levy a

37

tribute upon them. But the *Tejanos* of Goliad were indifferent to his arrival. They were of Spanish-Mexican blood, descendants of Spanish soldiers who had garrisoned the Presidio La Bahía, a stone fort built to protect the adjacent mission in the mid-eighteenth century. The town of Goliad had sprouted up around the old presidio. Its people had a sense of ownership and pride, and recently they had been as rebellious toward their mother country as the most troublesome An- glo settlers and land speculators, though with a different agenda. They protested Mexico's recent grants of large sections of land—their ranch land—to the Anglos. The territory had been theirs for nearly a cen- tury. Their cattle grazed the land. Their mud and moss jacales lined the river in town, and more commodious limestone houses, painted colors as varied as the wildflowers in spring, clustered around the pre- sidio. The wealthiest owned ranches which spread for miles along the banks of the San Antonio River.

They had a right to the land. Their Spanish ancestors had come to prevent the French and English from coming and to protect the king's missionaries from Indian attack. They stayed to fight the early Anglo- American filibusters. They witnessed the conversion of docile Indians and slaughtered those who stole from them. They took the native women to their beds and planted their Spanish seed and became a race toughened by the land. The *Tejano* citizenry of the towns of San Patricio and Victoria regarded the present generation of these Goliad peoples as gamblers, smugglers, and thieves, too shiftless to plant gardens but awe- some in their horsemanship.

And they loved their sport. The fighting cocks intrigued them more than did the Mexican general Cós, who wore gold earrings, was dressed too well for their liking in his blue military coat, and who demanded too much. His fingernails were manicured and very short. He wanted their money and provisions and their carts to haul his supplies to San Anto- nio de Béxar. He wanted their mules. One of his officers had struck the town's leader—the alcalde—and his soldiers insulted the women. Cós did not control his men, and though these citizens of Goliad were not a disciplined people, they admired force. At present they witnessed more force in the pit than in the general's handsome face. They had drunk his wine and listened to him tell how he had routed the state legislature of

Coahuila-Texas because some of the legislators had participated in fraudulent sales of Texas lands. And they knew while they listened that this tale was scarcely half true, that Cós had indeed vanquished the legislature, but not solely for the reason given. He had done it because it was Santa Anna'a policy to consolidate the government.

The people of Goliad did not like their Anglo and *Tejano* legislators' recent insidious land sales, but neither were they pleased with the supreme government's former *empresario* system, which awarded land to foreigners practically free. They were, in fact, not favorably impressed with the rulers of Mexico or General Cós with his Castilian blood and his speeches. So they rolled and smoked their illegal tobacco, placed their wagers despite the town council's ban on gambling, and encouraged the failing bird, a black Spanish cock still flurrying though his plumage hung in bloody tatters and his eyes were pecked away. *"El Corazón,"* they called him, "the Heart." He had fought and won before, which made his loss more bitter and more noble. The victor was an incongruous downy gray, like a dove, with the devil's eyes, blood-marked, flashing his needle spurs and cutting deep, and amid the noise and smoke that filled the crowded jacal a sadness hung. *El Corazón* would die. Crucita knew the sadness, for she knew these people, every one of them except the general and his officers and the great ranchero, Domingo de la Rosa.

His name, she knew. Don Domingo, he was called. His face she had seen many times; it was a long face with green Spanish eyes, dark mestizo skin, which proved his Indian blood, and a trim, triangular beard. It was like the face of the patron saint in her home, John with his cruciform staff. Crucita had noted before how plain his clothing was for a great ranchero. She knew his placid gestures. But his voice she had never heard, for he did not often address himself to women. Now as she watched him speak, the sound lost in the crowd, she saw his listener draw back and look at him intently.

The ranchero was a master at imparting information; he gave only what was relevant. Another informant might have intruded upon the cockfight and made a spectacle delivering his urgent news, telling the results of the battle and leaving General Cós to align scattered fragments of information. But Domingo de la Rosa had walked in, taken a chair beside the general, and stated simply, "The fighting has begun."

Cós queried, "Gonzales?"

"Yes."

"And do we have the cannon?"

"No."

"Does the fighting continue?"

De la Rosa did not say what he was thinking, that it was hardly a battle worthy of the Mexican nation. Instead he answered, "No," and related the particulars, how one hundred and fifty rebel settlers had blasted forth with their little cannon. *"Cannonito,"* he called it, with disdain. His custom was to relate information, not sentiments, but in pronouncing this diminutive word he did not hide his scorn. "We lost but one man," he concluded. "And we lost the ground. Our men are retreating to San Antonio de Béxar."

Cós fingered his glass of mescal, and drank it down. He watched the merciless bird slash his spurs into the dying Spanish cock. He knew what General Antonio López de Santa Anna, his brother-in-law, would say of the retreat, and that he, Cós, military commandant of the joint state of Coahuila-Texas, would be held accountable. This was a godless land, and these were godless people, but Santa Anna's cause was just. And there were those worthy of it, those, in fact, who made him feel unequal to it, such as this lean, solemn mestizo with Spanish eyes and hands calloused from three decades of roping and branding wild *mesteño* cattle. He did not look at the man. He did not like him. At last he said, "I, also, will proceed with my men to Béxar."

"The rebels intend to intercept you," De la Rosa replied.

"Let them try."

"You will leave a garrison at Presidio La Bahía?"

"Of course. Goliad and its presidio are the gateway to the sea."

"It will be difficult to hold."

Cós was silent. A vaquero reeking of sweat and tobacco and chewing a piece of sweet *leche quemada* stepped in front of him to watch the black cock's dying antics. The general was angered by this offense; he wanted to strike the man for standing so close. These people did not know their place. For an instant the odds of losing this war seemed very great, for even the *Tejano* population was indifferent and rude. But Santa Anna was coming, and Santa Anna did not lose wars.

De la Rosa watched the general's face, saw his contempt, and said in a voice so low that Cós was forced to lean toward him, "The Mexican army alone will not defeat the rebels. You can crush them in the state of Zacatecas, but not here. Some may be won to your side if given motivation, but they will not be forced to it. And this town will not be forced to it. We have made a country of our own here, and have little use for Mexico. She restricts our trade, and gives nothing. Santa Anna can march all of Mexico into Texas, and invade by sea, but without these people"—he made a gentle gesture that encompassed the room and again laced his fingers—"you will fail."

It was at this point that Cós drew back and looked at him. "Santa Anna does not fail."

The ranchero's face softened with a smile. "Ah," he said.

Cós stiffened. "It is our intention to return Texas to Mexicans. To drive out the Americans."

"Intention. Yes. I believe in your intention. I believe in Mexico. But I despise your Santa Anna, and it is despite him, not for him, that I will give myself to your efforts. God willing, the Moya brothers will supply you with horses from the wild *manadas*. De la Garza and Savariego will raise companies from the ranchos. And I," he said with a single tap of his chest, "I will supply the information. Without my knowledge of this country, you are blind. The rebels will fight you from the woods."

As he said this a young *cantinera* with black hair falling to her shoulders came to the table with a bottle of mescal and filled the general's glass. She was small, and had the features of the Coahuiltecan Indians who were her ancestors. De la Rosa watched her brown hands as she placed an empty glass before him. He covered the glass to prevent her from filling it, and looked at her. "Perhaps," he said, looking straight into her black, sloe eyes, "this woman will help me. Your name?" He spoke as if on impulse, but the general knew, and the woman knew as well, that he was not an impulsive man.

"María de la Cruz Pacheco," she answered without hesitation. "I am called Crucita."

"And you are the sister of Adelaido Pacheco?"

"Yes."

"And where is Adelaido now?"

She gave a hesitant smile, her lips parting over a row of teeth that were perfect but for a single chip. "He is with the horses. He is always with the horses, somewhere. I do not know where."

Domingo de la Rosa did not return the smile. "When you find him," he said, "tell him that his former employer, Domingo de la Rosa, to whom he owes so much, has work for him. Remind him of his debt to me."

"Yes, señor," she said, her brow creasing. "When he returns, I'll tell him."

Crucita stepped away to another table with the bottle of mescal.

De la Rosa leaned in closer to General Cós. "There's another man we should find," he said, "though I'll have to pay him for his help; he'll only work for pay. He's called Louie Métis, a half-breed, and it's possible he can bring the Indians over to our cause. He has connections with both eastern and western tribes, and can convince them that it's in their interest to side with Mexico. Which it is, is it not?"

General Cós was watching as the mangled body of *El Corazón* was tossed out of the ring. "Of course it is," he said indifferently.

A BABY

Gonzales, Texas

William disliked the colonists' bravado, but so far it had proved well founded. They had routed the Mexican force from Gonzales and kept the six-pound cannon, and on the night of the ninth a small rebel company from the coast, with the help of a few *Tejanos* from Goliad, captured the garrison General Cós had left at the old fort there—called the Presidio La Bahía—when he departed with his main force for San Antonio de Béxar. These actions gave the rebel Texans control of Goliad, which stood at the crossroads of Texas with access to the sea, and of Gonzales, which served as a buffer town to the eastern colonies where most of the Anglo-Americans lived. Now they wanted San Antonio de Béxar, the westernmost settlement between Texas and the rest of Mexico. Often called just Béxar, or San Antonio, the town was mostly *Tejano* and presently garrisoned by Mexican troops. The rebels intended to take possession before Cós arrived there with his reinforcements, or possibly after, or perhaps to intercept him in route, defeat him, and then move on to capture the town. They discussed a number of scenarios. They would have it in fewer than twenty days, they said. Some said a week. What these few hundred men and boys, scant of guns and ammunition, some armed only with long blades called Bowie knives, would do with almost one thousand Mexican soldiers as prisoners was not a question they seemed to ponder much. William did not ask. He did not particularly care, as he thought their victory was unlikely.

The Gonzales cannon was the rebels' only artillery. They mounted it on solid wheels sliced from a tree trunk and twice a day paraded it from the old fort through the jail plaza and down Water Street whimsically decorated with autumn sunflowers. They christened it "the flying artillery" for some reason William could not fathom, and painted a flag with this epithet, "artilery," spelled with only one L.

William kept to himself. He was in Gonzales only to find Sarah's baby. It was proving difficult in a town serving as headquarters for a reckless volunteer army silly with dreams and alcohol and, until yesterday, without leadership. Expresses sent out daily were eliciting new recruits from the colonies. Men came alone or in squads, on foot or horseback, on muleback, dressed in homespun and greasy buckskin with boots or moccasins. Everyone wore a hat to suit his own fancy, a military cap or animal skin or flashy top hat. Some wore Mexican sombreros.

And no one knew anything about a baby.

James W. Fannin, a plantation owner and slave trader from the coastal settlement of Velasco who had attended West Point Military Academy in the United States in his early years, was there with his "Brazos Guards." William B. Travis, on the run from Cós's underlings since summer when he'd lost his temper over a customs matter and organized twenty men to capture a Mexican garrison at Galveston, showed up and enlisted as a volunteer. He was viewed by most Texans as a hothead who had acted prematurely in the summer, but he had done it with flair, and success, sending forty of *El Presidente* Santa Anna's troops, disarmed, on a march inland. The rebels liked his style.

And Stephen Austin arrived, still sickly from his year's stint in Mexican jails. He was known to all Texans. Fourteen years previously he and his father had initiated the settling of Anglos in Texas. In the early years his policy was to steer clear of Mexican politics and instabilities in the government and he preached caution and detachment. For over a decade the people had listened. It was to their advantage to listen. Yet they wanted freedom of religion and trial by jury—familiar principles. They wanted repeal of the recent anti-immigration law that had halted friends and relatives on their way to Texas with wagonloads of slaves, or had simply caused them to cross the border from Louisiana as illegal aliens. And there was something else the settlers—mostly the Anglo settlers— wanted: separate statehood from Coahuila. Texas was not its own state, it was part of the state of Coahuila and Texas, and by the Mexican constitution did not have sufficient population to achieve statehood of its own. The settlers claimed that independent statehood would entitle them to "fair representation"—a phrase inherited from their revolutionary fathers. But William guessed that the request was more rhetorical than sincere. The Anglos here had come mostly from the United States, and their grandfathers had treated England the same way. Clearly the Anglo settlers, a recalcitrant people, wanted less to do with the Mexican government, not more. They wanted separate statehood because it was separate, not because it would entitle them to keener involvement. They wanted an identity of their own. They wanted to conduct their legal affairs in English. They wanted to keep their slaves.

And there was that which they did not want: a tariff. For seven years the fledgling colonies of Texas, with their expansive coastline, had been excused from tariffs. Texans saw no reason why they should start paying tariffs now that the arbitrary seven years was past. The fact that Mexico relied almost exclusively on tariffs for its revenue did not trouble them particularly.

It was Stephen Austin who had made the tedious journey to Mexico City to present this list of grievances. His negotiations were at first unsuccessful, and he took the liberty to write an impassioned letter home, instructing fellow Texans to prepare for separate statehood whether it was granted officially or not. In the end it was not granted, as Texas had less than half of the eighty thousand citizens required to qualify. But Santa Anna granted provisions for trial by jury and temporarily relaxed the tariff. He also repealed the anti-immigration law.

And Stephen Austin started home. Then his seditious letter fell into the hands of the law and before he reached Texas he himself was in those hands. Subsequent solitary confinement without trial, under the charge of attempting to incite insurrection among his Anglo settlers, did not ruin his spirits, but it did alter his thinking. Now he was free, and back, and for war in full. He retained his reticence; he was by nature a peace-loving individual, a bachelor, ponderous, pinch-faced and scholarly, devoted to Anglo Texans and their prosperity. War would ravage Texas, he knew, but without statehood, and without slaves, and with a despot such as Santa Anna in power, Texas would never realize its potential to be the world's cotton center, and that was Austin's vision. He believed in it enough to lift his narrow shoulders from their habitual stoop, assume a rebel's posture, flail his skinny arms, and spout revolutionary jargon.

Before Austin's arrival in Gonzales the rebels had organized what they called a "Board of War" for want of a better title, but could not agree on a leader. At last they had sent word to Austin; he came and was elected commander in chief. He was ignorant of strategy or weaponry but he knew the Mexican mind, he knew Santa Anna, and he could be trusted to act in the interests of Anglo Texans. William watched his affected military posturing and thought him a shy, unlikely leader for an army . . . if this assortment of individuals qualified as an army. To a man, they believed they did. They would not admit their limits, but they knew what they lacked. They wanted a company of lancers for their army, for they were sure the Mexicans would have lancers, and so they cut six-foot poles from the river bottom and strapped blacksmith files onto the ends. For practice, they lanced bales of hay behind the tannery. A graceless, bearded trapper from the Rocky Mountains named Scholar Tipton appointed himself captain of these lancers, and in search of more challenging sport took to spearing town cats. But the citizens complained they would be overrun with rats by spring and Scholar was forced to the woods for wilder game.

It was Scholar Tipton who finally led William to the baby. "Got a goddarn squalin' kid in that house way yonder at the other end of the street," he commented to his company during practice behind the tannery. The sun had descended behind the rooftops but its warmth still hung in the air. The odor from the tannery was strong.

A pimple-faced boy, poised with his lance to sprint forward and make his strike, said, "Was a man here lookin' for a baby yesterday."

"Well I found him one. A squalin' babe and an old woman holed up."

The boy launched himself forward with a guttural cry, plunging his weapon into the mutilated bale. Scholar nodded approval and turned to the next in line. "I warned her it were no place for a old woman and a babe, that the Mexicans was on their way. She said she's so fed up she'd welcome them Mexicans. Said she's tired of hoodlums pokin' around her property, huntin' out a place to bed down or for who knows what." He quirked his lip up and picked at a bad tooth. "Cats, I told her, just lookin' for cats."

The boy returned with his lance, its file tip askew. "That man askin' about a baby was a Englishman," he said, unstrapping the thong that secured the tip to its shaft. "Brown-headed, maybe that tall"—he pointed to a man just under six feet—"and a long nose. Or maybe it ain't long, maybe crooked; it was somethin' funny about his nose."

Later in the evening Scholar Tipton went in search of William, and found him, and took him to the house where Sarah's child lay sleeping under the watch of a white-haired woman.

Without any hesitation or apparent reluctance the woman agreed to surrender "Sammy," as she called him, to the stranger, whose English voice convinced her he was Sarah's brother. She was a midwife and had helped at Samuel's birth; he had come breech, "haunches first" she told William, "which means bad luck," she said. "It's why he lost his mama. Callum said he planned on coming back here for him, he's gone after one of them that killed this baby's mama."

William pressed for better details on the direction Callum had gone, but the woman did not know. She wanted to leave Gonzales and had waited until now, she said, only for Callum.

Scholar helped her load her belongings into a decrepit buckboard and hitch up a skinny ox. He tried to convince her not to leave in the dark, but she said darkness was safer than light, and that she'd risk Indians and Mexicans over the whites who had taken over her town and speared her cats for sport.

For the child, she gathered together remnants of a mashed sweet potato, a few bits of cloth, and a bottle with a rag teat. She said there was a cow out back and they could help themselves to milk.

Meanwhile William was holding Samuel, who was asleep. The woman had placed the baby in his arms when she began to pack her trunk of clothes, and William had not moved a step since then. He could not recall ever having held a baby. Finally he shuffled outside to give the woman proper thanks.

She was seated in the buckboard with the starry sky behind her and her belongings piled in back. Her mattress, with a small hole leaking feathers, sagged over the other crates, and Scholar was securing two chairs on top of it with rope. "One thing Callum did say," the woman volunteered, looking toward William, "is that the man he's gone after calls himself Maytee. It's French and spelled some way that ain't how it sounds. He was with the Comanches that had Callum's scalp with 'em, but the rangers and the Mexican ranchers that killed all them Comanches turned him loose for some reason."

When the old woman was gone, Scholar and William took a closer look at the baby. His clothing was fouled and one eye was clotted with mucous. He awoke and began to cry at once and they decided he was hungry. William had never milked a cow, so he talked the trapper into doing it. "So, that baby is your nephew?" Scholar asked, squirting the milk forcibly into a tin bucket.

"Yes," William answered, standing stiff-legged and holding the screaming child, who had worked himself into a frenzy.

Scholar's beard was brown and shaggy and his hair was twisted in a tangled braid. He wore a beaded necklace, moccasins, Indian leggings, and a buckskin jacket to his knees, fringed at every seam. From the belt cinched at his wide belly hung a knife and a small hatchet; slung over one shoulder was his bullet pouch and powder horn. He had propped his rifle against a nearby cedar and placed his smelly buffalo hide near it, and he kept his eye on them as if worried they would crawl away. Despite the warmth of the evening, he wore a red woolen hat, low-crowned and stained with years of sweat and Rocky Mountain snow. The hat was from St. Louis, he told William. "Nothin' like family," he said, speaking loudly to be heard over the baby. "I got some family myself, back in Arkansas. A wife and kids. I left 'em though." He took a noisy swallow from the bucket and wiped his face on his sleeve. "It just got in my head one day it was time to cut out and throw myself on providence," he said. "It's like gettin' caught in a river's suck—you just go with it. You know the feelin'?"

William did not particularly know the feeling. He was troubled by the child's hysteria and wondering what he would do if Callum had disappeared for good. He knew not one soul to turn to. Katie Kenner came to mind; he had not seen her since she brought him the blanket that night, for he had spoken to Hugh Kenner early the next morning and then left on foot in the fog and found his way to Sarah's home, with the two graves under a stunted oak tree in the back, where Miles and Hugh had buried Sarah and her daughter. In Sarah's house, with sunlight nosing through the weathered holes in the chinking, William had mourned for a week, nearly starving himself. Then he'd taught himself to shoot with a rusty musket he found in the barn, and the noise and power of it helped to jar the empty feeling out of him. At last he'd started for Gonzales in search of the baby.

"It's a powerful feelin'," Scholar said. The cow kicked one leg back and settled again. "I call it the Big Suck. Once you go with it, there ain't a chance it'll turn you loose or turn you around back home. It'll run you into a jam, maybe," he continued, "like it done to me, landin' me here in the middle of a war."

"You could leave," William remarked.

Scholar pulled at the fleshy bags, obviously enjoying their soft, giving feel in his hands, the thin stream of white liquid barely visible in the darkness. "I got no where else particular to go," he said. "The beaver trade's broke down 'cause of England shippin' in such a wad of silk from them Orients." Cocking up one messy eyebrow, he shot a look at William, who shifted Samuel in his arms. The infant quieted and began to snuffle and hiccup. Noises from town, of a volunteer army settling in for an evening of drinking, drifted from down the street. Cicadas were humming. William knew he should clean the child and change his clothes but did not know how. The baby seemed even more fragile now that it was silent. He guessed it should be bigger than it was, at four months old, though he had no idea if that was so. The flailing and fussing had been irritating, but now the sudden quiet opened William again to the feel of this bundle in his arms, the smallness of it and the tiny breath. He had never held anything so cumbersome and so piteous, and unless he could find Callum he was stuck with it. He wanted to feel tender toward it—Sarah's baby that he had not known she had, and that was named for him—William Samuel—and he took a look at it: the curve of the cheek, the wet eyes glistening in the darkness, staring up at him. The hair was downy red. Then he went around front to the water catch and stripped the child and submerged him, all but his head, several times. Samuel went rigid but did not cry, and William brought him out and laid him on his jacket. Samuel waved his arms and kicked both legs together, managing a kind of ineffective locomotion on his back and panting like a small dog. When William offered his finger, the child took hold of it with a grip that was astonishing.

Scholar Tipton came around with his buffalo hide over his shoulder, his rifle, and the bucket of milk. Hastily William tied a cloth around Samuel and held him up with both hands while Scholar inserted the rag nipple into the infant's mouth, and Samuel began to suck, twining his fingers around Scholar's fingers, which held the bottle at a tilt.

"His name is Samuel," William said. "William Samuel Mullins."

"Sammy," Scholar remarked.

"Samuel," William corrected. He wanted rid of the trapper, but owed him something. So when Samuel finished sucking and turned his head away from the rag teat, William asked Scholar to walk back to town with him. William carried Samuel against his shoulder and Scholar carried the wad of sweet potato in his shot pouch, for the next feeding.

Gonzales was in disarray. The camp was set up on the outskirts of town, but the inner village, built on the river near the old log fort and consisting of about three dozen structures, was headquarters. A handful of volunteers had taken over the abandoned homes and helped themselves to store goods. Austin had ordered that the goods be replaced and the homes left alone, but as yet it was not done. No one expected it would be.

Winslow Turner's hotel was an unpainted two-story affair in a cluster of Spanish oaks still keeping their summer green. Together William and Scholar made their way through a noisy group of men toward the entry door. Yellow taper light from the bar inside shone out through the windows. A tall man in Sunday dress with a sparse blond braid to his shoulders said, in perfect diction with a Southern drawl, "Well, god damn if that man has not brought a baby with him to war."

"You are right, he has, brother," said a shorter man with the identical low, soothing voice. His hair knotted his head with tight brown ringlets and his wide face was tipped with an immaculate beard.

Scholar said, "What goddarn business is it of yours?"

If not for Scholar, William would have ignored the comments and gone inside. But he could hardly allow the trapper to play his savior, so he turned and said to the men, "I beg your pardon, were you addressing me?"

They looked at each other, the blond feigning surprise, his gaunt and pitted chin pulled downward and his brows lifted. "I do believe it is a foreigner, Bull, dear brother," he said to the other, imitating William's English accent. A few in the group standing around laughed.

"I'm not looking for conflict," William said curtly, and continued toward the entry with the baby.

"You have come to war, but are not looking 'for conflict'?" the man's voice followed him. "We have a word for that here in Texas. We call it scared. Are you scared?"

When William did not answer, the other said, "My brother asked if you were scared," and William stopped and turned to look at him.

A silence settled on the gathering. Inside someone was squealing on a fiddle.

The blond man said, "I am Straw Hanlin and I asked if you were scared."

Scholar mimicked the sultry drawl. "Well, I am Scholar Tipton, and I asked what goddarn business it is of yours."

On the last word Straw Hanlin stepped forward and hit Scholar in the face. Scholar took the blow and stood very still, then laid his gun carefully aside and drew a knife and lunged forward suddenly with all his heavy weight, knocking Straw Hanlin to the ground and holding the blade to his neck. The others in the crowd stepped back.

Bull Hanlin, with the deliberation of an artist and in no apparent hurry, went to his horse, took from the saddlebags a bullwhip of braided cowhide, and unwound it. From a distance of five yards he whirled it twice above his head, cracked it on the ground with a sound like gunshot that brought the trapper's face around to look at him, and then with an easy snap of his wrist flicked it down onto Scholar's back with such force that the trapper arched and rolled sideways, his powder horn flung out beside him.

Straw used the instant to get himself on top, pinning Scholar's wrists to the ground. William could see the two men clearly in the light from the window, clasped together like lovers under the spreading oak, the man named Straw in his Sunday clothes with his long thighs straddling

Scholar's pelvis. They were not twelve feet away. But William held back, not knowing what to do with the baby. The crowd began pressing in, some shoving their way to the forefront but leaving clear distance for the whip.

"Let him up, brother," Bull said.

"But he has not had enough," Straw answered, deliberately drooling a viscid stream of saliva onto the trapper's face.

"I will give him more," Bull said. "First you must get off him." He swung the whip above his head, cutting the air.

"Let him go," William said.

Straw looked up and answered in a soft and mocking voice, "Oh, so now the nursemaid would like 'conflict.' Well, that's fine, but had not you better put the baby down?" He drooled again into Scholar's beard. "You don't think I would fight a man holding a little baby."

With a sudden movement Scholar thrust his wide body upward into an arch, launching Straw Hanlin forward, off him. But before he could stand, the whip came down on him. It coiled around his neck and sucked his breath and then let go. He tried to get to his knees but repeatedly the whip darted forward, curling around his chest and leaving him stunned and helpless.

William had never witnessed anything as brutal as this violence endowed with serenity.

Straw Hanlin pulled a pistol from his belt, leaned against a tree, and watched the whipping with an expression like benevolence.

William had no weapon, and saw that no one else would intervene. No one would look him in the eyes. He thrust Samuel into the arms of an old man and was advancing on Bull Hanlin when a gunshot sounded just behind him. Turning, he saw in the street a mounted man with a rifle. Bull also turned to look, and instantly the man lowered his gun on him. "Drop it, Bull," he said. "Drop it or I'll shoot your hand off."

Bull dropped it.

Straw cocked his pistol and stepped forward within three feet of Scholar, aiming at his head. "If you shoot my brother, Kenner, I will kill this man," he called.

It was only when he heard the name, that William recognized Miles Kenner on the horse. And it seemed Miles had not seen Straw Hanlin posing underneath the tree, until now. Miles was outmanuevered.

Then like an apparition from the trees behind Straw, a black-haired figure moved out with two pistols aimed at Straw Hanlin's back. "One move, my friend, and your life is over," the man said, and then, above the murmur of the crowd, "These at your back are the newest from St. Louis, two pistols with barrels of cast steel drilled cold from a solid bar. We call them pocket rifles. Pocket, of course, means they are very small. Rifle means they are very accurate." He laughed. "But you are a big man, *un hombre grande,* and are not afraid of small things. Now, drop your gun." Straw obeyed. "Drop your knife. Lift your arms."

Straw's compliance was hostile but complete. With his arms lifted he turned slowly to eye his captor.

Miles called out, "Pacheco? Is that Adelaido Pacheco?"

Adelaido laughed again.

William pressed through the crowd to Miles and said solidly as he stood looking up at him, "I'm very grateful."

"Don't take it personal," Miles said. "I was aiding that man there." He nodded toward Scholar, who was slumped on his hands and knees with his buckskin as bloody and torn as hide mauled by a mountain cat. "And paying my dues to my neighbors, the Hanlin brothers here."

He had done it for the fun. He had done it for the glory. Certainly he had not done it for William. He did not even know the trapper he had saved. And William understood that Miles was a man who was at his best in the midst of hazard. And also at his worst.

William said, "Callum Mackay is my brother-in-law. Your father told me you took him in, and the child. I owe you for that also."

Miles said nothing, and the silence suggested that the words had touched him. Sarah Mackay was rotting in a grave that he had dug. He had found her mutilated husband slumped over a horse's neck with the insects sticking in his blood and the baby Samuel wrapped in a blanket stiff with it, and had taken them in. He and his father had ridden over to the homestead and found the woman lying dead in the corner, stiff as wood, and her little girl beside her, and they had buried them both. And now he was learning that the Englishman was this woman's brother.

Bull Hanlin stood impotent without his whip. Straw stayed in the shadows with the *Tejano*'s pistols leveled at him. William went to retrieve Samuel from the old man and then to help Scholar Tipton, who was trying to stand.

HOPE

NOVEMBER, THE KENNER HOMESTEAD ON
THE SAN MARCOS RIVER

Callum Mackay did not return to Gonzales for the baby. William waited
for a week after the volunteer army of about two hundred restless men,
including Scholar Tipton, Miles Kenner, Adelaido Pacheco, and the Hanlin brothers, had moved on toward San Antonio de Béxar. Then he
began to worry seriously about what to do with Samuel if Callum never
came back. He could take the child to England, but there was no one
there to care for him properly.

William kept thinking of the Kenners. The mustang mare he'd ridden, and now owned, was still at their farm, so he used her as a reason
to go back. He started on the trail northwest along the San Marcos
River, with sweet potatoes in his satchel and Samuel strapped to his back
in a blanket. It should have been a day's walk, but with the burden of
the baby he lost time and had to camp for the night. Not bothering to
build a fire, he spread his blanket and stretched out beside the child. In
the night he awakened to the sound of cicadas and the rustle of a prowling animal. The child was nestled under his arm. William thought of
Sarah, who was the only person he had ever really loved and trusted,
and who was dead, and whose baby was so close with his baby-breath in

the darkness. And he felt more awe than sadness: how mysterious life was.

When he arrived at the Kenners' in the morning, Katie was outside in the sunlight washing clothes, plunging her arms up to her elbows in a murky tub of water that was white with soap scum. When she saw the child she dried her bleached, parboiled hands and reached for him. William marveled at her spontaneity; it gave her an ease and brilliance. "Father said you'd find him," she said, cradling the baby and petting him.

William accepted an invitation to stay for a while. Miles was still away with the rebel army, so Toby assumed the role of mentor and taught the Englishman farm work. Toby's patience was boundless. He taught by demonstrating rather than instructing; words were too abstract for Toby. He would place his hands around William's on the cow's teats to show exactly the proper grip and pressure, his mouth forming its lopsided smile and his eyes blinking with pride behind the round lenses of his glasses when William got it right.

They worked together training Loco, though Toby refused to mount her for fear she'd smash his spectacles again.

William decided to take Loco for a ride one day, and she behaved so savagely that he dismounted her and tried to lead her home. But she would not be led. She pulled against him like a mule, flaring her warty nostrils and laying her ears back flush against her head. When he swatted her with his quirt, she lunged at him and tried to bite him. He was considering the option of turning her loose, but then discovered she was willing to accompany him if the reins were slack. So they trod home with the reins draped loosely over William's shoulder and Loco's head bobbing very close to his.

"She's a packhorse," Toby said when they arrived, trying to make the best of it. "We'll just use her like a packhorse."

William more than earned his keep in the household. On one occasion he overheard the older Mrs. Kenner—Grand, they called her—remarking on his nice manners and saying he was a good influence on Toby. Though her tone was complimentary he felt oddly shamed. He did not want complicity with her, he wanted it with Rose, for despite Rose's shy, compulsive ways and her odd superstitions, she was a woman of tact and honesty. She let him have his privacy.

Katie cared for the baby. William was grateful, yet he kept his dis
tance from the girl. The fact that he liked her was no reason to seduce
her; it was a reason not to. He went about his work. He told himself it
was a matter of deciding what exactly he would allow himself to feel. His
composure was complete.

Katie's was not. She was falling in love for the first time, and she was
crushed. Her efforts to elicit some response from him were obvious, and
she knew her family thought that he would break her heart.

Grand told her to be less forthcoming. But Katie lacked William's
control. Love, for her, was not something one decided on; it simply
descended, which was the beauty of it. It had walked right down the hill
toward her at an unlikely time, and then gone away, and come back, and
she had given her heart. But William would not take it in. It didn't occur
to Katie that there was such a thing as an academic approach to love, in
which a man would refuse her because he thought circumstances inap-
propriate; romantic affection, for Katie, was so compelling she could not
imagine anyone willingly shunning it.

Had she imagined it, she would not have thought it very clever.

She felt at fault, perceiving herself as ignorant and inadequate. She
feared he would leave without warning.

With the first cold front William accepted Hugh's invitation to move
his pallet from the barn to the hearth in the family room. From then on
he slept there, with the smell of Samuel's soiled napkins, which Katie
dried by the fire before washing them.

Samuel slept in a crib beside Katie's bed in the adjoining room.
When Katie rose in the night to care for the child she would look
through the door at William's shape against the firelight. Sometimes she
saw him rearrange his body under the patched quilt or fling an arm out
toward the hearth. It was not propriety that kept her from going to him
in the night and asking him just to put his arms around her, but the
certainty he would not do it. In small gestures throughout the day she
offered herself and was politely shunned; if she abandoned herself and
went creeping to his bed and he did not receive her, the shame would be
too terrible. What Grand thought, and what the others thought, was not
of consequence, for Katie had her own pride.

And her limits.

Without knowing it, and without meaning to, William was testing those limits. He did not need her, and did not seem to want her, but he did give her the baby to care for. Her sense of justice was offended. Who was this man, anyway, to bring her an abandoned child to care for and offer nothing in return?

She did not know how to communicate her distress. She had always been the peacemaker in the family, standing between her mother and Grand, between her father and Miles, between Toby and his follies. She could be firm, even sharp, but always in the name of peace. Confrontations worried her. The role of pacifier was so inherent to her image of herself that she even feared grappling with her own emotions. She was caught in the dilemma of what to do with her discordant feelings for William. Her affection for him was turning bad, like a beautiful child grown ugly and unmanageable. She found herself fighting tears, and by the third week fighting William.

"Toby and I are going fishing," he told her one afternoon, standing just inside the doorway with his hat, one of Hugh's spare broad-brimmed felts, in his hand. The sun cast his lean shadow, from the shoulders down, across the puncheon floor toward her.

She looked up from her sewing. She was alone, since Grand was napping with the baby and Rose was outside grinding corn. She was weary of his formal manners. The needle pricked her finger and she licked the speck of blood. "You shouldn't have bothered taking off your hat," she said irritably, "since you're not coming in." She waited. "Go on," she added. "Go on fishing."

"Are you angry with me, Kate?" he asked. He always called her Kate, and she disliked it.

"Just go on," she said, and started sewing again, watching her hands at their task, her thumbnail with a bruise from the barn door swinging shut.

He did not invite her to continue, but said he would be with Toby at the downstream fishing hole, and then went out.

Katie decided she had had enough. After half an hour passed, she put her sewing aside, took up her shawl, and set out for the fishing hole. The sun was lowering in an empty sky and a breeze smoothed the field of tall grasses into glistening yellow sheets. Katie lifted her cotton skirt to be free of the grass. She felt as if the farm itself would suck her down. William seemed her only source of rescue, and she felt that losing him would mean never truly finding herself.

Pecan trees stood an acre deep along the bank in a gradual slope to the water, their autumn leaves pale brown, almost translucent with the late sun seeping through. It was the month pecan trees dropped their fruit. A black squirrel rose on his haunches beside a tuft of grass with a smooth nut in his mouth, stared at Katie, then went on burying his winter stash. A cardinal called; Katie saw him high up in the withered foliage. She was nearing the fishing hole, and slowed and quieted her walk, feeling in the effort new control and temperance. Crouching down so as not to be noticed, she gathered her skirt up over her knees and crept to the edge of the clearing, settling in behind a large boulder. The river before her spilled over a shoal of rocks, then widened and slowed into a deep pool reflecting a needled cypress tree that stood on the near side, its knobby roots partially submerged and rising from the water like the knees of crippled old men. Toby was sitting on a low limb of the cypress with his back against the trunk. His pants were too short and his skinny ankles seemed too fragile to support the heavy brogan shoes. His fishing line jerked suddenly, and he grew intent and jerked it once himself, then let it slacken. With a gesture of frustration, he pulled in a bare hook. Coon Dog got up on his hind legs to see what was happening, his forelegs braced against the tree trunk, and Toby said to him, "That big daddy stole my bait again."

William was seated on the bank at the foot of the cypress. Katie could not see his face, only the back of his head with the hair grown shaggy, and the curve of his back. She guessed from his posture that he was reading from a book in his lap. His fishing line hung slack in the water near the bank where there was not much current.

Toby took a chunk of pork fat from a small burlap sack he'd tied to a nearby limb, and ground it onto his hook. He swung the line out in a low arc, and it was pulled taut by the current. He fixed his eyes, not on where it entered, but down below the surface. The water was clear. He almost lost his balance when he jerked the line, then pulled it in with the fish, hand after hand, and let the fish dangle in front of William's face for a moment before bringing it on up.

William watched it ascend. "Is that the big daddy?" he asked.

"Big daddy's sister, I think," Toby answered, taking hold of the fish to extract the hook. "Big daddy's big sister."

"Dinner," William answered, and went back to his reading.

Toby pulled the hook out and tossed the fish down to the ground, where Coon sniffed it and took it in his mouth. Toby yelled at Coon to drop it, and the dog obeyed, though he circled around it, whining.

Katie stood up and stepped out as if she had just that moment walked down from the fields. "Catching anything?" she called.

Toby turned to look at her. The breeze made his hair stick up and Katie couldn't see his eyes through the wire spectacles, which reflected the bright foliage. He was just a homely, nearsighted boy with autumn all around him and a sack of pork fat in his hand, but there was something in his posture and his face that suggested wisdom. "I just caught that one there," he said, pointing down at it.

William said, "Hello, Kate."

Katie walked over to look at the fish. It lay in a patch of fading sunlight, one eye staring up at her, the red gills sucking and the fins moving slowly. It was a kind of perch which no one had ever seen anywhere but the San Marcos River, speckled black and white with an odd fleshy hump on its back like a bulbous nose. Katie wondered how she appeared to the glassy eye, with her face flushed and leaves sticking to her skirt. "Well good for you," she said to Toby.

Coon Dog wandered off into the bushes.

Toby wrapped his line around the pole and flung the pole and bait pouch to the ground, then dropped from the tree. He landed in a crouch and leaped forward. "I'm going back to help Father cut that cow's cyst," he said, taking up his gear and the fish and heading for the path with the pole bobbing over his shoulder.

William closed his book and started to get up. "I should go too," he said, but Katie sat down beside him and asked what he was reading.

"Poetry," he said.

"By who?"

"Shelley. Percy Shelley. An English poet. I should go help Toby and your father."

Katie noticed the edge of a loose parchment folded in the book, with charcoal lines and scribblings, and asked if it was Toby's drawing. William said it was.

Katie took it and unfolded it and saw it was a drawing of Coon Dog sitting in profile in high grass under a tree. "Toby could be a real artist," she said.

"He has a rare talent," William confirmed. "What interests me is his perceptions, rather than his skill. The distortions in his drawings are not a matter of fault but of perception, like his manner of enlarging objects and altering them strangely. Look here. Look how big Coon is in relation to the tree."

Katie said, "It's because Toby's eyesight is so bad. He wants to see those things clearly, up close. He lives in the moment, you know, and sees everything like you would see it in a certain moment. He drew me, once, but prettier than I am." And she added, "Do you think I'm pretty?"

A leggy brown spider dropped onto the parchment and started crawling across it. William brushed it off, folded the drawing, and put it back inside his book. "I think you're quite beautiful," he said.

For Katie, it came too easily and without emotion. "I think it isn't the sort of beauty that suits you, then," she said.

He looked away from her, out over the water. "You are lovely, Kate," he said gently. "Any man would find you so."

It wasn't what she was seeking. She wanted him to show some feeling for her. To be desirable but not desired negated everything. "Do you have," she hesitated, folding her hands together and glancing down at her bruised thumbnail. "Is there a woman you love in England?"

"No." Clearly, he wanted to close the topic, and chose a most final way to do it. "It isn't for a woman I'll be returning. But I will need to be going soon."

It was the worst thing he could have said, and Katie felt a trembling inside. She plucked a fallen leaf from the ground beside her, and with one finger traced its yellow veins from the center outward. "With Samuel?"

"I don't know."

"You've never told me anything about England, or your family there."

"There's only my father. My mother is dead. I don't remember much about her. And now my sister's dead."

Katie thought suddenly, and with a surge of hope: he is only afraid to love me. His mother died, and then his sister; it isn't any wonder he is afraid to love me. She gave him the benefit of a doubt, which William, had he known her thinking, would have spurned. She felt he needed reassurance and rescue. She didn't stop to wonder if he wanted it.

What he wanted was privacy. But there sat Katie, beginning to shred the yellow leaf and looking at him, wanting more, much more than he was willing to give her. The breeze tossed stray hairs across her face and she brushed them away with her wrist and went on tearing the leaf into bits, her face turned downward, the eyelids lowered in a lovely protest. Her dark hair formed a widow's peak that intrigued him. He could see a hint of her nipples, hard beneath the thin blue-gray blouse. Then her eyes shifted and she looked past him, upstream toward the tangled brush beyond the cypress, and her face took on a curious expression.

William turned to see what she was looking at, and saw nothing but dimming light resting on the riverbank, the tall weeds bending together as air pressed against them and passed through, moving up the slope and into the trees with mournful diligence. There was a fall of leaves, and a frog croaking; a turtle slid from its rock into the slow waters and for a puzzled moment William thought that ponderous creature was the object of Katie's interest. But Katie was getting to her feet and stepping forward, clutching the folds of her skirt and pulling it from the prickly weeds. William stood and followed her and when he reached her she was already bending, and then kneeling over the reeking body of a black man lacerated with fly-blown wounds. Coon Dog was hunched over the body, licking gently at the lacerations.

"It's Josh," Katie said, brushing away the flies and placing two fingers beneath the man's nose to feel for breath. Through the horror of it William saw her hand, a moment ago so childlike in its compulsive destruction of a fallen leaf, as a kind of graceful savior. He knelt beside her, fighting nausea from the stench of seeping wounds alive with gnats and white larvae; Katie made a hopeless gesture and appealed to him with her eyes. "It's Josh," she said again. "The Hanlins' Josh. He's alive. Bull's been at him with his whip."

Katie went for river water and brought it back in her cupped hands, but Josh would not part his lips to take it.

They carried him together. William squatted low and Katie helped him lift the body to his shoulders and drape it like a living cloak. She walked beside, talking in a low, slow voice, "You hold on there, Josh . . ." while William nearly withered with the weight, his legs cramping and his torso bent forward toward the ground.

Hugh was in the barn with Toby when William and Katie finally reached the clearing. Katie bolted forward through the field of high grass in the last evening light with her skirt lifted above her knees, calling out that William was bringing in Josh, the Hanlins' Josh, who had been whipped and was almost dead. "We found him near the water," she said, out of breath. "We gave him water is all. He couldn't drink it. The wounds are full of worms."

William staggered into the house and Rose helped him roll the heavy body off his shoulders onto Toby's bed. Grand stood in the door between the two rooms, watching. Toby and Katie brought rags and more water, and Hugh turned the body over, face down, asking for lard and turpentine. Katie brought it from the corner cupboard.

Toby stared at the body, the stained shirt adhered to gashes where swollen flesh parted into stripes crossing in a pattern like a patchwork quilt. One sock was missing, the other frayed with holes and dangling halfway off, and when Toby tried to help by pulling the sock off, red peppers, dried and crushed, fell out on the floor.

"To keep the dogs from following," Hugh said, looking at the peppers, easing the shirt from the gashes with lard and peeling it away. He studied the rotting cuts, dabbing them with warm water and turpentine. One cheek was pressed into the sheet like fallen fruit, bruised and flattened, and the forehead was swollen as if it had received a blow.

"The Hanlins'll come looking," Toby whispered.

"If the Hanlins come here they'll be told to leave," Hugh said. "This country still has laws."

Josh twitched and snorted once, his lids flickering, and William noted the foul ooze smeared on his own shirt from carrying the body. He watched Katie lighting tapers on the wobbly bedside table and Hugh pulling a hide-bottomed chair to the bed so he could sit and work more closely. It was a picture of humanity in all its impotence, he thought, for surely the Negro would die.

Shoving his hands in his pockets, Toby said softly, "If he dies I know where to bury him. Where he'd fish sometimes. I've seen him there a lot." Then he moved in closer and bent over Josh's face, looking at the protrusion on the forehead. "He looks like that baby with the big head," he whispered, and glanced at his father. "The one you brought to live with us."

A mute, frozen look came over Hugh. "You remember the baby?" he asked.

"I always remember that baby."

"I'm glad you do," Hugh answered him, then Rose said quietly to Hugh and Toby both. "I'm sorry you do. The poor thing is dead, and if you keep her living in your memory, it's like she's haunting us."

William didn't know what baby they were speaking of, but understood the baby had somehow changed their lives. He also had a sudden understanding of the woman, Rose. She believed the phases of the moon had meaning, she could count the stars within the ring around the moon—he had seen her do it—and predict how many days would pass before it rained. And for her, a troubling memory became a haunting.

Hugh went on smearing turpentine into a gash from Josh's shoulder to his buttocks. "I'll try to get him south, out of Texas, or maybe to Cós in Béxar," he said.

"But you can't get into Béxar." Toby said. "Our army's keeping everybody out."

"That isn't our army; it's your brother's army. I'll find a way through."

Grand stood silent in the doorway in her cotton frock. One of the tapers sputtered as the wick curled down on itself. Katie left the room.

"I'll go with you," William said to Hugh, and then regretted saying it.

Josh shivered, and for a moment William almost wished the life would go out of that grotesque black body stretched out on the bed. But Josh was opening his eyes.

"You have other responsibilities," Hugh answered William, and gestured toward the corner of the room where the baby Samuel was sitting quietly, looking at William and sucking on two fingers. Then Hugh's shoulders seemed to settle and his mind seemed also to settle, and he whispered softly to Josh, "Rest your mind. We're taking care of you." Turning to Rose, he asked her to bring the taper closer, and asked Toby to get the tweezers and help him pick the worms out of the wounds. Then he turned again to William. "Go out to the barn and gather up all the cobwebs you can find. We'll have to spread them on his back to hold the cuts together. And where's Katie? Ask her to bring clean water."

But Katie was already bringing in the water.

PASO CABALLO

SOUTH TEXAS, MATAGORDA PENINSULA ON
THE GULF OF MEXICO

The three men camped for the night at the end of the Colorado River, the last fresh water before it turned brackish at the bay. Adelaido Pacheco stripped off his clothes and walked out into it, letting the current wash him. Scholar Tipton crouched on the brushy bank in the evening sunlight and submerged his hairy face. Miles Kenner built the fire. They had made good time so far, covering almost two hundred miles by trace and trail in four days, Scholar and Miles driving an empty wagon pulled by two dray mules and Adelaido riding alongside on Donde.

Adelaido was pleased with their progress, and slept well.

But at daybreak his pleasure fell away completely when Miles Kenner said they would leave Donde and the mules on the bank and go on foot to the beach of Matagorda Peninsula. Miles said it through a mouthful of cold corn mush left over from the night before, and Pacheco felt his blood rise. He sat there on the soggy autumn leaves with his blanket around his shoulders and his eyes still gummy with sleep, and he almost defied the order. Donde was never left without supervision. But he ac-

65

cepted the plan without comment, and harbored his resentment. Miles was the designated leader of this effort: Stephen Austin had blessed him with the title. Austin did it, Adelaido knew, because Miles was Anglo. Adelaido would have been the better choice. The plan to leave Donde and the mules here at the river's mouth and walk so far down Matagorda to Paso Caballo was a bad one; they would have to come back for the animals when the ship came in. True, if they took them to the beach and the ship was late they would suffer for water. But another plan would have been better: the animals and the wagon could have been left at Linn's Landing just across the bay from Paso Caballo, and then the men could have brought a skiff over to Matagorda to wait for the ship. It would have saved time, and Donde would not have been abandoned on a riverbank with two inferior mules. Adelaido knew the area better than Miles did, and knew the investors they were to meet at the pass who were now making their way across the gulf from New Orleans in the schooner *Hannah Elizabeth* bearing illegal arms for the rebel army. Adelaido did not care who was assigned as leader, or even whether the job was done logically, but he cared whether it was done well. He was in this for the profit. He knew Miles to be a capable man, his equal in age and intelligence but certainly not his equal in experience. Miles had never run mule trains of tobacco into Mexico or escaped a Comanche attack or made or lost fortunes. He had lived in Texas less than a decade, and since his arrival with his family at age seventeen, had never been east of the Sabine River, south of the Nueces, or west of San Antonio de Béxar. Granted, Miles Kenner was remarkable with his hands. He had done impressive workmanship for Adelaido, building him a fine raft on the Kenner's property for use in smuggling. They had known each other several years. But as far as Adelaido could discern, Miles had never truly tested his wits or broken his heart or proven himself. He had not yet lived.

Adelaido had done it all. He had lost everyone in his family except his sister, Crucita, to the cholera of 1834, and in his grief had developed a passion for a married woman who did not love him, then for smuggling tobacco, and now for running guns.

And here was Miles Kenner with corn mush in his mouth, stating flatly that they would leave the animals and walk down Matagorda Peninsula to Paso Caballo. "Horse Pass," Miles called it.

Early, the three men set out walking—unhorsed or *sin pies*—without
feet—as Adelaido saw it—to Matagorda Peninsula. They turned south
down the beach. The peninsula was narrow, scarcely a mile across, with
a lagoon on one side and the gulf on the other—a thin wafer of land
that seemed to stretch forever. The men walked, hugging close to the
grassy dunes for protection from the eyes of Karankawas who inhabited
the area—a tribe of notably tall Indians known to cannibalize their enemies in rituals.

Scholar seemed to enjoy the cool, breezy day with the seabirds skim-
ming over the sand on their spindly legs. This change in landscape from
the mountains invigorated him. He remarked how he could see a long
way here without huge snowy bluffs hanging overhead and blocking half
the world.

Like a golden necklace draped out in multiple strands, the curving
line of six-foot dunes formed a gentle cordon between the inland bay
and the gulf shore. Out past the shore the gray-green water glittered in
the morning sun and then the noon sun, and the men placed their hats
to block the glare from their faces: Adelaido with an elegant sombrero,
Miles with a broad-brimmed felt affair, and Scholar with his sweaty red
woolen cap from St. Louis, with a low crown.

Adelaido watched the water beyond where a school of porpoises rose
to the surface, descended and rose again, beyond where the color slid
into a deeper blue, out to the horizon. He was looking for sails, a
schooner from New Orleans carrying loads of powder, lead, rifles, and
two small cannon. The men who had arranged the shipment—an Anglo
merchant and a *Tejano* native of Béxar who had studied in the United
States and shunned Catholicism to become a Protestant—were supposed
to be aboard. Adelaido knew them both. He had supplied the mustang
herd that they drove to New Orleans and sold in exchange for arms and
munitions. He had made profit on the deal. Now he had made a deal
with Austin and hoped to profit a second time by delivering the supplies
to the army, which he saw as grand and fitting irony. A closing of the
circle. He would use the money to make up for losses to Comanches on
the failed tobacco run.

"I have found coins on Matagorda," Adelaido said in his studied
English. He swung his water gourd to his mouth as he walked: it was a
Spanish gourd with two separate round bowls, holding a quart each,

joined by a single neck with a thong around it. "French coins." He shook the water from his mustache. His sombrero was resisting the wind and his black hair blew about his shoulders in glossy waves. "A hundred and fifty years ago La Salle buried a fortune somewhere in the dunes of Matagorda, and someday I will engage an expedition to search for it."

Scholar was impressed. He wanted to know more, and Adelaido satisfied him with a grand tale of La Salle's expedition and a grander tale of his own plans to find the buried treasure. Scholar walked with his buffalo rug and his rifle over his shoulder, stopping periodically to pick up seashells and put them in his pocket. Mid-afternoon he found a sea horse, a delicate, dried, dead, perfect sea horse the size of his little finger. Kneeling on his own shadow, he prodded the sea horse and asked Adelaido what it was.

"It is called a sea horse," Adelaido said.

"It swims?" Scholar asked.

"Supposedly." Adelaido pointed to the wings. "With these. Though no one has ever seen one swimming."

Scholar picked it up and held it in his sandy palm. "It's rare?"

"Of course it is." Adelaido said, setting his water gourd on the sand, retying the silk handerchief around his neck, and straightening the blanket around his shoulders.

Scholar tossed the sea horse aside. Miles was walking on ahead in his red plaid shirt and homespun trousers patched on the seat with buckskin. The breeze lifted the floppy brim of his hat, threatening to snatch it away and carry it off over the dunes, but the hat was shoved down firmly on Miles's head, making the hair stick out like straw beneath it. His saddlebags were over one shoulder, his coat and his rifle over the other. He stopped to put on the coat.

From the beginning, Adelaido had coveted the coat. It was a remarkable creation, made mostly of buckskin, fringed at the bottom and embroidered with patches of fur, each patch the shape of the animal it had belonged to. There was a jackrabbit on the right shoulder and an antelope on the left, a spotted panther on the front pocket and a furry bear on his hind legs sewn in the center, front, so that his two halves joined together perfectly when the coat was buttoned down. The buttons themselves were cut from cow horns. It was a piece of work: Miles considered it a piece of art. He had made it himself, and even now was toting in his saddlebags a swatch of hide he'd sliced from an old alligator he'd shot back on the Colorado. He had told Adelaido he would cut it in the shape of the alligator with its mouth open and sew it on one sleeve.

Adelaido said to Scholar, watching Miles, "He has never been taken by surprise, or he would not walk in that way: in front, and without caution."

"I think he's looking for the treasure."

"I think he is looking for glory," Adelaido answered.

"Well, there ain't a thing wrong with glory."

Adelaido said, "I don't trust it." He had found an audience. "I trust profit. And when there's trouble, I trust God. To find glory a person has to have a cause, or pretend to have a cause, and causes are never pure. They confuse. They burden. I prefer passions to causes."

Snorting out a laugh, Scholar said, "You prefer passions to darn near anything."

"No. Not to horses."

"Well, horses is your passion."

"No, they are my life." It was the truth. The passions came and went and were remembered fondly, but horses were different. He captured them, trained them, bred them, and sold them, but most of all he revered them. Never had he eaten a bite of horseflesh.

"Nope," Scholar said. "They're your livelihood. And it's a mean one. Give me a choice between a leg jaw trap for a day and then quick death, or bein' tied up and led about and rode till you're run-down, I'd take the first choice any day." He shook his head. "I was in that business of mustangin' for a few months on my way out to the Rockies, teamed up with a outfit that was makin' a mint. And I swear, one of ever three horses they got ahold of was dead before it was broken. And that was just the ones they got ahold of, there was plenty more that died before they was captured, havin' their pretty necks snapped nearly off when they was roped or bein' run so many at once into the pens after days of bein' chased that they trampled each other into such a pile of flesh flailin' against the fence that the pickets give way and the horses, them that was still alive and able, just trampled right over the dead ones and kept on goin'. I seen one stallion in a chase so set on keepin' his mares together that he forced 'em to leave their colts behind. He laid into some of them mares with his teeth and his hooves when they tried to wait on their babies, and I seen him kill one slow poke colt that was worn out and fallen in a heap; its mama would not go on without it and that stallion trampled it. You can't tell me it's a business you enjoy, if horses is your life."

Adelaido did not agree, but he had his sordid memories. There was one memory in particular that haunted him. During a chase, he had seen a mare drop her colt while she ran. She had been lagging behind and Adelaido was gaining on her with a rope when suddenly her hole had opened with a sacked fetus, the sack tearing open with a little nose resting on tiny hooves, dangling there from her hole. And then it tumbled out. The cord didn't break at once, so the mare dragged the little lumpy thing a pace or two before it broke off and lay there in a bloody lump, and on she ran with the cord still trailing out of her hole and the mess attached to the end, bouncing over the prairie. It was more horrible than an aborted fetus lying dead on the lush grass in the evening light, for the fetus had not been dead. Nor had it been mature enough to survive, and as the creature tried with an effort that was premature in its own life and primitive in the instinct that inspired it, to nose out of its sack and stand, Adelaido had shown mercy and shot it from his saddle. He knew that a mare's instinct to stay with the herd was greater than her desire for life and sometimes greater than her maternal instinct. But still he blamed her, for leaving her young.

It was easier than blaming himself.

And it was a story he never told.

Scholar said, "But I guess there's more considerate ways of catchin' horses."

"No," Adelaido answered. "The other ways all use betrayal."

Scholar shifted the buffalo rug to the other shoulder. "Horses don't care about things like that," he said. "If they're gonna get caught they'd just as soon do it the easy way instead of gettin' run till they can't go no farther or meet dead-on with a picket fence."

Adelaido maintained that the chase, at least, even in the spring when the prairie grass first sprouted and the horses were slowed by dysentery and newborn foals, did not invlove trickery. "I would rather run a *manada* to exhaustion than lure them with a belled mare they have begun to trust. And I detest the practice of enticing outcast stallions with gentle mares—making the mares into whores." He licked the salt taste from his lips, then said in a bitter voice, "I know a man who will dog a herd until they lose their fear of him and let him associate with them, and eventually they even follow him, and then he tricks them. He walks them into the pens. It disgusts me. The seduction of an entire herd is a sin impervious to a thousand confessions. Such an evil *hombre* is more surely damned than pirates out there in the gulf."

Scholar said, "How far is it to that pass anyway?"

"Too far. We should have crossed the bay on a skiff from Linn's Landing instead of walking all this distance."

"Well why didn't we?"

"Because Kenner's in charge. And he's afraid of water."

"Yeah?"

"I have seen his face when he runs his ferry across the San Marcos River, which is a narrow river without much current. And he's nervous. If the river is up, he's very nervous. And the river is nothing compared to the bay."

"Well, I'll be," Scholar said.

They watched Miles striding through the sunlight in front of them, leaving his boot prints behind, and Adelaido said, "He is in a hurry for his glory."

They walked on together, two philosophers on a cool and sunny beach waiting for the loot to come in, Adelaido searching the horizon for sails, Scholar Tipton searching the sand for bits of awesome color, and both of them peering now and then into the shade between the grassy dunes for signs of old buried treasure. Adelaido lifted his hat and ran his fingers through his glossy hair, then placed his hat back on at a tilt. "Matagorda is haunted by outcasts," he said in a quiet, dreamy voice with the precision of the artisan who considers his second language as important as his first. "In the bay there is a porpoise lacking the fin on his back. He has been there many years. I have never seen the bay without seeing the porpoise. Matagorda is his refuge: I believe he does not ever go out to sea. And also there is a horse, or the ghost of a horse I believe."

But Scholar wasn't listening. He had spotted a bubbled jellyfish the tide had left behind, and loped toward the water to shove it with his moccasin. So for a moment Adelaido was left alone with his story, without an audience to give it meaning. And it needed meaning. Adelaido could give it only drama and pathos.

What he saw in his mind was the killer horse—a pale gray pacer, almost silver like a smooth sea at twilight. He traveled only at a pace, with his quarters level and his neck arched, as if nothing was moving but the legs and the mane catching the wind and the tail streaming behind him like a banner. He was known to pace a mile in two minutes and outdistance running horses without breaking stride; he would swim the Paso Caballo and rise on the other side and pace off down the island without a rest or a falter. In the beginning, the pacer had a *manada* of over a hundred mares. But that was before Adelaido had become so eager to capture him that in the end he killed him. He had tried to run him down, but the pacer was smart and would split off from his mares and they would scatter and he would disappear. It was something Adelaido had never known another stallion to do, to abandon his herd. But the pacer always got them back. That was the mystery: nothing that was done to the pacer ever lasted. Not even death, for he had returned to life or some semblance of life: he had been seen several times since. But now he traveled alone. Once when some friends of Adelaido's were camped near the pass, the stallion paced through their campsite, directly, in the dead of night. They were all asleep but for one keeping watch, and he never saw the ghost coming and could not tell where he disappeared to in the dark, but all were awakened as he passed through.

The pacer had haunted Adelaido in life as his ghost haunted Matagorda now. Others had warned Adelaido that it was useless to want the pacer as he did, for pacers stumble with their riders and are worthless for work. But Adelaido didn't want the horse for a purpose, he just wanted him. He wanted him as he had wanted women. To touch him, that's what he wanted. To have him. He wanted to make the capture himself and would not let anyone help him, any more than he would let another man help him win a woman. But the pacer could smell a man three quarters of a mile away, and outran Adelaido's fastest horses as if he had wings. In desperation Adelaido decided at last to take the chance of creasing him, which meant nicking with a lead ball the nerve at the base of the neck where the silver mane tapered, stunning the horse just long enough to rope him. It was a violation of Adelaido's ethics to risk killing this creature in order to capture him, but the obsession had taken hold. He began waiting at the watering holes for a clear shot, and passed many opportunities for fear of shooting low and killing the stallion.

During the time of the obsession Adelaido was working for a wealthy ranchero named Domingo de la Rosa, who one day sent him to get a load of supplies from John Linn's landing. He was traveling the trace along Perdido Creek in an ox cart, and he left the cart a mile from where the gray pacer usually crossed with his *manada* and went on foot to the place. Fortune was smiling, and the *manada* was there, drinking from the creek in the sandy clearing surrounded by smoke trees. It was spring, and the smoke trees had their purple blooms, and it was evening, almost dark but not yet so, with a breeze blowing Adelaido's scent away from the herd. The pacer was apart from his mares, with his head lowered to drink. He was the color of evening and the smoke trees. He appeared a still and perfect target. If he had not lifted his head in sudden awareness, the ball would have missed him completely, because at the last second Adelaido could not stand to do it: he lifted the barrel and intentionally shot too high. But the pacer was alert and sensed Adelaido just as the ball was launched into the silver evening air, and he raised his neck precisely into it. He fell, and Adelaido thought that he had killed him. Never had Adelaido Pacheco been so wounded with remorse. He fell onto the sand, scratching at it with his hands and retching with sudden nausea, his back arched up like a poisoned dog, then ran through the brush toward the stallion with the mares lighting out in all directions. He was certain that the horse was dead. He flung himself down onto the body and wailed like a mother with a dead child, smoothing his hands over the ribs and belly.

And the horse came to. It was without warning and without a sound —he did not roll or flail his legs, but rose up in an even movement and reared with his ears laid flat against his head and his red mouth open and came down on Adelaido with all the wild strength of a stallion, but without a sound. The impact shattered Adelaido's shoulder, but he was able to pull his pistol from his coat pocket with the other arm, and fire. And even in the failing light he was certain of it: the ball entered the stallion's chest directly in the center where the soft hair fanned outward, making a hole the size of a fist. Adelaido saw the blood spew out, but the animal did not fall. He lifted Adelaido with his teeth and shook his mind into darkness like a dog shakes the life out of a rabbit, and then he reeled away, leaving a trail of blood—or so Adelaido was told later—for five miles to the prairies of Coleto.

The stallion's body was never found, but Adelaido still believed that he could not have lived, that the ball in his chest must have killed him, and it was certainly his ghost that ran off trailing blood.

Scholar Tipton came loping from the waterline and asked how far they had to go before they reached the pass. It was still a long way, and Miles was pushing on ahead, so they quickened their pace. When they arrived at Paso Caballo the sun had set and the gulf air was moist and nippy. There was no sign of the schooner or her crew. They chose a campsite on the beach side of the dunes, and Scholar and Miles hauled dried balls of mustang dung from the pass. Mustangs liked to mark their territory with lofty piles of excrement and had left several down at the pass. The dry manure was good fuel, easy for the men to carry in their blankets. Adelaido declined to help, not wanting to foul his blanket. Miles was angry, and Adelaido said, "Did I not save you both from the Hanlin brothers? The least that you can do for me is build a fire."

They were too weary then to shoot waterfowl and cook it, so they gnawed on strips of jerky and boiled water for coffee. Scholar showed Miles and Adelaido his scars from Bull Hanlin's whip, laced over his hairy back with older scars grown pale beneath the hair, and said his grandfather used to whip him when he was a boy. He also showed them his good luck charm, one of his daughter's baby teeth he carried in a tiny leather pouch around his neck.

After that, the men were quiet, and settled in to wait. Adelaido walked off in the dunes where he knelt and said his rosary. He returned feeling perplexed and anxious, wondering if Donde was all right beside the river.

Night pressed in from the west and the wind came from the sea, rolling over the men and over the dunes and over the inland marshes.

Chapter 8

KATIE

T HE KENNER HOMESTEAD ON THE
SAN MARCOS RIVER

The baby Samuel was a tyrant. Once again he had Katie up, the third time that night. She changed him, gave him a spoon to play with, and put him back into his makeshift crib beside the bed. Just when she was drifting back to sleep, he started fussing and she had to get up again.

She resented the extent to which William had surrendered all responsibility for Samuel, giving it all to her. But she did not want him to take the child away. She had fallen in love with both of them, the man and the baby.

When Samuel's head fell against her shoulder and his mouth parted with his sleeping breath, she laid him in his crib once more and got back in bed with Grand, settling into the hollow that her body made in the cornshuck mattress. Fearing her restlessness would wake Grand, she tried to be still. But she was tense and worried. Miles had been gone several weeks, and in the morning her father would start for San Antonio de Béxar with Josh.

Katie had always worried about disappearances. If the boys or her father were far from home she became certain that some tragedy would

75

pluck them from her life forever. If Toby just went out for kindling she worried that Indians would snatch him away. If she was sick she worried that someone would catch it and die.

Tonight she felt like everyone was leaving.

William would go soon, she could feel it. Lately that worry—that William would take Samuel back to England—had developed a sort of soul. At night Grand would breathe heavily in her sleep, Toby in the other bed would sometimes talk in his dreams, and in the loft above, her father often snored. And Katie lay in her cotton gown listening to the rustle of the corn shucks and growing accustomed to the worry. She even came to rely on it: it was familiar and dependable. It held her at night.

There was no moon yet to slip its light in through the slit between the shutters, so the room was very dark. A wind whistled outside, but the home that Miles had crafted was secure against it. Samuel was finally sleeping quietly in his crib near Katie's side of the bed, which was the side nearest the door to the adjoining room where William slept beside the fire. Sliding out from under the quilt and placing her feet on the cool planking of the floor, Katie looked at the child. His hair was sprouting out in silky patches. She loved him very much. He had begun to call her when he wanted her. He could not say her name but had mastered the last syllable, the one which William always refused to say. He would wail out "EEEEEE," when he wanted her. He could sit up, he could scoot across a room like a caterpillar, except he often trapped himself under the furniture. He had begun to hurl himself from chairs, and had to be tied in with napkins. He ate solid food and slurped milk from a glass if it was held for him. But he almost never slept. He redeemed himself by being exceedingly affectionate, especially to Katie.

She went into the next room to look at William.

He had made his pallet near the hearth, but the fire had burned down, leaving only smoldering coals of mesquite faggots. He was lying on his back under a woolen blanket. When she bent over him and looked at his face, the way he slept reminded her of Samuel, his fist pressed against his cheek as Samuel did when he was sleeping. What would he think of her if he woke and found her leaning over him? It felt like stealing something from him, to be watching him so closely. She could smell smoky mesquite, Samuel's wet and dirty napkins drying on the hearth. She put her nose down close to William and smelled his three-day sweat and oily hair: tomorrow would be bathing day. She did not mind his smell. She could barely see the rise of his pelvis beneath the blanket, and thought about that. It was a word she hated: penis. It seemed a small, insipid word for a thing so intrinsically important and mysterious. She had heard her father say the word once, when she was a child, and to this day the memory embarrassed her. Toby at age two had climbed out of bed one morning, lifted up his nightshirt with both hands, leaned over to look down at his little body and said to his father, "Yook. Yook that." Katie saw him through a doorway, and though she could not see her father she heard his response. "I see it," Hugh had answered mildly. "I see it." "What that?" Toby had demanded, to which his father answered, "It is called a penis." Toby had seemed satisfied to have the answer, and then lost interest and either forgot the word or had the dignity not to mention it again. But Katie, who was nine had not forgotten.

Samuel, from his crib, made a small and sudden panting noise and began crying for her with his extended vowel sounds, like a little bleating goat. She got him from his crib and carried him back in, laying him on the table to change his napkin, which was completely soaked. He grabbed his foot with one hand and a fistful of her hair with the other, and he yanked her hair. "Ow," she said, and tried to pry his fingers loose. But they had taken hold, and he gave another tug. "Ow," she said again, and he widened his eyes and squealed. She was too tired to play with him. He turned petulant and threw his arms open and began to work himself into a temper fit. "Please," she whispered. "Hush, please." But he did not hush. Frustrated, she wrapped him in his blanket, tossed him up against her shoulder, and headed for the door, to take him out, but when she opened it the cold wind gusted up beneath her gown. Samuel liked the wind: he quieted and was attentive to it. He would be warm enough outside, bundled in his blanket, but she would not. So she retreated back inside and shut the door and he resumed his bleating. She let him cry. She wanted to cry herself. She was tired, her father was leaving in the morning, there was a war going on, and life was feeling very tenuous.

William, beneath his blanket on the hearth, rolled onto his side and opened his eyes. When he saw Katie standing near the door with the noisy baby flailing around in her arms, he shut his eyes to pretend he was asleep.

Katie said, *"You* take him out. It's too cold."

William opened his eyes and appeared disoriented. "Out?" he said.

"He wants to go out. I always take him out so he won't wake everyone up. But I can't go out in this. It's too cold."

William groped sleepily for his trousers and maneuvered them on beneath the covers, then got up, his nightshirt hanging past his knees, took the child from Katie, and went outside. Katie stood with her bare feet on the puncheon floor and her arms hanging down, her shoulders a little slumped with fatigue, and waited for him to come back in. She was pent up and felt guilty about sending him out in the cold.

Finally she went out after him. He was pacing, the tail end of his nightshirt flapping in the wind, and Samuel was loving it. Katie said, "I'm sorry. I didn't mean it."

He stopped pacing. "Stop apologizing," he answered, annoyed. "You're *always* apologizing. You have a right to be unhappy with this situation. I've brought this baby to you and expected you to care for him, because I don't know how to care for him myself. It's a lot to ask of a woman I hardly know, but what else was I—"

"A woman you hardly know?" she interrupted in amazement. "You've been living here almost two months, and you hardly know me?"

He tried to explain, but she wasn't listening.

"Who *do* you know?" she asked. "I never heard you talk of friends you've got back home in England. Do you know Toby? Do you care about Toby? Do you care about Samuel, do you know *him?*"

"Kate, that's not the point."

"It is too the point. You don't care about your orphan nephew and you don't care about me and I can't figure—"

"You mean I don't care about you in the way you want."

It was true. But what was wrong with wanting? She was a grown woman, nineteen years old, stuck out here on this farm with nothing, no friends. "I don't know why you call me Kate," she said, "when everyone calls me Katie."

He did not respond to that. "You know I'll be going back to England some day," he said.

So he was leaving her. She wanted to beg something out of him, and felt the tears squeezing from her eyes and a child's voice whining from her throat, "I had just thought, maybe . . ." And then she sobbed aloud, pressing her forehead down into her palm and wiping her eyes with the back of her other hand. She knew William could not console her, because he did not love her and nothing short of that would help at all.

But he was not so destitute of feeling. "Listen," he said gently, and she looked at him. Samuel was grabbing for his chin. "I haven't been fair to you. I've asked a great deal of you, and you've been generous. I'm grateful for that. And I do care about you, more than you know. But I'm not the right man for you. I would never make you happy. It isn't feasible. And it isn't me you want anyway, I just happened to be the one who appeared."

She tried to regain some small degree of poise. "You can't tell me what I want," she answered. "You don't know."

But William had given all that he would give; she could see that. He was obviously cold in the nippy wind, and she was too. She turned suddenly and William followed, and when they were inside he gave her the baby without looking into her face, and went back to his disheveled pallet beside the hearth with the smell of mesquite logs and his nephew's dirty napkins.

Katie held the baby so close he fought against her. She put him in his crib where he settled in and babbled to himself but did not cry. Then she got back into her bed with the corn shuck mattress and the old woman, who pressed her cold feet next to Katie's warmth.

Chapter 9

THE SAINT

RANCHO DE LA ROSA, NINE MILES NORTH
OF GOLIAD ON THE EAST BANK OF THE
SAN ANTONIO RIVER

María de la Cruz Pacheco could not look at the great ranchero without seeing the patron saint carved from cottonwood, which stood on a pedestal in the corner of her home. De la Rosa and the saint had the same features, the same quiet piety and sad eyes. The ranchero's face was darker than the saint's because of his mixed blood, but it was still Spanish, narrow with a high forehead and waves of gray-flecked hair. His tapered beard was also flecked with gray.

De la Rosa's grave demeanor matched the room's austerity. It was a grander room, this *sala* of Domingo de la Rosa, than Crucita had ever seen in a home, though without luxuries. High sandstone walls were plastered so white they seemed almost to glitter in the candelabra's light, and formed a vivid contrast at right angles to the dark oak beams that spanned the ceiling. There were only three adornments: the Virgin Mary in her niche beside the door, a mirror framed in gold leaf on the far wall, and on the long table in the center of the room a small box covered in velvet the color of red wine. The mirror would have been a solitary touch of vanity had it not been placed to reflect perfectly the image of the Virgin.

The furniture—a dozen stiff chairs around the walls, a heavy Mexican trunk beneath the mirror, and a pair of Castilian *vaqueños* on tall legs with many tiny drawers and metal pulls for each, against the opposite wall—all was of dark wood, angular, massive, and without comfort: the formality of a church.

Crucita sat silently with her hands in her lap, breathing the clean, cool smell of sandstone. She had never been inside this house before, though she had been to the ranch while her brother Adelaido was employed by Domingo de la Rosa. She felt as if she had stepped into a tomb. Outside the sun was bright, the vaqueros were working mustangs in the corrals, the milk cows hawed loudly in their shed, and the pounding of the blacksmith's anvil rang through the crisp air from the shop beside the river. There was the noise of an imported population: De la Rosa had called for the citizens of Goliad—all those opposed to the Anglo rebels now in control of the town and its fort, the Presidio La Bahía—to remove to his ranch. They had come, and were camping on the riverbanks.

But here inside the patron's great house, inside the stone walls of three-foot thickness and the weighty paneled doors with iron hinges, where the light and sound were shut out and there were no windows and the fire was not lit, there was a resounding quiet, cold and intimidating.

Two loopholes on one wall—the wall that formed the outside barrier of the ranch compound—admitted each a handful of sunlight but no sound, as there was nothing out in that direction but a thorny rolling landscape of cactus, mesquite brush, and prickly pear with the gentle rustle of animal life and salt air from the gulf. The loopholes were round, large enough to shove a gun barrel through. Only once had the ranch compound suffered an Indian attack. Since then, Domingo de la Rosa kept at all times of day and night six of his twenty vaqueros on horseback patrolling the borders of his vast territory of five leagues. They were not merciful men, and after a few encounters the Indians shied clear of Rancho de la Rosa. Now, safe within the *sala* of his fortress, De la Rosa said in educated Spanish, in his placid voice, "María de la Cruz, did you have trouble getting out of town?"

"No, señor."

He was seated with unyielding posture, the black pupils of his eyes fixed on her, and she felt he knew and despised the tricks she had used to impress him. She had wanted, not to win him with beauty, for he was unattainable—but to astonish him with it. She had worn her silver earrings with turquoise stones that dangled down below her jaw. She had tried in vain to bleach her skin with a paste of powdered eggshells, and at last resorted to powdering herself with common Mexican white lead. It gave her an ethereal, ashen look, and she knew as she sat before this solemn, dark ranchero who was unmarried and not interested in female beauty, that he disliked the affectations.

He dressed plainly and carried his own dark color with elegance. But then, he had the Spanish eyes, and she did not. She was counted in the census as one of the many *colores quebrados,* with Negro blood from two generations past. Her brother Adelaido had golden skin and a hint of the lean Spanish shape to his face, but her own features were Indian. There were those who thought her beautiful, she knew, with her broad-boned face and sloe eyes and hair the color of shiny tar. There were those who admired her slender, perfect shape. There were also those too pure to speak with her. Always, she had considered Domingo de la Rosa among these last, but here she sat, alone with him at his own summons, in a chair by the high table in his *sala* with cold from the flagstones creeping through her best dress and the worn soles of her pigskin shoes.

"I'm told the Anglo rebels question all travelers, that they've declared a formal martial law in Goliad."

"The rebels own the town, if that is what you mean," she said. "But they didn't question me when I left. I took the old road."

"Ah. Yes. Well, I'm grateful you've come. I have some questions, and a favor to ask."

She nodded her assent.

"How many *Tejano* families remain in Goliad?"

"There are eight families, and me."

"Rebel sympathizers?"

"Not all. I am not."

"Good. How many rebels, do you think, in the presidio?"

"Eighty, maybe more than eighty. My home is on the slope between the presidio and the river, and I can see the rebels come and go."

"Do you speak to them?"

"They sometimes speak to me. Some of them bring me their shoes to repair. At times I mend their clothing."

"And they pay you?"

"Yes. They don't pay for the cattle and corn they take from the fields around town, but they pay me for my work. They pay me before I'll do it."

"Ah." He smiled. "Is that why you have stayed in town, instead of moving here? For their pay?"

"Yes. Señor, I noticed you have maguey growing in the field. Could I have enough to make some combs and sandals I can sell? I would pay you when I have the money."

He was quiet, looking at her, and then said, "You may have all of the maguey you can use. There's no need to pay me. Ask for Manuel when you leave, and he'll cut you some. But I need a favor in return. I asked you, before, to send your brother Adelaido to me. He owes me a debt. You have not seen him?"

"No, he hasn't returned."

"Then tell me where to find him."

"Señor, I told you the truth, I don't know where he is."

"I would pay you well to tell me."

"It's not a matter of money," she answered with resentment. She would not allow him to reduce it to money. It concerned something grander than money: it concerned her brother's honor, and her own, for the ranchero was doubting her honesty. "Adelaido always pays his debts," she said. "How much does he owe you?"

"He owes me everything. I taught him to read and to speak English, which is what allows him to conduct his trade."

"Of course I know you taught him; he's very grateful. He feels, I think, more than indebted. He feels devoted."

"No. Adelaido doesn't know the meaning of devotion," De la Rosa said, and stood and went to one of the tall pieces of Castilian furniture with rows of tiny drawers. From one of the drawers he took a glass jar no larger than his thumb, and returned to his chair, where he uncorked the jar and poured five glistening pellets into his hand. "Do you know what these are?" he asked.

The pellets in his calloused palm were identical to those she had dissolved in water and fed to her dying parents like liquid hope. "Calomel," she said. "To cure the cholera."

"No," he answered. "They are powdered oyster shells pressed into a bullet mold."

"But they're the same as what you gave to Adelaido for our family."

"Exactly, the same."

She did not understand.

"I bought them from a man named Louie Métis," he said, "who told me they were calomel to cure cholera. I believed him. I should have known they were a sham. But I was deceived and gave them to your brother like a gift of life, and he was deceived, and took them home to you, and you were deceived. Why do you think we were so easily deceived, Crucita? It's because we would rather have false hope, than no hope." He closed his hand around the pellets.

Crucita wanted, with a perverse instinct, to slip to her knees before him, as if he could give her peace. She craved peace. She craved it like a newborn needs the breast, the mouth beginning to suck even before it finds the nipple, and having no idea of the feel or taste of it.

There had been nothing sustaining to take hold of. When they were all dead, but Adelaido, Crucita had walked round and round inside the stinking, dark jacal of sticks and mud, taking hold of everything: her father's shoemaking tools, the comb with her mother's hair still in it, the patched blanket that had covered her infant brother, still smeared with his black vomit. She held in her hand the little clay doll Adelaido had brought to their sister from Colima. She lifted the hand mirror he had brought their mother from New Orleans, and studied her own weary, sloe-eyed face, and she set it down again and opened and closed her empty hands repeatedly. There was no one and nothing sustaining to hold on to. Adelaido had gone to the Anglo settlements in search of different medicine, and the other citizens of Goliad, those who had not yet abandoned the stricken town, were closed inside their own dim jacales and suffering their own losses. They were afraid to turn to one another, for no one knew who was carrying death with him in his clothes or in his breath. They were not even sure humans carried the disease; maybe the wind carried it, or the rain, or God inflicted it by choice or at random, or it lived in the pork or the fruit they ate or the water they drank or in food gone rancid or maybe in the dirt they walked on.

At first they had simply prohibited the sale of fruit and pork. But the disease kept on creeping through the streets of Goliad. So they banned public gatherings and kept to their homes, but the disease persisted until it seemed almost that the streets themselves were to blame, and the bewildered people of Goliad carried buckets of water from the river through the summer heat to pour onto the streets. And the disease flourished. So the citizens began to fear the water itself. They filtered cistern water through charred bread before they drank.

And the dying drank incessantly. Their intestines ran with water, and cramped, their bowels purged yellow liquid and blood, and they puked black bile and sweated and parted their scabbed lips to beg for more water.

Crucita had tried the mildest remedies first, her father at her side helping her with his shoemaker's hands and tormenting her with his limpid, grieving eyes. She stroked their bodies with wet rags and smeared poultices of mustard and strong vinegar on their tender abdomens. She fed them garlic and administered enemas of warm water and goat's milk, pressing the liquid into their bowels from the dried bladder of a cow through a hollow reed. Light hurt their eyes, even mild taper light, and Crucita tried to nurse them in the dark. She cut their arms and let their blood in the dark, and knelt beside her father before the patron saint of John the Shepherd, carved from cottonwood, his graceless arm crooked around his long cruciform staff, the lamb beside him with the same thin, devout face and eyes rimmed in black charcoal. For hours she knelt before the pedestal in the corner, staring through the darkness into the saint's black-rimmed eyes and begging him for mercy.

And so, when Domingo de la Rosa gave Adelaido pellets of calomel from the half-breed Métis, which were sure to cure the family, Crucita and her father believed their prayers were answered by the patron saint. They melted the medicine in filtered water and spooned large doses into the withered, birdlike mouths. And they stood quietly, waiting for the miracle which never came. The mouths still called for water; the tongues turned white. The breath came hard and hurried. The skin seemed to slip away from the faces.

She resorted to her own strength. She tried desperate methods, pressing hot bricks to their feet and scalding their abdomens with boiling water. Her father refused to help her now. He stayed on his knees before the patron saint with his narrow buttocks resting on his calves, the soles of his sandals turned up, with holes worn through: he who was a shoemaker. Crucita in her despair accused him bitterly of cowardice.

And she dreamed, each night, of death.

Her mother and sister were the first to die; they had suffered a full week. Then her sister's husband. The infant died within four hours of his first puking. Adelaido reeled from the doorway into the harsh sun and started to the Anglo settlements in search of laudanum. He had not been gone a day when the girl of six showed signs, and Crucita herself began to drip with sweat. She burned her own feet against the bricks and scalded her belly and inflicted the same loving torture onto the delirious child, Crucita with the tears streaming down her face and her father still kneeling in the corner before the patron saint.

One by one, they sucked the air and slid away from her. With each death, her father staggered from his knees, carried the fetid body out to his cart of saplings bound with hide, hitched the mule, and wound his way to the new cemetery, designated for victims of the cholera, down-wind from town. And then he returned and sank again to his knees before the saint and stared at him imploringly. Which was why, when the disease finally took him, Crucita's father died with his eyes open.

Crucita hammered down the coffin while Padre Valdez dug the grave, and together they buried her father. Then Crucita returned home, still hot with fever but having nothing now to do with her hands, and walked around picking up objects and putting them down again. At last she lifted the patron saint with both hands and without so much as a glance into his eyes she turned his face into the corner and set him down and stood there dripping sweat and staring at the carved robes of his back—the blue-green paint of copper ore now faded with the years —her bottom lip jutted out to show her scorn and her dismay, a hot, blue evening creeping in the doorway.

Fifteen months had gone since then, and she had not so much as touched his cruciform staff or wiped the dust away. She had not turned him around to look at his perfidious face, and she felt now, looking at Domingo de la Rosa seated in his high-backed chair before her, that she was seeing him again with all her awe and anger and all the bitter disap-pointment.

De la Rosa sat as placidly as stone, with the Virgin Mary in her niche behind him. Looking at the fist that held the pellets, Crucita said, "Why have you kept them?"

"To remember," he answered.

"Does Adelaido know we were tricked?" she asked.

"Yes."

"Does he blame you?"

"No. Do you?"

"I blame God," she said. "What do you want from my brother?"

"His duty as a citizen," De la Rosa answered, dropping the pellets back into the jar, one at a time, from his cupped hand. He shoved the cork into the neck, returned the jar to its drawer and closed it away, then returned to his chair.

"Do you mean the war? Adelaido is not motivated by patriotism."

"Then maybe he'll be motivated by loyalty, to me." He tapped one finger on his chest. "Or by his debt to me, for giving him language." Turning a small and knowing smile, he added, "Or maybe he'll be motivated by the risk, and the money; I could pay him for his work."

She had to smile at that. Domingo de la Rosa knew her brother well. But then he placed an elbow on the table and said with a look so suddenly serious that the expression itself, aside from the words, frightened her and her smile fell away, "Or perhaps he will be motivated by wisdom: it would be wise for him to help me. I like your brother, but he has disappointed me. He has few convictions that I know of. His career, aside from the time spent working for me, has been one of continual evasion of the law. Last spring he managed to avoid paying taxes on a number of cattle he sold in Béxar: it seems he didn't register the sale. Nor did he register the purchase of those cattle in the first place, and I have heard he bought them at prices well below the market value. He also ignores the regulations for exporting mustangs to the United States of the North, and avoids paying duty, driving his herds there along smugglers' routes." His voice was slow and very quiet; he tilted his head slightly. "As if that is not insulting enough to his country, he returns from Louisiana with contraband tobacco. Maybe he doesn't realize that Mexico is dependent on her customhouse money. Or maybe he doesn't care. He could be prosecuted, you know, if I chose to report him."

Crucita knew the truth of what he said. "And why would I tell you where he is, if you have so much power to hurt him?"

"Because if you do, and if he helps me, I will not hurt him."

"You want him, for what? To fight against his American friends?"

He gave another slow blink. "No, I want him to spy on them. I should say, I need him to. They know him, they accept him, he speaks their language better than they speak it themselves. And he knows the back trails and the roads from Louisiana to Tamaulipas, both the inland and the coastal routes. There's no one who can serve the Mexican cause better than your brother."

"And if the cause is lost? If the Anglo-Americans win, then Adelaido would have proved himself foolish to spy for you."

"I assure you, if the Anglo-Americans win they will not restore the Mexican laws or the Mexican constitution. They will make their own laws, or they'll join the United States of the North. And their laws will not favor the *Tejanos*." His anger could be seen in his expression. "Your brother, whatever his affinities, is still *Tejano*. He cannot bleach his skin. And I think it would benefit his soul, as well as his cherished future, to remember that. I despise Santa Anna, more than the Americans despise him. But Santa Anna, for now, is Mexico, and Mexico is my country. If the Anglos defeat Santa Anna they will withdraw Texas from Mexico, and you and I will find ourselves living in our own homes in a foreign land."

She was afraid of him, but drawn to his certainty. She wanted to believe in him. De la Rosa must have seen it in her face, for his expression softened and he said, "María de la Cruz Pacheco. Crucita. May I offer you a cigarillo?" She was hesitant to answer, and he smiled and added, "It's legal tobacco, that I've grown myself. If that concerns you."

His smile pleased her and she answered, "No, it doesn't concern me. I don't think about the Mexican treasury, I don't even know where it is. For certain, I've never seen a Spanish dollar of it, and none of it is spent on me."

From the velvet box in the center of the table he took two delicate cigarillos of tobacco wrapped in slivers of corn shucks. "And does that mean you want the cigarillo, or not?"

"Yes. Thank you, I want it."

He stood up and went to the candles in the tall iron candelabrum to light the cigarillos. She watched his movements and her wariness returned: he was too graceful and remote in his ascetic way. And he was beautiful, with his calloused hands. His stature was spare and strong. She saw the way the leather of his trousers fit, and when he lifted one cigarillo at a time to his mouth and sucked fire into it from the candle flame, she saw, beneath his arms, rings of sweat like crescent moons, on the linen shirt. The candles near his face gleamed as fierce and yellow as the candles she had burned around the patron saint of John the Shepherd while she prayed to him.

"I won't be tricked," she said. "If I decide to tell you where he is, it will be because you convince me. Not because you trick me."

He returned with his own cigarillo in his mouth, and gave the other one to her. She took a long and steady draw, savoring the flavor.

"And what am I to convince you of?" he asked. "That it's necessary for Adelaido to help me, for his own good? Or that it's right."

"Convince me of the first," she said, breathing out the smoke.

Domingo de la Rosa first smiled, then shook his head, and his expression fell away completely and he held the cigarillo idle in his fingers, staring at the glowing tip. "My father died when I was ten years old," he said. "He died wounded, in pain. I was with him. I asked him where he hurt the most, so I could try to ease the pain, and he didn't look at me, he just lay flat on the grass in the sunlight with his eyes shut and blood all over his face. And he said it was his soul that hurt the most."

The ranchero drew hard on his cigarillo.

For a while neither of them said anything.

Then, wanting to break his spell, Crucita said impatiently, "And why was your father's soul in pain?"

"He was Spanish. A Spaniard's soul is always hurting."

She hated him then. She hated his Spaniard's face and the taper of his beard and his green eyes, and she leaned and pushed the burning tip of her cigarillo into the cold stone floor then sat up again and placed the dead stub on the table. "I have Indian blood," she said, "And so does my brother. We have Negro blood. Do you see the color here?" She licked a finger and wiped it across her cheekbone, smearing the powder away. "Our Spanish blood is not as pure as yours, and we don't have the luxury of tormenting our souls."

"I think you do," he answered, crushing the burning tip of his cigarillo with his fingers. "The last time I saw your brother he rode up to that door over there, shouting for help. He'd survived a Comanche attack and left three comrades dead. I sent my best vaqueros, and they found the Indians, and Métis was with them. Your brother knew about the pellets of false calomel and how Métis had deceived us. But he let him go. Why? Because he prefers to torment himself rather than revenge himself. After revenge, there is no more torment. There is nothing. And yes, I see the color of your skin. I saw it through the lead. I have Indian blood, too. Forgive me, Crucita, but I'm offended that you seem to think your brother's safety is more important than his soul, and more important than his country. I hoped you'd see the importance of what I'm asking him to do."

"No," she said angrily, "you hoped to bribe me."

They stared at one another for a moment. Then Crucita crossed herself and said in a softer voice, "Forgive me, señor. But Adelaido is everything I have. You ask too much. Please don't demand it."

He leaned toward her and gently took one of her hands. "Crucita, listen to me. If these rebels were simply fighting Santa Anna, I would join them. But they are not fighting him. They're fighting Mexico. Do you know, Santa Anna has been to Texas before. Twelve years ago he came with the royalist army." She shook her head slightly: she had not known that Santa Anna had fought with the king's men.

De la Rosa stroked her hand as he would pet a dog's soft ear, seeming not to notice what he did. "My father and I fought with the rebels for independence from Spain," he said. "He died bearing arms against Santa Anna. I was compelled to take my mother and brother to New Orleans to elude persecution by the royalists. We lived ten years in exile there." She had already known that: the life of Domingo de la Rosa was a topic of great interest in the poor society of Goliad. He must have known she knew. But in humility or pretense of humility he spoke as if the details of his life were as unfamiliar to her as hers would be to him. "A decade is enough time to learn the Anglo temperament," he said. "Americans are lazy and decadent, and the United States of the North is vomiting the worst of them into Texas. For land, they swear their allegiance to our government and the Catholic Church, with no intention of keeping faith with either. Their race breeds vice and corruption: they have no discipline and no loyalties. Their influence has demoralized our citizens and corrupted us so that even native Coahuiltejanos in our state congress have voted to grant religious tolerance and soften the laws against slavery, and to allow English as a legal language of the state." He paused then, his face close to hers, the sweet smell of apple pomade that oiled her shiny hair drifting in the cold around them. Outside, a burro was braying repeatedly from near the corrals, the compulsive, monotonous noise barely penetrating the stone walls and sounding to Crucita like the labored breathing of an old, sleeping man. De la Rosa said, still in his soft voice, "These Mexican and Anglo statesmen are depraved speculators who are selling our lands—that we have nurtured for three generations and defended with our blood—to the Irish and Anglo-Americans. They would have Texas get rich on slave labor and cotton. They are as fat as cows, with greed. They want nothing from Mexico, but land." There were creases around his eyes, she noted. He was not old, but there were deep creases. His eyes were compelling. His voice, more than his words, moved her, and he gestured toward the Castilian *vaqueño* with its dark wood and spindly legs and the many drawers like secrets, one holding the little corked jar and the pellets made of oyster shells. "Deceit," he said. "And illusion."

He was winning her, and went on stroking her hand. She could not share his belief and certainty—she felt incapable of that—but she wanted just to touch it. With a small parting of her lips she let him know.

He smiled, his expression sad. "It is very difficult, Crucita. Texas is besieged by the flood of Anglo heretics from the north, and from the south by successive petty *caudillos,* vermin like Santa Anna who have nothing but each other to check their power. Mexico has become a whore, giving herself to depraved men. She has lost connection with God. *Tejanos* have cried like children for our wayward mother, Mexico, and she has paid no attention. She has allowed us to fall into spiritual chaos. We are neglected, and angry. But that does not mean we no longer need our mother. And it does not mean our mother no longer needs us. We have a duty." He pressed her hand and let it go, and added, "Where do you think the cholera came from, Crucita? It was from the United States of the North. It came on three ships from New Orleans."

He ended it there, and stood and went to the wide door made of oak panels, beside the Virgin Mary, and slung it open to the sunlight, the incessant braying of the mule, the hawing of milk cows, and the musical pounding of the blacksmith's anvil from the shop near the river. Vaqueros working mustangs were shouting to each other, and one laughed loudly with the wild abandon of a boy. De la Rosa said, "Manuel will drive you home. If you're questioned by the Anglos, tell them you were called to the bedside of your mother, who lives on a ranch outside of town, and who is dying."

Crucita sat looking at the man standing in his doorway with a placid expression and one hand on the latch, the noon sunlight behind him not daring to cross the threshold. Then she also stood and went to the door and said to him before stepping out into the light, "Adelaido will decide for himself. If I see him I'll let him know you asked for him." And she added, glancing down at the flagstones, the toes of her pigskin shoes under the frayed hem of her best dress, and then up at his face with the creases around his Spanish eyes, "I could be of better use to you than Adelaido could. The rebels would never suspect me, a woman, a seamstress who mends shoes. But I don't want Adelaido to know it, if I help you. And you have to promise me you won't tell anyone those things about him. If he decides to work for you, it has to be because he chooses to, not because you've threatened him. I would be paying his debt, for all you've done for him."

De la Rosa looked at her, his hand still on the latch. Then he answered, "You may pay his debt to me," and in a graceful gesture lifted up one finger beside his Spanish face and touched the air. "But only Adelaido can pay his debt to Mexico, and God."

L A Z A R U S

PASO CABALLO, MATAGORDA PENINSULA ON
THE GULF OF MEXICO

Adelaido Pacheco had refused to smear himself with rancid fish oil. He
would rather wear his thick hide gloves, wrap his silk handkerchief
around his neck, and suffer the mosquitoes to bite his face than to stink
up his skin with repellent fish oil.

Miles and Scholar did not share his conviction. They had lavished
the oil on their skin, and stank to such a degree that they could not sit
near each other. "Just keep the hell away," Scholar said to Miles, and he
was not joking.

But Miles had no intention of going near the trapper, for as well as
rancid fish oil Scholar had smeared himself from head to foot with a
paste of seawater and horse manure that clung to him in crusty globs.
He had spared only his beard. Though Adelaido was not close enough to
be sure, he believed Scholar's concoction was working: he had ceased to
slap and scratch. The fish oil alone was evidently not so effective, for
Miles was still plagued. But, Miles had said, a man should have limits,
and Adelaido agreed.

It was the only thing they agreed on. Scarcely one civil word had

93

passed between the two since their arrival at Paso Caballo—or Horse Pass, as Miles still persisted in calling it—two days before. It had come down to this: seabirds, the tides coming and going, two men who could hardly stand the sight of one another and a third who was covered in horse manure.

The ship had not come in.

Over the inland marshes the sun was beginning another descent, pressing shadows from the dunes out toward the sea and casting yellow waxy evening light along the waterline. Miles was sitting on the inland side of the dunes, out of the wind, in the last warmth of the sun, while Scholar kept the fire stoked against the wet gulf air and watched the horizon for sails. Their camp fire burned in the dip between two dunes. Adelaido, seeking respite from mosquitoes that drifted from the salt marshes when the breeze lulled, was situated in the wind on the shore side of a dune, and the fire's warmth could not reach him. When he craned his neck around he could see past the fire and past Scholar covered in crusty mustang dung, to where Miles's legs stretched out from the inland side of the neighboring dune. He could also see, in the blue-stem grasses, the knob of Miles's elbow in the plaid shirt, cocked over his face to shield his eyes from the light. Adelaido swatted mosquitoes with his hide gloves and smeared the dead insects on the sand. He was chilled in the dune's shade and drew his thighs up against his belly, pulling the striped blanket he was lying on halfway over his body. His concern for Donde was the worst of his agitation: the horse had plenty of water and pasturage, but three days was a long time to leave him staked on a secluded riverbank.

"Well," Scholar said, "life has got options."

The statement had no context, and neither Miles nor Adelaido responded to it. The trapper was evidently talking to himself. He was picking at his bad tooth, and the smoke blew in his eyes when the wind wavered, but he was apparently too comfortable to move back from the fire, nestled close to it as he was on his mangy buffalo rug between two dunes. He poked at the fire and tossed on a few dried balls of mustang dung to keep it burning, then contorted himself and scratched his back: the scars from his whipping were bothersome. But it seemed that his soul was at peace. "Life has got options," he repeated thoughtfully.

Adelaido said, "In the morning I am going back for my horse."

Miles answered, without turning to look at him, "If anyone goes, it should be Scholar."

Scholar turned his face toward Miles, the bits of crusty horse dung sloughing from his neck. "Not me," he said. "I waited this long."

"Adelaido needs to be here to deal with Kerr and Carbajal when the ship comes."

"If it comes," Scholar retorted. "But I ain't goin'."

"Look here," Miles said, suddenly swiveling his head around to look at his companions, "Austin designated me to be the leader. You don't like it, but it's a fact. So as long as we're in this, I'm gonna make the decisions."

Picking at his tooth, Scholar replied, "I bet it's hard to act so high and mighty when you stink like a dead mullet."

Adelaido chuckled. Miles said, "Go to hell, Tipton," and for a moment nobody said anything, until Adelaido made a suggestion. "Why don't *you* go back to check on my horse and your mules, Kenner. You're the one who said to leave them. There's no reason you have to be here when the ship comes in."

"Yeah, I'm the one who said to leave 'em," Miles retorted. "They're better off where they are. And I don't trust you to handle it alone here when the ship comes. You can forget that idea."

"Then I'll be going back for Donde at daybreak," Adelaido said. He took a small flask of *aguardiente* from the satchel he had been using as a pillow, flipped out the cork, and took a drink. Then he leaned back against the dune, watching as the shadows stretched from the dunes over the beach and the water glided in and out, leaving gentle curving lines of foam.

To the right was Paso Caballo, a treacherous entrance between Matagorda Peninsula and Matagorda Island, less than two miles wide, with shoals and risky currents. A continuous line of breakers washed over the bar. There were oyster reefs hidden underneath the murky green, though the only suggestion of their presence was a ragged turbulence on the water's surface. An abandoned pilothouse of stick timber, no larger than a toilet shack and with the roof blown off, leaned precariously in the salt grass near the edge of the peninsula.

Adelaido closed his eyes, and felt the sea air. The brandy settled into his mind. He listened to the waves. If there had been no interruption he might have gone on listening with his eyes closed until nightfall, but after a while Scholar slipped his low voice out against the sea air with such soft awe that his words were burdened with the weight of dignity. He said, "My God. It's Lazarus arisen from the dead." Adelaido opened his eyes, glancing first toward the pass, then to the north, where a horseman was approaching in open view, his long shadow reaching into the water and leaping with the little waves like a frolicking dog. Scholar had the field glasses pressed to his eyes and watched as the rider, as yet unaware of his observers, reined his sluggish mount, removed his hat, and wiped a hand across his forehead. As his hand passed his brow, he caught sight of the men in the dunes. Scholar crawled forward and gave the field glasses to Adelaido.

What Adelaido saw magnified through the lenses was a horror: a slack-jowled, grimacing face set against the yellow evening sunlight, staring at him with vacant eyes, above which a blackened strip of flesh covered what once had been a scalp. Stiff red hair grew on either side of the head and down onto the face, but on top there was nothing. It did not look simply as if the man was bald; it looked as if part of him had rotted away. The rider pulled the reins around and advanced slowly toward the dunes without so much as a nod or a lift of his hand.

"Psssst, Miles . . . Miles . . ." Scholar whispered. "Look here."

Miles roused from sleep and crawled to his comrades, the loose dune sand giving way beneath his elbows and knees. Adelaido already had one pistol ready; he handed the field glasses to Miles, who after a glance lowered them and said, "I know him. It's Callum Mackay. I know him well." And to Scholar he added, "He's the baby's father."

Adelaido knew the name: Callum Mackay. He had first heard it spoken on a field of dead Comanches, under a new moon, while a vaquero with a hare lip held forth a string of dried scalps and a ranger looked at one and said, "This one is not Mexican, it is Callum Mackay's, I would bet my life on it." And the half-breed Louie Métis had sat with his wrists tied behind him and his ankles bound, and had denied any knowledge of the withered scalp or its origin. Since that night, Pacheco had heard the story of the Scotsman, Callum Mackay, who had been scalped, left for dead, and then returned to life to save his infant son. He liked the tale. It was mythical and heroic. But seeing Mackay this moment on a decrepit horse with the lazy tide rolling in behind, the legend lost its bold and vivid color and its terror. There was only the monotonous shore with the tiny sandpipers racing on their stick legs, the cry overhead of a single gull circling, and the disfigured man replacing his slouch hat as he rode toward the dunes.

Callum Mackay did not offer his hand as he dismounted and the men stepped out to greet him at the edge of the dunes with the sun hanging low in the sky behind them. While Miles made introductions Mackay just looked at each in turn, first Miles with his greasy plaid flannel shirt and his blond hair dipped over one eyebrow, then Scholar Tipton encased in fringed hide with sweat stains in every crevice, a red woolen hat cocked back on his curly head and dry horse dung dabbed over his clothes. Last he looked at Adelaido, with his hide gloves and taut, golden skin, his green silk handkerchief around his neck and a striped blanket over his shoulders.

There was an uneasy silence, then Scholar said to the Scotsman, "I held your baby." Mackay did not answer. Scholar did not seem to expect an answer; he balanced on one leg to unlace and remove a moccasin and empty it of sand. "Fed him. In Gonzales." Brushing his knobby foot free of grit, wobbling for balance, he tugged his moccasin back on. When Callum still did not answer him, he added, "It was me who found him; your brother-in-law was lookin' for him."

Callum said in a dry brogue, "I've got no brother-in-law in Texas."

Scholar nodded. "William Mullins. A Englishman. He was lookin' for you and your baby."

Callum did not change expression, but turned his glassy eyes to Miles.

"He claims he's your brother-in-law," Miles said. "He showed up early in October on his way out to your place. We told him what happened and he went and got Samuel in Gonzales. That's the last place I saw him. He had Samuel, and was looking for you."

Adelaido could not read Mackay's thoughts, and did not try, for a man who looked as dead as Callum Mackay was unlikely to have thoughts of a human nature. Mackay just stood holding the limp reins of his mount.

They offered him salted pork and he squatted down beside the fire and stared out at the sea and ate the pork. A flock of brown pelicans walked clumsily, single file, down the shore toward the point and then lifted on unwieldy wings and headed south over the pass.

Rocking on his heels with his hands clasped behind his back, Scholar was compelled to fill the silence. "We're waitin' on a shipment from New Orleans," he said. "For the army at Béxar. There's supposed to be two cannons on board."

Mackay bit off another chunk of stringy pork. His shoulders were knotty beneath the frayed homespun shirt, and the freckled skin of his knee, with red hair, was visible through a tear in his trousers.

"It's a God darn shame," Scholar said. "We got a whole army just sittin' there outside Béxar, day after day, gettin' unruly and runnin' out of ever'thing and waitin' for somethin'. Them Mexican soldiers in there it seems don't care to fight."

A few moments passed, filled with Scholar's observations on the orange sun hanging over the inland marshes, the waterfowl, and the war. Mackay's sorrel horse stood with his head low and his hide quivering beneath droves of mosquitoes. Mackay himself let the mosquitoes light on him without seeming to notice them. Uneasy, Adelaido boiled a pot of water and stirred in some powder made from peyote cactus buttons. He always carried the powder, as well a sack of the buttons—hard, gray nubbins like ticks full of blood—in his beaded leather wallet, and used it to make a bitter Indian concoction known to inspire visions. Miles was the only one to accept a cupful, but he did not like the taste and poured it down a crab hole.

For Adelaido, the drug was a solace. He felt it lifting his mind, and stared boldly at Callum Mackay, who sat facing the water with a tense and stoic posture, his elbows on his knees and his slack face staring into the salty wind.

Before dark there was a flight of pink birds across a drifting sky. Miles shot and roasted two prairie chickens and the men ate them with corn mush and corn liquor, all except Scholar, who refused the liquor and drank water boiled with bitters instead. Scholar talked while he ate, sucking on his teeth between sentences and scratching away the last remnants of the noisome mustang dung. Dark set in and Miles built the fire to a blaze. The flames and the smoke leaned inland like the grasses

swept over by the trade winds. Only the yucca plants, the Spanish Dag-
gers, did not yield to the wind.

No glint of a ship's lantern appeared from the dark water, only the
wet wind shoving in twisted strands of clouds like winding sheets. The
sky seemed to roll over the men, and the yellow rim of the moon rising
over the gulf shone only for seconds at a time, spreading its eerie light
onto the troubled water and then blinking dim beneath tenuous, rushing clouds.

Scholar shook his buffalo rug free of sand and spread it against the
dune, near Miles, snuggling his back and bottom into it, his rifle
propped beside him. He and Miles sat leaning up against the dune,
facing the sea with their eyes closed. The wind was nippy, but its rising
strength kept the mosquitoes off and blew away the oily odor of mullet
grease. Eventually Miles slumped down on the flat sand and buried his
face in the crook of his arm. Scholar began to snore, and then his head
dropped forward and the snoring was choked off.

Lying on his back beside the fire, Adelaido drank more peyote tea
and felt the drug take over. He watched the sheets of clouds stretching
out above him and imagined he was under water looking toward the
surface. The thought of being out there in the deep, in the dark, dis-
turbed and intrigued him, and he rose to the surface and imagined he
was on the water, on a Mexican man-of-war sailing the dark, lapping
waters in search of schooners bearing arms from New Orleans to the
rebel army. Rustling night sounds of the land, of the varmints and the
marshy creatures, were smothered by the sound of the rising wind and
waves. Adelaido rolled over toward the fire, lifting on his elbow, and
plucked a piece of wire grass and held it in the heat above the flames to
watch it curl to ashes. Then with a glance through the flames at the
disfigured Scotsman, he said quietly, "Sometimes I have dreams about
the sea."

"Mae mother died in the sea," Callum Mackay replied, staring
toward the water. He had not removed his hat, even in the dark, and the
wind lifted the floppy rim. He said, "A man there is, known by the name
of Louie Métis. He were with the Indians which killed mae family. It
were said that ye be acquainted. I ask ye now to help me find him."

From far over the dunes a coyote eased his high-pitched howl into

the night and was answered with the lower howl of the wind rising with
the moon over the water. Mackay's horse pawed in the sand. "Louie
Métis," Adelaido said, staring at the fire and licking the salt from his
lips. "Yes, I know him." He slid three strands of wire grass into the
flames and added in his soft, meticulous voice with the precision of the
artisan, "I despise Louie Métis."

"Aye. So it were told to me."

"Who, who told you?" Adelaido asked him.

"I didna care to ask his name. A ranger, he said he was. Came to
Gonzales to tell me of the massacre of Comanches, the Comanches who
had killed mae family. He told me of the half-breed named Métis, who
claimed he were a captive taken on the week before, down below the Rio
Grande. Aye, it is a name I recognized: Métis. It is a name I heard the
night . . ." He stopped there, still staring at the sea, and added, "He
were not a captive. No. He were with the Comanches in the sommer.
And you let him go."

There was a sand crab probing with his tiny claws from his tunnel
near Adelaido's elbow, and not wanting to look at Callum Mackay, Adelaido watched the crab, then shoved sand into the hole and watched the
creature toss it out. At last he sat up, facing the fire, cross-legged with
his elbows resting on his knees, pulled a clump of grass up with sand
clinging to the roots and placed it on a lick of flame where it curled and
sparkled. The wind was colder and more urgent: it stung his face with
loose sand. "I don't know where to find Métis," he said.

Mackay turned his face to look at him across the tufts of firelight
blown all in one direction, and the glow lit his misshapen features and
seemed to pull them forward toward the fire, the sagging cheeks like pale
and yeasty dough, the hat rim blown back and a glint catching the eyes,
like a spark of life. Behind him, stringy clouds were flung across the
moon, and he said as if offering his chosen words to the wind, "For the
love o' God. This. The ranger gave me this."

And Adelaido saw that the man was holding forward, toward the
firelight, his flayed scalp tied onto a rosary, and he heard him say again,
"For the love o' God."

Something passed between them then. It was not fully understood,
but it was commitment. It was stated with a single nod, and another in

return, and not a word. Adelaido fixed his eyes on the awful remnant; he smelled the salty wind and felt the prickle of the sand blown hard against his skin. Then he turned away, brushed the sand from his mustache, twisted his blanket around himself, and plunged willfully into a restless sleep.

It was a blue norther pushing in, and sometime in the night Adelaido was aware that Scholar braved the flying sand and stoked the fire and lay down close beside it. Miles also moved closer and curled himself into a lump beside its meager warmth, which was all but blown away. There was no reason for them to stay awake watching for the schooner: Callum Mackay was awake and sitting as he had been all evening, now with the salt dusting his skin, his eyes squinting against the blowing sand.

In his sleep, before daylight, Adelaido felt something move. It was more a sensation than a dream, something dark and omnipotent turning inside him like a tide rolling in. He felt a warmth against his face and relaxed into it, but after a moment the warmth began to penetrate his groggy mind and feel insistent. He opened his eyes and lay staring up into huge, yellow horse eyes with the pupils dilated, soft and whiskered nostrils pressed close to his face and flaring rhythmically with each warm breath. He did not move at all.

Either it was a dream or a hallucination or a gray horse standing over him and breathing on his face. The creature pulled its head back as if lifting it a great distance, and stamped one hoof into the sand. Its silver mane hung down like silky tree moss and the ears were cocked forward over the wide breadth of forehead and the golden eyes. In the cleft of the chest Adelaido thought he saw a scar with skin splayed outward where the pistol ball had entered, but then perceived it was a shadow cast from the smoldering fire. His pulse was hard and quick, he raised slowly onto his elbows. Then a cold gust lifted a corner of Adelaido's blanket tucked around his neck, and the horse snorted and wheeled instantly into a pacing stride, gliding to the water and then turning down the waterline toward the pass and pacing down the shore. He tossed his head once with his red mouth flung open to the blown sea spume, as if calling to a *manada* of mares that was not there.

But nothing could be heard above the wind.

The fire had all but burned out, and Adelaido struggled to escape the vision. Miles and Scholar were asleep, Miles with his blanket over his head and Scholar with his face tucked into the buffalo rug.

Mackay was not asleep. He rose with the wind whipping at him, tugging at his hat, his long face invisible under the tattered rim, and with a soft gesture he lifted the palms of his hands toward Adelaido as if in supplication.

By now the stallion had already reached the pass and plunged into the waters.

Chapter 11

G R A S S

General Cós and an army of a thousand Mexicans were closeted inside
San Antonio de Béxar, and the rebel plan was to starve them out. Hugh
Kenner did not believe these unruly rebels were capable of that. They
had burned the pasturelands for miles around and were keeping scouts
on the roads to watch for any reinforcements that might try to steal their
way into the city, but it was obvious they were running out of patience.
And he could see, making his way through the camp in search of Miles,
that they were suffering from deprivations. Winter had crept in, and the
men were not clothed for winter. There was a shortage of blankets;
groups of men were bunched together under flimsy cotton quilts. An
emaciated horse was being fed corn off a saddle blanket, apparently to
prevent any waste of the precious kernels. And the only food that Hugh
observed on his walk through camp was beef roasting over camp fires.
There was no bread.

Under a blue sky the cold November wind was playing havoc with
the canvas tents; it lay low the golden grasses on the edges of the campsite and tangled the dry cornstalks, picked clean, in the fields that

103

stretched along the river tree line for a mile between the camp and town. It agitated the pecan trees near the water and roused the flocks of blackbirds seeking food in the grasses.

Chaos and clutter had descended into these hills north of San Antonio de Béxar. Offal from butchered cattle lay in piles. Hundreds of buzzards littered the morning sky and trash littered the camp. Hugh guessed there must be four hundred volunteer soldiers here, and their discontent was obvious. This was conventional warfare, and the warriors clearly did not like it. There were disgruntled farmers, who needed to go home and plow. There were volunteers from the United States, mere boys, who had come in regiments and uniforms to fight and not yet been granted permission—they had found a cause and a common language and had talked themselves into a premature frenetic state, and now had nothing to do with their enthusiasm.

They were shelling the stone fortress called the Alamo. Hugh had witnessed the scene from the hill before riding down into it: the rebel camp nestled against the river, the cornfield with a small redoubt dug in the center and two tawdry cannon set on the mounded soil, blasting away at the Alamo and the city with the river winding through. The Mexicans kept up a steady shower of retaliatory balls, grapeshot, and canister from eight or nine artillery pieces mounted on the Alamo walls, and the ground around the little rebel battery was pecked and dusty. Now and then a daredevil from one side or the other ran out through the cornstalks to retrieve one of the enemies' spent cannon balls for use in his own artillery. It was a deadly, ridiculous game. Hugh imagined Miles running that gauntlet for a four-pound ball of iron.

Miles would be here somewhere. Several times Hugh mistakenly thought he saw him. He asked a sullen group of men around a fire where headquarters was located, then picked his way in that direction through the disarray.

It was in a sugar mill, a small, round stone building resembling the turret of a castle, with a flat roof and shuttered windows—a rather affected structure. Behind the mill the man-made water tributary from the river had been shut off, and the water standing in it was shallow and stagnant.

Hugh went around to the front, where a sign above the door said "Zambrano's Sugar Mill." A few men seated on the ground were engaged in a serious card game, and a guard at the door with a fox-skin hat warned Hugh, "If you're here wantin' furlough, you gotta come back tomorrow, there's no more furloughs today."

"I was looking for General Austin."

"He's gone."

"Gone where?"

The man shrugged. "He got tired of us."

One of the cardplayers lifted his face and added, "We got tired of him."

"Then, is anyone in?" Hugh asked the guard.

"Yep. Go on in if it ain't furlough you want."

So Hugh knocked, and a voice within called "Open!"

It was dark inside, and smelled of cold limestone. In the center of the room was the mill apparatus, shut down. Two men were seated over a game of cards at a small, low table between the shuttered window and the door; one of them put his cards down and stood up, extending his hand and introducing himself as James Fannin. He was young and his face was pleasant though his head seemed a little small for his height and his features were small, the eyes very close together.

His companion was older and rougher-looking; he had his brogan shoes propped on the table, his legs crossed one over the other and the cards up against his chest. "Bowie," he said, with a nod, by way of introducing himself. "Jim."

It was arrogant, but it was enough. Hugh knew of James Bowie and his brothers: they had a lethal, criminal past and their exploits were famous. They had made their early fortune in the African slave trade and in land fraud. It was said they'd sold bogus titles to half the land in Arkansas and ended up with a lawsuit against them in the U.S. Supreme Court. But by then James Bowie was living in Texas, Mexico, speaking Spanish, married to the vice-governor's daughter, and borrowing money from his in-laws to finance speculations in Texas lands and a search for buried Spanish treasures.

Hugh took off his hat, introduced himself, and asked who was in charge.

Bowie set his cards face down on the table, yawned and stretched his arms, twining the fingers together. "Well, that's one hell of a question," he said, and Hugh noticed a nasty cold sore on his lower lip. A wad of

tobacco was stuffed inside the lip. "Seems to be the most primary question asked around Texas these days. If you mean who's in charge of this
camp here, it depends who you ask. Ask James Fannin there, he'll tell
you he's in charge. Ask the boys out there, and they'll say it's Ed
Burleson. Ask me, I'll tell you nobody. Nobody's got the first idea how
to run this goddamn war."

Hugh lifted the collar of his jacket against the damp cold and inquired where he could find Ed Burleson. Bowie said Burleson was making his rounds.

"Your interest, sir?" Fannin asked.

"I'm looking for my son, Miles Kenner."

"The proper procedure would be for you to place a notice on the
board outside," Fannin said, but Bowie was getting to his feet with his
wide and weathered face split open in a grin and his hand stretched out
to Hugh. "Miles Kenner is your son? Well, goddamn. Welcome. Sit."

While Hugh sat down in one chair and Fannin in another, Bowie
shouted through the doorway, the crystal daylight catching his blue eyes,
"Barnes, go get Miles Kenner. You know who he is; he brought that
powder in yesterday from Horse Pass." Then he shut the door, pulled a
third chair close to the table, and sat.

"Horse Pass, at Matagorda?" Hugh asked, fingering his hat in his lap.
A thread of light from between the closed shutters lay across the center
of the table like a statement of division between him and James Bowie,
and around them the room was dim.

"Paso Caballo," Bowie answered. "Yep. We sent him down with a
couple of men to meet a shipload of supplies. She was late coming, then
was run aground by a Mexican man-of-war right there at the pass, right
in front of their eyes, and her crew dumped most of the guns and goods
overboard before the Mexicans boarded and carried off prisoners. Three
cannon, dumped in the gulf. But Miles and his men were smart. They
waited till dark, when the powder kegs bobbed ashore, then fetched their
wagon, and carted 'em back here." Bowie reached for a tin cup on the
table and spat a wad of tobacco juice into it. "Six kegs of double Dupont, real fine stuff compared to that charcoal the Mexicans have got."

Fannin said, "So you just arrived?"

"Yes."

"Where from?"

"A little north of Gonzales." He added, "Not to join you, just to see my son."

"What's the mood in the countryside?" Fannin questioned.

"Business as usual. Most people still seem to be carrying on."

"So, what do you think of our little operation here?"

"I wonder if it's working."

"It's working. We hear that horses in Béxar are so short of provender they're chewing on the soldiers' uniforms. The Mexicans are short of everything, but water and time."

Bowie added, "And we're short of everything but water. It's a goddamn farce, in fact. Mr. Fannin here can afford to be complimentary about our little siege, 'cause he's got himself a honorable discharge and is leaving *mañana*." He took up the cup again and spat. "It's gettin' a little chilly and he don't like it much."

"Where did Colonel Austin go?" Hugh asked him.

"Stephen got full of bright ideas we didn't like much," Bowie answered. "He had a mind to waltz our men on in and take Béxar. Just, take it. Only problem was, some of our men weren't real enthusiasts about the idea of doin' it with them two dinky cannon we got. Said they'd like to have some real artillery, if you can imagine that. And the government of course ain't got any real artillery to send us, only what's been dumped in the sea at Horse Pass and one little six- or eight-pounder on a ship that was run aground out on Bird Island somewhere. So Stephen has hauled his bright ideas off to the U.S. to try to get us some money so we can buy us some real guns, and meanwhile Mr. Fannin here needs to go look in on his family. Mr. Fannin liked volunteer armies quite a lot, before he saw one. Now he is longin' for regulars. Of course there seems to be a dearth of regulars in Texas. Sam Houston is our only regular. He's major general of the regulars, in fact, elected by our brilliant little impromptu government sittin' over on the Brazos. Yep, Sam's commander in chief of the regular Texas army. But"—he shrugged his shoulders—"he can't find it. Now, me, I figure I reckon our boys out there can fight as well as any regulars. But then I've seen them do it on occasion and Mr. Fannin ain't often witnessed men in battle."

"And Colonel Bowie has never witnessed trained regulars," was Fannin's retort, with his tenuous smile.

"Mr. Fannin went to West Point," Bowie said amiably. "For a while."

There was no real animosity between them, Hugh observed. Bowie cleared his throat and spat in his cup. Outside, the cardplayers were having an argument.

Fannin remarked, "We would offer you coffee, but it's rationed, and since you aren't joining us officially . . ." He shrugged. He was a stickler for the rules.

Bowie added, "We would offer you a drink, but Mr. Austin ordered all our whiskey en route turned back." Then his tone became acerbic and he turned his face to Hugh with a brooding expression. "Our boys need action. If they can't have action, they need whiskey. If they can't have whiskey, they'll leave. Many of them have."

With his finger Hugh traced the line of sunlight across the table, between the cards.

"They have action," Fannin said placidly. "They're shelling the Alamo. Bill Travis's men have had plenty of action taking horses from the ranches."

"Mere recreation," Bowie said, still squinting at Hugh.

Fannin spoke to Hugh, and for the first time his remark was pointed. "That recreation is going to put an end to our beef supply; the Mexican ranchers don't feel so generous with their cattle when we're stealing their horses. Last week, Bowie and his friend Placido Benavides strung up an old *Tejano* and took his entire herd."

Bowie was suddenly friendly again. "We cut him down," he said, and smiled, favoring his puffy lower lip, which was burdened with the cold sore and tobacco. "Three times up, and down." He gestured with his thumb, the soiled, blunt nail jabbing at the air. "He lived. The third time up, he admitted he'd stolen those horses in the first place, so we relieved him of them, justly, and let him go. War has got its moments of virtue."

Hugh looked at Bowie's face with its deep lines and capricious expressions, the oily hair smeared over a heavy brow and furrows between the eyes, the chin receding slightly. There was something there to be despised and feared, and something to be wondered at. There was charm, wicked, mutable charm. There was the tone of evil, but not the look of it, and the wide mouth with chapped and blistered lips quirked up another smile.

"And its moments of folly, I suppose," Hugh said.

"Some folly, to be sure. But a hell of a cause, don't you think?"

"Not really, no."

Leaning back in his spindly chair, Bowie recrossed his legs, slid one brogan shoe off onto the low table, and scratched at the pads of his feet. "In case it slipped your notice, Mr. Kenner, we've got a invading Mexican army of about a thousand soldiers penned up in town less than a mile from here, with reinforcements on the way. Now what do you think we should do about that?" The tone was cordial but calculated.

Hugh said, "Ah. So Mexico is invading itself."

Bowie grinned and shook his head. "Seems like they're confused, I guess. Ain't it like the Mexicans to get confused."

"Well, somebody's confused," Hugh answered, and was quiet, listening to the players bickering outside. "I think Mexico's been fairly generous. I myself have enjoyed the freedom of conducting my affairs exactly as I please."

"In a foreign language," Fannin injected. "You have by law been forced to conduct your legal affairs in Spanish, and turn papist too."

"This is Mexico, Mr. Fannin, where Spanish isn't foreign anymore," Hugh said. "I've learned enough Spanish to get by with, it doesn't require much. It seems to me like you're trying to steal Texas, and I'm just trying to live here."

Bowie grunted amiably. Setting his shoe on the floor, he shoved his foot into it, spat into his cup, and said as if it were the last word, "But we came here under a federal constitution, and Santie Anna's done some pretty serious violence to that."

Hugh could see that Bowie didn't even believe his own rhetoric, and didn't care about it, and he answered him, "We came here under laws prohibiting slavery, and have ignored them altogether." It was widely known to what extent Bowie had ignored the slave laws: years ago he and his famous brothers had made an industry of ignoring the laws when the pirate Jean Lafitte delivered boatloads of Africans to Galveston and the Bowies escorted them in chains through the woodlands to Louisiana.

"Laws ought to be subject to change," Bowie said, unbothered. "But the constitution shouldn't. That's the point."

Hugh decided not to answer. He knew the point had nothing to do with the constitution, it had to do with land. Bowie owned title to hundreds of thousands of acres in Texas. His land was worth hardly a Spanish real on the Mexican market, but in the United States the fever was hot and property was selling for over a dollar an acre. Bowie was like all the other Anglo and *Tejano* land speculators in Texas: it wasn't the Mexican constitution they fought for, but independence that would likely lead to annexation to the United States, where slavery was legal and land was money. Bowie had a fortune to be made in this fight. Texas as a cotton kingdom offered endless opportunities for such an entrepreneur.

A silence settled in. Hugh picked the loose threads from a tear in one knee of his trousers, felt the rheumatism in his hands, and was rubbing his swollen knuckles when there was a knock at the door.

"Open!" Bowie called, and Miles was standing there.

He looked different. He was not wearing a hat. His hair was longer. He had not shaved in several days, and was wearing his jacket of animal skins. He registered Hugh's presence without betraying any emotion at all.

Hugh stood up and told Miles he'd like a private word. He suffered the notion that Miles might not grant it. Miles looked to Bowie, and Hugh had a reluctant, buried feeling that Bowie had stolen the father role. But Bowie's face was an implacable facade, and Hugh was grateful: Bowie did not command his men in family matters.

So Miles made his own judgment. "All right," he said.

Hugh followed his son outside. The men playing cards stopped to joke with Miles and compliment him on his job down at the pass. There was a low stone wall extending from the mill along the man-made waterway to the river, and Miles and Hugh walked down to where it met the river with the mist blowing under the trees, and sat side by side on the cold stones of the wall, though not close to one another. Hugh leaned forward with his hands clasped between his knees and watched the water sliding through the wooded banks like a snake that parts the grasses as it goes. "I'm not here to ask you to come home," he said.

"All right."

"You know what I think of this endeavor."

"Yeah, I do," Miles said, and the two of them were quiet for a while, the wind pulling at their clothes and sweeping the mist off the water. A heavy limb hung just above them, almost barren of its leaves, creaking in the wind and passing its shadow over their faces. Hugh shoved his hat more firmly on his head; Miles let the wind blow in his hair. They could hear, in the distance, the boom of cannon hurling metal through the blue sky over dry stalks of corn. And then Miles added, "I don't care what you think of it."

"I know. Where's your horse?"

"Sold him."

"Oh," Hugh said, then added, "I need your help."

"With what?"

"Josh Hanlin. Bull whipped him pretty severely and he ran away. He's mostly healed now. I left him in the hills north of here. I'd thought to get him in to Cós, but I can see that's not the thing to do. Josh never wanted to try that anyway: from the beginning he's just wanted to go south. But the roads aren't safe."

Miles considered for a moment. A pecan nut fell onto the wall between them, and before it rolled off Miles captured it and began tossing it aimlessly from one hand to the other. Hugh couldn't see his face, with the long hair blowing forward around it. "You on foot?" Miles asked.

"I bought a mule. We left Bay Mare at home."

"A good mule?"

"Apparently not so good," Hugh answered.

Miles said, "It's unlikely, any way you do it. We've got rumors of a Meskin mule train bringin' supplies and silver coin for the troops in Béxar, and we've got scouts out on every road almost to the Rio Grande. And there's a unofficial report that a Meskin detachment is on its way too." He glanced at Hugh. "Course you'd be better off if the Meskins caught you with Josh than if our boys did." He let that sit a moment, then added, "You've got him this far, why can't he go on by hisself? If he's found, with you, you'll both be turned in. They don't like men amblin' down toward Mexico with niggers. They'd take you for a spy." He kept on flipping his pecan from hand to hand. His timing was precise. "I saw the Englishman in Gonzales."

"I know. He's been living with us since then."

"Yeah? I thought he was looking for Mackay."

"He didn't find him."

"Well then he didn't look here."

"He's here?"

"I brought him here."

"From where?"

"Horse Pass. He was down there looking for a *Tejano* named Ade-laido Pacheco, who was with me. He'd heard Pacheco could help him find the half-breed." Miles tossed the nut high, caught it, and then held it.

"Did you tell him about William, and that he has the baby?"

"Yep."

"Do you think he intends coming back for the baby?"

"I think he intends killing the half-breed." Miles looked at his father then. The blond stubble on his face was still boyishly soft, the eyelashes very pale. He squinted slightly in the sun; a leaf was tangled in his hair. He said, "Believe me, the baby's better off without him; he's scary as hell to look at," then resumed his rhythmic flipping of the nut. "Hanlin brothers are here too," he added. "They know Bowie. They used to do the slave trade with him."

"Nice company you're keeping," Hugh said.

Miles shrugged. "Long as they're here, they ain't looking for Josh."

"Yeah." The cold was seeping deep into Hugh's joints, aggravating the rheumatism in his knuckles and his knees. He rubbed his chapped hands together to warm them, for he'd given his gloves to Josh. He could think of nothing else to say to Miles; he had not received the help he needed and saw he was not likely to. Miles had his own ventures.

Finally Miles said, "How's Mother?"

"She's fine."

"Tell her I would of helped with Josh if I could of."

Hugh was silent.

"How's Katie and Toby?"

"Katie's got her hands full with the baby. Toby's fine."

"What about the Englishman, on the farm? He work?"

"Yes, he works. He told us how you helped him in Gonzales."

"Yeah."

"How long do you think you'll be here?"

"Till the Meskins go home."

"And if they don't?"

"We'll rout 'em out. And if Santa Anna's on his way with a army, we'll have to whip him. If he ain't, yet, then some of the boys have got a plan to take the war down south instead of just waiting for it. Down to Matamoros. We could take that port, and be in a pretty fair position then. There's plenty of Meskins who hate Santa Anna and would help us out. They're scared now, that's all, but if we showed 'em, they'd catch on."

The naiveté offended Hugh. "You really think they'd take your side?"

"Seguín has. Navarro from Béxar. De Zavala. A bunch of 'em."

"Seguín has a cattle market in Louisiana," Hugh said. "De Zavala speculates in land. But the Mexicans in Matamoros don't have any reason to need your help. They won't trust you. And if they did decide to resist Santa Anna, why would they need you?"

Miles gripped the pecan in his fist. "They sure weren't so effective without us in Zacatecas," he said. "Santa Anna slaughtered 'em." Then he threw the pecan nut on the ground with a hard, defiant gesture and stood up to go. He shoved his hands deep into his pockets. The linen trousers he was wearing had been Hugh's, and they fit him perfectly, worn and ragged with the wind whipping them against his body in small rippling waves. His hair was tossed into his face; he seemed a dervish of motion with even the fur patches on his jacket—rabbit fur, bear fur— ruffled by the wind. The jacket was a testament to simple vanity, and Hugh had never liked it. It was not just youth that wore the jacket, it was Miles, and he would not outgrow it.

Hugh was still sitting on the wall rubbing his knobby hands when a distant shout came to him on the wind—"Reinforcements and a mule train coming northward on the Old Presidio Road five miles out! . . ."

When Hugh reached headquarters the men were already crowding around, and within a half-hour Bowie and the spy called Deaf Smith were leading one hundred mounted volunteers south on a trace toward the Presidio Road. Miles was with them, and Hugh watched him go. The men left behind were without horses, but they abandoned camp against orders and trailed out on foot in disarray: there was talk of silver, a "treasure train" of one hundred pack animals toting bags of silver.

Wind tumbled clothing and bits of garbage across the ground and whirled leaves and dirt into abandoned fires. One flimsy strip of gray cloth, carelessly anchored to make an improvised shelter, broke from its moorings and sailed through the air toward the river, where it lodged in the tree limbs flapping as if with some wild anger. Everything was in motion. It seemed nothing was so fixed that the wind could not carry it away. Even the men who had remained in camp scuttled about like blown and tattered objects, finally congregating outside the mill as if tossed up against the stones.

A slab of neglected meat was drying over the coals of a fire, but anxiety suppressed Hugh's appetite, and he could not eat. He thought he might see Callum in the camp, but did not want to, and did not look. He wanted to follow the army south and retrieve his son, but knew the impossibility.

He waited quietly on the edge of camp under a mesquite motte where the tall grass did not grow. He was facing south with a low grassy rise before him. Less than a mile away, though he could not see it, was the town of Béxar, a besieged city of mud and stone with a church spire under a sunny sky full of buzzards, and the river crawling through. Over to his left was a cornfield picked clean. As a small child he had been lost once in a cornfield, the stalks looming up so high around him that he could not see his way out, and he had charged through the stalks in a panic, going no direction in particular and always turning back, hearing the rustle of the hot dry leaves, tears marking paths on his dusty cheeks. He had been too shy and proud to call for help, and had looked to the sky—the only direction he could see—for guidance. But drifting clouds had further disoriented him, and it was only when his hysteria wore down and he stopped crying and became very still in his fear and re- signed to his defeat, that he perceived the order to the cornfield. There were rows to follow. They were haphazard rows, but with care and calm they could be distinguished, and he had found his way out by them.

Now he waited, looking at the timberline of the river and the golden grasses and the dry stalks of the field. From one of the mesquite branches someone had strung a wind chime made of rusty forks and spoons tied together with string. It was wild and tangled in the wind and the sound reminded him of the little girl baby he had brought into his home for care, those many years ago in Tennessee. The "big-headed" baby, Toby had called her, not knowing the word: hydrocephalic. Her name was Julie. She had loved the chimes. She had sat on a pallet in the Kenners' kitchen with her large, bald head scarred and blistered from the treatment of her doctors, and listened intently to Rose's chimes outside the window, and screamed hysterically if anyone came near her, fearing they would torture her poor head. Toby, five or six years old, had wept pitiably when she died, stroking her disfigured head and begging them to let the water out of it before they put her in the coffin. This was, in simple terms, the thing the doctors had attempted while she lived, with their bleeding and blistering, cupping her behind the ears, painting ether on her head to blister out the water, putting leaches to her temples and exciting hemorrhages at her nose. Other doctors, not Hugh Kenner. He had taken her away from all the treatment to let her die in peace in his own home. And because of that, he'd lost his reputation as a doctor, which was just as well for he no longer cared to call himself a doctor. It was not himself that he had grown to doubt, but his profession.

Soon the sound of distant gunfire carried from the south, lasting only briefly. A silence followed, with the wind chimes, then scattered fire, three separate volleys and the booming of a cannon, possibly two cannon. It must be Mexican artillery from Béxar, for the Texans had not taken any cannon. He listened, spellbound, picturing Miles in the heart of the battle. When his concentration finally gave way he realized he was cold and his joints had gone stiff and the chimes had persisted with their joyful melody. There were men dying less than two miles distant.

He did not have any medical supplies with him, but at headquarters persuaded an old man to give him some. Less than a hundred men had remained in camp. They were gathered around the mill, wild with talk. The old man guarding the medical chest made Hugh swear on a Bible that he was a doctor, before allowing him to take supplies. It was an uncomfortable gesture, since Hugh did not believe in himself as a physician. But neither did he believe in God, so he stood before the crumpled old man with the Bible in the dim light inside the sugar mill, with a single taper burning on the low table where he had sat with Jim Bowie and James Fannin, and casually placed his hand on the book and swore he was a doctor. He received scissors and salve and a bundle of cloth rags. Filling his water gourd in the river, he started southwest on the trace the men had taken, following the noise of intermittent gunfire.

Bright yellow, the sun floated on the horizon. Buzzards circled silently above the battlefield, which was a prairie between two dry creekbeds. The Mexican dead and wounded were still on the ground amid cactus and thorny mesquite.

Texans were celebrating their victory, though there had been no silver. The convoy was not a treasure train after all. It was not coming from deep in Mexico bearing the payroll for Cós's army. It was a foraging party from within Béxar which had gone several miles out to cut fodder for the starving horses, and was taking it back in when Bowie and his men attacked. The rebels had killed over fifty Mexicans, only to capture forty-three mules laden with bags of grass.

No rebels had been killed in the skirmish. When Cós had sent reinforcements out from town, even the canister and grapeshot from the cannon had inflicted only minor injuries, and the Texans were pleased with that. It was a testament to their bravado. But there was no silver. Bag after bag they ripped open with their Bowie knives and bare hands, and found only dry grass that glistened in the sunlight and blew off with the wind. The wounded Mexicans called for water and begged the Texans not to kill them, but the Texans had no interest in killing prisoners. They had no interest in prisoners at all, and released the few they had taken. The wounded who lay on the ground calling to them in a language they could not understand, embarrassed and unsettled them. They gave them water and left them there.

Hugh found Miles and asked him to help with the wounded. There were some delirious with pain, who would not live. Hugh and Miles came across one man with a bullet in his skull, who had fallen into a bed of cactus beside a dead mule. The mule was gut shot, his belly splayed open like the sacks of grass cinched to his sides, his entrails spilling out and mixing in a sticky wad with the golden fodder. The man, small and ugly with a pitted face and blood from his wound matting his black hair, was alive; he slit open his eyes. When Hugh cradled his head to give him water, he began to speak in Spanish. Hugh could understand only snatches of his words, and told Miles to get someone to translate, and Miles returned with the *Tejano* he had mentioned earlier, Adelaido Pacheco. Adelaido knelt and listened to the wounded man, then said to Hugh, "He wants you to cover him with a blanket and leave him here. He says if he lives, his comrades will come back for him. He asks not to be shot. He's afraid he will be shot." Then Adelaido removed the striped blanket from around his own shoulders and placed it over the wounded man.

Miles was standing up beside them. Hugh looked at the boots and the hem of the trousers that had once been his own, with the knee cocked out, then began pulling cactus thorns from the Mexican's neck. Adelaido helped him. The Mexican was now unconscious. "Will you help us with this?" Hugh asked Miles, not looking up at him.

"Yeah," Miles answered, but didn't kneel readily to help.

From the center of the clearing, behind Miles, came a slow warmth that grew into a blaze, and cheering from the rebel army lifted with the smoke. They were burning the grass, emptying the bags onto the flames, tossing armloads up to the last of the sunlight. Hugh looked up to see his son standing with his rifle against a torrent of light, and felt an overwhelming sadness. He knew Miles had no qualms about the workings of the day and did not see the price. What Miles saw was a victory; what Hugh saw was a bright field littered with mangled men and bags of yellow grass.

Jim Bowie rode up on his lathered horse and leaned forward against the saddle horn.

"Well, Mr. Kenner," Bowie said, "this should answer your question. The siege is obviously working."

Looking up at him, Hugh gestured toward the mound of fodder with the dead mule's entrails winding out onto it as if arranged there. "So," he said quietly, "your silver."

"Ah," Bowie answered, his voice both soft and hard, his arm reaching toward the edge of the clearing, the dry creek, and the golden land beyond. "It's better than silver, Mr. Kenner. It's gold, don't you see? Pure, bright, shiny gold."

Against his wrist Hugh felt the warm breath of the wounded Mexican, and went on picking out the thorns.

Chapter 12

A   CHOICE

T WENTY MILES NORTHWEST OF
RANCHO DE LA ROSA

Hugh Kenner's voice came so suddenly in the night from over the mule's shaggy neck that Joshua had the eerie impression it was the animal who had spoken. "I'm thinking you should chose a different name from Josh, for safety's sake," Hugh said. "And a surname with it."

Josh, they called him. He did not like it. But no one had ever asked what he preferred. His name was Joshua. He didn't know his age or date of birth or who his father was, but he knew his name was Joshua. His mother had been sold away when he was four or five years old, and he could not remember having ever seen her in the daylight. He had a vague memory of her body lying near him in the dark, with wide ribs and no flesh, sprawled on the corn shucks like a carcass.

And she had called him Joshua.

Now he was to choose a second name to end it off. He was to pluck it from the air.

The four men were traveling slowly in the night, Callum Mackay and the *Tejano*—Adelaido, he was called—both on horseback, Joshua and

118

Hugh Kenner leading the pack mule. The moon rose over them, rocking amid the clouds.

They weren't following the road. Maybe there was no road to follow. The territory was unfamiliar to Joshua, the trees were sparse and hostile, sprouting from the ground in thorny clumps. If there were nightbirds in these trees, they were strangely quiet. The mule's plodding seemed too loud.

Joshua distrusted the *Tejano*, Adelaido, who could be leading them anywhere. The hills were now mere swells of cold earth and the scorched prairie lands were washed in moonlight. There was nothing here to rely on. Adelaido had promised to lead them to a ranch where Joshua would be safe. Why would the *Tejano*, who was dressed so well and appeared so self-important, help a runaway? There was no profit in it, and the *Tejano* did not appear to be a serious man, motivated by a cause. He seemed like an adventurer. Maybe the *Tejano* was trying to trick him. He was gentle with the horse he rode, but gentility could be deceptive. The Hanlins always spoke with mock civility, even while they whipped him.

Joshua was not suspicious of the other stranger, Callum Mackay, who appeared too far removed from the world to bother about turning in a runaway. Joshua knew the man's despondent manner: nothing within sight on the open land mattered to this man. His body rocked in the creaking saddle with the horse's tired gait and the sway of the moon. He showed no concern of any kind. It was clear he had given himself to the *Tejano*'s lead, and was sunk inside himself. He was like the old slave at the river crossing when the whites feared alligators and sent him into the waters to test for them. The whites sat mounted on their fine horses in the spotty sunlight and spoke of alligators supposed to hide out in the waters beneath the swampy crossing, and they sent the old man in. If he did not go, they warned, they would shoot him. He went in, his gnarled feet sinking in the muddy banks and trudging out into the current. When he was up to his neck they called him back. But he did not come back. He kept on moving toward the bright center of the river until his head was almost under water, and then he gave a little flurry of movement and went under, and was not seen again.

And the white men never knew if there were alligators.

Mackay moved in the same manner as the old man: there was resignation in his movement, but nothing else. No fear.

Joshua was alive with fear. He was on the edge. He had made his bid for freedom but had not achieved it yet; he stood in the midst of it and saw only a moonlit prairie, scorched where the grass had grown and spread across with brushy shadows. A fluid pain ran upward from his swollen feet to the lacerations on his back where the scabs had not yet sloughed away. The only sensation of peace in his body was the warmth of his hands: he was wearing Hugh Kenner's gloves. He had taken the gloves when they were offered, having learned to take what was given. He did not know if he was meant to keep them or only wear them for a time, and hoped he wouldn't be asked to give them up.

No one spoke much, for Mackay's despondency imposed a silence on the group. Adelaido was in the lead with the moon shining on the folds of his white linen shirt and glistening along the dark stripe down his horse's rump. The horse had a silver streak in his black tail, like quicksilver in the light. Joshua could feel the moonlight on his own shoulders, a deceptive light which made things seem other than they were. The moon played tricks. It betrayed runaway slaves. It appeared like the devil's smile or the devil's face and lit the cotton fields so the slaves would have to work even after the sun had gone. The sun had no face; if you tried to look at the sun it would shun you. But the moon enticed your eyes to stare and stare, as if it were a human face. A white face. Joshua always felt the moon's presence. Now its light surrounded him like cold air and exposed him to the prairie; if there were enemies in the brush or the scrubby mottes of timber they could see him under the moon. Whites, Comanches, Mexicans, wolves—they used the moon to their advantage. But a nigger-man was better in the dark.

He took refuge in his name-searching.

Joshua Hall, he could be. Joshua Tyler. Joshua Wallace. He could be Joshua Morris. With his eyes open to the sky and a fear that any moment some creature would step from the shadows and deprive him of all hope, he went through a litany of familiar names. Within an hour of the mule's loud clomping in the still night and the pain swimming upward from the soles of his blistered feet, Joshua had made an obsession of the name-searching. He should find the perfect name. He would recognize it when he thought of it: his mind would belch it forth and he would know at once it was to be his name. But the names collected troubling memories of people he had known: the names took on white faces and spoke and punished him and sold his child away. They took on black faces with brands burned into them. He tried to make the names just names, to split them off from faces, but then they sounded all alike to him and he lost confidence in his ability to know the one. So he relied on chance, making a game of the search. "Joshua Calvert," he whispered, and watched to see if the mule snorted. It did not snort. "Joshua Long," he whispered, and counted the steps to the squatty tree up ahead; if it was more than twenty steps then he would keep the name. But it wasn't more. "Joshua Meeks." He looked to see if his fourth step would land naturally in the horse's print, and it did not. "Joshua Allen," he said, and waited to see if a wolf howled, as a sign.

A wolf did howl, long and painfully, and as the sound rose over the prairie Joshua's spirits fell. He did not like the name Allen. He would disregard the sign. But this might bring bad luck. He should keep the name. But he had always had names forced on him, the names of owners he hated. Why, now that he was free, should he give that power to a wolf, which was no better than a dog?

"Joshua Steen," he whispered to himself.

Ah, there was strength in that. It was solid. "It looks like this prairie land might be Mexico by now," he said to the doctor, and his voice in the open spaces sounded louder than he meant it to.

Hugh Kenner told him they were still in Texas, but Texas was part of Mexico, and Joshua said it couldn't be part of Mexico, because in Mexico there were no slaves. Hugh Kenner told him he was right, there were no slaves in Mexico, and all these years he had been kept illegally. "You were free when you crossed the border from the United States into Texas," he said.

Joshua refused at first to believe it, for it was hard to think that all this time he had been free and had not even known it. When he finally did accept it, his hatred for the Hanlins took new form. Not only had they used him like an animal, they had tricked him too. He suggested to Hugh Kenner he would choose the name of Joshua instead of Josh, and Hugh liked the idea and asked if he could have his gloves back for a while. "How about just one?" Joshua answered with a smile. "How about I give you just one glove, and we can switch 'em off?"

Hugh Kenner laughed quietly and deeply with his head tilted back, the light glistening in his sideburns.

Joshua said impulsively, "Steen. Joshua Steen. How about that?"

Hugh became serious, and looked him in the eyes. "How about that," he said, and nodded, and Joshua tugged off one of the gloves and gave it to him and they went on walking with the mule.

Adelaido slowed and waited, and when they were up with him he told a story. He told it while they traveled with the moonlight on their shoulders, Callum Mackay on his decrepit sorrel mare, Adelaido on his fine gelding, Joshua and Hugh walking with the mule between them. Adelaido stared across the prairie before him while he told the story. He said, "I have known horses to kill themselves. I've seen them starve themselves rather than submit to their captors. I've seen one mare die of thirst standing within reach of water, and another, who had escaped and run wild for a year, throw herself down from a bluff when we were chasing her, down into a mire of mud, without even breaking stride or looking back at us. And I know of a stallion that plunged his head into a trough and drowned himself."

Then Callum Mackay spoke. "And do ye think it be a noble thing?" he asked, and answered his own question, "No. It be a mortal sin. I meself were brought back from the dead, and I swear it were the hand o' God what brought me, and it were not allowed for mae own hand to send me back again. It was the mornin' when I come alive to find mae wife and daughter stiff in their own blood and mae Samuel skreelin' in his muther's arms and soukin' her dead breist through her bloody gown. Mae own horse, she comin' from the fields, and me with Samuel skreelin' like a banshee in mae arms and the blood pourin' down mae face so that I have no face, and mae mare she shied away from me. But the hand o' God, it stilled the mare for me, and led her through the trials in the grass with the insects stucken in mae blood and Samuel skreelin' in mae arms, and brought mae to the Kenners' home. And still it be the hand o' God, what leads."

He paused, and no one said a word. They kept on traveling, strung out beside each other. Then Callum spoke again, his voice spreading out across the moon-washed prairie like a breath of wind. "God let me hear the name, Métis. I thought it were mae daughter's name they said: Matty. Until the ranger brought me back mae scalp, I wondered how it were that the Comanches knew her name. It be the one thing I recall with perfect clarity—the name they said—Métis."

P O L L O   E N T E R R A D O

RANCHO DE LA ROSA ON THE
SAN ANTONIO RIVER

Morning broke. Domingo de la Rosa stood outside his doorway, conversing with a woman. His lean face was imperfect in the gray morning light; he stood outside the paneled door, his head cocked slightly to the side as he listened.

When he saw Crucita coming toward him, he turned his face to her and smiled.

The woman glanced over her shoulder at Crucita, then went on talking. But Domingo de la Rosa was no longer listening. She said something else about the games that were beginning, then went off to join the crowd of spectators.

"You've come," De la Rosa said to Crucita, seeming glad of it.

"The Americans questioned me when I was leaving town," she answered. "They asked where I was going. I told them my mother was ill. They almost didn't let me come."

"Have you seen Adelaido?"

"No, he hasn't been home. Has he been here?"

"No."

"I've heard some things, to tell you."

He led her through the side entrance of the palisade of strong pickets surrounding the compound, and there they encountered Padre Valdez, who knew them both. He was small with weathered skin and thick gray hair, and he was in high spirits, lifting a palm up to the misty rain and saying as he passed, "Fine weather you've arranged for us, Domingo."

"For you, Padre," De la Rosa answered, smiling.

The padre spoke briefly to Crucita. They were two among few who had survived the cholera in Goliad, and they had suffered it together. Valdez had not been quick to blame Crucita when she stopped attending church after burying her father; he, too, had fallen to despair for a time after the cholera, and ceased for a while to pray.

"Crucita," he said to her now, "you're happy today?"

"Yes, Padre, today I am happy."

He gave his blessings and moved on while Crucita and De la Rosa continued through the gateway.

Most of the livestock pens were protected within the palisade, but there was a large corral, about 150 by 100 varas in size, just outside of it. The crowd had gathered here, facing out across the prairie where the competition would take place, many of them sitting on the corral fence and others higher, on the palisade behind. Some had gained a clear but distant view by climbing to the sod roofs of the vaqueros' quarters, which formed part of the outer wall of the compound, where the stick palisade left off.

De la Rosa spoke about nothing of importance while they walked. He was not wearing a hat, and Crucita noted how much gray was in his hair. A matrix of deep crow's feet fanned out from his eyes.

Every year at the end of November Domingo de la Rosa hosted the *días de toros*—the days of the bulls—when his vaqueros and those from neighboring ranches tested their skills against each other and against the animals. They rode in the game of *pollo enterrado*—"buried chicken." They competed with the reata, roping livestock. On horseback they chased down running bulls, grabbing hold of their tails and flipping the animals off balance.

It was an honor to be walking beside the quiet ranchero who made the games possible and fed the people who had come. He was known to everyone. He led her to the end of the corrals, where the crowd was not pressing, and they stood side by side against the railings with the cold mist turning into rain.

"You've never played the game of *pollo enterrado?*" Crucita asked.

"No."

"Not even as a boy?"

"No, Crucita."

"Why?"

He smiled at her. "Because I wouldn't win."

She settled back against the fence, her elbows bent and resting on the middle rail behind her and her hands fastened together across her stomach. To the left, a track stretched out from the far end of the corral onto the flat mesquite lands and wound its way through cactus and dry winter brush, then back again. It was the shape of an irregular horseshoe. The track was partially cordoned off with red ribbons for markers, but the crowd ignored the markers and wandered back and forth through the center of the horseshoe. Three quarters of the way around, a man in festive clothing was shoveling out a hole where the chicken would be buried to its neck. He stopped shoveling and called for the chicken to be brought.

De la Rosa crossed his arms. "Adelaido won the *pollo enterrado* three years in a row, when he was working here," he said.

"I was here to watch him," she answered.

"Ah."

They were bringing out the chicken with its head hooded in white linen and ribbons dangling from the tail feathers. It was a large bird, rust-colored, and it struggled against its captor, who clutched it to his chest and held its feet together. The crowd closed in around, and Crucita could not see when the chicken was buried and the dirt tamped down around it. It would have an awful death, the riders descending on it one at a time and trying to grab its neck and pluck the bird out of the ground as if it were a weed. She had seen the head torn off before. She had seen the bird come out alive, only to be buried again for another game. Once she had seen every rider fall or miss in the attempt to lean and grab the neck, and then the bird was allowed to live. But that was only once.

"Now, tell me," De la Rosa said.

She answered, "There are eight hundred Mexican soldiers in Laredo getting ready to march to Texas, to fight the Americans besieging Béxar. The Americans heard about it from two foreigners, an Italian and a Frenchman who came through Goliad on their way north from Mier to Louisiana with a *caballada* of horses. The Americans disagree on what to do. Some think the Mexican soldiers are going to come through Goliad on their way to Béxar, and they want to stay in Goliad and fight them. But others say it would be suicide."

"What does their commander say?"

"I don't know. I've heard there'll be a new commander."

"Then what do you think most of the men intend?"

"To stay in the presidio and hold on to Goliad. They're almost out of corn, and some of the horses have died of sore tongue, but I think they'll stay. Most of them aren't Texan settlers, they're from the United States of the North, New Orleans and some other places. They expect to fight and to be paid with land."

"With this land," De la Rosa said. "The land you see before you."

She went on, "Some of them are tired of waiting, and talk about going south to Matamoros to incite the Mexicans there to start a war against Santa Anna, but I think most of them intend to stay in Goliad."

"Are the Italian and the Frenchman the only ones to bring word of Mexican troops in Laredo?"

"There were two Mexicans with the same news, but the Americans don't trust them. They think they could be spies."

De la Rosa said, "I would trust them more than I would trust an Italian and a Frenchman driving a *caballada* out of Mexico."

She smiled. "The Americans took the *caballada* and sent the foreigners away on foot."

"Well, good. I won't waste my pity on them. Crucita, who told you all of this?"

"Talk is free in Goliad."

"Tell me who you talk to."

"No."

"*Tejanos?*"

"I never agreed to tell you who."

"Are they spies for the rebels? *Tejano* spies?" His voice was very placid, and he lifted one palm to feel the drops of rain that had begun to fall.

Yes, they were *Tejano* spies for the rebels. She knew them, some of them she knew well, she had served them mescal while they watched the cockfights in the smoky jacal where she had worked as a *cantinera:* Manuel Escalera, Miguel Aldrete, Felipe Roque Portilla. They had rebel friends in San Patricio, Refugio, and Victoria—some of them Irish Catholics, some *Tejano*—who informed them, and they in turn informed the rebel garrison at Goliad, which sent word to the rebel army outside Béxar. All of south Texas was under their scrutiny. Domingo de la Rosa, she knew, was closely acquainted with many of these men, and would know them if she named them. But that was not her business.

She was mute, and twined her fingers tighter across her stomach.

"Very well, Crucita. You don't yet trust me. It seems you know the *Tejanos* siding with the rebels. I know them too." He began to list the names. "José Antonio Padilla. Sylvestre de Leon. Miguel Aldrete. Placido Benavides." He said the names carefully in a voice that would set them in her memory. While he said them she watched the crowd at the far end of the corrals moving away from the track, opening it to her view. Some, because of the rain, were leaving to take shelter in their lodgings near the river, but most seemed intent on the game about to start. The bird had been buried in the hole and its hood removed, showing that it was a rooster of remarkable size. Crucita watched its neck and head flailing from the fresh earth like a weed tossed by the wind, but there was no wind. The red wattles splayed against the dirt and the comb twisted with the bird's head: Crucita could imagine the watchful eyes. "Manuel Escalera of the De León family," De la Rosa continued. "Encarnación Vasquez. Felipe Portilla. Manuel and José Carbajal."

Twelve riders moved out from the corral in single file onto the track, the mounts stepping high and fast with their necks arched under a tight rein, and the preliminary procession began. From the corral fence and the palisade and the sod roofs of the vaqueros quarters the audience shouted their approval; children were lifted up to see. Even in the drizzling rain the scene was resplendent, the horses' tails braided with trailing ribbons and the contestants garbed in clothing with elaborate embroidery. One wore a woolen serape with coins dangling from the fringe, another wore pantaloons the color of blue midnight and embroidered with gold thread along the seams. The saddle leathers were all tipped with tiny metal trinkets that made a kind of music.

"Do you know the one riding in front?" De la Rosa asked Crucita.

"No."

"He's one of my best vaqueros. His mother died when he was an infant. His father was killed by Karankawas."

She studied the vaquero on his black horse. He was dressed all in black and white, wearing a black cravat tied at his neck like an Anglo-American would tie it. Though he was very young, he deported himself with composure and pride. His stirrups were each cut from a single block of wood and carved into the face of a lion. "Will he be first?" she asked.

"Yes. It cost him six weeks wages to be first, too much for a game." He shrugged and did not seem to care: the money would go to the padre.

"Do you think he'll win?"

"Last year and the year before, he won. There's a lot of money bet on him."

"Your money?" she presumed to ask.

"No. I don't like to gamble."

The procession wound its way around the track and back to the corral. The young vaquero's horse spooked from the people's raucous cheering and balked at entering, but he conquered it, causing it to step backward then turn in a sharp circle, after which he spurred it forward through the gate.

De la Rosa continued listing the *Tejano* rebels. "Even Salinas on the Atascosa is a traitor," he said.

It was clear that De la Rosa had a spy system as elaborate as the rebels', to know so much. Maybe he didn't need her information, Crucita thought. Maybe he already knew about the eight hundred Mexican soldiers gathering in Laredo, and only humored her by pretending not to. Or maybe he was testing her. She had offered him her services on impulse that day in the cold *sala* with the taper light, while she was under his spell, but now he stood in the rain with lines in his face and the odor of damp skin, and she almost did not like him. "You know everything already," she said. "You're like God. You think you are like God."

Suddenly the young vaquero on his black horse darted from the corral out into the prairie, taking the curve of the track at such a speed that the horse leaned almost on its side and one of the lion-faced stirrups dragged on the ground. The crowd cheered, then fell to an expectant silence as the horse and rider approached the buried rooster. Lithe and fluid in his movement, the vaquero leaned down against the horse's side, trailing his hand with languid fingers tilted like a dancer's. The bird saw him approaching and flung its head down against the wet earth. There was no sound from the spectators and nothing from the drizzling prairie but the beat of the horse's hooves and the small tinkle of metal tips dangling from the saddle.

The Vaquero fell. He leaned too far, and fell precisely on the bird. His horse kept running at full speed, veering off the track toward where Crucita and Domingo de la Rosa stood leaning against the rails, its mouth open against the bit, the tongue slinging bloody strands of saliva and the reins dragging on the ground. Crucita thought the horse would run directly into her, and almost turned to climb the fence to get away. But De la Rosa stepped in front of her and raised his hand with a calm and unaffected gesture, as if simply to dismiss the horse, and the animal wheeled and ran the other way.

"That vaquero has cost me another chicken," De la Rosa said, turning to look at Crucita through the rain falling in sheets between them. "He has broken its neck." She looked to see the rider, who was standing now and staring down sadly at what appeared from this distance to be nothing more than a rusty clod of earth.

The crowd was stunned to silence, then one voice carried from the rooftop of the vaqueros' dwellings: "Which one out there is the chicken?" A few laughed wildly, but most were not inclined to laugh. They had lost money. They climbed down from the fences and stood around shaking their heads, muttering, and no one offered to help the vaquero retrieve his horse, which was kicking and flinging up mud far out across the soggy prairie.

The man who had buried the bird walked out and began digging it up. Another vaquero ran toward Domingo de la Rosa, calling as he ran, "Don Domingo. May we have another rooster?"

De la Rosa shook his finger. "Not another rooster. A hen."

Crucita began to laugh, it was so ludicrous to replace the rooster with a hen.

"But, señor—"

"No. A *polla,* only." He was catering to her laughter.

The vaquero was angry, and dared to show it with his posture, but did not argue, and started back.

"Well, Crucita," De la Rosa said, turning to her with a smile, "we should go in from the rain."

She continued to laugh. It was very amusing to her: the expectation of the crowd and Domingo de la Rosa's praise of the flashy young vaquero, all ending in a limp rooster being dug out of the dirt. The bird had found a quick death and deprived them of their sport.

De la Rosa took Crucita by the arm, and he was laughing too. Together they went around the end of the corral walking very fast then stepping out into a run with the downpour spattering Crucita's dress against her body, tangling the skirt between her legs until she stopped to pull it free. They started on, and with the sudden feelings of a child she laughed so much that she could hardly run. But she was aware of the man and his wet trousers and his muddy cowhide boots splashing against the sodden earth. He was holding her arm tightly as they neared his doorway.

Someone, merely a blur of movement rushing through the rain in the other direction, called out, "Don Domingo, there are four men here to see you. I told them to go inside; they're waiting in the *sala.*" De la Rosa waved the man aside with the same gesture he had used to turn the horse away, and went on laughing with Crucita.

They were clinging to one another like children when they entered into the silence of the cold *sala* with the high-beamed ceiling and the Virgin Mary standing placidly in her gloomy niche beside the door. The quiet and the darkness overcame Crucita. She tried to stop her breathing, which was heavy from the running. Firelight from the far end of the room was shielded by four men grouped near the fire.

De la Rosa approached them and Crucita held back in the darkness near the door, stifling her breathing. When the voice from the far end of the room spoke out with clear and perfect Spanish there was such a sudden vacuum in her chest that she sucked a forceful breath and held it there. *"Buenos días,* Don Domingo."

"Adelaido."

"How are you, Sir?"

"Fine. I am waiting for the rain to pass."

"Señor. I've taken the liberty of bringing these men here, for your help."

She could not make sense of what was happening, a bizarre spectacle: Adelaido speaking from the other side of the long table with the flagstones echoing his familiar voice, the Virgin Mary smiling from the recess of her niche with painted lips. Crucita could see her own reflection in the mirror on the opposite wall as she stood wet and dismal between the Virgin and the dark paneled door. Adelaido was making introductions.

He spoke of a slave in need of temporary haven.

He spoke also of a man in search of the half-breed, Louie Métis.

Crucita, afraid that if she moved she would be noticed, stayed where she was, trembling in her wet clothes. If Adelaido saw her now—the woman who came running in from the rain, laughing with Domingo de la Rosa—he would demand to know the nature of her strange complicity with De la Rosa. If he learned that she was spying, and doing it for him, for Adelaido, because De la Rosa had threatened to expose his illegal exploits, he would be defiant and despise the great ranchero. And De la Rosa would then wield his power over him, which was power enough to ruin him.

She didn't move to the door, for fear Adelaido might see and know her. Why was he here? There was the runaway slave, stout and still against the firelight, and there were two Americans, one taller than the other, and there was the mention of Louie Métis.

Crucita looked at the Castilian *vaqueno* with the tiny drawers, remembering the jar with glistening pellets of false calomel hidden in one drawer. Was Adelaido planning now, after fifteen months had passed, after he had seen Métis and let him go, to find him once again and punish him?

Adelaido was in profile, his straight hair tied back. Crucita was as still as the Virgin Mary and coveted her dark niche and listened with disoriented fervor to Adelaido giving names again: Hugh Kenner, Joshua Steen, Callum Mackay.

At first De la Rosa said nothing. His shape was small beside the other men. His utter silence and lack of gesture revealed his strength. They had come seeking help: he had the power to give it. When he spoke it was in the perfect English he had learned during years of exile in New Orleans after his father died fighting the king's men. He had a heavy accent which Adelaido did not have, but his words were perfect, Crucita knew it from the poise with which he spoke. "Gentlemen, move these chairs up close beside the fire if you like," he said. "I will send a woman in, with chocolate and coffee. Her name is Anita; she will bring you anything you need. I would like for Adelaido to come into the hall with me, and speak in private. Ah, and I have cigarillos here."

When he turned to get the velvet box of cigarillos from the table, Crucita expected him to look at her and give some sign of what she was to do. But he didn't even glance in her direction. Then she understood: he was giving her a chance, and trusting her to take it. When Adelaido leaned to light his cigarillo in the fire, Crucita slipped out into the rain.

Adelaido knew these walls; many times he'd passed between them from the *sala* to the quarters of the great ranchero who had taught him to speak English and to read. This was the hallway to his education and his life, and he stood now beneath a single burning sconce, the smell of burning sheep oil mixing with the smoke.

De la Rosa said to him, "I've heard of your friend Callum Mackay. He was scalped by the Comanches?"

"By the Comanches that Métis was leading south. Métis is responsible."

"It's revenge he wants?"

"Yes. His wife and daughter both were killed."

"Then I can't help you, Adelaido."

"But I've brought him all this way. I promised him you'd help."

"I'm not responsible for your promises," De la Rosa said.

"Señor, God believes in justice, doesn't He?"

"No, I don't think He does." The ranchero's composure was like none Adelaido had known in any other man, the way he stood with his arms crossed before him as if he needed no one. The flame from the sconce on the wall above him cast shadows down his face, and the light rested on his shoulders like a blessing.

"But you know where Métis is," Adelaido said, drawing on his cigarillo.

"Of course."

"He's working for you?"

"He's working for Mexico."

"And you're paying him."

"Of course."

"Then it's you he works for," Adelaido answered, impatient with the game of words. The cold plaster wall beside him glittered in the flame like snow. He leaned one shoulder up against it and looked at the ranchero. "I had my chance to take revenge on Métis, and didn't. But you and I don't have the right to make that choice for another man."

"Of course we don't. And you don't have the right to make demands of me," De la Rosa answered, and Adelaido felt the ranchero's power taking hold of him in the way it had when he was younger. De la Rosa looked into his eyes and made his timing perfect. "Adelaido. Won't you come back, and work for me? Your country needs you. I could pay you well, if your patriotism failed to motivate you."

"My loyalty is to the Federalists," Adelaido answered steadily.

De la Rosa smiled. "Federalists," he said. "I find it amusing that they call themselves Federalists."

Adelaido answered in a biting whisper, "We're fighting for the Mexican federal constitution."

De la Rosa's green eyes were unmerciful. "You're lying," he said. "Do you know you're lying? Long before Santa Anna claimed royal powers the rebel Anglos were refusing to pay duties. They caused federal employees and federal troops to flee Texas, and they destroyed federal forts and properties. These are not the actions of people who are loyal to their federal constitution. The Anglos scorn everything Mexican—our religion and our laws."

"They do not scorn me," Adelaido answered.

De la Rosa stared at him, his lids just slightly closing down as if to draw a keener focus. "I won't help you find Métis," he said. "But I'll help the slave. He can work here if he chooses to, for the same pay I give my vaqueros, or I'll have an escort take him south into Coahuila if he wants to go."

The power was compelling. De la Rosa could take lives in his callused hands. And Adelaido could reach out to that power, he could hold on to it, there was safety in Domingo de la Rosa's kingdom. But there was no freedom; De la Rosa would own him.

Turning his back on the great ranchero, Adelaido spoke over his shoulder, expressing gratitude on behalf of the slave, and nothing on behalf of the pathetic Scotsman who was waiting in the *sala* with his own scalp tied to a rosary and tucked into a canvas bag hanging from his waist.

BOOK TWO

THE GATES
OF THE
PRESIDIO

THE VIRGIN OF LORETO

In that winter of 1835–36, the rebels carried on the war without an enemy. The enemy was gone, routed out of San Antonio de Béxar in early December when the rebels came down from the hills. General Cós with his fourteen hundred Mexican soldiers, like scarecrows, surrendered after five days of battle and were sent home on parole, walking the empty, frostbitten miles back to the Rio Grande. Some were willing soldiers, well trained: they were disdainful of the surrender. Some were Mexicans citizens, street people kidnapped by the army and prodded to Texas like cattle: they were glad to be going home. Six hundred others were convicts from Mexican jails, force-marched to Texas in shackles to fight, who arrived at the besieged town of Béxar just as the rebels attacked it. They were turned around with the others and sent back.

There was not a Mexican soldier left on Texas soil.

The war seemed to be over.

Sam Houston said it wasn't.

But no one was listening to Sam Houston. Once, he had been a great man: a congressman, a governor of Tennessee, Andrew Jackson's young protégé. But then his bride had left him, for no reason anyone knew, and he had fallen like a bird shot from a crystalline sky. He resigned the governorship and took a steamboat west to Arkansas, Indian territory, where he lived with a Cherokee woman, refused to speak English, and almost died of malaria. The word among whites was that he had gone to the Indians to organize them into a fighting force to take Texas from Mexico, and would reward the Indians with half the land; the other half he himself would rule, or give to Andrew Jackson and the Union. No one knew how true this gossip was, for Sam Houston nurtured his secrets. The Cherokees adored him and called him "Kalanu"—"The Raven." Sometimes they called him "Oo-tse-tee Ar-dee-tah-skee"—"Big Drunk." They sent him to Washington as their ambassador to his old friend President Andrew Jackson. And Andrew Jackson—so the rumor went—sent him to Texas, Mexico, to see if the ground was ready for the seeds of revolution.

Andrew Jackson wanted a revolution. He wanted Texas for his Union —divorced from Mexico and wed to him. So Sam Houston went to Texas, settled in and set up a law practice. He drank. He eyed the situation, and—so they said—spoke his secret schemes aloud to the wind in Cherokee tongue whenever storms blew in. He got himself elected commander in chief after Stephen Austin left the post. With stunning green-blue eyes he viewed the scene, and his voice was a voice to be heard.

He said in December while the wind wrestled with tufts of hair on his huge skull, that the war was not over, the war had just begun.

But no one was listening to Sam Houston.

No one was listening to anyone in particular.

The farmers went home to farm. The women made soap. It was hog-killing time.

There was a government, an impromptu, provisional affair made of a governor named Henry Smith and an elected council, but no one was listening to the government. They needed funds to finance the war, they needed guns and munitions, they needed fighting men. Stephen Austin went to the United States to get these things. He got promises and some money. He got a lot of enthusiasm. And he got in trouble, because the United States had a neutrality agreement with Mexico, and Mexico complained of the boatloads of armed mercenaries arriving in Texas from places like Paducah, Kentucky.

But he did not get in much trouble. Andrew Jackson—Old Hickory, he was called—was President, and he said Americans had a lawful right to emigrate and bear arms.

In January it snowed. There was dissension in the rebel government, the governor calling the council "a Damned corrupt council" and ranting that he was tired of watching scoundrels abroad and scoundrels at home. He dissolved the council, but members refused to leave. They called the governor a tyrant and impeached him. He in turn refused to accept the impeachment, and would not give over the executive papers, even when the marshal tried to force him.

There was an army. No one knew who was running the army. The governor said Sam Houston was to run it, but the governor had been impeached by the council. The council said James Fannin was to run it, but the council had been dismissed by the governor. The army itself wanted to elect its own officers: in San Antonio they elected Jim Bowie, who had a fandango and got drunk and unlocked the calaboose so the town prisoners could join in the dance. Houston ordered Bowie to remove all the cannon and blow up the Alamo, calling the fortress a trap and pronouncing that the war could not be won by small groups of men in isolated outposts.

Bowie ignored the order. He fortified the Alamo instead. It was a hard job, since San Antonio de Béxar had been robbed of its provisions by a freewheeling band of rebel volunteers from the United States who were planning to carry the war three hundred miles south and conquer Matamoros. If the war would not come to them, they said, they would go and find it. They would return with spoils.

"Piratical," Sam Houston called the proposed Matamoros campaign. "Predatory!" As the soldiers started south, Houston rode beside them for a distance on a long-eared mule, his feet almost dragging the ground, his huge voice bellowing at the soldiers that they were parading to their death, that a city of twelve thousand would not be taken by a handful of men who had marched twenty-two days without adequate breadstuffs.

Some of the soldiers started listening then, and dropped out.

It rained for days. The rivers rose.

The government was torn to shreds by dissension, and could not reach a quorum. It ran up a debt of twenty-eight thousand dollars. The people elected a new government, but time was sliding by. President Santa Anna had begun his march north from Central Mexico toward Texas.

When *El Presidente,* with his opium and cages of fighting cocks for entertainment, his silk tent and heavy carpets for comfort, and an army of six thousand freezing, underfed conscripts and their families—three thousand women and children—accompanied by a sprinkling of American and European soldiers of fortune with names like "Memory Johnson," started the long trek north to Texas, no one in Texas was listening to anyone else. No one could be heard above the din of voices; it was a war raging without the enemy in sight. Rebel mercenaries from the United States were testy, threatening to lay down their muskets and go home. They demanded to know what they were fighting for: was it the Mexican Constitution of 1824? If so, they were not much interested. They had wanted to fight for Anglo freedom, not Mexican freedom. Texas should declare itself independent of Mexico. There should be a proper declaration of independence.

On the down side, the people said, such a declaration might alienate the *Tejano* population and end hope for any cooperation from Mexican liberals. On the up side, it would attract more mercenaries from the United States. The debate waged. The ground froze. Santa Anna's army stretched out for miles, winding northward over the barren land like a mutant serpent, passing through the arms of the Sierra Madre and across the San Luis Valley, leaving behind a landscape marred with carcasses of livestock that fell from fatigue and stick crosses marking human graves. Oxen ran with blood. Mules drowned in a blizzard. Conscripts from the jungles of Yucatán froze to death. In villages along the way, the army kidnapped men and mules. Horses' tongues swelled and split open from the thirst, and many of the horses had running sores from the hoof and mouth disease.

Sam Houston rode east to visit people who would listen to him. Under the pine trees, around a camp fire and a common bowl of dog stew, he met with representatives of various Indian tribes and proposed they form an auxiliary corps of three hundred warriors to fight beside the rebels. They would be paid seven thousand dollars for six months' service.

They listened. They said they would think about his proposition.

The Raven ate dog stew and guaranteed them their lands and tax exemptions on trade. He put it in writing over his own outsized signature, and the chiefs signed the document under Sam Houston's name: Bowles, Big Mush, Samuel Benge, Corn Tassel, the Egg. . . . The Raven suggested that if they did not join the rebels, they should at least stay neutral. They said they would think about that, too. No one questioned if the Raven, with his steady green-blue eyes and the beads around his neck—intended to keep his promises to them. A few questioned if it was in his power to do so.

Sam Houston was a man on pilgrimage, a cerebral wanderer who had memorized most of Pope's translation of *The Iliad* and the poems of George Gordon Lord Byron. He was a man who had read *Gulliver's Travels* over again. He had questioned a lot of things in his forty-two years of life, but his power was not one of the things he had questioned. He was an optimist. He ordered from New Orleans one thousand butcher knives, one thousand tomahawks, well tempered, with handles, and three thousand pounds of Kentucky chewing tobacco for his Indian allies.

The Comanches were not present at Sam Houston's Indian meeting. They were positioned to make demands, and sent an emissary in a buffalo robe to Béxar demanding a treaty of amity, commerce, and limits.

In Laredo, General Cós and his scarecrow soldiers retreating from Béxar met head on with their President-General, Santa Anna, and his advancing army. He ordered them to turn around and fall in ranks and march back north to Texas.

The Mexican army divided ranks and crossed the Rio Grande, Santa Anna leading one division toward San Antonio de Béxar. The other, led by a shrewd Mexican general named José Urrea, advanced up the coast toward Goliad and its Presidio La Bahía.

There was a rebel navy. In the beginning, the impromptu government simply issued letters of marque to individual privateers allowing them to cruise the gulf and "annoy and harass the enemy" for prizes. But this made problems: most Mexican trade ships carrying valuables were owned by British and American companies who did not take kindly to the "annoyance and harassment," and would not surrender their goods to the privateers. Those ships owned by Mexicans were hauling mostly raw materials, and the privateers weren't interested in these.

So the rebel government had to get their own boats, four of them, and arm them too, and the Mexicans warned that they would treat these ships as pirate ships. New Orleans underwriters, on learning that the rebel Texans had bought a ship named the *Brutus* and were fitting it out in New Orleans with six small cannon and one big one on a pivot, for the purpose of capturing Mexican vessels which they had insured, wrote the United States District Attorney and asked that the *Brutus* be stopped from leaving port.

But the *Brutus* sailed, with the big one on a pivot, and the bitter winds carried her to Texas.

Santa Anna goaded his army onward.

The division led by José Urrea was maneuvering up the Texas coastline as the rowdy Matamoros expedition was maneuvering down. Local *Tejano* rancheros informed Urrea of the band of vagabond Anglo rebels, and Urrea set an ambush. Fifty-nine rebels were killed, a few escaped, a few were taken captive.

Thirty-two surrendered and were executed by Santa Anna's order.

Tied together and shot.

It snowed.

In rebel fortress strongholds—in Goliad at La Bahía, in Béxar at the Alamo—on farms and in the frontier towns, from one mouth to another the news passed, words falling with the softness of the snowfall and the awe of disbelief: Executed. Shot.

Santa Anna had said he would do it. He had said foreigners bearing arms against him would be treated as pirates and shot, as they were not subjects of any nation at war with Mexico and did not militate under any recognized flag.

He had warned them.

Nobody had been listening.

They panicked. It was to be a war of extermination waged upon them, they said: he would kill them all, women and children too. He would murder them all. His army of dark-skinned mixed breeds would rape the white women, they said.

Families began piling their children and belongings onto flatbed wagons and heading east for the border.

Then suddenly—as if the Mexican army had not journeyed for a month accompanied by whole families and two thousand mules and two hundred and thirty-three oxen and dragging twenty-one pieces of heavy artillery through frozen passes and baked flatlands and burying their dead along the way, but had sprouted from the muddy streets of town— suddenly the army was in San Antonio de Béxar. William Travis and Jim Bowie, with their rebel soldiers and a few civilians—Anglo and *Tejano*— scrambled into the stone walls of the Alamo and shut themselves in with a herd of beefs. In the dead of night they sent out dispatches written with a lilting, romantic melody and a minor quaver of desperation. They sent to the towns for reinforcements. They sent to the government for aid. They sent to Goliad for James Fannin to bring his five hundred men and come to their rescue.

In the confusion, one voice overpowered the others. Eccentric and verbose but surefooted as a marching band, Sam Houston spoke with a drumbeat. He had told the volunteers not to go to Matamoros: those who had ignored him were now dead. He had told them to blow up the Alamo and abandon San Antonio de Béxar: those who had disobeyed were now trapped like a nest of rabbits with the hole plugged up. He had tried to consolidate the army under his single command and drill for war: the soldiers had continued to act on whim and congregate at leisure, and were now facing an army of thousands led by a hard-eyed opium addict named Antonio López de Santa Anna Pérez de Lebrón, who would execute his prisoners without blinking.

Finally, the people listened.

The troops listened.

The leaders of the troops did not.

In the town of Goliad, at its presidio called La Bahía—a century-old fortress built by the Spanish, with barracks and a chapel, three and a half acres on the banks of the San Antonio River enclosed with stone walls almost ten feet tall and three feet thick and garrisoned now with five hundred rebels under James Fannin—the men were restless and uneasy. They were out of provisions. They wanted to pack up and pull out and head north along the river for San Antonio de Béxar, to rescue the men in the Alamo.

But Fannin was their leader, and he lacked Sam Houston's certainty. He equivocated. He had no food for the journey. Most of his horses had been confiscated by the men of the Matamoros expedition, and he had only a few left for scouting, so he was blind to the enemy. The *Tejanos* of the town had all disappeared to neighboring ranches, taking their wagons and draft animals with them, so there were scant means of transportation left in Goliad. With a good supply of provisions, he said—which might arrive from the coast at any day—he and his men could hold the presidio against attack. They had fortified the walls and burned the homes that stood within fifty yards, to open up the line of fire. Fannin was loath to abandon the place to the enemy after all the hard work.

Still, his friend Jim Bowie needed him at the Alamo, and the men were anxious for some action. So on February 25 he ordered sixty-seven soldiers to maintain the fort, and set out for Béxar leading the other four hundred and twenty on foot with unmanageable Mexican steers pulling four old wagons loaded down with cannon, with only half a tierce of rice and a day's supply of beef and seventy miles between this ragged wad of men and the rancho of the *Tejano* rebel Juan Seguín, where they could be fed. The wagons broke within two hundred yards of the fort, the ammunition wagon spending the night on one side of the river, the artillery on the other. The oxen broke their tethers and ran away and were not to be found in the morning. So Fannin ordered his men back to the presidio where they waited for another week, anxious for news from the Alamo. They bickered among themselves, shoveling dirt and inventing a new weapon called an "infernal machine," which was made of a hundred old muskets, mounted on a wooden frame, which could be fired off together with a single fuse.

Some of the men vowed to stay and hold the fort at any cost: it had become a home.

Some left: they called the fort a tomb.

Others came and went and came again. Among these, was Adelaido Pacheco. On the fifth of March, a cold morning that did not promise spring, he walked out of the fortress and down the muddy hill toward the river, to the jacal of sticks where he had been born and where his family had died of cholera, all but Crucita, who now sat on a straw mat, sewing beside a little fire that burned in the dirt in the center of the room.

"I'm not leaving Goliad," Crucita warned him as he entered. "Don't come in here to pester me about it."

He sat down in a chair and stared at her. The room was blurred with smoke. "Colonel Fannin is a human slug," he said bitterly. "He's incapable of taking action. Urrea isn't sixty miles from here, in San Patricio, drilling his troops which outnumber us two to one, and Fannin isn't giving any orders. He's scratching his head."

"What would you have him do?"

"Listen to Sam Houston. Whatever Houston says. But he won't listen, he's too proud, and he's fickle to his soul—either he's not thinking or he's thinking too much. He should stop trying to think, and listen, or we'll end up like those insubordinates trapped inside the Alamo."

Crucita put her sewing aside, rolled the leftover thread into a little ball for keeping and put it away in a box, then stood up and tidied the room, sweeping ashes into the fire and arranging her shoe-repair tools on a rickety bench at the foot of the bed in the corner.

In another corner was the pedestal and the dusty wooden saint, John the Shepherd, with his face to the wall and his cruciform staff reaching over his shoulder, the flicker of firelight casting a shadow of the cruciform onto the wall of sticks and patchy mud. A disorderly pile of men's clothing was heaped on the ground beside the saint, and another pile folded on a chair. "Has any food come in?" Crucita asked, folding the dirty pair of pantaloons she had just mended: red linsey-woolsey of the volunteers from Alabama. "I don't have any cornmeal left." He didn't answer her, and she looked at him and said, "What? What, Adie?"

"You are so pretty," he said.

"Adieeeeee—" she answered, flicking her wrist at him, "go and lie to someone who is not your sister."

He laughed aloud. "Yes, there is food on the road from Matagorda. We should have it by tomorrow."

Opening her eyes wide, she pressed the red pantaloons to her chest. "Can you get me some?"

"Of course. But you should turn the saint around. You're flirting with the devil." He nodded at St. John the Shepherd in the corner.

"Is there flour?" she asked.

"Flour, salt, coffee, beans, and six barrels of pork. Also soap and sperm candles."

"Will the candles be expensive?"

"I'll get you one. I'll get you two. I'll pay for them if I have to. Will you turn the saint around?" It worried him that she had spurned the Church.

"I'll pay for them myself," she said, and gestured toward the pile of folded garments. "I've collected almost twenty dollars American."

He did not congratulate her. He did not approve. "You'd better save it," he said, "there won't be anymore. A load of clothing is coming with the food. And shoes. The men won't need you anymore. Crucita, there isn't a decent woman left in this town, but you. You shouldn't be such an opportunist for American dollars. You aren't safe here with all these Americans coming and going from your home."

"I'm tired of listening to you bother me about that," she answered sharply, tossing the red pantaloons onto the pile of mended clothing. "And what do you call yourself, if not an opportunist? Fighting for the rebel cause. It isn't a cause you believe in. You think they'll win, that's all it amounts to, that's how you chose your side. I'll tell you what our friends are calling you, they call you traitor, many of them do."

He shrugged his shoulders. "And many of them do not. At least I haven't gone off to hide in the bushes, as most of our friends have."

"As you want me to do."

"You're a woman."

"Go back to the fort. Go shovel more dirt."

He changed his tone, becoming once again the little boy she had adored. Though she was not much older, she was as much his mother as his sister. "Crucitaaaa. Please."

"No."

"When the food comes, I'll get you some, and you can take it and the money you've made and go to the camp at Domingo de la Rosa's ranch."

"No."

"Then I'll take you there myself. De la Rosa would look after you, for me."

"No, Adie."

"You're a stupid woman." Walking to the chamber bowl beside the bed, he turned his back to her, unbuttoned his pants, and let a stream of urine into the bowl.

"Go outside to do that," she reprimanded.

"A witch, my sister is a witch," he muttered, loud enough to let her hear.

"I shouldn't have to clean up after you, just because you like the sound of it in porcelain. Are you too good to let your urine in the dirt?"

He finished and buttoned his pants and turned around to face her. "Yes," he said.

"Adieeeee—"

"Tomorrow I am going to take you away from here, if I have to tie you like a pig to do it."

"What makes you think Domingo de la Rosa would welcome me, your sister, when he knows you're fighting for the rebels, and maybe he's heard that I've been doing work for them. He would despise me."

Squinting his eyes almost closed, Adelaido studied her, and then said angrily, "You care what he thinks. You revere him, don't you?" He was convinced Crucita was deluded by the so-called great ranchero, a man who would employ an evil man like Louie Métis yet turn away Callum Mackay, a victim of a grotesque fate, who had come to De la Rosa seeking help. For Adelaido, it was not a matter of semantics or of patriotism, but of justice. It was a matter of how things should be, and how they should not.

"Revere him?" she said, defiantly.

"I doubt you've ever even met him, yet you revere him, just as all the peons do."

"No, Adie, what makes you say that?"

"Domingo de la Rosa is working for his own profit. He thinks if the Anglos win they'll rob him of his property, and he's trying to protect it. This whole town has been deceived by De la Rosa and his presumptuous piety—"

"Don't talk to me that way—"

"—the Great Ranchero, the Rich Ranchero who is too good to soil himself with women but would resort to any means to save his wealth—"

"Adelaido, what are you saying? I think your anger comes from jealousy."

"You've been taken in," he said. "Like all the rest of them. He isn't God. He isn't—"

"You're the one who thinks he is," she said. "You're the one who would hog-tie your sister and deliver her to his protection."

There was something in her voice he did not know, and had not heard before. She stood in the dim and hazy smoke with the saint behind her, her Indian face lowered with a look of defiance and her eyes cut up at him from beneath her black brows.

A knock at the door interrupted their confrontation. When Adelaido answered it, he found Scholar Tipton in his old St. Louis hat, out of breath from loping down the hill.

"Adelaido," Scholar panted. "Señorita." His pronunciation was very bad. He had recently shaved off his beard, and the skin was blue-white in the cold.

Adelaido turned to his sister, resorting to cool formality. "Crucita, this is my friend Scholar Tipton."

She said in her imperfect English, "I know him. I put a patch in his jacket."

Scholar's fleshy mouth was puckered with cold. He blurted out to Adelaido, "Colonel Fannin needs you, he asked me to come find you."

"What does he want?"

"Miles and them got back, and they've brought back a old padre from De la Rosa's ranch. They say he's a spy for De la Rosa. Fannin needs you to come talk to him, and translate."

"Is it Valdez?" Adelaido said. "Padre Valdez?"

"Yeah, the padre."

"He's not a spy."

"Well you'd better come tell Fannin that. They've got the padre tied and are askin' him a lot a questions and can't get what it is he's saying."

Adelaido said emphatically, "Tell Fannin I won't come. Tell him to let Valdez go, he's not a spy."

"I can't tell him. You tell him," Scholar said.

Crucita asked, "Where is De la Rosa? He is . . . all right?"

"They didn't get De la Rosa," Scholar said. "Just the padre, out at De la Rosa's ranch. Miles Kenner and four others got past the guard and stole the padre out of his bed. Bed," he repeated, uncertain from her blank expression if she understood. He pointed to her bed. "Padre sleeping." To Adelaido he said, "They couldn't get to De la Rosa hisself, because of too many guards around his house. It's like a fort out there."

"Tell him I won't set foot inside the presidio as long as the padre is held there," Adelaido answered. "I won't be part of an interrogation. Tell him the padre's not a spy."

Scholar mashed his lips together. "Well, hell," he said, taking off his hat in a gesture of frustration and scratching at the oily curls sticking to his forehead. "I'll tell him. He'll say it's insubordinate." Putting his hat back on, he stole a glance at Crucita, turned to go, and then turned back again. "Fannin got word from the government," he said. "The rebel government. He's gonna make a announcement later. The government has gone ahead and declared us independent. They did it on the second. Texas is a whole republic now. Though I can't see as it makes a lot of difference. Santie Anna don't care a fig for what our government declares."

Adelaido was unsettled by the news. It was not that borders were important to him; he could travel the land just the same, he could use it the same. He had always moved back and forth across the boundaries without consideration of the laws. But something was profoundly changed.

Scholar turned away, carrying the message about Padre Valdez like a burden up the muddy hill toward the presidio, his great hams flexing hard in their buckskin trappings with the fringe catching in the wind.

Crucita said, "Adie. What do you think they'll do to Valdez? He's a spy, you know he is."

Adelaido looked at his sister, and didn't answer her.

"Will they catch De la Rosa?" she asked.

"They'll try."

"I'm glad you lied for Padre Valdez," she said. "You fight your people, but you won't betray them. It's like the horses, I think. You would run them to exhaustion and take them in an open prairie, but you wouldn't win their trust and trick them into the pens. You're afraid of playing the belled mare."

"I am afraid of going to hell," he said. "I won't be the padre's Judas. But if it were Domingo de la Rosa they had taken, I might have acted differently."

Her voice was both critical and plaintive. "It's nothing but a game to you. You make your own rules, and they're meaningless. Is there nothing you believe in?"

"Yes," he answered, looking at her face. "God. And you. I've always believed in you, Crucita."

But doubt had crept in. She had said the name too many times: Domingo de la Rosa. She had said it with some care. She had been too eager to know about his safety.

And Adelaido doubted her.

In the evening, when the men of the presidio emptied into the streets of Goliad to celebrate the tenuous new nationhood of Texas, Adelaido told Crucita he would join them, and went up the hill in the cold, rosy evening light toward the presidio and town. But when he reached the northwest corner of the fort, where the stone walls met in a high bastion with the black barrel of a cannon peering over, he squatted with his back against the stones and a blanket wrapped around him. The ground was muddy and he did not sit, but squatted on his boots. There was a narrow picket gate in the wall behind him, locked. From here he had an open view of the jacales on the downhill slope and the river beyond.

Winding down the hill between the dilapidated huts was a trench the men had dug from the presidio to the river, about two hundred yards, covered over with boards, for access to water in case of siege. Winter rains had eaten at the hill and at the mud jacales, and the few civilians still living on the hill had used the mud dug from the trench to dab onto their homes and fill the chinks.

It was a bleak, cold, winter scene with a pale romantic wash of color in the sky.

From the *calle de villa,* the noisy celebration carried on with guns firing and voices belching out hurrahs.

When Crucita walked out of her rickety doorway and started up the hill, Adelaido moved to crouch behind a broken wagon which was near the narrow gate, beneath a willow tree, and never took his eyes off her. She walked so near the wagon that he saw the frayed hem of her brown skirt as she passed; he saw men's shoes on her feet—brogans with the toes worn out, so big they hampered her stride. Through the broken spokes of the wagon wheel Adelaido watched her feet passing in the hide brogans caked with mud, stumping along like the feet of a drunken man. Passing by two outhouses nestled close against the western wall, where the pink light cast a look of warmth on the stones, she rounded the southwest corner bastion with her clumsy steps, and moved on to the entranceway—the sally port, Americans called it, with its enormous gates opening like wings between the guardhouse and the stone room used as a jail. Adelaido followed, close to the wall, pressing up against one stinking outhouse then the other. He heard Crucita address the guard, asking for entry, and wondered at her purpose, knowing she had not entered the presidio since the rebels had moved in. She wished to visit the chapel, she said, while the men were gone to celebrate, and Adelaido thought it was a lie. When the guard was hesitant, she told him she was the sister of Adelaido Pacheco and worked as a seamstress for the garrison—though she confused the word garrison with garrulous and made the guard laugh. She laughed with him like a woman without a care, looking him directly in the eyes. The guard gave her entry and as she passed through, he apologized for the present untidy state of the chapel: it was being used for storage.

She did not seem to care.

Instead of going through the gate, Adelaido waited for the guard to go inside the guardhouse, then sprinted past to the southwest corner where a stone house neighbored the presidio wall. The rebels had commandeered the house, constructing a platform from its roof to the bastion and mounting a six-pound cannon on the roof. No one was inside. Adelaido climbed the stairs to the roof, then crossed the platform to the presidio compound.

The place was half in shadow, half touched with light that made the canvas tents look pink. Arranged along the walls, the tents were grouped by companies, nine companies in all. Long stone barracks for the officers formed the west wall. On the northwest corner was a small, separate compound and the gray stone chapel with its spire catching the light and stretching the slender shadow of the crucifix across the muddy ground.

And there she was, María de la Cruz, Mary of the Cross, passing in her clumsy shoes like an awkward spirit into the smaller, shadowed compound and the chapel. He had expected to see her lifted on her toes

in the heavy brogans and peering in the window of the jail, looking for
Padre Valdez. But she had gone to the chapel, as she told the guard she
would. She had not gone to pray; Adelaido was sure of that. Crucita had
not offered prayers to any saint since the cholera had crawled through
Goliad. Adelaido had the urge to call to her to wait for him, as he used
to do when they were children together playing on the bastions and in
empty corners of the fort. The walls had all been crumbling then, and
now were in a state of reinforcement and repair with the appearance of
activity halted in mid-progress: the men had simply laid their tools aside
and gone to town.

A single soldier in gray flannel walked from the shadows to the light
and crawled into a tent on his knees, and everything else was still.

When Adelaido reached the chapel yard, Crucita had already gone
inside and shut him out. The last of sunlight lay rosy-pale upon the
weatherbeaten wood of the doorway, two slabs closed together in an
arch. Adelaido feared Crucita would see the sudden light from the doorway if he went in, and turn on him. She would be a different person
somehow in her men's shoes with the soft sunlight shining down the
aisle and reflecting in her eyes. Some wicked whim or evil had possessed
her on this dark and cryptic errand, leading her in big shoes and a
crippled walk to the chapel where she had been baptized. Often they had
sat together there, Crucita and Adelaido Pacheco, when the chapel was
empty and also when it was full, at weddings and funerals and while
their parents made confessions.

A cloud passed over the western light. Quickly, without a sound,
Adelaido opened one of the doors and slipped inside. The chapel was
cold and absolutely quiet. A high, octagonal window, nestled on the
south wall beneath the arches of the ceiling, admitted a vague light that
barely glistened on the plastered walls and the painted panels of the
twelve stations of the cross, which lined the walls, six on either side. The
torches in the nave were not burning. One sconce burned on the north
wall near the sacristy, and though this single flame did not dispel the
darkness it tossed it back into the corners and beneath the benches.

Crucita was before the altar in the nave but she was not praying, she
was lifting the wooden Virgin of Loreto from her altar niche and tucking
her into her arms. She pulled her own shawl over the wooden hands that

were almost pressed together as if in prayer, covering the sad eyes and the painted lips, not with the care that one would take in covering a child and not with any show of reverence, but rather with a purpose to disguise.

María de la Cruz was stealing the Lady of Loreto.

It was an act of sacrilege, as Adelaido saw it, for the Lady of Loreto was never taken down and handled by the people of the town, only by the one old woman who made the Lady's clothes, for the Lady had saved the woman's son from death, and she had vowed to sew her dresses of fine cloth, and keep her clean, in repayment for the blessing. Crucita had no right to take the Lady. The French had brought her here a century and half before, and when they were all killed by the Karankawas, the Spanish had found the Lady in the ruins and had named their new fort after her: Presidio de Nuestra Señora de Loreto de La Bahía del Espíritu Santo.

Adelaido crouched down low on the dirt floor between two benches, and Crucita shuffled toward him in the big shoes, and past him, and out, closing the door behind her. She had not seen him. He could smell the barrels of gunpowder stored in the side altar, and the dirt. He could smell the cold and his own breath and taste the garlic from the stew he'd eaten earlier that day. "Blessed Virgin," he began to pray—

But the Virgin was gone. Stolen away.

Quickly he stood and went out and around the outside of the chapel in time to see Crucita shove her bundle through a low hole in the presidio wall that opened to the trench extending to the river. The chapel's shadow overtook her as she leaned with her brown skirt in the mud and pushed the brown shawl through the hole, her hair falling down across her cheek. And then she left, crossing back over the compound, speaking to the guard as she went out through the sally port where she had entered.

Adelaido also returned the way he had come, over the corner bastion. He guessed Crucita would go back along the south wall, the west wall by the toilet houses, and around the northwest corner and the picket gate and the willow tree to retrieve the Virgin, so he took the opposite way in the shadows outside the eastern wall.

When she came around from the northwest, he was already well hidden at the corner, and watched her struggling with the boards that covered up the trench. She retrieved her treasure, wrapped tight in the shawl, and was careful to replace the boards.

With twilight settling over the presidio and the sound of fire rockets popping in the town, she took up a broken shovel that had been left beside the ditch and started out on the road leading southwest toward Refugio. Adelaido was less cautious now in his pursuit of her: the night protected him. A few times she looked back, but there were several men in the streets and she did not notice her brother among them. He followed, past the charred remnants of jacales which had been burned by the rebels to clear the line of fire from the presidio, past a cluster of painted plaster homes. Night birds called to one another. When Crucita passed the dog-fight pit, Adelaido knew where she was going: with her odd and awkward gait, the shovel with the broken handle tilted over her shoulder and the bundle in her arms, Crucita was going to the cemetery. The road stretched out between them and the dark closed in. He recalled the teasing words he had said to her that afternoon while he let his urine in the chamber bowl—*"Una bruja, mi hermana es una bruja"*—A witch, my sister is a witch.

She was carrying the Virgin to the cemetery.

Crosses stood against the sky on the low hill with the winter trees, and Crucita walked among the crosses to her father's grave, which she had dug over a year ago with the help of Padre Valdez. All the Pacheco family lay buried close together there beneath the wooden crosses, all dead of cholera, all but Crucita, who had watched them die, and Adelaido, who had not.

There was no moon at all, but there were stars, a dense, disorderly array. The cold was sharp, and Adelaido shivered as he leaned against a knotty oak and watched Crucita dig a grave beside their father's. The splintered handle of her shovel seemed to hurt her hands, and she placed the Lady of Loreto upright on the ground and used the shawl to pad her own palms from the splinters. To Adelaido it looked as if the Lady of Loreto was a small and helpless child standing stoically and watching as her grave was dug, her little hands lifted and pressed almost together beneath her face as if in pleading rather than in prayer. Adelaido fingered the smooth beads of the rosary inside his trouser pocket.

Crucita knew exactly where her father's casket lay; she'd covered it herself, spreading grass upon the lid so as not to hear the thud of clods of earth shoveled onto it. Now she snuggled this new grave close beside it. When she finished digging she stood for a moment holding the shovel, among the many wooden crosses, the stars bright in the winter sky above the hill. Then she set the shovel down, lifted the Lady, wrapped her in the shawl, and laid her in the grave. As she resumed shoveling, scraping the dirt back in, she halted now and then to pick the painful splinters from her hands.

He followed her home. She left her muddy brogans outside and went in, closing the door behind her. The door hung so crookedly on its hinges that it left a wide gap, and Adelaido knelt beside the brogans and looked in.

Crucita was wearing her own shoes now, and had tossed fresh kindling on the fire, and was sitting cross-legged in the center of the room within the circle of firelight, writing in a tattered notebook which she had traded one of the men for sewing. There was a bottle of ink beside her. She leaned toward the fire of thorny mesquite, holding a quill pen thoughtfully above the open page, and wrote in hurried, agitated spurts like a student unhappy with her work. She dipped the quill, and paused to think, and wrote again. When she was finished she tore the page from the notebook and looked around her as if suddenly aware of her surroundings and concerned that someone might be watching.

On the shoe-repair bench at the foot of the bed was a pair of men's side-laced shoes that appeared like new. She took one of these and worked the pegs out of the sole, then slipped the folded page inside and pegged the sole back on again.

Crouching in the cold beside the door, Adelaido felt as if the ground were falling away. It had all come down to this: his sister had lied to him, hiding the truth inside of a shoe. He was embarrassed by the insidious nature of it, and offended. He was also deeply hurt. Still he managed not to show these feelings when he entered the jacale. He told Crucita that he wished she had come with him to the celebration.

"I had to work," she answered. "I had to mend some shoes." With a casual gesture, she flicked her wrist toward the pair of lace-up shoes on the end of the workbench.

"They seem like new," he said.

"They were defective. The soles were coming loose."

Walking over to the bench, he picked up the shoe which contained the parchment and carefully examined it, looking at the pegs and fingering the laces. "Very fine for a soldier's shoe," he said, holding it toward the firelight.

"It doesn't belong to a soldier, it belongs to Mayor Vasquez."

"Your pegs aren't very good. This one's broken."

"I was in a hurry; he needs them in the morning."

"You shouldn't be mending that man's shoes. He's possibly a spy for De la Rosa." These words he said without thought, but after he had spoken them their weight sunk in his mind like a stone in water and he almost guessed the truth, that Crucita also was a spy.

He put the shoe down.

Crucita pushed a chair close to the fire in the center of the room and motioned Adelaido to sit, saying casually, "I don't care whose shoes I mend, so long as I'm paid."

He sat and pulled off one of his boots, held his foot toward the heat, and stared at the black hairs on his toes in the glowing light, feeling the fire's warmth on the sole of his foot. He refused the food she offered. When she asked if he would not return to the fort for the night, he replied that he would not return there until Padre Valdez was released. She avoided the subject of the padre, and when Adelaido mentioned De la Rosa she did not respond at all, only tossed the hair from her face in the way she had done since childhood, and took up her sewing.

Four times she lied to him. While she stirred the fire with a stick he commented on the dirt beneath her nails, then took her hand and tilted the palm down to the firelight and asked her why her hands were raw. She said she had been digging for wild onions on the riverbank. She said she had used the onions in the stew she'd made at noon. She also said she had forgotten her shawl beside the river, and had returned to find it gone.

When he asked whose muddy brogans had been left outside the door, she assumed a puzzled look and said she did not know, then pretended to remember, saying, "Oh, a soldier brought those to be fixed, but they were so dirty I put them outside."

A strangeness settled in. Adelaido's thoughts were centered on the secret message hidden in the lace-up shoe. When he slid his other boot off and held his foot toward the fire, the warmth lay against the sole of his foot like the parchment in the shoe.

Crucita was obviously reluctant to go to bed and leave him sitting in the same room with her and with the shoe and its hidden parchment on the bench between them. So she sat with him by the fire until very late. "You won't go back to the presidio?" she asked again.

"I've told you, not until the padre is set free."

At last Crucita retired to the corner, undressed with her back to him, and slipped on her cotton gown. Usually she would go outside to relieve herself before bed, but tonight she used the chamber bowl. She was watchful of the lace-up shoe, like a vixen guarding her kill.

Without much being said, she got into bed and lay on her side with the blanket pulled up high, her cheek pressed into the mattress that was stuffed with Spanish moss, the firelight playing on her features. He did not know if she was asleep or only pretending.

For a long time he sat watching her, her face growing dim as the fire died away, as if she were withdrawing from him. When the fire was low he slid a narrow strand of mesquite out of the coals; the thorns were burning in tiny flames. Quietly, he went to the bench at the foot of her bed, took up the shoe, and carried it outside.

The night was cold and freckled with stars. Above Adelaido, on the hill, the presidio was dark. He could see the shape of the watchman moving on the northwest bastion. Down the slope the tree line of the river was unusually still since there was no wind, and Adelaido went around to that side of the house. Kneeling, he pressed the end of his mesquite wand into the mud, so it stood straight up burning from the tip and from the thorns with little wings of smoke dispersing in cold air, and he took out his knife and pried the pegs out of the sole.

The parchment was unevenly folded, with splotches of ink soaking through. He unfolded it, leaned close to his light, and read:

They now call themselves a country.

I have taken care of the Lady of Loreto as you asked me to. She is very safe. I buried her.

I have heard of the execution of the rebels going down to Matamoros.

Could you not have stopped it? Did you try? It is said it was your scouts who warned Urrea of these men, which means you are responsible for their capture. Could you not have used your influence to save their lives?

The presidio is still suffering from shortages, the men are very hungry. The cattle Señor Loupe sold them is all the food they have. There is no bread or salt. You said Señor Loupe had given his four hundred cattle to the rebels, but that is not true. He sold the cattle at ten dollars each, so he is not to blame. They would have taken the cattle for nothing if he had not agreed to sell.

The soldiers tried to go to Béxar to their friends in the Alamo, but the wagons all broke down and they have no horses, only a few, and so they are back in the fort preparing for defense and siege. They are digging a ditch to the river, and have placed large guns like cannons at the corners of the presidio, commanding all the main roads into town. They call the presidio Fort Defiance. They seem to have enough guns.

Their clothing is in threads, some are almost naked I would say and there is hardly a decent pair of shoes among them. I do not know of any food or supplies expected to come.

Fannin does not seem much in favor with the men.

Until later, God willing.

The letter was unsigned. If the script had not been so distinctly hers and if he had not watched her write it sitting in her circle of light in the center of the room, Adelaido would not have believed her capable of such a thing. He could not understand her motives. Was she in love with De la Rosa? Clearly, the letter was to De la Rosa, and familiar in its tone. Crucita and the great ranchero—the man whom Adelaido had once revered above all others, above his father, even—together, had deceived him.

One sentence Adelaido returned to, and read again: "I do not know of any food or supplies expected to come." It was a lie. He had told her of the goods coming from the coast. If she had told De la Rosa, his vaqueros would have started for the coast to intercept the wagons. But she had chosen not to tell.

For Adelaido, there was satisfaction in the fact that she lied to De la Rosa as she had lied to him, but there was no real comfort in it. The only comfort which he found to cling to as he sat with the parchment trembling in his cold hands and the little plumes of fire licking at the darkness, was the fact that she had not betrayed him. She had deceived him, but she had not used him: her letter contained no information which he had given her.

He was not among her sources.

Over and over, he reminded himself of that.

When Adelaido entered, Crucita was sitting up in bed.

He walked directly to the burning embers, squatted down beside them with his knees spread open and the red glow on his face and chest and inside his open thighs, and while he looked at her, and she at him, he dropped the parchment in the flames.

Neither said a word.

C O O N   D O G

KENNER HOMESTEAD ON THE
SAN MARCOS RIVER

Coon Dog's sudden barking made Katie sit up in bed, her heart beating hard. For an hour she had been awake with her monthly cramping, and now felt it clench her belly with new force. Grand sat up in bed beside her. Across the room, Toby was out of bed instantly and Hugh was coming down the narrow stairs from the loft. Reaching over Grand, Katie fumbled with the shutter beside their bed, but Hugh told her not to open it. He went through the door into the family room where Katie heard him speak to William in a groggy voice, and heard William answer him, saying there were two men in the yard.

The baby Samuel was sleeping. Katie checked on him before joining her father and William in the next room, and Toby came jostling by her in a hurry to see that Coon was all right.

Hugh went to the door and opened it a crack, then wider. He was wearing a long sleep shirt and had pulled on his baggy pants; the open doorway framed his body with the black night beyond him and the cold stealing in. There was no wind, but Katie felt the chill creep up beneath her gown. Rose and Grand came in, Grand looking small beside her daughter-in-law, her thin hair loose and trailing in silver strands around her face.

A voice addressed Hugh from the dark. "If you do not quiet your dog I will shoot him."

Toby pressed into the doorway beside his father. "Coon!" he called. "Coon, you come here!" But the dog kept barking, the sound descending to a growl and then rising back into a frantic yapping. Katie could not see him in the dark, beyond Toby and her father pressed together at the open door. But she could picture the dog, his face bristling, the hairs of his chin wiry and his eyes as bold as cats' eyes.

"Coon!" Hugh said with more authority than his son had managed, but still the dog did not obey.

Moving closer, to see around her father and over Toby's shoulder, Katie saw the Hanlin brothers mounted on their horses. She would not have known them in the dark, but for the voice. They had the same voice. It had always seemed strange to her that the Hanlin brothers were so different in appearance—Straw being lean and fair, his brother heavier and darker—and yet they shared the same voice and perfect diction. Bull had a rifle resting on his saddle horn with the barrel pointing at the dog. "I will shoot him," he repeated. Behind him the stars hung low in a black sky and the slope of the hill rose up.

Coon seemed to understand the threat, and would not be cowed. With a low growl he began racing back and forth between the mounted men, nipping at the horses and causing them to prance in place. The rifle barrel followed him. Toby continued shouting at the dog, then said to the man in a tone close to pleading, "Don't shoot him, he won't bite, he only barks—"

But as Toby spoke, Coon launched himself into the air and clamped onto Bull Hanlin's leg as if he had been fastened there. Bull kicked to shake him loose and the horse reared and pitched sideways, almost dumping Bull down on top of the dog. The gun went off. Katie felt her belly cramping hard, the warm blood inside her easing out onto the rag stuffed between her legs. She thought the dog was killed, and took hold of Toby's shoulder in front of her. But Coon was still clinging to Bull's trousers by his teeth, tugging down hard in steady jerks with his front legs off the ground.

Hugh stepped outside the door and Toby shoved out past him, into the yard, and threw himself down on the dog, trying to pull him from the leg. He seemed such a little boy for twelve years old, in his nightshirt that dragged the ground, his arms clamped around the dog's throat and his body hunched over. He did not make a sound, and somehow pried the dog loose and lay down in a heap on top of it; certainly Bull Hanlin would shoot again if he let go.

Walking up beside the nervous horse, Hugh said to Bull with apparent anger, "You can't blame a dog for barking at strangers in the middle of the night."

"We're not strangers, that dog knows us."

"It's the middle of the night," Hugh repeated.

"We were passing by, and thought it would be neighborly to stop and tell you where your son is, in case you had not heard from him," Straw Hanlin said. "He's with Fannin's men in Goliad. And we thought also, that as neighbors, you might tell us where to find our nigger Josh."

"I don't know where he is," Hugh said.

"We saw Thad Beale in Gonzales," Straw continued. "He said you stopped at Sullivan's last October, and had a nigger with you, and bought a mule. Knowing that you have no niggers of your own, and knowing this would likely be the place that Josh would come, we think the news means something."

Hugh was quick to respond. "When and where I buy my livestock, and who accompanies me, is my own private business."

Grand was standing so close to Katie in the doorway that a few strands of her silver hair trailed on Katie's shoulder. Rose stood at Katie's other side, very still. The house behind them smelled of spattered lard.

"If it was Josh you had with you, the business is ours," Straw answered.

"Are you offering a reward?" Hugh asked.

"Of course."

"For information, or for capture?"

"Both."

"Then maybe Thad Beale had good reason to lie."

Straw spat on the ground. Coon Dog struggled harder to be free of Toby.

Rose said in a voice husky with sleep, "Toby, bring your dog inside."

"I can't!" Toby answered in a mournful tone, wrestling with his dog. "If I get off him . . . Coon, no, bad dog, be still."

Katie trembled with the cold. She felt a hand against her shoulder, William moving her aside and stepping out under the glossy sky with his bulky nightshirt tucked into his trousers and a rope dangling from his hands. With Toby's help he tied the rope around Coon Dog's neck.

Straw Hanlin watched, remarking, "I know you," to William. "We were acquainted in Gonzales. You had a baby with you, and a trapper whom my brother had to punish."

William only nodded, appearing preoccupied with the dog.

"Do you know of a runaway named Josh?" Straw asked him.

"No," William answered, starting to drag the dog toward the house. Coon was stubborn and sat back on his haunches, causing the rope to tighten at his throat. His growling turned into a gurgling noise.

Then Bull Hanlin fired. Coon spun around like a wet rag, and Katie thought at first the dog had been killed. He yelped and seemed to falter, then got his balance and ran snarling at Bull, darting so rapidly through the darkness that it took Katie a moment to discern the injury: Coon's tail had been shot nearly off and was hanging limp, independent of the dog's movement.

William restrained him with the rope.

Balancing the gun across his lap, Bull untied a whip from the saddle leathers and unwound it. He snapped it once, cutting a mark in the ground in front of Coon.

With a rotation of his wrist he swung it in a circle over his head as if he were about to cut the dog in two. Hugh reached to restrain his arm, and instantly Straw Hanlin spurred his horse toward Hugh.

Toby stopped the violence. In a voice so calm and definite it did not sound at all like Toby's voice, he said, "I saw your nigger Josh."

Bull lowered the whip and Straw reined his horse. Hugh turned to look at his son. Katie felt the soft hair of her arms bristling, her braid falling against her neck with a touch of warmth. She saw Toby standing with the hill behind him and the stars glistening like snowflakes in the black sky; she saw him lift a hand up like an offering.

"When?" Bull asked.

"When you said. October."

"Was he here?"

"Yes sir."

The Hanlins looked to Hugh for confirmation or denial, studying his posture and leaning to see the expression on his face, but his manner revealed nothing.

"When did he leave here?" Bull asked Toby.

"About a day after he came. He was going to Louisiana."

Bull snapped the whip down on the ground, startling his horse and causing the wounded dog to snarl and strain against the rope toward him with his tail dragging on the ground. "You are lying, boy. He was not in a condition to travel."

Toby only shrugged.

"If you are lying, and we catch you at it, we will kill your dog," Straw said. When Toby did not balk, Straw said to Hugh, "You had better tell me what you know, or I will whip the dog to shreds."

"Do you think I'd trade a man's life for a dog's?" Hugh answered.

"A nigger's for a dog's, you mean. Your son seems willing to."

A silence settled over, with only Coon's low growling and the pawing of Straw Hanlin's horse. Bull kept his whip unwound, resting his rifle against the saddle horn. Then Straw's voice rang out, louder than before, "Woman, you there at the door, the young one; is this boy your brother?"

"Yes," Katie answered him.

"Is he lying?"

"No, he isn't lying."

"Did you yourself see Josh?"

"Yes."

"What condition was he in?"

"He was whipped."

"But fit to walk to Louisiana?"

"Yes."

"Did you take him in and tend to him?"

"No."

"Did your father?"

"No. Josh wasn't that bad off. He tended to himself."

"That's a lie," Bull said, and Katie didn't answer.

William was dragging Coon away, pulling him around the corner of the house.

Straw said, "Beale says that mule was notched on his right ear. If he is on your premises, Kenner, then your son and your daughter are lying, and I'll assume you are harboring Josh here, and we won't be leaving without him." Reining his horse around, he set out leisurely around the corner of the house where William had dragged the dog. Bull stayed where he was, the tongue of his whip lying in the dirt, his gun resting across the saddle horn.

Katie waited, thinking of the lazy mule sleeping in the barn with his head hanging low, one of his lop-ears notched at the tip. Straw would find him there.

But Straw didn't find the mule. He rode back around and told his brother that there was no mule. Katie thought it was a trick.

Grand, standing next to Katie with her knotty hands clasped together, tossed her silky voice into the night. "You men can leave us now," she said, as if they'd asked permission to go, and been denied, and now were finally granted it. "My family has told you all we know."

"You will pay for this," Straw said to Hugh. "You had a duty to report him."

Hugh did not reply.

"I should turn you inside out," Bull said. "That nigger's worth eight hundred dollars. If you have lied to us, we will retaliate."

"We will burn your house," Straw added. Then the two of them turned their mounts and rode out of the yard.

Toby was already heading around the house to see about his dog. Katie followed him. Coon was tied there. When he saw them coming, he pulled against his rope toward them, but he was weak and subdued. His breath was low and wheezy, his black lips stretched back, exposing his teeth like a crazy smile. The tail was severed but for a sliver of skin that held it. William was not with him. When Katie knelt beside the dog, he tried pathetically to wag his tail. Toby had to pull his legs from under him to force him to lie down.

"I should have just laid down on him right at first and not got off," Toby said.

"No, you did all right. You used your head."

Hugh came up behind and knelt to examine the tail. "We'll have to cut it off," he said.

"Can't it grow back?" Toby asked imploringly.

"No, son. It wouldn't."

The night was absolutely still, with the cold stars hanging low. Toby began petting Coon, at first with a tentative touch, then with more assurance, running a hand over the wiry fur from the shoulder down to the belly, back up to scratch behind the ears. "Aw, Coon," he whispered, drawing the words out like slow music.

Coon did not lift his head, but thumped his grotesque tail against the ground. Katie had to shut her eyes, it looked so awful.

William was coming from the barn. Toby looked at him and gave his queer, lopsided smile. "We have to cut his tail off," he said plaintively.

Hugh asked, "What happened to the mule?"

"I took him to the woods," William said. "I knew they might go searching in the barn."

Toby went on petting, leaning his face down against the dog's.

Katie stood up. She felt the cramping pain take over, so intense it separated her from her surroundings, the cold and the stars like snow-flakes, Coon Dog at her feet with his ugly crooked tail. She heard Toby asking, "Are you sure it won't grow back together?" and when no one answered, "If you stitched it here?" She heard her father asking her to get the sharpest kitchen knife.

HORSEMAN UNHORSED

M ARCH 6, TWO MILES SOUTH OF

RANCHO DE LA ROSA

The storm danced on the northern horizon high over the tree line. Lighting was so bright and so continual that Adelaido could see in bold relief the faces of the men who rode beside him and the break in the brushy timber up ahead.

He was guiding them toward the timber, the narrow parting of scrubby vegetation which was the back way to Rancho De la Rosa. Miles Kenner was the official leader of this group of thirty men, and Adelaido was the guide. They were playing out the old roles: Adelaido guiding but not leading, Miles leading but knowing absolutely nothing of the route to take.

Adelaido had cut a slab of leather and secured it around Donde's chest to protect him from the thorns. He himself was wearing buckskin *botas;* the Anglos called them leggings, and would covet them before the night was over.

Riding toward the storm put Donde in a spooky mood. "It's the wrong night for this," Adelaido told Miles.

But Miles was in good spirits. He told a story about a man who kept

167

boring his rifle out until the balls it used weighed twenty to a pound, then seventeen, then fourteen, then he shot his shoulder out at ten. After Miles finished the story, he was quiet a little ways, then said seriously to Adelaido, "I wish I knew how many men De la Rosa's got."

"They'll outnumber us, I'm sure," Adelaido answered. "He probably has some Karankawas; they're very loyal to him. And the Moya brothers with their men." Adelaido could see that this was a game to Miles, a grand adventure. Adelaido knew the art of grand adventures, but for him this was something different, it was his own private mission. He wanted De la Rosa in his custody. Maybe De la Rosa had, or had not, taken Crucita into his bed, but he had seduced her in some way. He'd stolen her from Adelaido and captured her loyalty so completely that she had endangered her safety by spying, and lied to her brother.

"If we can get ahold of De la Rosa, the war is over," Miles said emphatically.

"There's still Santa Anna with his thousands and Urrea with his, if you will remember," Adelaido answered.

"But they're blind, without De la Rosa's spies."

Adelaido disagreed. If De la Rosa were captured, Sabriego would take his place, or the Moyas, or Guadalupe de los Santos. The espionage would not stop with the capture of one man.

When Adelaido had last seen Domingo de la Rosa, in the cold stone hallway of his ranch home while Hugh Kenner and the runaway slave and Callum Mackay waited before the fire in the *sala,* he had felt the extent of the ranchero's power, and had defied it. There was nothing more between them: they had chosen different sides. For Adelaido, it was not without regrets: for many years he'd worked on De la Rosa's ranch and been his favored horseman. There was pathos in the present situation, which Adelaido recognized. There was mystery: he wondered how the great ranchero had seduced his sister, what promises he'd made. It was filled with drama, this story of the great ranchero and his woman spy, except that it broke Adelaido's heart to think of it. Crucita was not a woman to be bought, or threatened, but she could be won, and De la Rosa's winning seemed like robbery to Adelaido. Why would the man he had respected and worked for all those years repay him with duplicity?

As for Crucita, she had refused to give one word of explanation.

Thunder rolled over the voices of the men and the clatter of their horses' gear. The mounts were wary and recalcitrant, balking at the thunder, and though the men were making an attempt at stealth, they were not accustomed to it and could not stop themselves from talking. The night elicited their comment, with the spirit dancing in the sky. Someone said, "All that noise comin' from the clouds, when you can't see exactly what makes it, reminds me of when baby alligators start bellowin' inside their eggs. You can hear it but you ain't got any idea where it's comin' from." Adelaido recognized the speaker by his voice: he was Washington Bloom, who had a sense of drama Adelaido appreciated. Bloom had said he attributed his birth to the sun eclipse of 1806, which inspired seven pregnancies in his hometown alone.

"They don't bellow in their eggs," someone answered.

"I've heard 'em," Bloom said. "Ask Miller. He—"

"Quiet," Miles injected. "No more talking."

These men liked Miles. He had chosen them himself, mostly from the New Orleans Grays. There were two Germans among them who had signed on in New Orleans, and a few Irish Texans from Victoria.

Adelaido was the sole *Tejano,* and the Americans and Germans kept some distance from him. The Irish, being Catholic, were friendlier. At moments Adelaido resented the apparent prejudice, but at other times he liked being separate from these men. He was better spoken than they were. He was smarter than most of them, and more necessary to the rebel cause. So he said very little and took refuge in Donde's company, the sureness of the horse's footing and the warmth of his broad back. When the horse seemed skittish from the thunder and the brilliant lightning, Adelaido calmed him with his voice.

The group passed, two abreast, into the thicket, whacking at the shrubbery. Miles sent the message back along the line that the whacking was too noisy; they would have to pick their way. In some places the brush grew into clumps nearly fifteen feet high, transforming the path into a tunnel, and the men worked their way through by ducking and dodging errant vines. "God damn it, you stop it," Adelaido heard someone whine in a loud whisper.

Miles reined and turned around in his saddle. "Shhhhhhhh," he said.

"He's pokin' at my horse." The voice was a young voice.

"Who is?"

"Claiborne."

"That's a goddamn lie," Claiborne said.

"Shut up," Miles whispered more forcefully.

Bud Claiborne was known for his marksmanship and Cuban cigars, and when Adelaido turned to look, he saw the cigar tip pulse red in the darkness.

"Stop whatever you were doing, and take up the rear," Miles said, moving on. The others continued double-file behind him.

"Stop it, Claiborne," came the whine again.

"Stop what?" Claiborne demanded.

Miles reined in, whispering angrily, "Scholar, what's going on back there?"

"Fight," Scholar said.

"Over what?"

"Claiborne's pokin' this kid's horse."

"I am not, you pig," Claiborne growled.

"You sure are."

Miles said, "I told Claiborne to get in back."

No one answered.

"Stop it," the boy repeated, presumably to Claiborne, and Adelaido could not hide his irritation. *"Cállate, menso,"* he snapped, then said to Miles, "Make them quiet."

Thunder opened up the sky, and when it rolled away Adelaido heard something thrashing in the undergrowth and someone shouting.

Leaning low against Donde's neck, he pressed back through the crowd toward the noise. At first he could make no sense of it, but then a pulse of lightning shone white and vivid on the scene.

The boy was on the ground in the brush beside the path, with an ugly expression and holding his shoulder. Scholar was leaning over him, offering a hand, but the boy did not take it. In a needled thicket several yards farther from the path a panicked horse reared repeatedly, his mane and tail becoming so tangled in *huisache* and black chaparral that his movements were restricted. The vegetation seemed to suck him under.

Miles reined up beside Adelaido and together they dismounted, fighting the thorns and trying to calm the horse. But when the horse was finally still, sitting on his haunches like a dog with the brushwood high up around him and his stark ribs heaving with moans that Adelaido—

through his gloves—felt like tremors, his posture suggested he was badly maimed. He was an old, decrepit horse. Adelaido could not find the injury until he looked into the eyes, and saw they were gutted by cat-claw cactus thorns. Groaning heavily, the horse tried again to stand, its eyelids batting down the blood.

Against the lightning sky, Adelaido saw Bud Claiborne, barrel-chested, poised on his mount and studying the scene with detachment, his cigar sticking from his mouth like a cactus bud and his distinctive flannel cap, with visors of alligator hide attached to front and back, pulled down on his head.

When the sky went dark, Adelaido took his Bowie knife from the sheath at his waist and with a sawing gesture he slit the horse's throat, trying not to see the dark shape of the creature's head or feel how it lurched beneath the knife.

Miles was also kneeling. Touching the blood with his glove, he said, "God, Pacheco," and quickly wiped the glove against his trousers.

"His eyes were full of cat-claw," Adelaido said.

The men butted their horses together in the path, trying to see. A few dismounted to get a better look at the dead horse sprawled gro-tesquely in the undergrowth. "I never in my life," one commented sullenly. They also looked at Adelaido, and he felt they were blaming him.

"God damn it—" Miles was saying.

"It wasn't me," Claiborne said. "Thunder spooked that horse."

"Bullshit, *you* did," the boy accused, still sitting in the bushes near the horse and nursing his skinny shoulder. From his vantage he had not yet seen Adelaido's work, and that the horse was dead, and when he reached to touch the neck and felt the utter stillness of the body he turned and cried out to Claiborne, "He's dead! You killed him!"

"Not me," Claiborne said, drawing hard on his cigar. "The Meskin killed him. Slit his throat. Look at the blood."

The boy inched over, staring with loathing eyes at the wound and then at Adelaido.

"He slit his throat," Claiborne repeated.

"Shut up," Miles said. "The horse had cactus in his eyes."

Adelaido felt that Miles should show some gratitude to him for put-ting the horse down so quietly, without a shot. He had saved Miles from having to do it. But Miles said nothing else about it. It seemed to Adelaido that injustice was taking place: if his skin had been white, these men would not look on him now with such disgust. He imagined himself from their vantage, squatting in the prickly vines with scratches on his face and a wet blade glistening in his hand, his long hair tied back in a leather thong. He was a savage, a brown-skinned savage, in their eyes —not a man with a code of honor who told stories and loved horses.

Putting his knife away, he stood and fished his gloves out of the matted vines.

"Now what can I ride?" The boy was whining up at Miles, and again Scholar offered him his hand. This time he took it, then bawled out, "Owwwwwwww. It hurts. My shoulder hurts. I think it's broken. God, I'm scratched all over."

Scholar felt the shoulder blade and said it did not feel like it was broken.

"Who asked this boy to come?" Miles demanded in a whisper. Lightning played across the faces, the hats pulled low and collars turned up high.

"Claiborne did," someone offered.

"Kid's my nephew," Claiborne said, holding his cigar out and tapping away the ashes. "He goes where I go."

"Well he's going back to Goliad, so I guess you're going with him, then," Miles answered.

"No need for that," Claiborne said, stuffing the cigar back in his mouth as he dismounted and picked his way over to the boy. "He ain't hurt."

"Don't you touch me—" the boy warned. "I ain't lyin' that I'm hurt."

Claiborne took hold of his shoulder.

"Owwwwwwww—"

"There's nothin' wrong with you except you're a crybaby. Goddamn, look, now you've made me cut myself on that . . . plant. It's a goddamn . . . *sword.*" He swore and nursed his forearm, then turned to Miles and changed his voice completely, saying courteously, "Come on, Kenner, we don't want to go back."

"The kid's got no mount," Miles said.

"He can double up with me," Claiborne answered.

"Send them back," Adelaido said, but Miles ignored him and spoke to Claiborne. "All right then, double up. But if there's any trouble, you're both going back."

The boy did as he was told, favoring his arm and whimpering, and the men fell into line again, with Miles and Adelaido in the lead.

Everything seemed pending. Thunder was rolling closer. Adelaido's senses were so keen that he began to imagine sounds he did not hear. The horses from behind were crowding him and even the trees gave the impression of leaning in on him. Miles leaned toward Adelaido in the saddle and asked how long he'd known Domingo de la Rosa, and Adelaido answered warily that he had known him all his life, that everyone who lived in Goliad or the vicinity knew of Domingo de la Rosa.

"I mean, personally," Miles said.

"He employed me to train horses when I was twelve years old. He allowed me to live in his house and taught me to speak English. I respected him. He tried to help save my parents when they were dying of the cholera, and failed."

"Your parents died of cholera?"

"My entire family died of cholera, except my sister."

"So what made you turn against De la Rosa?"

"I'm not against him—against the man," he said. "We've only chosen different sides." But he was against him. His resentment had turned personal for it involved Crucita. Politics were tawdry in comparison.

They rode on as Miles continued to ask questions, though now the questions were not about Adelaido, but about De la Rosa's ranch, exactly how it was arranged and the most vulnerable points of entry. Miles was specific in his questions. Adelaido told him how the road forked up ahead—the left fork leading to the ranch and the right fork leading to a shallow crossing upriver and a path down the west bank to the ferry at De la Rosa's crossing. He estimated that twenty guards, at least, would be at the entry points and out patrolling the vicinity, and told of the *Tejano* refugees from Goliad camped on the east bank of the ferry crossing, which was the same side as the ranch. "If I ride in with just two men, I can bring De la Rosa out alive," he said. "You could place the rest of these men on the outskirts, at least four to guard the ferry crossing on the west bank, in case something goes wrong and De la Rosa tries to escape that way." Everything Adelaido knew of the ranch compound, he told: the measures the ranchero would use to protect it, the habits of the people living there, the location of the room where De la Rosa slept. "Cattle might be feeding in the bottoms," he said. "If some of us come in from that direction we should take care not to spook them on a stampede toward the compound."

"Hey, Kenner," someone whispered from behind. "How close do we get before we light these?"

Adelaido turned in his saddle and saw a man in the dancing light, slouching on his horse and holding up a slender mesquite branch.

Miles said over his shoulder, "Hold off. I'll tell you when."

Adelaido said, "We can't get anywhere near the compound with fire. We need dark."

"Look, Pacheco, there's no way we're going to sneak in and steal De la Rosa from his bed," Miles answered.

"It's what we planned," Adelaido said.

"No, it's what you planned."

Suddenly, understanding came to Adelaido. It came all at once in a bolt so bright that he perceived it like a vision: the burning of Domingo de la Rosa's ranch. His throat seemed to clog with cold air, and he reined Donde to a stop. "You plan to burn the ranch," he said with certainty.

Miles stopped beside him and had the courtesy to look him in the face. "We have to."

"To ride in with torches. Shooting?"

"If they shoot at us, we will shoot at them."

"Of course they will shoot at you," Adelaido answered.

Miles shrugged and said, "Then . . ." and didn't finish.

"These are not only vaqueros you'll be firing on. There are families living there."

"We don't plan to shoot women and children."

"And these men will take time to distinguish?"

"Look, Pacheco," Miles said impatiently, "it ain't right to ask you to go on in with us if you don't want to. You can stay here if you want."

"What I want is to capture De la Rosa alive, as we planned."

"Well the fact is, nobody else here cares a dollar for De la Rosa's life. Far as we're concerned, he's responsible for Urrea butchering our buddies on their way to Matamoros. Collins back there at the end of the line had a brother shot. Now you've got some respect for De la Rosa, but don't expect us to. We've just got a job to do, and we're gonna do it my way. Now dismount."

The word struck Adelaido like a blow: dismount. Miles intended to unhorse him, put him on his feet where there was only the hide of his moccasins between him and the dirt. He defied the order, sitting motionless on Donde's back.

"Dismount, Pacheco."

"No."

"Scholar," Miles called in a ragged whisper, "come up here."

Scholar edged his way up through the ranks, causing confusion and jamming up the narrow pathway. When he sidled up to Miles and Adelaido, Miles said, "Pacheco isn't going in. He's staying here. You better convince him to get off his horse."

Scholar sat in his saddle with lightning flashing on his fleshy profile and the misshapen hat pushed back on his head, and said, "How come you want him off his horse?"

"Because we're taking the horse with us."

"What about Horse Pass?"

"What about it?"

"Adelaido was loyal as you or me. On the same side."

With a note of exasperation, Miles said, "We had a job at Horse Pass. Now we've got a different job and Pacheco doesn't like it. De la Rosa used to be his friend. Personally, I think he's right not to like the job and not to go along."

"It's very kind of you to concern yourself with my honor," Adelaido interrupted bitterly, "after I've already brought you here."

"Get off your horse," Miles said, and drew his pistol from his belt.

"Come on, Kenner," Scholar said. "Let him keep his horse."

"I can't, when he knows every shortcut to the ranch."

"What, you think he'd ride in and warn 'em that we're comin'?"

"Maybe."

"Would you do that, Adelaido?" Scholar asked.

Adelaido only stared at Miles.

"I don't think he would," Scholar insisted to Miles.

Someone in the line remarked, "If he's turned tory, shoot him."

"I'll shoot him," Bud Claiborne said. "And I get dibbs on his horse."

The idea of that—of barrel-chested Claiborne with his alligator visor and cigars, riding Donde, put Adelaido into motion. He dismounted without a second more of hesitation and stood beside Donde, holding the reins of braided horsehair. "Shoot that greaser," someone said. "Do it in the thunder and nobody'll hear."

"No firing," Miles said emphatically.

Escape was impossible. The thickets on either side were like thorny walls. Adelaido did not know if Miles would shoot him.

"Can I have his horse?" Claiborne asked. "My horse can't take much of this doubled-up shit."

"Shhhhhhhh, keep it down," someone grumbled at Claiborne.

Thunder shook the ground at Adelaido's feet; he felt it pulsing from his soles up to his heart. He had not felt the thunder's strength when he was riding; there was elevation on a horse, emotional and spiritual. For Adelaido, the idea of placing Donde's reins into Claiborne's hands was worse than the thought of passing off a woman to another man. He thought: I will shoot Donde if Claiborne tries to mount him; I will shoot Donde out from under him. And beneath his blanket he cocked his pistol and aimed it at the leather thorn-guard strapped on Donde's chest.

"Scholar, take Pacheco's horse," Miles said. "And give Claiborne yours. Can you ride with just a surcingle?"

"I don't want to take his horse," Scholar said.

Miles turned on him. "I didn't ask you what you wanted. I asked if you can ride with a surcingle."

"Never have," Scholar said coldly.

"All right then. Claiborne? You want Pacheco's horse?"

But as Claiborne answered, Adelaido spoke to Scholar. "Take him," he said, holding out the reins. "He is a gift, take him."

Scholar studied Adelaido and the offering in his gloved hand, then stepped forward and took the horsehair reins. "I'll give him back next time I see you."

But Adelaido was unable to think of the future. For him, there was only the present moment when he stood in the narrow pathway on leaves decayed and soggy with the recent rains—the last remains of winter—and surrendered Donde to another man. He felt he had nothing left, no pride, and no choices.

Claiborne dismounted, giving his horse over to the boy, and grabbed the reins of Scholar's horse and swung himself up. Scholar took a blue canvas bag that hung from the saddle pommel and tied it around his waist, and with difficulty mounted Donde, his feet in moccasins groping for the rawhide loops that served as stirrups. Donde pawed the ground with agitation, and Scholar appeared uncomfortable and insecure with nothing but the reins to cling to.

"We aught to take the greaser's weapons and tie him up," Bud Claiborne said.

But Miles said no. He told the men to move on out, and led the way on down the path. Through the branches, lightning danced in erratic patterns across the sky.

On foot, at a distance, Adelaido followed. At first he had no plan, but then he came across a trace sprouting from the main path, and took it. Varmints were restless in the undergrowth and an owl hooted from a high limb, looking down with irridescent eyes. The trace was no more than a gash in thorny vegetation, a deer trail used by cattle now and then. Twice Adelaido encountered expansive walls of retama and prickly pear and had to cut his way around. His blanket kept snagging in the thorns, and finally he had to wad it up against his chest. Without the blanket around him, the cold stiffened his muscles.

The trace ended at the riverbank, where a mist lingered above the water, glistening like morning fog in the lightning. Evidently the rain had not broken upstream, since the current was slow and clear over the rocky bottom and the water was only three feet deep and within banks, no more than twenty yards width. Like a man walking in his sleep, Adelaido moved out into the water and trudged his way across with the cold numbing his legs. He began to recognize his surroundings and to plan where he was going. On the far side the trace continued up a brushy slope and opened to a dark prairie land. Adelaido could smell prairie roses and see pools of red when lightning flashed. Turning left down the tree line, now on the side of the river opposite Domingo de la Rosa's ranch, he followed the river for a mile until he reached a path that cut back to the river. Here, almost crawling, his hands in hide gloves grappling with the vines, Adelaido moved along the path to the river and the ferry crossing, listening for the voices of *Tejano* refugees from Goliad who had been camped at the crossing for months now. It was late at night, and possibly everyone was sleeping. He heard the water, and thought he was still hearing only water when he perceived another sound: music drifting hollow and serene over the river, silver notes of a guitar in the silver twinkling air. The notes seemed in rhythm with the lightning, the strings plucked separately, then played out to a low strum.

It was a song Adelaido knew, a Spanish melody. When he was close enough to hear the words, he recognized the voice. Since childhood he had known the voice, had heard the wind carry it on winter nights, and had known the summer heat to part and let the music pass from the jacal next to his jacal, when Louis Villapando sang late at night. Señor Villapando was an old man who made his living carting goods from the coast inland and back again, and who possessed more emotion in his voice than most men had in their tears. There were many nights in Adelaido's boyhood when his family grew melancholy listening to the music. His mother, instructing Crucita at her sewing, would rest the garment in her lap and lean her head back with her eyes closed and hum the melody, her lips pressed together as if she were feeling pain. Adelaido's father would set aside his shoemaker's tools to kneel before the statue of the patron saint John the Shepherd, and Adelaido would watch Crucita's bright eyes in the firelight, and listen.

Now the voice was muffled and distorted by the misty air which hung like a barrier between Adelaido and his people.

He thought of going over to them. Later, he would remember that: he would recall that he heard the singing of Louis Villapando and almost crossed the river. But while he crouched beside the path with one hand pressing the vines away to open his view to the river, the camp fires on the other side burning low under blankets hanging from the trees, and a dog barking lazily—he did not really think seriously of crossing over.

He had a different plan. He would capture De la Rosa on his own. If the Americans went riding into the ranch compound with their fire and their firearms, De la Rosa would outwit them. He would get away. He would come to the ferry crossing to escape, and Adelaido would be waiting there.

The song lilted through the mist, overcome at times by thunder rolling closer:

"Ese lunar que tienes cielito lindo
junto a la boca,
No se lo des a nadie cielito lindo
que a mi me toca."

Adelaido was still listening when the song stopped and another started. Then the firing of guns commenced from the direction of the ranch across the river. He waited. On the far bank, beyond the misty curtain of the river, silhouettes began moving frenetically around the fires under the trees, and soon there was shouting, Spanish words flung about the camp fires. The panicked refugees did not know what violent event the ranch was witnessing; they did not know whether to go there or flee into the woods. They called on God. They called to their children and their dogs. Some began to scatter. One group of ten or more boarded the ferry raft and pushed off to pole their way over. Others crowded into a canoe, which rocked in the current and almost capsized, but was righted. Order disintegrated into chaos, and as Adelaido watched and listened he began to pick out voices that he knew and names he had spoken a thousand times in casual conversations, before the Anglo soldiers came to Goliad and these civilians fled.

"*Soldados Americanos,*" he heard them yelling, over and over. "*Los soldados!*"

He noticed a certain little girl in a gown too flimsy for the cold and so loosely spun that Adelaido could almost see her tiny shape through it, with the river mists curling up around her body. She was small and placid in the turmoil, her black hair loose and floating down her shoulders and her back, and she did not make a sound when she was lifted to the raft. With her bare feet spread apart, she balanced as the ferry raft was poled into the current, which was deep and swift. Her arms were wrapped around her chest. He thought there was nothing there, in her arms; he thought that she held nothing but her own sense of self-possession. Her silence and her courage touched him. But as lightning opened up the scene and lit the shadows of her skinny arms against her chest, he saw a cat with glowing eyes struggling there. Her firm, maternal grip only scared the creature, and when thunder echoed down the river bottoms the cat clawed loose from her hold and flung itself into the water.

Falling to her knees, the girl reached after it and might have slipped into the water if a woman had not taken hold of her.

In the camp across the river a donkey brayed incessantly. Two pigs trotted to the water. A white chicken roosting in a tree spread its wings as if to fly, the last red remnant of a camp fire illuminating the white feathers from below.

Rain began to fall.

From the road that topped the slope down to the camp, three riders descended at a run, the chickens squawking around the horses hooves. They rode directly through the camp and to the ferry landing. One of them, in a black cape, with one arm lifted, leaned forward on his mount and called across the river to the group of refugees poling on the raft, and with the first word Adelaido knew him as Domingo de la Rosa.

"Ruiz, are you there?" De la Rosa called to someone on the ferry, his voice straining above the noisy river.

"Señor!" Ruiz called back.

"Hurry and see they're safe and bring the raft back over. We have to cross!" De la Rosa shouted. "They've set fire to the ranch!"

The canoe bumped up against the bank and refugees trailed off, pulling themselves up the muddy slope on roots and vines. A baby was squalling in a blanket. The raft also eased in with the little girl still on her knees and curled over the edge, the woman holding to her gown and restraining her. One woman dressed in blue stepped knee-deep into the water; a man lifted children from the raft to her arms, one at a time, and she set them on the shore. The little girl was handed over and stood trembling on the bank in the rain, her wet gown clinging to her legs, her eyes still searching the water where the cat had sunk away from her.

De la Rosa flung his voice across the river at the refugees, instructing them to take shelter in the woods and send word to nearby ranches. He wished them God's protection.

On the path, six feet away from Adelaido, they were passing with their children in their arms. Like a wood nymph with the rain falling in bright streaks on her hair, the little girl walked with her gown twisting around her legs. Thunder poured out of the sky and she stopped to cover her ears, but was hurried on.

With the rain now pouring steadily, muffling sounds and distorting distances, soaking the trees until they glistened in the lightning, Adelaido could not discern with any clarity what was happening across the river. But then he saw, through the water curtain, a vision of horsemen with lighted torches rushing toward Domingo de la Rosa and his two companions on the bank. In one flash of light he thought he saw Scholar Tipton riding Donde bareback, the thorn protector still strapped to Donde's chest, Scholar flinging out his meaty arms for balance with the fringe of buckskin flapping in the rain like feathers.

But he could not be sure.

There was a volley of gunfire.

A torch was lifted to a blanket that was strung between two limbs, like a roof; for an instant it caught fire, than went limp and soggy.

Ruiz, on the ferry raft, was poling back across the river for Domingo de la Rosa, but there was no time. De la Rosa pointed toward the path that led upstream, instructing his companions to go in that direction. Then he reeled his horse around, leaned over the neck, and headed off the other way, alone. Adelaido guessed where he was going—toward the shallow crossing half a mile downstream.

The Anglos pursued the two *Tejanos* on the route upstream. Adelaido began groping his way back through the brambles. He reached the prairie before the refugees. There, with the rain pelting his face, he turned along the tree line at a run, heading for the crossing downstream. With the river winding as it did, he could cut across the bend and travel half the distance De la Rosa had to take to reach the crossing. Rain pricked his face with cold. Lightning washed the prairie in white light that shone vividly on red prairie roses spread between clumps of scrub oak and mesquite. He knew the river would be rising and imagined he could hear it rolling through the bottoms with increasing speed, gathering into a wall of water that could flood the shallow crossing and cut him off from De la Rosa.

When he arrived, the crossing was still passable—swift and turbulent but only shoulder-high. A worthy horse with a skilled rider could cross easily unless sudden floods descended from upriver.

Adelaido waited, breathing hard and picking thorns out of his leggings. From his hiding place he could see across the water to the sloping bank. He felt certain De la Rosa would come, and was so familiar with the route along the river that he knew the timing of it, and expected the ranchero at precisely the moment he appeared through the mist on the far side, his black cape dragging wet around him, his horse slipping slightly in the mud as he ventured from the sodden trees down to the water's edge.

De la Rosa studied the water currents, looking both upstream and down, the lightning flickering on his profile.

Crouching in the bushes, Adelaido smelled earth and the musty odor of wet bark. He could hear nothing but the river tumbling with the rain. When De la Rosa urged his horse into the current, Adelaido removed his gloves and drew his pistol. Patiently, he waited, watching as the horse and rider crossed with the dark and frenzied water peeling off around them. They kept their balance in the tumult, and the horse maintained its footing, straining up the slope with De la Rosa bent low over its neck to help with the momentum, the cape hanging down below the horse's flanks and the rain beating down as if melting everything into the sludge. They topped the slope.

Quickly, Adelaido stood up from his hiding place and stepped into the path, his pistol aimed at De la Rosa's chest. For an instant only, the ranchero seemed surprised and unable to discern who it was that blocked his way; he showed uncertainty, reining with an awkward gesture. Then, regaining calm, he spoke as if this were a casual, expected meeting. "Adelaido."

"Dismount." Adelaido said the word, and felt an odd remorse.

Looking at him as if he were a snake that had crawled across his path, De la Rosa dismounted. But his voice was one inquiring of a friend. He said, "I see that you are *sin pies,* Adelaido. Where is Donde?"

"I've lent him to someone," Adelaido answered over the noise of the rain.

De la Rosa smiled. "Lent him? I see." Letting his sarcasm linger, he added, "I thought I recognized him a while ago, with a gringo rider, when the rebels set fire to my fences. Yet I didn't think you would allow a gringo to ride Donde. I misjudged you. You are more generous than I supposed."

He knew Adelaido far too well. Adelaido looked at De la Rosa, at the rain beating on his aging face and dripping from his hair, and said to him, "I used to admire you more than my own father. But you've used my sister for your purposes and I will not forgive you."

A brief respite in the lightning shrouded De la Rosa in such opaque darkness that it seemed he'd disappeared. But his voice spoke: "What has your sister told you?"

"Nothing. But I know." The rain washed his voice away.

"You know what, precisely?"

"That you've used her as your spy. And I suspect you've used her as your whore."

De la Rosa did not call him foolish. He said he was deceived. "You have deceived yourself," he said. "All your life you have known her, and you think her capable of whoring? She is not a whore."

He had turned everything around, Adelaido saw. It was De la Rosa who defended Crucita's honor now. Adelaido stood in the mucky rain with his pistol cocked, and it was the other man who honored her. He felt his own convictions dissolving in the downpour, sloshing down around his feet in turbid pools of water. His hand that held the pistol lowered at his wrist and his arm seemed to sag in its socket. "She is in love with you," he said bitterly.

"If she is, I am not aware of it."

"Why else would she spy for you?"

"For me? You're not as smart as I believed," Domingo de la Rosa said. "It's for you she does it. When the war started, I wanted your help, and asked Crucita to find you. She wouldn't do it. I told her that you owed me a debt for my help and my belief in you, and for teaching you to speak English. She acknowledged that you owed the debt, and said you would pay it, that you always pay your debts, but that you'd choose your own method of repayment. So I told her I would turn you over to authorities, for your smuggling, if she didn't find you and convince you to help me." He paused, and added, "She said that she herself would pay your debt to me. Which she has done."

"By informing you of rebel movements, and of mine."

"Of the rebels', only. Never yours."

"But I am with the rebels."

The horse shook its head against the rain, rattling the bridle. De la Rosa looked at Adelaido, his eyes hollow in the dark, then he glanced around the woods and said with heavy sarcasm, "Are you with them? I don't see them here."

The mockery offended Adelaido, and he resumed his pistol aim.

Looking at the gun, De la Rosa said, "Yes, you'll have to shoot me if you want to take me. It's your decision, Adelaido." Then he swung his soggy cape around himself and mounted his horse like an eagle settling onto a rock. Placidly he sat on his Spanish saddle, looking at the trees and the sky with water pouring from it. "I hope this is the last cold weather," he said. "It should be spring by now. The anaqua tree beside my door is in full bloom, at least it was an hour ago. It may be in ashes now. Well, perhaps the fire has been blighted somewhat by the rain." He was quiet, then added solemnly, "God's will," and Adelaido did not know if the ranchero was referring to the hope that the rain would blight the fires, or to the choice which Adelaido had to make.

It seemed the choice was not his own, that it was made before he made it.

He stepped aside and lowered the cold metal of the gun down against his thigh.

De la Rosa then moved forward on his mount. As he passed, he looked back through the wash of rain and said, "You can tell Crucita to stop sending the letters; there's nowhere she can send them now. And consider your debt to me as paid. But remember, Adelaido, *Extra Ecclesiam Nulla Salus.* There is no salvation outside the Church. Will you not change your mind, and come with me?"

"No," Adelaido said emphatically. "You have nowhere to go."

Waiting for a burst of thunder to roll away before he spoke, his shape indiscernible in the black cape with the rain beating down, De la Rosa answered, "I would rather my ranch burn, than my soul."

Adelaido took shelter in the woods until the storm had passed. Before dawn he ventured back onto the prairie, to a round hill topped with white oak trees. There he knelt and said his rosary.

He was wet and cold. He was without a cause, and felt without a friend.

But he had Crucita back.

At first he thought the orange glow on the horizon beyond the tree line of the river was De la Rosa's ranch on fire, but it became the sun. The clouds rolled away and morning light poured across the prairie land of red flowers, where a solitary bull grazed on new mesquite grass. In the dripping branches overhead, a flock of noisy birds showered droplets down on Adelaido, and they glistened on his face like tears.

He saw no sign of flames on the horizon, and no smoke. But when the spring breeze shifted, he perceived, mixed with the fresh scent of prairie roses, the certain smell of something burned or burning.

That was how he told the story afterward.

Chapter 17

LEAVING HOME

M ARCH 12, THE KENNER HOMESTEAD

There was the storm, a day of light, then four days of rain. It seemed the rain had settled in around the Kenners' house for good. The roof leaked, the yard became a hog wallow, the river bulged from its banks.

A leak above one corner dripped dirty water down on Toby's drawings and his drawing paper, and he became depressed and quiet.

Before dawn on the fifth day, in a north wind, a rider came, all bundled up and sopping wet. He was very young. Before a new fire, with his teeth chattering and his clothes dripping on the hearth and one of Rose's blankets wrapped around his shoulders, he told his tale of carnage.

This is what he told: the Alamo, reportedly, had fallen. Santa Anna's army of several thousand men had made brief work of it on the morning of the sixth, breeching the fortress walls and killing all within but the women and the children—almost two hundred men—and afterward burning all the bodies. Travis, Bowie, Crockett were all dead and burned but they had taken many Mexicans out with them. The reports were not confirmed: General Houston, with his army in Gonzales, had sent out scouts for that purpose. It was not yet known what Houston would do if reports were true, and if Santa Anna started marching eastward toward Gonzales. Houston was calling on all able men to join him; there could be no more apathy in the countryside. Every family leaving home and evacuating toward the east was entitled to one armed man for protection. All other men should join the army—armed, but not mounted, since there was not grain enough to sustain horses. Houston had sent to Colonel Fannin by express, an order—a second order—to remove his five hundred men from the fortress at Goliad, dump in the river whatever artillery could not be hauled along, and blow the fortress up, but it was feared that Fannin had delayed too long and already was besieged by Mexicans. Two months previous, Houston had issued the same orders to Travis at the Alamo and the result of disobedience was now disaster. Houston stated that the rebels must not depend on forts: roads and ravines would suit them better.

The women of Gonzales were frantic: thirty-two of the Alamo defenders were Gonzales men, nearly the entire male population of the town, and if reports were true that all were killed, Gonzales would be nothing but a town of widows.

Santa Anna was threatening to sweep the country free of all Anglos.

The Texan government was still writing a constitution at Washington on the Brazos, far enough east for safety at present.

East was the way to be going. Of course there were dangers in the east; it was said the Mexicans had infiltrated the Indian tribes there, particularly the Caddos, and were inciting them to rise against Americans. But this was only rumor, and therefore insignificant compared to the certain danger of Santa Anna's armies advancing from the south and west.

The vision settled over them.

The story had been brief, but the images were full: not far away were charred bones of men whom they had known. No burial, no meager semblance of honor for the dead, no rites of passage to another world.

Rose was the most offended, for Rose had the most belief in the other world.

Charred bones, was all.

Rose asked the question, her voice low and her demeanor watchful, like someone waiting for a judgment or a quietus. "Do you know who died? Do you know the names?"

"Some of them," he said.

"Miles Kenner?" she asked, and her voice did not falter, though her freckled hands made little anxious gestures in her lap, picking at a loose thread of her woolen shawl. She did not wait for him to answer, but went on, "The last we heard he was with Fannin down in Goliad but he knew Bowie, he'd been with him before, in the siege last winter"—and she looked to Hugh.

"I've heard of a Miles Kenner down in Goliad," the messenger broke in. "If he's the same one. He must be, 'cause my cousin was down there two weeks ago and talked about a man named Miles Kenner who was scouting for Fannin, that most of Fannin's men are U.S. volunteers and Miles Kenner was one of the few Texans, so that's why he's a scout. Him, a few of the Irish from the settlements, and a couple of *Tejanos*."

A silence settled, with the ticking of the clock and water dripping at odd intervals from the leaking roof. Rose's gray cat rubbed up against the messenger and he leaned to stroke it, asking, "Is he your neighbor? Because I'm looking for a doctor named Kenner—"

But she corrected him. "He's my son," she said, and Hugh said, "Fannin is trapped too, at Goliad?"

"We don't know it for sure," the man replied to Hugh, then turned to Rose. "If he's your son . . . I'm supposed to find a doctor named Hugh Kenner but I thought he was on up the road, and—"

Rose's gaze went back to Hugh, and he felt it like the kiss of Judas, and he said his name out loud, still looking at his wife, her red hair twisted in a single wave and hanging down between her breasts, across the cotton gown.

"I thought you lived on down the road, I was sent to warn everyone around here but especially to find you," the young man said, and pulled a soggy hand-drawn map from out of his coat pocket, unfolded it and turned halfway around to hold it to the firelight, a few rough lines so wet they ran together and so darkly drawn that Hugh could see them through the parchment.

He saw a bold cross, circled, and guessed it was to mark his home.

"Ah, this is wrong then," the messenger said. "The fellow who drew it thought your place was farther north. I'm lucky to find you." Refolding the map and tucking it back in his pocket, he took out an envelope sealed with a blob of common wax, and handed it to Hugh. "This is from General Houston. He said he hopes you'll answer it in person."

Hugh opened the envelope and found the page inside so wet it nearly melted in his hands. He neared the fire and crouched to turn it to the flame light, for the dawn was dark and no light came in through the window shutters. The dripping messenger stood near him with the fire steaming his wet clothing, and Grand sat upright in her rocking chair. Cats lay about the room like rags. The family all stood around—Toby in his nightshirt and the women wrapped in shawls. William, with his pants wrongly buttoned and his shirttail hanging out, was holding the baby.

Hugh read the letter to himself only. The script, on both sides of the parchment, was jagged with the wet, but large and bold enough to be easily discernible.

Headquarters, Gonzales, March 11, 1836

Sir. You will receive this letter at the hand of Mr. John Vance. I pray you that you will extend to him your kindness.

As he will tell you, I am induced to believe from all facts communicated to me that the Alamo has fallen, and all our men are murdered and their bodies burned.

Our army here is in need of men. We will be in need of doctors. It has been told to me that your sentiments are not with us. It has never been intimated that you would be disposed to aid the enemy in any way, and those few who know you have declared to me that you would not. They call you passive. If this is true, may I assure you that I care nothing for your sentiments, it is your skills I need. I would not presume to trust you if I did not know you by reputation. There is a friend of mine in Nashville—and of yours, I believe—most reliable and good—Dr. John Shelby, who during your ordeal over the death of the disfigured baby, spoke most highly of you to me. He said your humanity was not at question, and your methods were correct. You will recall that he spoke on your behalf when the baby died. He encouraged me, as Governor, to do so also. I was prepared to do, but you moved away, and directly I was involved in my own misfortune and my own act of conscience, and censored by the same populace that censored you.

Sir. The army needs you. I urge you to repair to this point forthwith. Take what precautions are necessary for your family—remove them for God's sake as Santa Anna is sure to advance this direction. But come.

Sam Houston

Beneath the signature another line was added:

Do not rely on the ferry at Gonzales—we may burn it to slow Santa Anna's crossing.

Twice, Hugh read the letter to himself with the flame light washing the page in yellow, then looked around at the anxious faces of his family, still puffy from sleep, and said simply, "He needs doctors."

A quiet followed. Katie started to put water on to boil, but left off before the pot was swung over the flames, and just stood there.

Hugh thought of Bowie with the cold sore on his lip, their meeting last November, and the image of the cold sore mingled in his mind with the image of the burning bodies, flesh puckering in bubbles. He had seen burned human flesh before. He had treated fire victims and seen dead bodies charred down to the marrow.

The messenger handed Rose the blanket she had given him, and said he should be going. Katie gave him food to take along, bits of jerky tied together with a string. Hugh asked him which river he had forded, the San Marcos or the Guadalupe, for Gonzales was nestled up against the east side of their junction, extending down the Guadalupe for a distance.

"San Marcos. Someone else was sent along the Guadalupe."

"Which crossing did you take?"

"The one on that bend two miles up from town. But the water was real high, and pro'bly worse by now. I had to swim the horse. You could maybe still get across on horseback, but if everybody goes—" He glanced around the room at all the people. "Well. You'd never get any kind of wagon across. You ought to take that ferry flat that's just north of here; that's what I plan doing on my way back down."

"There isn't a ferry north of here," Hugh said.

The messenger was standing near the door holding his hat and the small bundle of jerky. Stuffing the bundle in his hat and setting the hat down on the floor, he pulled out the map again and bent close over it. "Well, this fellow was wrong about your home, so he could be wrong here too, but according to his map there's a ferry right near here, just north." He looked at Hugh. "He said it's hard to find, tucked back in the bushes near where a stream butts in."

Hugh shook his head.

"You sure?" the man asked.

"Yes."

"Then I don't know of any way you'll get a wagon over." He studied his map again. "It's very definite here. And the man who drew this seemed real sure about it. Maybe you've just never seen it."

"I've lived here seven years," Hugh answered. "I'd know about it."

Then Toby said, with obvious reluctance, his head ducked slightly and the shadow of his pointed face thrown huge above the doorway to the sleeping room, "Father, I think there is one."

"Where?"

"Pretty near here."

"On the Hanlins' property?"

"Not that far up."

"On ours?"

Toby nodded.

"Whose is it?"

He shrugged.

"Who uses it?"

"Nobody, I guess."

The visitor spoke up. "Smugglers, maybe, if it's that well hidden," he said offhandedly, and then to Toby, "A mile up, you'd say, or farther? Would I see it from the path?"

"Probably not. Look for the stream coming in from this side. The river's pretty narrow there. There's a cross hammered on a oak tree, but you can hardly see it. I'd say it's almost two miles up."

Hugh, in all his shock about the Alamo and the burning of the bodies, noted only vaguely how strange the boy was acting: clearly, he was quite familiar with the ferry flat and felt some shame about it. If it was a smugglers' he should have told when he found it. But that seemed of little relevance, a minor trespass. Abruptly, Hugh offered his hand to the messenger and walked out into the rain with him, telling him to help himself in the barn if the horse needed anything.

Waving the offer aside, the rider mounted and set off toward the road. The rain closed in around him.

When Hugh went back in and shut the door, there was unnatural quiet, everyone just looking at him, waiting. The room, which had been a home for seven years—a solid place of refuge—seemed no longer to offer any sanctuary. Already Hugh was taking leave of it. He did not go to warm himself beside the fire.

Toby said, "You think that man in Gonzales who made my hat is dead?"

"I don't know," Hugh answered. "I don't know if he went to the Alamo."

"You think he did?"

"Probably."

"Then he's dead," Toby said, and there was something adult and disturbing in the finality with which he said it. "And Mr. Miller, too, I bet he's dead."

Hugh turned to Rose and asked if he could talk with her alone.

Inside the dark sleeping room, with the door shut, Rose sat down on Toby's bed, which was still unmade and rumpled with a red patched quilt and a brown spread. Hugh was reluctant to show her the letter. He felt distant from her. The letter would only call forth memories unpleasant for them both, of a child, who was not even theirs, who had entered their lives like a disfigured curse and changed everything.

But there was not time for sensitivities. Hugh gave the letter over and lit the taper on the wobbly table. When Rose finished reading, she looked up at him.

Hugh said, "We should go, I think, all of us. And I should try to find Miles."

"You should go find Miles," she said. "But we should stay here."

"It isn't safe to stay."

"It isn't safe to leave, either." She added, "This is my home. The war is out there." She gestured toward the closed shutters. "And it isn't our war, that's what you always say."

"If the soldiers come they aren't going to ask whose war it is."

"You believe they'll murder helpless families?"

"No, but I can't leave you here," he answered her.

She was angry. "You brought us here. I never wanted to come, you know that. I didn't want to come out to this place and live in terror every minute thinking Indians would come and steal my children. But I did it, for you, and now I've made a home of it."

"We've all made a home of it, Rose, but—"

"That's a lie," she said, her voice a whisper, her green eyes stunning with their anger. "You never have. You never put your heart into it. You or your mother. Your heart is"—she made a sweeping gesture with her hand—"I don't know where it is." He looked at her, a red-haired beauty who was losing her whole world. He had never heard her speak this way, he had not known the full extent of her resentment. She said, "And if we left, how would we go? The wagon's nearly rotten. The oxen are too old to be pulling it through this . . . bog. You think we're better off out there in this weather, with the rivers to cross, and Samuel—remember we've got a baby to look after, and a very old woman—and a broken-down wagon to pile everybody into?"

He, too, had his anger, but he held to his composure. "You won't be managing alone," he said. "There's William. You would go with other families toward the border, and on into Louisiana if you have to. We'd arrange a meeting place, like at my uncle Jason's in New Orleans—"

"We're not going to Louisiana," she said. "I'm not leaving home."

"This is about Miles, isn't it," he said. "You don't want to leave because if he came back you wouldn't be here."

"Don't patronize me, Hugh. Of course I worry what would happen if he couldn't find us. But I have other children, too."

"Yes. We do." But Rose had always favored Miles, with Toby like a lost soul and Katie longing for more mother than she ever had.

"Don't accuse me of playing favorites," she was saying, "you're the one. You've never cared for Miles, just because he's not like you. You favor Toby just because he is."

He resented how she had to simplify. She never saw complexities. "Toby's not like anyone," he said.

"But he's more like you," she insisted, and she was right. "You should go. We should stay. God will protect us here."

He saw her reasoning, and strength, but still he disagreed. "Should we ask the others what they think?" he asked, and his voice was not harsh now, for he did love her.

But the question—to go, or stay—was never presented to the others. When Hugh and Rose entered the family room they found Grand and Katie unloading the fine china from the corner cabinet and stacking it on the floor. Katie, still in her gown with a shawl draped over her shoulders, was standing on a chair and handing the pieces from the top shelf down to Grand. Baby Samuel was awake and secured to a leg of the table with a strip of sheeting long enough to let him crawl about, but not long enough to let him reach the dishes, and he was straining for a stack of saucers. The fire was blazing. Katie turned and said, "Toby and William went to fix the wagon."

Hugh glanced at Rose's profile, saw her close her eyes in a weary blink. He thought he saw the hope slide from her face; it seemed to him that something fell away, though her jaw was lifted. "We don't have room for dishes," she said quietly.

So she was going. That would be her way of saying so: to decide about the dishes.

"We're going to bury the dishes," Grand said. "And Hugh's books. We'll wrap them up the best we can and put crosses at the mounds to look like graves so no one will dig them up."

Rose said, "But it's your family china."

Holding the platter to her fallen breasts, Grand answered, "I don't care about the china. We're going home."

"No we're not; we're leaving home," Rose said. "And we'll be turning back before we reach the border."

Grand held the platter from her chest and looked at it, speaking as if to the platter, "I never will. I never, ever will." Then she looked up at Katie standing on the chair, and said decisively, "I'll take this one with me. Just this one," and she turned to Rose and in a gesture of rare generosity told her she could dig the others up if she came back, and keep them as a gift, from her, and pass them on to Katie.

Toby would remember that day—when he dug the holes—as the day he made a place for himself in the world.

There was not much blending of the dawn into the morning, for the gray would not give way to light and a misty rain persisted steadily. Toby himself chose the place to dig, beneath a stand of stunted oaks between the river tree line and the house. The yellow grass lay flat and sodden like wet hay, and the soil was closely packed and pebbled. A growth of weedy roots from the grasses defied the shovel blade to cut them, lacing each scoop with a stringy, clinging matrix. Even the dirt itself was heavy, it was so burdened with water, and Toby's arms began to ache before one hole was halfway dug. He left that hole unfinished and started on a second just to vary the task.

At least three holes were needed, deep enough to lodge dishes in, and possibly a box of tools if there was room. They were to look like graves.

Toby had volunteered to do the digging. He wanted to be alone. He'd always thought of Miles as safe, untouchable somehow, and now he knew how wrong that was: even Jim Bowie, and David Crockett—a congressman—had been touched: burned up in a fire. Suddenly, with this news about the Alamo, his fears for Miles became so troubling that his mind refused them and kept jumping off to smaller worries. Toby thought of how the cats were all mewing about inside the house, rubbing on everybody's legs, and the poor creatures did not know they were about to be abandoned. He thought about a book he'd stolen from the shelves a month ago and had not yet returned. It was titled *Aristotle's Masterpiece* and was filled with woodcuts of the female body depicted in detail and very large, with whole paragraphs describing "Female Anatomy" in scientific terms. The book was in the barn hidden underneath a rusty pail. Toby had spent hours sitting on the ground in the dim light tracing the drawings with his fingers and squinting at the text.

And now his father, packing up the books, might notice it was missing. He might also ask about the ferry flat. These worries crowded Toby's mind, and Toby welcomed them so they could push aside the image of the bodies burning at the Alamo.

The truth was, Toby didn't want to go. And the whole truth was, he didn't want to go and he didn't want to stay: he could not figure what it was he wanted. Just a place, maybe. A safe place.

At least Coon could come along. He'd get to sleep with him at night. But the thought of fleeing seemed worse than staying home. There was a sort of fear that was inspired by the act of running. At a younger age, Toby had felt it in the games of chase. When the pursuer, usually Miles, was closing in on him, Toby would stop suddenly and let himself be caught rather than experience the fear of being overtaken. Miles was always angry with him when he did it.

Coon Dog watched each dump of earth expectantly, sitting on his haunches and wagging his poor stump against the earth.

The drizzle continued, a chill creeping into Toby's insides, up against his stomach. His stomach rumbled, though he didn't feel hungry. His hands hurt. He could barely see anything, his glasses were so spotted with the rain—only the dark hole with its musty smell, the rusty shovel blade plunging and lifting methodically, the expanse of yellow grasses with the gray shape of a house on the slope and, in the other direction, the long tree line of the river.

Then Hugh came out, approaching through the muggy light, and offered to spell Toby with the shoveling.

"Is it all torn up in there?" Toby asked, glancing toward the house as he handed Hugh the shovel.

"Yeah," Hugh nodded. He sliced the shovel into the pebbly earth with a grating sound. "I feel torn up myself."

"Mother doesn't want to go, does she," Toby remarked.

"No, she doesn't."

Toby squatted beside Coon Dog with his elbows on his knees, and glanced up to see his father's face, which was shielded from the drizzle by a floppy hat. When Hugh met his eyes, Toby looked away, off toward the trees along the river, all blurred and hazy with the rain. "I wish I could go with you," he said. "Mother doesn't need me. She has William."

"She needs you, all right," his father said, jabbing the shovel down hard with his foot.

Toby smelled the dank earth and the dog beside him. "There's nothing I can do that Mother or Katie can't," he said.

Hugh stopped shoveling and looked at him. "You can swim," he said. "Better than anyone. You'll have to cross at least five rivers and some bayous between here and Louisiana. They're likely to be flooded and the crossings and the ferries washed out. If there's a way to cross, you'll be the one to find it."

That was true: Toby could swim. It was the one thing he could do better than Miles, who had always been uneasy around water. And it was the one thing Toby could do perfectly without his glasses. The underwater world was all a blur and was supposed to be, it was a blur for everyone. It was, for everyone, what the outside world had always been for Toby; it did not play favorites.

Hugh resumed his shoveling, then stopped again and asked directly, "Whose ferry is that, on our property?"

So there it was, a matter of loyalties, and Toby made a choice. He needed to feel solid, with his father, so he told. "Miles made it," he said, and added, "It's just a little raft."

"What for?"

There was some release in telling. "For smugglers."

"Smugglers?"

"Tobacco smugglers."

"And Miles knew them?"

"Yeah."

"And he built the flat for them?"

"I guess." Silence followed, with a bird winging low overhead. "Yeah, he built it."

Coon Dog sensed the disconcerted tone and looked attentively at Toby, then laid his wiry muzzle on top of Toby's shoe and cocked his eyes around in their sockets, looking up at Toby then at Hugh as if waiting for someone to speak.

Toby said, "I guess I should of told before."

"I don't know what I would have done about it if you had," Hugh answered, scraping a clod of mud from the toe of one boot with the other, then staring at the ground for a while, leaning on the shovel handle with the blade shoved deep in the earth. Toby was uneasy with the silence by the time Hugh finally looked at him and said, "I remember once when you and Miles were little, and we found a clump of shiny stones in the woods. You both thought they might be gold. Miles studied them and decided they weren't gold, and went off and left them. But you felt how smooth they were, the way they curved, and you couldn't decide if they were gold or not. So you took some just in case and because you liked them anyway." The tone of voice, the keen look in his father's eyes with his hat brim pulled down low and his old brown jacket missing two buttons on the chest, the grave partly dug—all of it together entered Toby's mind in a picture he would not forget. He might forget the story, but not the image—through smudged glasses with tiny specks of dirt—of his father leaning on the shovel handle in the misty rain. "And you're still the same," Hugh said. "If anyone has any gold, in the end, it'll be you. But meanwhile you're carrying around a lot of worthless stones."

Toby hesitated. He wanted to know more. There was something here, important. "Is that good, or bad?" he asked.

Lifting up his hat to shake the water off, Hugh said, "It's good," then put his hat back on and went on digging for a while, grunting occasionally with the labor, talking about the rising river and how he hoped to have the wagon loaded up by noon.

Toby stroked Coon's face with one finger, following the nose upward between the eyes, the way the fur grew. He thought about the story of the gold. He thought about the men he knew in Gonzales, Mr. Kimball and Mr. Miller and Johnny Kellogg, who had stolen Mr. Miller's wife, and how they might be dead, thrown into a pile and sizzled down to bones. He thought about those bones. Then he thought about the dog. "I wish Coon would stop trying to wag his sawed-off tail," he said. "You think he's a ugly dog?"

Hugh kept on shoveling. "Yeah, he's on the ugly side."

"Yeah, without his tail," Toby remarked sadly, and stood up. Coon stood up too. "I'm rested," Toby said. "I'll take it over."

"William can come spell you in a while; he's loading things," Hugh said, handing him the shovel, then started toward the house.

Toby glanced down at the rusty shovel blade with the mud sticking to it and a few strands of yellow grass, a brown beetle crawling along the jagged edge of violated earth, and looked up and ventured the hard question. "You think Miles is all right?" he called to his father.

His father failed him then, or Toby thought he did. "I don't know," was all he said, and went on up the slope.

Coon Dog cocked his ears forward, cocked one paw off the ground and watched him go, but stayed with Toby.

Toby plunged the shovel deep. The roots were fewer now and did not cling together. After ten minutes of hard shoveling, he saw, suddenly, that he had dug a hole. A place which had not been before. At sight of it, something in him lifted and took flight; despite everything, the war and everything, he felt a pride in the creation and a sweet, momentary urge to lie flat down inside it. "Look here," he said to Coon, breathing hard. "A hole."

Baby Samuel was trying to walk at nine and a half months of age. That afternoon he managed his first series of swift steps. Katie, to keep him out of the mud, placed him in the center of the little two-wheeled cart which was to be drawn by the sorry mule. For just a moment she turned her attention away to help her mother carry a heavy bag of corn, and Samuel stood up and walked right over the lumpy floor of the cart, which was made of ropes and rawhide woven together, and Katie looked in time to see him stepping off the tailgate into the air with his arms spread out like wings. He looked exhilarated, almost beatific, like a flying angel, until flipping forward in midair and landing face down in a mud puddle and horribly bruising his head. For an hour afterward he screamed, clinging to Katie but glaring up at her face if it were her fault, and she was terribly upset. Rose tried to comfort her, saying Samuel was a headlong child without the natural fear of falling that most babies his age had, and that Katie shouldn't blame herself. Katie blamed herself anyway.

It was late in the afternoon by the time the family wheeled out of the yard, with the mule pulling the cart loaded with provisions, the two oxen pulling the wagon loaded with bedding and people and two trunks of clothing. William and Hugh took turns driving the wagon and walking beside Loco, who was laden like a packhorse. Toby, with his knapsack and Coon Dog on the seat beside him, drove the cart, since he was patient enough to handle the mule. Bay Mare's lead rope was tied to the tailgate, and she was led along behind.

Grand sat beside Hugh in the shotgun seat of the wagon wearing a

green bonnet and holding an umbrella over her head, while Rose and
Katie entertained the baby in the back of the wagon. William had secured Grand's rocking chair and another chair with a cane-bottom behind the driver's bench for added seating, and Katie tried to rock Samuel
to sleep in her lap with a section of white canvas draped over her for
protection from the rain. But Samuel screamed so hysterically underneath the canvas that Katie thought she would go deaf, and gave it up.
The canvas was too small to extend over the entire wagon back, so she
draped it over the two trunks, making a low kind of tent between them,
and she and Rose lay down under it on hay spread over the bed of the
wagon. Samuel crawled out into the drizzle and played pee-pie from the
edge of the canvas, attacking the tent with a series of rapid slaps and
waiting for Katie to respond from within. If she did not respond at once,
he repeated the assault, and Katie would finally lift the edge and tiredly
sing out "Pee-pie!" This made Samuel scream with laughter. His face
was joyous with a blue bruise on his forehead and mud smeared into
one nostril.

The ferry flat was secured under the low canopy of dripping leaves.
It was smaller than Toby remembered.

Before loading, Katie dug through the huge, wet trunk covered in
bull-hide with the glossy hair still on it, where she thought she had put
Samuel's extra nappies, and discovered that in all her worry she had
failed to pack them. For Katie, after all the trauma of the day, this was
too much, and she slammed the trunk closed and leaned her face against
the black bull hair on its lid and wept.

It took two hours to get everyone across the river. The pole and
paddles were gone, and had to be improvised. The ferry was too small to
carry the oxen and the wagon together, so the oxen had to be unhitched
and ferried over separately. Then came the mule and Loco with the cart.
Loco was nervous about water, and troublesome. The crossing required
three trips in all, using clumsy branches for poles and a flimsy piece of
driftwood for a paddle, through a rising current littered with debris.

Dusk was moving into dark when the family started down the meager trail along the east bank toward Gonzales. The rain was still falling.

Through that night and the next wet day and into the night they
traveled. When they reached the prairies north of Gonzales the sprin-

kling rain ceased for a while, opening the sky to a few stars behind a wash of silky clouds.

Toby was in front driving the cart pulled by the notch-eared mule with Loco clomping along beside. Behind him, Hugh was riding Bay Mare. The sky in front of them was tinged with red. It seemed to Toby that sunset lingered on the horizon over Gonzales. But night had settled. Gonzales was southeast, not west where the sun would set. Placing a hand on Coon Dog's chest to steady him, Toby reined the mule and turned on the seat and saw that William had stopped the wagon. Rose or Katie, he could not tell which in the odd light, was standing on one of the trunks in the back of the wagon and staring down the trail past him, toward the reddish glow.

Hugh dismounted from Bay Mare in the middle of the trail and said in a voice that drifted hollow through the wide expanses of the prairie night, "Gonzales is on fire."

William rode ahead to see the burning town.

There were several guards posted west of the Guadalupe River whom the army, in its haste, had failed to inform of the departure from Gonzales. They learned of it when the town went up in a blaze and they found the ferry had been sunk and they had to swim the river.

There was a woman, a widow of an Alamo defender, who had refused to leave the town and hid in the roots of an old tree on the outskirts in a daze.

There were a dozen men who had stayed behind, under Houston's orders, to set fire to the town when the army and civilians left, so that Santa Anna would find no food or refuge when he got there, not one ear of corn. There was one man who had put the torch to his own home.

These people, one by one as William came across them with the yellow flame light tossed across their features like wind, the men all breathless with their labors, the woman in dull recitations, told pieces of this story: a Gonzales woman had been within the Alamo walls and seen her husband, dead. She had seen Buck Travis and Jim Bowie and Crockett, the congressman from Tennessee, and the Gonzales volunteers, all dead. This woman had appeared in town at twilight in bloody clothing with her baby in her arms and the slave of Buck Travis at her side. She was bearing a message from *El Presidente* Santa Anna to Sam Houston, which Santa Anna had told to her while the bodies burned: the Mexican army, having been victorious at the Alamo in San Antonio de Béxar, would immediately advance on Gonzales; three thousand Mexican soldiers would be camped on the Cibolo River by nightfall.

Sam Houston had received the news and promptly given orders to evacuate the town by midnight, stating he would not hazard a contest at present, in Gonzales, with fewer than four hundred effective men, short of guns and ammunition and ignorant of the first principles of drill. So he was leading them in retreat from Santa Anna, heading east for the Colorado River where he planned to concentrate the entire army—Fannin and his men included, if they arrived in time from Goliad. On the Colorado he would drill his troops, and make a stand when Santa Anna came. Four oxen, Houston had. One wagon. He had given the other three army wagons to civilians who had no transportation, and ordered that the army baggage that could not fit into the single wagon should be burned, and the only artillery—two small cannon—should be thrown into the river. This was all done. The baggage and many of the tents went up in flames. The ferry on the Guadalupe River was loaded with stones and sunk. Three hundred dollars which Sam Houston had in cash he distributed among civilians. And the exodus began: an army of four hundred, mostly on foot, and a trail of refugees without a soul among them who had not lost family or friends at the Alamo.

William took the news back to the Kenners, and they moved on together in the wake of the retreat.

In the middle of that night, just east of Gonzales at Kerr Creek, Toby saw Sam Houston for the first time in the light of several torches, the black smoke billowing up under a canopy of dripping leaves. Hugh and Toby had left the family farther back in traffic and walked ahead in search of Houston. They found him crowded in by men. He was on foot, having given the little yellow mustang he'd been riding to an old man with stomach cramps.

Houston was big, bigger than any man around him. He wore Indian moccasins and a slouch hat creased in the style of a Revolutionary War tricorner, with a feather sticking from one side. His black frock coat flashed open when he walked, and Toby saw, beneath a buckskin vest, a pistol stuck into the belt and a long saber dangling.

The task at hand was to get the solitary army wagon, pulled by a yoke of oxen, over Kerr Creek. The water wasn't more than a foot deep at the crossing place, but several carts and wagons belonging to the refugees had already crossed and rutted up the riverbed, so the army wagon stuck before it reached the center shoal, which was a brief, narrow island of loose pebbles. The driver was putting the whip to the oxen vigorously but without effect, for the animals were too weak. Sam Houston waded out and put his hands to a hind wheel of the wagon, saying, "Come on, boys, let's help these poor creatures," and those men nearest sloshed out and started shoving.

Hugh and Toby waded out, leaving Coon Dog on the bank. By this time there were enough men pushing from the rear, so Toby slogged on toward the front of the wagon with the water filling up his boots— Miles's outgrown boots, and still too big for Toby. Then he took the headgear of the failing ox and coaxed the animal forward.

"You get away from there, boy," the driver called above the water sounds and the groaning of the men, but Toby kept on speaking to the ox and tugging lightly on the headgear, and the ox responded, pulling steadily and gaining better footing in the sludge.

The water was very cold, sucking at the boots. For two full days Toby had been chilled, and now his teeth began to chatter and his shoulders drew up almost to his ears, giving him a backache. He looked back at the men, all grunting and shouting at each other and sinking in the mud. They were sinking so deep even Houston seemed reduced in height before the wagon was dislodged and rolled onto the shoal in the center.

There was a moment of reprieve, a shout of victory. Then the driver, who had done so little good during the ordeal, climbed down off the wagon onto the shoal, careful not to wet his boots, and leaned down for a long draft. The delay blocked passage of the men behind, who had done the work and now stood round bathed in mud and glaring at him while he took his drink.

Too long, he drank. Foot traffic stopped completely and started bunching up along the bank. The torches belched their black smoke upward and the low limbs showered droplets. Houston's yellow pony, with the sick old man, pranced at the edge of the water. The oxen groaned heavily, and one man shouted, "Move it!" to the driver, who only cut his eyes over and gulped slightly faster, though no less fastidiously, from his cupped hands.

Sam Houston, in muddy water to his knees, extended a finger and said in a voice so resonant and full it seemed like an echo and so well projected that it carried like a shout, though it was not a shout, "Knock him down, God damn him! Knock him down! Standing there holding up the whole army! God damn him! Knock him down."

No one had the chance to do it, for the man rose quickly like a chastened dog and started climbing back onto the wagon. But Sam Houston said, "No, God damn it, you walk," and moved his finger, still extended at arm's length, till it pointed straight at Toby. "You," the general said. "You take his place."

Toby sought his father's face but couldn't find it, there were so many men so close together on the bank and trailing out into the water amid the black smoke of the torches. So he did as he was told. His boots were so heavy with water that he had to curl his toes in them to keep them on while climbing into the driver's seat. He took the reins and tried to keep his teeth from chattering as he called, "Hi-yah!" The oxen moved laboriously forward.

Then there was Coon, hurling himself into the water and bounding like an otter to the buckboard. He leaped and took his place beside Toby and sat there, shaggy wet, looking straight ahead but leaning with one bony shoulder blade pressed against his master.

From behind, Toby heard a voice call, "Got your girlfriend with you?"

"Down, Coon," he whispered. "Down, boy. Get down. Bad dog. You swim." But the dog only laid his ears down flat and turned his face away from Toby.

The sarcastic voice began to call the dog. "Here, pooch, poochie poochie. Here, girl." Coon did not even turn to look, but Toby did, and recognized the former wagon driver slogging through the turbid water, taunting him. He concentrated on the men ahead of him trudging up the sloping bank and disappearing on the path into the trees, and made good time with the oxen. Sitting close like lovers seeking warmth—Toby so aware of the insults from behind him that his back muscles knotted up with tension, Coon with his ears flat against his head—they crossed Kerr Creek and pulled up beside the trail on the eastern bank. There Toby waited stoically for Hugh.

Instead, Sam Houston stepped up to the wagon in his frock coat smeared with mud, and said with a forward motion of his hand, "Is there some goddamn problem with this wagon? Let's get it rolling."

Toby was at a loss. There stood General Houston with a wad of tobacco in his lower lip, a hat like one Toby had seen in a drawing of Napoleon Bonaparte and a voice like God's essentially giving Toby a man's job with the army. Toby couldn't refuse him and say he was going east with his mother and couldn't join the army—not when he was sitting in the driver's seat of the only army wagon and had earned respect by crossing without sticking it. So he started to shrug the reins forward.

But before the oxen responded, Hugh appeared like a voice of conscience from in back of the wagon and introduced himself to Houston. "You sent for me," he said. "This is my son, Toby."

Sam Houston turned to Hugh, and his sour expression eased. "So, sir. You came. Was I right about your sentiments?"

"Yes. But the army needs doctors, and I need to find my son. My other son. He's—"

A gun went off.

Houston turned and shouted, "God damn it, who's firing?"

"Just someone shot a possum!" came the answer from across the creek.

"Well tell him to save his ammunition," Houston called back, and had turned again to Hugh when another answer came through the cold air from the creek, "It was a woman. Her kids is hungry."

Houston closed his eyes. He sighed deeply. "Yes, I need doctors," he said to Hugh. "I've only had one, up to now, and he looks to be a hazard." A torch bearer was passing by with a shotgun over his shoulder, holding the flame up high so the smoke did not blow back into his face. The light briefly illumined Houston's features in relief against the passing crowd: a large, dissipated face but clean-shaven, with a deep cleft in the chin and eyes that seemed to catch the light and hold it. "Do you have your family with you?"

A young man with narrow eyes and blond hair so thick and cropped that it lay on his head like a bowl, stopped and said to Houston, "Now the lock came off," and held out his gun lock in one hand and the stock and barrel, tied together with buckskin strings, in the other.

"That gun's more goddamn trouble than it's worth," Houston said, but took the lock and shouted, "Do any of you men have any sturdy string?" and then asked Hugh, "Your family is heading for the border?"

"Yes."

"Good. Some are heading for the coast to avoid east Texas Indians; there's a rumor the Mexicans are trying to incite the Caddos. But I've got a treaty with most of the tribe leaders for neutrality. A solid treaty; their word to me is good. That's the direction to be going. There's chaos on the coast."

A man trotted up with a long sliver of rawhide and Houston took it and hurriedly secured the lock in place, his broad hands working with agility, like the hands of a seamstress. "Now don't let that hide get wet and stretched, or you'll be blowing pea-pods through the barrel," he said, handing it back over to the owner, then turning back to Hugh. "There's a woman on down the trail in front of us, about to bear a child, who lost her husband in the Alamo. Someone told me she's been vomiting since nightfall."

Hugh said he would look in on her and then be heading south to Goliad. "I have a son with Fannin's men down there. They'll need doctors down there too, so I'd rather put in my duty there."

Houston stared at him with concentration, the slight breeze touching his scant hair. "You know it's likely Fannin's got himself surrounded by Urrea's forces," he said. "There could be another battle, in the fort there, like the Alamo."

"Yes, I know," Hugh answered.

The line kept trailing by: a black man pulling a water sled with a little white child on it, an old man missing one eye, a boy toting a brass pistol.

"It's possible Fannin's left the fort," Houston said. "I sent an order several days back for him to blow up La Bahía and bring his force to join me on the west side of the Cibolo, so we could relieve Béxar. But two days ago when I first suspected that the Alamo was lost, I countermanded, telling him to send a third of his men to me in Gonzales and fall back with the rest to Victoria, and hold Victoria. So I have no idea what he's doing. The last letters he sent, or the last I got from him, said he intended to march on San Patricio and possibly try to take the port of Cópano. I don't know if he's insubordinate or indecisive or just hasn't received my expresses, but he certainly hasn't obeyed them up to now." He paused. "I'm telling you I don't know where you'll find him."

Hugh listened carefully, took from his coat pocket a thin notebook bound in hide and a small piece of charcoal, scratched the names of places Houston had mentioned and said that he would go generally south and try to find him. He offered to take any messages Houston might have for Fannin.

"If you find him in the fort and he's not yet besieged," Houston said, "tell him to move his ass out of there and meet me near Burnham's Crossing on the Colorado. He's got more men than I do, and I need them. Tell him I don't care how long he's spent fortifying La Bahía; troops shut up in forts are useless. We need them here, where they can fight from the trees. Tell him I don't give a goddamn about his West Point training; you might as well take dunghill fowls' eggs and put them in eagles' nests and try to make eagles of them, as to try to make generals of boys who have no capacity by giving them military training. And he falls into the dunghill category."

"Would you like to put that message into writing?" Hugh asked, with a flicker of a smile.

Houston spat a stream of tobacco juice. A burdened mule passed by with his load drooping on one side, and Houston said to the man who led him, "You're going to lose that load," and then, with irritation, "Look here. Can't you tie a rope?" and he untied the rope and cinched it so tight with an upward yank that the mule was lifted inches off the ground. "That's better," Houston said, slapping the mule's rump, and the man and the beast moved on. "What about the boy?"

At first, still seated in the wagon with the reins in his hands, Toby did not realize that Houston meant him. "I could use him," Houston said. "I have men deserting by the minute, to get their families out."

Toby's teeth began to chatter. He put his hand on Coon Dog's back and braced himself to be humiliated by a father who was sending him off toward the border with three women and a baby and an Englishman who could help them out just fine.

But Hugh glanced at his son, and hesitated, and to Toby's plain astonishment said directly to Sam Houston, "No, he's going along with me."

THE FIRES OF GOLIAD

Mᴀʀᴄʜ 17, ɢᴏʟɪᴀᴅ

Crucita was very ill, sweating with a fever, when they came to burn her home.

Adelaido had abandoned her. Since the night he found her letter to Domingo de la Rosa sewn inside the lace-up shoe, and took it out and brought it back and dropped it in the fire without one word to her, he had not returned. She had feared going to the presidio to ask for him, and sat for days in her jacal sewing on men's garments and working on men's shoes while rain ate patches of mud from her walls and weighted the straw roof so heavily that the edge above the bed collapsed and she had to drag the bed out toward the center of the room. Her food gave out, and she bartered work for food. Her hands were chapped with cold and blistered from the tools, the marking wheels and cobbler's hammer and the files and awls.

Then she got the fever, and with it came the fear she always had when any kind of illness struck her: she thought it was the cholera, returned, or resurrected from her body like a buried curse. Aloud, with no one listening, she told herself that it was not: "It cannot be the cholera, no one near has cholera, the men do not. They have the ague and influenza, but no one has the cholera." But her heart was not con-

vinced. She turned the patron saint around and looked into his eyes for
the first time since her father's death, and she knelt and tried to pray.
But the painted face only reminded her of how the saint had failed her
and how her father died on his knees in this very spot where she was
kneeling, so she shunned the saint and ceased to look at him, though she
let him face the room.

Leaving him there, facing out, was not concession but a kind of
punishment: he should view the dismal room without the family whose
pleadings he'd refused to answer, the roof now falling in and the woman
left alone.

More than ever, now, Crucita needed to place blame.

From her doorway, at moments between chills and fever, she
watched the presidio for any sign of Adelaido. She saw men going out in
squadrons. She saw riders going out alone. She saw the narrow picket
gate in the wall that faced her house—the north wall of the chapel yard
—thrown open, and seven cannon dragged out and taken down beside
the river. The next day she saw the cannon brought back in, covered in
slimy mud, and knew they had been buried and dug up again. She saw a
group of thirty riders whom she hadn't seen before, cantering in from
the coastal road to a shouting welcome.

Twice, she saw Adelaido's horse led down to water at the river, but
not by Adelaido.

One old man who came to buy a pair of sandals she had woven from
maguey plants saw that she was ill and suggested that she leave, if she
could travel, and find someone to care for her. He said that the commander, Fannin, had received orders to burn the fort and evacuate the
town and had prepared to do so, but was waiting for the return of two
groups of men who had gone down to Refugio. The first had gone to
escort some Irish families out, since Mexican forces and rancheros were
swarming the countryside. The second group, of nearly one hundred
and fifty men, had gone to see what happened to the first group when
they did not return. It was feared the Mexicans had got them all. But
Fannin would not leave until he knew.

"Was my brother Adelaido Pacheco with these men?" she asked, but
he didn't know. He wasn't sure he knew who Adelaido was.

And so Crucita had no idea of Adelaido's whereabouts when she
heard the men approaching from the presidio and went to the door and

watched two of them setting fire to the abandoned home of Louis Villapando, next to hers.

She stepped out in the drizzling cold, her face red hot with fever,
and tilted back her throbbing head and called as loudly as she could,
"Adieeeeee! Adieeeeee!" then waited, watching toward the fort to see if
he would come.

But he did not come.

The men with torches looked at her as if she were a witch, and one
of them she knew: she had patched the hat he wore. He said, "We've got
to burn your house, it's Fannin's orders, we have to burn all of them to
clear our line of fire in case the Mexicans surround us."

She stared at him with fevered eyes, and howled again, "Adieeeee!"

When the sticks of Louis Villapando's walls finally sparked and
started up a smoky flame, and the second man held the torch to the wet,
drooping straw of Crucita's roof, swearing at the flame's reluctance to
take hold, she stopped calling for her brother. "*Madre de Dios*," she
whispered.

Then she went inside to gather her belongings.

First she took her father's tools and tossed them out the door. Then,
in a large burlap sack, she put her box of thread and needles, the hand
mirror Adelaido had brought their mother from Colima, one brush for
her hair and a small one for her teeth, the last remnant of dried corn,
and two woolen dresses with cotton undershifts. Over her shoulder, she
put the blanket from the bed and beneath her skirt she tied her leather
pouch of money, which had but two coins in it.

She left the shoes and clothes belonging to the soldiers. They could
burn.

When she was prepared to leave, the roof took flame, and she looked
into the eyes of John the Shepherd and said with scorn, "I have turned
you around, and you can watch it burn." But when she was outside, she
turned and went back in again, and brought the saint out in her arms.

They watched it burn, together, Crucita and the shepherd saint and
his single sheep, until the roof caved in, sending little sparkling bits of
straw floating through the mist and turning to black ashes.

The chills had overcome her now, and her sick body took great
pleasure in the fire's warmth, though the tears ran down her face. She
did not care if they were tears of sickness or despair, and put the saint

down in the mud, gathered up her father's tools and took them down beside the rushing river, where she hid them under a pile of twigs and rotting leaves.

Then, because she had no other option and nowhere dry to go, she went up the hill to the presidio and asked for Adelaido at the entry gates. She was told he was not there. The guard made inquiries while she waited in the guardroom, which was a small stone room with straw spread across the floor. Men came and went through the gates; she saw the two with torches who had burned her house passing back in through the gates into the open yard where anaqua trees were blooming in the center, with white blossoms.

She smelled cold stone, and straw, and smoke, and the fragrance of anaqua.

And then the guard returned and said that Adelaido was not in the fort, and had not been there for ten days, since he went out with an expedition to set fire to a nearby ranch where spies were hiding.

Crucita's shaking almost took her off her feet. She asked which ranch it was. He said it was the big one on the river, nine miles north. The description was enough. And why did he not return? "Nobody knows, they say he just split off," he answered.

She did not understand his meaning. "Split off," she pressed, "what does that mean, split off?"

"Abandoned," the man answered. "Left. He argued with the leader, and split off."

"But two days ago I see his horse."

The man would not be pressed. He motioned her to leave.

"I wish to speak to Mr. Scholar Tipton," she said, but the man picked up her blanket and her burlap sack and took her by the arm, leading her out of his small guardroom to the outside of the fort. There he gave her the belongings, and went back in.

"Mr. Tipton!" she called, trying to lift her voice above the walls and growing faint with the exertion. She called repeatedly, but no one came.

Miles Kenner was another name she knew, though she had never met him, and she called him, too. A man passing by the gates looked at her with an ugly smirk on his chapped lips, and winked at her, and she was going to show him her disdain when he said, "All right, lady, you're looking for Miles Kenner?"

She felt such gratitude she almost knelt. "Yes," she said, and he said he would look for him.

The air was gray with smoke. Nine houses were on fire on this side of the presidio. From where she stood Crucita could not see the flames of her own home. When the Anglo-Americans had first come into town and inhabited the fort, they had burned many of the buildings, and had since pried several homes apart to use the sticks for firewood. But this was a clearance, a creation of charred prairie land around a fort of stone. Crucita felt she should grieve heavily for the final desecration of her town, but her physical discomfort and great worry for her brother were all that she could feel at once, and she witnessed the destruction without mourning, clenching her teeth to stop their chattering and wrapping her arms around herself for some small warmth.

After several minutes, when the worst of the chills had stopped and left her so weak that she had to sit down in the mud with her whole body aching, Miles Kenner came. He was a handsome man, and young, with yellow hair and boyish eyes and a coat of rare patches. Crucita stood up from the mud and tucked her hair behind her ears. "My name is María de la Cruz Pacheco," she told him. "Adelaido is my brother. I remember that he mention your name. I am very sick and I need to find him. They tell me he was going to burn the ranch and he was . . . split off."

"That's true," Miles Kenner said. His voice was not unkind. "He left us before we reached the ranch, and I don't know where he went. He hasn't been back here since then."

"Did you went with them to burn the ranches?"

"Yes," he said. "Look, I can give you some food, and bring you in here where it's warm." He made a gesture toward the gateway.

She shook her head. She didn't want food or shelter with the Anglos, she wanted Adelaido. "But two days ago I see his horse. He doesn't like to . . . borrow . . . his horse. I think he must be hurt."

Miles shook his head, "No, he's not hurt."

"The ranch was burn?" she asked.

"Yes."

"And somebody kill Domingo de la Rosa?"

"The ranch was burned but De la Rosa got away," he said flatly, and wiped his hair out of his eyes. "He escaped. *Vámonos.*"

"With Adelaido, together?"

He shrugged. "No, I don't know what happened to Adelaido." He gestured with both hands before his face, the palms toward her and the fingers spread as if to make a little fence between his eyes and hers. "I do not know where Adelaido is," he repeated.

With all her feeling, she said, "Please, mister, help me to find him."

Miles Kenner lowered his hands and looked at her in such a way she thought that he would help her. But then he said, "No, I can't find him. It's impossible to find him."

His tone was very final, and she stood seeking something from his eyes that he refused to give her, or could not, so she ceased to look at him and looked instead across the view of burning houses with the flames like angels' wings fanning out against a misty sky.

She thought of De la Rosa, his corral where she had stood beside him, laughing when the flashy young vaquero leaned too low and fell onto the rooster—the corral in ashes now. She thought of the grand *sala* and wondered if the glistening walls were soot-blackened and the tall *vaqueños* reduced to ashes. From the corner of her sight she saw Miles Kenner shrug his shoulders and press his boyish lips together. "Don't you have anywhere to go?" he asked her gently.

Sudden anger overcame her. She began to shake with chills again. She wanted to shame him, to say, "Yes, I have somewhere to go, I can sit in the ashes of my home." But she did not know the word for ashes. "I can sit in my burn house," she said with spite. "Or go to Señor De la Rosa's rancho and sit in his burn house."

And she took up her belongings from the trampled mud and started for the river.

THE   RABBIT

This was enemy territory. The first two days, traveling south from Gonzales, Hugh and Toby had encountered only refugees and volunteers in search of Houston's army. The third day they saw a single rider in the distance and could not discern the color of his skin. But now, nearing Goliad on the fourth day, they entered country overrun by Mexican soldiers moving on horseback in small numbers and in larger forces on foot, the red of their uniforms showing up against the stunning green of spring, even through the drizzle, from a distance.

If Goliad had not yet fallen to the Mexicans, it was at least surrounded by them.

Repeatedly, Hugh and Toby found themselves crouched down in briery vegetation by the road while the birds sang all around them, Toby chewing his lips until they bled, his arms clamped tight around Coon Dog, his voice cooing at the dog to keep him still while mounted Mexican soldiers passed along the road, one wearing his uniform jacket against bare skin, another with bare feet perched in the heavy stirrups. These soldiers were accompanied by *Tejano* vaqueros dressed in serapes and heavily armed. Hugh recognized one of the vaqueros, very tall for a Mexican, as the employee of Domingo de la Rosa's who had escorted

him, with Adelaido Pacheco and Callum Mackay and Joshua, into the
rich ranchero's parlor that rainy day.

De la Rosa's ranch was not far off, and Hugh wondered how the
ranchero had played his hand in this war up to now, and what had
become of Josh.

He asked Toby to recite again Jason Kenner's address on Milly Street
in New Orleans, near the Holford Inn, where the family was to meet or
write if they were separated, and he called out words for Toby to practice
in Spanish.

"Food."

"*Comida.*"

"Please."

"*Por favor.*"

"Friend."

"*Amiga.*"

"*Amigo* if it's a man."

"*Amigo.*"

Hugh thought constantly of Miles. Their last meeting, in November
in the army camp near Béxar with scavengers floating on the wind like
omens, had been a sort of playacting in which each of them performed
the part assigned, a drama of misunderstanding. Hugh could not accept
that such a barren encounter might prove to be the last time that he ever
saw his son alive.

The muddy path that Hugh and Toby traveled now cut through a
thicket loud with spring. A hazy rain was falling. *Huisache,* with deceptive fernlike leaves, so delicate, disguising thorns, was everywhere in
bloom with tiny yellow puffs of flowers, like berries but furry to the
touch. They gave the woods a yellow wash like sunlight, though the day
was wet and gray. Ahead, the thicket opened to a prairie, and far beyond
that was a smudge of smoke blending with the solid sky. The trees and
tangled vines were so crowding and disorienting Hugh could not discern
the direction of the smoke. He guessed it came from Goliad, which
made him feel so sick at heart that nausea hit him like a gust of wind.

In his mind he saw them: burning bodies.

"They're burning something," Toby said warily.

"Armies are always burning something," Hugh replied.

Maybe he'd been wrong in bringing Toby. But when he'd seen Toby holding the reins in that wagon at Kerr Creek he had known with certainty that if he didn't take the boy with him, Toby would somehow end up with the army, and he had acted on instinct. Perhaps the reason he had brought him here was not to keep him out of peril—they were walking face on into peril—but to guide him through it and determine his responses to it. Certainly Hugh could have traveled more discreetly without Toby and his dog, for he had to stop repeatedly to help Toby pull last year's hardened stickers out of Coon Dog's paws. They had to keep the dog on a rope and he kept fighting it, getting it between his jaws and chewing it. But Hugh had made a choice: if they were captured, the presence of the dog would help them prove they were not soldiers: they were a doctor and his son and dog traveling south unarmed.

Unarmed, but like fugitives.

Toby said, looking at the smoke, "They burned bodies at the Alamo," and Hugh saw from looking at his profile, smudged with dirt, the lips bleeding and one eye leaking out a tear, that Toby was near breaking. "Maybe we should turn ourselves in," the boy stammered. "Then if they took captives, we'll find Miles. They'll see we aren't armed."

But no captives had been taken at the Alamo. The widow who had brought the word to Houston in Gonzales said those few who had surrendered had been cut to pieces. So far, Santa Anna had held to his policy of no quarter. Santa Anna wasn't here, in Goliad, but whoever was in charge of this division would be operating on his orders. If Goliad had fallen, Miles was probably dead.

The rolling prairie opening before them was green with new grass, but there were patches of red and coral paint brushes sprinkled with tiny white blossoms, like snow, and clumps of purple phlox and a blue wash like a lake of water. The path continued across, curving slightly or appearing to with the low swells of the ground, but Hugh and Toby kept within the trees, turning in tandem to the left to skirt the open spaces.

Coon Dog did not turn. A rabbit, a small cottontail, took fright and leaped out from the cavities of wood into the open spaces, and Coon Dog lunged so suddenly with his fierce instinct that the rope leash snapped in two where he had chewed it, freeing Coon Dog to his whims. Coon chased the rabbit out a distance in the field, snarling and trailing twelve inches of frayed rope, missing his prey repeatedly between his paws as it crisscrossed through the flowers. Toby pleaded with him, whispering loudly, "Come here, Coon, come *here*," but the dog was possessed by impulse.

The rabbit made it almost to the patch of blue before Coon pinned him down and grabbed him in his mouth. Oblivious to his masters on the edge of the clearing and to the whole misty, fragrant world, Coon shook the squealing bunny until it was limp. Then his bright eyes caught a movement on the far edge of the clearing. He froze for an instant with the lifeless wad of fur stuffed in his mouth and one paw cocked off the ground, his eyes fixed across the field on two horsemen who had reined their mounts and were looking at him. Then the riders disappeared back into the trees.

Coon Dog trotted his kill back to his master and laid it at his feet like Judas with his kiss.

Hugh looked at the rabbit, its soft fur all damp, and then across the clearing.

"They'll catch us now," Toby said, still holding his end of the severed rope, and Hugh heard in his voice a semblance of relief, the perverse and childish urge to have it done with. Hugh looked deeply into Toby's eyes, through the spattered lenses of the spectacles into the brown irises so like his own. "If they catch us," he said, "we'll ask for De la Rosa. If they're about to catch us, and we're sure of it, we can do it then. But we aren't going to give up just because we fear they'll catch us." He wasn't used to platitudes, but the world in which they trespassed was a world at war.

They had made it around the clearing into a solid mass of green mesquite and sow thistles. The yellow thistle blooms were alive with insects and agitated sparrows and a green lizard bloating his throat into a bubble. Hugh whacked out a place in a patch of yucca spears and honeysuckle and crammed Toby in it, then got in himself. They waited there with twigs poking in their backs, their knees pressed up against their chests and their hats wadded in their laps. Coon Dog stood across their feet with his ears erect, and would not sit down, though Toby pressed down hard with both hands on his rump, saying, "Sit, *down*."

They might have been safe, if not for the hounds. There were two hounds, from the sound of it, and they fastened on the scent, following the exact route along the tree line. Their deep, incessant baying was like a mournful dirge, imparting such sensation of approaching death that Hugh and Toby felt an overwhelming dread.

Coon could barely be controlled. He trembled with the effort to obey his master and stay still, emitting one long high-pitched whine after another and watching fixedly through the little door Hugh had carved out of the brush.

Through this opening Hugh and Toby could see only brush and yellow thistles glistening with water, nothing else, no stretch of the prairie, no advancing dogs and riders, which made the baying seem unreal and strange, supernatural somehow and more frightening even than reality.

When the dogs were close, Hugh picked his medical satchel and drawstring bag out of the vines and crawled out of the wet and thorny womb into the painted prairie, telling Toby to stay hidden.

The dogs were bearing down. There were two hounds and a huge, silent dog, black as pitch, loping beside them. Hugh watched them following the tree line directly toward him, about thirty yards away, the hounds with their noses to the ground and the third dog bounding shadowlike on his tall legs and sniffing the air. Behind them rode four horsemen.

Hugh stood among the purple flowers, took a breath, and willed his heart to slow. A feeling consumed him then, of peace and utter calm. It seemed the world went still and quiet, all but the hounds. Catching sight of him, they raised their noses from the ground, their pace quickening and their ears flopping in the air. The deep baying from their lungs seemed to overcome the prairie, though Hugh was vaguely aware of Toby's voice imploring from the bushes. Placing the bag and the satchel at his feet, he hailed the riders.

Then Toby appeared beside him. Hugh hadn't seen him stepping from the bushes, he just perceived his sudden presence: a boy wearing a floppy hat that was too big for his head, standing beside him with a gnawed-off rope attached to a barking dog whose fur was speckled with cockleburrs.

"*Párate! Párate!*" The riders shouted at the dogs. The hounds froze almost in mid-step, lolling their tongues out and falling silent, while the black dog loped on a pace or two like an elongated, runaway shadow, before circling back.

Near the bushes, the bees were buzzing in the drizzle, feeding on the honeysuckle. Hugh raised his hat, calling to the riders, "I am looking for Domingo de la Rosa," and then, in the best attempt at Spanish he could make, *"Yo quiero Señor Domingo de la Rosa!"*

The vaqueros reined their mounts and consulted each other on the edge of the prairie. One vaquero shouted back, "Put up the feet!"

Coon paced back and forth in front of Toby as far as the shortened rope would allow, his wiry hair on edge all the way down his spine, and Toby started to lift one boot from the purple phlox.

Hugh said quietly, "I think he means for us to raise our hands," and lifted his.

Toby raised one hand, the other still gripping the frayed piece of rope with Coon Dog at the other end.

The birds chattered from the brush; a robin lighted on a flimsy twig of the mesquite and bent it almost to the ground.

Two riders of the four, one wrapped in a red serape with a knife dangling at his side and a rifle gripped in his left hand, the other in buckskins with a pistol cocked, ventured closer on their mounts. Their faces were dark beneath the wide sombreros. The one in the serape, who was older, and thicker through the chest with gray in his mustache, said, *"Señor De la Rosa es mi patrón. ¿Por que está usted preguntando por él?"*

Their fates were about to be placed like trinkets in De la Rosa's hands. Hugh said, *"Mi nombre es* Hugh Kenner. *Éste es mi . . ."* he did not know the word for son. *"¿Hermano?"*

The vaquero looked doubtful, and Hugh tossed out the next word that came to mind, *"novio,"* knowing at once, even before the two vaqueros glanced at each other with amusement, that the word was wrong: *novio* meant "boyfriend."

The vaquero dressed in buckskin shouted back across his shoulder to the others, *"El dice que éste muchacho es su novio,"* and they chuckled and rode closer at a trot.

Hugh said directly, *"No, perdonen me. El no es novio, pero* . . . son. *¿Cómo se dice,* son?"

None of them answered him. The old man pulled his red serape up around his chin, studying both the father and the son. His horse, a lanky dun, pranced impatiently.

The dogs came sneaking forward, but the youngest of the four vaqueros, dressed in black and muddy white, rebuked them harshly. *"Párate!"* he shouted, and they sat on their haunches.

Coon, still pacing, began to growl. The sound of it anguished Hugh as much as anything so far; if the dog cut loose, this encounter could turn bloody very quickly. Hugh and Toby scolded him together, and he quieted.

Toby spoke slowly to the old vaquero in the red serape, "Sir, I am not armed, no guns, no guns," and opened the palm that was not holding the rope leash, indicating he was empty-handed. With his eyes still on the old man to watch for any harsh reaction, he squatted very carefully, his hands trembling, and retied the piece of rope around Coon's neck, this time in a slip knot. Pulling the rope taut, he stood and raised his arms again, though the rope was so short that he could not raise that arm as high.

The four horsemen formed a circle around their captives. Coon began circling Toby protectively, with a continual growl, and Toby had to switch the rope from hand to hand.

"¿Por que está usted preguntando por el Señor De la Rosa?" the old vaquero demanded again of Hugh, and Hugh answered, "I know Señor De la Rosa. I am a doctor."

"¿Médico?"

"Sí." He nodded toward his leather satchel on the ground, and the young rider in the black and white dismounted with his spurs clinking, and squatted down beside the satchel, between Hugh and Toby. He was so near, they could have touched his hat. He unwound the strip that tied the satchel closed, laying open the two halves against the flowers and a patch of soft new stickers, the tiny vials and instruments secured in rows.

The old vaquero said, *"¿Médico, y espía?"*

"¿Espía?" Hugh asked, not knowing the word. *"¿Qué es, espía?"*

"Espía. Espía," the old man repeated.

"Spy," another vaquero said.

"No. *Yo no espía,"* Hugh answered emphatically. *"Médico solamente."*

The old vaquero said, "*¿Cómo conoce usted al Señor De la Rosa? ¿Es él su amigo?*"

"*Sí.*"

The old vaquero held his reins with a fleshy hand, leaning over the saddle pommel and scrutinizing Hugh. His horse was shod with squares of rawhide covering the hooves and tied below the fetlocks like a drawstring bag. The man's boots were patched with rawhide. His skin was deeply lined and coarse, overweathered in the sun, and unkempt strands of his mustache hung down over creases that bracketed his mouth. There were fatty bags beneath his eyes. He stated his suspicion: "*No lo creo. Pero vamos a ver. Señor De la Rosa es mi patrón. Nosotros se los llevamos a él. Ahora, baje las manos.* Put down the feet."

As Hugh and Toby brought their arms down to their sides, Coon let loose a sudden, vicious snarl and lunged against his rope toward one of the vaqueros in back of Toby, almost pulling Toby off his feet. The slip knot tightened at Coon's neck and he began to choke, but he continued straining, his nails digging muddy claw marks in the purple phlox. Hugh could not discern which had happened first: the lunging of the dog or the flying of the lariats that circled in the moist air just above him with a whirring sound. The lariats descended with the grace of mist. In an instant Hugh and Toby both were bound, their arms cinched to their sides so violently by the ghostly ropes that Toby lost his balance. He could not reach to break his fall, but instinctively he opened both his hands to catch himself, and the leash he held slipped away like a grass snake set free: Coon was loose. Coon flew directly toward the mounted man who had roped his master, his canine mind perceiving even in the turmoil of two ropes descending from mid-air, which man that was, among the four. But before Coon reached him, a third loop was cast out in the air, tossed like a fishing net, and fell around his neck as easily as in a game of horseshoes, and the dog was flipped high off the ground and thrown down on his side.

One man cheered his comrade in the black and white for his fast action, and the young vaquero made a formal bow from the waist in his saddle. Wrapping the lariat around the pommel, he took a small rope in his hand and dismounted with the grace of a dancer. While the horse stepped slowly, artfully, backward, keeping the lariat taut and Coon Dog gasping at the other end, trying to gain footing, the vaquero walked over to the dog, leaving boot prints in the fragile flowers, and knelt beside him.

Toby got to his knees, then to his feet, saying in a trembling voice, his spectacles askew, "It's all right, Coon. Be still. Good dog."

The vaquero spoke to the dog in soft tones, in Spanish, and gradually Coon ceased his struggling and began to wag his stumpy tail. *"Dáme la mano,"* the vaquero said, holding out his palm, and Coon, accustomed to responding to that gesture to have stickers taken from his paws, offered his front paw.

The young man laughed. *"El es un perro Mexicano, él habla Español,"* he told his friends, gently shaking Coon's paw, and they laughed.

Coon seemed uncertain of their mirth and pulled his paw away. He lay his pointed ears down flat against his head. But when the young vaquero reached to scratch behind his ear, he allowed it, then sat and scratched himself behind the other ear, his mouth drawn back and giving the impression of a smile.

Toby stood biting on his lips, squinting through his crooked spectacles. One of the vaqueros went to him and jerked his arms backward, crossing the skinny wrists and tying them with strips of hide. Hugh watched the boy's fingers, with their bitten nails, twine themselves together at his back.

Hugh asked while they were tying his wrists, too, "Will you fix his spectacles?" and nodded toward his son.

They did not respond. The young one went on stroking Coon, the older one sat his mount, and the other two argued between themselves, something to do with how the knots were tied.

"Por favor," Hugh said.

The old man dismounted heavily, hitching up his pants over his wide belly, and walked over to Toby. With a single hand, almost timid in its gesture, two fingers only, he lifted the slender metal arm and draped it over Toby's ear. Then he stood back and looked at Toby's face, as if to see if all was well.

Hugh saw a flicker of a smile beneath the gray mustache.

He thought of the dead rabbit, a mere lump of wet fur, lying still and cold as stone at the far edge of the brush across the prairie.

He thought of Miles in his coat with the patch of rabbit fur smoothed by the wind, the blackbirds circling in a blue sky.

The two hounds and their lanky shadow sat obediently on their haunches in a patch of clover.

The dun shook his head and snorted, jangling the bridle.

The mist was falling and the air was cool.

Chapter 20

SEEING THE LIGHT

PERDIDO CREEK, TEN MILES NORTH
OF GOLIAD

When Crucita first awoke she thought the warmth was only from the fever. She tried to open her eyes but the light, even so soft a light, made her eyes burn and water with a flutter of vibration inside her head, and she caught only a glimpse before she shut them: the timid sun that follows rain, hazy-wet and greenish-yellow through the leaves, blotches gliding across her fingers with the breeze.

The warmth was from the sun.

She heard the birds. She heard a voice speaking in Spanish, soothing and familiar and also vaguely troubling: "How far away from town?" and let it linger there close upon the humid air with its touch of light, a question. She lay very still but felt as if she moved, and thought it was the sunlight moving over her that gave her the sensation. Slitting her eyes open again she saw through a watery glaze that in fact she was moving, rocking gently in a woven hammock beneath a canopy of limbs and leaves like ferns with spots of yellow and tiny gnats gliding all around. A spiderweb stretched across the green above her, glistening with drops of water. She was so relaxed that there was no real feeling in

225

her body, except the breath of air across her skin, and she had to move her fingers to know exactly where her hands were, how they lay one upon the other on her stomach.

"Not far from the lower ford, off the road, in the grass. We thought she was dead. We almost didn't see her, the grass was so high."

She remembered the grass, wet ribbons curling over her, the fresh, pale smell, soft stickers not firm enough to puncture her palms as she crawled, but clinging to her hair and dress like children. As if she were their mother.

"She asked for you," a third voice said, "in her sleep."

"He didn't want to pick her up," the second voice cut in, with an edge. "He heard her saying something about cholera, that she had cholera. He would have let her die in the grass like a rat."

There had been a tiny yellow flower no bigger than her smallest fingernail, which had seemed to her as big as the sun. She had put her ear down against the grass and the grass had made a pillow and a blanket too, closing over her, and the yellow flower on its stem was leaning toward her face, and she had rested her head on the grass, staring deep into the yellow center of the flower as if there were a world in there that welcomed her.

Grass insects had waded through the moisture on her sweating face as if they cared for her.

She had shunned the open road, afraid of . . . something.

She had refused the woods with their deceptive light, so plush, the birds all calling to her: if she entered the woods alone she would not come out again. There were thorns in there disguised as blossoms, the petals growing right out of the spikes, and there were flowers full of poison.

But the grass was a savior.

The grass, and before the grass, the river with its cool waters twining all around her body, pulling out the fever and washing it away like dirt. She had put her face down in it and cooled her burning eyes and let it tug her hair like river grass floating just beneath the surface.

She lay very still in the hammock, not a finger moving. The leaves did not make any noise, so there must be no wind. The hammock rocked her and supported her like wings. Someone else must have made it start its rocking, but she felt certain now that it was rocking on its own, and she trusted herself to it, resting into it as if it were her father's arms and she were still a child.

They were saying something else. There was an offering of food. It was Domingo de la Rosa's voice. There was not a certain time when she recognized the voice, she simply knew it or had known it from the moment of awakening, very calm, very sure, not the slightest tenor of regret or worry. Only Don Domingo spoke that way.

What had become of the John the Shepherd? He was saved from the fire, she remembered. She had saved him, it was her strength, not his; when the fire ate away the roof she'd brought him out, him and his black-eyed sheep, and it was such an irony that she had prayed to him all that time when her parents were dying of the cholera.

She remembered the cholera. She had burned her feet and belly and seared the cholera down deep inside her, and the roots had taken hold in there like the dark kernel of the corn, and flourished through these years.

De la Rosa was beside her. Her eyes were closed but she could feel his presence blocking the sun specks and their tiny warmth, and she said, "It is the cholera."

"No, it is the ague," he said.

"You can't be sure," she said, her eyes still shut against him. "You always pretend to know."

She wanted him to touch her, if for nothing else than some assurance that she was alive. But he was not a natural man, he was a voice blocking the sun. "I can't find Adelaido," she said, opening her swollen eyelids to the shadow leaning over her.

His face was just the same, just as placid. There were gnats around him too. She remembered, the Anglos had burned his home. Yet he was untouched by them, his Spanish eyes still slanting downward with the lashes and his hair combed back from his forehead, the brows and the mustache flecked with gray like the spattering of white flowers in the grass. The rhythmic rocking of her hammock made him seem to come and go, closer and then back again, a reluctant presence. She could smell his breath with the taste of wild onions from the riverbanks, and she felt his plain humanity, and said, hearing her own words as someone else's and not feeling any effort in the speaking, "If you know where Adelaido is, please tell me. The Americans have his horse. I know he wouldn't give it to them willingly."

He said, "I saw Adelaido, the night they set fire to my ranch."

"He did not return to Goliad," she said.

"I didn't think he would. They'd robbed him of his horse, and also, I presume, of his convictions. The few he had."

She shut her eyes again, hating his cold certainty, knowing if she continued looking at him with the fragile green of spring above him like a light from heaven and the gnats circling him as if they worshiped him, she would come to hate him. "You don't know where he is?" she asked.

"No."

"You haven't seen him since?"

"No. He wouldn't come to me, for anything." Pausing for a moment, he added, "He knew you were spying, and I confirmed it," and he chuckled softly. "You see, he had a pistol leveled at my heart which inclined me to be truthful. He would have discerned a lie. Of course I don't know what he's thinking now, or where those thoughts have led him."

"What did you tell him?"

"That everything you did, you did for him."

She felt the fresh air fill her lungs. "I've been afraid it's cholera," she said, seeking consolation. A sudden fluttering of wings in the leaves spilled drops of water down.

"No." Again, the certainty and faith: he lived on faith. She distrusted him, but he was all she had, for Adelaido had abandoned her. So she reached for him with one finger only and felt him twine one of his own fingers around it and let go.

He would not hold on.

There were voices not so far away, but Crucita did not listen to them. A dove was cooing, and she listened to the dove. When De la Rosa spoke again, he said, "Adelaido was inclined to think that you were doing it for me," and the statement sounded like a question.

She slit her eyes to see him.

It was the closest he had come to her in all the months of their acquaintance, even closer in a way than the time he put his arm around her in the rain, and she felt as if the swing had brought her right up next to him and left her there, his face bent over hers, his eyes as green as foliage, the whites showing white against the transparent light like a disfigurement. She almost reached her arms around his neck, but felt too weak to lift them.

He said, "You're safe with me, Crucita." She wanted to believe him but his voice was plain and distant and he added, "When you left the town, what were the Anglos doing?"

"They were burning my home," she said, then added bitterly, "Have I not been your spy for long enough?"

For a while he didn't answer, and she closed her eyes. She knew his motives so completely and despised them: he would use her endlessly if she allowed it, until she was used up. She perceived it as a visceral sensation, De la Rosa stealing all her strength and giving it to God.

He was speaking now to someone else, and someone tucked a hand behind her head and lifted it, touching water in a vessel to her lips. She took the hand to steady it and felt it was a woman's, and let a drop of water ease into her mouth.

"Were the Anglos preparing to leave Goliad?"

She was so tired that she gave him what he wanted. She tossed it out to him like a child who throws the ball back to its owner when the game is done, and walks away. She knew she would not get it back: the hope, the feeling. If he had given her the drink himself, with his own hands, or if he had shown human worry and concern, she might have gone on giving to him—information, anything he wanted—and gone on waiting for him to give her something in return. Affection, maybe, or some meager care. But it was over now, as easily as that, and it seemed in her exhaustion there was nothing there to bid for any longer. Perhaps there never had been. He had no heart. He would sacrifice her on the altar if her blood would please his God. "I don't know if they plan to leave," she answered distantly, "they seem . . . to change their minds. An Irishman came from Refugio asking for help to get his children and his wife out of town. The woman was with child, he said. And there were others to get out of Refugio, who had waited too long; the Mexican soldiers were all around Refugio. Forty Americans went, almost forty, some on horses. And with carts. To Refugio to help. But they didn't come back." She had to pause before she could go on. "More than a hundred were sent after them, and they did not come back either. I think there was talk of everyone leaving the presidio then, I don't know where to. A few came to get their clothes from me and took them away, though I hadn't mended them yet. So I think they were planning to leave. But they didn't leave. They were waiting for the others to return. Thirty men came on horseback, but not the same ones who had left. Those never did come back."

"And they will not," he said softly.

"They are dead," she said, not as a question: she knew.

"Most of them, yes."

"And it is your doing."

"And God's doing."

"One and the same," she answered wearily, still not looking at him. "Though God's breath doesn't smell like onions, like He has been rooting in the woods."

De la Rosa let the insult pass, and asked, "How many men were left, then, at the presidio?"

"How am I to know? I never saw them all at once, and counted them."

"More than three hundred?"

"Yes. More."

"Four hundred?"

"No. Go away, señor. If you won't help me find my brother, I have nothing more to say."

"It isn't a game, Crucita."

She opened her burning eyes and stared at him. "You think that I play games, señor, when they have burned my home?" Then she closed her eyes again and felt his shadow on her skin, cool and dark, and longed for him to go away so she could feel the airy flecks of sunlight. She lay drifting, thinking of the grass and its green light.

She was sleeping when a vaquero came seeking De la Rosa, saying two Americans had been captured and brought in.

When Hugh and Toby were presented to Domingo de la Rosa, with their hands still bound behind their backs, the ranchero showed no recognition. He was seated on a blanket beneath pale foliage with the late sun seeping through, and he was braiding strips of rawhide and smoking tobacco rolled up in a slice of corn husk.

His vaqueros spread the travel gear they had confiscated on the ground before him, and reported on the capture. De la Rosa listened, then laid his work aside to sort through Hugh's medical satchel. In English, he said to Hugh, "You are a doctor?"

Hugh reminded him that they had met before, when he brought the slave to him for escort south, but the ranchero cut him off. "I remember our meeting," he said abruptly. "My question to you now is if you are a doctor."

Coon Dog sat at Toby's feet with his eyes fixed on De la Rosa.

"Yes," Hugh answered.

"And the boy?"

"He's my son."

De la Rosa took a piece of charcoal out of Toby's knapsack and some dirty parchments folded over several times, and unfolded the parchments, and saw Toby's sketchings of a river and a cow. "Did you draw them?" he asked, glancing up at Toby, who nodded hesitantly. The ranchero folded them and put them back and gave the knapsack to Toby. To Hugh, he said, "You were traveling toward Goliad. Why?"

"I have a son there. Unless the men there have gone elsewhere."

"The men there have gone nowhere. Most of them have gone nowhere. Some, I have captured. If your son was one of these unfortunates, then he is no longer living. General Urrea has executed others. Are you carrying papers from Houston?"

"No."

De la Rosa ordered his men to search the prisoners, which they did. When he was satisfied, De la Rosa drew hard on his corn husk cigarillo and said, "No doubt you have the message in your mind."

"I'm here as a physician, not a courier," Hugh answered.

"Well, that is very good," the ranchero said, his sarcasm evident only in his words, not in his voice, "as I have many here in need of a physician."

Hugh was silent.

De la Rosa said, with his placidity, "Why is the dog staring at me in that manner?"

Hugh looked at Coon. "I don't know."

Toby said, "Coon, stop it." The dog glanced up at him then went on staring fixedly at De la Rosa.

"The slave was sent to freedom," De la Rosa said to Hugh. "I sent him south with the army of General Cós when they retreated to the Rio Grande. A strange circumstance: I saw him yesterday. The slave. He has come back. He is a servant to General Urrea." He paused, put his cigarillo between his lips, and took up his rawhide pieces to resume his work. "If you will take care of my sick, here, this evening, I will release you after dark." He nodded toward the satchel. "We will keep your medicines, of course."

"What about my son?" Hugh said.

"Of course he will go with you," De la Rosa answered, and added without a trace of humor, "The dog also. I do not want your dog."

In Crucita's dream, the darkness seemed to be inside her and all around her as if she breathed it in. The stones were cold, and there was dirt; she felt its presence on her skin and also in her hair. She recognized the window of the chapel, a circle with the sides sliced away to give it corners, but there was no light coming through. The moon should be out there, but there was no moon, there was no light at all.

Our Lady of Loreto was still gone. Her niche within the altar was empty. Crucita could not see the altar in the darkness but she knew the Lady was not there.

She would be returned.

The stones were very cold, the painted stations of the cross were lost in darkness or were gone. There were no benches on the floor, only bits of garbage and the ashes of an old fire in the center of the chapel, and ashes everywhere, and the walls were blackened; she could tell it even without light because the walls were an extension of the dark: they did not shut it out or shut it in but allowed it to pass through, and outside were anaqua trees with rough sandpaper leaves and dark air passing through them, and no noise at all.

Adelaido would come to bring the Virgin back.

She waited.

There was not a sound, or if there was a sound she could not hear it, as if her ears were filled with mud.

She did not see him enter through the door, she did not feel the door at all or recall which wall it penetrated, but there was a door and he came through it in the dark, and at the altar lit a single candle.

He carried the Virgin in his arms, wrapped in Crucita's shawl.

"Who do you light a candle for?" Crucita tried to ask, but she couldn't make a sound. She felt as if the words would choke her, trying to escape. They filled her up inside like cholera, like weeds in a fertile garden. She opened her mouth the way that black crows open their shiny beaks with nothing coming out, no sound.

Yet he seemed to know her question, and he answered her. "For Mary of the Cross," he said.

He spoke in English, with his hair tied like an Indian's and his eyes shining.

For Mary of the Cross.

For the Virgin.

The Virgin of Loreto.

Our Lady of Loreto.

And then the Lady spoke.

Cradled in his arms, her small hands with mud upon them almost touching at the palms as if she were about to pray, but not touching, Crucita's shawl around her caked in mud and falling away from her face, the Virgin spoke without moving the wooden painted lips and with no gesture, though the gentle voice was surely hers, "It is not for me."

Adelaido did not turn to see Crucita, though she was wishing to be noticed as if she'd spread her arms and waved them high and slow above her head. "Adie," she tried to call to him, "Adie!"

He took the shawl from around the Lady, and her clothes beneath were clean. He rubbed the dirt off her hands and face and stared awhile into her brilliant eyes, then lifted her so gently to the niche that Crucita thought her heart would break with watching it.

She was looking straight into his eyes, so close she saw the water in them and the flecks of light, the way they shone, a crease of thoughtfulness across his forehead and a shimmering of oil on his golden skin.

The single candle cast a shadowed light.

He touched her face, saying, "Now you will be safe," and then was gone, and everything was sliding into darkness, the candle flame burning in the distance very far away, a lilting speck of light. "Adie," she tried to call, but her voice was lost.

And then there was the light.

It was an evening light, gray-green and cool, and a man was leaning over her, not Adelaido but an Anglo man whom she had never seen, his eyes staring so intently at her face that she was frightened. He said quietly in English, "You were dreaming," and tried to speak her language. *"Tiene una . . . vida . . . in su dor . . . dormir . . . dormido"*—she was having a life within her sleep.

But it was not a life, it was a death, and she could not shake free of it. I am going to die, she thought, and said aloud, *"Me voy a morir,"* feeling how her lips were parched with thirst. *"Del cólera."*

His eyes were solemn and his face was good. He had full sideburns and soft hair receding from his forehead but falling to his collar, and stubble on his face. "No," he said directly, "I am a doctor, *un médico. Y su no tiene* cholera. Señor De la Rosa told me your symptoms. You have the ague. Influenza." He offered her warm liquid from a gourd, lifting her head and touching the gourd to her mouth. "This is tea, made from sage. It cools the fever."

She took a sip of the bitter liquid. He assured her once again that what she suffered from was not cholera. "Your fever . . . it is . . ." He groped a moment for the word, then said, "It is going away . . . *va* . . . go," and gave a dismissing gesture with one hand.

But the dream was still with her. She told him that her family died of cholera, all but her brother. He encouraged her to take another drink from the gourd. "No, thank you, mister," she said. "Does Señor De la Rosa tell you to take care of me?"

"Yes." He was noticing her feet. Someone must have removed her shoes or maybe she had lost them at the river. She could not remember. He touched one foot, the sole of it all scarred from when she burned it at the time of cholera, and the pink scars creeping up along the edges like pale blood that she had stepped in.

"I burn my feets before to take off the cholera," she said.

He knelt beside the hammock and placed his hand on her forehead. "How do you feel?"

"I feel nothing. I have tired. Like air." She could not see the spider's web above him, the light had grown so dim.

"The cholera doesn't come back, when it's gone," he said, "unless it is a new . . . epidemic. And no one else here has it. *Nunca aquí tiene.*"

She told him she had dreamed of death, and was worried for her brother's life, and the doctor told her it was natural she would dream of death when it was everywhere around.

"But I feel, it is real," she said. "I feel it is more real than when I am awake." She wanted to explain the dream to him and ruin its magic and its power, bringing it into this world where the evening was the way that evenings always were, with the nightbirds starting now to call to one another and a drop of water from the fragrant branches falling on her neck. But the man was an American and a doctor, far above her in his education, and she did not dare to share her superstitions. She noticed that his wrists were raw with bloody rope burns, and asked, "Did Señor De la Rosa find you?"

"His vaqueros found me."

"Señor has mens in all areas. Do you come from the presidio?"

"No. I was going there."

"I did not remember seeing you in the presidio."

"You were there?"

She nodded.

"When?"

"Before today."

"My son is there," he said.

"In the presidio? The Americans in the presidio burn my house," she answered.

"I'm sorry," he said.

"You are going to see him?"

"Yes." He added, "Your English is very good."

"Thank you. My brother teach me to speak English. He speak perfect English. He is with the Americans, but I cannot find him."

"Did you know the men in the Presidio?"

"I fix their clothes and shoes," she said. The dark breeze flung drops of water from the trees and lifted the American's soft hair around his face. "I do not know all the names of soldiers," she went on. "Many times they don't say the names. But some I know."

"My son's name is Miles Kenner," he said, and suddenly, very strangely, she felt his worry for his son as if it were her own; it seemed to enter in a shiver like the shiver of mesquite leaves, as fragile as the ferns beside the river and the rippling current.

"I see your son," she said. "I talk with him, today. I ask him for my brother because he know my brother. It was your son who burn the rancho of Señor De la Rosa, your son and my brother they did it. Is possible maybe my brother . . . split off . . . from the Americans before they burn the ranch. I don't know the truth. I know they took the horse and your son won't tell me where is my brother."

"It was today, you saw him?"

"Yes. I think it was today."

"What is your brother's name?"

It gave her hope to say it. "His name is Adelaido Pacheco."

"I know your brother," the American said. "Once, he helped me. He did a favor for me."

She looked at his kind face against the twilight and the foliage, noting a small pit in the skin of his left cheek, the hair at his temples lifting with the breeze. "What favor does he do for you?"

"I was taking a slave, an escaped slave, deeper south in Mexico to secure his freedom, and your brother guided us to Señor De la Rosa's ranch."

"For freedom, he does it?"

"Yes, we were taking the slave to freedom."

"No, my brother, does he do it for freedom? Do you pay him?"

"You mean, for free?"

"Yes, for free. My brother is very interesting in money. But he does have feeling."

"Yes, I think he does have feeling. He did it for free."

The approval made her proud of Adelaido. "When?"

"In November."

She remembered. It was November when Domingo de la Rosa hosted the *días de toros,* and Adelaido appeared in the *sala* with two Anglos and a slave. They had asked safe harbor for the slave. "Did Señor De la Rosa help the slave?" she asked.

"Yes."

"So Señor De la Rosa does a favor for you too? And now you are his prisoner?"

He nodded. The last of twilight faded as if the breeze swept it away, and locusts sang among the trees. There were voices of De la Rosa's men not far away. "What is your name?" the doctor asked her.

"María de la Cruz Pacheco, but they say Crucita. You can say Crucita. Do you have medicines?"

"Yes, a few. But I don't have much faith in medicines. I believe in setting . . . fixing . . . broken bones and pulling teeth and cleaning out infections. But that's all."

She was listening to the crickets. "Will Señor De la Rosa let you go?"

"Yes. Tonight."

"But they are going to find you again."

"I hope not."

"Hope? And what is hope, if you have many enemies in the area?"

He didn't answer her.

"Will you take me back to Goliad with you? I need to find my brother. You can be safe when you travel with me."

"But my son told you they don't know where your brother is."

"I don't believe your son."

He was quiet, and tucked his hair behind his ear. "You can't travel tonight, you're too tired, you're safer here with Señor De la Rosa."

She was very tired. "Señor De la Rosa, he is not responsible for me," she said. "He is . . . *devoto* . . . very religious, he keeps all the law of God and of Mexico, but he doesn't love anybody."

The throbbing of cicadas in the trees around them seemed to isolate them there together, Crucita and the doctor. She closed her eyes. She could smell the thorny *huisache* blossoms, and still taste the bitter sage.

COLD FEET

B URNHAM'S CROSSING ON THE
COLORADO RIVER

Katie felt her past slipping off behind her like the miles along the muddy
trails, trampled down in wagon ruts by all the blistered feet. Her life
became the journey, a test of faith and fortitude, and she felt strangely
liberated. Having learned to worry back at home on her corn shuck
mattress in the nights, she now did it with a practiced grace and shouldered burdens that would have crippled women less accustomed.

She dropped her childhood fears in the mud along the way. At last,
at least, her new fears were valid, not just lurking down inside like mere
sensations of the heart. They had faces now, Indian and Mexican and
faces of the crazy drunk Americans in Houston's army, bristling faces,
maimed and twisted, a foul smirk and narrowing of clumsy eyes. Indians
were said to burn off captives' noses and char their feet night after night
with flaming logs so that they couldn't run away, and were rumored to
be east along the border.

The Mexicans were to the west, advancing.

And the Anglo soldiers were everywhere. There had been a rape. It
was spoken of along the line of refugees. The men spoke little of the

rape itself, they spoke of how Sam Houston hanged the man. Houston, who reprieved deserters and neglectful watchmen, strung the rapist from a limb for everyone to see. It was a lesson for the men and a gruesome promise to the women: the rapist dangling from a stunted oak and looking ten feet long. What it was to Houston no one knew, but it was more than discipline and more than a warning: it was personal, religious.

He damned the man.

And there were more men, hundreds. Some were desperate with killing on their minds, and some were just plain evil with the bloodlust gurgling from their throats like phlegm, and Katie feared them all.

The rain had ceased for now, but a slow mist hung in the dusky air. Katie's arms were damp and rough with chill bumps. She took the sleeping child from Rose and pressed her chin down over him.

Grand and Rose were bedding down beneath the wagon to keep dry, and Katie carried Samuel with her to the cart, which was a little distance off, near the edge of the clearing, so Samuel wouldn't keep the other travelers awake all night.

There were people scattered everywhere around the clearing, squatting around fires and bundled up beneath the trees. The river was out of its banks and Katie could hear its impatience. There was only one ferry raft for public use and a long waiting line. An old man had built another raft and was charging cash money for its use, double price at night. Most people could not pay the price. Rose could, but refused. William said he'd build a raft, and then recruited two boys to help him.

Katie spread her blanket on the soggy grass beneath the cart and placed Samuel on it. Lightning bugs were drifting silently about the field, pulsing yellow light, and they made Loco nervous. She was hobbled near the cart, for she would tolerate the hobbles better than a tether. Katie had torn some strips off an old blanket to use for nappies, and she rolled Samuel over as she tied a clean one on him. He had a rash from not being changed enough. At home she would have scraped the nests of mud daubers off the barn wall and mashed the chalky mud into powder for the rash, but out here there was nothing.

She sat down beside the child, unlacing her shoes and pulling them off, placing them very carefully beside the blanket so she could get them in a hurry if she needed to. Running her hand across the blanket, she felt for stones, and reached beneath to pull them out. Water from the grass was soaking through.

She did not unbraid her hair, she was too tired, though she would have liked its warmth around her shoulders. Sometimes she would dry her shoes by the fire before retiring, and put them on still warm, but tonight there had been crowds around the fires and she and Rose were too tired to build a fire of their own. They had eaten cobs of raw corn standing up with their elbows on the sides of the wagon truck and their eyes staring off at nothing.

Now Katie sat on her feet, letting her toes soak warmth from her thighs while she tied a rawhide string around a spoke of the wheel and another around her waist. Both strings, she looped around Samuel's little torso in loose slip knots, then snuggled down beside him with her muddy skirt wadding up around her. If he tried to crawl away, which he did sometimes when he woke up in the night, she would feel the tugging like a fish upon a line, and gather him back in. His restlessness always kept her wakeful, but night after night she refused to let Rose or William keep him. He was her charge. He was her baby.

And he was so warm. She thought of tucking her feet under him for just a moment to steal some of the warmth but was afraid of waking him. If he woke up he would fuss for an hour, keeping everyone around awake. Some old man or woman would yell at him across the prairie grass. So Katie tried to warm her feet with her own body, lying on her side, one foot and then the other tucked into the bend of the opposite knee, her toenails, which needed cutting, burrowing into the soft flesh like chigger-bugs.

But while one foot gained warmth the other one grew cold, and Katie was still wide awake an hour later. She entertained herself by squinting one eye closed and then the other, which made the neighboring camp fires appear to jump around between the spokes of the cart's wheel, and made the flight of lightning bugs seem skittish and erratic. It was early in the spring for lightning bugs. Rose would say they were an omen, to come so early. Katie listened to the voices from the river, the coughing of sick refugees, the croaking of an old man singing "Springfield Mountain":

"On Friday morning he did go
Down to the mountains for to mow
He mowed, he mowed all around the field
With a poisonous serpent at his heel."

With her eyes shut, Katie recalled a drawing Toby had copied from a book on ocean whales: a huge whale's head emerging from a placid surface and blowing out a spray of water, to the clouds almost. She shut her eyes and imagined her head as the whale's head with a hole in the top and all the worry forced out just that way. She pictured her head empty. But this imagining just waked her even more, and she opened her eyes to look at Samuel's sleeping face and pet his downy hair.

She was startled to see a man squatting, looking under at her, one hand on the cart for balance. Then she realized it was William.

"We got it built, Kate," he whispered, his hair ruffled up with sweat.

"You did?" She lifted on her elbow. "Already?"

The camp fires were winking out. A slender shape, perhaps a child, was feeding one of the fires with brush, which caught and flamed. Loco wandered over to sniff and nibble William's hair, and he stroked her warty nose. "I had assistance, quite a lot. They'll be using it tonight. But we have first reservation for the morning." Reservation. He picked such words. "I've never seen so many fireflies," he added, awed, then, "Stop that, you crazy horse, that hurts."

"Fireflies?" Katie said. "We call them lightning bugs. I can't figure why they're out so early. It's usually summer when we have this many. I can't sleep, my feet are freezing."

"It's not extremely cold," William answered mildly, sitting on the wet grass.

The old man singing from across the field began a different tune, an anti-British ditty called "American Taxation." He'd been harassing William ever since he heard his British accent on the day before, and William ignored him completely. Now the old farmboy flung his verses out amid the lightning bugs:

"While I rehearse my story, Americans give ear
Of Britain's fading glory, you presently will hear

I'll give a true relation, attend to what I say
Concerning the taxation of North Americay."

Evidently he did not know the second verse, for he began the first one over again. William seemed not to be listening. He wasn't looking at Katie, he was looking at Samuel, she could tell by the tilt of his head. "He resembles Callum," he said.

"No he doesn't." Callum's face was like the faces of her fears, so pitiful with no soul behind it.

"Perhaps not like Callum now, if he's so greatly disfigured." And then he asked, with caution, "Is he, Kate?"

She said the truth. "Yes. He is."

Loco wandered off with hobbled steps, grazing as she went. They could hear her chewing.

William stared across the field at the lightning bugs and shapes of vehicles and livestock. "Samuel resembles Callum in his youth," he said. "It's the way his face is shaped. I often notice it. And of course his hair."

"His hair's the color, but I don't see anything else particular like Callum or like Sarah either," she said.

William said, "You knew Sarah?"

"I met her once. They called on us."

"Why haven't you ever told me?"

She wasn't sure exactly. "I thought you didn't want to talk about her. And later it seemed too late."

"What did you think of her?"

"I envied her," Katie said. "Sometimes I still do. I don't like to think about her much, I guess."

"Kate?"

"Yes?"

"Would you tell me about when you met her?"

It was such a personal request, and unlike William. She was touched. "They came one afternoon," she said. "I remember Sarah was wearing a blue ribbon in her hair. She had Matty with her, and Samuel too in a way; he was several months from being born. Callum was worried the whole time that Matty was too near the fire, so Father put the screen in front of it."

"And what did Sarah talk about?"

Katie sat up, dragging the cover up with her. Beneath the cover she looped her arms around her knees and took hold of her feet to warm them. "She asked Mother what to do for earaches, because Matty got them sometimes. And Mother—you know Mother with her cures—she said to find a Bessy bug and mash it up and squash it down inside the ear. And that would draw out the infection." Katie stroked Samuel's wispy red hair with her thumb. "I could tell Sarah wasn't going to try it," she said.

William said, "I think she must have liked you." He plucked a lightning bug from mid-flight and cupped his hands around it.

"No, I don't think she did. She never came back for another visit."

The bug's light shone pale yellow from between his fingers, and he parted them for Katie to look in. "Maybe she was waiting for you to call on her." Opening his hands, he let the bug crawl out onto his knuckle and launch into a silent flight.

"They would have had to pass our house any time they went to town," she said. "And we never had to go that far upriver, and she didn't invite us."

"She probably expected you to come, but didn't want to make you feel obligated. Sarah always felt herself an imposition. And she wouldn't have thought it proper to call on you a second time before you called on her."

That had not occurred to Katie. "I just thought she didn't like us. I hate to think she was waiting . . ."

"It doesn't matter now; you've made amends. You've taken in her child."

Her child. Sarah's.

But then William gave Katie the child back again with such a simple statement. "She'd like it that you have Samuel now. His devotion to you is so extraordinary. She'd be glad."

Katie felt a sudden strange affinity with Sarah, and an inclination to know more. It now seemed that knowing of the baby's past and parenthood would admit her closer to him rather than—as she had thought—shutting her away. "How did he know her?"

"Sorry?"

"How did Callum meet her? In the beginning."

The camp fires and the lightning bugs were winking on the prairie behind him. The sound of voices drifted from the river. Katie sat with her knees pulled up and her arms around them and her hands holding her cold feet. The dirty blanket was pulled up to her chest and stretched out over Samuel.

William said, "Callum was driven from his home in the Scottish Highlands when the people were displaced by sheep." He paused as if to find his voice, and then went on. "His family were poor farmers, Gaelic —they spoke Gaelic, and they'd rented the same land for generations. But then it grew more profitable for the Highland chieftans, who owned the land, to raise sheep than to lease the land to farmers, so the people were removed. Their homes were burned, and they were forced off to the sea. Many took ships to America, but Callum and his parents stayed and tried to make a living in the herring industry, fishing. One day when Callum and his mother were out collecting plovers' eggs on the cliffs over the sea, his mother fell from the edge, or the wind pushed her, and she was thrown down. She died either on the rocks or in the water, I don't know which; Callum never told me. Sarah only told me that.

"Later, the father died of typhus and Callum earned passage to England, where he took employment in Liverpool, on the coast, as a ship hand on a coastal trader. But he hated the sea. He came to Manchester a short time later and worked as an apprentice in my father's factory, which makes cotton machinery. 'Mullin's Machinery,' it's called.

"Callum had grown embittered against everyone of rank and privilege; he had a determined bloody-mindedness, and my father's factory made his anger more emphatic . . . It was . . . my father was . . ." and here William faltered, then said outright, "Mullin's Machinery employed laborers for dog's wages and ten-hour days, and children were exploited. Overworked entirely. Callum stood against it. He joined a group called Owenites, who were active for social reforms, and he became the spokesman for the group in Manchester. Of course my father dismissed him when he learned of it, but that was after Callum was acquainted with my sister. They met outside the factory one day, Sarah and Callum, when she had come to call on my father, and after a few clandestine meetings he won her to his cause. She married him. Father disowned her for it and never spoke to her again, and she left with Callum for America within the year. I wanted to go with them. But Sarah refused to take me. I was too young and had an education to get. I did go with them to the boat. She wrote to me on occasion. They lived for a time in New Orleans before coming here, but Callum wanted land of his own."

He stopped with that. Katie knew the ending better than he did, for he had not seen Callum with the blood clotted on his face so thick that he could not be recognized, and the baby in his arms.

She felt as if the story opened up a window to another world, where people were displaced by sheep and blown from rocky cliffs into the sea and children were penned up in factories for all the daylight hours. But the strangest thing to Katie, as she sat there with the bugs flashing their brief fires in the dark, was not the strangeness of that world, but its proximity: it was Samuel's grandmother who spoke another language and was collecting eggs—a kind of egg which Katie didn't know of— when the wind tossed her away.

She reached out for William's hand but he did not take hold, so she took her hand away. He did not like to be comforted. Or maybe it was just that he had told her more about himself, in this story about Sarah and Callum, than he had yet done, and now was uneasy.

He looked away again. Catching sight of the rawhide string tied in a double knot around the wheel, he gave it a gentle tug, then followed it beneath the blanket with his hand, discovering that Samuel was tied to the other end and that there was a second rope around the boy. He seemed to know, without groping, that the second rope was tied to Katie, and he removed his hand and gave his soft, deep laugh, which always seemed, to Katie, slightly tardy or delayed. "My dear," he said, "what do you think, Samuel would go crawling off and pull the wagon with him while you're sleeping?" The way he said it made her laugh. The foreign world subsided. "You've worked it out so nicely, Kate, with Samuel. I bet you'd like us all secured to you with strips of hide so no one could escape or get himself in situations."

"Shhhh, he's moving," she said, and he said "Kate, I wish you'd let me take him tonight. I found a good dry place right there in the trees and you could get a better rest."

She shook her head.

William added, "You're quite obsessed with him, my dear. Isn't it overdone? The strings, I mean. One would do. No wonder neither of you sleep, you can't even turn over without tangling in the strings."

Impulsively, she pulled the cover back and said, "Get under here by Samuel and get warm."

"It isn't such a good idea," he answered.

"Then go away. Freeze. I want Samuel with me," she answered, and nestled down, tugging the cover up. She could see the dark shape of Loco's belly and her hobbled fetlocks, and hear her rhythmic cropping of spring grass.

"It isn't you I distrust," William said. "It's me. I'm not a man of steel."

"I think you are, you seem to be."

"I'm not, Kate. It isn't easy to resist you." On his own, he said it. She had not even prompted. It was as if his statement came from nowhere.

"Don't tease me, William."

"No," he said, "I won't. But you . . . But I . . . I care about you very much . . . very much more than I intended to."

She was quiet.

"I meant not to tell you. Nothing good can come of it."

"Because you're going back to England."

"Probably. Yes."

She kept very still, looking up at him, her head propped up with her cheekbone resting on her palm so heavily it seemed the world would all collapse if her elbow should give way. "You're still invited in," she said.

He obliged quite tenderly but with some awkwardness; he crawled beneath the cart and bumped his head. "Ow."

Katie pulled his head down close to feel for blood. There was only a small lump and the warmth of his scalp and the faint smell of oily hair. "It's all right," she said. "It isn't bleeding." Her skirt was tangled around her waist and she tried to straighten it without making a fuss of it; the hem was caked with mud. She was not clean. She feared she might smell of mashed-up sweet potatoes, which Samuel had smeared on her dress when she fed him breakfast. And she'd been so damp and sweaty on the road, her clothes wet and drying on her body. But William wormed in close to her, as close as he could get without smothering the child between them.

Samuel stirred, making little sniffing noises and sucking with his mouth, and Katie put her thumb in his mouth to let him suck on it a moment, until he drifted back to sleep.

William whispered, "I want over there," and pointed to the other side, where Samuel wasn't.

"You'll wake him up if you crawl over."

"I'll get out and go around."

"All right."

He crawled out and went around the cart to her side. This time he took his boots and socks off. To Katie, he seemed cumbersome and large when he got under the blanket, and he took up more than half the room under the cart though he was evidently trying to stay near the edge. At first Katie felt he was like a stranger: she had never had him up against her, and he was different up so close. He'd always intimidated her but this was not intimidation, this was just plain clumsiness on both their parts, and she left it up to him to make it right.

He didn't manage that, but the rain did. It started slowly, then increased, falling in a curtain down around the cart. William moved in closer to keep from getting wet, and his arm slipped under Katie's neck in such a natural way that she nestled close and laid her head against his shoulder. They lay on their backs with their sides pressed together and stared up at the underside of the cart, which was caked with dry mud. Katie aimlessly reached up and touched the mud, accidentally causing a small piece to fall off onto William's cheek. "Oh, I'm sorry," she whispered.

"It's all right," he said, but then began squinting and poking at one of his eyes.

"Did it get in your eye?"

"Just a bit."

"Come here, let me see," she said, and he rolled over toward her.

It was far too dark for her to see a speck of dirt in someone's eye, but she tried, pulling on his lid, and soon it watered itself out, which left her lying face to face with William. He kissed her cheek and she moved closer to him, her breasts against his chest. He kissed her on the lips, softly at first, then harder, and though he'd shaved his face that morning it still rubbed her skin like sanding paper. Her body started to respond and she gave herself over. His hands passed from her face down across her neck and to the bodice of her dress, and he rubbed his thumbs across the fabric where the nipples were, and undid the buttons. She wanted him to talk to her but he didn't, and she could think of nothing right to say, so there was only the sound of their breathing and the falling rain and a little cooing noise that Samuel made while he was dreaming. When the buttons were undone and the drawstring of the thin chemise pulled loose, William moved down slowly with his kisses until his mouth was on her breasts and on her nipples, one and then the other, and they became hard as if they reached inside his mouth. He sucked gently like a baby, and the feeling of it went straight into her heart, then down between her legs with such intensity that she opened all of it, her heart and body, to welcome the feeling, and wrapped one leg over William's legs and pushed herself against him. "We shouldn't," she whispered. "Someone might see us."

With one hand he untied the rawhide string around her waist and undid the fasten of her skirt, and it fell loose, allowing his hand to slip inside and feel her undergarments. It seemed to Katie that the hand had taken on a life and was acting on its own, fumbling with her drawers, finding its way in. She wanted his clothes off. He was taking hold of her; it felt astonishing and good, but still she had the feeling that he did it without giving himself over in return, and she murmured anxiously, "Would you take off your clothes?"

Ah, she owned him now, he was doing what she asked, he was taking off his clothes. She had seen him many times without his shirt, the scanty hair of his chest and stomach retreating down into his trousers. She had imagined the rest, she knew it would grow hard and big, but when she touched it now, with hesitation, just the tips of her fingers glancing over its exquisite smoothness, she felt a sudden horror. She could see it only as a vague thing with the dark wash of a rainy sky and no other light.

"Please wait," she said.

He was on his knees, the trousers open and pulled down, and he sat back on his calves, then began undressing her completely, gently pulling down her drawers and slipping them off. She helped him some. He took both her hands and pulled her to sit up, folding her bodice back from her shoulders as if removing angel's wings. She raised up her arms when he lifted the chemise over her head, then sat back with her buttocks on her calves. She was completely naked.

He slid a finger from the hollow of her neck down between her heavy breasts and said her name, the way he always said it—"Kate"—but with a reverence now.

"Am I pretty?"

"More than pretty. Lie down, allow me to look at you."

She lay down on her back but felt too vulnerable that way, so she rolled over on her stomach. Her braid fell across her neck and she brushed it away, folding her arms before her face and resting her cheek on them, her head turned to see William there beside her. She pressed her pelvis hard against the ground for the sensation of it and he caressed her back, feeling all the curves and the ridge of the backbone. She wondered how her body looked to him, and asked him while he studied her with his head dipped slightly to one side, "Is my bottom big?"

"No, Kate," he said, stroking one side of her fanny. "No, it's a perfect size." She felt the warmth wash through her like the tides, far down into her toes, and then he said in mock surprise, "Oh, but then it has another half!" Laughing, she rolled over and brought herself up against him and kissed him on the mouth. He was laughing deep beneath her kiss, and his arms went clear around her as he laid her down again and moved on top of her. He was kicking his pants off, she could feel him doing it while he kissed her face, and it seemed a bit like trickery to her, as if he were trying to distract her up above while he did something sneaky down below. But his body felt so good on top of her, its solid weight, that she allowed him liberty and spread her legs so he could rub against her. She was both enamored and ashamed. She should worry about getting with his child, but she didn't worry. When he started pressing in, the sensation was so dear she welcomed it, the pain and all of it. His face was solemn and intent above her, his lids half-closed, a blue vein on his forehead and the scar that Loco made.

Then from the corner of her sight she saw another face appear, like a moon in orbit, as Samuel rolled and bobbed up suddenly and sat looking at her with his little grumpy visage. Her heart faltered. "William," she whispered, "stop it, look," and he followed her gaze and met Samuel face to face.

"Oh God." But he ceased his movements only for an instant, then resumed, whispering, "As long as he'll be quiet—"

"But he sees us!"

"It's not as if he can report us—"

"William, he's upset—"

"No he's not—"

"He will be, he'll remember, look at him."

The child was staring at William. His bottom lip stuck out and his pouty face was puffed with sleep. He did not make a sound but he seemed not to like what he was watching. Drawing in a little snorty breath because his nose was plugged up with a cold, he studied them both, William and Katie.

Katie could not stand it. All the feelings in her body disappeared with her desire to protect the child from seeing such a sight as two unmarried grown-ups rutting there so close to him, so close he could have reached and grabbed her naked breast or reached the other way and put his little hand on William's sweaty rump. It was too disgusting. It was awful. "Get off," she said to William, and he could tell she meant it now, and did as she commanded, pulling on his pants and boots but leaving off the socks. While he was buttoning his shirt and she was searching urgently among her wadded undergarments for her drawers, he said, "I'm sorry, Kate. It's my fault entirely."

Samuel, with a sudden, baby laugh, hurled himself on top of her and kicked his body over to his uncle like a puppy jumping headlong in the middle of a frolic, and there he rolled around giggling, snorting through his stuffy nose, swiping at them both with both his hands, the rawhide strings tangling up around him.

"Goddamn," William muttered.

Loco pushed her big head, with water dripping from the nostrils, down beside the cart to look under at them all. Then she wheeled and trotted for the trees for cover from the rain.

Katie continued getting herself dressed, but she felt suddenly, quite strangely, light and happy, as if she had received reprieve, perhaps forgiveness too. She had been rescued from her folly. Had they gone through with it entirely, she would have felt a hold on William like a desperate need. But the baby had saved her.

She began to giggle; she felt it rising in her like a wellspring. Samuel kept on kicking wildly with his feet and gurgling with wild baby laughter, and she grabbed his ankles with both hands to stop him. "No, honeybear," she laughed, "you must not kick. Shhhhh, hush, you'll wake up everyone, be still."

William folded his long body down across the child to smother the wild noises, and Samuel squealed. "You scoundrel," William laughed against the baby's belly. "You bloody little scamp, I'll hang you by your toes, I will, I'll plug your mouth up with my socks!"

N I N E - M I L E   P R A I R I E

G OLIAD , MARCH 19

Toby and his father waded the river at a shallow crossing in a morning fog a mile below the town of Goliad, everything emerging from the burdened air in front of them like quiet semblances: the water, the trees, the muddy bank. It was a feeling Toby knew; it was like being under water. He could hear the noises of the army in the direction he was going and only hoped it was the right army. He heard explosions, too. The word that finally made his mind leap forward through the fog toward the destination was a word in English which defined the speaker as American and the army as the one they sought: it was a name shouted in a hearty voice, padded by the dampness of the air, but discernible. "Jim?" Toby heard it; Hugh did not.

So the rebels were still holding the presidio.

On the far bank of the river three rebel horsemen greeted them with two rifles and a pistol aimed to fire, and Hugh spoke directly to tell them who he was, and that he wished to see James Fannin. They lowered their guns at once.

The stone presidio of La Bahía, in the ruins of Goliad, rose above them through the smoke of burning buildings and the solid morning fog. If stones could seem ethereal they would be these stones, pale and damaged. The men were knocking them down. It was a scene of harried and deliberate destruction.

In torn trousers wet with river water Toby pressed up the hill with his father and his dog and one man in a gray uniform on horseback, toward the stone walls of the fort.

In his pocket was the folded parchment from Señor De la Rosa—safe passage scribbled out in Spanish.

In his memory was the great ranchero's face and his voice in Spanish then in English, to him and to his father both, *"Vaya con Dios.* Go with God. And may He protect you."

And in his heart was doubt, of everything.

But out there, outside himself, in the streets of Goliad and the fields around, there were angry men with whips and lances chasing oxen, shouting to each other that these goddamn oxen had been trained by Mexicans, and didn't understand English commands. There were cannons being fired at the walls of the presidio. There were ruins of homes and foul remains of slaughtered steers and scattered piles of human dung. A stench was potent in the fog, and everything smelled like an ending—of life, and of an era.

The army was preparing to abandon Goliad.

The gates of the presidio were open.

"The colonel's over there," the guard told Hugh, pointing across the muddy compound within the walls, toward a bastion. "Did you just get here, from out there?"

Hugh declined to answer, and put his hand on Toby's shoulder, ushering him in. They went directly to James Fannin, who was helping three men roll a cannon from the bastion down a double plank to be hitched up to a steer.

Hugh introduced himself, reminding Fannin that they'd met before, in the old mill in the camp outside of Béxar.

Toby stood beside the steer, and couldn't tell if Fannin recognized his father. Fannin seemed suspicious and confused. His oily hair was plastered flat against his head. He was wearing a gray mackintosh made with India rubber, and his skin was gray against the colors in the compound: a group of leafy trees with white blossoms in the northwest corner and the uniforms of the soldiers, some of them a brilliant red though muted by the fog. Toby felt isolated from the men, like an intruder. The men seemed made for war. They were real soldiers, not like Houston's bunch of boys and aging volunteers. He knew his father's attitude that these soldiers of fortune were not all honorable in their motives: many of them had come from the United States to fight, not for a cause, but for land. But Toby was in awe of them. It made things worse that his father seemed all at once oblivious to him, so that he had no ally but the dog. He kept looking around for Miles.

Hugh stepped aside with Colonel Fannin. Toby watched them talk but could not hear them, because the soldiers were making so much noise. He watched Fannin's pale face, like a dead face in the fog. Men grunted at their labor with the cannon and instructed one another—"tie it there, ass head, right there." Along the walls were rows of canvas tents hanging limp in laden air, half disassembled, and from the pole of one of them a blackbird took sudden flight, soaring off beyond the walls. There were fires in the compound, near the chapel, and Toby could smell burning meat.

Coon Dog sat on top of Toby's boots, his eyes shifting left and right. It was Coon Dog who saw Miles, or simply caught his scent, as Miles was such a distance off across the compound and looked so different in his ragged clothes and with a stubble-face. Coon was suddenly attentive: he cocked his ears and clamped his mouth shut and stared, then began to whine and tremble. He cast his eyes at Toby and across at Miles. Toby followed the dog's glance and his heart jerked as erratically as Coon's pathetic tail, for there was Miles, standing with one foot planted before the other and handling someone's gun, an old musket. He was studying the gun's lock. He was so changed Toby felt betrayed, as if Miles had transformed himself into one of these intimidating foreigners. His hair was longer, his face thinner, he seemed taller. And Toby, with all his love for him and all his overpowering relief to see him alive, felt oddly isolated from him. He didn't want to go to him, he had a strange impulse to hide. After all, he and his father had not really come to rescue Miles, they had brought nothing. They had come to share his fate, and Miles now seemed like such a stranger that he might not want their company.

So Toby stood beside the trembling dog, both of them suffering the same awkward blend of urgency and reluctance.

When Miles saw them, he brought the gun down to his side. His head cocked slightly: he was disbelieving. So Toby lifted up his hand as he always used to do when greeting from a distance, not a wave, just all the fingers spread, the gesture frozen in mid-air.

Miles gave the man his gun and came striding toward Toby with a disbelieving look.

Toby said, "Hey, Miles," trying to sound casual, noting a new scar on Miles's jaw, still pink with healing. Miles looked too different from how Toby thought of him.

"Toby?" He spoke so tentatively and with such warmth that Toby almost flung himself into his arms.

"Yeah, hey."

"Where'd you come from?"

"Home."

"How?"

"With Father."

"With Father?"

Hugh had stopped talking with Fannin. He stood with his satchel still strapped to his back, and was looking at his sons. Miles followed Toby's glance, and saw him.

"Why'd you come?" he asked, his voice turned hard, more an accusation than a question.

"It was my choice, Miles," Hugh said.

Hugh and Toby and perhaps the other men around who had been sons and fathers and now stood in this stone fort, in a prairie, hemmed up and surrounded by the enemy, scared of dying, missing their families —they knew what Miles was feeling. Miles had become a man, and it was hard for anyone to be a man when his father was around, and he resented Hugh for coming. But there was also a meager glint of gratitude. He said, "You shouldn't of brought Toby."

"I wanted to come," Toby answered, offended.

"It was his choice, Miles," Hugh said. "It isn't your responsibility."

"Yes it is."

"No. You didn't ask us to come, I'm sure you didn't want us to."

"Where'd you leave Mother and Katie and Grand?"

"East of Gonzales. William is with them. Everyone's moving out with Houston's army."

By now about two dozen men had abandoned their chores and crowded in. They fired questions off at Hugh: Where was Houston?

Where was Santa Anna? Was it true the Alamo had fallen? Fannin had received Houston's orders to abandon Goliad and fall back to Victoria on the Guadalupe, and also Houston's letter telling that the Alamo had fallen. But when Houston wrote that letter, he didn't know the details of the battle—only rumors that the men had all been killed and their bodies stacked with wood and burned.

Was it true?

Hugh answered the questions and told the men Gonzales was reduced to ashes. Then he took his leave. Miles led him and Toby over to a fire and a skewer of charred beef: there was no other food but beef, and no salt either. The balance of the corn and surplus meat—that of several hundred steers—had all been piled up near the chapel and set on fire so as not to fall into the hands of Mexicans. Somewhere there were rations for the journey to Victoria, but these were packed away in one of the wagons.

Miles sat down across the fire from his father, and started sharpening his knife on a whetstone. "Fannin's incompetent," he said. "Some say he can't ever make his mind up, but it's more like he makes it up fine, then just changes it right away, like a one-man committee all to hisself making all these decisions, and every one of 'em a contradiction. We get told we're leaving: blow up the fort, tear the walls down, bury all the extra cannon. Then we're staying: build those walls back up, fortify, dig up those cannon. We were supposed to be out of here yesterday, then this morning by daybreak. But all the oxen ran off this morning. It's one thing or another. And nobody's got the first idea what's going on in that man's head. We sent a bunch of men out to Refugio to help some families there evacuate, and none of 'em came back, so now our force is cut down by a third and sprawled out and Fannin either doesn't want to leave until they get back or he's afraid to."

Toby knew that these pronouncements were too easy and dogmatic. Sitting beside the fire and chewing on burned meat, he watched his brother sharpening the knife and talking, and his father listening, and he felt a kind of wisdom but without the sweet detachment that such wisdom should imply; he was with them both at every word and every turn.

Miles said, "Pacheco told me you got Josh to De la Rosa's ranch all right. But I'm not sure you did him any favor. We had to burn that ranch 'cause De la Rosa had spies swarming all over us. It's him who's pro'bly spelled the death of all our men the Meskins have caught. He's working for the army. He even used a old padre for a spy, but we caught him though. The padre. So I can't tell you what's become of Josh."

"He's with Urrea's army," Hugh said. "We saw De la Rosa on the way, and he told us."

"You saw De la Rosa?"

"His vaqueros captured us a few miles north and took us to his camp."

"And he let you go?"

"Yes."

"I guess he didn't know it was your son who burncd his ranch."

"If he did he had the good grace not to mention it," Hugh said.

"And he just turned you loose? Where's his camp?"

"It's moved by now, I'm sure."

Fannin interrupted and joined them. Hugh spoke his regret that Fannin hadn't followed Houston's orders sooner, and confirmed that now the Mexicans wcre everywhere in the countryside around. It would be unlikely for an army of this size to travel to Victoria unnoticed, he said, but it would also be impossible to hold this fort forever. He assured Fannin that Houston would not come here to rescue them: Houston did not believe in isolated outposts. Also, Houston's army was a ragged one, untrained, undrilled, primarily unarmed, a mere impromptu gathering strung out and heading east. Fannin had only himself to rely on.

Fannin, listening to this assessment of the situation he had made, never lost his poise. He was barely over thirty years of age, in a critical predicament, but he maintained composure—as if he were detached somehow from all the turbulence around him. He said, "They won't attack an army of our size, with all our cannon. And if they do by chance, we have enough artillery and powder to kill thousands." It was arrogant, and naive. Even Miles saw the folly of it and said so to Hugh when Fannin left them.

They passed through the sally port gates under cover of the fog and began the twenty-five-mile journey to Victoria, where Houston's last letter had instructed them to go, almost three hundred men on foot, others so sick with fevers and infections that they had to ride in carts, and thirty mounted. All of them were edgy and disgruntled, and Toby could not quite discern who they all were—the different groups with their different uniforms. The Red Rovers were distinct; they wore red jackets with long fringe, though some had cut the fringe off, and some wore white pants while others wore red ones to match the jackets. They wore different kinds of hats. Besides the Rovers, there were evidently two groups called "The Grays"—one from Alabama, the other from New Orleans—who wore a mix of blues and grays with hats that Toby had never seen the likeness of. The New Orleans Grays fought a lot among themselves, and some had heavy accents Toby did not recognize. There was a group from Kentucky, and these men had no uniforms, but they had good rifles and they called themselves the Mustangs. There were two small groups of Texans. One called themselves "regulars" and their captain was a man named Westover; the other was a handful of Irish Catholics from Refugio. Last, there was a spattering of men who weren't attached to any group. Miles was one of these. He had an acquaintance named Scholar Tipton who was a trapper from the Rockies with short legs and a round face. Scholar explained to Toby that these soldiers had come all the way to Texas for a war and spent most of their time sitting around camp fires and waiting for it. At least now there would be action, he said. They were going out to find the war. He personally was not too eager for it, he said, and speculated they would be attacked before they reached the lower ford a mile below the town.

But there was no sign of the Mexicans.

They were halfway to the ford, Toby walking between Miles and his father, when a man on horseback sauntered up beside them and told Miles to report to Fannin. Miles left and soon returned on a fine horse, reining in beside them from a canter.

"That your horse?" Toby asked.

"Nope, I'm just riding him."

"It's Adelaido Pacheco's horse," Hugh said.

"Yeah, it's Pacheco's horse," Miles answered. "Pacheco deserted us several nights ago. Listen, Fannin's asked me to ride ahead with Horton and his men, and scout around to check for ambush. There's four of us, mounted, left to watch the rear." Then he touched his hat and galloped off ahead, the horse's hooves flinging wads of mud.

The passage of the vehicles was laden and unwieldy. Exasperated with the pace, men began to swear at the draft animals and at each other. They swore at their six prisoners tied together in a line, *Tejano* spies taken from Domingo de la Rosa's ranch the night it was burned, and the small old padre named Valdez, whom they had captured from the same ranch, earlier. They swore at Fannin, too, though not so he could hear. He had delayed at the fort too long, they said, and now had started out too burdened with his guns, dragging along nine brass cannons including several small field pieces for lauching musket balls, a few howitzers, and a mortar. "My cannon must go with me," he'd pronounced. "I cannot do without them."

"Horse shit," the men grumbled. "They'll slow us to a crawl."

An Irish woman from Refugio named Mrs. Cash traveled with the ranks. She drove a patched-up cart and had her son along, a boy Toby's age, and they were armed with sawed-off muskets and a blunderbuss which the boy said he would pump full of blue whistlers if there came a fight.

Most of the soldiers were armed with their own knives and pistols, some had tomahawks and many had rifles, and six among the rifles were percussion. One thousand extra muskets, in crates, were loaded in a single cart. The cart broke down before it even reached the river ford and the guns had to be transferred. Far too much baggage was stacked in too few vehicles with too few mules and oxen, some wagons so ludicrously overloaded the oxen could not budge them. The men argued hotly over which objects should be left behind. Some men persuaded a dark man named Hews, an octoroon who had come as a tourist from Georgia in a white frock coat with a horse and gig, to carry their personals in his buggy.

The other irritation was the local oxen, who with some perversity kept trying to go backward, shoving their bony rumps against the carts they were to pull, presumably because they had been trained to different commands of the whip and a different language. The men grew impatient and stabbed at the oxen's rumps with lances and whipped their backs raw.

It was an unpropitious start, a slogging pace. The road was littered to the ford with abandoned baggage and flimsy vehicles that had crumpled under heavy loads.

The crossing proved a hazard. They took the lower ford since it was judged the least conspicuous, but the banks were steep and muddy. The water was deep enough to flood the vehicles, which had to be unloaded and the contents carried over singly by the men, then the carts drawn over by unruly steers and loaded up again. Many crates fell in the river during passage and were left for ruined.

While the six-inch howitzer was maneuvered down the bank on a flatbed truck it broke from its moorings and bolted down into the water, where it lay like an alligator, all but the barrel submerged in the turbid flow. Alabama's Red Rovers broke ranks to wade in and shove the cannon back up the bank, clambering to get their footing in the mud. Their captain was a tall and skinny doctor by the name of Shackelford.

When the river had been forded, Hugh took charge of four sick men who were traveling in the foremost wagon with their belongings piled practically on top of them. One had consumption and was coughing blood, another had a form of dropsy which Hugh called hydrocele, his scrotum bags so swollen they were blue. A third patient had been crippled by a night guard who mistook him for the enemy and shot him in the leg. The fourth suffered heavily with an infected hole between his ribs where a steer had gored him two weeks before. The driver of the wagon was a local *Tejano* who spoke no English but had managed to communicate a high price for his services. At times Hugh walked beside, and now and then he rode on the edge of the tailgate for a distance, leaning in to spread a blanket out or swab the blood away.

Toby followed, not too far behind, with Coon Dog and Scholar Tipton. The trapper had a mangy buffalo rug over his shoulder, which started smelling bad as the day grew warm.

The others walked in columns, the Red Rovers in the vanguard and Kentucky Mustangs in the rear with Fannin.

Six miles, they traveled, stretched out in a line with the mules and oxen hawing and the morning passing into noon and the fog lifting to a humid day with dark and heavy clouds and not a breath of air. The soldiers ate their knapsack rations as they walked. The chill wore off, and they removed their jackets and the dray mules drew a sweat. Gnats loitered in the muggy air, so tiny that the soldiers sucked them in their nostrils with the slightest breath, and ate them with their food. The Grays, the ones from Alabama, started up a round of tunes to lift their flagging spirits, someone tapping the handle end of a bullet mold against a metal clevis taken from a wagon they'd abandoned. But the singers had to keep their voices low for safety reasons, and it was so disheartening to be dropping their voices down around their knees that they trailed off on the second round of "Yankee Doodle."

One man named Melvin, just a few rows back from Toby, took it on himself to serenade in solo. He sang a backwoods tune in a tenor voice:

> *"Then come on, my dearest dear*
> *And present to me your paw*
> *For I know you've got tobaccer*
> *And I'm bound to have a chaw.*
> *I'm bound to have a chaw*
> *And I'm bound to have a chaw*
> *For I know you've got tobaccer*
> *And I'm bound to have a chaw."*

Disgusted with the creeping pace, the men shoved unmarked boxes off the wagon trucks to lighten the load. They crossed a creek and stretched out down the road through a string of narrow, open prairies and scattered oak woods where the trees grew far apart and there was not much undergrowth, just green, lush grass and flower patches blanketing the earth.

The soloist continued singing in a clear voice above the jangling gear and tromping feet and the creaking of the wagons. He had an air of drama which Toby found confusing and a little womanish. Scholar told Toby not to look at Melvin: "Just better not to," he explained. Some of the Grays began to say, "Shut up, Melvin," and "God Almighty," and "Would you listen at that, it's goddamn pitiful." But Melvin kept on singing, dancing in the median between the wagon ruts.

Soon after noon, the column entered Nine Mile Prairie and Fannin called a halt beside a swath of earth where a recent prairie fire had burned the old mesquite grass and fertilized the land for new and tender sprouts. He said to graze the oxen there, or they'd be useless.

His order traveled up and down the line, and commotion rumbled from the ranks and spread from the New Orleans Grays to general discontent: there wasn't time to stop. They should be pressing toward Coleto Creek where they'd find refuge in the timber if attacked. Several of the officers—Shackelford, Duval of the Kentucky Mustangs, and Ira Westover—protested at the stop. Hugh went forward also, and spoke against it, though some wags among the ranks made gibes and catcalls and accused those urging to move on of simple cowardice and fear.

They had stolen a march on Urrea under cover of the fog; Urrea was outwitted, they said. He would never catch them now.

Fannin listened to the arguments. He listened to Hugh Kenner's talk of De la Rosa's spies, how no army could traverse this open country without being seen. He stood leaning back against a wagon with one boot planted in the grass and one cocked up on a tailgate hanging limp from broken hinges, and looked at his pathetic oxen and ordered that the oxen be unlimbered. He said the Mexicans were nowhere near, and would not dare attack an army of so many men with such intimidating firepower.

Cursing burst forth from the ranks, but the oxen were unlimbered and turned out to graze. The clouds hung low and sullen and there was no sign of how the day was passing, no shadows shortening or lengthening, only the quiet, grassy landscape and the bitter voices of the men.

The group was growing frayed about the edges.

After an hour's rest they moved on. Another cart broke down, causing a delay while the load was redistributed to other vehicles. Horton and his riders, Miles among them, circled back then rode ahead to scour the Coleto timber to the left and front.

The four horsemen who had stayed behind to guard the rear, showed themselves and signaled from the woodlands to the rear and right that all was well, then disappeared back in.

When the army had advanced to where the river tree line was not two miles distant, in clear view across the rolling of the landscape, there appeared from the trees to the rear and left—quite far away—what seemed to be two horsemen clad in Mexican regalia, who hung there on the outskirts for a moment, then retreated back into the foliage.

Toby did not see them, but Scholar did.

The arguments began. Some said, with certainty, that what they saw was only cattle loitering beside the trees. "Yeah sure, dressed up in uniforms," the others said.

Forward, they kept inching, though everyone was glancing backward at the trees which had produced the enemy. Their pace was like a crawl, moving toward Coleto Creek and the safe embrace of its protective trees. Presently the same rear belt of timber glittered once again with armaments; six horsemen this time, reconnoitering. Toby saw them. Then again they melted back into the trees.

They had been found. And where were Horton's men, who were supposed to warn them? Who was it, anyway, who said the enemy was up ahead when in fact it was behind?

Fannin, someone answered. Fannin said it. He'd left four horsemen —only four and all together—to guard the woodlands of the rear.

Fannin pressed his army onward.

When Toby saw the Mexicans again, they were a dark and solid line detaching from the same trees to the left and rear as one would peel the skin off of an orange. In lines four riders deep, without the sound of any bugles, they spread out their line, advancing steadily. They could not be counted individually, they were a single creature, the men blending with their horses and the horses blending all together as if skewered on a four-prong spit. They cast no shadows, there was no sun, they seemed to be the same as shadows: silent, solid, moving.

From the adjacent timber to the rear and right, four horsemen bounded at a dead heat and advanced along the tree line. It took a moment for Toby to discern that these were their own scouts. "A tad tardy," someone drawled as the men stood viewing the four horsemen spur and whip their mounts to a full stretch of speed along the timberline in an effort to reach them.

Or it seemed at first they did intend to reach them.

But when the four riders should have started turning inward, they kept alongside of the trees, riding full speed toward where Horton's horsemen had disappeared into woodlands of the river up ahead. Only one reined sharply to the left and whipped his mount toward the rebel column.

"God damn them, they are cowards!" a Red Rover shouted, and others shouted insults at the disappearing riders. "Cowards! . . . Goddamn craven bastards! . . . Thank you very much for nothin'! . . ."

The single horseman dashing toward the column on his winded horse was wearing the uniform of the New Orleans Grays; he rode up and panted out as he dismounted, in an accent Toby thought was German, "Zey has lefts us."

The cavalry of Mexicans continued to advance at a well-regulated canter. When they'd come within a quarter mile of the rebel column, close enough to show their banners, they split in two divisions, bracketing the rebels from behind and moving forward on both sides to cut them off from the Coleto timber.

It was ominously quiet. The clouds hung very low.

The captain of the New Orleans Grays called for "The Poles," and Toby thought it was a kind of instrument until he saw four tall men rushing forward from the ranks, and he guessed in his distracted mind that they were called the poles because they were so tall. But then he heard them speak, and discerned that they were foreigners, and at last it came to him that they were Polish, blood-related too because they looked alike. They unlimbered a six-pounder and shoved a ball and bag of powder in and blasted a reverberating shot across the prairie grasses.

The earth trembled and the air was dense with smoke. A flock of startled quail ascended and descended. The ball fell short and did no harm, but it shattered the quiet into fragments which did not settle back again. Toby had never heard anything so loud. The Grays and then the others began cheering, and the Poles swathed the cannon's throat and fired off another cannon ball.

Fannin was still ordering them onward. He allowed them one more cannon blast, then had them form themselves into a hollow square and keep advancing slowly. He said that Horton's men would hear the firing and circle back to help them.

But there was not a sign of Horton's men against the tree line of the Coleto.

Launching their third shot, the rebels scrambled for their places in the square, three lines deep, New Orleans Grays and Red Rovers making up the front, Duval's Mustangs in the rear with the Poles and all the heavy guns, the Alabama Grays along the right-hand side and Westover's Texan regulars along the left. Those not attached to companies fell into line wherever they were standing. The carts and powder magazine and the six prisoners were kept on the prairie road in the center of the square, which had high grass growing solid in between the ruts.

Hugh stayed with the wagon of invalids in the center, and Toby stayed by Scholar on the outskirts of the square.

They were moving toward the timber of Coleto Creek. The steers were jaded now. One yoke lagged, refusing to go on no matter how the driver laid the whip, so the driver left the cart and the decrepit steers on the prairie in full harness.

The advancing Mexicans stretched out their lines, moving along in double files about five hundred yards from both sides of the rebel square, and Toby saw that they would pass the rebel square, then turn inward to join their mounted lines together and cut the rebels off. Toby could see what quick time the Mexicans were making, and that it would be impossible to beat them to the trees of the Coleto.

Fannin climbed onto the crates of muskets in the center cart, shouting to his square of men to turn obliquely to the left toward a commanding eminence of high ground three hundred yards away and the nearest trees beyond it, which were closer than Coleto Creek. He flung his hand out that direction and stood in his gray mackintosh against the grayer sky, in the rigid posture of a signpost, one knee cocked up on a crate, keeping perfect balance while the cart began to turn.

Like an unwieldy beast, the army veered and lumbered off the road into a gradual depression of low ground, six feet beneath the area around which swelled into a grassy rise. They were moving cumberously across the lowland when another cart broke down. The axle split in two.

"We fucked it up," Toby heard someone say in a tone of disbelief. "We loaded all the ammunition in one goddamn wagon."

The broken cart contained the ammunition.

Many met the news with bitter blame. How could it be, that all the ammunition had been loaded in a single wagon? Who loaded up the wagon? Who loaded up the goddamn wagon? It was the Grays . . . the Texan regulars . . . it was not *either*, by God . . . it was not, *goddamnit.*

The question was flung round and round the hollow square, bouncing like an echo. "We ain't started out that way, there was two other carts that had some ammo in 'em," someone said emphatically, and someone answered, "There was one that broke down at the ford when the wheel hit that big rock, and I think that wagon Tom left over yonder on the road on account of the steers had one big box of cartridges at least."

The thing was done. The battleground, if there was to be a battle with guns and ammunition, was chosen by the breaking of the axle. And it could not have been a worse one. Even Toby, who knew nothing about battle, understood that much. They were in the low part of the center of an oval prairie without a rise of ground to fight from or a stick of timber to take refuge under, and surrounded by an enemy that far outnumbered them.

"Here's the place, men," Fannin said, standing on his crates of muskets with the sheathed point of his sword showing from beneath the bottom of his rubber mackintosh. "We fight here."

"We do not, sir," one of the Red Rovers shouted back. "We ain't stopping nowhere in the open such as here."

Another insubordinate agreed. "We'll just do without the ammo and fight our way on over yonder with our bare hands to those trees if we got to. That's what I say."

Fannin called his officers together for a consultation. They gathered by the cart, and Fannin sat on the crates to talk. The square collapsed. The men among the ranks shoved in.

Toby stood back from the crowd with Scholar Tipton. The trapper, picking at a tooth and staring at James Fannin, said, "That man has got himself a death wish and he means to take us with him."

Fannin, sitting on the crates, defied the anger of his men. He called for a vote among his officers. He did not lack courage. Some of the officers consulted with their men, others cast their votes outright, and it appeared that most were in favor of remaining on the prairie with the ammunition.

A few of Duval's Mustangs began unloading all the ammunition and loading it in other wagons in case the vote should change, but the time was running out.

The Mexicans continued with their tactics.

Toby felt his heart pumping and his bowels clenching down. He could not see his father in the pressing crowd. He stared across the prairie to where Miles, with Horton's men, had ridden off into the trees.

While Fannin held his consultation and men stomped and spat and shoved their rifle butts against the grassy earth, defying him and cursing God and watching fate descend upon them like the clouds, the Mexican dragoons were finishing their expert tactics. Two double lines of cavalry turned inward, toward each other, at right angles and keeping to a canter, and closed in ranks around the stranded rebels, cutting them off completely from the protective timber of the Coleto, which lay so close ahead of them, and from the line of trees on either side.

From the same ripe woods behind, which had produced the cavalry, the infantry appeared, spilling from the trees and fanning out to close the rear gap which the advancing cavalry had opened.

Fannin's army of three hundred was surrounded utterly by an open field of grass, a double line of mounted Mexicans, and another column that advanced on foot and spread like liquid.

So they prepared for battle. They defined the square at about an acre and a half by placing the artillery at the corners. Two oxen liberated from their yoke launched themselves out toward the enemy: three Grays raced after them a ways but were fired on by sniping horsemen and retreated.

The Mexican dragoons began to circle, and their bugle blasts split open the wide prairie and roused the beasts of burden within the rebel square to a fevered panic: a mule kicked out across the grassy prairie and one of Duval's riflemen fired off a ball that dropped him in his tracks.

"That'll teach him to turn traitor," someone said.

Toby found his father with the sick wagon, swathing blood from his consumptive patient, who was coughing it in mouthfuls. When Hugh saw Toby and stepped toward him with the blood smeared to his elbows, the *Tejano* driver of the wagon, still seated on the driver's bench, saw his chance to break and whipped his yoke of oxen to a sudden bolt. The wagon lunged forward, overturning a box of two-pound cannon balls that spilled beneath the wheels but did not stop the motion. Out through the grass, lashing at the oxen, the *Tejano* deserter headed for the enemy.

Not knowing his purpose, Mexicans opened fire on him. Toby had never seen men make a target of another man. The *Tejano* leaned down low against the bench to escape the musket fire, and tore his white shirt from his back to wave as a white flag. His sombrero, anchored with a string, blew back from his head and flapped against his shoulders.

The rebels watched, mesmerized at the wild spectacle. The wagon cut a waving path that left the tall grass flattened down behind it. Then a single head lifted up above the tailgate of the wagon.

The sick were being carried to the enemy.

Grabbing a loaded musket and two packs of cartridges which a soldier had put down, Hugh said to Toby with an urgency oddly blended with civility, "Please wait here," and headed out into the prairie at a run, after his sick men. At twenty yards he paused, took aim, and fired on the oxen dragging the cart. One stumbled and lay kicking with the grass partly obscuring him, and his antics almost pulled the other down. The *Tejano* sprinted from the driver's bench and bounded from a squat into a run, straight toward the Mexicans, waving his white shirt above his head and yelling. He was not fired on again: the sniping cavalry turned all their skill on Hugh.

Toby watched his father run, bent over low against the ground, and reach the wagon, taking cover by a wheel. He heard him shouting to the sick men in the wagon to keep their heads down low, and saw him crawl up to the wounded ox. Hugh must have drawn a knife and cut the creature's throat, for it kicked a moment, bellowing, and then was still. The other ox was still straining forward, and it was strong enough to drag its dying partner and the wagon a few yards farther before Hugh rammed another cartridge in his gun and shot him in the head. Toby saw the second ox fall.

The scene grew still. Toby could not see his father in the grass. "Please wait here," he'd said, so formal in his manner that he might have been a stranger.

Here. Toby stood with his toes to some imaginary line and gnats lighting on his spectacles. The weedy grass grew to his knees and men jostled up against him. They were shouting of such things as canister and round shot and passing out the guns. It was an acre and a half of land inhabited with warriors and nine pieces of artillery and a dozen beasts of burden clamoring at all the noise.

He felt dumb fear rush over him.

Out there, the mounted Mexicans were spiraling their circle inward. Some wore red and some wore blue. They had tall helmets crested with long shocks of horse hair. Several rode in close enough to take possession of the wagon abandoned on the road, and whipped the steers to haul it toward the trees. Duval's marksmen asked if they could open fire on them, but Fannin wouldn't allow it. He said he wouldn't start the fight before he was prepared.

Out in the opposite direction, one Mexican horseman veered and rode directly toward the stranded sick wagon.

Toby saw his father raise his head and place the barrel of the musket on the ox's ribs. He saw a tiny cloud of smoke burst from the gun. He saw the rider fall, swaying in his red jacket with green epaulets, then lean back against the horse's rump like a trickster in a rodeo, and slide off to the ground.

At such a distance human death was strangely interesting and brightly colored, but Toby did not wonder at the death. He wondered at the killing. He wondered at his father shooting someone from his saddle, and searched his mind for anything to set things right again.

Four men were running out to join Hugh Kenner. One was Hews, the dark-skinned Georgian tourist in his white frock coat. He was carrying a rifle, sprinting from the square with lightning speed. They all four made the distance in about fifty reaching strides, taking refuge there with Hugh and the dead steers.

One of the sick comrades—the blond boy wounded by the night guard—tried to crawl out of the wagon, but before his feet had reached the ground the first line of advancing infantry opened fire on him and he fell like a limp doll dropped from the wagon by a child. Someone beneath—Toby could not tell if it was Hugh—maneuvered over to him on his elbows but evidently found him dead, for at once the man returned to the others hiding in the grass beneath the driver's bench. One man beat the bottom of the wagon truck with his musket butt, shouting to the sick men left within to keep down out of sight, that Solomon had just been killed.

Toby stood transfixed and squinting. The Mexican dragoons were circling closer at an even canter to the sounding bugle, buying time for the infantry to assemble triple deep. One rider galloped to a spreading live oak just a stone's throw from the wagon. The tree limbs were so low they touched the grass, and the horseman dismounted and secured his horse and disappeared in the frothy leaves, then climbed the limbs and scattered down a well-directed fire on the wagon. He aimed first at the sick within and evidently killed one, for only two were seen to pour themselves over the sides and find refuge with the gunmen underneath.

The rebels launched a double load from the mortar in the closest corner of the square, but it overshot the tree and fell without effect, raining down between the tree and the circling cavalry.

Presently the Georgian's rifle bullets, fired from beneath the wagon, hit their mark. The Mexican came crashing to the ground. His startled horse, secured beneath the canopy of limbs, reared and pulled against the reins that held him.

Toby was still standing with his toes to the imaginary line, oblivious to Coon Dog at his feet, to gnats working in and out the open slit between his lips and the sound of muskets blasting all around him as those who'd loaded their guns early fired them to clear the mucky powder out. He saw a group of half a dozen riders glide off from the cavalry and charge toward the wagon, and two horses dive against the ground, and one dragoon mount up behind another, and another never rise, and when they were repulsed and reeled around he saw one of the rebels—a Red Rover, by his uniform—rise from beneath the wagon and venture in a loping gait to the fallen Mexican dragoon, and take his gun, and move on to the body underneath the tree, and mount the horse tied there and ride out holding forth a bulging coin bag, six inches long. When a cavalryman charged him with his lance lifted to full tilt, the Rover simply turned in the saddle and drew a pistol from his belt and shot him down. The horse ran free, dragging the dead body several paces by a boot caught in the stirrup, and the Rover seemed to hesitate, desiring to capture that horse too.

But when he turned again it was too late. It seemed that the entire cavalry descended on him.

A morbid fascination clamped on Toby's mind; he felt compelled to watch. He felt as if he drew in close and shared the Rover's fear while he was hacked to pieces.

Someone laid a hand on Toby's shoulder and shoved a wide gun stock in his palm. "Stand here," the man said, spitting out a brown glob of tobacco juice. "Hold your fire till they get in close."

The gun he was gripping was a flintlock blunderbuss with a short but fat brass barrel. It was primed to fire. But Toby made a calculation: if he fired off the blunderbuss the kick would knock his shoulder nearly out. So he gave the weapon to a larger man, scrambled to the musket crates and chose a long-barreled Springfield which was lighter than the blunderbuss, though still heavy. When stood on its butt, it was taller than Toby was. Some of the Grays were loading up with buck and ball together, so Toby did the same for this first shot, three buckshot shoved in atop a .64 caliber ball. With two packs of ready-made cartridges and extra flints, he went back to the line, fearing now to look out toward the wagon and see how it had fared in the moment of his absence.

It was enveloped in a cloud of gunsmoke, since there was no breeze to blow the smoke away, but no Mexicans were besieging it at present.

Toby heard his name called from within the square, and answered, and Scholar Tipton came and found him. By then, he was shouldered in between two men twice his size, with Coon Dog running, panting, up and down the line behind him. The men were jammed in tight and trying to form triple deep, but the volunteers along this side were unpracticed in maneuvering together. Toby was jostled out in front, where it was just as likely he'd be injured by fire or percussion from the man behind as by fire from the enemy. Scholar said, "Give this kid some room, Gus. Gustavious, you deaf? You've got him all squenched in," and the man named Gus opened up a space for Toby. Scholar took a stand on Toby's left, spreading out his buffalo skin to mark his spot. "Toby, that's Gus," he said, pointing to the old man on Toby's right. "Gus traveled around Pennsylvania in a road show with a stuffed whale on a wagon back in 1818. Maybe later on he'll tell you how they stuffed it." Scholar was bluffing his way with drivel. Gus ignored him and Toby hardly heard, though the thought of the stuffed whale brought to Toby's mind a drawing that he'd made of a whale shooting water from its blow hole. Against this new uncertain image of a whale, stuffed, the drawing took on odd significance and seemed violent and lewd.

Two by two, the mounted Mexicans were circling. Out past, in lines three deep, the infantry was wrapping itself around the valley like a rope laid in three coils, then severing on two sides to group in regiments. The bugle called a new tune, and the fighting force turned inward.

"What are they doing?" Toby asked.

"We're about to pay the piper," Scholar answered in a voice turned deadly serious. He bit off one end of his paper cartridge and spat out the acrid taste.

Fannin's voice rang out above the turbulence. "Hold your fire, men, hold it till I tell you!" He moved around the square, calling out the order, and the men nudged in along the line and fell to silence. They were listening to the voices from within.

It would not be long.

Still Toby held out hope. He disbelieved the inevitable. While everyone was gearing up for battle, he denied in his own mind what was about to happen. It could not be like that, that the Mexicans would just surround them, then just ride in shooting.

Scholar Tipton tapped some powder from the cartridge to the priming pan and snapped the frizzen shut. "You hear?" he asked Toby. "You hold your fire till he says." Turning the muzzle skyward, Scholar set the butt against the ground and poured the remaining powder down the muzzle. He pressed the ball and the wadded cartridge after it, and shoved the ramrod down. "If I get killed, you let my family know it. My wife's name is Mary Tipton. She lives in Memphis with her mother who's named Sally Grimes. Grimes, like grime, like this grime here," and he rubbed the fingers of one hand together, smearing the black powder into his skin. "Can you remember that?"

"Yes sir. When do you think Horton's men are coming back?"

"Never, if they got a lick of sense," Scholar answered. "Not unless they find some reinforcements in Victoria."

"My brother'll come back. He'd never leave us stranded."

But Scholar wasn't listening. "From the looks of it, the Meskins will be comin' in from all four sides. Most of the cavalry are set to come in on our rear around the corner there and the infantry on these three sides. With their lines this tight, you shouldn't take much time in aimin', just fire off as many shots as fast as you can load. The cavalry will prob'ly ride in first to soften us a little, then pull back and let the footmen do their deed. You know how it's done?"

He knew about volleys, he had read about them in books. He had seen drawings. "I know about volleys," he said. "But isn't there something else, first?"

Scholar looked at him. "Like what?"

He didn't know. Just anything else.

"Volley's first," Scholar said, looking back at the Mexican lines. "Then they'll maybe try to move on in and carry us by storm."

"How long does one last?"

"One volley?" Scholar shrugged. He was eyeing the enemy, and was sweating hard. "Seems longer than it is," he said, handing his rifle and his musket to Toby and unbuttoning the fly of his buckskin pants to let his urine in the grass. "But they've got no cannons, that I've seen. They've got a lot more men, but we've got bigger guns." When he finished, he buttoned up his pants and took back his guns.

"So that gives us a kind of an advantage?" Toby asked.

Scholar turned to face him. Black powder from the cartridge he had opened with his teeth was smeared across his bottom lip and peppered on the scruffy growth of his new beard. "Ain't no such thing as a advantage when you're hemmed in on four sides," he said, then turned to look across the prairie at the enemy and uncorked his water gourd and took a swig. Toby did the same with his canteen. " 'Ccpt, you yourself have got one, bein' shrimpy," Scholar said. "Fat me, they'll shoot me like a cow. Now make your dog behave."

Toby had forgotten about Coon. He ordered him to "go lie down," and Coon slunk away with his chin nearly dragging in the dirt, and lay down beneath the powder magazine, staring at his master watchfully.

Toby leaned on his musket and looked out toward the wagon and past it, where the colorful line of foot soldiers was facing him. The cavalry was assembling on the slope of ground over to the left, opposite the square's rear, the horses' heads bobbing and legs stomping down the grass that tickled at their bellies. Slightly to the right was the wagon. "That's my father out there at the wagon," Toby said, balancing his gun between his knees and taking off his spectacles to wipe them on his shirttail with his shaky hands.

"Yep."

The enemy was beating on a drum. The notes tapped out as light and innocent as raindrops on the tin roof back at home. "I should have gone out there with him. He told me not to, though."

Scholar wasn't listening. He remarked, "I'd just as soon of stayed back in the fort."

"How close in will they come?" Toby asked.

"Depends when we start shootin' and how scared they get."

"One hundred yards, you'd say?"

"You're askin' me what's gonna happen to your daddy. If they'll be overrun."

"Yeah." He felt a kind of numb fear that was not like real fear.

But then the trapper said, "Well look ye there. Your daddy's a smart man."

Hugh and the defenders and the two sick ones who were still alive were crawling from beneath the wagon with their arms twined all together to support each other in a line. They took advantage of this moment when the enemy was off a distance and assembling for the charge to run the grassy gauntlet.

Toby felt as if he dragged them forward with his eyes. He saw one stumble; the line buckled but was strong enough to hold. One of the men was almost carried on the arms of his comrades, his feet were trolling out behind, and as the line drew closer Toby saw it was the young consumptive, smeared with blood. The man with dropsy had also survived, and was within the line.

Their hampered journey seemed to take forever. When they were halfway, peppered rifle fire erupted from the enemy and the line swerved and leaned as if it moved against storm winds, and so avoided being a sure mark, and no one was hit.

The men in camp were cheering, and Toby sobbed aloud with the sensation of relief. He turned to run and greet his father, down beside the cannon on the corner off to the right, but the Mexican bugle blared and the cavalry began their charge against the rear, down the line from Toby to the left.

Toby turned to look. The horses sprinted forward to a run. Their motion was precise and beautiful. The lances were full tilt against the sullen sky and the banners took on wind. The horsemen fanned out so they curved around two edges of the rebel square, and the rebels wheeled the howitzer and mortar through the center to the rear to command the broadest view of the attack, leaving wheel marks swerving through the grass around the vehicles and crates and the cluster of the six *Tejano* prisoners who squatted, bound together with hemp ropes.

Toby was positioned at a place that would receive the charge; not the hottest place, along the rear, but at the flanks. When Scholar placed his musket to the firing position, Toby did the same. He sighted down the barrel and pulled the hammer back. The ground under his feet trembled with the weight of horses coming at a stampede pace. The long musket, which would usually have felt so cumbersome, felt light as air. Scholar had said not to bother aiming once the shooting had turned general, but on this first shot, waiting for the word, everyone was staring down his sights.

When the horses were in close, Fannin called out "Fire, now!" above the thunder of the hooves, and Toby took his aim at the broad part of a uniform—a swath of red—and pulled back on the trigger.

There was the little flash of fire catching in the pan, a small delay, then Toby was shoved backward by the blast into a burst of noise so loud and so prolonged that he dropped his gun and thrust his hands against his ears. He didn't know if he had hit his mark. The artillery was touched off all at once with loads of grape and canister, belching smoke so black it turned the day to night. The rifles and the musketry were so persistently reloaded and fired it seemed the noise was solid, all one piece, like the foul smoke. Toby could not see in front of him. Groping in the shaggy grass, he found his musket and the cartridge box. He took a cartridge and tore it with his teeth, the gritty powder with its sulfide taste causing him to spit and retch and giving him a sudden painful thirst. The smell of powder was like rotting eggs, and the taste was even worse. Toby was enveloped by the smoke, and tried to wave it from his face. He felt he could not breathe. Still he managed to ram more ammunition down the musket's throat, point the barrel outward in a general direction, and fire off again.

And once again. And once again. He knew now why the soldiers carried shot pouches designed specifically for these premeasured cartridges; it was because in war one had to load by feel, not sight, with the smoke so thick. The first few times he fired, he had to feel the ground to find his cartridge box lying in the trampled grass before he could reload.

The green grass was contaminated with spilled powder and the sulfide smell, but there was still the scent of spring down against the dirt. A spotted beetle worked into the soil and a tiny spider jumped from one blade to another. There was a living world down here. Toby took a kind of refuge in it, for seconds at a time, then ascended back into the smoke.

After his fourth shot, he shoved half a dozen cartridges into his shirt, against his stomach, and no longer had to paw the ground. His movements gained rhythm and efficiency.

Presently the solid firing became scattered, as if crumbling into pieces, and Scholar said, "Hold your fire, they've turned tail." The murky smoke began to dissipate. Toby removed his spectacles to rub them free of powder smudges, and when he put them on again a scene came into focus that made his heart surge up and nearly choke him. He gagged on his own breath.

"Hell of a assault," the trapper said. "I thought we'd turn 'em sooner."

Most of the cavalry had fired from a distance of about two hundred yards, but thirty or more had come within sixty paces of the rebel lines. There were piles of horse and human flesh. Living wounded writhed in their own blood, and the fallen horses tried to stand, grunting and squealing at the sky. At least a dozen horses, riderless, some gutshot and others with faulty, crippled strides, blundered here and there between the rebel square and the retreating cavalry. One, still shaggy with the russet remnants of a winter coat, stumbled blindly right up to the rebel lines and stopped just yards away from Toby, his head hanging and blood running from his eyes and coursing down his ravaged face; he could not see to move, and eventually he folded on his knees with a slow groan and lay down on his side. Once, he moved his head, but not again.

The noises of the wounded were grotesque.

Four Red Rovers dashed out in the wake of the retreating cavalry to gather weapons from the fallen bodies, but their captain called them back, for many of the Mexicans were still alive and could shoot upon approach, and the balance of the cavalry could still turn back and charge again. Still, the temptation was great, and a youth clad in poor home-spun and good boots, who was with the Irish contingent from Refugio, crept out and stole two pistols, returning at a run with one in each boot leg and a Mexican on horseback chasing after.

The pursuing rider was hunched over in the saddle and charging toward the line not far down from Toby. Westover's regulars opened fire on him, but he never fell. When the horse reeled through the ranks behind the boy, who was running at a rapid pace, it was seen the Mexican was dead and must have been dead from the start. He had strapped himself into the saddle. The men parted for the entrance then closed in around and unstrapped the soldier and pulled him off his horse. They stood looking at him as if he'd dropped out of the sky. One used a rifle butt to toss the dead man's arm back from his face, and said, looking at the Irish youth, "You had a dead man after you."

The boy appeared more frightened by this fact than if the Mexican had been alive, and put a finger to his bottom lip, a child's gesture, and stared with incredulity at the bloody warrior lying at his feet.

Toby stepped in close enough to see.

The uniform was blue and shot with many blotchy holes. The helmet, adorned with black hair from a horse's tail, dangled from a thong around the throat. He was a man of middle age, with a trim mustache. He had closed his eyes before he died. "Guess he rode to battle with his eyes shut," someone joked. "No wonder he ended up in the wrong camp."

But this dragoon had been no coward and no fool. He might have strapped himself into his saddle for any one of many different reasons, but cowardice was not among them.

A plain-clothed soldier calmed the spooky horse and took a Pagent Carbine from the saddle ring. A Mobile Gray unstrapped the saber from the body and claimed it for his own. But when the dead man had been robbed of all his weapons, and his boots, there was still the body, like a final statement of a grievance that would not be put to rest. Westover told three men to drag it off to where the prisoners from De la Rosa's ranch were sitting with the padre.

None of the rebels was severely wounded in the charge, though many suffered powder burns and bruises from their own musketry and one had a shallow rake across his forearm from a Mexican carbine ball. Some credited their good fortune to God. Others bantered about how Mexicans were sloppy marksmen, too craven to take any time to aim. Scholar said, "They're just burnin' sorry powder, else we'd half of us on this side have been hit."

"Long as we've got Dupont powder and can fire the big guns, we'll keep 'em off," Gus stated, sucking his sore thumb. He was very old. His white hair trickled long and sparse from beneath his Gray beret, his small head jutted forward with the bottom lip hanging loose and flaccid. He was wearing some strange uniform from an ancient war, and out of place along this line with the Texan regulars.

Then Toby saw the infantry advancing.

He felt the sweat ease out beneath his arms and trickle down his sides.

Fannin shouted from across the smoky square. He was standing on a crate beside a cannon and using a sawed-off cow horn to project his voice. "They're coming on three sides," he called above the din. "Take your places. Hold your fire till they get in close."

The men started toeing up against the lines again, two- and three-deep in some places, sparse in others, more ragged toward the corners. The Polish gunners wheeled the big artillery around and repositioned it at all the corners, using sponge-tipped rammers to cool the metal throats and extinguish deadly sparks that lingered down inside. A large water barrel sat on the tailgate of a cart in the center of the square; the Poles refilled their buckets from it and took bags of powder from the barrels in the magazine, loading up the several cannon with canisters of musket balls, and the howitzer with grist.

Toby dashed twice around the square, his faulty vision sweeping left and right to find his father, but Fannin was ordering everyone to fall in line, and Toby returned to take his place beside the trapper. "I can't find him," he said breathlessly.

"Well, he ain't gone far, for sure," the trapper answered.

"Hold your fire till they get in close," Fannin spoke again, his voice projecting through the horn, and the officers repeated his command to their own men on each side of the square.

The men rubbed mucky powder from their priming pans and cursed the humid air. They gulped water with metallic taste from canteens warmed by their own body heat, and some drank from natural gourds. A few sprinted to the water barrel on the cart for refills, returning to their places to stand and watch the enemy advance.

The Mexicans marched three lines deep, in perfect rhythm to the drumbeat.

"Hold your fire!" Fannin shouted through the horn.

At three hundred yards the Mexican footmen halted and the first line knelt.

Two riderless horses, a splotchy dove-colored animal running with its stirrups flapping, and a small black horse picking its way delicately through the green grass, favoring a foreleg, moved into the line of fire between the armies.

Toby stared out past the horses, at the lines of infantry, and started to take aim. But Fannin's voice slid through the cow horn, careful and emphatic: "Hold it, men, not yet, this round won't touch us." So Toby

lowered his gun and stood with the butt planted in the grass and listened to the far-off voices of the Mexican officers shouting commands.

The Mexicans did not take careful aim and their timing was imperfect. They fired, one line and then another and another. The two horses
fell, which gave the strange impression that this whole endeavor was
merely for the execution of the horses, as the volley fell short of the rebel
square. Only about a dozen spent balls dropped down within the lines,
with less force than hail. A man two down from Toby reached out and
caught one as it fell.

For a moment the Mexicans' own smoke obscured them from the
rebels, then they stepped out with the drumbeat, advancing for another
hundred feet through the tall grass with their pennants hanging limp in
the soggy warmth of spring and their gun barrels resting on their shoulders, pointing skyward to the dreary overcast which hung so ominously
low. It seemed not only that the enemy was closing in, but the sky was
falling down. Flies buzzed and gnats drifted aimlessly and several bleeding horses continued to flounder close to rebel lines.

A trooper who had been wounded in the cavalry charge was lying
sixty paces out and to the left of Toby, and started shouting in delirium
and trying to crawl out toward the advancing infantry, waving with one
hand, but a shot exploded from the rebel square and he was swallowed
by the grass, either dead or hiding.

"I said to hold your fire!" Fannin called.

The Mexicans marched on, then halted for a second time.

"Still hold it, through this volley," Fannin said.

The officers did not repeat the order.

A murmur moved along the lines instead.

Toby doubted this round would fall short, and had an urge to lie
down in the grass. But he stood his ground. He did it because everyone
was doing it. He locked his knees and rested on his musket, but rested
very lightly, ready to lift it and take aim. He was so focused on the
enemy, he failed to see his father step in close between him and the
trapper, and was unaware that he was there until Hugh spoke to him.

"Son?" was all Hugh said, touching him lightly on the shoulder, but
he said it with such feeling and such wonder that Toby flung himself
impulsively into his arms, musket and all, and didn't say a word, for fear
that he would choke on it.

For just that instant, with his cheek against his father's shirt, flat against a brown patch on the shoulder which Katie had put there, he convinced himself that all was well.

But the drums were beating. He pried himself away. He saw Hugh had a musket, like his own. "Maybe Miles is coming back with help," he said, and Hugh answered him with certainty, "If there's any way at all, he will."

The words gave Toby back his hope.

Side by side, with Gus over to Hugh's right, Scholar standing with his moccasins flat in the center of his rug, close to Toby's left, and a stranger pressing in behind, they stood and watched the Mexicans lift their guns to fire.

A yellow butterfly flittered low to the grass over Toby's boots with a movement that seemed oddly serene and yet precarious, and Toby watched it cut a zigzag course across the open field.

"Keep holding," Fannin called.

A rifleman near Gus yanked down his pants and half-squatted, passing a stream of liquid defecation in the grass, barely pulling up his pants before the guns went off.

The Mexicans turned loose their volley and were lost in smoke. The noise rocked Toby backward on his heels but he didn't fall.

At once the rebels turned to one another to see that all were standing. No one had been hurt, though an Alabama Gray had a torn sleeve and a Rover shouted that he'd heard a ball whiz by and had turned to see one of the oxen kick as if it had been hit. Jogging in to take a look, the soldier yelled excitedly that it was true, in fact; the creature had what looked to be a rifle bullet sticking in his neck, though it had not gone deep enough into the hide even to draw blood, and fell out with the light thump of a finger.

The Mexicans continued their advance.

The rebels sighted down their barrels and shuffled in their places, but Fannin ordered them to hold their fire.

Scholar said, "If he thinks I'm gonna stand here through another volley with my hammer parked on safety then he's crazy." After a moment more of watching the advance, he added plaintively, with less bravado, "When is he gonna let us fire?"

"You tell me," Hugh said, deadly serious.

The grumbling spread on down the line in both directions. One man from the far side of the square, probably an officer, shouted at Fannin, something unintelligible to Toby, but Fannin continued speaking calmly through the cow horn: "Hold your fire, men, we have to make it count."

"Is he joking?" Scholar said, and spat. "Is this a fucking joke?"

The Mexicans were close enough that Toby, squinting through his dirty spectacles, could see the drummer's drum, though he couldn't see the sticks that were beating out the march. Nor could he see the feathers on the helmet.

The first line was almost to the stranded wagon—one hundred paces out—when a halt was called.

"What's the goddamn point in stayin' with our ammo when we ain't allowed to use it?" Gus muttered bitterly.

Hugh sat down in the grass and motioned with his hand for Toby to sit too. "There's no point in standing," he said. "If we're called to fire we can do it sitting down."

Toby sat.

Then Scholar also sat, and Gus lowered on one knee.

Diagonally across the square, Dr. Shackelford had the same idea. He shouted to the Rovers, "Boys, if we're to take another volley at this range, we'll do it sitting down. Go ahead and sit."

They obeyed, going down at once.

Fannin called again, "Hold your fire, men."

Duval ordered his Kentucky riflemen, the Mustangs, to sit down.

Westover told his regulars to do the same.

The New Orleans Grays were next, then the small Refugio militia and the Grays from Alabama.

Within a moment all the men who made the square, all but Fannin on the right flank and the gunners at the corners, were sitting in the damp grass with insects crawling on their trousers, the sounds of anxious breathing and the click of hammers pulled back to the ready mark, seeming loud enough to echo through the long blades of the grass.

The Mexicans' front line knelt, and on the order, fired. The second line fired above the shoulders of the first, and the third between the shoulders of the second.

Toby twitched and squinted with each fire, fingering the smooth cool metal of his musket lock.

The Mexicans continued their advance.

"God damn," Scholar whispered, watching them.

Hugh turned and looked behind him and said, "Fannin's hit."

"What?"

"He was hit."

They turned to look, and Fannin was still standing, but he had come down off the crate and was holding the gray mackintosh open in the front and staring down along his body as if puzzled by it.

"The gunner, too," Hugh said, glancing at the corner nearest Fannin, where a gunner leaned half over, gripping his stomach.

Handing his musket to Toby, Hugh got up and crossed the square toward Fannin. When he passed the cart which Coon was lying under, the dog came out and followed him.

When Fannin saw Hugh coming, he motioned him to go back to the line, then brought the cow horn up against his lips and said with utter calm, "I was scratched by that one, men. It's time for us to fire. We'll turn the big guns loose." He reached his rifle toward each corner of the square like an orchestra conductor, getting everyone's attention. The wounded gunner tried to take his place beside his cannon's touchhole, but a comrade stepped in for him.

Then Fannin, with his hand still holding up the rifle, gave the word.

The several cannon fired off at once with a noise that made the prairie shake, and again the smoke obliterated all the world.

But the smoke was not a cushion from the danger, nor a nightfall that would bring an end to things. It was merely Dupont powder burning with the smell of rotting eggs.

While the booming of the cannon was still rolling toward the edges of the tree line on all sides, Fannin shouted through his cow horn for his men to fire off their musketry and rifles.

And so began the battle that would last until the clouds were leeched of all their dismal light and the scattered oak trees lost in darkness. There was not a moment in that afternoon which was not clouded with the sulfide smoke. It plugged the rebels' nostrils and lighted on their clothing, so sticky and opaque that men appeared like charred survivors of a city caught on fire, they were so black with soot. The animals turned black. But by then, many of the animals were dead: it was known

in the first hour of the battle that Urrea must have given his men orders
to aim first at the draft creatures, as well as the artillerists, and so prevent the rebels from attempting to move their square toward timber.

One by one, the oxen were picked off. They bellowed in their blood.
Their deaths became so horrible and frenzied that one Red Rover took it
on himself to finish off the job, and went around shooting every animal
not standing on four legs.

Toby saw it happen through the clouds of smoke which parted inter-
mittently as mist will sometimes do. He saw a mule led over to the
corner, when the other mules were dead, and three men strapping a
small cannon to its back. Since the mule would soon be dead, they
would make use of him in the killing, transforming him into a living
carriage for an iron gun. The mule was jaded and complied with the
procedure, allowing the tube of iron to be strapped on his back with the
cannon mouth facing out over his rump; it weighed less than many
loads he'd toted. The men turned him inward toward the square with
the cannon mouth out toward the enemy, and the touchhole was ig-
nited. The cannon blasted grape effectively against oncoming infantry,
and launched the living carriage to his knees, bent practically in two
with a broken back. Just once the bloodied creature tried to lift his head
and see what thing had done such damage to him, but rightaway he
died, and several soldiers rolled the body sideways, with the cannon still
strapped to it, and dragged it to the line. They could use it as a breast-
work now.

By now the assault was general, the Mexicans coming in on every
side, mounted and on foot. When they couldn't break the rebel square
with the military tactics of Napoleon, some of them dismounted and
fought the rebels in the grass, crawling, with their lances and their
sabers, until the combat in some places became hand to hand with
bayonets.

They retreated, and regrouped, and came again. The rebels rolled the
lightest wagons from the center of the square to the outside lines to use
as barricades, and piled their baggage up for breastworks.

More than once in the beginning when the cavalry was charging, the
rebels caught a flash of color or a movement distorted by the distance
and the smoke, and one would shout, "Don't shoot, they're our horse-

men coming!" and the word would spread across the square in hopeful tenors, "Horton's men are coming, hold your fire!" But Horton's men were not coming.

Repeatedly, Toby's heart flopped open with the hope, and the loss of hope—they were coming . . . they were not coming.

How could Miles abandon him?

The emotions faded, though. There was silent fear and screaming fear and there was also hope, and dread, and stunned despair, all like fickle specters shimmering illusively against the billows of black smoke.

But the images, unlike the feelings, were neither shimmering nor fleeting. They were clear and intricately drawn. They came with living color, and penetrated with the drumbeat and the blasts of the artillery and the rattle of the smaller arms. He longed to shut his eyes against the scenes, and at last he coveted the moments when the sulfide smoke encompassed him. When it parted, it became a frame around a picture, each picture a story all its own.

There were the prisoners in the center of the square who with the prayers and guidance of the padre named Valdez got their hands untied and used discarded bayonets to dig three foxholes in the ground, between the carts, for their own protection. No one stopped them.

There was the ancient Gus, who had traveled with a stuffed whale on a wagon, who had a watch hitched to a bob in his pocket and was saved from injury when a rifle bullet hit the watch and did not penetrate. Gus was so grateful that he wept, and sat weeping, hammering a lead ball against a broken musket lock with a metal bar, pounding it into the round shape of the crystal and fixing it against the enameled face, with the bold numerals, to protect the hands. When he finished, the watch looked blank and blind, like a dead eye covered over with a coin.

There was Mrs. Cash firing her blunderbuss loaded with blue whistlers, her hair turned loose and wild.

There were two men famed as braggarts, one self-named Blackhawk and the other with a name that Toby never knew, who were discovered hiding under blankets down beneath a baggage cart. They were beaten out with oxen whips.

There was the freckled Rover who went within the square to lean against a cart and smoke his pipe and take a respite from the killing. The air was so humid that he couldn't get his pipe to light, and used a few grains of black powder from his pouch as kindling, which caused a large explosion that charred his face and caught his clothes on fire and nearly ripped his arm out of its socket. The fragments of his powder horn were blown clear to the edges of the square, igniting several fires in the grass which the men had difficulty putting out.

Though Hugh tended to the man at once, he could not save him.

There was the ruffian, Bud Claiborne, who fell down on his knees and set up such a howl of grief when his nephew was shot dead beside him that the men all thought they would lose their minds just listening to him howl, and one beat him on the back with a rifle butt.

There was the ramrod flying like an arrow shaft when Toby in exhaustion rammed the cartridge in and fired the gun without pulling out the rod.

But there were rods to spare, and he got another.

There was Coon, covered in black soot and nicked by a ball, gently as a caretaker licking blood off a man who had a hole shot in his cheek. The man came back to consciousness with blazing eyes, and flung the dog away.

There were Toby's own hands blackened with the powder and bleeding from small sores and cuts received from quick, careless handling of the guns, the red blood drying underneath his fingernails and turning brown and flaking on the back side of his hands.

He knew the blood was on his hands. He'd killed at least one man, he'd pulled the trigger at close range and seen the body fall.

There was Scholar beside him with his leg bleeding buckets where a copper ball had gone in just below the knee: Scholar speaking calmly through a twisted smile, "Go get your daddy, boy. I need him now," and muttering while Hugh was probing in the hole, "God damn them Orients. Them slanty-eyes broke down the beaver trade with their silkworms. If not for them, I'd be a long way west of here. Agggghhhh!"

"It's deep." Hugh said. Gnats were swimming in the blood.

"I know it's deep. Them Orients, agggghhh, Doc. . . . Fuck them Orients."

The picture, though, that hung most heavily in Toby's mind was the empty water barrel.

He saw it midday when he went to fill up his canteen and Scholar's too, and a bucket Hugh was using for the sick. The big barrel was perched on the tailgate of the wagon, empty but still damp inside, and someone had rolled it over on its side to get the last drops out.

"Where's the rest of the water?" Toby asked a soldier who was propped against the wagon wheel chewing a tobacco wad, his pants sliced off around a wounded hip, showing one bare buttock.

"Is none," the man said, and spat.

"No water?"

"No water."

He did not believe it. "Only that one barrel was all we had?"

"That one, and one over there in that painted wagon, but it's empty too. We had more startin' out, but someone pro'bly dumped 'em 'cause they're heavy." The man gestured toward the nearest corner. "You noticed we ain't firing any big guns anymore, and it ain't just 'cause the gunners have got shot. It's 'cause we've got no water for the sponges. We got some fools around, but no one fool enough to shove them bags of powder down a hot barrel." He leaned and stared down at his bleeding hip and drooled a brown stream in the grass. " 'Less Fannin might. He's fool enough I guess."

Toby listened for the cannon. It was true, they had stopped firing, only the rifles and the musketry were popping, but he still doubted what the soldier said and went off elsewhere to ask about the water. He asked four other men. Three told him that there was no water. The fourth said he had heard a rumor that there was no water. Not a drop, nowhere.

Coon was suffering with thirst, trotting alongside Toby and casting his eyes up at Toby's face to communicate his need. Toby's own thirst began to haunt him. For the first moment since the fight began, he felt an overwhelming panic start to blossom, and almost lay down to surrender to it.

But he had to find his father with the wounded: Hugh had sent him for the water and he had to go and tell him that there was no water.

After that, he quit the line and gave his efforts to the wounded, watching their agony through the smoke and the sticky film of blood and powder residue smeared on his spectacles. Again, and once again, and once again he had to tell them that there was no water, though they begged for it. They lay on their sides, wrapped around their knees like embryos, and begged for it. Toby crouched beside his father in the gore and did exactly as Hugh told him: tying, cutting, probing. When dusk crept in he felt the battle to its very core: he felt a soldier die beneath his hands, his breath just slip away.

Sometime afterward, the Mexicans drew back within the woods along Coleto Creek to wait for morning, and the guns stopped firing. Night descended on the prairie, black as death, and the camp fires of the enemy began to twinkle from the trees. A stillness and an awesome beauty settled over everything, marred only by the groaning of the wounded and their futile cries for water.

The dying Mexicans left in the field were also crying out for water, some in Spanish, some in English, and the rebels plagued with their own gruesome thirst shouted angrily into the darkness, "There is no water! ¿Comprende? No agua," and the Mexicans, not understanding, thinking the Americans were simply being cruel, repeated their pathetic cries for water.

G E N E R A L   U R R E A ' S
B I R T H D A Y

General José Urrea was eating his late meal in the woods of Coleto Creek. He ate standing up, leaning his back against the gnarly bark of a spreading oak, one knee cocked and the bottom of his boot planted firmly on the tree. He was in full uniform but without his hat, his jacket red and blue with piping and lace epaulettes and heavy bullion fringes. His lapels were embroidered in gold. In one hand he held the tin plate, and with the other he ate his hardtack and a bite of beef cooked from two steers the enemy had abandoned on the road when their column was surrounded. Behind him, the creek trickled through the darkness of the trees.

Urrea's aides were crowded at the nearest camp fire over forty feet away but still beneath the tree's expansive canopy. With them were three women who had followed their men on the long campaign, and who were smeared with blood from caring for the wounded.

Joshua sat on the ground, apart, between the fire and the general, in the darkness of the people's bulky shadows, which spread outward from the fire and stretched high into the foliage.

The voices were just whispers, for this was a night of death. There were more than fifty soldiers dead and two hundred badly wounded, and there would likely be more killing in the morning.

Camp fires were strung along the tree line, nestled beneath the twisted limbs, each with groups of people pressing in and sharing meager rations, wearing bloodied clothing and speaking in soft tones. Ghosts were in the woods tonight. Souls hung about the shadows and flitted through the firelight high up in the branches. Apart a distance to the right was a clearing where the wounded had been carried, and where the sounds of agony and death were so appalling no one but the bravest would go near.

The only blood on Joshua was Urrea's blood, a tiny blotch on his sleeve smeared there when Joshua was wrapping gauze around the general's wounded wrist. The general had been nicked and the lock shot off his gun when he led the first charge of the cavalry. Joshua was not ashamed to wear Urrea's blood, for the general was so great a man. It was troubling to admire him so much, but the general, once again, had proved his brilliance. He was a clever general. He was a politician too, the governor of a state in Mexico. He had marched his army up the coast and fought small groups of Anglos and taken ports and left his soldiers stationed all along the way at places called St. Joseph's Island, Cópano, Refugio, and San Patricio. He had won each battle that he fought and executed most rebels whom he captured bearing arms. All his men adored him. Often they spoke ill of Santa Anna, the supreme commander who was somewhere to the north and west, but they loved Urrea, and Joshua was proud to serve him.

He watched the general leaning back against the tree and putting his last bite of hardtack in his mouth. Firelight reflected on the metal buttons of Urrea's jacket, reminding Joshua of long ago when he was a boy hunting after dark with his master: he would carry a pine torch and a deer would be attracted to the light and its eyes would catch the glow, and the master's gun would drop it dead. "Shining the eyes," they called this kind of hunting. The eyes were golden like the buttons on José Urrea's jacket.

Joshua had met José Urrea in a town south of the Rio Grande called Leona Vicario by some, and by others called Saltillo. He'd traveled south from De la Rosa's ranch with the retreating army under General Cós, and crossed the Rio Grande on Christmas Day with the depleted army. By then he'd learned the language well enough to find employment, and stayed in Leona Vicario to work on a ranch outside of town. But on his second day of work the rancher had tried to treat him like a slave and so he had walked out on him. Next, he took up with a muleteer who made his living driving mule trains through the desert between Monclova and San Luis Potosi. But before they started south, General Urrea arrived in town with his division of the army, moving north to Texas, and drafted the muleteer to go with him and transport provisions.

Joshua began to look for other work, but Urrea learned of him, and that he was a runaway, and being liberal in his views Urrea asked to see him and to question him on slavery.

No one had ever asked Joshua to tell the story of his life. But Urrea was a man of curiosity. Joshua distrusted him at first, and stuttered with the language, but he told his story. Urrea listened closely, his eyes slanting upward at the corners and keenly focused and his stunning widow's peak of hair jutting far down on his forehead, black as pitch against his skin. And before the army left that town he had developed such a fascination with the story that he offered Joshua employment. "You would not be working for the army, but for me," he said. "You would be one of my personal servants. I myself would pay you. If I'm pleased, I'll pay you well."

With the army, Joshua decided, he'd be protected from the Hanlins if the brothers were still hunting him. And if he made enough money, he could return to the United States and search for his wife and child in Louisiana, and maybe find a way to buy their freedom.

Once he had devised this plan, he fastened on it with such urgency there seemed no other choice: he would not live his life alone in Mexico where there was no society for him. The Mexicans were mostly predjudiced against him. In Mexico the shades of skin determined shades of worth, the same as with the whites, and his shade was still the darkest. He could change his legal status here from slave to freeman, but he could never change his caste. And though there was no glory in the work of manservant, there could be something kin to glory in proximity to so great a man as José Urrea, and certainly there would be privilege.

So Joshua had crossed the Rio Grande again and the frozen desert,

and now was sitting in a haunted wood on a spring night with the damp
air turning cool but no breeze at all. There were men dying in the little
clearing in the trees off to the right, and also on the grassy prairie
bordering the woods, and José Urrea's buttons glinted in the firelight.

A foot soldier, wet up to his knees and leading a horse, approached
Urrea from the creek. The soldier's pace was weary and his sandals
dragged the ground, but the horse was not jaded, and walked with his
head high, his hooves clomping softly. The soldier, with the accent of a
farmer, gave his formal greetings to Urrea and then said, "We found this
horse in the woods. The saddle is American."

Urrea set his plate down on the ground. "He's very fine," he said,
running his hand down the neck. "And he has no wounds?"

"None," the soldier answered. He seemed so weary he could hardly
speak and was wobbly on his feet.

"I've always loved the *bayo-cabos-negros,*" Urrea said to him.
"They're always strong. Take this horse to Colonel Nuñez, with my com-
pliments. His mount was killed today."

The idea came to Joshua that he had seen this horse before. He knew
the markings and the size, but at first he was uncertain why he knew
them. Then the man turned the horse fully around to lead him off and
Joshua saw, in the firelight, a narrow streak of silver flowing down the
tail.

Astonished, he set his plate aside.

He had seen that streak in moonlight along his route to freedom.
This was the *Tejano*'s horse.

And there was something in the sudden recognition that unnerved
him—a connection with the past, a circle closing when he had not
known that he was traveling in a circle.

Life brought things back again. It brought reunions, unexpected.

He stood, and in imperfect Spanish told the general that he knew the
horse, that it belonged to the *Tejano* who had led him to Señor De la
Rosa's ranch.

The soldier stopped, and stood holding the reins.

Urrea looked at Joshua with curiosity. "You're sure this is the one?
The saddle is American."

He was sure, he said. The horse had had a Spanish name he could not remember, but he knew the markings, the streak of silver down the tail—he remembered that. He had walked behind this horse for . . . he paused, not knowing what the distance was. "For all the way," he said.

"Well, if you're sure, then we should return the horse," Urrea answered. "I'll have him taken to Domingo de la Rosa, and maybe he can find the owner. And if he doesn't find him, he can keep the horse, himself, an expression of my gratitude, and yours."

Joshua was deeply touched that Urrea would believe his word and act upon it. He was only a servant—he did not delude himself—he was there to set the general's tent exactly to his liking and to shine his boots —but he had been believed and given power: the *Tejano*'s horse would be returned to him, or given to the rancher, De la Rosa, and either way a debt would be repaid. And when he thought about it then, the name occurred to him. "The *Tejano*'s name is Adelaido," he said aloud.

Urrea told the soldier to secure the horse and leave him. He summoned his aide from beside the fire, Lieutenant Colonel Pablo Ferino, instructing him that the horse should be delivered to one of De la Rosa's riders and given to a man named Adelaido. He said that most of De la Rosa's riders had pursued the Anglo cavalry that ran off through the woods toward Victoria, but they would be returning by the morning.

After giving these orders, Urrea walked out to the edge of the woods to think, and stood staring into the black night that had settled on the prairie, his hands clasped at his back. The darkness was so deep the rebel camp almost a mile away was lost in it, marked only by brief flashes from the intermittent fire of Urrea's snipers in the grass around it, and the return sniping of the rebels from within the square. A body of Urrea's infantry was situated to the left, blocking the road to Victoria at four hundred paces from the rebel square and protected from the rebels by a gentle slope of ground. The soldiers in that body were all resting on their arms in utter darkness. Even Urrea, who knew exactly where they were, could see nothing of them.

Joshua stood back behind Urrea, in the trees. He knew Urrea's need to be alone. There were grim decisions to be made, for the situation here was precarious.

It had been late morning when Urrea learned the rebels had abandoned the presidio under cover of the fog. He had sent Colonel Francisco Garay to take possession of the fort, and he himself led the forced march to catch the rebels, leaving baggage wagons and artillery and surplus ammunitions with a guard of one hundred infantry to follow as quickly as they could. But the wagon convoy had never arrived at the scene of battle. In desperation at midday Urrea had sent horsemen back to rush them, but the horsemen did not return. Evidently, the convoy was lost out on the open landscape. By the time the daylight faded to a wash of gray Urrea's army had been almost out of ammunition and he drew his soldiers back into the woods to wait, bringing with them all the wounded they could carry, and even now his bravest troops had gone back out to comb the grass for other living souls. His scouts were creeping close enough to watch the slightest movement of the rebels, and his best marksmen, including the Karankawas and the Cerise Indians of the Rio Grande, were keeping up an intermittent fire on them. But many of the rebels could escape right now, one by one in the cover of this darkness, if they chose to try. If they did not try, morning could bring cannon to Urrea, and victory. Or, if God had different plans, it could bring rescue reinforcements to the rebels, though De la Rosa's spies had not reported any reinforcements on their way.

They were fools, those rebels out there on the prairie. If they had left the fort just two days earlier Urrea could not have stopped them; his army was too small. But while the rebels had delayed, Urrea had received five hundred men.

Urrea turned and beckoned Joshua, but then said nothing to him when he came, just stood staring out at nothing, and Joshua began to think he had misunderstood and had not been summoned. At last he asked the general if there was something that he needed.

"Cannon," Urrea said, not looking at him. He pulled his watch out of his breeches pocket and stared closely in the darkness to discern the hands. Then he snapped the watch shut, put it back into his pocket, and said gravely, with his eyes fixed on the darkness out beyond, "I was born exactly to this minute thirty-nine years ago."

Joshua did not know his own birthday, and it seemed astonishing to him that anyone could know the moment of his birth, that there could be such continuity and sequential order. Certainly the general had done honor to his birthday.

The moments ticked away, and the two men stared into the darkness with the damp air turning cold. It seemed that they were watching something, some performance of great interest, but there was nothing there to see except the intermittent popping of the snipers' guns, small, brief flashes like pulsing lightning bugs. They could hear the sound of camp behind them, and after several minutes the clear notes of a bugle rose above the tree line to the left in a tune that sounded like a soul ascending, a brief and lovely melody. Joshua's heart moved with the sound, lifting and falling, holding steady as the music died away. "I've ordered that the bugles play out different calls throughout the night, at five-minute intervals, to keep the enemy confused and continually alarmed," Urrea said, not looking at him. The call was answered by a bugle from the infantry camped four hundred paces from the enemy, and another from an outpost on the far side of the rebel square playing *"Centinela Alerta."* From this music, the rebels would discern that they were still surrounded, and by more than darkness.

Urrea listened quietly, and when the call was done he said, "It is a herald to your freedom, Joshua," and turned and went back to the woods toward the clearing where the wounded lay.

Joshua, left standing alone on the edge of the prairie, felt sadness falling on him as heavily as darkness. He allowed it there; the sadness anchored him to life and let him know he wasn't merely passing through. He was living, now, and free. He could allow himself to feel. His melancholy could become a rueful friend. He listened to the Mexicans grouped around the many camp fires in the woods behind him, and he stared across the prairie where the white men were huddled far out in the darkness, speaking his own language. He despised the arrogance and common cruelty of whites, he despised the way that they would treat him if they had him in their custody. But he listened for their voices, and took a few steps out onto the prairie with his boots swishing in the meadow grass. He was wearing boots Urrea had provided, better than the shoes and sandals which the soldiers wore. Better, too, than what the whites out there were likely wearing.

He went a little farther still, into the blackness, until he stood a ways out in the open, and tuned his ears far out across the distance. Sound carried through the open spaces. He saw a tiny flash and heard the sniper's fire, and the fire in return. He kept on listening. He closed his eyes, though there wasn't any need, for the darkness made him blind. And gradually he fancied he could hear the crying of the wounded from within the square, frantic bleatings or slow wailings that lingered in the cold and humid air and seemed without an end, as if the wailing would go on forever in the prairie.

It could have been a trick of wind passing through the grasses. Except there was no wind tonight.

He refused to feel the pain he heard. He refused to care. But his sadness kept him standing there.

A   N I G H T   W I T H O U T   W A T E R

The rebel square had caved in on itself. The men were bunched close together in the dark. Nine dead were covered over with their blankets, men with names like George McKnight, Archibald Swards, Conrad Eigenuer, John Kelly, and Captain H. Francis Petrussewicz of the artillery. Three other men were sure to die, sixty were severely wounded, and everyone was suffering intensely from the thirst. Their ammunition was depleted. They had no food, not a drop of water, and few medical supplies. Their bodies were a mass of cuts and powder burns and bullet wounds that left the flesh splayed open and the bones severed and spilled so much blood that the trodden grass was sticky with it. Their bowels ran with fear.

Even their bravado was disfigured and seemed to lie in heaps amid the crippled bodies and the stacks of empty musket crates. Some said that they had won the battle of the day and kept the Mexicans from breaking in the square, and they could do it on the next day too. Some said that they had killed the Mexicans ten for one, and with those numbers could defeat the enemy in one more fighting day. But most took quiet stock of their blighted situation and said nothing, just grabbed for an elusive thread of hope, or courage, or a thread of resignation.

None of it would hold for long.

"Them sons of bitches is *talented,*" Hugh heard one Red Rover, struck down by a sniper, bluff while sitting on the ground with his legs splayed out before him and one kneecap hanging loose. "It's a goddamn turkey shoot."

But it was worse than that, worse than anything most of them had ever been a part of: no one could have thought of such a debacle as this, to be surrounded, without water, and friends dying all around. A Polish veteran whose brother had just died told Hugh in his stilted manner, "Me and Francis fought wars with Napoleon, and we never had a fighting day and a whole bloody night without no drink of water."

Some began to speculate that water could be reached by digging, and roused one *Tejano* prisoner out of the foxhole he had dug with his hands and a discarded bayonet, and set to work on it with a shovel and three spades. The hole became the only hope for water. Many crowded around to watch and peer down in the blackness and to say, "Is it muddy yet? . . . How's it look down there, any sign?" But after it was dug down past five feet without a sign of mud, the endeavor was abandoned and the spectators wandered off and the prisoner was given back his hole.

Fannin was to blame for everything, some said. But tonight they did not damn him audibly, for he had damned himself. He was badly wounded. He had two wounds in one arm and a deep one in his thigh where he had taken the third volley standing up. The ball that hit his thigh had not lodged there: it had put a hole clean through the pocket of his mackintosh and through his denim trousers but had not penetrated the silk handkerchief tucked inside his trouser pocket, though it had rammed the green silk deep into the flesh. When the silk was pulled out of the hole, dripping blood, the ball had come out with it and fallen in the grass, and the men had fished it out and passed the ball around with a questioning kind of murmur, not because it failed to penetrate the silk —providence or luck made strange things happen—but because the ball itself wasn't made of lead. It was a copper ball. A four-ounce copper ball. They had heard of this invention, but had never witnessed it.

Before the evening passed they knew the horror of it: copper was a poison. Those with balls embedded in their flesh sweated all their moisture out and raged aloud with fever; they grew delirious and called for

God and for their mothers and begged for water even though they knew there was none to be had. They tried to crawl away and leave the fever off behind them; several now were tied like dogs to wagon wheels and bound about their wrists to stop their crawling toward Coleto Creek. They wanted water, at all cost. They would crawl right through the infantry assembled out there on the prairie, and the camp along the trees, to get it.

Hugh Kenner and Jack Shackelford and several medics dug deep and mercilessly in the flesh of many wounds to extract the copper balls. At any risk, they had to be removed: the pain and loss of blood did not cause half the agony or danger that the poison caused. There were not instruments enough to go around, so some used pocket knives, working in the dark, guided only by their hands and intuition, for if a single light was used they'd make themselves a target for the snipers.

Hugh was probing the leg wound of a young boy named Harry Ripley when the first call of the bugle rang from the trees along Coleto Creek. Harry's bone was splintered just above the knee and the wound was large enough for Hugh to get his thumb inside and feel the ball and start to work it out, but when the bugle called, the dazed boy tried to twist away and drag himself back to the lines to meet the heralded attack. Others of the wounded did the same, some crawling, if they could no longer walk, and Hugh was at a loss to stop them. But this one boy he could. Toby was there with him, and they talked and tried to reason with the boy and then used force to hold him while he begged, "God, sir, don't." After Hugh had worked the ball out with his thumb, the boy, disoriented from the pain and the work the poison had already done, dragged himself a few feet over to Mrs. Cash and called her "mother" and had her fix a prop up in her cart, which was on the line, for him to lean against. She helped him up and set his rifle up beside him and he asked her if the padre was nearby. She answered that he was, for all the citizens of Catholic towns—Refugio, Victoria, and Goliad— knew the old padre Valdez, who had been in Texas since the Spanish owned the land, chaplain of the Alamo for several years, then chaplain to the garrison at La Bahía almost twenty more.

"Go call him for me, Mother, just in case . . ."

"But he's been spying for Urrea and the rancher De la Rosa."

"Go call him for me, Mother, please."

Hugh stayed beside the wounded. He had done his share of killing. The ease with which he'd done it had numbed him earlier that day, and now he could not let his qualms crowd in.

Toby stayed there with him.

The men along the lines fell quiet then, all lying in the grass or in the carts drawn to the line, staring at the darkness with their fingers on the triggers, waiting for the charge. After several minutes they perceived that there would be no charge—there was only sniper fire, and one man hit—and their muscles went slack and their readiness fell away and they withdrew inside the lines again to try to make some sense of things.

Fannin called a meeting in the center of the square. But before the officers assembled there, another bugle call was made, and answered with the bugles all around, and the effective officers all dragged themselves back to the lines.

This call, also, was a false one.

At the third call, they began to speculate that the enemy would keep this up all night, and though that idea did not stop their hearts from quickening at every tune the bugles played, it did stop men from running for their places on the line. They withdrew within and made their square smaller still—a quarter of an acre, and they took cover from the snipers who were doing more injury to morale and spilling more blood than all the volleys and the charges of the day.

Duval's marksmen made the snipers pay for every casualty. "Give them greasers a drubbing," Duval told them when the snipers shot his finger off. "Make them have regrets." And his Kentucky riflemen lay waiting to see the flashes in the grass, then aimed just above the flash, and many of the snipers out there never fired twice.

Captain Ira Westover was helping Hugh and Toby wrap a patient's arm. The patient was Westover's nephew, Lucius Gates, shot in the upper arm. Though the bullet had found exit through the flesh and the wound did not need probing, Gates was losing consciousness from loss of blood and dehydration, and his uncle was recalling to him in emphatic but disjointed speech how Gates could live through this, for they had lived together for five days on Padre Island without water when a score of others died of thirst. "Don't you faint on me now, boy," Westover said. But Lucius Gates was drifting off. He asked where the Mexicans were, and Westover told him they were everywhere. "I'm so glad,"

Gates said dreamily, drawing out his words in whispers. "Do they have the water?"

To Toby, Westover said quietly, "When we came to Texas, our ship was wrecked at Padre Island and the Mexicans rescued us and gave us water. An irony, I guess."

More than an irony, Hugh thought, tying the rag to stop the bleeding. It was a tragedy. There was not a single element in this affair that would leave a man's heart whole. Every nook and cranny of the rebel square, every factor that had led each man in this army to this night, had a sadness and a gruesome twist about it. What in God's name were they doing on this prairie without water? Hugh had never hated anyone the way he hated Fannin at this moment; he saw him as a kind of human slug. Fannin wore the trappings of the aristocracy, he played their games and spoke their rhetoric, he owned and traded slaves and more than once had brought shiploads in from Cuba, sailing on the voyages himself. He was a dreamer, an adventurer, he knew the strategies of war and was composed enough to act the part of colonel. But he had no soul down underneath the trappings, no central core. He was a man on the make, looking for his fortune, changing bets on each roll of the dice and pretending to believe in something. He was committed to his fortune, to his family, to his image, and to Texas, but not to his beliefs, for those wavered with the wind. When there was no wind, when the stillness sat upon him like the damp night air, he could not think, or move. He was completely paralyzed. What Hugh had first seen when he met James Fannin in the abandoned sugar mill in the camp outside Béxar, was an opposite of Bowie. Fannin was a man of caution, given to pondering. Hugh had liked him more than he liked Bowie, though not much. He now knew it was those very qualities of caution and reserve that had led these men to this disaster.

It was time to make a plan. Hugh told Toby to stay with Lucius Gates and went to speak to Fannin. He found him on the ground near the powder magazine, lying back against a bundle of pillaged haversacks with his injured leg stretched out. Dr. Jack Shackelford, captain of the Rovers, was sitting on the ground beside him. Shackelford was a tall man with an air of dignity. Throughout the day he'd shown a courage and commitment to his men—the young men of his hometown of Courtland, Alabama, his son and two nephews among them—which Hugh found touching. Hugh could not conceive how any man in his right mind would purchase arms and uniforms and bring so many youths to a foreign land to fight, but Shackelford possessed an unaffected gentility and a seeming honesty that he admired.

When Hugh approached the two, Fannin peered up at him in the dark, saying, "Is that Dr. Kenner? Join us."

Shackelford, evidently trying to wrest Fannin from his indecisiveness, said to Hugh, "We have to make a firm decision before the men start acting on their own. The Grays think we should move our square toward the trees over that way at all hazards." He gestured toward the tree line where no fires burned. "And some are saying we should fight our way on the road, over to the creek. They're threatening to go on their own if the colonel doesn't agree to it."

"It would mean abandoning the wounded," Hugh responded at once. "There's no way to take them."

"Yes, it would mean that," Shackelford said gravely. "I'm opposed to it."

Fannin said, "Under no circumstances will I leave the wounded."

"You are among the wounded," Hugh retorted.

"I could walk. But I'm not going anywhere."

"Nor am I," Hugh said, and sat down on the ground beside Shackelford. His joints ached from exhaustion and the cold. "But I think the rest of the men should have that option if they choose, and shouldn't be disgraced about it," he said, thinking of Toby. "To stay is likely suicide."

"Not if we get those reinforcements from Victoria," Fannin answered. "There's still a hope for that."

"I doubt Horton even made it to Victoria," Shackelford said.

"I believe he did," Fannin answered. "He knows the way like the back of his hand, and all the hiding places in the woods, and so do all his men. At least some of them would make it. But there's a chance, even if they get there, they could find Urrea's troops instead of any of our militia; Urrea might have garrisoned it days ago."

The sniper fire was growing more sporadic but the sounds of torment filled the square and did not ease at all. Between his fingers Hugh could feel the sticky blood of the men, and could smell it too, and tried to wipe it on the grass.

"We only have two rounds of ammunition left for cannon," Fannin said, glancing toward the shape of the powder magazine looming up beside them and the empty wagon parked nearby, with the empty water barrel turned over on the tailgate. "And not enough for a protracted fight with small arms."

"So we couldn't win a fight tomorrow," Shackelford concluded.

"We wouldn't last a fight tomorrow," Hugh said. "Not without water." The wounded were already dying of their thirst, and though the others might hold out a little longer they could not fight effectively for long.

"Urrea's likely short of ammunitions, too," Fannin offered, trying to adjust his leg and wincing at the pain. His pants had been split open from the hem up to the thigh, and the wound was wrapped in someone's extra shirt, with the sleeves tied in a knot.

"He'll get some more," Shackelford replied. "He has time, and water on his side."

"And we have many brave men," Fannin answered.

The bugles sang to one another in the distance.

"And many wounded men," Hugh said. It seemed impossible that just that morning Fannin had been stating that the Mexicans would never dare attack a column of such size, and if by chance they did, there was artillery and powder enough to kill them by the thousands. His miscalculations were astonishing; he had mismanaged everything from the beginning. Yet Hugh himself had recommended that the force abandon Goliad, and now suffered the haunting recollection of the fort as it stood, ten miles away, encompassed in its stone walls. If they had stayed within the walls, they might have died like those men at the Alamo. Or they might not have. A man could easily misjudge.

Hugh could almost have forgiven Fannin for his faulty judgment, if it had not come from weakness. "We'd be wrong to underestimate the Mexicans again," Hugh said.

For the first time Fannin showed annoyance. "So what do you propose we do, Dr. Kenner? Turn ourselves over to their gruesomeness? They shoot their prisoners."

"I propose we let anyone who wants to try to get away, go ahead and try it. And the rest of us stay here with the wounded and hope for the best."

"They'll butcher us," Shackelford stated.

The cold was getting more severe. The air was leaden with moisture.

"If only it would rain," Hugh said, draping his arms around his knees for warmth, leaning his head back and staring up at nothing.

"And ruin our powder?" Fannin snapped.

"And quench their thirst," Hugh answered quietly, still looking up.

Moments passed. Again the bugles sounded in the distance, answering each other on three sides. Shackelford asked Fannin how his leg was doing, and Fannin said that it was doing fine considering it had a hole clear to the bone, but that the bandage was a little tight, and together Shackelford and Fannin loosened up the shirt sleeves tied around the wound.

Shackelford was packing wadding into Fannin's shirt against his other wounds, in his arm and shoulder, to stop the loss of so much blood, when a man appeared beside him. The fringe hanging from his jacket hem identified him in the darkness as one of the Red Rovers, and he addressed his captain, not his colonel. "Sir, Blake and Jim Bob say they're headin' out alone if we don't all get movin'. They won't stay 'till mornin'."

"They will stay until I tell them they may go," Shackelford responded calmly, squatting back on his heels and looking at the man, the doctor's thin face jutting sharp angles of his chin and nose against the blackness of the night. "Who started that malarkey, of threatening to leave?"

The man shrugged. "I can't say there's much of anybody wants to stay."

"They'd leave the wounded?"

The man shifted his stout weight and set his musket butt against the grass. "I guess they plan to take the wounded with 'em," he said.

"I'd like to know how," Shackelford responded. "Go ask them how."

The man just stood there.

"Go ask them," Shackelford repeated, and the man turned and left.

Two of Duval's marksmen appeared out of the darkness and spoke to Fannin, the tallest of the two saying, "Meskin snipers ain't fired once in ten minutes. Either they've retreated or we've picked 'em off." His companion added, "Either way, they've quit us."

Together the five men fell silent, listening. They heard no sounds of gunfire, only the voices of the men, now and then one voice rising up above the others from one part or another of the square, disjointed sentences with tones of pleading or defiance lifting in the cold night air, "Give it here, Lou" . . . "Like hell it is" . . . "You touch that you're a dead man," and "Do like I told you, brother." Gradually the sounds began to change and shift over to the right and to focus somehow and evolve into commotion, a single rifle shot and a voice from a brief distance, and a closer voice saying, "Ain't nobody," and others saying "Yes it is . . . Look yonder . . . hold your fire . . . He's speakin' English," and "Back off . . . God Almighty . . . Back off . . . God Almighty . . . God Almighty, it's Miles Kenner."

Hugh felt something hard and cold pulse through his blood, and instantly was on his feet, bounding to the line. There was a mob around, and they were saying "Give him room," and "That's his daddy, give him room," and "How'd you get here? Where's the rest? They all comin'? What'd you do, crawl clear over from them trees?"

That was exactly what he'd done. Hugh had never seen Miles look so wild or so disoriented. His clothes were torn and all the buttons of his shirt, but one, were gone.

"Where's Toby at?" he was asking frantically of everyone, "Where's my brother and my father?"

"Here," Hugh answered him at once. "And Toby's here; he's all right."

"I could hear the fighting all day long," Miles said, pressing toward him, "I was off in those trees over there, but I had to hide inside a stump and I couldn't see nothing of what was going on and I tried gettin' up in a tree but the Meskins were everywhere and even when the fighting stopped and I started crawlin' out here they were out there everywhere, dead ones too, I crawled on top of two dead men before I even saw 'em. And then there were those snipers and the goddamn bugles and, where's Toby? He get hurt at all?"

"No, he's fine, he's here—"

Toby appeared within the crowd, soot-blackened. Miles opened his face in such grin of sheer relief it was like madness had come over him. "Brother? Brother?"

Toby broke down with the first tears Hugh had seen him shed all day. He put his head back and opened up his throat to the cold night air and sobbed out loud. Miles shoved his way up to him and they stood looking at each other, Toby with the tears rolling down his blackened face and his whole body shaking with the sobs, Miles just grinning stupidly and fingering the only button on his shirt.

Fannin struggled his way over through the crowd and questioned Miles. "How many of you are there?" He had to ask it several times before Miles turned a baffled look on him and said, "How many?"

"How many men are coming?"

"It's only me, sir. The others rode on toward Victoria and I ain't seen them since."

Fannin was confused, he did not understand that Miles had never left the woods or ridden toward Victoria, that he had spent the day hiding in a tree stump two miles off, and the evening crawling alone through the prairie grasses. "Not any of them?" Fannin asked.

"No sir. But they were going for help. At first when we heard all the firing we turned back but then we saw so many Meskins and you all surrounded, and there was no way possible for us to get to you. Horton and me, we wanted to try, but the rest said we'd be cut off sure as anything and they weren't coming. So Horton rode on with 'em to Victoria. I ain't seen them since." As he spoke, he uncorked his water jug and took a drink and everyone fell silent watching him, and he brought the jug down from his mouth and saw their eyes intent on it and looked around their faces and was puzzled. "What? What are you all staring at?"

"We're out of water, son," Hugh answered softly.

"Out?"

"Yeah."

"Completely out? None to drink?"

"That's right."

And Miles had just had his last swallow right before their eyes. It seemed he wanted to apologize in words but was unable, and his attempt seemed more defensive than contrite for he was just now taking in the fullness of the situation. "I . . . I was savin' that last drink in case I didn't make it here . . . I didn't know . . . I figured there was plenty . . . We started out with plenty, didn't we?"

But no one cared to talk about it. They had done their blaming and were tired of it. What they longed to hear—that Horton's men were coming back with reinforcements—were not words that Miles could give them, so excitement at his presence turned to disappointment and the men got very quiet and began to shuffle off. Their instinct was to drag their feelings off and suffer them alone, but there was nowhere they could go, so they milled around the square and peered down at their wounded comrades and remarked in monosyllables.

Fannin called them all together then.

They assembled in the center of the square with the wounded spread out on the ground among them, some resting their bruised heads in the laps of friends and others propping themselves up against piles of baggage. The Kenners sat on the clammy grass together.

Fannin stood despite his wound, and used the cow horn to project his spoken voice. But his strength was failing and the men farthest away had to strain to hear and often had to ask their neighbors what exactly had been said. Fannin said the picture here was simple, but the decision would be hard. They could reassemble now and leave everything behind and try to cut their way through all together in a night battle. He thought they could succeed, though they should know the ammunition was running low. But this action would necessitate abandoning the wounded, because there was no means of transportation. Fannin said that he himself would not go, but would stay with the wounded. He said that if the men chose to go, they would leave behind a piece of their humanity. The other option was to wait for morning and hope that Horton would appear by then with militia from Victoria. If Horton didn't come, they would have to decide in the morning whether to fight or to attempt an honorable surrender. They would not surrender except on promises of fair treatment. Fannin added that the men had fought so well throughout the day that he was sure they could hold their square together for another day at least and severely reduce Urrea's numbers, if only they had water and sufficient ammunition. But their shortages would preclude a protracted fight. He added that whatever the men chose to do, it would be done as a unit. The majority would rule. No one should act on his own whims or convictions; no one should try to make it through the lines alone. If they stayed, they stayed together. If they went, they went together, all but the doctors and the officers who chose to remain with the wounded.

So the choice came down to this: to leave the wounded and try to save themselves, or to stay and share a common fate, which could be death, but would not be dishonor.

Saying that, Fannin lowered the cow horn and sat down on the grass and waited while the men grouped around their officers and fell into emotional discussion.

Miles went around to see some of his wounded friends, then returned to Hugh and Toby and the three of them sat together with their arms looped around their knees and blankets draped about their shoulders. Coon was wide awake and watchful, snapping his head from side to side at every sound and craning his neck to lick his shoulder wound. Toby's teeth were chattering. Several men came over to speak to Miles. Scholar Tipton struggled over, dragging his bad leg, and Miles stood up when he saw him.

"Tipton? What the hell—"

"Shot," Scholar said, easing himself down beside Hugh. "I been playin' target all day long. But your daddy here," he laid a hand across Hugh's shoulder, "he dug out the ball. Else I'd be a maniac like them poor bastards over there. Them Meskins is shooting copper balls. Big ones." He held his hand up with the tips of his thumb and forefinger touching in a circle, to illustrate the size, the circle punctuated with the blackness of the night.

"Copper?" Miles repeated.

"Poison," Scholar said. "We got ourselves into a difficulty here without you."

Gus straggled over and sat down. He was still wearing his beret. "How long it take you to crawl all that way?" he asked Miles.

"Since dark. I started crawlin' when the Meskins took off for the woods."

"Well, you got in," Gus said. "Could we get out?"

"Likely. I think the question that the colonel put to us is if we want to."

"I sure don't want to if it isn't feasible; I have no hankering to crawl into a death trap." Gus turned to Hugh. "How about you, Doc?"

Hugh said that he was staying with the wounded, but he didn't think that everyone should stay.

Miles took offense at that. "You think you have more honor than we do," Miles said.

"No. But I'm a doctor and have a duty to the wounded."

"And I'm a soldier and have a duty to my comrades."

"So if you have a duty to them, that means you'll go with them if they vote to go," Hugh said.

"No. It means I'll put in my two cents to talk them into staying."

It really was that simple. And Hugh saw the honor in his son and understood what he had somehow overlooked before: Miles was the kind of man to count on. He was a difficult son, but a good brother and a good friend. Hugh had been so bent on perceiving him as a son that he had failed to see him as a man.

"We couldn't hold together even for a hundred yards in this dark anyway, I guess," Gus said reluctantly. His hair was wispy white against the blackness of the sky, and he shook his head. "If anybody tries to go, it ought to be each his own, and without a ruckus."

"Nah," Scholar said, sucking on his teeth, and did not elaborate.

Toby petted Coon and seemed not to be listening.

"I imagine that we'll all be staying," Miles said. "But if Fannin even thinks about surrendering tomorrow he can just forget it. Nobody here will stand to be humiliated."

"Well, I don't know, nobody's gonna stand this thirst long, neither," Scholar said. "You stay around a few more hours here without no water and suffer through a fusillade like we had poured on us today, before you make such speeches."

"I'd prefer dyin' in battle than execution-style," Miles reaffirmed.

Scholar said, "I don't think they'd execute this many of us."

"I do," Miles said.

Gus said, "Tipton, you know they shoot prisoners. It's just what they do."

"Well if that's for certain, I'm not long for this world, either way. With this hole in my leg, the chances are, I'll end up as a prisoner, unless we all die fighting or some damn thing like that, or unless a miracle comes 'round, like the Meskins just get up and go on home. Or Horton rides in with a awful lot of help."

"So what's your vote?" Gus pressed.

He shrugged. "I'm just sayin', if the vote is to go, I don't guess I'll be goin' with you, for the simple reason that I would not get far on this leg. But if I was whole, I guess I'd go. And I don't think Miles should go around shaming every man who sees things different than he does. Why should all these boys sacrifice their own lives for those of us already goners?"

"You're not a goner," Toby said.

The bugle off along the road played *"Centinela Alerta,"* and was answered by two others not too far away, and Scholar said, "That noise makes me crazy. What are they tryin' to do?"

"Make you crazy," Gus said. "That's what."

Hugh was trying to decide what was the safest thing for Toby. But Toby spoke for himself. "I think I'll stay here too. I haven't joined this army, so even if they vote to go, I guess I can do what I want."

Miles said softly, "That makes me real proud of you, brother."

Which was, Hugh thought, Toby's motivation. Hugh would stay for duty, Miles would stay for glory and for friendship, and Toby would stay for Miles, to make him proud.

Miles said, "You're entitled to your own opinion, Tipton. But I have my own, too," and got up and walked over to the dozen men of Frazer's Refugio command, and said, "How do, Nick? Where's Billy Gould?" and pretty soon was saying, "Well if I was shot, I'd sure be glad if my friends didn't leave me here for Meskins to come butcher in the morning."

Hugh and Toby sat listening to Miles and to the other voices. Some wounded men were begging friends to leave them and to save themselves. Others asked their friends to stay.

Scholar peered down at his bandage, and Gus took out a large twist of tobacco and chewed a piece of it.

"They're pretty goddamn mean," Scholar said.

"Who?" Toby asked.

"Meskins."

Twenty minutes passed. The bugles of the Mexicans sang at every five. Hugh got up and checked on a few patients, then returned. Miles visited a number of the groups and returned with the news that three Grays had gone out on their own for the timber where he'd come from.

"Which ones?" Gus asked.

"Tom D. and those two always with him."

"The one of them with that big mole?"

"Yep. And the other with the pigtail."

"Figures."

"Yep."

"You see them go?"

"No. But I was told. The men are basing part of their decision on whether or not those make it. If we hear shots, we'll assume they didn't. And if they do make it, the Grays and some of the Rovers say they're gonna vote to go. And some say even if the vote don't pass, they might leave anyway."

"So some of them have got some sense," Scholar said.

Pretty soon a volley sounded from the direction in which the men had gone, and a silence fell with everyone within the square just listening, and then there was another volley.

"Well, two of them are dead, at least two of them," Miles said.

"Let's hope one of them dead was Tom D.," Gus added.

In the end, when the officers all gathered around Fannin and related their vote count, the decision was to stay and prepare for a battle in the morning. It was partly bravado and partly fear of ambush that made them vote that way. But it was mostly a reluctance to leave the wounded, for there was not one man in the ranks who did not have a relative or close friend lying in a fevered heap on the sooty grass in the center of the square. Even the New Orleans Grays, who kept on threatening to make an exit on their own if the others would not go, could not justify it in the end, and their declarations dribbled off to mere wishful thinking. They could not, really, leave their wounded. Their camaraderie sustained them. It gave them grace.

They began by digging trenches. Their square had fallen to a quarter of an acre and they dug four extended trenches to define it, shoveling dirt and tossing it on the outside to form a bank. Vehicles and dead draft animals were piled on top as barricades. Even many of the wounded worked to build the makeshift walls of dirt, for these would be their sole protection in the morning. They could only use the cannon once or twice before they got too hot to load, and the small-arms ammunition would give out, but they would have these trenches and these walls. They made a prison for themselves, walling themselves in. The digging was an act of desperation and also an escape from cold, for only those who could stay active were spared the numbing temperature.

Hugh's arthritic joints were stiff with pain but he did his share of digging. Once or twice he tried to lie down on the ground to rest, but the cold was so damp and severe that he returned to his labors. Every man who could worked diligently but with intermittent rests on the cold ground, and when they were not digging with their shovels and their bayonets and makeshift implements—some with their bare hands—they were keeping watch against a night raid, positioned on the inside of the wall, each with two muskets and a third one with a bayonet attached. At any moment Urrea's cavalry could come reeling in. If they did, the rebels were to hold their fire until they were in close, then make each shot count, then use the bayonet.

But it did not come to that. The Mexicans made only false alarms brayed out by bugles on all sides, and now and then a lone picket out on the prairie would fire off a shot to make known his location or to rid his gun of dampened powder, and now and then a crippled horse which had fallen out a ways toward the farthest timber whinnied in the dark.

Before daylight a soft rain fell, and Hugh and Toby lay down side by side flat on their backs and stretched open their jaws to catch the droplets. Men dropped their shovels in the dirt and every face within the square was turned up to the rain; and when Hugh rose to make his rounds he found another man had died, staring straight up at the sky just like the living were, except his eyes were open and the rain had washed them like fish eyes. Tin drinking cups and all receptacles of any size were set out to catch the water, but what was thought to be a blessing turned into a nuisance: the rain died off—it was just a spattering—and left hopes blasted, and mucky powder in the guns. Everywhere was heard the clink of metal as the men unscrewed the breech pins of their rifles and scraped the soggy powder out.

Hugh's body had been so abused in battle and the night of labor that he felt a kind of dullness far deeper than exhaustion. The dullness blunted his emotions as he watched his two sons digging what could be their graves. Finally he drifted off to sleep with Toby nestled next to him for warmth. Even in his sleep, he felt his thirst. His throat was dry and sore and he could hardly swallow. When he awoke, the noise of labor had dropped off. A different mood had overcome the men. They were grouped along the western barricade, staring down the road toward Goliad. It was still dark along that far horizon, but a touch of early morning red shone through the trees over to the east along the timber of Coleto, and just enough of it crawled out across the prairie to the west to show a moving line. Hugh climbed up on an empty cartridge box to see, and Toby woke and climbed beside him. They could not tell what they were looking at exactly.

"Horton's men," someone said. "It has to be."

Of course it did not have to be. As the line drew closer, everyone accepted what it was before they could admit it to each other. Urrea had a mule train of at least a hundred burdened mules, plus a long line of soldiers, plus three cannon—what appeared to be two four-pounders and a howitzer—winding their way from west to north to east around the outskirts of the prairie. As the morning light lost its reddish tones and turned to yellow through the wispy clouds, the mule train made its way and the rebels watched it with their souls bleeding out. Their night labors were a waste: with cannon, these embankments made of dirt piled four feet high were useless. The carts and dead animals they'd dragged with so much effort to the top of the embankments, for use as breastworks, would now serve against them. The Mexicans' artillery could reach every corner of the camp. It could slash through the breastworks, sending bits and pieces flying back through the square like missiles: splintered truck beds and dismembered oxen.

They had built themselves a death trap on the prairie.

Some broke down and cried.

Others wandered out a little from the square, stooping carelessly to pick up battle remnants lying in the grass. One found a Mexican banner under a dead horse and rider, and brought it back and tossed it down amid the camp debris. Duval's snipers shuffled through the chilly light in search of the dead marksmen they had killed, and robbed them of their weapons, though no one seemed to think they'd have a chance to use them. If there was a battle, it wouldn't be a long one. The rebels were outnumbered, outsupplied, outgunned, and outmaneuvered.

And they were dizzy with their thirst. Their swollen tongues made speaking difficult and their dexterity was so impaired they fumbled with their weapons. They began to drink their urine.

Urrea marched his soldiers from the trees to meet the reinforcements. They formed into an imposing battle array, with the rifle companies advancing along the open country and the cavalry, in two wings, positioning to charge both flanks of the rebel square. The cannon were unlimbered and positioned several hundred paces from the rebels, protected by the rifle companies with infantry assembled to the left. The cannon then belched out two rounds of grape and canister, and the rebels had to scramble to their ditches, dragging the wounded with them. If the cannon were brought any closer and aimed a little lower they would prove deadly. These initial shots were just for show, a demonstration of new firepower.

Hugh and Toby hunkered close together in the ditch with men pressed close on either side. They smelled fresh dirt and fouled bodies. Spent grape rained down on them like hail. After that, they emerged with all the others to stare out at the Mexicans assembling—well over one thousand, they estimated, two thousand, some insisted. Then another blast of cannon sent them ducking down again.

But this second shot did not consist of grape. A long, high whistling noise spun toward them and they turned their faces up to see a silver length of chain tear and wrinkle through the placid morning light. It passed over them and fell clanking beyond the breastworks on the far side of the square.

Toby had chewed his lips so raw the blood ran down his chin. He stayed down in the ditch this time when the others emerged. Hugh stood up in the ditch and saw a rider with a white flag lunge from the line of Mexicans and gallop several paces toward them, then rein suddenly and ride back to his line.

Miles said, "They're inviting parley."

"Fuck them if they think we'll parley," one Gray croaked.

"No fucking chance of it," another one confirmed, slurring all the words.

But there had been the chain, and there it lay, coiled out in the grass. And over in the center of the square there were the wounded, flushed with fever and mumbling nonsense words. And everywhere, like a demon God, was the agonizing thirst destroying the morale.

The decision was to parley. Fannin asked his officers, and they asked their men, and the vote was almost, but not quite, unanimous: there were those among the Grays and Rovers who proclaimed they'd rather go down fighting, and one or two who still said they could win.

Hugh went back to the wounded, then. Toby followed him, stumbling as he walked, and said, "Father, they're bringing us some water," and repeated this twice more, emphatically, pointing out across the

morning landscape toward the Mexicans, his bleeding lips so swollen
that he looked like someone else's child. Hugh's heart froze nearly solid
at the sound of such disoriented talk. He did not know if Toby was
hallucinating from the thirst and mental shock of all that he had seen, or
if he was just hopeful beyond reason. He made him sit down with his
dog, and sitting side by side they seemed more like two dogs, Toby was
so black and mangy with the grime.

Hugh's hands had lost coordination, and the ground with all the
writhing wounded seemed to fly up in his face. He was only distantly
aware of what was happening—Fannin stating audibly that he would
make no capitulation which did not guarantee their lives and property,
and sending out an officer and two men who spoke broken Spanish, the
parties meeting in the field halfway with their white flags in the morning
sun. Back and forth, the messengers of each party went—the Anglos on
foot and the Mexicans on horseback, then Urrea rode out on the field
himself on his fine sorrel gelding, and Fannin was conveyed out between
his two interpreters, his arms around their shoulders for support. After
that, two Germans were called out on the field, one from the rebel side
and one from the Mexican, to help translate better what was being said,
so that part of the negotiations were done in yet another language.

Hugh crawled among his patients, and did not even try to comfort
them. He tied rags around one torso to keep the entrails in. Then Fannin was escorted back between his two interpreters and the word was
sent round that an honorable capitulation had been reached. The rebels
were to lay down all their arms and surrender themselves as prisoners of
war, and would be treated according to the usage of civilized nations.
The wounded would be taken back to Goliad as soon as carts could be
gotten to convey them. They would be properly attended to at La Bahía.
All private property would be respected.

Hugh saw Fannin's adjutant, Joe Chadwick, get out a writing desk
and paper and proceed to write the terms as Fannin spoke them, while
three Mexicans came into camp and set to writing also, so that there was
a copy done in English and another done in Spanish.

The men stood round and suffered silently, and many sat down in
the grass and wept without a sound.

Toby stroked his dog.

Miles stared off toward the eastern horizon as if he still believed that Horton's reinforcements would come riding in.

A rumor started that they'd all be marched to Goliad and then on to the coast, and there be put on ships and sailed back to New Orleans. Hugh heard the German colonel who was with the Mexicans and in charge of taking all the rebel arms, say, as soldiers stacked their muskets at his feet, "Well, gentlemens, in ten days, liberty and home."

They laid down their arms, the muskets in one pile and the personal property—dirks and pistols—in another. With them, they laid down all their pride and surrendered all their hopes. They avoided looking into one another's eyes. One man who had no teeth was allowed to keep his dirk, so he could eat. The officers were told to place their arms in a separate pile, and these were tagged with the owners' names and placed in wooden boxes and the lids were nailed down.

The Mexicans impatiently barked out orders, gesturing when they were not understood, and the rebels stared at them with hatred, their eyes burning with the lack of sleep and many with their faces glowing blood red from the fever.

At last Urrea rode into the camp with several of his officers and Fannin stood up long enough to unstrap his sword and hand it over, sheath and all.

Hugh did not even watch, nor did many of the men. They had few opinions left to state. They wanted water, and sleep. They wanted to go home. They appeared to be an army of men walking in their sleep, guided by some distant mental power that was not their own. Somnambulists, they were. Sleepwalkers, full of hate.

They were hearing other voices.

An alarm was trumpeted among the Mexicans. The rebels regarded it with little interest, for they'd heard the bugles playing all night long. It seemed without significance when they saw a line of Mexican cavalry reel off at top speed toward the eastern tree line toward a small band of horsemen.

It was Horton's riders, who had come. But they retreated back into the trees. They'd come too late, and too few. The brief event was tawdry and the rebels shrugged it off, though it meant their last chance, blasted. They needed water more than hope.

Mexican soldiers began wandering into camp to see the men and cannon that had rained such death among them on the day before.

Only one event roused the captured rebels from their trances, and only for a moment: someone tossed a lighted cigar into the powder magazine and blew himself to bits. The detonation shook the ground. Three Mexicans were killed in the explosion, and it was only after careful scrutiny that the culprit—almost charred past recognition—was identified as Bud Claiborne of the New Orleans Grays.

It was an accident, some said. Others called it suicide and an attempt to murder everyone within the square, Fannin and Urrea too. Claiborne's blackened body was wrapped in a blanket and placed beside his nephew's in the eastern trench, and all the rebel casualties were covered over with the grassy dirt, and that became their grave.

The wounded were left on the field, and the doctors, Hugh among them, stayed to care for them. Carts were sent for, to transport them back to Goliad.

All the rest were started on the march in the afternoon with the warm sun on their faces. They were not provided water, yet. The light was bright across the prairie. When Hugh last saw them trudging off in double file, Toby and the dog were swaying like drunkards. It seemed an afterthought when Toby, walking beside Miles, turned back for a last look at his father and raised a hand, a gesture slow and dreamy in the sun.

Hugh felt a hand upon his shoulder. He was being offered water in a yellow gourd. It was a black man, offering the gourd. An impression drifted in Hugh's mind. It was Josh Hanlin, Joshua, offering the gourd. Hugh took hold and drank without reserve, the liquid sliding down his ravaged throat until his throat cramped on itself and gurgled water out, and sour vomit with it.

E X O D U S

MARCH 21, EAST OF THE COLORADO RIVER

The sunlight was in motion with the March winds whipping it about. Everything and everyone was on the move. Santa Anna was rumored to be only fifteen miles west and advancing on Houston's army, which was perched on the east bank of the swollen Colorado. The refugees were pressing eastward toward the Brazos River. River after river, they would have to cross. William and the Kenner women were with a group of nearly fifty traveling at a steady pace. Bay Mare and one of the oxen had been requisitioned by the army, and now the mule was going lame and stumbling with each step. Finally Rose unharnessed the mule from the cart and turned it loose beside the trail, where it stood blinking in the bright sun, its head hanging and its notched ear twitching. William and Katie transferred baggage and provisions from the cart into the over-loaded wagon.

Katie especially was demoralized by the abandonment of the cart. It had sheltered her at night and been a kind of home for her and Samuel. She knew every notch and nail of it. She didn't even try to keep her spirits up, for her sleepless nights had worn them too far down. She had given her bonnet to an old woman and the morning sun had burned her face. She hadn't taken time to comb or braid her hair in days; it hung in matted knots.

William also was worn down. His hands were blistered with a poison ivy rash that had crept up to his elbows, and between the loads he rubbed his hands and forearms on his trousers to try to satisfy the itching. Katie annoyed him by saying he would only make it spread by doing that.

The line of refugees filed by, moving up a low rise in the open land. Many of them William knew by name. Baby Samuel watched them passing by his wagon and was so excited and unruly Rose had difficulty holding on to him.

When all the baggage had been transferred, Katie got up in the driver's seat of the wagon and shook the reins forward. The ox budged only a few inches, then balked at the new weight, and William had to whack his rump with a stick to get him going up the slope.

William was walking with Loco, who was burdened like a pack mule. William's hat was pulled down against the breeze, and the ox labored beside him. The wagon's wheels were creaking badly and needed to be greased. Grass beside the trail was up to William's knees, and he glided Loco's reins gently in and out between his fingers to scratch the oozing poison ivy blisters as he walked. In front and back of him the refugees moved steadily. When he glanced back down the sloping land behind him he saw an old man stopping to eye the mule, and shouted against the rising breeze, "Wesley, that's our mule, he's lame! He cannot travel any farther!"

Wesley's face was shadowed by a black hat with a bowl crown. He shouted back at William, but William couldn't understand him.

"He's too lame to be of use to you; leave him where he is!" William yelled.

Lifting a hand to acknowledge he understood, Wesley nonetheless bent down to lift one of the mule's front legs and probe the hoof with a stick.

Katie, looking back from the driver's seat, said, "Poor mule," and Rose said, "That old fool. He'll try to ride that mule."

"He won't get far," Grand said in her sweet voice, smiling like an angel.

William turned away and continued up the grassy rise of land. He let his thoughts take over.

These refugees were heading toward the border or the coast. Some had not decided on a path any more specific than just "east." They could travel through the redlands or turn southward toward the coast and hope to find some passage there at Galveston. William didn't know where he'd be stopping in the end. These muddy traces through the woods and weedy trails across the prairies could be leading him full circle to the sea, and England. Or he might be stopping somewhere on the shore, and turning back.

A two-wheeled buggy pulled by a mousy mare sped up from behind and careened into the open land beside him, fifteen yards or so. Its passengers were three motherless children whose father had remained with Houston's army on the Brazos. The oldest, a buck-toothed boy named Jeffrey, called out to William, "That your mule back there?"

"Yes, it is."

"Why'd you leave him?"

"He's lame."

"That old man's riding him."

William turned and saw the mule stumbling up the trail with Wesley on his back holding his bowl hat on with one hand and flailing at the mule's rump with the other. The sight irritated William: the man would ride the mule until it dropped down on its knees. William started down to talk to Wesley, but Rose said, "It's not worth it."

Katie said, "Yes it is."

William looked at Samuel, who was clinging to the side of the wagon making happy snuffing noises in the breeze and trying to climb out.

Forget the mule.

William kept on tramping up the hill beside the wagon until he topped the rise. There the green land stretched out before him like an open hand. The spring breeze laid the grasses low. Downward sloped the curving trail with the line of refugees pulling and prodding their beasts forward through the sunlight, veering off the road and cutting many paths through the grass. One woman's skirt was sliced off at the knees because the fabric had become so caked with mud and so encumbering. Her calves shone starkly white in the vivid sunlight. Another, young and fat, carried on her hip a small, square-headed child with glossy curls. Rose had offered this woman a ride, but she had declined. There was a family of eight, all on foot carrying provisions, and a family of four on a flatbed pulled by a pony no bigger than a big dog. Three dogs trotted in a pack: the female was in heat. The males had given her no peace since morning, trailing with their noses to her tail. A lone rider on a sorrel horse plodded at a slow pace in the shadows of the tree line over to the left, keeping at a distance. Leading, in the center of the prairie road, were nine ragged slaves and their mistress, a woman of middle age named Iris Parton who was transporting all of her fine china and her linens and two bedsteads in three wagons and a buckboard. Two of her slaves—a man and woman—had escaped into the dark the night before.

From this vantage there appeared to be a kind of order in the exodus —a progress and a rhythm that resembled music moving toward a denouement. The prairies were the breezy places in the music, but the music had its hard beginnings and sad movements in the passage. These refugees—all but Iris Parton—had lost most of everything along the way. They had left their homes and their belongings; some in the greatest hurry had left chickens in the coops and food on the table. Some had left graves beside the road. Oxen were left to die, bogged in mud beside the river crossings, their heads and backs protruding from the mud like the monsters William knew in Scottish lore, the flesh split open and the flies settling in swarms.

But the land from here was so expansive that the human plight looked trivial, a mere outing on a placid surface of grass and flowers.

William thought of England. He recalled the night when he had told his father he was leaving. A cold fog had descended on the streets outside and hung so heavy William could see nothing past the leaded windowpanes. He had stood at the window looking at his own reflection and the reflection of his father behind him, who was sitting by the fire in a wing-backed chair with his pipe and his newspaper. The room was silent but for the steady ticking of the mantel clock. William spoke without turning, watching his mouth move in the panes, his voice coming as a shock to the quiet room, saying he intended to go abroad and see his sister. His father folded up his paper and removed his pipe, very slowly, then spat his words out, "Sister! She has tainted this family and still you call her sister!" Then he'd raved about how Sarah was living among savages with her bloody Scottish socialist, a papist, in a Godforsaken land. William kept his posture with his back turned, and he kept his stoicism. The mantel clock chimed the late hour. Samuel Mullins spoke of how he'd built Mullins Machinery with his own sweat, and how he'd done it for William. "I didn't sacrifice everything to watch you board ship for another country," he had said, and William stood looking at the windowpanes and answered, "Had I never been born, you would have done the same. And it wasn't your sweat that built it, but the sweat of laborers you hire for dogs' wages."

"Leave the socialism to your sister; it doesn't become you," the old man said. "You care not one bit for the laborers. At most you are embarrassed by them, as their labor has financed your education. And fed you, for that matter."

William had denied it at the time, his breath so hot and forceful that it misted on the window glass, obscuring the image of his father, small and aged, folded into the protective wings of the chair. But he had not looked his father in the eyes while he denied it. As the mist began to dissipate from the pane, William saw his father, in the pane's reflection, stand and turn his face full on him and tell him softly in the Irish cadence of his ancestors, "William, do not go."

Here, the sun was out. The land was endless. Katie was speaking to him from the wagon, and when he gave her his attention she was in the middle of a sentence, ". . . and Grand says they were in the hide trunk this morning and she thinks someone must have taken them while we were fixing breakfast because unless you moved them, she didn't, and neither did Mother and I haven't see them since yesterday when . . ."

Seen what? What was she talking about? She was sitting up there in the driver's seat, bumping along and saying something had been stolen, and she had draped a linen tablecloth over her head and shoulders to protect herself from sun. It fell in soft white folds about her face. Samuel was crouching in the wagonbed in back of her, tugging on the tail end of her hair that showed beneath the tablecloth, and Rose was trying to pry the twisted hair from out of his small hands. Grand, on the seat by Katie, on the far side of the wagon, leaned down and rustled on the floorboards and came up with a sweet potato in her hand, and Katie took a look and then turned back to William, saying "Never mind, we found them."

Rose took the potato from Grand and fed part of it to Samuel. He spit most of it back out into her palm, then lay back in her freckled arms in the shadow of her bonnet, his eyelids batting down with sleepiness.

The trail of refugees slogged onward, eastward, down the sunny slope toward the tree line on the far horizon. Past that boundary there were other boundaries, rivers to be crossed, an ocean, another continent, and a quiet room on a foggy English night with an old man reading from his paper, drawing deeply on his pipe, and a clock on the mantel ticking steadily.

In the shadows of the trees along the north side of the prairie a lone horseman, who had dogged the line of refugees since Burnham's Crossing on the Colorado, turned his mount inward toward the Kenners' wagon. William watched his slow approach and wondered who he was, and what he wanted, and felt a certain dread; the slow, methodic pace was ominous. The rider was slumped forward in the saddle, his long back in a curve, as if he had lived many days in that same posture and his body had assimilated the rhythm of the horse's stride. The broad brim of his hat hung limp from days of wearing in the rain; his clothes were torn and he seemed shrunken down within them.

Katie had spied him, too. William glanced and saw her with the white cloth draped over her head and a little frozen look on her face, the folds falling down around her as if she were the Virgin Mary draped in her mantilla.

"It's Callum," she said, and gently reined the ox to a stop. It almost seemed she had been waiting for him, the way she knew him instantly. Grand Irma peered around from the bench beside her with her old face shadowed by her bonnet, and Rose's face was also shadowed and uncertain.

Callum rode up close, and reined the horse. He must have been aware of how he looked to them, his face falling off beneath the sagging hat brim like sap dripping from a wounded tree. He had been living with the dead and was half rotted, and he had no use for courtesies.

The last time William had set eyes on Callum they were standing amid stinking fish on a cold dock before daylight, and Callum was taking William's sister to America. William was but fourteen years of age, and in awe of Callum, and had asked again to go along. But Sarah cupped his cheek inside her palm and said he had an education to get.

Callum wished to take him, and he said so. There was more to be learned in America, he said, than in elitist schools in England.

He was now proven right. There was more to be learned in America. And more to be lost.

William now looked Callum in the eyes, not allowing his own eyes to betray his shock. There was neither blame nor pity in the firm expression that he held, though he was feeling both. He looked for Callum there behind the grotesque visage, and saw a remnant, only. Callum was a walking shade. "I have been looking for you since October," William said.

"Aye," Callum answered him. "So I were told."

William looked at Katie and saw that she was frightened. Her eyes darted over to the baby. Katie was the one who had cared the most for Callum when he stayed for days out in the Kenners' barn with the dusty hay clinging to his scabs. Hugh had tended to his wounds, but it was Katie who persuaded him to eat. Now it was the baby whom she cared about; it seemed that she considered Callum lost, and in some buried way she wanted him to be.

"I have come to see mae son," he said.

Samuel was sleeping. Rose had him in her arms. She invited Callum over with a gesture of her finger. He got down from his horse, gave the reins to William and walked over to the wagon. Rose held the baby out for him to see.

The breeze lifted Samuel's hair to glimmer in the sunlight. The little skull was perfect, the lips were full. He was peaceful. There was no disfigurement, for Samuel. There was no memory. His tragedy required nothing of him.

Only Callum carried markings of their past. He placed his hands on the railing of the wagon bed and looked in at the child in Rose's arms, but was hesitant to touch him. Katie climbed back from the driver's seat, the linen falling down around her shoulders. She was protective in her movements, and huddled over Samuel like a mother. Her gestures were so blatant.

Rose's face was tilted up to look at Callum, and she struggled to her knees. "Hold him," she said. Her face was sweet and friendly. The sun shone on her nose and on one freckled cheek. "He's a good boy, Mr. Mackay."

Katie made a little gasp of apprehension and her hand fluttered in the sun, then rested on her lips. Strands of her dark hair were tossed and tangled by the wind. When Callum reached to take the child, Katie cried aloud, "Don't take him off; he doesn't know you anymore and he'd be scared without me—"

The words lifted in the air and fluttered down around them all. There was a wagon passing by. A cloud ran across the sun. Samuel stirred in Rose's arms and rolled against her breasts, throwing one arm up against her neck. When he opened his blue eyes, they settled fast on Callum. For a long time, Samuel lay blinking sleepily and looking at his father, then saw Katie waiting there. He broke into a smile and reached for Katie.

She took him without asking, as if it were her right, as if she were his mother, and he put his little perfect head against her neck and snuggled in and clung to her as if he were her child. She pulled the linen table-cloth close about her shoulders and around the child.

"Are you hungry? Come ride with us," Rose said to Callum.

Watching Callum's face, William saw a twist of pain unfurling deep inside him like a banner taking wind.

"Aye," Callum said, and nodded.

Samuel raised his head from Katie's neck to look at Callum once again, and Katie's hand that held the linen slipped and lost its grip. The breeze grew strong and lifted up the strip of cloth, flinging it into the sunlight like a ghost taking sudden flight. Callum reached both hands to catch it, but the same breeze lifted off his hat, and he instinctively took hold of that instead.

The linen sailed out over Callum, startling the horses, and tumbled out across the prairie grass with William chasing after.

Chapter 26

THE ANGEL OF GOLIAD

MARCH 22, PRESIDIO LA BAHÍA

A moon just shy of full was haunting the presidio when the last carts of rebel wounded crossed the river at the upper ford. The water was just shoulder high, but Hugh sank his head and body down beneath the surface to let the current wash him clean. The water numbed his tired limbs but waked his mind from its exhaustion. From underneath the rippling surface he could see the misshapen moon and hear the muffled splashing of the men and oxen dragging through the current.

He could escape from here, if he wanted to. He could let the water carry him downstream. The guards were not so watchful of the doctors and the night had lulled them all into a state of reverie and he could simply slide away. But he had no desire to; he wanted to be with his sons. He rose back to the surface and emerged on the muddy banks with water tugging at his clothes. The carts carrying the wounded were rumbling up the slope. There were so many wounded, both Mexicans and rebels, they lay on top of one another. This haul was the third and last from the Coleto battlefield to Goliad; the first two hauls had brought in mostly Mexican wounded, who far outnumbered the rebels, and in this caravan of six carts, two wagons, and a flatbed there were all the

325

wounded who remained—over sixty rebels and forty Mexicans who had stayed out on the field since the battle Saturday.

Fannin was among them, riding on a horse with his bandaged leg cocked forward on the saddle pommel and his arm with two bullet holes pressed against his side.

Since the morning of surrender, Hugh had stayed three days and two nights on the field, allotted only meager ears of corn to eat and three bites of bull beef. He was so depleted physically his eyesight and his hearing were distorted, but he did not feel hungry. Nor did he crave sleep. He was nourished by anxiety; it kept him moving and also in a strange way kept him sane, for it linked him to his sons. While he nursed the gruesome wounded on the field, the memory of Miles and Toby and the dog stumbling off toward Goliad under heavy guard had settled on his brain like a malady. Fannin had assured him that Urrea would protect the prisoners and see that they were fed, but Hugh himself had seen Urrea ride off toward Victoria, not Goliad. The rebel prisoners were in another's power now and subject to the whims and the discretion of other officers and commandants.

The moon hung high above the chapel. The air was crisp and full of spring and the frogs were chirping. Many of the Mexican soldiers were camped outside the fort in tents or on the open ground. Some of the stone houses near the fort had not been burned and were alight with torches and activity. Hugh guessed the officers were quartered in these few remaining homes, and maybe wounded soldiers too.

Two cannon flanked the sally port and the gates were open.

The rebel prisoners would be within the fort.

Hugh's clothing dripped with river water. His joints ached with the cold. His mind, deprived of sleep for three nights now, was ill at ease with its perceptions. The officers in charge, out on the field, had ordered that all wounded Mexicans be tended before the rebel doctors were allowed to see to their own men, so Hugh with two other doctors and several aides, including a man from Hamburg known as Vosz and a Creole from Louisiana who spoke Spanish, had worked through the nights with only moments of sleep.

Passing through the gates of the presidio, Hugh stumbled and was almost unaware that he had stumbled, for the chill of his wet clothes had numbed his legs. The carts and wagons halted just inside the sally port and the scene became confused. Here within the fort were more soldiers bedding down along the walls, but no sign of the prisoners. An officer who looked no more than twenty-five years old stepped forward, and Urrea's German colonel, Holzinger, who was riding beside Fannin, presented the young man to Colonel Fannin as the commandant of La Bahía—Colonel José Nicolás de la Portilla. Wincing with pain, Fannin dismounted and requested Holzinger to ask Portilla where the prisoners were being kept.

Portilla's voice was high and grainy, and though he was young his shoulders were hunched like an old man's. He was full of energy and flung his arm out toward the chapel, saying, *"Adentro de la capilla."*

"All of them?" Fannin asked incredulously.

Holzinger related this in Spanish and Portilla nodded. *"Todos,"* he said.

Hugh felt a wave of nausea. He was dizzy and disoriented. The voices sounded hollow and distorted. The chapel stones, which he'd seen only through a morning fog, were now radiant in moonlight, as white as bleached linen. How could the chapel hold so many men? From this vantage he could only see the side of it that had a room attached like a square stone box flush against a larger box. The side room, in the moonlight, cast a stark and slanted shadow to the ground. There was a single window way up high, near what must have been the altar, and the yellow light of a fire wavered from within. A wooden cross rose plain and vivid from the roof above the other end, above a smaller courtyard. On the center of the roof two cannon stood in stark relief against the sky, positioned to command the river roads. The building seemed all angles in the brightness of the moon, a flat roof and flush sides and a flawless order to the structure.

Hugh went over to see Scholar Tipton, who was propped up in the corner of a cart with his back against the flimsy picket rails. "They're inside, in the chapel," Hugh said.

Scholar eased his inflamed leg down over someone else's knee, but the man jerked up in the darkness and pushed the leg away, so Scholar tried to settle it again. It was stiff and would not bend. The cart was crowded with eight other men. One spat out through the rails.

"Can't be," Scholar answered Hugh. "Ain't room in there."

A raw-boned man within the cart awoke and sat up slowly. Realizing where he was, he said flatly, "Does this place by any chance look familiar to you boys?"

"Did at first," one answered. "But the soldiers has all shrunk and is wearing the wrong uniforms."

Only one man laughed. The others rearranged themselves like squirrels in a nest, bickering and shoving for more room.

"Can we get out, Doc? My butt hurts," someone asked. It was one of the Red Rovers, and Hugh had noticed in the daylight that his face was flushed so red with fever it almost matched his jacket. His cuts and gashes were also vivid red, and some had turned a putrid yellow. "Look here at this, Doc," Scholar said. He had removed his bandage, crusty with dried blood and filth. The wound spread out across the flesh below his knee and up the fatty part beside the kneecap like fingers of a hand that had laid claim. Even in moonlight Hugh could see the putrid yellow color of infection, and the stink was strong. "I bet you're thinking you can take it off," Scholar said. "But 'tain't so. It's my leg. *¿Comprende?*"

"Your leg," Hugh answered, "and your life. Let's just see how bad it gets." Urrea, it was said, was sending instruments for amputation.

Hugh turned and went to Fannin, who was still conversing with Portilla. Portilla didn't speak a word in English and relied completely on the German, Colonel Holzinger, a young man with pale skin and hair so blond his eyebrows were invisible. Holzinger spoke sufficient Spanish and enough English to interpret, and from listening to him Hugh understood that all the wounded rebels were now being relegated to the chapel with their comrades. The German motioned the *carreteros* to drive over toward the chapel, and they made a slow and jagged route across the center of the compound, past the three anaqua trees in bloom, and halted at the entry to the chapel yard. The *carreteros* were civilians, and they got down from their vehicles and stood together smoking cigarillos while a few Mexican soldiers and the rebel doctors—Hugh and two others—unloaded wounded from the carts. The forty wounded Mexicans were carried in a doorway to the barracks on the west wall of the compound, but the rebels were transported to the chapel doorway and placed on the ground. Some of them refused to be aided by the soldiers and crawled the brief distance on their hands and knees. One man with a broken rib lay down on his back in the cart and struck at every Mexican who tried to touch him.

The chapel doors—two large paneled slabs that fit together in an arch—were closed. Two cannon were arranged before them, commanding the interior, and guards stood by with blazing torches.

Hugh saw the waxing moon as motionless as stone above the walls. All the rest in sight was in frenetic motion, the weighty forms of injured bodies twisting to find comfort. The languid branches of a tall willow tree that grew outside the chapel yard, near a narrow picket gate in the north wall, were draped across the wall by breezy gusts and ventured down like nervous fingers on this side, caressing the cool stones.

Hugh listened for the prisoners within. At first he only heard a low and muffled rumbling of their voices, but then the noise grew louder and developed rhythm, as if the edifice had come alive and its heart begun to beat. He thought the men were singing. But then the rhythm hardened and became a kind of chant. While heaving stinking wounded out of carts, he listened to the pulsing beat within the doors and tried to make out what it was the prisoners were saying. When the cadence grew so strong and so insistent that the words came through, Hugh felt the nausea hit him hard, and sat down on the ground beside the chapel doorway staring at the glistening stones. Despair was taking hold. Hugh fingered the torn cuff of one wet sleeve, then set his hands within his lap to try to stop their shaking. He recalled a line that he had read somewhere, or heard . . ."If stones could talk . . ." but he could not recall the rest of it. If stones could talk . . . what? What would they say? "Feed us," they were calling. "Feed-us, feed-us, feed-us . . ."

His boys were in there, crying out for food.

The chant became unstable and seemed to wobble on itself, then assumed another pattern and another language and grew strong again. *"Co-mi-da, co-mi-da,"* they were calling. Food. They had been so proud and held the Mexicans in such contempt and now were forced to use the foreign language to sing for sustenance.

When the doors were finally opened the noise erupted into cheering; perhaps they thought they would be fed, or maybe it was only fresh air that they wanted. The yellow light of sconces with the stench of burning sheep oil and of soiled and sweating men washed out into the courtyard with the cheering.

Fannin stepped up to the doorway. Chadwick stepped beside him. Those just inside and closest were the only ones to see their colonel, for the others were packed together, back to chest, less than one third finding room to squat down on the floor. Those who saw him standing in the open doorway with his aide beside him and the moonlight and the cannon hovering behind him fell quiet and their silence rolled on backward toward the nave.

Hugh pressed inside in front of Fannin, easing in between the bodies crammed together. He could not have fathomed men in such proximity. It was difficult to breathe because their bodies gave off so much heat. Their dirty faces were a waxy yellow in the light of burning sconces. Most of them were very young, but sallow in the light. Hugh jostled through the mass of flesh, asking repeatedly for Toby and Miles. He found them shoved against each other near the railing where the altar would have been, though there was no railing and no altar. There was no furniture at all, as the men were jammed from wall to wall. Hugh's emotions were so blighted from the lack of sleep that tears rolled down his face. When Miles and Toby saw him coming, they tried to move to meet him. Miles's chest was pressed to Toby's back. His face with a rash of pimples and a new growth of blond stubble was perched just over Toby's head, and the brothers moved in tandem but got nowhere, there were so many men shoved in between. At last a narrow path was opened and Hugh was pressing up against his sons. He was distantly aware of the dog crouching at their feet with his ears back flat against his head and his tongue hanging out, his sides heaving as he panted from the heat.

It was difficult to hear above the noise, for the voices around started up again when Holzinger escorted Fannin and Chadwick into the square room off the main chapel and shut them in. Holzinger barred and locked the door, then made his way back through the crowd and out to the fresh air. Hugh knew from the commotion that the wounded were now being carried in and situated there beside the door, causing all the prisoners already wedged inside to shove in even closer. The few that had succumbed to sitting in the close air near the ground were forced to stand up and relinquish what small space they had.

Hugh asked, "Have they fed you yet?" and Miles answered him above the din that echoed up against the stone coves of the ceiling, "Not today. Yesterday they gave us water and each a piece of meat no bigger than a turkey egg. Toby gave half his to Coon."

"Not the water, just the meat," Toby said defensively. "Have they fed you, Father?"

Hugh nodded, moving even closer up against him, smelling Toby's boyish smell and oily hair. He felt a mildness drift across his mind like a waft of scented air. If he could just hold on to it, and sleep for just an hour. There were men who needed care, but he was wedged between his sons and wanted to surrender to exhaustion.

Miles was saying, "We got rowdy yesterday and the commandant sent his peons in to tell us there's a shortage, they ain't had food either. I think it might be true but some think the Meskins are just trying to incite us to a riot so they can turn those cannon loose in here."

Hugh tried to answer him. He meant to say that he believed that they were short of food, for there had been a shortage on the field for Mexicans as well as rebels, and it was only because Josh had procured corn and bits of beef that Hugh had eaten anything at all. But what he said instead was something about Josh, nothing to do with food, and Miles looked at him with puzzlement, as if he did not trust him, and said, "Josh? Josh Hanlin? Josh is with the Meskins?"

"With Urrea," Hugh answered him. A boy with snaggle teeth was shoving up against his ribs. Someone stepped on Coon Dog's foot or stub of tail and Coon let out a yelp. The sound was muffled from below. The voices and coughing of the men sounded hollow and remote as they lifted to the ceiling, and Hugh looked up at all the space awash in yellow light. The arching of the stones was beautiful. "He gave me food," Hugh said.

"Josh was fighting?" Miles inquired.

"No, not fighting. He's one of Urrea's aides."

"His valet?"

"Something like that," Hugh answered. The men around were packed so close he didn't have to use his energy to stand. He would not have fallen even if he'd tried.

"That's right neighborly of him," Miles said, "after you saved his life."

"You talked to him?" Toby was asking.

Hugh's mind was playing tricks on him. He recalled the cornfield he'd been lost in as a child, when the stalks all hovered close around him and denied him sight of everything except the sky. "Briefly, I did," he said. "Then he left with Urrea for Victoria."

Some of the men were shouting at each other, and the sound was magnified, echoing against the walls.

"If they put more men in here you're gonna have to get rid of that fleabag dog," someone from behind complained to Toby.

"He stinks," another added.

"You stink, Evan," Miles said.

Toby asked where Scholar Tipton was.

Hugh told him he was here, but didn't say how bad the wound had become.

A shaggy man who was stripped down to his trousers, his chest a mass of hair glistening with sweat, inquired about a friend of his, named John Brooks. Hugh knew of Brooks. Brooks had a shattered hip. He'd spent two nights in an open cart because there was no ox to pull it. Hugh related this and the man said, "God bless him then. I know his sister from back home—" and started nudging through the crowd toward the door to find him.

Toby scratched his head, his blistered fingers lost in the dirty shock of hair. There was still a paste of black gunpowder matted in the sweaty strands around his temples.

"That goddamn Fannin and Joe Chadwick have got a whole room to themself," a bald man with a red scarf tied around his head was grumbling, and Miles responded with a note of plain annoyance, "I doubt they had a lot of choice about it."

"Don't defend that jackass, Kenner. He's why you're stuck in here."

"I'm why I'm stuck in here," Miles answered.

Hugh had the dim sensation that his thoughts had gone astray and were trailing aimlessly amid the warm breath of three hundred men. The wounded evidently had been placed beside the entry door, and though Hugh couldn't see them from this vantage he could hear the repercussion of their delirious voices. He felt that he should go and care for them but had no strength to do it. His boys were looking at him, from so close, as if he puzzled them. He closed his lids and rested back into the steaming bodies and let his mind lift upward toward the wide expanse of air.

Standing up, he slept, dreaming he was carried in a boat which traveled with a current in a dark corridor of water, swinging in and out against the ragged, narrow banks and ramming into jams of logs but with the current always pulling onward, down over waterfalls and out into midstream where the land was beyond reach. At moments he was jostled into wakefulness and saw things which his mind could not make sense of. He saw the room awash with light from sconces hanging high against the stones, and red meat passed from hand to hand and red blood on the lips of those who ate it. He saw Miles perched up on a stranger's shoulders and lifting down a painted panel from the white stones of the walls. There were other panels on the walls, figures of Christ's journey on his way to crucifixion. The one which Miles removed while balanced on the stranger's shoulders was a faded painting of a lovely woman leaning over Jesus, who was carrying His cross on His back and was bent beneath the weight of it. She had wiped the face of Jesus with a linen cloth and on the cloth a likeness of His face appeared within the folds. Painted in blue on the bottom of the panel were the words *"Veronica limpiando el rostro de Jesus."* "Veronica wipes the face of Jesus." Hugh stayed awake just long enough to see the panel stomped upon and broken up and used to feed a small fire built within a foot of space near the center of the chapel, the pale dress of Veronica burning in the flames and the men all crowding in to roast their meat on skewers made of splinters from the panel's wood. He felt the press of bodies moving him like water currents, and drifted off again. When he woke, the arches of the ceiling were washed gray with smoke which traveled from the little fire upward in a path that wavered, and from a second fire closer to the entry doors, like souls ascending to the arches and lingering to view the scene below.

Miles fed him meat cooked warm, but raw inside, apologizing for it being bloody and explaining he could not stand near the fire long enough to cook it better, for the heat was so unbearable and there were so many men waiting for their turn to cook. Hugh tried to give his meat to Miles or Toby but they had already eaten theirs and wouldn't take it. While he drifted back to sleep he felt Miles take his jaw and pry it open, pushing bits of meat inside, and then instinct took over and he chewed and swallowed it and took the rest in his hands and ate it with his eyes still closed.

The sounds all seemed to fade to nothing but a murmur. The fires died away. The sheep oil in the sconces burned away and several of the flames flickered down to nothing, darkness where there had been light, and Hugh suffered from his thirst and saw the dog crouching in the dark down at his feet and Toby squatting with an arm around the dog and his head against it like a pillow, and Miles standing up asleep, his head cocked sideways on the shoulder of the old man, Gus, who had his head thrown back, his throat ribbed and wrinkled in the dark shadows. There was still the sound of coughing, men hawking phlegm and now and then a tired voice or startled cry and groaning from the wounded who were lying near the doorway, but sleep had claimed the chapel. Hugh fell asleep again and didn't know what time had passed when he was jolted into watchfulness by a voice calling his name.

At first he thought that he had dreamed the voice, for it was Dr. Kenner that it called for, not Hugh Kenner but a name out of the past, and it reverberated with an echo. But when it called a second time Hugh knew he wasn't dreaming. It was not a dream, it was a man's voice with a Spanish accent calling from the doorway. Hugh strained to see above the heads pressed in around him, through the remnants of the smoke and toward the entry of the chapel where the doors were open and the soft beginning light of dawn had washed across the sky outside.

The men around began to wake. Toby came up from below, his eyes clogged with sleep and his hair sticking up on one side of his head. Miles opened his blue eyes—Hugh could see their color even in the faulty light —a dreamy and bemused expression lingering behind the stubble on his face.

"They calling you?" he asked.

Hugh nodded, remembering how Miles had fed him like a baby in the night, and something passed between them at this moment, some understanding or perhaps forgiveness of a kind for sins that neither of them could define. Then he briefly set one hand, heavy as a stone, down on Toby's shoulder, and made his way with difficulty through the bodies toward the doorway.

The wounded, more than sixty of them, were spread like corpses near the door. Some spoke to him as he went past, asking him to bring some water. He had cared for most of them at one time or another in the last two days, and knew many of their names. Scholar Tipton was jammed in between two brothers who had come to Texas with the Mobile Grays. The guard asked Hugh's name and motioned him to go outside.

A Mexican woman was standing in the gray morning light, wearing an old faded frock that hung too loose about the shoulders. She seemed no bigger than a child. She had brought an offering, and held it out to him.

"The wax of bees," she said. "To stir with grease and make medicines." She was the woman who feared cholera. But now it seemed she was completely without fear, standing like an angel in the hazy courtyard and holding out the canvas bag of wax, her dark eyes watching Hugh intently.

He took the bag and thanked her, more touched than he could say. He noticed the willow branch still tapered down across the wall from the other side, damp and placid now against the stones, the night breeze having died away completely.

The woman was looking at his hand that held the canvas bag, the knuckles swollen red with rheumatism, and she said, "Today I'll boil red ants in water with vinegar, for your hands. It's necessary that you have your hands, to be a doctor." When he did not respond to her she added in a voice as tenuous and gentle as the hazy light, "It's possible for me to get more wax of bees. I am not afraid of bees."

THE HIDING PLACE

March 23, victoria, twenty-five miles northeast of goliad

Dusk was coming early with the rain.

Joshua built a fire in the sooty fireplace of Urrea's headquarters, a one-room stone house on the square. It took a moment for the draft to pull correctly and the smoke to rise up the chimney; at first the smoke blew inward with the sparks from the shaggy cedar bark and rose to hang about the rafters, which sagged from one side to another of the slanted ceiling because the roof was so uneven. The plank floor slumped the other way, giving one end of the room a ceiling height of almost seven feet, and the end with the fireplace a height not more than six.

When the fire caught, Joshua set Urrea's muddy boots on the hearth to dry.

General Urrea was seated on a dirty, rumpled bed in the corner near the door, his legs stretched to the floor and crossed at the ankles, his bare feet splotchy-white from being wet so long. The door was open to the rainy twilight, and a portly lieutenant entered with formality and launched into a story of events that had taken place in Cópano the day before. Urrea listened. Joshua put water on to boil for chocolate, then started polishing the sword that Fannin had surrendered to Urrea. Urrea wanted the blade so clean it would reflect the light.

The lieutenant, dripping wet, the droplets lingering within the folds of his fat face, said a shipload of Americans had sailed into the port of Cópano, unaware that Cópano was garrisoned by Mexicans. Before they had laid anchor, most of them jumped overboard to wade ashore. They were splashing in the water like children when the soldiers came out from the bluff and took them by surprise. They had no choice but to surrender. The ship, however, got away.

"Were they bearing arms?" Urrea questioned him.

"The ship was bearing arms, I'm sure, but the men did not have weapons in their hands."

"Then they're fortunate," Urrea said. "Send them on to Goliad, but keep them separate from the other prisoners. Mark them in some way, to designate that they weren't bearing arms."

The lieutenant walked over to the fire and stood with his back to it. He mopped his wet face with his palms. "The others at Goliad, are they to be shot?"

"Not by my order, no."

"But by the law, they should be."

"Of course. But it would be a stain on Mexico if Santa Anna executed so many men together who surrendered honorably and placed their lives at his mercy."

The lieutenant stood with his arms crossed. Finally he said, "There was another incident near Cópano, this morning," and he told Urrea of a slaving ship that had dropped anchor offshore just south of Cópano that morning in the rain. The crew had been unloading slaves onto the rainy beach—sixteen male adults, thirty females and their small ones, all in chains—when the soldiers came out from the dunes and took the slavers captive. The slaves were all wild Africans who spoke a foreign language, and the Mexicans had left them in their chains for now, on the beach, under guard. The slavers were imprisoned on board the boat they had sailed in on: one was English, three were Cuban, seven were Americans. Most of them were just the hired crew, but two investors were on board. Or so the Cubans said.

"Turn the slaves loose," Urrea said.

"They're wild Africans," the lieutenant repeated.

"They were," Urrea corrected him. "They are now free Mexicans. Give them food and turn them loose. If they want to stay with us for sustenance, then let them."

"But they speak only gibberish."

"Then let them speak it freely," Urrea said.

"And the slavers?" the lieutenant asked.

"They're prisoners of Mexico. Chain them and bring them here to me."

"But they weren't bearing arms."

"No, they were bearing slaves, which is against the law."

"There are two other prisoners we captured near the landing sight," the lieutenant said. "Americans. One was armed and one was not. They don't speak any Spanish and we didn't have an interpreter with us, so I brought them here and put them with the captives we took yesterday."

"Go and get them," Urrea said. "The one with arms is of course a prisoner of war. But I hope you didn't mistreat the other one. We need allies here, and anyone who isn't violating laws or bearing arms should be treated with respect."

As the lieutenant left the house, a gust of damp air from the open door played havoc with the fire. The sound of rain beat steadily against the roof, drowning out all other sounds. The pan of water on the fire started boiling, and Joshua dropped a cube of bitter chocolate in a cup and poured the water over it and gave it to Urrea, then went on polishing the sword. The rag that he was using caught against the tip and ripped in two, and he cursed beneath his breath and set the cloth and sword aside. He needed to relieve himself, and asked permission. Urrea, who had taken up a book with leather binding and had lost himself to reading, nodded absently.

The rain was a nuisance. Joshua took off his boots so not to get them wet, then tugged his collar up around his neck and sprinted barefoot just a short way down the side street to the woods. The street was empty but for two horses hitched at the railing near a ratty dry-goods store. Returning in a moment with his head ducked against the chilly rain and his feet sloshing in the mud, he saw a group of men coming toward him from the square. As they came closer he saw they were the prisoners

Urrea had called for, with their guards behind them. The lieutenant walked in back, shaking water from his boots.

It was only at a glance he saw them, and with all the downpour in between and the dusky light, but he recognized them instantly. There was not a second when he thought a trick of rain or distortion of the light deceived him. It was the Hanlin brothers, Bull and Straw, bound in ropes, making their way toward him at a steady pace, not looking at him and not knowing him.

He turned and ran back down the street and to the woods, his sight blurred by the rain. When he was deep in the woods he veered into a thicket overgrown with honeysuckle vines and tore his way inside it with his hands. He was breathing so hard he could hear his breath above the rain. He crouched and wrapped his arms around his knees and buried his face into the space between his chest and thighs and took refuge there, smelling his hot breath. The panic almost choked him.

But in a moment he became aware of light. It was gray twilight filtered through the trees and rain but strong enough to see by. His breathing slowed and he could hear the rain again. He took possession of himself, and staring down into his lap he turned his panic into something still and solid. He thought: they are at Urrea's mercy now. Urrea despises slavery and he can punish them. If he would have them shot or put in prison, my freedom would be certain. No one would come looking for me then.

And so he crawled out of the brush and walked back through the downpour. Three guards stood outside the stone house in the rain. When Joshua stepped in, he saw the Hanlins there before the fire he had built, and thought of all the fires he had built to warm these men. It seemed from how they stood with the ropes that had been tied around their torsos now lying near their feet, their hands behind their backs and their backs to the fire, that they might have been free men; he could not see the ropes that tied their wrists. But he trusted that the ropes were there.

They did not recognize him, with his jacket. Urrea was still sitting on the bed, barefooted and impatient, the book now set aside, and he asked Joshua why he'd been gone so long.

"I was in the woods," he said.

And that was when the Hanlins really looked at him. Straw knew him first. Then Bull parted his full lips and his eyes froze over. His dark ringlets dripped with water.

Urrea said to Joshua, "Ask these men what they were doing on the beach."

Joshua addressed the questions to the Hanlins in English without a word of recognition.

Straw recovered his composure. He stood sopping wet, squinting with his narrow eyes as if still uncertain this was Josh, and said directly, like a challenge, "Tell him we were traveling south to Mexico."

Joshua told this to Urrea. The firelight played on Urrea's face the way that lightning dances on a landscape of pure stone. And Joshua added then in his best Spanish, "That is what he says. But he's lying."

"Lying?" asked Urrea.

"They were on the beach to purchase slaves," Joshua said.

Urrea studied him, and then the men. "How do you know?"

"Because I know them. I was their slave. They used to go to Cópano for slaves; once they took me with them."

The Hanlins couldn't understand what he was saying but they understood that he possessed their fate. Anything they argued in their own defense would be translated through his voice.

Urrea said, "It is an irony," his voice as hard as it had ever been.

Bull said to him, "The nigger is lying."

Urrea said to Joshua, "Tell him that I do not understand a word of English."

Joshua told him.

Urrea said to the lieutenant, "Which of these men was armed?"

"The blond one."

"Put him with the prisoners we took yesterday, to go to La Bahía. He's a prisoner of war. The other had no weapon of any kind?"

"No."

Joshua spoke on his own, "Did he have a whip?"

"A bullwhip," the lieutenant said.

"The bullwhip was his weapon, then," he said, and began to unbutton his own wet shirt and peel it away. Then he turned his back to let Urrea see the scars. The rain was beating down with force he had never heard. He could feel Urrea's eyes. He draped the shirt back on and turned to face him.

Urrea said to the lieutenant, "Execute these men. They are pirates bearing arms."

Straw Hanlin's eyes were wild, but when he spoke to Joshua his voice was soft. "What is he saying?"

Joshua was silent.

"What is he saying? Will you not tell me what the Mexican is saying?"

Straw's voice still held its power over Joshua. If Joshua spoke now, it would be with fear, so he did not speak. He buttoned every button of his shirt, watching how his fingers pushed the buttons through the holes. The Hanlins then began to speak in gibberish themselves, demanding and then pleading that he "tell the Mexican that we weren't fighting in the war, we've been neutral from the very first, tell him we were traveling south . . . tell him . . . tell him . . ."

But he told him nothing.

The guards were called inside to take the prisoners away. There was discussion of the weaponry, wet powder, and the rain. The guards were told to go and get dry guns. They left and came back with more men, bearing muskets bundled in a tarp. The Hanlin brothers promised Joshua they would set him free, if he would help them now. But he just sat down on the floor and went on polishing the sword while they were taken out in the rainy street.

Urrea remained sitting on the bed. In a moment Joshua stood up and went over to the door and stood beside the fat lieutenant.

Through the dusky rain, he watched. Three men spread the tarp open in the muddy street, three others knelt beneath, loading their muskets, and four men strapped the Hanlins to a tree, both together on one tree just ten feet distant from the men beneath the tarp.

The lieutenant walked out in the street and gave the word to fire. The guns were fired from beneath the tarp. Joshua heard the sound and saw the sparks and stood peering through the darkness that was falling and the rain running off the roof in torrents. Only when the bodies were unstrapped and dropped in the mud like butchered hogs, did he turn back to his general and the room all washed in light.

A   PETITION

MARCH 24, PRESIDIO LA BAHÍA

Crucita boiled honey and wild onions for their colds, and sage tea for their fevers. She was at Hugh Kenner's side through days and nights. When the prisoners were moved out of the chapel into the compound yard, she brought armfuls of lush grass from the prairies to spread across the ground along the barracks of the western wall, where the prisoners were to sleep out in the open under heavy guard.

She brought grass into the chapel, which was transformed into a hospital for the wounded, the Mexicans on one side and the rebels on the other.

In two days' time she became so accustomed to and so comforted by the doctor's presence that she sought him out like grace. His gray hair, thin and wet with rain, was long enough to curl up gently at his collar, and his arthritic hands were visibly inflamed, and both these things endeared him to her. She had never known such kindness. Together they could nurse a naked man without embarrassment. And so when he came looking for her in the chapel on one afternoon, she followed him outside and said she would do any favor in her power.

They stood together in the chapel yard, beside the picket gate, in gray light under heavy clouds. They could hear the echoes of the wounded from within the chapel.

The rain would start again.

Hugh Kenner told Crucita he had spoken with the other doctors, and they'd come to a decision. If Colonel Portilla continued to insist that all the wounded Mexicans be treated every day before the doctors could attend to their own men, the doctors would refuse to tend to any Mexicans at all. They were too exhausted. They could not continue to administer to Mexicans all day and to the Anglos all night. They wanted to give equal time to their own men, and have some rest at night.

Crucita felt a moment of discomfort and divided loyalties. He was an Anglo. But she trusted him.

"I need your help, Crucita. I need to see Portilla, and explain to him. Can you arrange for me to see him?"

She told him that she did not know the colonel, they had never greeted one another, though she saw him often with his officers, and some of these she knew. She said his lodgings were with other officers in the stone house outside the wall, and she motioned toward the southeast corner and offered to go speak to him. Then she took Hugh Kenner's hands in hers, touched his bloated knuckles with her fingers, and turned to leave the churchyard and go into the larger yard with the prisoners and guards and all the trampled mud.

José Nicolás de la Portilla was standing at the window of his office on the second story of the house just outside the southeast corner of the presidio. He was looking down over the wall into the chaos of so many prisoners inhabiting the ground along the western barracks.

An officer escorted Crucita into the room, and closed the door behind her, and she waited for the colonel to turn away from the window and acknowledge her. She had fixed herself for him; she had washed her hair in the river and combed it tight against her head while it was wet, and braided it. It wasn't long enough to hang across her shoulder, but it glistened, thick and black, against her neck.

Portilla turned, and recognized her, for he had seen her before. He had watched her from this very window bringing grass in from the prairies, bunches of it draping from her arms for the prisoners to sleep on.

He introduced himself, and with a sudden gesture of his hand he invited her to sit. She gave her name—María de la Cruz Pacheco, "Crucita," she said, and sat down in the chair against the wall to the right of his desk, sitting with her hands in her lap and her face turned slightly to look at him.

To her, he seemed unlikely for the office which he held. He was a small and barrel-chested man with fierce, exaggerated features and a neck so short his shoulders seemed to hump around his ears. His voice was high and boyish.

He said, "I've seen you before," and his tone was so emphatic that it almost seemed he was accusing her of something.

A gust of wet air came in through the open window, ruffling a stack of papers on the desk, and he set a bar of lead down on the papers so the air would not disturb them, then leaned back against the windowsill to feel the freshness on his back. "Do you live in Goliad?" he asked.

"I did until they burned my home," she said. "All my life, I lived here." And she added, "You're very young to be the commandant of such a place as La Bahía, with so many prisoners."

"I'm older than I look," he answered, his irritation evident.

So he is a man of insecurity, she thought. A boy who feels the need to prove himself. She was not intimidated by such temperaments. "You aren't thirty, yet," she remarked.

"No."

"Your duties must be tiresome."

"I haven't slept a full night since the prisoners came," he said.

She said, more seriously, "No one sleeps in La Bahía, with the wounded so pathetic, crying all night long. It must be terrible for you, with so many men to care for."

"It is impossible to do right by God, in such a place at such a time," he answered.

"You can only try," she said. "I'll help you any way I can. That's what I came to say: I know the local people and also I speak English."

"I speak English too," he answered, "though I don't admit it to the prisoners. If they knew I speak English they'd always be coming to me with all their demands, and I can't answer their demands. They're underfed because we don't have any food to give them. They're without medicines because we don't have any medicines. I can't sit and listen to complaints." Then he observed, "I've seen you with the American doctors. Did you come to ask for medicines?"

"No. I've come to tell you something I overheard the doctors saying. Some of them were saying if they can't be given equal time to care for their own wounded, they'll refuse to treat your men."

"I never said they couldn't care for their own men, each day," he said.

"They think you did."

He was visibly angered. "I said they were to care for both, but I never made any other stipulation. I used to be a prisoner myself, a wounded prisoner, and I would never deny physicians to a prisoner."

"Probably the doctors just misunderstood," she said.

"No. I think my officers deliberately misspoke my orders." He turned back to the window. "Several of them just pretend obedience, like dogs, but sneak behind my back and do just as they please."

There was a fluttering of wings outside the window, two doves in sudden flight from the roof top.

Crucita said, "There will always be men who act like dogs."

"I'll countermand their orders to the doctors," Portilla answered, turning his strange face around to look at her, the March breeze lifting up his hair. Then he said, "You're thinking how ugly I am, aren't you? With my twisted back. It's true, I'm hideous. But I would never deny physicians to a prisoner. I have more humanity than you would guess."

A   BLESSING

M ARCH   25,   ONE   MILE   WEST   OF   THE
BRAZOS   RIVER   BOTTOMS

They were down to rationing the corn, and had to feed three ragamuffin children who had no parents and no food. It was raining too hard to sustain much of a fire, but Rose had laid a little mound of twigs beneath the wagon, and had gotten it to burn even though the grass was wet. She was determined that the corn be roasted. The children were hungry and begged to eat it raw; they had had it raw for breakfast and for lunch. But too much raw corn wasn't good for them, Rose said. So they squatted underneath the wagon staring at the corn shucks curling in the heat and the frying pan of stringy rabbit meat.

The light was gray. A steady rain persisted. Everyone was wet and chilled and crowded close for warmth. Only Callum had not come to join them. He ate his meals alone. Rose had placed a board on the ground for Grand to sit on, and Molly, a little thin-faced girl wrapped in a cotton shawl, had nudged in beside her.

William turned the meat, and then the corn. The buck-toothed boy named Jeffrey pulled an ear of corn out of the ashes with his fingertips, and Rose said, "It's not ready yet." Molly tried to entertain Samuel, making babbling noises and pulling on her lip, but he was only irritated by her antics.

The other child, Joel, was a sullen boy not more than six years old. He stared down at the frying pan, swabbing the smoke out of his eyes.

Samuel was wearing booties made of hide, like moccasins, and was trying to kick them off. Katie was battling to keep them on. Her temper had been short ever since Callum's appearance. With every misplaced gesture Callum made, she was more convinced that he could never care for Samuel and more determined he would never have the chance to try. He rode along the fringes in the day and camped outside the fire's light at night, and when he tried to enter into conversation he was unnatural with his words. Grief hung about him like drawn curtains. She saw him lose his temper once when his sorrel mare was spooked by a bird taking flight from the grass, and Callum leaned forward in the saddle and slapped the mare's nose so hard with the reins the force raised a welt. Katie didn't think that he would ever harm his child, but Callum was so strange and unpredictable, she wasn't sure.

The water from the grass was seeping through her skirt while she sat beside the fire now, with the baby fussing in her lap. She waited for the corn husks to curl. At last William rolled two ears out of the flames into the grass. Jeffrey burned his fingers prying at them, and reached his hand out to the rain to cool them.

Rose told him she could talk the fire from the burn, and took his hand and held it to her mouth and whispered something. When he looked, the redness was gone.

Molly swatted her corn out in the rain to cool it, then unwrapped it from the husks and started eating with both hands, her hair a dark and soggy mass around her narrow face.

The rabbit meat began to sizzle.

Grand said, "We need a blessing," but the girl continued eating.

Callum in his trousers with the knees torn appeared around the tailgate and squatted down, looking under at the group of people, water sliding from his hat.

Rose plucked a handful of fresh grass and used it like a rag to give an ear of corn to Callum, saying as he took it, "Would you ask the blessing for us?"

His knees protruded from his trousers, his twisted face was prickly with red hair, the sideburns gnarly and uneven. A wild expression glinted in his eyes, and Katie pulled the baby closer to her. Callum noted what she did, how she coveted the child. She started tying Samuel's booties tighter, saying, "There now, sweetie, I don't want your feet to get too cold."

The smell of rabbit meat washed through the air beneath the wagon. Callum moved in from the downpour, just halfway.

Jeffrey started gnawing on his corn. His younger brother said to William, "You seen that wolf came into camp last night?"

"No," William answered him.

"There weren't no wolf," Jeffrey said scornfully.

"Was too. Molly seen him too."

"No I ain't," the girl injected.

Rose was still waiting for a prayer.

Callum looked at Katie and she felt her heart jolt to a different rhythm, deep inside her. Callum's eyes, through steamy smoke, were like ghosts' eyes, the features twisted in the rainy light with the hat brim pulled down low to cover the disfigurement. She felt he wanted something from her and was trying to communicate it with his eyes. When he finally spoke, it was to pray. He was still looking right at Katie while he prayed. He gave an ancient blessing in an ancient language and a voice so burdened and so solitary all the wash of rain could not disguise the lonely feeling there—

> *"Some ha'e meat*
> *and cannot eat*
> *And some can eat that want it.*
> *But we ha'e meat*
> *And we can eat*
> *And so the Lord be thank-ed."*

Samuel kicked his legs in Katie's lap and struggled in her arms, grunting at her rigid hold on him. She bent her head down over his. Rose pushed the last ears of the corn out of the fire with a stick.

William stabbed a piece of rabbit meat in the skillet and plopped it on a tin plate, slicing it in bites for Grand. The children ate their corn, the boys peeling back the brittle shucks with expressions of absorption, then staring at the meat while they gnawed the corn, waiting to be served.

Finally Samuel stopped his fidgeting and settled into Katie's lap, blinking at the dying fire like an old man dropping off to sleep.

Callum ate his ear of corn, still squatting only halfway underneath the wagon, the rain still running down his back and pouring off his hat brim like ornamental ribbons. It was the first time he had eaten with the family since the day he joined them.

Rose talked about it afterward, before she fell asleep. She told Katie there was hope for Callum now.

Katie said she didn't think there was. "His soul is gone," she said. "He might still have his heart, but I know his soul is gone."

And in the morning it was found that he had disappeared.

THE GRAVE

MARCH 26, PRESIDIO LA BAHÍA

The night sky hung down low, with clouds covering the stars, and the air, though damp, was not as cool as it had been.

As Crucita moved across the compound she glanced up and saw the dim light of a taper glimmering from the window of Portilla's office.

Portilla must be sitting up tonight, she thought.

Along the barracks of the north wall many of the prisoners were sleeping. There were more now than before; Urrea had laid hold at last of the straggling group that Colonel Fannin had sent down to Refugio two weeks before, and now they were returned to Goliad—almost eighty of them—under heavy guard. Another group had been taken by Urrea's soldiers on the beach at Cópano. These last were harbored in a gutted house outside the walls, with white bands tied around their arms to signify they were not bearing weapons at the moment they were captured.

The total number of the prisoners was now almost five hundred.

A few were still awake tonight, sitting up in their designated area along the northern wall, around the fires they had been allowed to make. They seemed in better spirits than before. It was rumored they would be escorted down to Cópano one morning soon, and put on ships and sent back to New Orleans. Fannin, with his wounded leg, had ridden horseback down to Cópano with the German colonel Holzinger to see if there might be a vessel there to take them. Though Fannin and the colonel had returned today to say there was no vessel, Fannin remained hopeful that there would be soon. His optimism lifted many of the prisoners from despair.

They would be going home.

As Crucita passed across the center of the compound now, carrying a blanket bundled in her arms, she listened to the music of a flute. One of the prisoners had kept the flute, though he could have bartered it to the women of the town for food. The prisoner was seated by a little fire with his friends, just their silhouettes showing around the twinkling of the flames. While he played, they sang a song about sweet home, the music drifting in the sultry air.

And where would she be going, then, when all these men went home? She had no home to go to. She would find no peace in Goliad. She had separated from the people here by staying when the others left last fall; her work for De la Rosa had a price. The women who had left the town had said that she, who stayed, had stayed here as a whore for the rebels. Now they had returned, and they would never understand why she had not left. She would not try to make them understand, for she had come to feel she did not need them. She was strong, alone.

But where would she be going?

She held the blanket to her chest and moved on toward the gates, grateful that the drizzling rain had stopped. She was going to the cemetery for the Virgin. When the sun rose in the morning, on Palm Sunday —the Day of the Palms, the Day of the Branches, it was called—the first day of the holy week—she wanted it to light an open grave. The Virgin should be placed back in the chapel, for all the wounded Mexicans who needed her.

The odd thing was, Crucita also felt in need of her. She pictured her beneath the dirt, wrapped in the thread-worn shawl, with her hands beneath her face in an attitude of prayer. She hoped the constant rains had not harmed her. It might be that the water had chipped the paint of her red lips, or warped the wood. Her clothing might be spoiled.

I will make new clothes for her, Crucita thought. The danger that the Virgin would be desecrated by the Anglos was over now.

Glancing at Portilla's window once again before she reached the gates, she saw a shadow there.

Behind her, at the north wall, the song about sweet home was lilting through the sodden air, and she wondered if Hugh Kenner was awake to hear it. She knew nothing of the home that he would be remembering if he were listening to the song, or of the woman who lived there, who had borne him both the boys. Sometimes Crucita thought Hugh Kenner must have had a wife who died, then been married to a second wife who bore him Toby, for Miles and Toby were so different she could not imagine they had come from the same womb.

Two cannon were positioned at the gates, guarding outward down the road both ways. Several soldiers slept on blankets on the ground against the walls. Four guards were smoking cigarillos. One greeted her as she passed through, but she held her blanket close and hurried on, not wanting them to notice, when she came back this way, that the blanket would be shielding something new. She intended to return the Virgin secretly.

The stone house where Portilla stayed was to the left and near the walls; the old cemetery was beyond it. But the cemetery she was going to was to the right, and down the road. She turned and started out that way. There were few houses that remained along the route; most had been destroyed. Ashes of the fires were all melted down to mud, and here and there charred pickets stood erect like old dried stalks of corn. An old dog guarded one place where a house had been, and stood up slowly, growling, when Crucita neared. But she knew his name and spoke to him. He followed her a short way with his head down and his tail between his legs, before turning back.

The sky was so low that she felt the weight of it. Out past the noise of insects in the trees she could hear the howling of a distant pack of wolves. Behind her the faint glow of camp fires from the fort cast eerie light against the clouds, and she wondered if the flute beside the little fire was trailing out a different song by now. She feared that someone might be watching her, as there were many soldiers in the town and many citizens who had returned to live among the ruins. But the soldiers were all quartered near the fort, and the citizens were camped beside the river. This side of the town was desolate.

When she reached the cemetery she went directly to her parents' graves. On the Virgin's grave beside her father's, the ground was wet and spongy but the grass had sprouted. She would have to dig with sticks and with her hands, so she started looking for a sturdy stick.

That was when she saw the figure coming toward her on the road from town, padding up the mild slope like a misshapen child. It was the commandant, Portilla, she could tell as he came closer. His shoulders were hunched up around his head and his walking gait was odd, one foot turned out, his broad sword swinging at this side. She might have hid from him if she were not so certain he had seen her, and when he neared he raised a hand and said her name.

"I saw you leaving the Presidio," he said when he was close to her. His voice was strange tonight, unnaturally slow.

"I came to see my parents' graves," she answered. "They both died of the cholera, and are buried here."

"Which graves are theirs?" he asked, and she pointed to the graves. He stooped and picked a clump of yellow flowers at his feet and took them over to the graves.

She followed, touched by his kind gesture, and arranged the flowers as he set them down, at the bases of the crosses. The bodies would be so decayed by now, she thought, and then she thought of all the wounded in the chapel and how some wounds had larvae crawling in them, for the men had been left too long on the prairie and the flies had laid eggs in the open flesh. Scholar Tipton's leg wound was alive with worms.

"You're not afraid to come alone?" Portilla asked her in the same methodic voice, and without his usual chaotic gestures.

"There is nothing I should fear," she said, rising from the grave to look him in the eyes, and then, when he was silent, "Do you think that I should fear your soldiers?"

"No." He stood looking at her in the dark, his hair cut short on his high forehead and his eyes set far back in his skull. "You should fear the dead."

She held the blanket close. "I have no reason to be afraid of the dead, I never did them wrong."

"And if you had?" he asked, still staring at her with his homely and exaggerated features. "If you had done them wrong, then would you be afraid?"

"I would be more afraid of my conscience."

"And God's retribution?"

I am afraid of *you*, she thought. His questions were too strangely intimate, his manner too intense, and on impulse, with defiance, she said, "No, I'm not afraid of God."

"You believe that God is merciful."

"I believe . . ." She hardly tried to think what she believed, she was so distracted by his presence: the Virgin rotting in the grave beside them and the strange, misshapen colonel standing with the light of La Bahía's camp fires shining dim and golden on the clouds behind. "I believe—" and then she shrugged, a flippant gesture of dismissal.

He was quiet for so long that she began to doubt that time was passing. The wolves stopped singing in the distance. The clouds were steady and the night was still; only the pulsing of cicadas in the trees gave a sense of time. Then Portilla said, "I'm certain God is merciful. I told you I was once a prisoner myself. They beat me, which is why I can't walk with both my feet turned straight. I thought I would be executed. But God was merciful, and I was spared. He had other plans for me."

"And why were you imprisoned?" Crucita asked him.

"For my beliefs. And for Santa Anna. Four years ago Santa Anna tried to overcome the government's corrupt administration, and failed. Those of us who had conspired and participated in his cause were punished. I was twenty-four years old. They put me in a dungeon." While he spoke his face contorted into strange expressions. "I've sacrificed a lot for Santa Anna, but he still wants more. I think he wants for me to sacrifice my soul as well."

The throbbing of cicadas was loud and so invasive to her thinking that it seemed in rhythm with the beating of her heart. "What is it he wants you to do?" she asked.

He was hesitant, then shattered the strange spell that he had cast, shrugging his humped shoulders and fidgeting with buttons on his jacket. "It's a matter of logistics, only," he answered in a different tone entirely.

But it was more than that. She watched the way he fidgeted and heard the weight drop from his voice, and knew that he was harboring a secret. "Maybe you should talk to the Padre about it," she suggested cautiously. "He was in the chapel when I left there just a while ago."

But Nicolás de la Portilla was no longer listening to her. He turned his face away and stared at nothing she could see, as if he were now listening to voices from the dead, and when he spoke his own voice seemed to come from very far away, "Tomorrow is Palm Sunday, and I wish with all my heart that it were not. Walk with me, María de la Cruz Pacheco, back to La Bahía."

Without a word, reluctantly, she went with him, noticing his odd and tortured gait and thinking how the Lady of Loreto would sleep Palm Sunday, buried in her grave.

THE DAY OF THE PALMS

M ARCH 27, PALM SUNDAY,
PRESIDIO LA BAHÍA

Toby was asleep when the light of morning, as soft as a gray dove, filtered through the heavy clouds.

Coon was sleeping with his bristly chin on Toby's chest, and Miles was on the other side sharing the same blanket.

A Mexican soldier stepped lightly in between the sleeping prisoners and leaned down to awaken the two carpenters whom Toby knew as White and Rosenburg. They got up sleepily, took up their haversacks, and went away with the soldier.

Toby turned over on the ground, pulling a stone the size of Samuel's baby fist from underneath his ribs. He wadded up his cotton knapsack for a pillow, placed his head down against the initials he had written on the knapsack in black charcoal—"T.K."—and drifted back to sleep.

Then the bugle sang.

He had not heard a bugle call since the battle on the prairie, and the sound jolted him awake so forcefully he sat up swinging both his arms.

Coon jumped up beside him with his prickly hair on end. Miles awoke more slowly, and sat up with a dazed expression.

356

Toby looked to see if his father was there by Miles. But it was only Gus crammed up against the wall. His father must have stayed another night inside the chapel with the wounded.

The ground was hard beneath his buttocks, and Toby sniffed the morning dampness. The clouds were as thick and heavy as the night before. His stomach hurt. In the full week of imprisonment he'd eaten nothing but small portions of bull beef and three tortillas that his father and Crucita had obtained for him. His head itched from the lice, and he rubbed the scabby sores. He and Miles had spent the morning yesterday picking lice out of each other's hair, smashing them between their nails and scraping tiny eggs off the single hairs, until Crucita, in the afternoon, had brought some scissors and clipped their hair off near the roots. Now his head felt odd and prickly, and he ran his hand back and forth across the crown.

Four hundred prisoners were waking, piled practically on top of one another. "What's the goddamn noise?" a slack-jawed man near Miles complained. "What's the goddamn trumpet for?"

No one knew.

The music stopped as suddenly as it had started and about three dozen Mexican soldiers, twice as many as had stood guard on the prisoners until now, marched in among the bedrolls and the filthy bodies and started shouting orders, gesturing with muskets. *"Levántense!"* they shouted. *"Recojan sus cosas y formense! Rápido!"*

"Goddamn greasers," Gus mumbled with a froggy throat. "What are they jawin' about?"

"They want us to line up for roll call or some damn thing," Miles answered.

"You'd think they'd get somebody who speaks a little English to let us know," Gus offered, picking at his hair.

"Levántense!" the soldiers kept repeating. *"Rápido!"* Slowly, prisoners rose and milled around grumbling.

In a moment Colonel Holzinger, speaking English with his German accent, ordered the prisoners to pick up their belongings and fall into ranks. Toby bundled up his knapsack and Miles slung the blanket they had shared across his shoulders. They had slept in all the clothes they had; Miles still wore the shredded shirt with just one button, but had sold the decorated coat for food. Toby's feet were bare since the guards had robbed him of his boots while he was sleeping two nights earlier.

When the prisoners had grouped themselves in something that resembled order—the Grays together, the Rovers, and the smaller regiments with haphazard knots of individuals—Holzinger walked among them, drawing out three German prisoners, two of whom were Prussian, and leading them off toward the heavy entrance gates of the sally port.

"Wonder what that's all about," Gus said.

"He wants 'em to switch sides," Miles said. "He's been badgering them since we got here, to join the Meskin army."

Looking in the direction where the Germans had been taken, through the press of ragged men, Toby noticed that two cannon, previously situated just outside the sally port to command the road, had been wheeled around and aimed within. Beside the cannon, guards were standing by with lighted torches.

"Brother—" he whispered.

Miles whispered back, "I know. I see them."

Gus said, "They've got those cannons pointed at us."

"I see them," Miles repeated in the same flat whisper.

"God damn," Gus said.

"God damn," a man named Curtis echoed.

Three names were called by an officer in uniform. Two prisoners answered and were summoned forward, but the third man did not answer.

An Irish Texan named McKinny, who was standing behind Toby, asked above his shoulder, "Did he say McKinny?"

"I think so. I don't know," Toby answered. McKinny was one of Frazer's company from Refugio, known for his good looks. Like almost everyone, he had stubble on his face, but his black eyes were stunning and his hair fell in black waves around his angled features.

"Was he calling me?" he asked again.

No one knew, the accent was so strong.

"I wouldn't go," Gus said.

McKinny hesitated, then started to go forward. But the officer was already turning to escort the other two away, so he stopped.

The two were taken off across the compound, toward the cannon, through the sally port, in the wake of the three Germans.

"Papists." Nat Rollins spat. He was standing in among the Grays. Toby knew him by his reputation as a bully. His temper often flared without any provocation, but mostly when he was awakened from his sleep. Even other Grays regarded him suspiciously, his moods were so intense and unpredictable. "Both of them, papists," he said, then broke off coughing, thumping at his chest, and saying, "Guess they're taking them to mass, some shit like that, since it's Palm Sunday."

"Shut your mug," McKinny said defensively.

Rollins broke into a grin, his fleshy cheeks bunching up around his eyes. He had a blond and bristly widow's peak extending too far down the center of his forehead, with the rest of his thin hair receding on the sides. With feigned, exaggerated sweetness, he said, "Oh, I'm sorry, I forgot you're papist too."

McKinny let it pass.

Colonel Garay of the Mexicans called for Colonel Ward, and sent him with a guard to the workshop in the northeast corner.

The *commandante*, Nicolás de la Portilla, was coming from the other way, through the sally port between two officers. They crossed the yard and stood before the prisoners. Drawing his sword, Portilla pointed with it toward the gates which he had just come through. "*¡Marchen!*" he commanded in Spanish.

No one did. They balked. If they obeyed, they would be marching face-on toward the cannon. The officers among them motioned for the men to stand their ground. But as the prisoners' many voices rose in speculation and suspicion—"Where do they aim on takin' us?" . . . "Where are we fixin' to go?"—a single word began to pass among them: Cópano.

Cópano, they said.

They're taking us to Cópano.

It must be that the ship came in.

Then other words descended like a flock of birds alighting: Parole, New Orleans, Home.

They're sending us back home.

And with the buoyant tread of angels they marched forward, bearing haversacks and hugging wadded blankets to their chests. They called to one another joyously, a phrase in French they had grown fond of,

"*Sauve qui peut,*" which meant essentially, they thought, "the devil take the hindmost."

Toby fell in line beside his brother, walking almost on McKinny's heels. They were going toward the gates of the presidio. This was liberation. They would have to pass the cannon, and then they would be out there in the open. He glanced back toward the chapel where his father was. He was leaving him without permission and without good-bye. He wished to see his father coming after him; he had never spent a night out of his father's care. But he had suffered through a battle, and survived. He had lived through the imprisonment, among these men.

Now they were so full of hopes they had abandoned all their caution; they were prancing, ragged, nearly naked, in between the cannon, out through the sally port with the gates that opened outward on their iron hinges. They were like children going out to play.

Toby passed out through the gates on his bare feet, close among the men with Coon Dog right beside him. On one side was the guardhouse, on the other was the jail—the *calabozo* it was called.

A mob of people waited just outside the gates: several hundred soldiers wearing their dress uniforms, dirty and ill-fitting but complete with brogans rather than the sandals which they usually wore. They even had their shakos on, strapped beneath their chins, and they were armed with muskets with fixed bayonets.

It was a stunning escort for a march to freedom.

There were also soldiers' wives and people from the town. Some civilians carried branches of soft leaves; Toby did not know the reason. "*Pobrecitos,*" one old woman said repeatedly, looking at the prisoners— "poor babies." They had become so thin on their short rations. Another woman offered Toby a strip of salted pork for something in his knapsack, but he refused to bargain. All he had inside his sack was an extra shirt, a tin cup, a spoon, a piece of charcoal, and a small round stone he had found and kept because it was so smooth. He did not want to part with any of it. He'd already sold his drawings of the river and the cow, and he had liked those drawings, the way the shadows fell across the water, the way the cow was standing in soft grasses to her belly.

Nat Rollins said, "These greasers all have fleecing dispositions."

Out beyond the people were the rolling prairies in full bloom and small detachments of the cavalry galloping about.

The ranks of prisoners collapsed to chaos in the pressing mob. Their leaders tried to get some order back, calling names and designating space. Miles and Toby placed themselves with some of Frazer's Texans from Refugio, and Gus stayed with them instead of standing with the Grays. Almost half of Frazer's men were missing; Frazer himself was in the chapel, badly wounded. The Fagans—Nicolas and John—as well as Edward Perry, James Byrd, John James, and Anthony and John Sydick, had been present on the night before, and now were gone. No one knew where they were. William Gould and George Carlisle kept puzzling over it; John Williams said that he had slept between the Fagans, and found them gone when he woke up. Fitzsimmons was the only one who thought they would appear in time to go along to Cópano.

Coon Dog trotted off and had a hostile, brief encounter with a bigger dog, and then came running back.

The crowd was closing in. The heavy sky was pressing down and threatening more rain. But this was freedom, too: they were outside the walls. An open sea was waiting, and a ship to board, and the city of New Orleans.

Toby was thinking of New Orleans when someone jostled against him, and he turned to see his father standing there.

Crucita walked up from the river where she had been bathing, wondering at the activity in the streets so early. When she turned the corner from the west wall toward the entrance gate she was astounded by the mob of people. She saw that some of them were carrying the branches in celebration of Palm Sunday, and thought they were demanding to be let into the compound and the chapel for their worship.

But there were a lot of soldiers, too, and these were not assembled there for worship.

Then she saw the prisoners file out, and the crowd close in, and the soldiers try to hold the people back.

Pressing her way through, she searched for Hugh Kenner but couldn't find him. She thought that he might still be in the chapel and tried to shove her way in through the gates, but the guards were letting no civilians in.

She thought to climb a little stunted tree that grew along the wall down near Portilla's quarters, and to get up on the wall where she would have a better vantage point from which to search the crowd. But when she hurried off in that direction, she was shocked to see Domingo de la Rosa standing near the stone house of Portilla's quarters, with a face that had grown old.

He had not come to town in months. He had been operating from the woods, riding with his horsemen and patrolling all the land between Victoria and Goliad and on down to Refugio and over to the coast. His reputation was like God's. But here he was, in person, with his rawhide boots and Spanish face and his calloused hands. He was standing alone. She felt the sharp unrest inside her heart. But he no longer had the power over her, he no longer needed it. He had used her all he could.

Slowing her pace and approaching him more calmly, she greeted him. She asked him where the prisoners were being taken.

The stone house was behind him, framing his dark face. She knew his soul, too well. But she had never known the man.

"To the prairies to be shot," he said.

The sultry sky turned cold.

De la Rosa cast his eyes out past Crucita toward the people. "Portilla sent a message to me in the middle of the night that Santa Anna ordered him to shoot the prisoners here."

Her hand went to her face, trembling like a leaf caught in the wind.

"He received the order at the hour of seven last evening," De la Rosa said. "One hour later he received a contradictory order from Urrea, telling him to treat the prisoners well, to feed them from the steers sent from Refugio and to use them to rebuild the fort. Urrea didn't know of Santa Anna's order, and probably still doesn't. Portilla has decided in favor of the executions. He decided in the night."

In the night. She remembered it as if she were reliving it, how he had stood above the Virgin's grave and said that Santa Anna had requested him to sacrifice his soul. He had talked of mercy, and the dead. He had spoken of imprisonment, and life. He had feared damnation. And then when he had walked beside her back to La Bahía, he had made her stand an hour in the street outside the gates—just there where all the prisoners were standing now—and he had told her of his childhood and his parents, who were dead. And then he had retired to the house, because, he said, he had decisions he must make. She was glad when he had left, because he tired her with his extreme intensity. But she had watched until he was inside the door, and felt almost a fondness for him, because he was eccentric and so young, and because he had confided in her.

In reality, he had confided nothing.

She began to plead with De la Rosa as if it were his doing.

"There's nothing to be done," he said. "Portilla is afraid Santa Anna will have him shot if he doesn't obey."

But she knew what Portilla feared even more than that. "More than death, he is afraid of being damned," she said. "We should go to Padre Valdez. He can convince Portilla."

De la Rosa blinked so slowly, with such hard regret, it seemed that he had shut his eyes against the world. "Portilla has spared the few he knows are Catholic, and thereby hopes to save his soul. Yet he will forfeit Mexico. The world will turn against her after such a massacre."

"But only, just a few, are Catholics . . . And four hundred to be shot?"

"The men captured down in Cópano, wading from their ship without weapons in their hands, they will all be spared. They've been taken to the peach orchard. And Portilla has agreed to spare seven men at my request—the Fagans and the others who have been my neighbors and my friends. He's made arrangements for them. Colonel Garay saved the carpenters who did some work for him. He called them to his tent in the orchard and hid them there."

But she was hardly listening. Hugh Kenner slipped into her mind like the presence of a ghost. "The doctors . . . will he kill the doctors?"

"He intends to save the doctors, and their aides. Two have been removed to Garay's tent out in the orchard. Some are in the chapel, still."

"But the prisoners . . . the rest . . . four hundred . . . more than that—"

"They are doomed, Crucita."

"But if I find Padre Valdez and he persuades Portilla . . . ?"

"The padre has no influence. He already tried. I saw him on his knees before Portilla."

She turned around to look at all the prisoners assembled underneath a sky that threatened rain. "And they have no idea what is to happen?"

"If they did, of course they wouldn't go. We would have the bloodshed here, in the town. The cannon would be fired on them." She looked at him. He ran his tongue across his lips and kept on staring at the prisoners. "They'll be separated into three divisions and taken out on different roads. The time to open fire has been set, so it will happen all at once. It is less than thirty minutes off. Crucita, there is nothing you can do."

She felt her skin turn damp and cold and her whole body shake. But she did not believe that there was nothing she could do. Toby was a boy, and she could not believe the soldiers would execute a boy. Turning from Domingo de la Rosa, she ran back to the crowd and pushed her way through, calling for Toby. She saw Miles first with his torn shirt and the blond hair she'd cropped so close to his skull; he was laughing and punching playfully at another prisoner's arm. Toby and Hugh Kenner were beside him. She made her way and put her hand around Hugh Kenner's wrist. "The doctors need to stay here," she said.

He shook his head. "Crucita, no, I'm going with my sons."

"But the wounded men, they need you here."

She could see in his eyes that he wished to say good-bye to her in a different way. "You've been so kind," he said, adding something that she couldn't hear because the men around were talking loudly and the women were bartering their wares in broken bits of English. She stood mute before him, harboring her secret like an illness, and then said, "It's important. Do not go. For me, you don't go."

Miles and Toby were looking at her; she could feel their puzzlement and scrutiny.

Hugh Kenner said, "I have to go."

She turned away and felt that he was watching her and tried to disappear into the crowd so he wouldn't see that she was going to the guards who were lined up near the gates. It was a guard with a cruel face whom she chose to speak to. She said the man with gray hair and a sty on his right eyelid, who stood beside the young boy with cropped hair— and she pointed to be sure he understood whom she was speaking of— he was a doctor and was not supposed to go. He should be taken back into the chapel.

The guard was quick to do his duty. Crucita stared across the road at the Mexican soldiers. Would they all be executioners? They were only boys themselves. Many were the Mayan Indians who hardly spoke the

Spanish language. They'd been kidnapped by the army from their homes in the jungles of the Yucatán, and force-marched here to Texas with Urrea, and now were being sent out in the prairies to shoot four hundred men. They were as small as boys, stocky with wide faces, and they looked on white men as superior. But the Mayans were accustomed to blood sacrifice. They were a people dedicated to religion and its hard demands. They had claimed the Catholic faith and mixed it with their own beliefs, and though they might be troubled at the killing of so many men on a religious holiday, the men they were to kill were heretics who had burned the stations of the cross.

Crucita watched while Hugh was shoved back through the jostling crowd, toward the gates, with his wrists tied at his back. He was calling back across his shoulder to his sons with an awful turmoil in his voice, saying something about New Orleans and a street address—a place they were to find—a family name. Miles stared after him with parted lips and not a word, and Toby looked down at the ground. Their heads, with all the hair cut off, seemed naked and pathetic.

The guards were trying to impose some order on the mob; they forced the citizens to move back across the road. "¡Muevanse!" they shouted, "¡Muevanse del camino!" Crucita moved where she was told, but kept her eyes on Toby. It was difficult, as he was small. The soldiers closed completely in around the prisoners, and the prisoners were falling into columns six men deep. Too quickly, they were marching out, and the guards were forcing them to break up their formation of six men to a line, and to form instead in double files, so they were strung out for a distance.

Crucita singled out an officer whom she had seen before, with a mustache and a square face that reminded her of Adelaido's. She crossed the street to go to him. He motioned to her angrily not to cross the street, but she called out, "There's a boy going with the prisoners who is too young, and Colonel Portilla designated that he should not go. My name is María de la Cruz Pacheco, and I know the colonel well. It's that boy, there—" She pointed. "He's only twelve years old."

The officer was hesitant. He motioned her to come to him. His face turned solemn and he said, "Do you know where they are going?"

She slid her voice down low. "Yes, I've been told."

"The colonel wanted us to spare the boy?"

"Of course. He wouldn't execute a child."

Still he seemed uncertain. "No one told me anything about the boy."

Her words fell to a whisper. "Would you shoot a child, señor, on the morning of Palm Sunday?"

In his eyes, she saw how he regretted everything.

He turned away and shouted an order for the boy to be removed from the line.

A soldier shoved his gun at Toby and ordered him in Spanish to step out of the line. Coon showed his teeth, and Crucita was afraid he would attack the soldier. Miles had moved on several steps ahead, and did not see, but Gus stopped and spoke some words to Toby, evidently trying to help Toby figure out what the soldier wanted him to do. But then the soldier said in English, "You halt, come," and Toby understood, and with a look of sudden panic on his narrow face he did as he was told.

The dog ran after him.

Gus shouted to Miles, and Miles turned to see his brother being taken off, and called out, "Brother . . . Brother—"

The soldier had his hand on Toby's arm, and Coon Dog, following, began to bark and snap at him. Toby jerked his arm away and turned back to his brother with a face so utterly forsaken that he seemed not eight years old.

Miles tried to break free of the line and go to him, but he was threatened by another soldier, who aimed his musket at his face and shouted at him to be quiet and keep marching. "*¡Callate!*" he shouted, "*¡Callate, hombre! ¡Marcha!*" Miles continued marching, backward though, and with the barrel in his face, and calling to his brother in a string of words like a bird launching into sudden song, "Remember Holford Inn in New Orleans on Milly Street—if we lose each other contact Father's uncle Jason there like Father said—" And then he was cut off by Gus, who saw the guard cock back the hammer of his gun. Gus flung himself at Miles's back, buckling his knees and dragging him down backward just to quiet him.

The guard kept his gun on them as they fell to the ground.

Toby folded in against himself and bent over hugging his knees, and Crucita went to him and smoothed her hand against his back as if she smoothed the wrinkles from a bed. She could feel the ribs and spine protruding underneath her palm. "Toby, you listen to me," she said. "Look at me. Stand up and look to me. It is important you trust me."

Miles and Gus had risen from the ground, and the soldier ordered them to fall in line. Miles still was looking back, but marching on now, passing by the stone house of Portilla's headquarters.

The file of prisoners was split. The first half went to the left on the road toward the lower crossing and Victoria. The second half was cut off by soldiers and forced over to the right on the old road to Refugio and Cópano. The split was so well orchestrated that Crucita, watching from this vantage, wondered if the prisoners in the first division knew the second half was going off a different way.

Miles was with the Grays in the front division which went left. They disappeared from view behind the corner of the wall. Crucita was aware of Toby on the ground and the dog beside him. Kneeling down, Crucita took the boy's face in her hands and made him look at her.

The third group of the prisoners had been escorted off the other way, back along the western wall toward the road that headed northwest to San Antonio de Béxar; she could see the last of them disappearing around the corner of the fort. She would take the boy this way. "Put your hand in my arm and walk with me, *rapido*," she said to Toby, and took his hand and put it there and almost dragged him to his feet. She guided him beside the western wall with the dog trotting at his heels. She told him to look only at the ground. "Look in the floor," she said. "Walk fast." He did as he was told, his scabby head tucked down and his hand holding to her arm just where she had placed it, his bare feet padding softly in the dirt. He had regained composure and now started asking questions. He asked where she was taking him, why he'd been separated from his brother, and if his father was still in the fort. She answered nothing, telling him not to ask those questions and to walk more rapidly. She told him to trust her. "Later if I take your dog," she said, "you trust me?" It would be too difficult to hide him with the dog.

"He won't go with you," Toby said defensively.

On their right side was the wall. On their left was the road, where citizens of Goliad whom she had watched grow old were carrying their branches on Palm Sunday, some walking close to her and crying *"Pobrecitos."* She could see their shoes upon the ground, and some of them were shoes she'd watched her father making with his tools. Children ran along beside their parents. They were following the prisoners along the road to Béxar who were marching to their death and did not know it. The air was wet and gray, the grayness so rich and heavy it was like a color. The flowers grew in random patches, and though there was no order to their boundaries, the boundaries were definite, the blues did not trespass upon the reds, and the yellows kept themselves apart entirely. The grass between was lush and green in contrast to the sky.

Crucita ordered Toby not to look out that direction. She said to keep his head down and to walk more quickly. She made him keep his hand upon her arm, as if he guided her, and she kept to the outside, near the road, making him walk so close to the wall that his shoulder brushed against the stones. They could smell the odor of the urine in the outhouses against the wall. They could hear the prisoners talking to each other, speculating why they were being taken on this road instead of on the road to Cópano, and why the others had been led away in separate groups, out of sight now back around the southeast wall. At the forking of the road they were guided left, and Crucita ushered Toby to the right, around the northwest corner of the fort, past the willow tree that reached its branches out across the wall into the chapel yard. She led him past two wagons parked beneath the willow tree, and on along the wall which was the north side of the chapel. Farther down, they reached the shallow ditch extending from beneath the wall down past the ashes of Crucita's home and toward the river. It was the same ditch where she hid the Lady of Loreto before she took her off to bury her.

The ditch was covered over with wide planks of wood, and she dragged two boards away to make a space for Toby to slip in, and told him to get down inside the ditch.

He balked, and then refused. "Tell me why," he said. She was on her hands and knees, waiting to cover him when he got in the ditch.

"Because your father wants," she lied.

"Father stopped me from going?"

The prisoners who were being led along the eastern wall on the route toward Victoria—with Miles among them—would come into sight at any moment from the other way, appearing at the corner not a hundred paces off. She could hear their voices now.

"Yes, your father," she answered him emphatically, looking up at him, his little face against the wide expanse of gray clouds rolling over-head, "your father made this plan. He thinks it is more safe than if you go to Cópano."

She shoved her palm down toward the ditch. "Come and go in here and I will cover you, *por favor*, Tobito," she said, begging him with her eyes.

"What about my dog?"

The dog was sitting as if waiting for her answer, but before she gave it he leaped into the ditch and stood with his bright eyes peering up at Toby and his stump tail wagging. Toby tossed his knapsack in and crawled in after. The ditch was only deep enough for him to crouch, and he settled in with one arm looped around the dog.

She couldn't take the dog; there wasn't time. She dragged the boards across and spoke between the slats before she went away, peering down at Toby's homely face with just a stripe of gray light slanting down across his chin. "If you hear anything, you need to stay in there and don't come outside until I come back," she said.

The lead guard of the group which traveled on the road down toward Victoria was coming into sight around the corner of the wall. Miles would be among them. She stood up, made the cross upon her chest, then turned and hurried off, watching her shoes glide along the ground beneath the frayed and dirty hem of her brown skirt.

He heard singing. He lay with the gray light glancing through the slats like ladder rungs, the ditch rising to the fort on one end, sloping to the river on the other, and he smelled the damp, fresh earth, remember-ing the holes he had dug two weeks ago back home. He listened to the singing. He knew it was the group that Miles was in. He recognized the voice of Melvin, singing the last verses of the tune he'd sung on the same road just a week ago, before the battle on the prairie—

"Then come on, my dearest dear
And we all will fight and scratch

We'll all root together
In the sweet potato patch—"

And the others joining in with tuneless grunting—

"In the sweet potato patch,
The sweet potato patch
For we'll all root together
In the sweet potato patch."

He could hear the liberation in their voices.

Coon Dog also listened. His breath came hot and fast with excitement, his tongue dripped with saliva, but he snapped his tongue inside his mouth and held his breath for seconds at a time to listen. Then he cocked his head, whined, and turned in a cramped circle.

"Be *still*, Coon," Toby said, and when the dog stepped on his hand with his sharp nails he snatched his hand away and whispered, "Ow! Sit *down*."

Miles would not be singing, Toby knew. Miles would be worrying about him. And what would Miles think if Toby suddenly appeared out of the ground like a magician? Miles would have a look he sometimes got when something pleased him, his eyelids opening so wide the irises were like something floating in a pond. He would drop his jaw right down.

Toby placed one palm against the plank that stretched above him, and pressed until he felt the plank give way, and after that there was no going back. He shoved the plank aside, and the one beside it, also, and Coon Dog leaped out of the ditch as though he'd been freed from a dungeon.

With his knapsack slung across the shoulder, Toby crawled out just behind his dog, and strode out toward the column and his brother.

He thought the Mexicans might try to stop him but they didn't. They looked askance and one questioned another, but then they let him pass into the ranks where Miles greeted him with open arms. Gus shook his hand and Melvin turned to smile at him while everyone kept singing—

"In the SWEET potato patch

The SWEET potato patch

For we'll ALL root toGETHER

In the SWEET potato patch."

They jabbed their fists into the air with the emphatic words.

"Crucita tried to hide me in a ditch," Toby told his brother. "She said that Father wanted me to stay with him back at the fort, but I'd rather go with you so I waited till she went away and then I just crawled out—"

Miles kept his arm around his brother's shoulder and called in a rollicking, exaggerated southern accent, "Gentlemen, lead your partners. Them that's got on shoes and stockings will dance the cotillion; them that's got on shoes and no stockings will dance the Virginny reel; them that's got on nairy shoes nor stockings will dance the scamper-down!"

Someone farther toward the front called in answer, "Well, hos, let's take a trot and make them splinters fly!"

They were moving in a sloppy double file; the Grays out in the lead, about one hundred and fifty men in this division all together, with twice as many soldiers walking close on either side. Some prisoners were now noting that the back half of the column had gone off down another road, and they tried to step just slightly out of line and glance back down the road to see them. But the soldiers forced them back into their lines.

Toby's bare feet felt the rocky road at every step, and he walked carefully, laughing at this brother's antics, favoring a stone bruise on his heel. Miles was right beside him, with Gus lagging just behind. They were near the rear with the half a dozen Texans from Frazer's company. Mark McKinny and his friend O'Bryan marched side by side in front of Miles and Toby. McKinny's hair was shiny black and oily; he had tied it with a shoelace. He wore no shirt. Toby watched his bare back and a flat mole beneath the shoulder blade.

"Bye, bye, La Bahía," someone way up toward the front called out, and Miles answered in a loud, deep voice as if it were the walls that spoke, "Bye, bye, *los hombres Americanos*," which made everybody laugh. "Sauve qui peut!"

In front of Mark McKinny was Nat Rollins with the Grays. "This ain't the way to Cópano," he said. "Don't these greasers know the way?"

"Cópano isn't the only port we got in Texas," Pat O'Bryan answered, adding that he'd never seen so many flowers on the prairies. O'Bryan had a broad, pale face and a pleasant manner. "I think they're taking us to Matagorda, through Victoria," he said.

"Right through Nine Mile Prairie and the battlefield," Gus said.

But it hardly mattered. They were going to the sea. The prison was behind them.

"It's because of all the rain," a New Orleans Gray said back across his shoulder, in response to the comment on the flowers.

"Or," McKinny added thoughtfully, "there's a little trail up here on the right that circles back and joins the road to Cópano, and they could be taking us that way just to separate us some from the others that they took straight on the Cópano road, so we won't so many of us be together. See, yeah, if they marched a third of us this way and cut us back through on that little road, the rest of them that they peeled off behind would have a head start, since they're going straight, and then the Rovers they were taking north might be supposed to cut back on that road beside that cemetery and fall in, in back of us a ways. Like a detour."

"I bet that's it," O'Bryan said.

"That way, they play it safe," McKinny finished. "We ain't all together like a army."

"It makes more sense they'd take us through Victoria," Gus said.

Someone farther up the line, whom Toby knew as Evan from New York, was wondering aloud where Miller's New York volunteers were quartered. Miller's men were the ones who had been captured on the beach unarmed. Evan, who had come with the New Orleans Grays, knew one of them from school back home. He'd been surprised to see him here in Texas. They hadn't been allowed to talk, since Miller's men were housed outside the fort with strips of white cloth tied around their arms to separate them from those captured bearing arms.

There was no sign of them this morning. Evan turned and asked McKinny if he thought they might have been escorted down to Cópano in the middle of the night. McKinny said he didn't think the Mexicans would take them in the dark.

"They might," Gus said, and added, "Wish I hadn't sold my hat," and then said, "I had me a chance to take French dancing lessons once."

"*Sauve qui peut*," someone answered him.

That was when Miles started acting strange, and quiet. He touched a finger to his lips and gestured with it, very quickly, cautiously, toward a Mexican soldier who was marching on his left. Toby looked past Miles to see.

The soldier's face was dripping wet with tears. He was walking steadily and looking straight ahead. He had his musket at his shoulder with the bayonet, but he was shaking and his face was all awash with tears. He was not more than seventeen years old; he had no facial hair. His uniform was dusty and ill-fitting, with the tall shako sitting on his head askew. He looked like he was playing dress-up in a borrowed costume.

Toby studied other faces of the Mexicans and began to feel uneasy. The people of the town were no longer following along.

Miles said beneath his breath, "Drop your knapsack in the road."

Toby dropped it without asking why.

Someone far up in the line was singing loudly, badly:

> "*Rose, Rose; coal black Rose*
> *I nebber see a nigger dat I lub like Rose—*"

and the man beside him started on an imitation of the Juba dance, but was reprimanded sharply by the soldiers.

Melvin was unruly. He sang a bawdy solo with his tenor voice:

> "*Eighteen pounds of meat a week*
> *Whiskey here to sell*
> *How can the boys stay at home*
> *When the girls all look so well?*"

But his tone was growing strident now, no longer lilting or appealing, and when he finished that one verse he broke off into silence.

The singing stopped entirely.

A feeling passed among the men. They began to turn and meet each other's eyes. They could hear the insects in the grass. A sudden flight of birds from a small mesquite motte near the road startled them and several drew their breaths in hard and faltered in their stride. The soldiers did not even glance at them, but kept on marching steadily. Some cavalry were cantering along the right side of the column—the side where Toby was—and the tread of horses prancing was so loud it sounded like it echoed.

Toby's breath came faster than before. He stared hard at the mole on Mark McKinny's back, and knew that something of importance had gone wrong.

Gus said to Miles, beneath his breath, "What's going on?"

Miles said to Toby, "Get prepared for anything. Be ready to run."

The silence of the Mexicans was ominous. It was like a living creature had settled in with wings. The prisoners were skirted on both sides by the soldiers and not a word was being said among them.

Then Nat Rollins blurted out, "Are you taking us to Cópano?" and jabbed his finger at the soldier beside him. "You."

The soldier glanced at him and kept on marching.

Rollins asked again, *"Voy* Cópano?"

"Sí, Cópano," the soldier said.

"We're going to Cópano?"

"Sí."

"To a boat? A ship?"

"Sí."

"To New Orleans?"

"Cállate."

"Comprende, New Orleans?" Rollins insisted. *"¿Parole?"*

"Sí."

"But this ain't the way to Cópano," Rollins said.

The soldier didn't answer.

"This road goes to Victoria." He waited. There was no response, and he demanded, "Are you taking us to Victoria?"

"Sí, Victoria," the soldier said.

"Which is it, goddamnit, Cópano or Victoria?"

The soldier did not look at him.

"You goddamn monkey," Rollins said between his teeth. "Cópano? Cópano, or Victoria?"

Miles said, "Shut up, Rollins."

But Rollins kept on badgering the soldier. "You stupid little brown *pendejo*. Cópano, or Victoria?"

Another soldier turned and shouted at Rollins in Spanish, and Miles intervened, leaning up between McKinny and O'Bryan and saying to Nat Rollins, "Cut the bombast, you idiot, or they'll be down on us like ducks on june bugs."

Rollins swung around to answer him, his pale widow's peak jutting like a barn owl's, but his attention was arrested by the soldier who was crying. The blood came to his face. "What's he crying for?" he asked Miles.

Miles didn't answer.

"Where are they taking us?" Rollins asked, more plaintively.

Miles ran his tongue across his bottom lip. "Just control yourself," he said.

Rollins eyed him with wild, squinting eyes, then did as Miles suggested and continued walking forward.

McKinny had turned back to Miles, and Miles said beneath his breath, "They ain't got any camping gear."

McKinny looked to see. "Ah, God," he said.

"They what?" O'Bryan turned and asked.

"They don't have any camping gear," Miles repeated steadily.

"They never have much camping gear," Gus said, from just behind.

"They would have some food at least, if we were going on a march," George Carlisle, who was walking behind Gus, observed. His tone was so forboding that it seemed the voice had come out of the burdened air.

"Ah God," McKinny said again, this time not looking back, but stepping forward, slowly, looking to the left and right.

The road was chalky white, with little pebbled stones. The solid sky was rolling overhead. Toby stared at Mark McKinny's mole, as perfect as a coin below his shoulder blade. The men all smelled of sweat. The horses' gear was jangling in the silence. Coon Dog trotted in and out between the double files. Toby couldn't see much past the soldiers, who marched two deep on either side, but he glimpsed on his left a mesquite hedge jutting from the road in a straight line to the river. The river was about a quarter of a mile away. When the column had gone past the hedge, a Mexican officer on horseback turned and rode back down the line, calling "*A la izquierda, a la izquierda,*" and waving his long sword, telling them to turn left off the road, along the hedge, toward the river.

The column buckled as it turned.

O'Bryan began whispering, "The Lord is my shepherd. I shall not want. He maketh me to lie down in green pastures. He leadeth me beside still waters. He—"

"They won't shoot us," someone whispered. "Not this many of us."

"They might," Miles answered quietly. "Our lives ain't worth a snap."

Toby watched his brother's profile, searching for denial of those words. Miles had no expression, none at all. He said, with just a glance at Toby, "Brother, see if you can step back out of line, they might let you."

Toby kept on walking. His bare feet carried him. His gaze settled once again on Mark McKinny's back.

"Do it," Miles said. "Now. Step out of line. Tell them you are ten years old."

He wasn't ten years old, he was twelve. His mind took hold of that thought with a fierce obsession. The voice inside his mind kept saying, "Does Miles think I'm ten? Does he think I'm ten?" though the words really had no meaning to him. They were something for his mind to say. And his feet kept stepping forward and his eyes kept staring at the mole.

"Do like I told you," Miles said.

But he didn't.

Miles looked straight ahead and closed his eyes down tight, the lids squeezing hard together. "Toby. Please," he said. And then he said, "Think about our mother."

But Toby couldn't think of her. He just kept stepping forward in the grass, among the flowers, toward the river, and staring at the mole. He heard O'Bryan whispering and starting over once again and getting all his words confused this time as if he didn't know the way they were supposed to fall, "The Lord is my shepherd, I shall not want. He maketh me . . . to lie down in . . . He restoreth . . . He leadeth me beside the paths . . . of righteousness, and yea though I walk through the valley of death . . . of the shadow of death, He will . . . He is my shepherd, I shall not want . . ."

Without the prisoners knowing how it happened, the soldiers on their left flank slowed and then ceased marching and maneuvered over to the soldiers on the right, so that no soldiers were between the rebels and the hedge, and out ahead of them was the river snaking through the trees, and back behind them was the road.

"Halt!" An officer on horseback shouted at the column, reining in his mount. "Halt!" The column turned to face him. The officer spoke Spanish phrases, pointing his drawn sword against the sky and turning it as he would twirl a lasso, but slowly, drawing a circle with the sword's point in the heavy air. "*¡Dénse la vuelta!*" he commanded. "*¡Dénse la vuelta!*"

From the gestures, they began to understand. They were being told to turn around and face the hedge.

An infantry officer, standing in the flowers with the soldiers around him and the cavalry behind him, pointed at the ground and said, "*¡Dénse la vuelta, y arrodillense! ¡Rápido! ¿Comprenden? ¡Rápido!*"

They were being told to turn around, and kneel.

The soldiers were lined up in front of them in their blue uniforms, not ten paces distant, so the prisoners were trapped between the soldiers and the thorny hedge.

"They're just trying to scare us," someone said.

And they clung to that last hope and to each other in a way, reaching without knowing it to touch someone beside them with a glancing of their arms together or a meeting of their eyes, drawing closer in until at last they bunched up like spooked cattle in a pen, against the thorny hedge.

From the distance back behind them came the rumble of the thunder which the sky had threatened through the morning, but it wasn't thunder after all, it was volley fire coming from the road which led off toward Refugio and Cópano, and then it sounded from the Béxar road too, closer, and Toby heard the shouting and the screaming follow—and then the soldiers out in front of him, standing in the prairie underneath a sky of stone, raised their guns to fire.

"Miles? Miles?"

"Toby? Brother?"

Many of them reached for one another, several of them lunging forward in a unit just before the guns went off as if to rush the line of soldiers with nothing but their hands. These took the volley in their bellies and their faces. Others turned and flung themselves into the thorns of the mesquite and took the volley in their backs. Toby fell down on his knees and twisted his face back around to see his brother. He watched Miles toss his arm against his head as if to cover it, then lean to cover Toby, or Toby thought it was to cover him but then saw Miles was shot with holes and that his ear and pieces of his skull were gone away. And Miles fell down on top of him. Toby thought Miles wasn't dead and then he thought he was. There was no movement. Nothing. Just the solid weight. The smell of blood. Everyone was screaming. Toby tried to crawl. The powder smoke was thick and smelled of rotting eggs. The guns went off again . . . again . . . and men impaled themselves against the thorns and tried to climb the hedge, and others turned back toward the road, and some ran for the river.

Toby stumbled to his feet and headed for the water. He felt his bare feet stepping on the bodies. He saw the back of Gus's head lying in a patch of blazing flowers. After that, he did not once look down. In the partings of the powder smoke he saw the line of trees that grew along the bank, and got his bearings, and ran along the hedgerow, crouched down against the grass, crawling and then running. He was aware that blood was smeared across his face and chest and that his hands were sticky with it but he did not know if it was his or if it came from Miles. When a soldier on horseback rode at him through clouds of smoke, Toby kept on running and the rider must have veered away to chase down someone else. Toby never did look back. He skirted straight along the hedge a distance with cool grass and flowers underneath his feet and then he heard a rider coming up behind him, and cut out to the field, zigzagging like a rabbit. Others ran beside him and many were shot down or driven down with lances. Once when he was fired on at close range Toby threw himself down on his back and spread his arms and lay as if he had been killed, and even when a lancer galloped over him and crushed his hand, and the horse's hind hoof grazed his nose, and a soldier darted through the smoke and stabbed a bayonet into the soft flesh where his arm joined to his body, then ran on, Toby did not move enough to let them know. He told himself that he was dead, and made himself believe it.

Then he was alive again, and running toward the trees, and he could see the water twisting through the foliage in a ribbon of dark green.

Sticks and twigs were breaking underneath his feet.

The bank was high and steep. Without breaking stride, Toby stepped off into air.

The silence stunned him.

And the cold.

He sank down deep in turbid green and let the current rock him, pulling him downstream. "A thousand one . . . a thousand two . . ." he began to count, as he always did beneath the water, the numbers speaking in his mind like a strain of music. The water was still murky from the rains, but he could see the river weeds below him, down too far to touch, and the shapes of lazy fish weaving slowly in and out among the stones. A large stone sat among the weeds, and Toby swam down to take hold of it, trailing blood behind him. When he was anchored to the stone, he rolled to look up toward the surface and could see, as if through a pane of glass, the limbs all cragged and rippling green against the stony sky.

A soldier stepped into view, standing on the bank beneath the limbs in his blue uniform, his shape distorted by the water flow. He aimed his musket down at Toby and fired one shot into the water, the ball hitting with a force and then sinking like a pebble carried gently by the current.

There was a louder splash upstream, and the soldier, like some vague figure in a silent dream, turned and loped away in that direction, disappearing out of Toby's sight.

Turning over, Toby hugged the stone a moment, then let go and let the current carry him. The hand that had been crushed beneath the horse's hoof was numb, as if it wasn't there. He touched his face with his good hand, and felt his spectacles were gone. "One thousand sixty-two, one thousand sixty-three," he counted, and his sides began to heave for air. The current rocked him like a baby. He saw his own blood darkening the waters. A churning sound aroused him and he swiveled on his back and saw the water on the surface up above him broken in a mass of swirling bubbles. At first he thought the water agitation was an odd phenomenon of fish. But then he saw the paws and hairy underbelly thrashing in among the bubbles, and remembered Coon.

"One thousand eighty-three, one thousand eighty-four . . ."

So much noise was echoing around the walls inside the chapel that Hugh hardly heard the volley of the guns. He paused and listened for a moment, thinking it was distant thunder, then went on rolling up a dirty wad of bedding for a man with broken ribs.

A soldier named Martínez, who had attended school at Bardstown in Kentucky and spoke English, was standing above him, saying, "It is a feeling very strange to me, that I should share a room with him in school, and five years later we are shooting at each other in a battle, and he is taken prisoner. I haven't known what to say to him. I'm relieved to see him go."

Hugh did not reply. There was something in Martínez that he didn't like. He did not even look at him, but kept to his work; he was in charge of moving all the rebel wounded out into the yard. There were more than sixty of them. He'd been told they would be loaded into vehicles and driven down to Cópano, and he was hoping to go with them and meet his sons that way.

There were orderlies to help him move the wounded, since the other doctors had been taken somewhere else. Fannin was shut inside the stone room over to the right. Up to now, Fannin and his aide, Joe Chadwick, had been free to walk within the confines of the chapel and the chapel yard, but this morning Chadwick had been taken out and marched off with the other prisoners and Fannin was locked in alone.

Those wounded who were capable were moving outside on their own, some with splints made out of boards strapped on their arms and legs, others bound with grimy strips of bleached domestic.

Hugh was on his knees, folding up the blanket, when the second volley sounded from a closer range.

He sat back on his heels.

Others stopped to listen also.

Martínez said to him, "It is only soldiers cleaning out their guns." But his voice rang false.

Hugh set the blanket down and walked between the rows of pallets to the door and out into the crowded chapel yard. There were women and some soldiers on the northwest corner bastion and the walls, looking toward the river. There were wounded, rammed like cattle in the southwest corner, guarded by more soldiers. He saw Scholar Tipton standing just apart, against the wall, his weight on his good leg and his broad belly sloped against the stones. Scholar was listening to something. He turned one ear up toward the sky, as if to hear out past the wall.

Everyone was listening.

The guns went off again, this time from the road down to the lower ford that led off toward Victoria.

Slowly the knowledge came to him. He saw the women on the walls in their sandals and their flowing skirts, some standing, some crouched down, their scarves and black hair draped across their shoulders, down their backs like the branches of the willow tree that ventured to cross over.

He saw Scholar Tipton look in his direction, his curly hair so oily it seemed wet.

A child was playing on the wall—a little boy in a big hat who aimed a stick as if it were a gun, pointing with it toward the river.

More guards were entering the chapel yard, some coming in from the compound, others filing through the picket gate beside the willow tree.

They latched the gate behind them.

It seemed as if the churchyard had gone silent and the only sounds that he could hear were outside the walls. The gunfire now was steady but the shots were individual.

And screaming could be heard.

Someone close behind Hugh said, in a voice of utter calm, "We might as well stop bringing out the wounded. We will all be shot."

And Colonel Garay, of the Mexicans, passed in front of Hugh and said as he walked by, "Keep still, Doctor, you are safe. This is not from my orders, nor do I execute them."

Crucita was before him then. Her hair had come down loose. Urgently she said, "They are killing the prisoners. But Toby, he is fine."

Hugh stood like an empty body in the chapel yard, and spoke as if the act of speaking was a simple placement of the tongue within the mouth, with no inspiration from a living mind, "Where is he—where is Toby?"

"He is . . . you can't see him. He is safe. I put him in a safe place."

"But where—"

"You can't go to him in this moment."

"Where is Miles?"

So slightly that the movement almost could not be perceived, she shook her head. "He is gone," she whispered.

Hugh spun around toward the picket gate and tried to force the latch. The guards who tried to stop him had no effect at all; he flung his arms against their guns, shoving them aside as if they were mere sticks of wood. Crucita followed shrieking like a witch at all the guards and saying that he was a doctor and they must not shoot him. The women on the walls all turned to look. Crucita thought Hugh Kenner would break the gate in pieces with his force, but instead he reeled around and ran out through the entry to the compound and past the three anaqua trees. The guards positioned at the sally port saw him coming and took aim, but she came running after, screaming that he was a doctor and they must not shoot him, and she became his guardian of passage.

They let him through the gates, and once outside, there in the street, with a few old women wailing, waving branches, an old man sitting on a bench beside the wall, a group of soldiers and a dog with just three legs, Hugh stopped and tried to get his bearings, listening. His face was turned up to the sky; his hands were flung out on each side of it as if he called on God, and the sound of gunfire came from all directions. Four soldiers started to approach him, but Crucita shouted at them, "¡El es un médico; no le disparen!"

Hugh Kenner turned in one full circle, listening far away. The sound of gunfire and of screaming came from three directions and blended in confused and distant echoes. Following the sound would be like following the dead; there was no path at all. It was everywhere around.

She ran to him and tried to get his eyes to look at hers and told him once again that Toby was alive and safe within a hiding place.

He shouted at her, "Tell me where," and "Which way did they go?

Which way did Miles go?" She knew that if she even glanced down one road or another he would run in that direction without any heed for his own life. And the soldiers standing by or the hundreds of assassins in the prairies and along the roads would shoot him as he ran.

She made her eyes look only at his eyes, though they were so tormented and so lacking in a focus that she wondered if he even saw her there, or if perhaps he was just shouting at the air. "Which road did they go on . . . Where is Toby? Where is Toby?"

She promised he was safe, that she had hidden him, and then Hugh Kenner started calling for him and for Miles, and the sound was so excruciating and so powerful Crucita thought that Toby would come running from the far side of the fort where he was hidden.

Or that Miles would answer from the dead.

But there was only distant screaming of the living from out across the prairies and over toward the river, and Toby did not come, and Hugh Kenner took her face in both his hands and started begging her with almost more emotion than she could withstand. He begged in Spanish and in English. He pressed her face between his hands and pleaded with her to tell him in which direction Miles had gone. She pulled away and fell down at his feet and put her face against the dirt and sobbed aloud, and he got on the ground beside her, shaking her with both his hands. Still she did not tell him of the hiding place. Nor did she lift a finger toward the road down to the ford. She lied, and cried out that she did not know on which road they had taken Miles. But he did not believe her, and he went on shaking her with both his hands, his face down close to hers against the dirt.

She began to scream.

The guards came forward and the group of soldiers moved in close around. When she saw them put the muzzle of an *escopeta* at his head, she shoved it off with both her hands and flung herself across him. "*No le disparen, él es un médico. Ustedes no deben de matar a los médicos,*" she cried up at them. "*¡No le maten!*"

Two of them took hold and dragged her off him. She struggled to get free. A voice was shouting, "*Traigan una cuerda. Rápido,*" and she recognized it as Holzinger's voice, and a guard was shouting, "*Está uno en el calabozo.*" She could see up close the dark blue of the uniforms and the shiny buttons and the faces of the guards who held her, one with heavy brows and pitted skin—and both of them were shouting at her to be still.

They let her go. She lay there on her side. The dirt clung to her face. The dog with three legs came to look at her; his fur was long and dirty white. Several women stood around and stared at her. One of them she knew by name: Rosita. Rosita with her close-set eyes. Another leaned to help her stand.

Then the sound, behind her, made her lift her face up from the dirt.

He was on his knees surrounded by the guards and soldiers in blue uniforms, his arms strapped to his sides with rope and a leather belt. His eyes were tightly closed, his head was tilted so far back his soft hair fell against his shoulders.

He was calling out the names of both his sons with such a voice it was as if he cast the life out of his body with his cries.

After that, she went back to the chapel yard.

It had become a place of slaughter. The wounded prisoners were summoned from the corner, two by two, to face the executioners. Most of them came forward in a state of silence, crippled and bent over. They spread their blankets out and sat down on them with their backs against the wall.

In the beginning there was order to the killing: three executioners for two victims at a time, the third to fire only if the first shots did not kill. The victims were blindfolded before being shot. The cloth the soldiers used for this was torn from sheets of bleached domestic which Crucita had procured for Hugh two days ago to use as bandages. But there was not enough of it, and so the later victims were told to turn around and face the wall, and some refused to turn, and some refused to sit, and the shooting then became less organized and grew into a frenzy involving many soldiers. The wall was covered with the victims' blood and gore and all the chapel yard was filled with powder smoke, for there was not a breath of air to blow the smoke away.

Those who could not walk or sit were carried in their blankets from the chapel and placed down on the ground and shot at close range in the head.

Crucita did not stay there for the dead. She stayed there for the living. She took the scraps of paper they thrust at her, with the names of loved ones whom they wanted notified, and took their few belongings for safekeeping and made promises and gave them all the strength she could to face the guns, and many looked to her, through all the smoke, while the guns were blasted in their faces, and she did not look away as long as they were living.

But when the guns were fired and the bodies fell she turned her back upon the dead.

Scholar Tipton took his place against the wall when he was summoned. He leaned awkwardly, favoring his wormy leg, to spread his rug of buffalo hide on the bloody ground. Then he turned and limped back to Crucita with his hands working to untie a thong that was secured around his neck. He could not untie it so he jerked on it and broke it. A small pouch dangled from the thong, no bigger than a finger, and he tried to tell her something about what it held inside. But he could hardly speak in sentences and she could barely hear above the voices of the soldiers who were shouting at him to get back against the wall. Scholar fumbled with the thong to open up the pouch and show her what it held, but his hands were shaking so that he could not. She tried to help by taking it to open it herself, and while she bent her head and pried it open he was shoved out by two soldiers and shot down against the wall.

A baby's tooth was what it was, inside. A broken baby's tooth. It dropped into her palm. She heard the yelling and the guns. She put it back inside the pouch and tied a firm knot in the broken thong. Then she slid the thong around her neck, with care, as if it were a lovely necklace, and she wore it there.

The little boy was watching from the wall. The women were all gone. The willow limb was reaching down within, and the picket gate was opened, then. Outside, was the willow tree with two wagons parked beneath it.

The soldiers stripped the bodies of their bloody clothes before they dragged them to the wagons, so the soldiers, too, were washed in blood.

More men, and more—more than sixty all together—were shot within the chapel yard.

Colonel Ward, sent to La Bahía by Urrea just two days before, was brought in from the compound by two guards. He was told to kneel, and he refused. He was told that if he kneeled his life might then be spared, and he said his men had all been shot and that he wished to die. And then he was shot down.

Smoke hung murky in the humid air. It was a scene no artist could have rendered. The sound of death was permeating everywhere: the pleading of the victims—those who pleaded—and the shooting, and the awful silence of the dead.

Fannin was the last man to be shot. He was brought out from his room within the chapel, his wounded leg so stiff that he leaned heavily against his guards. He had heard the shooting but was not prepared to face the scene before him when he stepped outside the chapel doors: the bodies of his men stripped naked, tangled in a pile beside the picket gate, to be carried out and heaved into the wagons waiting. His mouth contorted and he made a sound that was not human; then he gained composure, and held to that composure, as if it were the last sustaining thing he knew.

It sustained Crucita, too. Her mind was giving way. She could no longer think about the blood and all the bodies and the way the men had looked to her like children looking to their mother, the crippled ways they moved out to the wall and spread their blankets so as not to sit down in the blood. She had grown numb to everything, incapable of pity. Fannin was a man whom she had not respected and had never liked, but she understood the manner that he had when he was facing death, his stoicism and his stunning calm. She stood there in the corner where the prisoners had been, and watched his final moments with detachment, as if she were not standing there at all.

A Creole, very young, named Joseph Spohn, whom she had spoken with when they were working as assistants to the doctors, was summoned from the *calabozo* where he had been sent. He spoke Spanish very well, and the captain of the Tres Villas battalion, who was in charge of all the killing of the wounded, told him to inform Fannin that since he had led an armed band to commit depredations in the attempt to revolutionize Texas, the Mexican government was about to chastise him.

Fannin stood beside the chapel doors in his overcoat made of India rubber, and heard the sentence spoken in Spohn's Creole accent. Then he turned to the captain of Tres Villas and asked to see Portilla. The captain questioned why he wished to see him, and Fannin pulled a gold watch from his pocket, saying that he wished to leave it for his wife, in Portilla's care. The captain reached for the watch, and said that he would give it to Portilla, adding, "Thank you, me thank you." Fannin then said he could keep the watch himself if he would have him buried after he was shot, at which the captain bowed and smiled and said he would, *"con todas las formalidades necesarias."*

Fannin then made three more gifts to the captain: a small beaded purse of coins, a handful of dollars, and a stained silk scarf which, he said, had stopped the copper ball from lodging in his body. A chair was brought and placed there in the corner by the doors. Fannin was told to sit, and he did so, and his eyes were bandaged by the captain, with a handkerchief. As the captain stood behind the chair and tied the handkerchief he asked Fannin if he was tying it correctly, saying, "Good? Good?"

Fannin answered, "Yes, yes."

In a moment, when Fannin heard the executioners—there were six of them—approaching close to him, he turned his blinded face to Spohn and said, "Ask them not to come so close that they will burn my face with powder."

But even while Spohn turned to make this last request, the captain of Tres Villas gave the sign to fire, lifting the silk scarf in the leaden air, and the muskets fired from two feet away.

Fannin died at once, his face so scorched that he appeared to be a black man. It seemed as if he had been waiting there for alms beside the open chapel doors, had laid his head against one shoulder, and gone off to sleep.

Crucita then felt free to go. She went out through the picket gate, where the wagons, filled with naked bodies, were parked beneath the willow tree. The spattering of gunfire in the distance was becoming more sporadic.

She went over to the ditch where she had hidden Toby, and saw two boards were moved aside, and knew.

He had been found, or he had gone away.

She knelt and looked inside, and said his name, and when she knew for sure he was not there, she walked away.

There was nothing in her left to feel.

She found Hugh Kenner in the *calabozo,* sitting silently on a bench with three other men, all four with their arms bound against their sides. The light was very dim. Soldiers were bringing in the clothing and belongings they had taken from the dead out on the roads, and piling it up in the corner. There was a pot of soup for them to eat. Crucita did not know if this was for the noon or evening meal. She had no knowledge of what time had passed.

None of them were eating. Some sat and stared down at the floor, which was made of brick and strewn with dry grass. A boy not eight years old was crouched before the bench, offering a wooden bowl of soup to the four prisoners. He held it out to one and then another. But their expressions were like those of dead men. The boy shook his head and pointed at their foreheads, trying to communicate to them that they would not be shot. They did not seem to care.

Hugh stared at the corner where the bloody clothes were piled, and at the floor where pieces lay amid the hay. A red jacket of the Rovers lay rumpled at his feet. Beside it was a green knapsack embroidered with the name of Wingate.

When he saw Crucita, he did not seem to know her.

She said only, "Toby, he is not here. He is gone."

At first she thought he did not hear her. Then he gave a slight nod over toward the corner, and she turned to see what he was looking at.

Toby's knapsack, with "T.K." written on it in black charcoal, was lying in the dim light near the base of the pile. The strap that she had seen him wear across his shoulder was tangled in the moldy grass.

She walked among the soldiers to retrieve the knapsack, and brought it back to Hugh. He asked if she would see what was inside. She sat down on the floor and pulled a soiled shirt from the sack, then poured into her skirt a tin cup, a spoon, a small brown stone, and a piece of charcoal.

Silently, she sat fingering the stone. She did not look at Hugh, but she could see his feet on the floor beside her, in old shoes with the buckles both undone.

His voice was hoarse and low. "Did he have it when you hid him?"

Yes, she nodded, still not looking up at him.

The little boy came over with his bowl of soup and sat cross-legged facing her, his bare feet black with dirt. He watched her crying, and he made a little pitying expression. He offered her the soup, and she shook her head. He watched her fingering the stone, and showed some interest in it, leaning forward toward her lap to see it better. With a flicker of his finger toward the stone, he asked her timidly, and formally, if he could hold and keep it. "*¿Me puedo quedar con la piedrita, por favor?*"

T H E   P A L E   M I M O S A S

It was not the dead that haunted Toby through the misting night, it was the wolves feeding on the dead. They were scavenging the prairies for the bodies not burned in the funeral pyres. Though he was now across the river and half a mile downstream, and could not see from his hiding place in the honeysuckle vines the pillars of the smoke rising on the prairies, he could see smoke easing its way down to the river, and could smell the burning flesh. The wolves had smelled it too, from far away. They crept in like the fog, as Toby lay all night with Coon Dog, hidden in the vines and shrubbery beside the water, listening to the water and their wretched mournful howling out on the open land. They snarled at each other as they prowled through fields of dead and waited for the fires to go cold.

All night he trembled from the cold and his emotions. His body wound itself into a knot of anguish so intense he was incapable of movement. With one arm wrapped around his dog, he sat with bracken and honeysuckle all around him, twigs poking in his face. His clothes were dripping wet. His nose, where the hoof had nicked it when the horse passed over like a shadow, swelled large and bloody, throbbing with the rhythm of his heart. The bayonet wound in the soft pit of his other arm bled every time he moved; Coon spent the whole night licking blood away.

At first he thought his father might come looking for him, but after dark he knew he would not come.

A chill, wet norther moved in with the smoke, quiet as a cat, without a breath of wind.

Perhaps his father had been killed.

Perhaps Toby was the only one alive. He had seen others running for the river, but most of them were hunted down. He remembered how they fell in wild contortions, their hands snatching for the sky as if to grab hold of the spirits that were leaving, and he recalled his brother's face with one side of his skull not there. How heavily he fell. But Toby's mind began to numb and he could not remember how it happened, and he thought maybe he was shot dead too, and this was just his spirit crouching in the woods, and there were spirits of the others all around him which he could not see. He began to think that he was breathing ashes of his body, which was burning on the prairie, and the dog beside him was a ghost.

But he could feel his wounds. The pain was real. The blood flowed. The dog beside him smelled of fur and river water and his breath, and whined and turned around in circles in the brush. The vines and shrubbery still made a rustling noise against his movements, and the air was cold.

A whippoorwill alighted in the tree above and eased its soft and filmy strands into the smoky air.

Rose had always called the whippoorwill a messenger of death.

Up above, beyond the canopy of leaves, the drizzling sky was tinged with orange from the fires.

Northeast was the way he should be moving: a stretch of grassy land with creeks and rivers to be forded. He could not safely stay along the roads. He would have to travel through the brush in daylight and the open prairies in the dark, and without shoes. He had no way to carry water. He had no weapons and no food. And he was almost blind without his spectacles.

He had his dog, was all.

Coon Dog could chase rabbits down for food.

But the thought of rabbits chased and murdered in the prairies made him cover up his face with both his hands, and the thought of roasting meat above the flames made his stomach swell. He smelled the smoke again—his brother's skin and hair on fire—and held his breath— "A thousand one, a thousand two . . ."

The whippoorwill above was answered by another, off across the river, and the duet was so mournful and forboding that it plucked at Toby's heart like nothing had before. He bent his head against his knees and continued counting till he had to breathe, then he sucked in smoke —pale and limpid with the sweet and horrifying taste of burning flesh— and he gagged it out and started counting over.

His lungs would never empty of the smell.

All night long the whippoorwills called and the wolves out in the prairies skulked around the fires, howling at the sky. Then the rosy light of fires died away and the night was black and wet and the dawn began to ease in through the honeysuckle vines, gray and chalky as the dawn before it.

With it, came the lancers searching for survivors, riding out along the tree line and picking their way through the foliage in the river bottoms, up and down along both banks. He could hear their voices coming closer and receding and approaching once again, speaking to each other, calling to each other across the water, echoing like voices down a canyon. He heard a shout, and then two shots.

If they found him, they would shoot him where he sat.

Coon began to tremble there beside him.

His shirt was stiff with blood.

A beetle crawled across his feet.

He eased the shirt off, put the shirttail in his mouth and tore a strip off with his teeth, then wrapped the strip around the wound and put the shirt back on.

The lancers in the bottoms were not coming any closer, but there were others wending their way from the open field on this side of the river to the trees. Where the foliage was too thick they dismounted, so close that Toby heard their conversation.

They were talking about horses: he heard the word *caballos.*

They were talking about home: he heard one saying *"mi es- posa . . ."*

Most of the other words he did not know, but he could hear the soldiers hacking at the brush. Any moment they would find the deer trail he had crawled along and it would lead them straight to him. It was possible, if they were careless, and he was absolutely still, that they might pass him by; he was a few yards off the trail and hidden in the vines.

They found the path and turned to follow it. They came so near that he could hear the twigs and branches snapping underneath their feet. He placed his hand on Coon Dog's back and felt the hair stand up along the spine, and then from deep inside, the slow vibration of the lungs. He could see the water through the trees in the muggy morning light, a drop of thirty feet. His fear was so consuming that he almost stood up and surrendered, just to have it over with. Often he had done that as a child when playing hide and seek with Miles, and Miles had never understood.

He stayed there in his hiding place.

Then the slow vibration deep inside of Coon began to rise and quicken. Toby whispered to the dog to hush, and looked him in the eyes, so shiny black and with the vines reflected in them like black lace, and begged him to be still. But Coon began to bare his teeth. The tremor grew into a rattling growl, as if a rattlesnake were making its way out, and Toby wrapped his bloody arm around the dog and clasped one hand around the prickly muzzle to hold the mouth closed shut. He placed the other hand gently at the throat, feeling the rattle of the snake inside, the bony ridges of the rattle in the throat. "Shhhhh," he said, his voice soft and reassuring. His heart was so loud he could hear it. Then he was tearing his way through the undergrowth toward the water and slipping down the muddy bank. He felt the water closing cold around his body. He looked to see if Coon Dog was behind him, but he wasn't.

For a while the passage led him through a corridor between high banks, but then he left the river and started out in the direction he guessed to be northeast. It was a long passage, through wet days and frigid nights. Now and then the sun came through, and now and then the stars, but mostly everything was blanketed with rain and the world obscured out on the far horizons, over in the ridges of the trees or the swales of flowered meadows. He lay for two days in a shallow creek and let the minnows nibble at his wound to clean it. He thought that maybe Coon Dog would appear, and waited. Then he had to travel on. Other days he traveled through the rolling prairies without water. Some nights he tried to gauge direction by the stars, and stood there squinting up at them with his myopic eyes, barely making out the bright ones. Then the clouds would come, or rain, blending everything to gray, and night would come, and he would walk in darkness and at daybreak find himself back in the place that he had started from.

There were cane brakes with black soil and cane fifteen feet high, matted up with greenbriers and extending miles along the creeks without a passage through, alive with bears and rodents and the wolves.

Along the Guadalupe there were Mexican patrols, and Toby could not sleep, for fear.

Few wild fruits or berries were growing in this season, and the nuts and mast down in the river bottoms were all eaten by wild hogs and deer. The bulbous tunas of the prickly pear were not yet ripe. He ate wild onions and elm buds and mesquite grass, and picked the undigested seeds out of dry varmint droppings. He ate the snails that he found crawling on the prickly pear, and plucked long Spanish moss from live oak trees to make his bed with. One day at dusk he came across a prairie set on fire, and climbed up in a tree to let the flames pass under. From this vantage in the leaves he watched through his blurred vision the rabbits and the deer and antelope running from the flames. A doe and fawn ran right beneath him, then the fire also passed beneath, and he held his breath against the smoke and felt the heat of it. The flames rolled on across the prairie like troubled waves rolling on the beach. He watched after for a while, then dropped down from the tree and walked across the charred stubble with his bare feet, and by nightfall he was leaving tracks of blood.

After that, he wrapped his feet in Spanish moss tied on with strips of cedar bark and pieces of his trousers. On the days the sun was out he draped the moss across his head and walked across the prairie like an old and crippled woman with her hair down loose.

One morning, passing through a deer trail in a thicket, he came across a large nest of a cactus wren woven in the tangle of mesquite thorns, with two eggs nestled in it. When he cracked the eggs he found the birds inside were nearly hatched, and snapped their heads and ate them anyway, and even ate the shells, watching as the mother wren flitted in the brush.

On the next day he ate purple flowers of the prairie spiderwort, but he did not eat the roots, for he recalled his father told him they were poison.

He thought about his father through the days.

He thought of Coon, and longed to know where he had gone, and always looked behind to see if he was coming. He believed that he was coming.

He often thought about the stuffed whale Gus had told him of.

At night he thought about his mother, and once he dreamed of her and Katie. He was awakened from the dream in the light of dawn by a band of mustangs running through mesquite grass underneath the rising sun.

One afternoon he found fresh water mussels in a stream, and stayed for two days and two nights, feasting on them. In the days he propped himself against a tree and watched an army of large cut ants stripping leaves from a massive oak that stood nearby and carrying the green leaves down the bark, like banners. His vision was so blurred that he could hardly see the ants against the bark, and he imagined that the leaves were moving on their own, as if the tree were disassembling one leaf at a time.

The yucca plants were all alive with bugs.

The prickly pear were knotted up with vines, and when he tried to make his way through narrow varmint trails the thorns stuck in his legs, and he was often forced to turn back on the trail and wend his way around the tracks of cactus and large prickly pear.

Thorns worked their way into his flesh and it swelled up with poison, and Toby stripped down naked and spent hours lying in the waters of a creek to let the current wash against the sores and numb the pain.

Hackberry trees that grew along the waterways were infested with ball moss and speckled with small berries, but he couldn't reach the berries without climbing, and his legs were swelling with the thorns, and his wounded arm was stiff.

The whippoorwills stopped singing when the moon went down.

The mourning doves would then begin their cooing, the sound of it so soft it fell like dew, and cardinals streaked across the sky in brazen red.

He found the dried-up hide and bones of a large stag that had been killed and partially consumed by a panther or a Mexican lion, and he soaked the hide in a shallow stream to clean and soften it, then cut it with a stone, which took him all day long. He wore the largest section wrapped around him as a cloak against the sun out on the prairies and the thickets full of thorns and the rain at night. The smaller strips he tied around his feet, using Spanish moss for padding.

Sometimes when he lay out in the prairie in the day to sleep, the buzzards circled overhead. Once he woke to find them on the ground around him like a council of old men.

When he walked, the grass was matted at his feet, and he had difficulty getting through it.

He saw the signal smoke of Indian fires in the distance.

On a river that he thought to be Cow River he saw a drove of razorbacks down in the bottoms, and found that he was salivating at the sight of them just as wild animals would do.

He came across a house that had been looted of all edibles and clothing, the habitants long gone, and on the door was written in black charcoal, "Thomas Camp," and "Herman Ehrenburg."

So he was not the only one who lived, and passed this way, and under those two names he carved his own with a piece of stone, cutting deep into the wood. It was a statement of his whole existence. He slept that night beneath the roof, then started out again.

The prairie hens made lowing sounds like cattle, and strutted through high grass. The turkey were so tame it was as if they spoke to him when he was near; they lighted in the scattered mottes of timber as the sun went down, flocking in from four directions. He slept beneath them just to have their company because the wolves were howling.

He chewed his lips so much he tasted blood all day and night, and when he wasn't traveling he tried to pick the thorns out of his legs, squeezing at the sores, but most were so embedded that they drew out lumps of flesh.

It was the homing instinct, like a runty pig's, that kept him moving mostly in the right direction. He smelled salt in the air. He entered a small forest of mimosa shrubs which towered nine feet high, and as he brushed against the hairy leaves, they folded in against themselves, withdrawing from his touch. He observed that those in front of him were folding up their leaves before he reached them, like the women waving fragile ferns in Goliad as the soldiers had passed through. When he looked behind, he saw the trail that he had left, the pale mimosas hesitant to spread their leaves again, and he imagined that the path was a corridor behind him, through the wild mimosas and the grasses and the rivers, back through miles and miles to La Bahía and the charred bones of his brother scattered out among the prairie flowers.

D E S A G R A V I O S

Good Friday, April 1, Goliad

Adelaido Pacheco returned home from his wanderings on the morning of Good Friday. He did not plan the day for drama, he did not even know what day it was. Simply, a sadness, far deeper than mere loneliness, had descended on him in the three weeks he was gone. He had firelight and warmth, and he had food. But he had no country and no friend and nothing to believe in.

He had started talking to himself. He told stories and told lies. He said he was immortal, and that he needed no one. He said he should be moving on, and he made plans of where to go, two ideas specifically of how to make a living. He could market corkwood from the Brazos bottoms to be used like cork in floats for fishing nets, and sell it both in Mexico and in Louisiana, and he could also start a business with the Spanish moss that grew along the river bottoms near the gulf. He could build a gin to bale the moss for use in packing crates and for stuffing beds and sofas.

So he made his plans.

But he had lost his heart. He longed to see Crucita. He continued thinking of the night beside the river when Domingo de la Rosa sat his mount with the rain falling down in torrents and told him in a voice ascending up above the water sounds, "She said that she herself would pay your debt to me. Which she has done."

So it wasn't that he had nowhere to go that kept him lurking in the wilderness those three weeks, in the rain.

It was his shame.

He had thought Crucita was in love with De la Rosa; he had thought that she was De la Rosa's whore. He had spoken both these thoughts aloud to De la Rosa, and been proven wrong, and worse than wrong—he had been proven frivolous. Crucita risked her life for him, and he had called her Whore.

He thought of never going back. He thought of making fortunes out of nothing: out of wood and moss. He told himself there were no boundaries out along the far horizons that he could not cross.

But then he came to know, through the nights alone, and through his wretched sadness, that there were boundaries in his heart.

He allowed himself to cry, and felt as if it were just yesterday when his family died. For days he sat cross-legged staring at the muddy water of a ditch and watching how the insects skittered on the surface, and he experienced a melancholy he had never known.

And on the morning of Good Friday he went home.

He had no idea what he would find when he reached Goliad; he did not know if rebels were still holding La Bahía. He had spoken neither with the Anglos nor *Tejanos* since the night he was unhorsed, for he trusted no one.

He did assume, however, that De la Rosa's riders would discover him before he reached the town, for though the great ranchero's home had been burned down, the man himself had ridden off into the night, and surely now was operating from the woods. Often in his wanderings he'd seen the great ranchero's horsemen passing by. Most of them he knew by name—some he knew quite well, from the time he was employed by De la Rosa. But he always hid himself when they were near, for to them, he was a traitor.

So much time had he spent hiding, he began to think he was a traitor, to himself.

Walking into town was like surrendering. He did it without care. Nothing mattered now but that he see Crucita. His past was like a long adventure that meant nothing in the end: he had nothing to his name, and no one, but Crucita. The games he'd played with fate were not endowed with all the meanings he had given them in stories: he had believed in destiny and all the grand ideas; he had believed in making fortunes. Now all of it was blown away and scattered out across the prairies, pelted down in mud, and he had nothing left to lose, but her.

He heard the bells of La Bahía tolling long before he reached the town, and it surprised him that no soldiers stopped him on the road. The road was uninhabited. The sky was filled with scavengers and gray clouds driven by the wind. The taste of salt was in the air, and rain to come; the wind was from the east. He wondered at the circling of the birds, and knew that something ominous had happened. He saw one muleteer with a cart, who did not stop to speak with him. Crossing at the upper ford, wading waist-deep in the frigid water, he came across an old man whom he knew from long ago sitting idly on the south bank with a fishing cane across his knees, the line not even in the water, but coiled beside him in the dirt.

Adelaido asked the old man if the Anglos were still holding La Bahía. The old man looked at him as if he did not know him, and touched one finger to the wind.

Adelaido heard the wailing, then.

He heard the bells of La Bahía.

The old man said, "The bells are tolling for the dead."

Adelaido stood and listened to the wailing carried on the salty wind, and heard the sound of music intermingled with the sound of suffering: the *matracas* rattling to no rhythm in particular, the beating of a raw-hide drum and the whining of the many fifes cut out of river reeds. "It is Good Friday, then," he said aloud, and the old man answered him, "It is Good Friday, following Palm Sunday, when four hundred men were killed out on our prairies."

He was very still, and withdrew within. The wind blew his wet clothes against his skin. And then he said, "Who are the dead?"

"Heretics. Americans."

"There was a battle here?"

"There was a butchery." The old man paused, still staring at the water. "They led them out along the roads and shot them in the fields. Fannin and his whole command. They tried to burn the corpses, but the air was wet. Our town is now surrounded by the corpses, charred to bones without the flesh, and wolves come in at night and drag the skeletons around and gnaw them in the fields. There is no sleep in Goliad, but the sleeping of the dead. There is no peace, not even for the dead. I tried last night to go into the fields and bury some of them, but the wolves were there," he said. He looked at Adelaido. "So I sit here fishing, on Good Friday."

Fannin and his whole command, the man had said. So Adelaido, once again, had danced along the edge of death. The wind was playing with his hair; he felt it like the touch of God. He had been spared. And yet he had returned out of the wilderness into a another wilderness so bleak and empty that it leached the blood out of his heart. The scavengers were calling from the sky. In a voice he hardly heard, he said, "And my sister, María de la Cruz Pacheco, she is here?"

He nodded. "She is here."

"She isn't harmed?"

"Ah," the old man sighed, and gestured with a gentle movement up the slope toward town. "We've all been harmed far past redemption. But still the people go on with their rituals. The commandant Portilla won't allow them in the chapel. Since the chapel yard is stained with blood, he's closed it off. The gate's locked, and the doors into the chapel have a board across them. So the people of the town, who have been living in the ruins of their homes, have assembled in a gathering of protest. They've been walking with the *penitentes* since dawn in a procession around the walls of the presidio—you can hear them now—bearing crosses and the image of the Christ, and dressed in black with thorns wound around their heads. It's just the same as always on Good Friday, except they can't go in." He paused, and sighed, and said, "God has shut us out," and then he spoke into the wind, "Domingo de la Rosa leads the *desagravios.* He has taken off his shirt for everyone to see his skin, and while he walks he whips his back with a scourge of hide and thorns, and all the *penitentes* who are following him do the same, encircling the presidio with tracks of blood. But their supplications are in vain. Our town is damned, and all our souls, and no amount of penance will prevail."

When the old man finished speaking, Adelaido heard the sound of water splashing and looked back toward the river to see three horsemen crossing with the gray light on their wide sombreros. They were De la

Rosa's riders, he knew by the authority with which they rode. When they had crossed the river, they realized it was Adelaido waiting there, and reined their horses in.

It was then that Adelaido recognized Donde. The horse's winter coat was starting to shed and he was thinner than when Adelaido saw him last, but Adelaido knew for sure that it was Donde. Looking at the young vaquero who was riding him, Adelaido felt that he was seeing an old image of himself, as if in some time past he'd crossed the river riding Donde, casting his reflection on the water, and now the same reflection had come back to life, emerging from the water after all these years. The young vaquero's hair was tied back with a thong and he was dressed in black and white with a black cravat tied at his throat. He had the same style Adelaido might have worn at such an age. He was the same young man who won the *pollo enterrado* two years in a row, after Adelaido ceased to play the game, though last November he'd disgraced himself by falling on the rooster.

It was not until this moment Adelaido knew how utterly he'd changed while wandering without a horse, without a country, three weeks in the wilderness. He said to the vaquero, "That's my horse you're riding," and Donde heard his voice and tossed his head with recognition.

The vaquero stilled the horse and answered, "The *jefe* told me I could ride him."

The man who rode beside him was an old vaquero who had taught Adelaido with the lariat when Adelaido came to work for De la Rosa. His name was Manuel Sanchez. He said, "Everyone is calling you a traitor, Pacheco."

"They may call me anything they like. The horse is mine, Manuel."

"Did you come here as a spy?"

"I came to see my sister."

"They'll shoot you if they catch you bearing arms."

"Do *you* think I'm a traitor, Manuel?"

"Are you?"

Adelaido shrugged. "I'll give my pistols to the *jefe*. I only came here for my sister. And my horse."

Tilting back his face, the old vaquero looked at Adelaido down his nose. "Then I'll take you to the *jefe*, now."

Donde pawed the ground and tried to go to Adelaido, and when the young vaquero drew the reins back tight, Donde arched his neck against them, opening his mouth against the bit and stepping backward, almost back into the water.

The old man with the fishing cane said to the vaqueros, "You can't talk with De la Rosa now; he's leading the *desagravios*. When I saw him he was striped with blood." He gestured with one hand toward Adelaido. "You should let him go and find his sister. We've had enough blood in Holy Week."

But the third vaquero would not have it so. He took a long drink from his water gourd and shifted in his saddle, saying, "If we can't take him to the *jefe*, we'll take him to Portilla. The dead are stinking in the fields, but the war isn't over." Then he spoke to Adelaido. "You became a traitor, Adelaido. You can't just change your mind now that we're winning. There's a price for bearing arms against your country, and you're not above the laws. Though you've thought so, all these years."

God had spared him once. God had spared him many times.

It had not occurred to Adelaido, ever, that he would not be spared. It occurred to him now.

Two days after the killing, Hugh had gone searching among the dead to find his sons and bury them. The horrors of it were unspeakable. Crucita was there with him. The bodies had been stripped of clothes and were too burned to tell one from another.

It was not until the third night that Hugh slept, and found an hour's respite from the howling of the wolves. He spent the long nights in the *calabozo* with the other doctors and their aides—seven all together, and in the days he tended to the wounded Mexicans housed in the barracks of the western wall. Each morning when he stepped into the daylight he could see the buzzards circling in the sky above the fields.

His movements were an old man's. His hair was thinner than before, and his eyes were vacant.

On the morning of Good Friday he at last accepted food—a small tortilla and a cup of coffee—and crossed the courtyard to the barracks of the west wall where the wounded Mexicans were housed. There were soldiers in the courtyard wearing clothing they had taken from the executed men: the fringed red jackets of the Rovers, bizarre hats of the Grays, and boots too big to fit their feet.

The clothes were torn with holes from musket balls. They'd been washed in the river the day of the executions, causing the river to run red—but they were still stained with blood.

There was a guard who went about in Miles's patchwork jacket. Hugh saw him every day. The jacket was not shot with holes, as Miles had sold it in the week of the imprisonment.

In the barracks, Hugh attended patients until noon. Many of their wounds were fly-blown with large worms, but he was long past pity or revulsion and he nursed them with the manner of a farmer examining the broken pieces of a plow. On the day before he'd amputated someone's foot, which was alive with gangrene. He had cut it just above the ankle. Crucita was beside him while he cut.

She was beside him now, though she left him to go out and climb up on the bastion of the southwest corner and watch the *penitentes* circling. The wind whipped at her skirt. She saw the *penitentes* coming toward her down the western wall beneath the driven clouds, a group of thirty dressed in black, the *penitentes* leading, followed by the faithful. The *penitentes* were not men of Goliad; they were eccentrics, excessive in religion and reclusive. They lived among themselves like monks in lodgings down the river.

But the faithful were the women of the town.

Usually the roads were crowded on Good Friday with the vendors plying wares, but there was no festivity today. A few citizens were strung along the road to watch the *desagravios*—the public penance—but a kind of stillness and a silence hung about them. The wind blew the music of the *desagravios* back along the wall, so it sounded feeble to Crucita until the long procession was beneath her.

They bore three crosses of cragged tree limbs out in front. Their lines were triple deep, ragged and irregular behind the crosses. They carried high an image of the tortured Christ, painted garishly on charred remains of someone's door. A few of them wore crowns of thorny vines, and blood ran in their eyes.

De la Rosa was the leader, just behind the crosses, his face lifted to the wind. He did not wear a crown of thorns, but as he whipped his arms and back, the thorns tied on the scourge flung drops of blood in such erratic patterns that his face was speckled with it.

He passed beneath, so close he might have touched Crucita's hand, had she been reaching down. He saw her standing on the bastion with the March wind pulling at her hair; he saw her, but he did not recognize that she was there. And when he'd passed by, the thudding of the drums filled her heart. She turned away.

Goliad had lost its soul.

When Hugh went to the *calabozo* while the others drank their bowls of rancid soup, Crucita followed him. They sat together on the cold brick floor and listened to the *penitentes* circling around the fort, the noise coming and then fading off and coming around again.

"I know it was you who made the guard take me from the line," Hugh Kenner told her, in the quiet of the room.

She waited a long time before she answered. It was not a favor she had done him. He had no wish to be alive. "Yes. I did this for myself," she answered. And then she said, "I must tell you the truth. I was a spy for Señor De la Rosa for a long time. Without De la Rosa and his spies there would be no fighting at Coleto and no prisoners to kill. I think I am responsible your sons are dead. Not alone responsible, but some."

They were seated side by side against the wall. He took hold of her hand. She made a small sound, like the whimper of a wounded dog, hung her head, and gripped hold of his fingers. "De la Rosa goes in the front of the lines of the *desagravios*," she whispered. "I have never seen him do this *penitencia* in public."

The procession was coming around again; they could hear the fifes and drums. There was no window to the road, only one grate high up on the wall, so sounds were muted by the stones.

"The *penitentes* are dressed in black clothes like to bury people, and some wear on their heads sticks like Jesus," Crucita whispered with remorse, still holding to his fingers. "De la Rosa has no shirt, and whips his back. He has no shoes. The blood falls down his back and he leaves blood on the ground. All the women are the ones of faith who believe very much in Jesus, very *religiosas*, and every year on Good Friday they carry the Virgin de Loreto dressed in blue. They take her from the church the night before, then they take her back to the church at *medi-*

odía on Good Friday. But now Señor Portilla, he closed the doors and the church is locked and they can't find the Virgin." She paused, and said, "I buried her. She's in the cemetery buried by the side of my father. Every day I think I will go get her. I'm scared her paint is already gone and she looks bad. I buried her to save her from the Americans. It was the wish of Señor De la Rosa. Yesterday Señor De la Rosa asked me, where did you bury her? And I didn't tell him."

Hugh Kenner turned his gray, unshaven face to look at her, and pulled her against his shoulder. She felt his grief, so pure and painful it was kin to beauty, and wrapped her arms around his neck. The beat of drums and the piping of the fifes passed along the road outside, followed by the rattle of *matracas* and the hollow wailing of the faithful.

The tribunal judging Adelaido on that evening was an odd assembly, and a tired one. They gathered in Portilla's office in the stone house by the fort. There were the three vaqueros who had brought him in, and the old man who came with him with his fishing cane. There was the padre, and Portilla, dark and troubled, with his shoulders drawn up to his ears, and De la Rosa with the blood soaking through his shirt. De la Rosa was unsteady on his feet.

Adelaido stood before Portilla's desk, and said, "I came to town to see my sister."

Leaning backward in his chair, Portilla clasped his hands behind his head and asked him for his sister's name.

"María de la Cruz Pacheco. We are citizens of Goliad."

Portilla looked at him awhile with expressions flickering across his face, intense but transitory, then called sharply to a guard outside the door to go and fetch María de la Cruz Pacheco. As an afterthought, he ordered that they also bring the doctor by the name of Kenner. "We'll wait until your sister comes," he said to Adelaido, and turned his chair around to face the open window with a grating sound against the floor. He leaned back in his chair again and propped his feet against the sill and stared out at the sky. A wind was scudding dark and salty clouds across the view, with scattered drops of rain. Dark was blowing in.

The others in the room stood around in silence, the three vaqueros holding their sombreros. The youngest was uncomfortable with such a silence and loosened his American cravat, then spoke about the coming rain, saying he could smell it in the wind.

"It's blowing from the sea," the old man said, fingering his fishing cane. "Maybe it will bring a storm and scare away the wolves, and I can sleep tonight."

"Nothing will scare away the wolves," the padre said.

Portilla turned and took a quill pen from his desk, then turned back, propped up his feet again, stared out into the twilight, and ran the feather through his fingers in a nervous manner.

The old vaquero's stomach started growling and he cleared his throat to cover up the sound, shifting weight from one leg to another and flinging his serape tight around his shoulders. Quiet settled once again.

Crucita stepped into the room, wary and uncertain why she had been called. The room had grown so quiet that the gathering could hear the little gasp of air she took when she saw Adelaido.

Adelaido went to her and took her hand.

In the shadows of the doorway, Hugh Kenner stood with one hand on the frame. Adelaido glanced and saw him, but at first he didn't know him, he had changed so much. When he recognized the doctor, he said softly, "Is Miles dead?"

Hugh answered plainly, "Both my sons are dead."

The room was dark enough to need a light but Portilla did not call for one. Turning his chair back around to face the room, he spoke to Crucita first. "Please translate to the doctor. Tell him a message came from General Santa Anna today, asking me to send him the best surgeon we have here." He gestured toward Hugh. "They tell me he performed an amputation on a man who was dying, even without having proper tools, and saved his life. So I'm sending him to Santa Anna. Tell him he'll be leaving in the morning under guard. If he wants to, he can choose an aide to take along."

Crucita nodded, looking at Portilla, but didn't do as he instructed. Impatiently, he flung his hand out, saying, "Tell him, tell him," and Adelaido whispered to her, "Shall I tell him for you?"

Then Hugh said, "Crucita?" and she heard his voice and seemed to come back from a reverie, and turned to him and told him the entire message.

Before Hugh could respond, Portilla said to Adelaido, "So is it true what these vaqueros tell me, that you lived with the Americans here in the presidio, as a traitor, bearing arms?"

Adelaido was still holding Crucita's hand. "I was with the rebels, here," he answered. "But I left them."

"And what inspired the change of heart?"

"Betrayal," Adelaido said, and did not explain.

There stood De la Rosa, whose ranch had been burned down by the rebel Anglos, and the padre close beside him. There stood Dr. Kenner, whose son had taken Adelaido's horse and set the torch to De la Rosa's ranch, and now was dead. There stood three vaqueros who could not forgive, and a fisherman who cared for nothing but to sleep without the howling of the wolves. And there he stood himself, holding the hand of a sister he had loved, and wronged, in front of a young commandant who had ordered that four hundred men be shot down in the fields.

It was betrayal that had changed his heart, but he could not say whose.

Portilla tossed the quill down on the desk and stood up. "Explain to me what happened. Why were you fighting with Americans? Don't you know you're Mexican? Why wasn't your heart with your people?"

Adelaido smiled. "My heart was traveling," he said. "I had to go and find it. It wasn't with my people; it was in the rain beside a muddy ditch."

Portilla did not understand the allegory. "You're very clever, but your life is in the balance," he said harshly, stepping from behind his desk and walking over to address Padre Valdez. "Do you know this man?" he asked the padre.

"I've been giving him the sacraments since he was a child."

"Is he a man of God?"

"Yes, he is a man of God," he said.

Portilla addressed the great ranchero. "They say he worked for you. Do you know him well?"

The room was all in shadow now. Wind gusted through the window. De la Rosa's hands were clasped before him; he stood very straight, his hair damp with sweat and his forehead beaded with it. Blood soaked through his shirt in patches at his shoulders and his back. "I know him very well," he said. "He was a son to me."

"And if you stood here in my shoes, would you judge him as a traitor?"

De la Rosa answered with his Spanish eyes unblinking and no blood in his Spanish face, for his blood was dried in footprints on the roads around the stone presidio. "If I stood there in your shoes, I would be loathe to judge another."

Portilla tried to answer with a bold and livid stare, but his hands began to fidget with his buttons and his foot turned out, as if he were a nervous child. It seemed that in that moment his eyes opened and he understood that this tribunal wasn't for the man, Pacheco; it was his own tribunal. He was judged. And in his guilt he turned away and went back to the window and stood looking down.

He saw a group of soldiers loitering around a cookfire in the compound with night descending and the dark wind whipping at their clothes—the tattered clothes of the rebels with holes from musket balls and stains of blood. How grotesque it was, this nightmare, La Bahía, and he pronounced his sentence with his back still turned.

"I'm in no mood to punish your transgressions," he said, with irritation. "I'll send you with the doctor, and his guards, to the *presidente,* Santa Anna. He can be the one to judge you."

Crucita's cry was plaintive, "No, señor, *por favor, no se lo mande a Santa Anna, déjelo ir, por favor*—" but Portilla did not turn to look at her.

Adelaido did not move. The padre crossed himself. The three vaqueros stood holding their sombreros, waiting for dismissal from their *jefe,* and the fisherman moved toward the door.

De la Rosa turned to Adelaido, but then he wavered on his feet and slowly folded on his knees as if to pray, his arms stretched out before him on the floor, and it was not until he laid his head against the boards that the others in the room knew what was happening. His mind was shutting down; he was losing consciousness.

The padre went down on his knees beside him.

Portilla started toward the door, calling to the guard to bring a doctor, his voice so raw and anxious it seemed he thought that God had fallen, rather than an old ranchero. But Hugh Kenner was already on the floor beside the padre, leaning over De la Rosa, and seeing him, Portilla was embarrassed by the way he'd lost restraint. Why should he be worried for the man who had just spoken to him without even any pretense of respect?

Adelaido and Crucita also went down on their hands and knees beside the *jefe* and the three vaqueros stood back in astonishment and fear. The great ranchero was like Mexico, to all of them, and he was lying on his side on the dusty floorboards with his shirt soaked through with blood, and he was hardly breathing anymore.

Hugh Kenner felt his pulse and also felt his heart, then leaned back on his heels and said, "He has collapsed from loss of blood." He sent the guard for whiskey. Crucita put her hands on De la Rosa's face and spoke to him. Padre Valdez was also speaking to him. De la Rosa moved, just slightly, and Crucita cradled his pale face in her palms. Her eyes were wild and weeping and she asked Hugh, "Is he dying? Is he dying?"

"I don't think so," Hugh responded.

She was losing the composure she had held all through the week, and she cried aloud to Hugh, "Tomorrow I am going with you, with my brother. You cannot say no to me, you cannot say anything."

Adelaido said, "Crucita, *mi hermana*—" and she answered him in Spanish, "I am a citizen of Mexico, and free, and there is not a man within this room allowed to stop me—"

"Crucita, listen to me, listen—"

But she was far past listening. She put her fingers to his mouth and flung her head back in despair. "I have to go with you, I have to go with you—"

Portilla buttoned his coat and then unbuttoned it and flung an arm up in the air, a gesture without meaning, and the padre stared at him with scorn.

The young vaquero turned his black sombrero slowly in his hands, and the other two stood by while the old man with his fishing cane watched from the door.

Wind brought the dusk in through the window with the salt taste of the sea, and with it came the woeful howling of the wolves.

"I can't stay another night here, with the wolves," Crucita cried in Spanish, above the whispers of the padre. There was something kin to madness in the blackness of her eyes, her hair fallen in black waves around her shoulders. Her hands fluttered from her brother's lips to De la Rosa's face, then gripped Hugh Kenner's arm. As if he anchored her to sanity, she stopped her crying, and was calm, and spoke with love and hatred both at once in plain defiance of the pain that she had suffered, "I am leaving Goliad, I am going with you. *Yo me voy contigo.* I'm not staying here. *Yo no me quedo. No te vayas, por favor,*" and she let go of his arm and placed both hands again on De la Rosa's face, repeating her words once again while staring with an odd, remote expression toward the gray light lingering outside the window. It wasn't clear to her or to the others if her words were spoken to the doctor or to Adelaido or to the great ranchero lying with his face pressed in her palms—"I am leaving Goliad. I am going with you. *Yo me voy contigo. No te vayas, por favor*—" Or maybe they were spoken to the wind.

SONGS OF THE DISPOSSESSED

Callum Mackay rode eastward to the gulf at a slow pace on the jaded mare, a man in utter darkness. He traveled like a lost dog trailing his own scent to find his way back home.

At Horse Pass on Matagorda he built himself a fire in the dunes and sat staring at the water while the night blew in. After dark, the ghost horse swam the pass and paced along the water's edge before him with the wind tangling his silver mane and the salt spume blowing in around him. He paced northward on the shore, and Callum watched until the darkness swallowed him.

Loosening the drawstring on the canvas bag that hung around his waist, Callum took his rosary and scalp out of the bag and held them to the firelight. The scalp was coarse and withered and the hair was falling out. He dug a hole there in the dry sand of the dunes with a flat shell for a spade, and buried the scalp and the rosary together, and stared at the sea with the sand still clinging to his hands, beneath his nails.

He hated the sea. His mother had died in the sea. Or rather, on the cragged rocks of Scotland near Strathy Point under a blue sky when the wind lifted her from the edge of the cliff and tossed her down—so far down onto the rocks that she was like a fallen piece of clothing with the water tugging at it. They'd been collecting plovers' eggs together, Callum and his mother, and had spied a nest at the same time, and she had made a little sigh of discovery which he hardly heard above the wind, and leaned to take the eggs, and then been lifted away. It seemed she had gone willingly. Perhaps she put the basket down before reaching for the nest, but in his memory the gesture was after the wind had already plucked her tiny feet from off their purchase on the rocky incline, as if she left the basket upright with four perfect eggs, for him.

He stood there, twelve years old, braced against wind from the Arctic Circle, clutching his own empty basket and staring over the black bluff and knowing she was dead. Within minutes his emotions went from panic to a hatred as solid and tenacious as his own footing on the rocks. She would not have been on the cliff collecting plovers' eggs if she had not been driven from her home in the Highlands to make room for the sheep. And she would not have been driven from her home if the English factor Patrick Sellar had not ordered his twenty-four constables and shepherds to set the house timbers on fire even while she sat on the sod roof and spoke her protest in Gaelic. It was Callum who had forced her from the roof. She would not have gone otherwise. And she would not, two months later, have been tossed by the wind like a piece of rubbish, into the sea.

He would never stop hating the salt smell of it. And here it was, rolling toward him like life itself, onto a different landscape in a different country, but still with the salty smell of exile.

"It shan't be buried till I'm buried," Callum said aloud, and dug the wretched scalp back up again. "We'll fit into the same patch of the earth," he said to it, and shoved it with the rosary back in the canvas bag.

In the morning he left Horse Pass, following the tracks of the ghost horse, and traveled northeast on the shore. He then journeyed up the Neches to Coushatta territory where he found a camp of friendly Indians cooking at a fire in the piney woods. They told him that they knew the half-breed named Métis, who had tried to win them over to the Mexicans, to fight. Métis had come to them as a paid emissary from a *Tejano* rancher named Domingo de la Rosa who was very powerful and wished to gain the trust of eastern Texas tribes. Métis had told them that the white men wanted to exterminate the Indians, and that Sam Houston's promises were lies. He said his *jefe,* De la Rosa, wished to earn their trust, on behalf of Mexico. Promising free plunder, he called for men and horses.

But they didn't want to sell their loyalty. They had retreated to the woods and scattered there. Métis had lingered for a while, then gone northward with his message and his offerings, searching for the leaders of the Kickapoos and Kichais. He traveled with a band of twenty Caddos on their yearly trading expedition.

Into the northland, to the Red River, west to the land of Wichitas, Callum Mackay followed the elusive half-breed, harboring no fear and carrying his own scalp in the canvas bag that dangled like a totem from a thong around his waist. Sometimes while he rode he spoke aloud in Gaelic to the dead who kept him company, his voice rasping with the slow and rocking gait of his sorrel mare. He rode into the mountains and recalled the Highlands of his youth, chanting sluggishly the Scottish songs of exile, the songs of all the many dispossessed—

> *From the lone shieling of the misty island*
> *Mountains divide us, and the waste of seas—*
> *Yet still the blood is strong, the heart is Highland,*
> *And we in dreams behold the Hebrides.*

THE ROAD NORTH

Hugh's parting from the other doctors was a painful severance. Shackelford, particularly, seemed an aged and fallen man. He had furnished uniforms of fringed red cloth and raised a company from his hometown to wear the uniforms. He had furnished guns. His son and two young nephews were among the company, and all of them were dead now.

It was raining on that morning when Hugh Kenner and the aide whom he had chosen said good-bye to the others and went out through the gates to where Crucita, Adelaido, and the guards were waiting. Hugh knew he was blessed to be going, yet he felt it like a banishment, for he was leaving Miles and Toby and the place where they had spent those last tormented days together. He remembered those days now with longing and a sadness that was kinder than his grief; a poignant feeling that would never leave him. He was to ride away and leave their bodies on the soggy prairie as carrion for vultures, and this because Portilla chose him as the surgeon best at amputations, best at severance.

He could refuse to go, and stay here with his dead. There was a moment in that morning, in the rain, when he placed his foot up in the stirrup just outside the gates of the presidio, that he almost said he would not go.

Yet he pulled himself into the saddle.

Despite the shortage, De la Rosa had procured five mounts—the best that he could spare, though they were old and thin. Hugh knew that De la Rosa did it so Crucita would not have to walk. Though De la Rosa offered to give Donde back to Adelaido, Portilla intervened. Adelaido was a prisoner. He would ride in handcuffs, double with a guard, since his talent as a horseman was well known and he might make a wild escape if given means.

They crossed the river at the place where Hugh had crossed with Toby just two weeks before.

Only once he looked back, but the rain obscured his vision. He saw nothing of the fort once he had left it. A curtain had been drawn.

Adelaido rode with one of the two guards, behind the escort on his pony. The aide whom Hugh had chosen was a man named Hopkins, spared by the Mexicans though he was not a doctor. Hugh had chosen him to go along because he wished to save him from insanity: Hopkins was so haunted by the violence he'd seen he was withdrawing from reality. He rarely spoke, and since the day of the massacre he had refused to wash himself or clean his clothes. It was Hopkins and another whom the Mexicans had sent to carry drinking water from the river on the evening of Palm Sunday, and they returned with empty barrels saying that the river was too stained with blood to draw clean drinking water, for the soldiers had been washing out the dead men's clothes.

Hopkins rode in silence now, brooding. Neither he nor Hugh were required to be handcuffed during any of the journey, though the guards were armed and under orders to shoot them if they should attempt escape.

They traveled slowly, sometimes in the road and sometimes on the trails, twenty miles a day, mostly in the rain. On the second day they met a rider coming down from Béxar, who told them Santa Anna had moved his army eastward out of Béxar, toward Gonzales. Hugh was surprised to hear it, since Houston's army had believed two weeks ago that Santa Anna was en route behind them moving eastward in their wake. As he listened though, he learned the truth: Santa Anna had sent two divisions in pursuit of Houston, but he himself had stayed in San Antonio de Béxar, planning strategy.

The escort and the guards conversed with the rider awhile, sitting on their mounts in the road with a tepid sun hanging low on the horizon. Then the rider left them, going south toward La Bahía, and the travelers veered northward toward Gonzales.

The escort was a heavy, verbose man with a bulbous nose and a friendly manner. He was *Tejano*, from a ranch near Béxar, and knew of Adelaido's reputation as a horseman. He treated Adelaido with respect, sitting his own saddle in a sloppy way and gesturing while he spoke.

There were many rumors about Santa Anna's plans, he told the guards as they rode on. Hugh listened, comprehending only half of what was said. He understood that many of the officers had turned against their president-general, who was often high on opium and raging. It was said among the officers that Santa Anna thought the war was over, with Sam Houston in retreat and the country cleared of the Americans. It was said he spoke of going home, and it was said he would have done it if his pride did not prevent it. It was said that Santa Anna's victory at the Alamo had cost him more men than he could afford to lose—hundreds still lay maimed in Béxar, in need of surgery—and that it gained him nothing but a devastated chapel. Urrea was the general who had won the victories that mattered. If Santa Anna turned south and went home, while Houston fled into the east, history would determine that Urrea won the war.

It was said that Santa Anna would go east and follow Houston toward the border, for no reason other than his pride. The government, the people, and the army of Americans in Texas, all were flying for the border of Louisiana in a frantic route, and they would likely keep on going whether Santa Anna followed them or not. So the escort said.

The guards asked many questions on the four days of the journey, but the prisoners didn't speak much. The rain drained all the clouds, the nights descended and the mornings rose, and then more clouds came rolling from the west, with rain. Hugh felt the rocking of the horse beneath him, the cool and timeless air and the silent presence of Crucita on the tired mare beside him. She wore her brown dress and a striped serape which Domingo de la Rosa gave her for the journey, a black hat with a flat crown in the Spanish style, which was also a gift from the great ranchero.

Sometimes Adelaido told his stories, but his hands were bound behind him and his voice was flat. At night his feet were hobbled. He was riding to his judgment, and maybe to his death. Crucita never spoke of it. Her eyes were vague and did not seem to rest on anything too long. When she looked at Adelaido her sadness was so visible it was as if she had already lost him.

On the third morning Hugh awoke beneath a blanket wet with dew. The sky was balmy gray. Crucita was not beside the cookfire with the others. Adelaido, waiting by the fire for his food, saw the doctor's eyes in search of her and told him she had gone into the trees to dress herself.

Hugh thought of how Crucita had stayed beside him while he was at La Bahía; sometimes even when he didn't feel her presence, she had been there. Sometimes he had felt her presence almost eerily, with such intensity it was as if she were the only other person left alive. In the moment when he held her in his arms inside the *calabozo,* he had felt a sharp and stunning severance from the life he knew, the people he had known, from Rose especially. Rose had borne the sons who were now dead. She did not even know that they were dead. His life with Rose had been a different life from what Crucita gave him when she saved him from the massacre. Rose did not know him, now.

Crucita knew him perfectly. In the days between Palm Sunday and Good Friday, he had never felt that there was anything he needed to explain. She had been with him while he performed the amputation, her broad features and small hands, the front tooth with the chip, an endearing flaw. The circumstances of their daily lives had been unspeakable, working with the loathsome, worm-infested bodies and the memories, and their only comfort came from one another.

Through the rolling plains and the mottes of live oak and mesquite, they rode, Crucita on the weary mare beside him. When it rained it seemed to Hugh they were alone together in the landscape, pocketed by rain, for she rode very close to him. He was aware of every movement that she made, every word she said, her graceful posture and the way she held the reins. He wanted more than anything to have her next to him, and closer still, to talk to her in private and to comfort her. His longing was the only feeling that he knew besides despair, and on the last night of the journey, when they stopped to sleep, he dared to lie so close he heard her breathing.

Adelaido lifted on his elbow, a silhouette against the night, and whispered, "If I'm condemned and shot, will you take her to Domingo de la Rosa. She has no where else to go."

"I'll care for her," Hugh said, not even knowing what he meant.

A low mesquite limb overhead, shaggy with its fragile growth of spring, dangled its new leaves into the dark and humid breeze.

They said nothing more.

In the afternoon of the fourth day when they neared Gonzales, Hugh began to feel his former life confronting him. He recognized the landmarks of the town: he recognized a stand of oaks where he and Toby had stopped to pull some stickers out of Coon Dog's paws, on their way to Goliad. He felt so sick with grief that nausea turned his stomach.

The buildings of the town lay scattered in ashes from the fires set by Houston's men, and muddy streets were lined with canvas tents. There were so many soldiers Hugh could not estimate the number. Many wore their jackets on bare skin and had no shoes. Some wore moccasins and sandals, and stopped their activities to watch the group of travelers riding in on Water Street, winding their way through the tents with the escort leading on his pony. They stared at Hugh—a foreigner, a spectacle. It was noon, and damp, and there were cookfires blazing. The canvas tents were full of holes and frayed along the seams and the soldiers seemed an army of forsaken orphan children.

Hugh hardly looked at them. What he was seeing, was the town. He saw it like the disfigured body of a dead friend. Thomas Miller's store, where he had purchased farm tools and house supplies and fabrics for Rose, was ashes now. In the hat factory of Almeron Dickenson and George Kimble, where Toby had been fitted for his first good hat when he turned ten, there were stumps of burned furniture still placed where they had been. Winslow Turner's inn was a blackened shell with the fireplace still standing and the spreading oak charred black but upright like a monument to all that had been lost. Hugh thought of how the men of this town all were burned to ashes too, in pyres at the Alamo. His mind played tricks on him. He remembered phrases of the Christmas songs the pianist at Turner's inn had played one winter afternoon when he and Rose had spent the day shopping for a Christmas gift for Katie. They had bought a pair of kidskin gloves and talked of how they wished that Katie had more opportunity to wear them, and they had passed the inn and heard the singing of a solo—"What child is this, which laid to rest, on Mary's lap is sleeping?"

He began to think that Adelaido would be executed. He thought there would be nothing left he cared about, except Crucita. He felt that Rose was dead, that Katie would forget him, that his mother would not make it to the border. He rode like one who has been banished and returns at last, an old man, and finds that everyone he ever knew is dead and everything he ever touched is gone.

The escort led them to a group of soldiers gathered around a piglet roasting on a spit, and the soldiers knew the escort and called him by his name, asking where he'd been. "La Bahía," he said soberly. "The orders of *El Presidente* were obeyed, and all of the Americans were shot."

The soldiers stood in silence with the smoke and smell of meat hanging in the air. The oldest shook his head. "Beast," he said. "He's not a president, he's turned into a king."

The escort asked where he could find "the king," and was told that Santa Anna had moved east toward the Colorado with a picked division. Generals Tolsa and Ramírez y Sesma were supposedly already at the Colorado.

The soldiers were looking at Crucita. She ignored them, tilting her head back to look up at the blackened branches of the tree against the drizzling sky, then turned to watch a barefoot soldier chasing a chicken through the wreck of fallen, sooty boards where the inn had stood, the bottom of his feet flashing black with soot as if they had been charred.

The escort asked where he could find General Filisola, and the youngest of the group brushed his hand through the air, saying, "Filisola is unreasonable today. He's had three men whipped for no reason. You should go to Cós instead."

This statement got Crucita's full attention and she turned to look the escort in the eyes, saying she had met Cós once, when he passed through Goliad—it was October last, she said. She met him with Domingo de la Rosa at a cockfight in the town. "If you take Adelaido to General Cós, can I go with you?" she asked.

The escort leaned back in his saddle. "You want to speak on his behalf?"

"Yes."

He shrugged. "Then come," he said, and turned to Hopkins. "Señor

Hopkins, you stay here. Adelaido, Doctor, and Crucita, come with me
and let's be done with it."

General Cós was in a tent with General Filisola near the outskirts of
the camp, and when the escort called him out to see the doctor and the
prisoner, Cós said he had no time for trivialities. He stood inside the
entry to the tent, looking at the group of travelers who had dismounted
and were waiting in the misty rain. He glanced at Hugh, and told the
escort he would find a way to send the doctor on to Santa Anna later.
"The prisoner, was he bearing arms against us?" Cós demanded.

The escort knew that Adelaido's fate could be determined by the
wording of his answer, and was hesitant to place his words. "It's said,
that for a while, he did. But only for a while, and then he had a change
of heart and he came willingly to Goliad when—"

"Did he carry arms against his country?" Cós repeated sharply.

The escort turned to Adelaido.

Adelaido raised his chin. His hair hung damp and glossy to his
shoulders, and all his pride shone in his eyes. "I did," he said. "And by
my choice, I do no longer."

Cós stood scrutinizing Adelaido, a bitter look on his pale face. It
seemed from his expression Cós was likely to condemn the prisoner,
with just a word and gesture. His hand was resting on the tent flap in
such a way that he could pull the flap down, closed, with a single finger,
and Crucita noted dimly how his nails were manicured, and recalled
how gracefully he used his hands to hold the glass of mescal she had
brought him on their meeting in the dim jacal back in Goliad. She read
the general's face and looked to Hugh, but there was nothing he could
do, for any word Hugh uttered in defense of Adelaido would implicate
the proud *Tejano* as a friend of Anglos.

Crucita stepped forward. She had taken off her hat and was holding
it against her skirt. The mist was speckled on her hair. "I've met you
before, General, in Goliad with Domingo de la Rosa at a cockfight, in
October," she said quietly, and with formality. "Since then I've been
working as a spy for Señor de la Rosa. This is my brother, Adelaido, you
are judging, and I ask you with respect to be merciful."

Cós looked at her, annoyed, impatient. He was in no mood for complications. Someone from within the tent was calling him, and he sighed heavily and looked out toward the trees as if he longed to walk away from everything. Then he turned his attention to the escort and said with irritation, "I can't think about this now. I have important matters. I can't condemn a man to death without the time to think. Bring the man along, and keep him tied. *El Presidente* can decide, later, when we join him." Then without another glance at anyone Cós flicked his finger, pulling down the flap.

Chapter 36

THE RUNAWAY SCRAPE

WASHINGTON ON THE BRAZOS

The ragamuffin children had the pink-eye and had given it to Samuel, who passed it on to Katie. She got it first in one eye, which ran so watery at night the liquid slid across the bridge of her nose when she was lying on her side, and dripped into the other eye, which turned so red and puffy on the next day she could barely see.

Grand's throat was white inside with pus. She had ulcers in her mouth and couldn't wear her dentures.

Rose had an ear infection and had stuffed a wad of damp tobacco in the ear to draw it out.

Only William seemed immune to the diseases, even to the whooping cough and diarrhea, but the poison ivy blisters were still torturing his hands.

They arrived at Old Washington, on the Brazos River, in the wagon, in the rain.

Up to now the exodus had been a line of straggling refugees but here there was a throng like nothing they had seen. Rumors said that Houston and his army were downriver several miles and heading east pursued by Mexicans. Anybody left behind was left to Santa Anna's mercy.

The people were in panic and the thoroughfares were jammed. Families lost their kinfolk. Kinfolk lost their faith. Houston was called coward. Whooping cough and measles and the pink-eye spread like flooding waters; rumors gusted through the camps on stormy winds.

There was the story of Comanches who attacked a group of refugees and killed two men and took a woman and two children captive. Reportedly the infant had its brains dashed out against a tree. The mother got away and wandered on the Colorado until she found some rangers camped on Brushy Creek. The rangers led a rescue raid upon the Indians at Walnut Creek and retrieved the woman's son—a child not four years old.

It was said another band of Indians stole seven horses from a camp at New Year Crossing. A different rumor said it was white horse thieves not the Indians.

There was the story that a man named King was eaten by an alligator on a tributary down near Lynchburg with his family witnessing. The alligator, fifteen feet in length, appeared in dusky light to be a log, and Mr. King, who had bad eyesight, carelessly stepped on its back and was attacked.

Another tragedy happened at the crossing there in Washington the day before when a baby crawled off the raft and drowned before it was discovered missing.

Other children had been separated from their mothers or abandoned, and one old man had hauled three of these orphans on a sled the whole way from the Colorado to the Brazos.

It was also said a lunatic with yellow eyes was preying on the slaves who tried to run away, tracking them and torturing the ones he captured. Three dismembered bodies were discovered near the mill on Yegua Creek in John Cole's settlement.

Every vehicle with wheels was rolling east. The movement had two names. Some were calling it "The Runaway," others christened it "The Scrape." By the time the movement reached the Brazos the two names joined into a phrase that held the terror and the sickness of the fleeing multitudes, and the flight came to be known as the fearful and profoundly shameful "Runaway Scrape."

It seemed the land, prostrate all these years, had had enough of rain and people and war and lifted on its haunches to spill out the entire mess in a wash of water toward the border and the sea. The government was on the run. Deserters from the army who were searching for their families fled eastward spreading rumors of the Texan army's weakness and ineptitude, and spreading word that Fannin and his men had been defeated in a battle, though no one knew for sure if it was true.

Grand said it was not true. It could not be.

Rose said very little.

Katie fell to such an anxious state she hardly got an hour's sleep a night.

It was a land without a law. Horse thieves posed as press gangs working for the army requisitioned steers and horses in Sam Houston's name.

Sam Houston and his name were cursed.

On the Brazos, at Old Washington, William and the Kenners had to wait three days for their turn on the ferry. Five hundred people crossed the river every day. The citizens of Washington and the government, with all its papers and the Declaration stuffed in several saddlebags, had fled. The street—the only street, a swath cut through the woods with stumps still standing in it—was filled with frantic exiles and the smell of excrement and the litter of a mob.

The flooding river ran two hundred yards across, brimming out of banks in a bloated six-mile current. Most refugees had dumped their tools somewhere along the roads to lighten their wagons, and had no means of building boats or sturdy rafts. Hundreds scattered to find cover in the cane growing in the bottoms.

The rain was God's own curse upon the people, and all of nature was against them.

The owner of the ferry cut his rates in two—fifty cents per wagon, thirty for a buggy with two horses, ten cents for adults, and five for children. He and his three helpers ran the ferry without interruption, using torches in the nights, but it could carry only passengers with their draft animals—no extra cattle—and many of the refugees had cattle with them. The bank was lined with people herding cattle in the bulging river. The strongest cattle swam across but others bogged down in the marshy bottoms on the eastern side, among the cane, and were left to die. The weakest were swept away in crossing. Calves drowned, bobbing with the driftwood toward the sea. News that one division of the Mexicans had come as close as Bastrop and was marching east, while the infamous Urrea was approaching from the south, caused such alarm that some abandoned their belongings and their cattle on the bank and spent the balance of their money buying ferry rides across. Houston's army, said to be downriver, should protect them from Urrea, but with Houston in a mind or mood to run. . . . the Coward.

The Yellow Dog.

A petition was composed insisting that the folk with slaves should leave the slaves behind at the mercy of the Mexicans—that all the whites should be allowed to cross the river first. It claimed that slaves might have to be abandoned at the border anyway since U.S. laws prohibited importing foreign Negroes. It warned it was too dangerous to travel with so many slaves and few white men, in case the slaves should get it in their heads to turn against white women and the children.

The petition was presented to the Kenner women to be signed while they huddled underneath the wagon with their clothes soaked through. The bedraggled woman who delivered it squatted down beneath the wagon in her soggy brogans, pulled the parchment from her coat, and handed it to Rose, explaining what it was. Rain was pouring down in torrents and she had to shout above it with the flooring of the wagon leaking water on her head.

Rose said, "The slaves would be set free?"

The woman shrugged and answered, "The point is there ain't room or time to cross 'em over."

"I know the point," Rose said. "I asked if they would be set free."

"They'd be left," the woman said. "I reckon that's free."

Rose was hesitant.

Grand said bitterly, "Left naked, without food, I imagine, to be tracked down by the slavers or the lunatic."

The woman snatched the paper back from Rose and sloshed back out into the rain with it.

"We should have signed it," Katie said regretfully. "They'd be better off left here."

"I just don't know," Rose answered. "I don't know. They would be left with nothing."

On the next day Katie and William went down to the meeting tent beside the ferry landing to see how fast the ferry line was moving. The tent was a weathered tarp strung in the trees, crowded with more than a hundred steamy bodies. Pressing his way in, William reached for Katie's hand to pull her with him. She was reluctant to take hold, since his hand was scabby with the lumpy poison ivy blisters and she feared contagion.

Names were scrawled in charcoal on large boards at the front of the tent; each name was marked out when the family was crossed over on the ferry. The boards were made of shutters from a barn, and eight of them were used completely, covered front and back with names marked through, and thrown down in the mud beneath the tarp as flooring. The ninth was nearly full down to the bottom and propped against the wide stump of a sycamore. Someone was supposed to be in charge of writing down the names and calling the families with a cow horn when it came their turn, but the post had been abandoned. It was to each his own. There had been some cheating—insertion of new names of late arrivals thinking they could cut in line. These names were nestled in small print between the others, and William took the liberty of scratching out a few in front of "Kenner" and replacing them down near the bottom of the board.

From the look of it, the Kenners had at least another day to wait. Katie knelt and started counting down the names, pointing with her finger at each one and moving down, and William recognized the full extent of her fatigue and disappointment in the automation of her voice and movement, the low, quick slurring of her counting—"fifty-five, fifty-six"—and the angry look she gave an old man who jostled in front of her—"Can you just wait a minute, sir, I'm trying to count." Her generosity was worn down to a frazzle.

William put his hand across her shoulder, saying, "Kate—" and she swung a warning look around and up at him with the awful pink-eye seeping from both eyes, and continued counting, louder, "fifty-eight . . . fifty-nine . . . no . . ." And she paused. "It was sixty-eight . . . was it sixty-eight?" She looked up at him again, saying, "Now you made me lose my place."

The old man was kneeling and pushing in between the board and Katie with a chunk of charcoal in his grizzled hand. William tried to rescue him from Katie's wrath by taking the wrath himself. "Don't turn those awful eyes on me," he said to her, in the manner of a joke.

But it was not a joke to her. She was ugly, she was tired, she was frightened for her father and her brothers. Standing up, she shoved her palm at William's chest, which in her state of weakness did not budge him. "Let me *go*," she said as if he held her.

"Kate, I was only joking," he appealed.

"Just stop it then. All right?" She saw his eyes were watering because he looked at her, her own eyes being truly ugly and inflamed. Repulsive, truly. She stepped around him, through the crowd, and went out toward the riverbank.

The landing for the ferry raft was on a steep slope at the tail end of the road that passed through town, so vehicles could drive straight down the road, and down the slope, onto the raft. The road was crowded with pedestrians and vehicles. There was a squealing pig and some commotion; the pig had been injured by a vehicle. Katie shoved through the mob and on across the road, through a herd of several dozen cattle. Lifting her skirt so as not to drag it in the water puddles, Katie picked her way downstream in the misty rain along the bank toward a stand of cottonwoods on a sandy point. The bank was soft with loamy mud that sucked her shoes, and she left footprints like deep postholes. When she'd labored only thirty yards, the mud, like quagmire, tugged her left shoe off her foot and she turned back to pick it up, but saw that William was behind her following so close in the misty rain he could have heard the noise the sludge made sucking at her shoes. His soggy clothes stuck to him and his hat sagged down on either side like floppy ears.

She left the shoe and wheeled around and kept on toward the point, imagining how clumsy and how ugly she must look to William from behind, without any grace at all, her hips too wide and one shoe off and one shoe on, like some big child who never learned to walk. She yanked the second off, and carried it. Glancing back, she saw that William had retrieved the other shoe. He waved the shoe and called out, "Kate, slow down!"

The stand of cottonwoods out on the point seemed like a kind of refuge but the nearer she got, the deeper the mud, and she saw the point was precarious since floods had washed the bank away below it. It was a steep drop of several yards with water flowing rapidly beneath. She walked out on the point to the cottonwoods, which were tall and leafy and shedding stringy cotton fluff. They grew without much grass or vegetation at their roots, and Katie leaned against the biggest one and said to William when he got up close, "I came out here to be alone."

He settled back against a tree beside her. "If this ground gives way, don't expect me to save you," he said, and dropped the shoe and crossed his arms, looking at the water.

Side by side they stood with the drizzle quickening to rain, large drops falling on them through the trembling leaves. She recalled how Toby used to say the raindrops on the water were like fairies dancing. She was cold and dropped the shoe beside the other, crossed her arms beneath her breasts, and snuggled her fists into the warm flesh underneath her armpits. Her eyesight was impaired by the pink-eye and the rain but she watched the ferry toiling in the brown water forty yards upstream, returning from depositing a load of refugees, the paddles of four rowers lifting and plunging down again. She could see out on the eastern bank where swampy yellow cane grew tall and thick.

William said, "I wasn't serious about your eyes."

"It's true though. I look horrible."

"Not so bad," he said.

The drops against her face annoyed her and she tried to shield her eyes against them with her hand, placing it against her forehead as if scrutinizing off across the river. She thought of that day in October back at home when William was beside her staring at the river and she'd looked past him up the bank and seen Josh Hanlin lying in the bushes with Coon Dog licking at his wounds. "I'm just worried about Father and the boys," she said. "I can't sleep."

"I know," he said. "I can't either."

Her anger slid away. "Do you wish you'd gone with them?"

"No, I promised your father I'd stay with you."

And she ventured it. From a heart accustomed to its restless ways, she flung the words out: "Do you love me?"

He tucked his hands in his pockets and looked out at the water. "Yes," he said, "but you give me pause."

"What is that supposed to mean?"

"Just that I don't hope for things the way you do. You take hold of things and then you have this fear of losing them, and that fear gives you passion, but it doesn't give you any sense."

"And you just don't take hold," she said. "You get *pause* and don't take hold."

He sighed and crossed his arms again. The rain was easing back into a mist. "I don't want you to get hurt. And I'm afraid you will."

"Maybe you're afraid *you* will," she said.

He looked at her as if she'd slapped him with her words, then she stepped up next to him, took hold of his crossed arms, and uncrossed them, pulling them around her like a coat. He took her braid and tugged it gently so she'd tilt her head to look at him, and when she did—even with the ugly pink-eye weeping down her face in tears—he smiled at her and picked a wad of cotton, fallen from the tree, out of her hair. "Maybe so," he said.

They were distracted by something taking place upstream at the ferry landing. Iris Parton was boarding the ferry with three slaves, a mule, and one cart hitched up to an ox. Assembled on the landing were the rest of her belongings, including six slaves, two horses, two mules, a milk cow, and three yoke of oxen hitched to wagons.

"Her name wasn't on the board," Katie said.

"No, it wasn't."

"I bet she's bribed the ferryman. She told Mother she had a thousand dollars sewn in her corset."

"Evidently."

"It'll take three runs to get them over."

"At least."

The crowd on the landing was angry. A woman waded to her knees and started screaming after Iris Parton.

"It was her who brought us that petition," Katie said.

"It was *she*," he corrected.

"What?"

"She is the predicate nominative."

"Oh, stop it. I don't like that."

The ferryman was moving out to meet the current and the scene was washed in rain. Iris Parton in a blue dress climbed up in the cart beside the driver, a small black boy. Suddenly the woman standing in the water raised a gun and shot the mule on the ferry, and the mule fell to its knees beside one of the rowers, rolled on its side and began kicking its hind legs. The rower kicked the mule until it rolled and flopped into the water.

Iris Parton was screaming at the woman, who was holding up the pistol like a torch of light.

The body of the shaggy mule slid by the point of cottonwoods, close enough for William and Katie to see the floppy ears. It floated like a drifting log, riding just below the surface and then bobbing up again, rolling so that now and then the hind legs or the tip of the nose parted the water's troubled surface.

"Is it dead?" Katie asked. "Its legs are moving."

"It's just the water moving them," he answered.

They stood in the rain entwined together on the precipice beneath the leafy cottonwoods, watching as the body slid downstream. William thought about the woman with the gun and all the deep depravity that humans had created, and Katie said, "For sure it's dead by now," and William said, "It has to be."

On the next day a newly married couple cut some cane with a machete and secured it in a framework tied with rawhide thongs, then killed a cow and stretched the hide around the frame to make a boat. It was flimsy but it got them over.

A group of women and young boys gathered pieces of loose floatwood and tied the corners with hemp ropes, placing cross-sticks in both directions. Then two women and a boy climbed on and shoved into the current and the raft broke in pieces. All the luggage sank. One of the women couldn't swim, but wore a riding skirt of camel's hair impervious to water, which buoyed her until three boys swam out to rescue her.

William and Katie helped others construct rafts, but didn't make one for themselves, deciding it would be too dangerous to cross Grand and Samuel that way.

A steamboat called the *Yellow Stone* was plying down the Brazos River on that afternoon, hauling bales of cotton toward the sea as if there were no war. The boat had been in Texas for two months or more;

it had brought the Mobile Grays and now it stopped and loaded up with refugees who'd had enough of traveling by land and wished to go by sea. It would carry them downriver to Velasco and to Galveston. William and the Kenners talked of boarding, but space was limited and costs were high and hazards even higher, as Santa Anna and Sam Houston would be crossing somewhere downstream on the Brazos and no one could predict exactly where. The steamboat, a sidewheeler with a deep draft, two stacks, and a keel of a hundred and thirty feet, could achieve impressive speed. But William estimated it would burn six hundred cords in passage to Velasco, meaning frequent stops to chop and take on wood, and this set Rose against the thought of going.

So for another day they camped in muddy Washington waiting for their turn on the ferry raft. When it finally came, they crossed without an incident, then had to journey through the swampy snake-infested canebrakes, littered with bogged cattle carcasses, and wait a day in line beneath dripping sycamores to raft the Navasota. For miles they slogged with others through the turbid bottomland so flooded that the water came up in the wagon bed. The cane pulled at their clothes and scratched their faces. Where there was no cane, the current was so strong it parted in a wake around the wagon and at places it was easier to swim than walk.

Grand and the youngest of the ragamuffins—the sullen boy named Joel—rode together in the wagon, which would bog with any other weight. Grand sat in her rocking chair with water swirling at her ankles and the soggy strip of canvas draped above her head. Joel sat beside her on the cowhide trunk, trembling with chills and hugging in beneath the canvas while the older brother and the girl trudged beside in river trash and rain, and Rose and Katie took turns carrying Samuel. Samuel's blankets were so wet he was a heavy load. William sloshed beside the ox, coaxing it along, sometimes toting Samuel on his back.

Several times the wagon stuck, and the trunks and chairs had to be unloaded, and Grand was lifted from the wagon to the stack of baggage. Then the others set their weight against the rear wheels and the tailgate, shoving from behind.

It took a full day to travel just four miles.

They reached Cow Cooper's flooded farm early the next morning.

Cow had got his name from his extensive herds of cattle, now loitering in water to their bellies. Several hundred refugees were camping in the barns and sheds of Cooper's settlement. The smokehouse was opened to everyone. Some took far more than their share, hauling ribs and haunches eastward on their sleds. "Just leave enough for me," Cow Cooper said repeatedly, standing in the smokehouse in a throng of people with the roof dripping water on his shoulders and the chickens roosting in the rafters.

The Kenner women took the children to the mule shed and crowded in around a smoky fire, turning front to back to dry their clothes. They took their shoes off and their feet were shriveled white with water log, the dead skin sloughing off in grisly patches. Katie's eyes were globbed with mucous. The smoke clogged in her throat. Noise beneath the shed was deafening with children howling and the sick coughing and rain beating on the tin.

The buck-toothed ragamuffin, Jeffrey, stood by Katie in wet trousers shredded by the cane, saying that his throat hurt when he swallowed.

"Then don't swallow," Katie answered. She was tired of the children. She had the pink-eye, thanks to them.

By evening they were camping with a dozen other families on high ground along the western bank of Clear Creek, which seemed more like a river. They had no way to get the wagon over and Rose and William strolled a distance in the woods to make a plan while the others slept practically on top of one another.

They could leave the wagon but for Grand, who had a fever and difficulty walking on her swollen ankles. The rain had stopped for now but it would start again, so the creek wouldn't go down by morning. They returned to camp without a plan. Rose leaned back against the muddy wagon's wheel and said good night to William, the soft glow of the camp fire flickering across her tired face and on the wild limbs of the buttonwood behind the wagon.

William felt very tender toward her. In a gesture that was rare for him, he put his arm around her shoulders. He could smell the damp tobacco she had stuffed in her bad ear, and her warm skin. "Try to sleep," he said, and stepped back, looking in her eyes. "I'll keep watch."

With a look he never would forget, she said, "One of them is dead."

A whippoorwill was calling from across the creek. The frogs were chirping and the breeze was rustling the leaves.

"One of them," she said again, "is dead. One of my boys is dead."

In the morning Rose was up before dawn, sitting with a quiet woman by the name of Francis Sutherland, brewing coffee at the camp fire. Thunder pounded the horizon and a mist was falling. A rider rode into camp and said that Santa Anna, with a small command, had crossed the Brazos down near San Felipe.

They would have to move on and leave the wagon behind, since they couldn't cross it. While the women unpacked trunks and chose what objects could be left, William hammered the tailgate loose to use as a raft. He chopped three low limbs from an ash tree and secured them to the bottom of the gate with ropes. It was painful work with blistered hands.

Rose and Katie loaded the gate with all of the provisions it could bear without submerging.

Stripping to his trousers, William waded to his waist in the cold water and shoved the burdened gate in front of him. It was six feet long and three feet wide, unwieldy in the current. He swam the thirty yards across, pushing it before him.

The other refugees made rafts from boards and floatwood. William made two trips across and back, then got out and tied a lead rope to the ring that pierced the ox's nose and led the ox and Loco into the water. Since most of Loco's back was under water, she let William mount without reacting much. Coaxing Loco to swim, William trailed the clumsy ox behind, and with only a little difficulty in mid-stream he got the creatures over.

When it was time for the children to cross, Molly and Jeffrey insisted they could swim the distance, and William made them hold on to the gate on either side of him and use it as a float, treading with their legs. He placed Joel, who could not swim, on the center of the gate, and they forded safely. Grand Irma, when it was her turn, balanced in the center holding her fine china platter and a bundle of damp blankets in her lap. Her skirt trailed in the water and her hairpins had come loose beneath her bonnet. Strands of gray hair hung about her face like weeds. William tried to keep the gate from rocking, scissoring his legs without splashing on the surface of the water, but his progress was erratic due to his fatigue.

He returned to find Katie in an anxious state, holding Samuel on her hip and insisting that she go along to help in crossing him. She reprimanded William for not checking on the knots that held the pine limbs to the bottom of the gate, and then apologized and waded out and took her skirt off under water while standing with her feet sunk in the bottom sludge. Dragging up the wet wad of material, she sloshed it onto the gate beside Samuel. Then she helped propel the gate by kicking, one arm wrapped around the screeching child. Her eyes were running with the pink-eye, her bare legs parted underneath the surface in rhythmic sweeping movements, and her braid trailed out behind her. She had so many splinters in her arm by the time they reached the other side, she did not even try to pick them out, and William handed her the skirt to put back on.

Rose waded out and swam across alone, her thin skirt twisted by the current like a winding sheet.

In the clearing on the western bank underneath the spreading buttonwood, the wagon and the bull-hide trunk sat empty and abandoned. The rocking chair, the only thing left in the wagon, rocked slightly in the breezy morning drizzle, as if the ghost of some poor woman were still sitting there.

With fever and raw throats and eyes weeping infection, they pressed eastward, deep into the piney woods toward the river called the Trinity. Through forsaken settlements they journeyed with the stream of refugees. The people of this area had left their homes in such a hurry many left their meals spread on their tables. Pans of milk were molding in the dairies of the farms and cribs were full of corn. Feathers from torn mattresses lay trampled in the mud. Dogs sat on the porches howling at the refugees and sometimes trailed a distance after them. Garden truck and young corn flourished in the rain. There was food here for the taking and shelter in the nights, but a mood of slow despair descended on the people. What they found to take from others, they had also left behind. Someone else was eating poultry they had raised and sleeping on their linens in the homes which they had built. Someone else was butchering their hogs. There was no ownership but what the people toted in their arms or dragged along behind on sleds made out of sticks and river wash.

The roads were strewn with objects which they could no longer carry, and along the way were crosses where the dead were buried.

Chapter 37

A VILLAGE OF COTTON

Past creeks named Tejocote, Vaca, and the Navidad, General Filisola led his army eastward in the wake of Santa Anna, the soldiers and their wives all sick with colic and the dysentery, sick for home, sick of rain and mud and rationed bites of bull beef without salt. Hugh Kenner grew so weary nursing them through day and night his movements were a drunken man's and he was clumsy with his hands. He hardly ate, and was so thin his clothes no longer fit him. His beard grew chalky-white. Crucita helped him all she could and pitied him his pain, doing seamstress work to buy for him a shirt that wasn't torn. Hugh stayed among the sick at night and when Frank Hopkins tended them Hugh dropped into a sleep so deep the world all fell away. Crucita spread her dirty blankets on the ground and spread out Adelaido's too, since he was kept in bondage with the handcuffs on his wrists behind his back. At night Adelaido suffered the discomfort and the shame of hobbles on his ankles, a humiliation he himself had never imposed even on a worthless pony. Without his hands he was dependent on Crucita for his food, his rest; she fed him like a child. He could not even work the buttons of his pants without her.

Days passed into nights without much telling of it and when morning came the light was wet and morbid. But the air was always cool and smelled of spring. The birds sang even in the rain.

Hugh was well acquainted with these roads. He passed tilled fields of families he knew, their houses burned to rubble, a forsaken sawmill where he'd purchased boards with Miles to lay the flooring of their home.

At the Navidad, Filisola got word that Santa Anna now was camping on the Brazos in the ruins of San Felipe, which the Anglos had burned. Houston, it was said, had crossed the Brazos just before him, running like a hen.

On the Colorado there came word that Santa Anna was now chasing Houston on across the Brazos and Filisola should follow.

It took three rainy days to haul the baggage and artillery across the flooded Colorado. The cattle had to be abandoned on the western bank, so fifty steers were slaughtered and the meat cooked all night over smoky flames of many fires that sputtered in the rain.

The army then continued past the Colorado to Arenosa Creek and east through flowered swales and woods and slow acclivities between valley passes. In the middle of the month they marched through fields of wild rye and wild indigo and reached the burned remains of Stephen Austin's town, San Felipe, on the west bank of the Brazos River, in a dreary rain.

San Felipe was the center of the mother colony of all the Anglo colonies in Texas, which Stephen Austin had once dreamed would be the cotton capital of all the world, and it was lying prostrate veiled in sooty black like a ravaged widow. Austin's home and office had been burned and the fence posts plucked for fuel. What had been a town strung half a mile along the road beside the riverbank was now inhabited by ghosts. The Peyton tavern had the remnants of one wall. The tools within the blacksmith's shop remained in order in the open rain, and tins burned black were scattered in the ashes of Dinsmore's Dry Goods Store. There was nothing left of Whiteside's story-and-a-half hotel but rubble. Gail Borden, owner of the printing press—an inventor and a dreamer— would have nothing to come home to.

The cotton gin was standing, that was all.

And up and down the streets there was the cotton, armfuls of it strewn like snow among the ashes. The rebels had stacked bales of pro-

cessed cotton for a quarter mile along the loamy riverbank. Evidently
they had planned to hold the town and use the cotton as a breastworks,
then changed their minds and burned the town instead. Santa Anna's
army had come through and used the cotton for their beds. Filisola's
now did the same. The women with the army carried bundles of it in
their arms and spread it out along the banks so they could bathe and
climb out of the water without stepping in the sand. They used it to fuel
fires and wrap wounds. They used it wastefully, a luxury to handle without care when all else in their lives was spare and rationed, and when
they pitched their tents at night the town was cloaked in rain, and cotton lay in sodden piles.

In the morning of the first day in the town of cotton, Hugh awakened to a squadron of the cavalry charging toward the river where a
foreign boat was passing, belching smoke. He and Adelaido went down
to the riverbank and watched the boat go by. It had the name *Yellow
Stone* painted on its side. Filisola, ignorant of such machines and the
speed the engines could achieve when moving with a current, ordered
the battalions of Guerrero, Aldama, Toluca, and the first active of Mexico, as well as a six-pounder, to fire on the steamboat as it passed. The
firepower was to no effect. The cannon plopped one ball into the water,
jamming on its second shot, and passengers stood on the deck and
jeered, shouting insults through cupped hands.

They were Anglo-Americans, of course.

It felt to Hugh as if his life and all the memories connecting him
with Rose were streaming down the river past him.

Later that day he set up his hospital with fifty patients in the cotton
gin at the end of town. The gin was a three-story wooden structure
untouched by the fire. He placed his patients on the dirt floor of the
bottom level where the wheel was circled by the tracks of mules, since
several officers had claimed the second story for themselves. The third
floor was divided into stalls packed full of raw seed cotton, and would
have made good lodging, but portions of the roof were gone and the
stalls were flooded.

He knew that he would likely lose two of his patients before morning. One of them was dying of lockjaw. The other was a woman from
Toluca who had walked to Texas. She had followed her husband and her
son who were conscripted into the army, and while crossing the Brazos

she was bitten by a water moccasin, a deadly cottonmouth. She had tried to cauterize the wound herself by igniting it with powder, and her foot came nearly off.

There also was a man who shot himself by accident and severed all the leaders of his toes, which meant that he could only balance on his heel. He had fallen into melancholy so intense he would not speak. There were soldiers with teeth so rotten they couldn't chew the stringy beef, which was the only food, and others doubled up with cramps or bloated with colic. Hugh rubbed camphor on their bellies and their swollen gums to ease the pain and pulled teeth by the dozens.

In the middle of that night, when it was Hopkins's shift on duty, Hugh retired to the lean-to propped against the backside of the gin. It was a simple storage shed, a halfway place where processed cotton could be loaded into baskets to be hauled off to the cotton press for baling. There was no entry from the gin into the shed, except a wooden chute running from the second story down through the tin roof of the shed, used to drop the cotton down after it was processed by the gin. So Hugh had to go outside and wade through sludge around the gin to reach the shed. The rain had let up and a moon three-quarters full shone stark white in between the scudding clouds. It glistened on the tin roof of the lean-to and on the standing water in the furrowed fields of cotton, the shoots now sprouting from the mud but not yet showing buds. Cotton fiber lay thick on the ground beneath the shed like lint, some of it raked into baskets ready to be taken to the cotton press, the rake still leaning as it had been left against the side beam of the shed.

There, Hugh made his bed. The moon shone on the cotton as it shone on rippling clouds, and Hugh took off his clothes, which had the smell of blood, and sank his naked body in the silky floss, spreading it across him like the waters of a bath. His knees and shoulders ached from stooping over patients on the ground, but while he lay there looking from the darkness of the rafters to the brightness of the cotton covering the ground around him, he felt soothed and weightless. He looked out past the roof edge to the moon between the clouds. It hung down low enough to shine on him and on the cotton he lay buried in, but shadows crawled about the corners where the moonlight did not reach.

His mind was grappling with these shadows and he closed his eyes, and there were shadows in his mind. He felt the shadows were like faces in his childhood and he doted on them, fixing them in memory like butterflies pinned on a board in groups according to the size and color of the wings, without motion, fading with the dusty colors of the wings smudged half away by too much morbid handling. These were not the shadows he had lived with and had come to know as one becomes familiar with the light and dark that moves across his garden with the passage of the day. These were shadows cast by nothing solid, without meaning, without shape or form that he could name. He sank down into them, and then he slept, and felt her hands upon him parting all the shadows and letting in the light.

"Rose?" he said. "Rose?"

But it wasn't Rose, it was Crucita kneeling in the moonlight, on the cotton, her dark face framed but not illuminated by the light. She said, "Do not say anything."

He was so in love with her and so in need of her he could not separate one feeling from another. He touched her cheek and moved his finger down her neck and lay there looking at her face framed by the moonlight, and she leaned forward, sinking down into the cotton next to him, and laid her face against his arm so close to him their breathing came together. He spread the cotton over both of them and she wrapped both her arms around him and they lay there, very still.

Close against his soft beard, she whispered, "I think you don't forgive yourself for being alive, when Miles and Toby are dead."

"It's that I don't forgive myself for wanting to," he said.

"Ah, *entiendo*," she sighed. "*Entiendo.* I have the same feeling when my family died."

Gently, with his hands, he started taking hold of her, exploring how her body curved and folded into his, the way her lips were parted. With his thumb he felt the jagged edge of her chipped tooth, and touched her face, and smoothed her hair. When she began to touch his skin he lay very still again remembering the movements of her hands against the sick and wounded with such vivid recollection that it almost seemed he was familiar with her touch, it was not new. He listened to her warm breath in the cotton and the small sounds that she made, and felt her lips against his own, his tongue against the chip on her front tooth, the warm taste of her mouth. It was life that he was feeling, as holy as the resurrection, after death. She gave it to him with her breath. She took his hands in hers and kissed the fingers, then undid the buttons of her skirt and blouse herself because his hands were swollen with the rheumatism and she knew it even in the dark of all the mounded cotton, for she knew his hands as intimately as she knew her own.

He did not lose himself in her calm presence, though he might have if he'd been a different man. Instead he found himself, allowing the discovery, choosing and pursuing it, slow and careful with his thoughts and with his feelings. He thought of Rose and how he loved her. He thought of Miles and Toby shot down in the prairie and the columns of black smoke rising from the piles of burning bodies. He felt Crucita's living body with his hands and thought of things which he had not been willing to think of for some time, and thought how kind Crucita was and how she knew him perfectly, and he took comfort knowing there was nothing to explain. She knew, of course, he was in love with her. She also knew the love would bring her pain. Yet still she wanted it, and both of them took hold of it, as if he gave his grief to her and she gave hers to him and both of them accepted willingly. He held her face within his crippled hands, her cheekbones nestling perfectly into his palms, as smooth and delicate to touch as his mother's precious china teacups. He did not want to kiss her now, but simply to brush his dry lips against hers, to feel the breath once more drifting back and forth between their parted mouths. They whispered to each other with their lips still touching, speaking of sadness, of departure and death. He felt almost a gladness with Crucita in his arms that he could not bear to acknowledge, because it was a gladness that came to him after so much suffering, and the full cost of it, he knew, was yet to be reckoned. He traced the contour of her trembling lips with his tongue, then whispered her own name into her ear like a secret sound. She whimpered as he said it, as if it broke her heart, then pulled her skirt and blouse away and stretched her naked body down his side and wrapped her legs around his thighs.

Gropingly, though not so haltingly, their movements came together and they whispered things that neither of them would forget. When he pressed his body into hers there was nothing left to say, but everything to feel at once, a kind of urgent tenderness.

He released inside her all his grief with all its terrible intensity, and she received it all together, took it in and sobbed it out and lay beside him, weeping in his arms.

In the morning, in the cotton gin, they were told that they and Adelaido were to march ahead with General Cós and his five hundred men, to Santa Anna, who was to the east near the town of Lynchburg, beside the river of St. Hyacinth, known in Spanish as the river and the plains of San Jacinto.

CROSSING OVER

TRINITY RIVER

It was a night crossing on the Trinity. The river was spilling out of banks, spreading two miles out on either side and filling up the caney bottomlands between the hills. The rain had stopped. The moon, three-quarters full, shone bright enough to light the way.

They would have liked a daylight crossing better but the rain would start again by morning.

They had seen the ferry pathways from the hills, swaths cut through the mass of swampy cane, winding in between the sloughs like paths carved by worms in soft wood, intersecting one another here and there but mostly running parallel. Where the canebrakes met the river channel, trees and willows grew along the banks, their trunks now under water so that only leafy branches showed above the rushing current of the river, fifty yards across of muddy water burdened with debris. On the east bank were more willows and two more miles of cane and then, off in the distance, hills again.

All day from the hills through misty rain they'd watched the ferries come and go in the distance, poling through the pathways in the cane, disappearing underneath the trees along the bank and launching out into the littered current to cross over. Now when it was their turn Katie had an odd sense of detachment, as if watching her own journey from the vantage of the hills.

The raft was only twelve feet square and overloaded, water running over it three inches deep. The larger ferry was a sturdy scow, but the owner had reserved his services for families with sick children and the waiting line was long, so several men were running makeshift ferries of this size, constructed hastily of flat boards roped together—and without rings to secure the oars.

The raft was short one oarsman, having only three: a ghostly looking man named Luke, a boy named Brad, who seemed to be related to him, and the owner, called Joe B., an intimidating, unkempt character with bad teeth and sour breath. William substituted as the fourth, working from the left rear of the raft with a piece of driftwood for a paddle and a thin branch for a pole.

The raft was crowded with the Kenners, the extra children, Loco and the ox, as well as a two-wheeled cart. Rose had bought the cart on a bargain of ten dollars from a man whose steer had drowned when a bridge collapsed, and William had replaced one wheel to make it mobile. It had taken him most of one day. He had chiseled out the broken spokes, carved new ones out of hickory poles and driven them into the hub, then heated up the tire and molded it around again.

Katie, standing ankle-deep near William with her feet slightly apart for balance, one knee then the other bending with the gentle rocking of the raft, held Samuel in her arms. He had drifted off to sleep with one arm flung out in a casual way, relaxed as long as Katie held him.

Rose was sitting with the children on a pile of baggage in the cart. Just above her on the driver's bench Jeffrey sat backward holding the smoky torch which was the only light besides the moon's, his legs dangling from the bench and his face lit yellow in the ghoulish flicker. Grand sat beside him facing forward in the driver's place with a sack of cornmeal and the platter in her lap. She was looking out the other way, across the sea of cane. Cool and steady moonlight lay upon her profile in a striking contrast to the dancing warmth of firelight that played upon the boy.

Rose turned to Katie and said quietly, "Do you remember crossing here, the other way?"

Katie kept on swaying side to side with Samuel. Her back hurt with the baby's weight, her feet were numb with cold and her shoes were water-logged. "No," she answered, watching torchlight play on William's hair, down near her skirt. William had to kneel to row, his trousers wet up to his waist. She watched the movement of his arms and how the yellow flicker wound its way into the soft folds of his ragged shirt. She also watched for snakes down in the water; they were known to float aboard and would be difficult to see with so much cane and river drift littering the raft, the water shining yellow like spilt gold beneath the torchlight and reflecting walls of cane.

On either side, the cane grew close and high. The moon was in the northeast nestled in between the folds of clouds. Camp fires flickered from the hills both east and west and far-off voices from the camps wafted from the hills like soap bubbles on wash day, clear and hollow orbs drifting aimlessly, mingling with the closer voices of the crewmen on the big scow toiling westward back this way through a different avenue within the cane.

"The water was low then," Rose said. "We drove our wagon through this cane."

"Toby had the influenza when we crossed the Trinity," Grand offered, turning her face around toward the torchlight. Her fever was returning with the night and her flaccid cheeks were purple. She hadn't worn her dentures in days since her mouth was swollen with sores. It was obvious to Katie that the single thing that kept Grand moving was direction: east. She was taking with her one fine platter of her china and only half her family, but she was going home.

Rose said dreamily, "Toby was just five. Or was he six?" and stroked the forehead of the boy named Joel beside her, who was about that age.

As the big scow inched closer through the cane, nearing the place where its own path intersected theirs like the junction in the middle of an hourglass, both crews hugged close against the walls of cane to give the other passing room. There was just six feet between them.

The scow had torches mounted high up on its bow and several on its rear casting lurid light upon the crew. Three oarsmen manned each side. A stout, bald man who was rowing on the near side called over, "You're riding a little low there, ain't ya, Joe B.?"

Joe B. was rowing just in front of William. He had taken off his shirt and tied the sleeves around his spreading belly; his suspenders cut into the flesh and black hairs of his shoulders. "And you're ridin' way too high," he mumbled, not looking at the scow.

"Joe B.? You hear me?"

Joe B. flung his words across at him. "What the hell am I supposed to do about it? Dump these kids off in the water?"

The crewman wheezed a laugh, and called out, "Joe B., ridin' low down in the water! Low, low down." And then he chanted, "Joe B., What ya see? Blub Blub Blub. Joe B., Look at me! Blub Blub Blub."

Joe B. muttered and went on rowing, his back and arms so covered with black hair it looked as if a horde of long-legged spiders crawled across him.

The scow eased by, the crewmen jeering and the one still hailing, "Joe B., How are ye? Blub Blub Blub."

Joe B. hurled his oar aside, startling Loco, and stood up from his knees swiveling his bearded face around, sloshing between Katie and William toward the rear of the raft. There he stood with both feet planted on the edge, and belted at the scow a string of nonsense and profanities.

The crewman shouted with exaggerated sympathy, "Joe B., Feels crot-che-ty," and his crew all sang together, "Blub Blub Blub."

Even the two oarsmen on his own raft were laughing at Joe B., and he turned his wild profanities on them. "God damn you, Luke, you think it's funny? You goddamn idiot. It ain't funny." The other was still laughing, and Joe B. said, "You fucking better shut your mouth."

"Aaa, sit down, Joe B.," Luke said.

"You go to hell. It ain't funny. I ain't gonna put up with this shit."

Katie said, "Be quiet or you'll wake the baby up."

Joe B. made a gesture toward the sky and stomped by Katie, splashing water on her skirt. He retrieved his oar and flung himself into his work. "Fucking baby," he said.

After a while, when the scow had disappeared around a slow bend in the cane, the tension eased and William started asking questions of the crew about the Indians between the Trinity and Nacogdoches. He wanted to know if it was true the Mexicans had tried to pay the Indians to attack refugees.

"Yep," Joe B. answered, "though it ain't took yet in a general way. A occasional kidnap and horses stole, is all."

Luke, the lead man on the right side, rested on his oar and said, "Ever'body's got theirselves deluded if they're thinkin' to outsmart them Indians by passin' rumors round about which tribes will be attackin' where. You can't outsmart a Indian. You just never know, that's all. I've got me some scars to prove that for a fact. They're wily, I tell you. Best thing is to go about your business like they ain't around, 'cause if they want ya, they will come and get ya, ain't no foresight gonna stop 'em. I tell you. And the truth is, we have took their land, and who's to blame 'em if they join up with the Meskins? It's Meskins clearly winnin' in this war. If I was them, I'd be doin' depredatin' on both sides of this river, and I bet ya forty dollars they will be pretty soon. Them Caddos know these rivers, I tell you for a fact."

"Sam Houston cut a deal with them," Brad said. Brad was the youngest of the three and had no facial hair. His face was pale and carried a perpetual look of surprise, the eyebrows slanted upward toward his temples. "Them and Cherokees."

"Sam Houston," Luke injected, spitting in the water, "is running with the Meskins on his tail. Yellow fool. Gonna beat a path to Andy Jackson's arms."

"Ain't a word of truth in that," Joe B. sputtered. "He's got him a plan. He ain't runnin'."

"Sure is movin' fast."

"But he ain't runnin'."

"I was speakin' of the current, ass head," Luke proclaimed.

"No you were not speakin' of the current, this here is a aimless current. Sam's got him a plan," Joe B. repeated. "He's gonna string them Meskins clear across, let 'em draw out their supply lines and get all wore out, then he's gonna turn and fight 'em. He's discombobulatin' 'em right now, that's all."

"Horse shit," Luke retorted. "If he's stringin' out the lines it's just so he can get to Andy Jackson's troops over on the border and have them fight the Meskins for him. And they would too, ya know," he added, now addressing William. "They've got their toes just about hangin' over the east bank of the Sabine, just itchin' to cross over, just waitin' for a excuse. That's the truest answer to your question on the Indians. I dare say the U.S. Army *wants* them Indians to do a little deprecatin' so they can send in troops on pretext of subduin' savages, and hang around for long enough to fight the Meskins too and go ahead and capture Texas for theirselves. Or if Sam Houston dragged his army on across the border with the Meskins hot behind him, then no doubt the U.S. Army would just call it a invasion of the Meskins and just start a war right then and there. Andy Jackson, he would seize that opportunity."

"That's plain ridiculous," Joe B. said.

Brad stopped paddling to dig a finger up his nose. "You're so keen on Sam, Joe B., then how come you're not with him?" he asked.

"Got to be somebody get these women and their little ones across."

"What a heart you have, Joe B.," Luke said sarcastically.

For a while they rowed in silence, only the sound of the oars in the water and the sloshing sound when someone tossed away a piece of cane or river trash that scudded up onto the raft. The stars were visible beyond the clouds. The moon sat stoically between the folds.

William laid his paddle on his knees and stared down at the broken blisters on his hands. He wondered if his hands would ever heal. When he looked up at Katie she smiled and leaned down, holding Samuel against her chest, wadding up her skirt around her knees so not to dip it in the water on the raft. "Look at Grand," she whispered.

Grand was staring at the moon again, sitting on the driver's bench of the cart with the sack of cornmeal and her precious platter in her lap. Her profile showed a chin caved slightly in without the dentures, wisps of gray hair like fine cobwebs in the moonlight. She seemed to be remembering. Her face was very pensive.

"She was a beauty," Katie said to William. "Father told me so."

The sound of the oars in the water was like music. Mosquitoes had come out now the rain had stopped, but not as many as there might have been if the air were warmer. One was humming near William's face. The children bickered sleepily for room inside the cart, "You're hoggin' it—" "*You're* hoggin' it—" and Rose, to quiet them, suggested that they look for faces in the clouds. They found a bear's face, and a dog's. Joel found an armadillo, the whole body nose to tail humped up across the western sky above the hills.

The pathway narrowed and the current quickened as they neared the channel, and several times the raft brushed up against the wall of cane.

Joe B. blamed the other two for not rowing steadily. They ignored him and tossed a twist of tobacco back and forth between them, spitting in the water that swirled around their feet.

"You kids up there have a vantage, so keep a watch for snakes down here," Joe B. told the children in the cart.

When they neared the tree line of the channel where the leafy trees grew in among the cane with water clear up to their branches, Joe B. said, "When we get through these trees and in the channel we'll have a rocky ride across for maybe fifty yards. You kids and ladies just stay put. Miss, if it gets rocky you just grab ahold of that cart and give that baby to your mama." He shoved his finger at William, "You paddle like hell."

Rose and the children, in the cart, lay down to avoid the branches, and the boy gave up the torch to Luke. It had burned down to a stub and Luke lit another with it and dropped the used stub in the water, where it hissed and flickered out. He jammed the new torch in between two boards at the rear of the raft and resumed his place rowing.

Katie leaned back against the tailgate of the cart, her head bent over Samuel to protect him. He was heavy in her arms. He smelled of hominy and rancid sweet potatoes. Her feet were numb with cold. Loco and the ox were both uneasy, pawing in the water while the low limbs scratched across their backs. Weeping willows trailed soft fernlike limbs across the cart and over everyone, and entangled vines snagged hold of everything they touched. Snakes dangled from the vines, black water moccasins and others of a brownish hue; William spotted two entwined together hanging from a vine looped through the branches of a cypress tree, and the oarsmen shifted course around the tree.

This passage through the swampy trees took on an eerie feeling with the frogs and insects chirping and the moon shining through the leaves. The torch was knocked down by a low limb and the flame almost went out, but Brad was quick to set it right.

Katie could no longer see the fires twinkling in the hills, nor hear the voices of the refugees camped there. The branches closed around her like a cage. William fended off the branches with his floatwood paddle, sometimes grabbing a low limb and pulling under it. A sharp twig sliced across his cheek. The sound of water rushing through the channel up ahead grew louder, and when the raft broke free of the trees the current caught it and swung it around like river wash.

Katie felt the current at her feet, circling around her ankles. She felt the strength of it beneath the boards, rocking her whole body, and she bent one knee then the other, riding with it, clutching Samuel like a talisman and leaning back against the cart. Rose and the children lifted from their prone positions, taking stock of the increase in speed, and Grand sat straight up on the bench again.

Katie looked upstream at the moonlight on the moving waters of the river, dizzied by the sudden rush of current coming toward her. They were past mid-river when a pile of brushy driftwood washed aboard and nudged between the forelegs of the ox. Katie felt the cart lean back against her like a living presence seeking out her warmth, the wheels creaking in the water as the ox backed up a few steps in the effort to escape the pile of brush. Grand took up the whip and reins and snapped the ox across its back. Two steps forward, and the pile of driftwood tangled in between its legs like snakes gone stiff, terrifying it and causing it once more to back away. Loco reared and snorted at the sudden backward motion and the creaking of the wheels. Katie stepped away. Rose shoved the oldest children out of the cart and grabbed Joel, tossing him onto the deck, then climbed out behind him. The oarsman near the ox stood up and took hold of the yoke, but the ox was moving with an instinct beyond reckoning, and continued backing toward the edge. William stood and moved out of its way. Katie saw the wheel William had constructed, turning by her. Everything was shifting. The raft was tipping with one corner rising like a creature from the sea. The clouds lunged forward and the moon jerked in the sky. The muddy water rose up with the moon, and there was nothing to hold on to. She saw William leaning toward her, both arms reaching for her. She was sliding with the baby in her arms. Then the water swallowed her. She held the baby at her chest and felt the cold waters closing around her. Samuel struggled, squealing out his breath in bubbles. The current swept the bubbles like leaves driven by the wind, and Katie realized she was being carried underneath the raft. She fought the current then. Her shoes were water-logged and heavy and she couldn't reach to pull them off, or she would drop the baby. Her skirt was tangled at her legs. She scissored both legs, kicking frantically to gain the surface rushing over her. When she broke the surface, all she saw at first was the moon gliding way up high. She could not defend herself from the debris on the surface. The

raft was tipping at an angle, dropping oars and baggage in the water as
gracelessly as one would plunk small stones. She had surfaced close beside the raft but the current was still sweeping her away. William was
suspended at the edge with one hand reaching for her. With the other
hand he held on to the driftwood paddle, which he'd wedged between
two boards for leverage. But Katie could not take his hand or she would
lose the baby, who was screaming in her arms, his head above the surface, at her throat. William yelled things that she could not understand
above the water sounds. She kicked to stay afloat, choking on the water,
and jerked her body forward toward the edge and William's hand. "Take
him, take him," she was gasping, thrusting Samuel at him with an effort
so profound it forced her deeper in the water, and she felt the burden
lifted from her hands as if by grace of God, and then was free to swim.
William had the baby. Rose was leaning forward with the moon behind
her and her arms around the youngest boy, sliding. Everything was sliding now. Loco's hooves were sliding. The torchlight was drowned out.
Katie, treading water, heard one oarsman shouting out to everyone to
shift weight over to the other side and balance out the raft, but the
flooring of the raft was slick and no one had a footing. Rose was calling
to the children. Loco's hind legs buckled and the water swirled against
her withers. The water was opaque with mud and trash and the cart was
sinking in a slow submergence while the ox, with Grand laying on the
whip, strained to pull it forward. But the wheels were over. Katie saw
them dip into the water.

William, tucking Samuel underneath one arm, lunged and reached
for Grand. Grand turned her face around and down toward Katie struggling in the water and laid the whip with all the force in her frail arms;
she knew the only way to keep the raft from turning over was to make
the ox go forward. Katie, fighting with the current, saw the moonlight
on Grand's face, like plaster, and shouted to her to get out, the wheels
were over now.

But Grand had turned her back. Repeatedly, she laid the whip. The
old ox squatted on its haunches in the effort to go forward, and
floundered in the water to its shoulders, its bony rump now totally
submerged. One oarsman grappled with the yoke and horns but he was
sliding forward in the effort, and let go.

The cart then backed into the water and sank out of sight, and

Grand went down beneath the surface with it. The hind end of the ox descended with the weight but the creature tried to keep its head above the water, straining with its awkward forelegs for a hold, and the raft continued tipping, spilling everyone into the turbid flow.

The last part of the ox to disappear was its black nose ashine in moonlight. The raft fell flat again against the current with a slapping sound, and beneath it passed a clattering of hooves as the ox swept underneath, still trying for a foothold on the only solid object in its reach, and Katie plucked her shoes off her feet and sucked in air and plunged down deep and sightless in the water, groping frantically for Grand. She came up screaming William's name, and screaming for her mother. She clutched at driftwood and the shifting waters. She grabbed for anything in reach. "William—William—"

"Kate—"

"William, do you have him—"

"Yes I have him—"

"Where is Grand? William, where is Grand—"

"Kate, swim to shore—"

"But where is Grand? Mother? Mother?"

"Kate, swim to shore—"

"Where is Mother—"

And then her mother's voice called from the water, "Kate? Do you have the baby?"

"Mother—"

"Kate, swim to shore—"

"But where is Grand?"

"Grand—" She heard Rose calling. "Grand—" and Rose was calling for the children and the men were calling out to everyone at once, and Katie saw the girl clinging to the raft with the current washing everything away.

And then she saw the plaster face lift through the surface near her, full of terror now and gasping hard for air, the mouth thrown open, full of stringy hair.

"Grand—" she screamed. "Grand—" and fought the water to get to her. Grand stared at her with eyes gone blank, and Katie looped an arm around her waist beneath the water. "Kick your shoes off, Grand, kick them off—" she shouted. But Grand wore lace-up shoes. They would pull her down. Grand's plaster cheek was up against her own; her hair had come down loose. She did not speak a word but trusted all her fragile weight to Katie's strength and Katie struggled toward the eastern shore, swimming backward with her face out of the water and her arm around Grand's chest, Grand lying back against her, as thin and pliant as a river weed. There was a moment in the passage when it seemed that Grand was dead, she was so limp and silent. But with one hand she clutched Katie's skirt, which billowed full of water. Grand's silver hair was trailing in the current. Katie's braid was wrapped beneath her arms. She let the current carry them but angled for the shore, breathing hard and choking, brushing river trash away. She felt as if her clothes were pulled away. Her strength was going with them, down the river. Everything was pulling from her clutches. Grand was almost torn out of her arms. The ferry raft washed by, the little girl now up on board and lying flat with someone—Rose?—draped over her, and others clinging to it, though not William—not so she could see—and Katie screamed out "William?" and felt Grand lurch in her arms.

"William—William—"

If he answered her, she could not hear. She thought she heard the baby, but water filled her ears. She sobbed and called for Rose, her calling now descended to a whisper almost like a prayer, "Mother, Mother, Mother—" But there was no one there. She was going under now, stroking with one arm and choking on the water with each breath, and Grand still lay against her with no movement and no sound.

Then the cypress tree reached out for her with prickly arms. She turned and wrapped herself within its branches, taking hold with one hand, taking Grand's hand with the other while the river clutched at Grand to drag her off. Grand reached to grab the branches but she had no strength, and Katie knew that if she let her go, then she would go forever.

She was unaware of anything but holding on. She held her grandmother by one hand and clutched the limber branch within the other, feeling the soft needled leaves inside her grip, the limb giving with the weight as if it would stretch out forever, all the length of that long river to the sea. The water was a force of evil with its awesome power. Katie sobbed aloud, "I can't, I can't," and felt the current stretch her arms, felt the bony grip of Grand's white hand between her fingers like the hand of death. Grand never looked at her. She never, ever did in that long time they clung there strung together like cut paper dolls with the water tugging them apart. Grand was looking at the moon. She fixed her eyes on the light between the spiny branches and she clung to Katie's hand.

Grand was still looking at the moon and gasping at the air when Katie's strength gave out, her fingers letting go, and Grand sank underneath the muddy surface with her face still turned up toward the light. Katie called and called, but she knew then, and always afterward believed, Grand never heard her calling.

And even while she clung there in the branches of the cypress tree and saw Grand fly away beneath the littered surface of the Trinity, Katie thought how horrible for Grand to know, the final human touch she ever had, was someone letting go.

THE FACE OF EVIL

A PRIL 21, THE PLAINS OF SAN JACINTO

The cold night of April 20 lifted to a blue and breezy morning with the march still underway. Cós and his five hundred were now walking in their sleep. They arrived to find *El Presidente* and his army camped in a grassy prairie with a swath of marshland and the river of St. Hyacinth— the San Jacinto River—at their back. At their front, was Sam Houston's army, not one mile away in a stand of massive live oaks draped with moss along a high-banked waterway called Buffalo Bayou. The two armies were nestled into the bend where the bayou flowed into the San Jacinto River, with nothing but sage grass prairie and a stretch of trees dividing them. The trees did not reach all the way across the field, but left a gap a mile long in the center, so the armies would have had a clear view of one another if not for a gentle hill—a mere swell of ground— between them.

There had been some skirmishing between the armies on the day before with two of Santa Anna's mules killed and the cannon's carriage damaged, and it was fortunate for Santa Anna that the skirmish hadn't grown into a battle, as he needed Cós and his five hundred men in order to outnumber the rebels—the land thieves, as he called them.

The grape that Santa Anna showered down on the land thieves holed up in the mossy live oaks had proved useless. The trees were like a fort. Santa Anna bragged that he would have to coax the cowards out to fight, but it was evident he thought it possible they would attack him in the night, for he'd kept his army busy building breastworks and resting on their arms till dawn.

At nine in the crystal morning when Cós arrived with reinforcements, Santa Anna greeted him with a roll of drums.

The land thieves would be listening to the drums. From their perches in the trees they would be watching as the lines filed in—the mules and all the men.

Hugh Kenner halted with the soldiers in mesquite and sage grass to his knees in the hog-bed prairie with the drums still rolling, and saw *El Presidente* Santa Anna, the man who had ordered Miles and Toby shot, standing in the sunlight thirty yards away. Hugh's blood ran through his veins with such a force the ground welled up and the sky seemed to recede and he had to catch his balance. He could hear birds singing in the grove along the marshlands of the river. He felt Crucita's hand against his arm to steady him. Adelaido, beside him, said, "He's much younger than I thought," in a voice of quiet poignance.

El Presidente was a young, handsome man with excessive gestures and black hair tousled in the breeze. He wore a heavy blue frock coat that hung below his knees with red lining and gold embroidery radiant in the sun. When the wind gusted, his blue coat peeled open down the front and showed his sword dangling from his belt and the glimmer of gold buttons down his shirt. He wore black boots and white trousers without mud and stood there with a gentle slope of ragweed and the tents behind him, the grass swept down around his boots by spring winds and the officers gathered around. He flung his arms about and seemed to be berating General Cós, his lone voice high and puny from this distance above the rolling of drums, and with the wind. Crucita listened closely and then said to Hugh, "He is angry because General Cós has brought to him men in bad condition. He says they are going to take the supplies and food and they are not good for fighting."

After his abusive reprimand of General Cós, Santa Anna strutted to his tent and from there issued orders to his army to rest in preparation for a battle. He did not say, nor could his soldiers guess, when the battle might take place, but it did not appear that Santa Anna intended to engage in fighting on that day.

Beef was boiled in pots of iron. Cards were taken from the saddle-bags for games of monte. Officers retired to their tents. Cós and his division, having neither slept nor eaten in twenty-four hours, were granted permission to stack their arms and retire to a grove of trees at the north end of Santa Anna's camp, near a marshland which bordered on the river. Mules and horses were led back and forth through swampy grass to water in the river, and everything was quiet in the rebel camp across the way.

But judgment hung in the sky that day, with bird song and the breeze. Adelaido would receive his judgment from *El Presidente:* he likely would be shot. Crucita did not speak of it, but clung to him with little soothing sounds and gestures like a mother with a dying child.

Hugh could think of nothing but Crucita and her safety. They were a country to themselves, the three of them, and slept beside each other on a mound of dry grass in the morning sunlight, and stayed together in the afternoon while warmth crept over the marshes, Adelaido following behind the other two with hands cuffed at his back, standing like a guardian and watching while they tended to the sick. He tried to keep his nerve and now and then showed false bravado in his manner, tilting up his chin. But it was pitiful the way he twisted his bound hands together and was always glancing everywhere to see if anyone was coming for him.

He was living on the fringes, all that day.

When the sun had lowered past its zenith and the camp had fallen quiet in late afternoon siesta time, the three of them sat down to eat their meal together at the base of a twisted mulberry tree on the farthest northern outskirts of the grove, spreading Crucita's striped serape on the ground to sit on. The ground before them sloped to sunny marshes with waterfowl standing in the boggy grass, a line of trees along the riverbank—magnolias blooming in between the bearded oaks—and then the river, full of floating hyacinths, just a glimpse of it between the trees. Soldiers grouped together in the grove behind them, closer to the main part of the camp, a few women scattered in among them. Many sprawled out on the grassy ground beneath the trees and slept. Others ventured to the edges of the grove to feel the sun, nursing little fires in the wind.

A lull fell over everything and intermittent sounds took on that sharpness that implies disturbance of the natural order of the world; sleepy voices punctuated the crisp air inside the grove, and the crackle of the fires carried loudly on the breeze.

Crucita fed her brother spoons of beans from her own cup since he couldn't feed himself, his fine wrists bruised and scabbed beneath the metal cuffs, the nails with dirt beneath them. She could see that he was trying hard to lift himself above despair. She knew she was his only comfort but could also see how his complete dependence on her dragged his spirit down. She'd shaved his face and tied his hair back with a thong, but he was dirty from his inability to bathe himself. Her hand shook when she fed him one more bite of beans, so the juice got on his mustache and dribbled from the spoon onto his shirt. With the edge of her skirt she wiped it off his mustache, but the brown stain on his shirt remained, and Crucita knew that Adelaido, so fastidious by nature, saw it as a blot upon his pride. He was embarrassed to be spoon-fed like an infant. He was in some pain and tried to twist his back to stretch the muscles, and Crucita set the food aside to massage his shoulders. He shrugged his shoulders from her grasp and said that she should eat.

Hugh ate an ear of corn in silence, leaning back against the stringy bark and watching Adelaido and Crucita. Then he gazed across the marshland toward the river and said quietly, "We could crawl away in that high grass, after dark, it's possible."

Crucita set her ear of corn down on the striped serape, her dark face shadowed by the wide brim of the Spanish hat Domingo de la Rosa had given her. She listened to the sound of someone snoring in the grove and the hushed tones of a woman's voice beside a nearby fire. Then she looked at Adelaido. Half in sunlight, half in shade, he was staring down at strands of fluid grass curling at the edge of the striped serape, the part of his black hair running jagged toward his forehead where she had not taken care to comb it evenly. "How can Adie crawl, with his hands tied on his back?" she said.

Adelaido answered, "If I were to try it, I would try it on my own."

"Impossible," she answered. He was quiet, and she knew his

thoughts and said to him in Spanish, "You're afraid you would hinder us if we all went together, and you want me to consider leaving you, and I won't."

"But I could make it on my own," he said. It was a lie. They all knew it was a lie. He would be caught, and shot as a traitor. "The two of you could go together and hide out in the country for a while until the battle's over."

"No," she said.

"Crucita, listen to me—"

"No. You listen. You can't make it on your own. Look at you, you can't even unfasten your pants. They would catch you."

"Well I won't go if you're going," he said. "It's too dangerous for you. They'd punish you for helping me escape."

She brushed the air with a dismissing gesture. "They wouldn't punish me. How dramatic you are. Pure theatrics." But then she realized it was possible that they would punish Hugh, and she wavered.

Hugh guessed what she was thinking from the way she looked at him. "I would take the risk," he said.

"Then we go together," Crucita whispered, unable to express her gratitude. "All three." She stood and started pulling berries from the lowest limbs. Hugh watched the way she moved her arms, the turning of her waist, the way she plucked the berries with one hand and held a fold of her brown skirt out with the other hand to make a place for them. The berries weren't yet purple ripe. They were not even red. But when she had about a dozen in her skirt, Crucita knelt and held one out to Adelaido's mouth.

He turned his face away. "I won't risk taking you," he said.

She sat and gathered up the berries in her lap and looked at him. "If you try to go alone, I'll follow you," she answered.

Adelaido said, "If I ask you, Crucita, for the love of our good mother, to let the doctor take you—"

"No," she said, shaking her head. "I will not." She took up an ear of corn and gnawed a bite off the cob and stared at him defiantly.

"There will be a battle here, Crucita," Hugh said tenderly.

She swallowed her corn and answered with an edge, "I know it's a battle. But it's not possible I leave my brother. And you don't ask me to do that."

He looked at her in the sunlight filtered through the downy mulberry leaves. "Yes, I do," he said. "I ask you to."

"Then you don't give me respect," she answered him.

Adelaido spoke to her in Spanish, a string of desperate words, saying she would be in danger in a battle and would serve no purpose here by staying. He said he did not want her here for him. He tossed his head to throw the loose hairs from his face and said that if he was condemned he didn't want her here to watch, and if the battle should begin he didn't want her in it. He wanted her to go away with Hugh.

She listened and then said, "But I'll be here with you, if you want me to or not."

"Crucita, please—"

She made a gesture as if parting the air with both her hands, and silence fell between her and her brother. One by one she plucked the berries from her skirt and tossed them in the grass.

Adelaido said to Hugh at last, "If she won't go, then you should go without her. I think if you go alone your chances are good. You could make it to the rebel camp." He looked across the sunny grasses, the clumps of yellow thistles and white ragweed. "There isn't any reason for you not to."

But there was a reason, they all knew. Hugh wouldn't leave Crucita. He thought of Rose and all that he had lost and all that he had yet to lose.

"Go," Crucita said, as if she wanted him to. "It is the right thing to do."

Hugh shook his head. "You know I won't, without you."

Adelaido threw his head back in despair and his long hair hung down against his back, oily in the shifting sun, coal black and tied back with the thong Crucita had secured. He said he could not bear to have their blood upon his hands, and asked Crucita if she thought herself so charmed that even in a battle she would not be harmed?

She dismissed his words and ate her corn and tossed the cob in the grass and said in Spanish, "I won't go, unless you will go with me."

Adelaido stared at her so hard his eyes filled with tears that swelled and trickled from the corners, down his face, which she had shaved for him, and she leaned gently forward, reaching out a hand to wipe the tears away.

He struggled to his feet and looked at her, then shook his head and said to Hugh, "What is your preference? To go, or stay?"

Hugh knew for certain Adelaido did not have one chance in ten of being pardoned. And Crucita would be better off away from here. The risk was mostly his. "We'll go," he said. "Tonight."

Adelaido took a breath and rolled his head back as if searching through the branches. The wind was playing with the leaves. Adelaido then looked down at Hugh sitting placidly beside Crucita with his back against the tree, and said, "With all my heart I thank you." To Crucita he said nothing, but looked at her then turned his back and walked off down the tree line to the right, half in shadow, half in light, his dirty hands clasped underneath the metal cuffs.

Hugh uncorked the water flask suspended from his belt and offered Crucita a drink. She shook her head and watched him closely, thinking that his silence was a condemnation, and she was angry with him for the first time ever. "Adelaido is my brother," she protested. "How can I leave him here to die by hisself, or let him crawl by hisself in the grass like *una vibora* on his stomach with no hands."

"You can't," Hugh said, and smiled sadly and touched her cheek with one finger. "Maybe another woman could."

She lowered her face to where he could not see it underneath the hat. But then he said her name in his soft whisper, and she looked at him and let him see that she was crying. She did not even wipe away the tears. "Please don't say anything more to me," she said. "Every word you say, it hurts my heart." She stood and shook a few last berries from her skirt, lumpy orbs of reddish-green, and gathered up the tin cup and the spoon and started off along the tree line where Adelaido had gone.

"Crucita?" Hugh called after her.

She stopped and turned around and stood holding the cup with the spoon about to fall, her head tipped to the side and her brown dress speckled with dry mud and spots of sun. He smiled at her. She returned the same sad smile then turned away again, gathering up her skirt with her free hand and walking very quickly so as not to let her brother too far from her sight.

Hugh sat there on the striped serape, the gift Domingo de la Rosa gave Crucita, in the speckled light. He watched her walking in her brown dress through the sunlight and the shadows of the tree line with the grass up to her knees, and imagined what she must have been like as a child, how happy and how strong she must have been and how she loved her brother. The thought that he would lose her was so painful that he ceased to look at her, and stared down at the stripes of the serape, brown and indigo against the green of grass. He wondered if Domingo de la Rosa loved Crucita, and feared he did, and hoped it too, and yet the idea tortured him, to think that she might ever be in someone else's arms.

Hugh was still sitting with his back against the tree when a barefoot officer in a shabby uniform came through the grove behind him and stood before him, pointing back where he had come from, through the grove, and trying to say in English that Hugh was wanted in the main camp. The officer was young and had large eyes with straight lashes. Hugh stood up and spoke to him in faulty Spanish and the officer introduced himself as Colonel Pedro Delgado, of Santa Anna's staff. He told Hugh General Castrillón had called for him.

"*Quien es* General Castrillón?"

Delgado answered in fluid Spanish, saying Castrillón was acting major general, and Hugh asked other questions, seeking any information that could help him in his plans for after dark. Delgado told him General Castrillón was an old, beloved Castilian, a proven veteran—"Much different from the President," he said pointedly. Castrillón cared for the soldiers, "unlike the President," and had designated a tent in the main camp for use as a hospital since many of the men had influenza. Hugh asked how many men were in the hospital, and Delgado shrugged and said the tent was not large enough to shelter more than twenty, then pointed down at his big toe on his left foot, and Hugh leaned down and saw an ingrown toenail caked with mud and thoroughly infected. He told Delgado he could cut it out, but this would mean removal of a large part of the toenail. Delgado shook his head. "Another time. Let it stay," he said, and motioned Hugh to follow him.

Hugh took up the serape, leaving in its place a square of flattened grass, a brilliant green, and turned to follow Delgado. Then on further thought he tossed the serape down beside the tree, thinking that Crucita would return and find it there and know that he intended to come back. She would wait for him.

They walked together through the grove, past Cós's men, who were around their fires sleeping off exhaustion from the night before. Hugh asked Delgado if he thought there would be fighting soon, and Delgado said he didn't know.

On the outskirts were the bulk of the reserves—Hugh estimated maybe seven hundred—camped in regiments on the open ground. Passing by a woman who was stirring a pot of soapy water with a stick, Delgado told Hugh they'd acquired large supplies of soap and white flour in New Washington two days before. They wound their way on through the men and baggage, crates of squawking chickens, ragged, hobbled mules, and piles of offal from the butchered beefs lying near the boiling pots. The cavalry was out along the far side where the prairie opened to the south; Hugh estimated there were eighty horses and at least three hundred mules, half now being led or ridden bareback to water at a little lake that bulged off the San Jacinto. From what Hugh had seen of the land, it seemed to him a bad location for a battle. To the north and east were boggy sloughs and prairie with small groves of trees, and then the river curving in a loop around, closing it all in. The open land was to the south, and this was grassy prairie without cover, and to the west, where the rebels were.

In the main part of the camp stood about a dozen officers' tents. A few entry flaps were open with officers inside sitting on their pallets playing cards, but most of the tent flaps were closed. It was siesta time.

Delgado pointed out two tents erected in the center, one larger than the other, both made of red-and-white-striped silk. He said derisively, "These are the lodgings of *El Presidente.*" The tents reminded Hugh of carnival tents or those at a Baptist revival. Stacked outside the entryway of the larger one were several crates with roosters staring beady-eyed through the slats, and Delgado waved a hand toward them and said, "He loves his sport. His temper is short because the war has gone on longer than he'd thought and he's running out of cocks to fight. He only has seven left and we started with forty-nine."

"So *El Presidente* enjoys fighting," Hugh said.

Delgado shrugged. "He enjoys blood."

"Do you think he'll fight tomorrow?"

Delgado studied him a moment, then shed a piece of his reserve and said, "No one knows the answer, except *El Presidente*. And probably he doesn't know. He'll let his opium decide. He has lost his wits in this campaign. He smokes his opium and has his fits of temper, with me, with everyone." He gestured broadly with his arm. "His Excellency listens to no one and blames everyone for anything not to his liking. And here we find ourselves in a flooded prairie, with a river at our backs, a camping ground of His Excellency's choice and against all military rules. We outnumber the rebels two to one, but we are sitting in a trap." Hugh did not understand every word of what was spoken, as Delgado spoke in rapid Spanish, but he knew the essence of it.

Not twenty yards away from Santa Anna's tents the barricade stretched out a hundred yards along the west—the front line. The barricade was three feet high, a sturdy construction of pack saddles, baggage, sacks of beans, and hard-bread, the gaps filled in with dirt and brush. If the rebels came out of the trees and fought in military squares from open ground, this barricade could give the Mexicans a clean advantage. Ten or fifteen soldiers were still working to improve it, shoveling grassy dirt and tossing bags around. In the center was a single cannon, a brass twelve-pounder with the carriage splintered. Three men were trying to repair the carriage. They seemed diligent but oddly quiet at their work, as if they slept and dreamed while sawing wood and hammering. From a stand of tall pecan trees to the left, five men came dragging more limbs through the grass to pile up on the barricade.

But that was all. Aside from these halfhearted labors of exhausted soldiers, it seemed *El Presidente* had prepared for battle all that he intended to prepare. He had his barricade. He had his numbers. And he had his arrogance.

"He is in his tent, asleep," Delgado said scornfully. "But here is the hospital. Ah, and here is General Castrillón."

An older man with square shoulders and heavy gray hair stepped out of the canvas hospital, stooping beneath the tent flap and then rising with a military bearing. He addressed Delgado formally as "Colonel," and Delgado introduced Hugh with a slight bow, his pronunciation of the name "Kenner" so corrupted that the general turned to Hugh and asked him in good English for his name.

The officers exchanged some words in Spanish, Delgado asking Castrillón if he believed the barricade extended far enough down to the left. Castrillón frowned and said he had instructed some of Leulmo's men to lengthen it, but that Santa Anna had reversed the order. "Nothing avails here against the caprice, arbitrary will, and ignorance of that man," Castrillón said. He didn't raise his voice above its natural tenor and he evidently didn't know that Hugh could understand his Spanish, for he was not a man to criticize his President in front of strangers. But neither did he make an effort to drop his voice down out of range of Santa Anna's tent. He was as angry as Delgado, and evidently did not care if Santa Anna knew.

Turning to Hugh, he said in English, "You will find the hospital to be crowded, and also many sick with influenza out on the camping ground. Please go first to those inside the hospital; they're the most severe. There is a man just to your left beside the entryway with—" He paused. "Have you no medicines?"

"None," Hugh said.

Castrillón addressed Delgado, telling him to go to the supply tent, but before he finished his instructions the sudden notes of a bugle split the April air. He paused, his face lifted in the sun as if to sniff the wind, and then his eyes fastened for an instant on Delgado and the two men wheeled around and charged past Santa Anna's tent toward the barricade. Hugh ran with them.

The men dragging limbs from the pecan grove to the left dropped their loads and ran toward camp, shouting—"*Los Americanos, los soldados Americanos*—"

Hugh reached the barricade and climbed up next to General Castrillón on a stack of ammunition boxes, squinting in the sun, and saw advancing through the prairie, directly toward the barricade, a long, single line of silent figures moving at a steady, loping pace. They ascended from the far side of the gentle slope of ground. They came out of the sun. They did not make a sound. Their line stretched out a thousand yards across the field to the groves of trees along the reaches. On the far left side a group of nearly forty cavalry was coming at a gallop, closing in against the south side of the camp. In the center of the line were two small cannon, shoved forward by six men, and one flag with indistinguishable markings and something like a glove on top—fingers reaching for the sky. Down along the far right of the line, opposite the northern grove where Hugh had left Crucita and Adelaido, the line was thick and wavered forward with a red flag. There must have been eight hundred men spread out across the sunlit prairie, bearing arms, moving forward like a pack of silent wolves. They wore everything from frock coats to buckskins, hats of every style in hazed relief against the sun behind them. A few were wearing U.S. Army uniforms. Twenty yards in front a rider on a dappled gray galloped up and down the line, moving northward and then wheeling and proceeding back the way that he had come, his saber held up high and glinting in the brilliant sun. He wore a black tricornered hat, and as he rode along the line he started calling in a slow and steady voice—"Hold your fire, men, hold your fire—"

Houston. It was Houston.

Behind Hugh and beside him the camp sprang into life. Officers sprinted from their tents in confusion, pulling on their jackets and their trousers. Castrillón was shouting orders. Santa Anna stood beside his tents, bareheaded, flinging out his arms. The cannon was touched off not ten yards down the barricade from Hugh, but it shot high, falling behind the advancing line, and Houston kept on coming, calling, "Hold your fire, men, hold it till you see their eyes." To the left the rebel cavalry was closing in and cutting off the open, southern fields.

The Mexicans touched off their cannon once again and black smoke rolled onto the prairie, billowing and creeping like a living thing.

Sam Houston swung his dappled gray back toward the center of the line, his gray coat flapping open in the wind, and pointed with his saber toward the two small cannon. Both were touched to fire, one and then the other, and when the smoke had rolled away a gentle song was piping in the air. Hugh saw beside the cannon on the right a small boy with a flute. He was playing an Irish love song with a calm, sweet melody, a tune Hugh knew by heart—"Will you come to the bower I have shaded for you? Our bed shall be roses all spangled with dew"—and then his song was muffled in the roll of a drumbeat to double quick time by a black man trotting beside him.

Mexicans flung themselves on the barricades, shoving in by Hugh, and fired their muskets at the line. But the rebels seemed impervious to fire and the music kept on playing. The Mexicans touched their cannon off again, and once again shot high. Castrillón was yelling a name— "Arenal! Arenal!" and Delgado was rallying the men.

Hugh swung down from the ammunition boxes and launched himself northward, past the cannon, past the tents, running pell-mell with the barricade toward the grove. He moved on instinct, only dimly noting his surroundings. From the left corner of his sight he saw out past the barricade toward where the quiet rebel line advanced with its red flag of death. And then the barricade was gone, it tapered down to nothing. Hugh reached the end of it and there was nothing but the field of bright green grass between him and the rebel line. He had at least two hundred paces yet to go before he reached the grove. He heard the scattered notes of music drifting over on the breeze and the spring wind passing through the prairie grass—"There under the bower on roses you'll lie, with a blush on your cheek and a smile in your eye." Lush grass tangled around his legs as if to bring him down, but was powerless against his stride. The rebel line was curving at the end, advancing on the grove; it would be there when he reached it. It would catch the drowsy soldiers by surprise.

In silence, but for the music of the flute and tawdry drum, the rebel line moved forward at a trot. When the line was only sixty yards away Hugh was still running at full speed with the wind on his face and the song in his ears—"Will you, Will you, Will you, Will you—come to the bower?" He glanced and saw Sam Houston signal with the sword. Pushing himself faster, he saw the rebels halt, sink down in the grass, and lift their weapons to take aim. He dived flat on his stomach in the grass, heard the fire of the guns, the whistle of the balls in the air above him, and lifted up to see the rebel line had disappeared in smoke.

When the rebels burst out of the smoke they came like demons out of hell, shouting, firing at random, plunging forward with such noise they shook the earth. Hugh rose and ran on toward the grove, picturing Crucita's face, the striped serape on the ground, the dappled sun beneath the tree. He looked behind and saw the line had flung itself onto the barricade, the men there fighting hand to hand, the rebels turning the twelve-pounder on the Mexicans and touching off a load of grape into the camp. Ahead of him, the rebels on the north end of the line rushed into the grove before he reached it, and Cós's men were just now charging out of it in total rout and wild confusion, rushing southward toward him, toward the main camp and the barricade. They were men whose faces he knew, men he'd nursed in San Felipe in the cotton gin or on the riverbanks along the way, running past him now in utter terror with the rebels on their heels.

He started yelling for Crucita. The soldiers running toward him jostled into him and knocked him down. He tasted his own blood, and rose up from the grass as if he flew through air. The guns were going off around him. The screaming was so loud he couldn't hear his own voice calling for Crucita. He felt invisible, for none of these white demons with their beards and red eyes and their ragged clothing cast him even one clear glance. He was a phantom to them. They were killing only men with black hair and brown skin. He was searching so intently for her face, imposing it on every face he saw, his cognizance of all the carnage and the screaming was more distant than a dream. Above the chaos and the yelling a howling cry ascended, echoing among the leafy branches, shouted out a hundred times before Hugh listened to the meaning: as the rebels slaughtered Mexicans—shot and stabbed them, splayed their throats wide open with their Bowie knives, beat their skulls against their pallets on the ground with musket butts—they howled the battle cry as if the cry itself empowered them to deeds of such atrocity— "Remember the Alamo—Remember Goliad—Remember—" They named their friends who were now dead at the hands of Mexicans, names winging through the branches like birds—"Remember Buck Travis! Remember Andrew Kent!" Hugh heard some crying out *"Recuerden La Bahía . . . Recuerden* Gregorio Esparza . . ." for *Tejanos* were among these rebels who were plunging out of hell.

It was revenge they sought. It was annihilation. It was a sacrifice of blood in the names of those shot down at La Bahía and the Alamo. Many of the Mexicans fell on their knees and begged for mercy—"Me no Alamo," and "me no Goliad—" to claim they had not been there.

But mercy was not in the wind that day. The executioners were working with the fervor of fanatics—using tomahawks and knives, squirrel rifles, musketry and pistols. They fought with sawed-off shotguns, buck and ball, they killed at close range and were bathed in blood. Their hands were slick with it; their beards were spattered. It was butchery at fever pitch. The howling and the screaming were like sounds of animals. Blood clotted in the fur of their caps and on their waistcoats and buckskins.

Hugh tripped on dying men, and left them there. His arm was cut by someone's sword, and he didn't care. A splotch of blood obscured his sight so he could hardly see; he groped his way from tree to tree, shouting wildly for Crucita. When he reached the edge he found the blanket as he'd left it, but Crucita wasn't there, so he wheeled around and ran in the direction she had gone when he last saw her, to the right along the edge, then back in the direction he had come, toward the camp, the way that everyone alive was running. Back across the crowded sunlit field the Mexicans were shot down as they ran, falling in heaps and begging him for mercy as he ran, as if he were the enemy, *"No me maten, no me maten, por favor—"*

In the main camp he found smoke and fire and the scream of horses smelling their own blood, for rebel cavalry had thrown themselves onto the south side of the camp where Mexicans were taking horses down to water, scattering the horses into panic and stampeding them into the camp. The camp was like the clashing point of two wild storms—Cós and his men rushing from the north, the horses from the south all boiling in together with such turmoil that it was impossible for officers to form their men into their ranks or rally for defense.

They collided, then surged eastward toward the river. Castrillón was dead beside the cannon. The barricades were blanketed with dead. The cannon, full of grape, was fired on the fleeing Mexicans, who fell like grass beneath the wind. Santa Anna's tents were shot with holes. Sam Houston's dappled gray lay dead. The hospital tent had crumpled down on top of those inside. Wounded horses stampeded over dying men, and the mules in hobbles leaped like crippled rabbits through the fray.

Hugh ran eastward with the body of the people, searching for the movement of her brown dress in the crowd and searching bloody faces. He was running with the rebels now and had the strange sensation he was one of them, as if he'd charged the barricades and now pursued the Mexicans toward the marshes of the little lake that bulged out of the river.

There was a boggy slough to cross, and this small crevice—six feet deep and ten yards wide and stretching down the center of the prairie— meant the doom of hundreds. They trampled one another trying to get over. Some went underwater but were shot when they came up for air. The water and the marsh were red. Horses struggled in the mud along the edge. The slough filled up with dead. Hugh ran up and down the length of it, searching for Crucita, looking for her hat or her brown dress in the muddy, bloody water and the thrashing bodies.

Sam Houston, with blood trailing from one boot, galloped on a pony with his sword drawn from the scabbard, shouting, "Take prisoners, men, God damn you, stop your shooting and take prisoners. God damn you, hold your fire!" A voice screeched in reply, "Boys, you know how to take prisoners, take 'em with the butt of your guns, club guns and remember the Alamo, remember Goliad, and club gun left and right and knock their goddamn brains out!"

Sam Houston and the other officers who tried to halt the massacre had less control than birds caught in a tempest. Houston whipped his pony toward the drummer in the open field. "Beat a retreat!" he ordered. "God damn you, beat a retreat!" The drummer did as he was told, setting crooked branch sticks to the little drum, but the sound was puny and the army had become a mob. The killing moved on eastward over the green prairie with the speed of a cloud's shadow on a windy day.

At a narrow bend in the boggy slough several horses were mired in the mud, and the rebels crossed on the horses' backs, one behind the other leaping from the bank onto the saddles or the bare backs of the struggling creatures and then over to the other side, splashing in the marshy grass and rushing on after the Mexicans, on toward the shaded tree line of the lake that bulged out of the San Jacinto.

Hugh didn't wait his turn to cross over on the horses. He flung himself into the water with the Mexicans. Bodies fell on top of him and he went under. Beneath the water's surface there was respite from the noise, a muffling of the sounds, but the bottom sludge was writhing underneath his feet—he could feel the movement and the struggle, could see the bubbles rising up, and clawed his way to the surface, spitting bloody water, flinging out his arms to throw the bodies off. He could taste and smell the bloody water. When he wiped the water from his eyes he saw a bearded rebel in a top hat and an Eton jacket, squatting in the bullrushes over a Mexican soldier who was begging, *"No señor, no, por favor—"*

"Remember Wash Cottle at the Alamo," the rebel said, and cocked his pistol and pricked the man's face with his knife, then fired one ball point blank in his head.

Wash Cottle. It conjured up a face, a place—George Washington Cottle of Gonzales, who had once sold Hugh a plow. And then Hugh recognized the butcher in the Eton jacket as the small-eyed Jimmy Curtis, father of Wash Cottle's wife, who had never cared for Wash, in life.

A hand was clawing at Hugh's face. He grabbed the wrist and saw he was holding to a wounded soldier stripped naked to the waist. He tried to pull him to the other side. Jimmy Curtis started laughing with a high pig's squeal, and Hugh saw him take the black hair of his victim and slice the Bowie knife along the scalp. Jimmy Curtis yelled, "I'll make me a razor strop out of your hide—"

The soldier in Hugh's arms was bleeding from the mouth. His hair was dripping murky water. Hugh hauled him through the twisting bodies, and when he got him to the other bank he felt the body lurch in his arms and looked to see a hole gaping where the face had been. He then let go. Clambering for footing in the grass, groping with his gnarled hands, he rose out of the sludge and started sloshing eastward through the open field with Mexicans and rebels running in the same direction out on either side, the rebels shooting as they ran.

At the marshy lake there was another jam of people, hundreds bogged in sludge and hyacinths with purple blooms and waxy leaves, hundreds farther out in water to their necks swimming eastward toward the river through the tangled weeds. The rebel cavalry was galloping in both directions on the bank, shooting at the heads of soldiers in the water. It was a sport to them, at that grim hour. It was like shooting turtles in a pond.

Hugh would not have noticed Adelaido on the bank if he hadn't seen the handcuffs at his back. Adelaido was not running now. He had stopped there at the edge. He had no hope of making it across the water without arms to swim. They would shoot him in the head. He chose to stand there on the bank and be shot in the chest, instead. He stood in boggy grass up to his knees, looking out across the lake, the crowd in panic pushing past him to the water. As he turned his face around, Hugh saw his dark eyes squinting in the slanted sun. He had a calm, perfect dignity; he expected to be shot. When his face came full around, Hugh saw that one half was disfigured to a bloody mass.

Hugh's boots were full of water. He could hardly run. He stumbled on a soldier—a dead man with a gun. Grabbing up the musket, he lunged toward Adelaido. Adelaido did not seem to know him. A rebel in a planter's hat lunged toward the crowd near Adelaido, swinging his broad sword, and Adelaido leaped sideways out of the blade's path yelling in English on behalf of everyone around him, to try to save their lives, "We surrender to your mercy! Take us—we are prisoners! None of us are armed!" But the sword went slashing on. It cut an old man half in two then beat the water in a frenzy, butchering the fallen soldiers.

Adelaido hurled himself against the man who swung the sword, knocking him down sideways in the marsh. The blade sank in the grassy weeds. While the rebel floundered, groping for his sword with one hand and holding a pistol with the other in a fixed attempt to keep it dry, Hugh splashed into the water in between and stood in front of Adelaido with the musket barrel aimed at Adelaido's stomach. "He is my prisoner," he gasped, glancing over at the man then back at Adelaido and his bloodied face, the black eyes just now showing recognition.

The man rose up with murky water draining from his homespun clothes and dripping from his chin. He had the sword in one hand and the pistol in the other. "No he ain't," he said. "He's mine."

"He is my prisoner," Hugh repeated. The man stepped forward with the sword, but Hugh swung the musket up against the blade and knocked it aside. Looking at the musket for the first time since he'd plucked it from the soldier's hand, he saw it was not primed, and placed his other hand in such a way the rebel could not see the gun was useless, and turned the aim on him.

The man cocked back his pistol and pointed it at Adelaido's chest. "You can't knock off a bullet," he said evenly.

"I will shoot you if you shoot him," Hugh responded, cocking back the safety on the gun.

Two mangled soldiers sloshed their way toward Hugh and crouched beside him. "*Ave María purisima!*" they cried, holding on to his legs, "*Por Dios, salva mi vida!*" They were badly injured; one had lost an eye. "*Ayúdame . . . Sálvame!*" they cried.

Adelaido, back behind him, was asking Hugh if he had seen Crucita, and Hugh shook his head, staring at the man before him, the hard blue eyes. It seemed so long since he had seen blue eyes. Miles had eyes this blue.

Adelaido's whisper had grown frantic in Hugh's ear. "I thought she was with you—"

The rebel said to Hugh, "You would shoot me, for that greaser, you're in earnest?"

"Yes."

Something passed between them, then—not an understanding, but a blessed whim, and the man blinked his blue eyes and said, "Take him then," and turned and fished his hat out of the water.

The soldier at Hugh's right moaned fretfully, casting his blank, mutilated face up toward the light with one eye gashed away, *"Gracias a Dios, señor, gracias a Dios. Señor todo poderoso, gracias—"*

The soldier at Hugh's other side whispered, *"Oh, Dios mio, gracias, señor,"* his voice no louder than a sigh of breath, and then released his hold on Hugh's left thigh and leaned and sank his face down in the water. Hugh grabbed the collar of his shirt and tried to lift him, but the weight was like a willing weight, as if the man now wished to drown himself. Hugh couldn't get a better grasp unless he let go of the gun, and this he did not do.

Adelaido squatted down to where the water swirled around his chest; he turned his back and tried to get hold of the soldier with his tethered hands, his face turned sideways and his bloody cheek resting on the surface, his fingers groping underneath the water at his back and trying to find purchase in the man's thick hair.

But the breath was rising from below in crystal orbs, crystal jewels released and given to the April air, a parting gift of life. The man was dead, and sinking.

The other soldier was still staring upward with his one good eye, staring at the blue, blue sky, speaking to his God in a voice so low and slurred that Hugh could only recognize one word, *"Dios . . . Dios . . . Dios—"*

The last of the late shadows stretched long across the marshy meadows and grew thin, like old and withered men, and then joined all together in the grasses and purple twilight settled on the land. The rebels, sickened of the blood, began to take live captives and escort them to the camp on the far side of the prairie in the bearded oak trees by the bayou.

Crucita lay flat on her stomach in the grass beside a little boy, holding the boy's face tight in both her hands. The boy lay on his back, shivering with cold and staring at the rising moon, a dusty-looking moon veiled in thin clouds. A ball had shattered the bones of both his legs below the knees, and he shook violently and eased a high-pitched whine into the purple air, his arms outstretched, his small hands gripping fistfuls of green grass, as if he had been pinned there on the ground beneath the moon like Jesus on the cross, his skin turned white and ghostly cold.

"My skeleton is coming through," he cried aloud with horror. "I can feel the bones sticking out of my legs—" The fretful whine eased from his throat, water slid out of his eyes and ran across his temples to his ragged hair, and blood boiled from the wounds and made a sticky, pungent mass, clotting in the grass. It seemed the earth would claim his body droplets at a time.

Crucita got up on her knees and looked again and told him no, his bones were still inside. She said she could not see the bones within the wounds—the skin still covered them—which was a lie. She tore her brown dress at the hem, all the way around, and wound the strips around his legs. The boy was near delirium with pain, and shook so hard his legs began to spasm. Crucita lay her weight against his thighs to make them still, and he lay trembling underneath her, staring at the dusty moon, his hands still plucking at the grass and a wild look in his eyes. She moved her body over all of him except his legs and held his head against her breast as if he were her child. She made him say his name—Manuel. She asked his age—he said that he was seven. She asked him how he came to be here when he was so young, and only for that instant he stopped trembling and he said it was because he learned to play the drum.

"You are a drummer boy," she said to him.

"*El Presidente* says that I am good."

And then his spasms started up again, and the rattling whine from all the way inside his lungs. "Is *El Presidente* dead?" he said.

"I cannot say, Manuel. I do not know."

"The Americans, are they still looking for us? Will they come back again?"

Yes, they were still looking. She raised her head and saw the torch-lights moving on the twilit prairie. They were taking prisoners now but evidently they had not stopped killing altogether, for now and then she heard the distant popping of a gun, the echo ringing hollow out across the marshes.

She could not see beyond a rise of ground off to the west where their camp lay—she estimated that the camp must be three miles away. A trail ran from a stand of trees through the open prairie from the south, curving to the west and up the slope, and Crucita watched the rebels bringing in the prisoners on the trail. There were fewer coming in, now that it was dark; most had gone back to the camp before the light had faded. Now they came at intervals, sometimes only two Anglos on horseback goading several Mexicans along in front of them. When they topped the rise they seemed to sink and disappear as if the ground had swallowed them.

Perhaps the prisoners would all be shot, together, in the morning, in retribution for the massacre at La Bahía.

In the stand of trees, near where the trail emerged, Crucita saw a torchlight casting its bright flicker on the branches and its pale smoke into shadowed evening light. She watched it move onto the trail and out onto the prairie, and she heard a voice, then, from over the western rise, calling out against the wind, "Lem? Is that you, Lem, with that light?"

"Yeah. Who's that?"

"It's me, Peter."

Crucita watched the dark shape loping down the rise along the trail toward the man who held the light, and the two met midway on the trail beneath a small mesquite tree only thirty yards from where Crucita lay.

"Have you found many live ones?" the man with the torch—the one named Lem—asked the other.

"Not 'live enough to give us any trouble. Goodson brought in twelve all by hisself."

A silence settled in. Wind whispered through the grasses. Crucita's dress was damp and cold and underneath her ribs she felt the tremors in

Manuel's small body, felt the long, high whining pressing from his lungs. She looked straight down into his eyes and whispered to him softly, "Manuelito, try not to make the whining noise, you must be quiet now, you must be calm, your bones have not come through, these Americans, they will not hurt you. I will not let them hurt you."

The moonlight glistened in his eyes.

"I'm goin' back to camp," the man named Lem announced. "It's gonna be completely dark in thirty minutes."

"Ever' Meskin we let go is one more Meskin who can fight us later," his companion answered.

"I pretty much doubt that, Pete. They've had their fill of us."

"Don't be so sure. If Santie Anna gets away and rallies 'em—and hell, he's got thousands more, all over—there's no tellin'. This battle could mean nothin'." He paused, then said decisively, "I sure would like to be the one to get my hands on Santie Anna. He can't of got too far."

"Somebody said they saw him on a black horse headin' off toward Vince's bridge."

"Now how the hell would anybody know what Santie Anna looks like?"

"That's just what I heard."

"From who?"

"God damn, I don't know who. Just somebody said he heard it from somebody."

"Yeah, well, I ain't goin' in yet, not while that son of a bitch is out there somewhere. Millard said he saw some rustlin' over in that area, before where it gets marshy." He brushed a hand toward where Crucita lay. "Said he bets there's twenty at least hunkered in them grasses."

"Millard's a goddamn liar. He can't tell the truth for nothin'."

"Well I intend to look. You go on back if you want. But gimme your light."

"I ain't givin' you my light."

"There's plenty light to get you back to camp. There's half a hour yet till dark."

"I said I ain't givin' you my light. Go get your own."

"Why, you spooked?"

"You bet I'm spooked. There's dead ones ever' where."

"You're scared of the dead ones?"

"Hell yeah. If you had a lick of sense—"

"Shhhhh—you hear that?"

"What?"

"Somethin' in them grasses. Over there."

"You're just tryin' to spook me."

"No. Shhhhhhh."

Manuel had let out his long trembling whine. His teeth were chattering. Crucita placed her palm against his mouth. "Manuel, Manuelito —" she whispered, and looked to see the man named Peter lift his arm beside the torch and point in her direction. She leaned her head into the grass beside the boy's shoulder and tried to steady her heart. *"Madre de Dios. Ruegale a tu hijo por mi."*

"I don't hear it."

"I did. I heard it. Come on, let's go see."

"I'll be damned if I intend to grope around in that grass for live Mexicans—"

"Set it afire, then," the answer hastened. "Just move downwind and put your torch to it; they'll come out. Go on over there a little ways, and the wind'll push the fire toward the lake and trap 'em in the marsh."

"We ain't had orders to be settin' fires."

"We ain't had but two orders all day long: first to fight—and that one come about a month too late—and then to halt our fightin'—and that one come too soon, before the job was done. We'd of lost this battle, they'd of turned on us if we'd of stuck to orders." Lem's silence said he disagreed, but the voice went on, "I say to hell with orders. Put that torch down to the grass. Hell, I'll do it. Give it here."

A night bird flew low down against the grasses, so close Crucita heard its wings, and then rose over near the moon and lighted in the timber to the south. To the north was swampy ground with bullfrogs chirping in the marsh, and then the dark lake and the river. Crucita felt the boy's frail body shake beneath her own. He tried to ask her what the men were saying but she hushed him with her finger on his lips.

Her instinct was to crawl off toward the river, but the boy would never make it through the marsh. She could not drag him either—not that distance, without being seen. If they lit the fires she would have to bring the boy out of the hiding place and appeal for mercy from these men.

She saw the torchlight passed from one man to the other, watched the figure striding east into the gusting wind. She watched him lean and gently touch the fire to the grasses, just as one would lean and stroke a dog. The tips of grass furled in the light and barely caught and almost flickered out, but then took root and fire started spreading on the ground. The figure watched a moment, appraising what he'd done, then strode farther, curving northward, touching fire to the field in a dozen places.

The flames were moving toward her, driven by the wind. She could smell the smoke as it blew over in a haze. "Manuel, Manuel," she whispered, "they've set fire to the grass. I'll have to call on the Americans to help us. I speak English; they'll understand me and have mercy because I'm a woman and you're a child. You shouldn't be afraid."

But she—herself—she was afraid. The butchery that she had witnessed on that day had shattered her last faith in human grace. She had seen, from close up, something worse than war: she had seen the face of evil. She'd watched an Anglo rebel call a halt upon the firing, shouting out across the water that all Mexicans who would surrender to him would be spared, and when a few who understood complied and started swimming back to shore, the man had raised his hand and thrown his head back with a laugh and cried aloud to his companions, "Give it to 'em, boys!" and six or seven opened fire.

This, she saw while she was running with a mob of others down the shore in slimy, heavy mud that sucked the shoes off her feet and caked around her ankles.

She had no faith in pity now. She wished for Hugh. She wished for Adelaido though she thought he must be dead. But as the flames rolled toward her the only one to call on was the stranger who had held the torch at first and who was tired of the killing and the hunt and was reluctant to set fire to the grass.

"Señor, Señor Lem?" she called, at first in a whisper, then with more insistence. "Señor Lem?" She could see him through the misty smoke, standing underneath the lone mesquite. She saw him turn his face in her direction. She stood up, calling once again, "Señor? My name is María de la Cruz. Please, señor, I need you to help me. You please come help us."

The man stood without moving, listening to her words, then turned eastward calling his companion in a shaky voice, "Peter? Peter?"

"Yeah," Peter answered from beyond the smoke. "Lem? Where are you?"

"I'm still over here. Did you hear someone calling me?"

"Calling you?"

"Yeah. I thought I heard my name."

"Spooks. Maybe spooks."

"No, Peter. Where are you? I can't see you. It was my name, a woman called my name, for help. Peter? Are you there?"

But the flames were rising and the smoke was black and Peter did not answer from beyond the wall of fire.

"Please, señor, my name is María de la Cruz and I need you to help me." She was yelling now, throwing her voice out with the smoky wind. "Here is a boy with me and his legs are bad. The fire is coming fast. Please hurry." She was searching for the words. "Please rush," she said. She waited, hoping, staring at his smoky shape. She saw him take a step, and stop. A gust of smoke obscured him, and she called again, unable to disguise her fear, "Señor, the fire is coming fast!" Leaning down, she struggled to take Manuel in her grasp, clutching his frail body underneath the arms and moving backward with him toward the trail and the mesquite tree. If she could move him twenty, maybe thirty yards—as far as the mesquite tree—then she might possibly escape the fire's ragged path. He tried to fight her off with his thin arms, and howled in pain, but she dragged him with her, his broken, bleeding legs trailing limp and mangled through the grass.

The light still lingered in the air but smoke had washed it gray. From the marsh that wound around the lake several other figures, dark and silent, rose, half-stooped, and sprinted toward the water like mute, crippled ghouls. She no longer heard the croaking of the frogs. Back across her shoulder she glimpsed other figures, three Anglos, "Americans," against the purple sky along the rise, running toward her—toward the fire—with their guns. She was no longer calling for the man named Lem, for all her energy was used in speaking to the child, and pulling him. The smoke was thick and sharp and stung her eyes. Above the crackling of the burning grass she heard scattered yells and gunfire. Dark shapes ran like phantoms all around her. The boy was weeping with bewilderment and rage at the intensity of his pain, his tears grimy from the smoke, and Crucita let him rest for just a moment, kneeling down beside him. She heard the sound of boots thudding on the grass and looked up to see a man looking wonderingly down at her, his face obscured by the growing dark and by shifting bands of smoke. The face was young, framed by a widow's peak and downy sideburns. "How did you know my name?" he asked her, lifting his voice above the crackling of the burning prairie.

She looked into his kind and troubled face and answered him. "Because I heard your name; I heard him say your name."

Bits of burning grass danced above his head like fireflies borne on the driven winds. He waved the smoke away and blinked painfully, rubbing his knuckles in his eyes and glancing at the coming fire, now not far away.

"Can you please help me?" Crucita said to him, "I need you to help me. This boy, look, his legs—" The strips of cloth that she had tied were torn away and bone was visible again. The man leaned over, placing his hands on his knees and staring down. A shiver wracked the boy. *"No me maten, por Dios, señor!"* he cried, and Crucita spoke to tell him that the man had come to help him, not to hurt him.

The man then knelt and took a closer look, and slid his hands beneath Manuel and lifted him and carried him swiftly toward the lone mesquite, Crucita trying to support the broken legs, but Manuel's shrieks of pain were unbearable to hear and Lem set him down before they reached the tree. "The fire's veering off," he said. "It looks like it would miss us here but we should move him farther if we can. We need some kind of splint." He hurried over to the tree for limbs which he could break and use to hold the legs in place. But the mesquite limbs were contorted and too springy with their April sap, and Lem called over to Crucita, "Wait here with him; I'll be back," and turned to run off toward the stand of trees.

A man was coming toward them from the trees, and seeing him, Lem stopped and called, "Bring some sticks for splints! Over here!" and pointed toward Crucita and the boy. But the man did not bring any splints. He ran along the trail toward Lem. His hair was red and wild, his legs were bandy and he wore large spurs, the rowels caked thick with mud. In one hand was a sword drawn from its scabbard, in the other was a pistol. "Have you seen my horse?" he said.

Lem shook his head.

"God damn it to hell," the man responded, and walked quickly over to Crucita and Manuel, looked at the boy appraisingly and shot him in the head. A piece of the boy's skull struck Crucita on the cheek, and she felt blood brimming there—hers, or maybe his—cool against her skin. She touched it with her fingers. The air around was hot and dense with smoke, but there against her cheek the blood felt cold.

The officer—he seemed to be an officer, to her—turned briskly and walked over to Crucita. She was weary with her horror; she could not command herself to run.

"She's a woman!" Lem was shouting, running toward him, and his voice rose high and querulous above the crackle of the burning grass. "She's a woman, sir—"

The officer said nothing. His eyes were wild and narrow as he plunged the sword into her heart. She saw his ruddy coloring turn white, the pale skin of his cheeks begin to ripple. The pain was quick and blunt, as if a horse had kicked her. But when he pulled the sword out of her body she could feel the rending of its blade.

The face of this man was as blanched and indifferent as the face of the dusty moon hanging just above the limbs of the mesquite, as remote and unconcerned as the wooden visage of St. John the Shepherd when she turned him to the wall. She fell forward with the green grass cool and moist against her cheek, then turned onto her side, watching toward the burning light and groping in her failing memory for a kinder face, a face with a benevolent light in his eyes, the face of someone who had loved her. Perhaps she found him there, for the worry seemed to seep away and she grew lazy, watching the curling strands and flecks of light, the windborne sparks swirling around her head.

A   B O Y   B E S I D E   T H E   F I R E

Someone had set fire to the grass about three miles from camp, and Sam Houston, on the edge of consciousness from loss of blood, had seen the light on the horizon and smelled the smoke and was not pleased. He lay sputtering profanities beneath a spreading oak in the rebel camp beside the bayou, a saddle for a pillow. Disoriented and disgruntled, he called for Santa Anna to be brought before him, though Santa Anna had not yet been captured. He heard the intermittent firing of guns out in the marshes and demanded that the killing stop.

But no one in the camp was listening to Sam Houston and his dream-infested ramblings. Those who had returned to camp were listening to the voices from within. They gathered underneath the oak trees by the bayou and stoked their fires bright to keep away the souls of seven hundred dead out on the fields. They sat in awesome silence, caked in blood and tired now to tears. Some smoked cigars and milled around the heaps of spoils—crates of wine and food, soap and candles, stacks of weaponry and blankets, and a military chest with an estimated twelve thousand dollars in specie. No one spared the wine. Men claimed whole bottles to themselves and drank and crowded in to stare at Santa Anna's saddle, which was richly mounted in silver. One man in a fur cap spat on the saddle, and soon it was an obligation for every man to make a pilgrimage and spit on Santa Anna's saddle.

It was a victory, which they had won. But it was something else, which they had lost, and their voices had a hollow ring beneath the high and massive canopy of branches. They told stories of the day. Spanish moss dripped from the gnarled limbs like gray clumps of fog and the moon hung bright and almost full, glaring through the leaves at the men beneath the trees, glaring at nine miles of prairie sedge and intermittent woods littered with the dead, the slough and lake both tinted red.

Shortly after dark a man named Peter dragged into the camp and said a woman had been killed. Those around the fires lifted their faces from between their knees and felt the heat on their cheeks and stammered out their disbelief.

A woman? A woman had been killed? What man would kill a woman?

It was a sin, they said: it was a sin far greater than the ones they had committed on that day. They had won a battle, they had won a bloody battle, they had kept on killing after they had won. They had shot men on their knees. They had shot them close range in their heads and hammered out their brains. They had mutilated many of the dead. They had lost but six men on their side and killed an estimated six or seven hundred. It was a massacre, in numbers, but no one said the word aloud, for massacre was not a word men could apply to war when God was on their side.

And no one—no one—would have killed a woman.

No one but the man who did. He was somewhere in the camp or on the prairie—a murderer who ought to pay for such a sin, and they began, with their fatigue and tired hearts and gruesome memories to call down judgment on his soul. They demanded answers and told lies. They named the man though no one knew if he had really done it, and heaped their own guilt on his hide. His name was Forbes; he was a colonel and the commissary general whom they all despised, a red-haired Irishman with Scottish blood, famous for his temper and his acid tongue and for withholding of supplies.

"Who killed the woman?" one man shouted from his camp fire to the next, and the answer echoed through the trees, several voices in a chorus—"Colonel Forbes!" "Colonel Forbes, he done it!"

The story grew. A strange hysteria grew from it. Someone said they'd seen the colonel drop out of the rebel line and lie down in the sage grass while the rebels marched upon the barricade. The coward. Someone else had seen him hidden in the trees. Another man had seen him half an hour into battle with no blood upon his sword, eating stew from the iron cook pots of the Mexicans while the battle swept off eastward across the boggy slough.

"Who killed the woman?" one voice queried.

"Colonel Forbes!" a hundred answered, tinged with laughter now and giddy with the game.

"Why did he do it?"

"To bloody his sword!"

"Who hid in the grass?"

"Colonel Forbes!"

"Who hid in the grass and ate the stew?"

"Colonel Forbes!"

"Who hid in the grass and ate the stew and killed the woman to bloody his sword?"

"Colonel Forbes!" "Colonel Forbes, brave he!"

They disguised their troubled hearts in reckless laughter. As long as they could call down judgment on the colonel they could suspend it from themselves. Their moods were fickle and their voices rose and fell from revelry to anger at the man who killed the woman. They all could kill, they said—sure, they could kill, they could kill brutally and in mass numbers, but they could never kill a woman, they weren't capable of such a deed. The colonel, he should pay for his atrocity.

It was after dark, long after dark, when wolves had started prowling on the battleground, that Hugh and Adelaido reached the camp. They had talked themselves into believing they would find Crucita there among the prisoners, for they'd been told there were some women captured. If they couldn't find her in the camp, they'd get a blacksmith to remove the cuffs from Adelaido's hands and get a hat for Adelaido and place a wand of cardboard in the band such as Juan Seguín and his *Tejano* rebels wore to separate them from the Mexicans. Then they would return to the fields and search for her again. It would be a risk for Adelaido to be walking in the fields of dead; there were rebels, mad as rabid dogs, foot loose on the prairies shooting anyone they came across who had brown skin, and in the dark a piece of cardboard sticking from a hat would likely not protect him. But Adelaido was in such a state of wild anxiety about Crucita that the risk meant nothing to him. The right side of his face was peckered with a powder burn from someone's gun exploding at close range, the wound so deep the flesh was stiff with blood and speckled black with the embedded powder. The eye was blistered red, though the vision seemed to be intact, and Adelaido cast his glance around so strangely and with such a haunted air that to look at him was almost more than Hugh could bear.

Hugh carried his strain differently, within. His hope was sliding to despair. He searched the shadows for her eyes, her hair, the way she moved and held her head. He saw her brown dress everywhere, in every crevice, every bunch of grass, floating with the dead all tangled in a mass. Three times after twilight he had waded out among the water hyacinths to drag a body up and see its face.

His clothes were dripping wet. His hands were bloated stiff. He'd bound his arm above the elbow where the saber had sliced through, and though the wound was shallow it still bled. Deeper, deeper down he shoved his fear. He'd grown dependent on Crucita, and his eyes would not accept she was no longer here.

They were moving from the prairie to the trees, shivering with cold from their wet clothes. The moon shone on their shoulders, white as chalk. Three men were entering the trees together fifty yards down to the right leading half a dozen mules and horses loaded heavily with spoils. To the left the road wound from the slope with several horsemen riding down it toward them, goading ten or fifteen prisoners before them.

The wolves were creeping in.

Hugh could see ahead the light of camp fires in the woods. He could hear the voices and the murmur of the wind. He heard a chorus sung out in a burst of unison: "Colonel Forbes!" The name meant nothing to him. Once again he heard it, "Colonel Forbes!" Then he heard a lone voice trailing through the trees, lifting high above the branches on the breeze—"Who killed the woman?"

"Colonel Forbes!"

Hugh stopped there, suddenly. Adelaido also stopped, and looked at him, his mangled cheek caked black with blood. Adelaido said, "There were many women that it could have been."

"Yes."

"There were at least thirty with the Mexicans."

"Yes."

"They wouldn't kill a woman who spoke English."

"No."

They were lying to each other. There were not thirty women with the Mexicans, there were probably not twenty. And it could have been Crucita. They had called, and called . . .

They went to where the prisoners were kept—a clearing in the woods—and found about two hundred men and almost twenty women crowded in a pen built out of hemp ropes and pack saddles. There were thirty guards around tormenting them. A bonfire burning long and leafy limbs sent sparks clear to the moon, it seemed, and all the guards were bearing candles in their hands like schoolboys on a Christmas Eve. The clearing was awash in festive light. The guards were armed so heavily the weapons were like decorations, bags of bullets, powder horns, and knives strapped on their clothing. Each had a carbine or a musket, some had rifles, some had pistols. "Where's Santie Anna? ¿Comprende?" they shouted. Seguín's *Tejanos* shouted in Spanish, telling the prisoners they would be executed in the morning, burned alive in retribution for the funeral pyres at the Alamo and La Bahía. Many of the prisoners were on their knees, begging in the name of God for mercy.

Hugh and Adelaido circled around the pen, searching frantically among the sweating faces in the firelight, Adelaido in his handcuffs asking of the prisoners in Spanish if they'd seen a woman in a brown dress and a hat. But they were leery of him, in his cuffs, walking free among the Anglos with a face burned black with blood, and either did not answer him or said they had not seen her. One who recognized him spoke to him and called him by his name, but said he had not seen Crucita once that day.

Hugh asked of her among the guards, but they said Mexicans all looked alike to them, they doubted they'd remember if they'd seen her. They did not care about a woman in a brown dress and a hat; it was Santa Anna whom they wanted.

"Where's Santie Anna? You. Mongrel. You—"

"Dead," the prisoners would answer, backing off and crowding up against the corners. "He is dead."

"He ain't dead, you goddamn liar."

"Dead. . . . Dead, señor. . . ."

"Liar. Goddamn fuckin' liars, every one of you bastards. Where's Cós at?"

One guard bragged to his companions, "I seen Santa Anna."

"Bullshit."

"Then it was Cós. He had him a uniform with gold dangles on the shoulders."

"Then for a fact it wasn't Cós. I seen Cós in December in San Antonio and he's nothin' but a sorry little scrub. And he ain't wore no gold."

The breeze licked at the candle flames the guards were holding and the bonfire's heat melted wax onto their hands and they shook their hands to fling the wax away.

"You, fat woman, *donde es Cós?*"

"Dead, señor. I see his body, he is dead."

"Yeah? Then let's you and me go see."

The woman backed away, not understanding all the words but knowing his sly look, and a prisoner—a man—stepped forward and said calmly to the guard, "I will take you there."

"Liar—he ain't out there. He ain't dead," the guard said, and sucked one cheek between his teeth.

"Perhaps you fear to go where there are wolves," the prisoner said, and the guard took note of the embroidered shoulder-straps on his blue jacket and his cold dignity in bearing, and demanded, "Are you Santie Annie?"

"No." The prisoner's face was cool, his voice was hard, there was no fear at all.

"Is he Santie Annie?" the guard began to shout at all the prisoners, leaning over the pack saddles and the rope that formed the corner of the pen and aiming his rifle at the man. Some of the soldiers cried aloud, "No, señor . . . no . . . him no es general . . . no es Santa Anna—"

Hugh was passing by and saw the prisoner looking down the barrel of the rifle with a cold abhorrence in his face, and he recognized him as the colonel who had fetched him from the woods and taken him to General Castrillón. Delgado was his name. "He isn't Santa Anna, he's a colonel," Hugh said tersely to the guard, remembering Delgado's greeting underneath the mulberry tree in the speckled light a thousand years ago, his bare foot with the nail ingrown, the toes caked thick with mud against the striped serape which Domingo de la Rosa gave Crucita.

"Adelaido!" he called suddenly, turning from Delgado and the guard. "Adelaido! She's not here."

Adelaido came to him with smoke blown toward him in a gust of wind, and together they went back through all the camp fires scattered in the woods and took a hat out of the spoils and stuck a piece of cardboard in the brim, and then searched out a blacksmith willing to remove the cuffs from Adelaido. Hugh left Adelaido with the blacksmith.

"Who killed the woman?"

"Colonel Forbes!"

"Who hid in the grass and killed the woman?"

"Colonel Forbes!"

The voices came from all directions in the camp and echoed with a strangeness through the mossy limbs, so it was hard to follow them. But Hugh, his clothes now only damp, his joints oblivious to pain, stumbled past the fires, in among the drunken men, asking them: "What woman has been killed? Who saw the woman? Was she young, or old? Is there anyone who could describe the woman?"

"Peter Benson—"

"Peter Benson?"

"He ain't seen her but his friend did, his friend talked to her, his name is . . . What's his name, Matt?"

"Lemuel Metcalf. They call him Lem."

"Yeah, that's him. He saw her killed. He's one of Burleson's I think. But he ain't sayin' much. Who are you?"

"Where's Burleson's camp?"

"Over by the water. Direct through there. But he ain't sayin' much. Who are you?"

Hugh found him sitting on the bank of the bayou staring at the moon's reflection on the sluggish water. He was about the age of Miles with longish hair and full sideburns cut far out into the hollows of his cheeks. He sat hunched over with his arms folded on his knees. His hair stood straight up from his forehead where he'd shoved his fingers through it in a nervous, repetitious gesture, accentuating a deep widow's peak. He glanced at Hugh and then continued staring at the water.

Hugh asked him if his name was Lem.

"Yeah."

Hugh sat down on the bank beside him. The murky water of the bayou was so slow and lazy that it hardly made a sound, but the frogs were croaking with the pulse of insects in the trees, and the howl of wolves was carried over on the breeze. Behind, the camp was finally settling down, as the men curled up beside the fires on their beds of Spanish moss and sank out of the world. "They say you saw a woman killed," Hugh said.

"I didn't."

"Your friend Peter says you did."

"Peter ain't my friend."

"I was told you spoke with her."

Lem pushed the fingers of both hands back through his hair and left them there, resting his forehead wearily in his cupped palms. "Go away."

"Did she say her name?"

"Look, I ain't seen any woman killed."

The moon's face wavered on the muddy water and shimmered on the far bank thirty yards across, with ghostly live oaks dripping Spanish moss, and Hugh said quietly, "There was a woman with the Mexicans, a friend of mine. I can't find her on the field, and she isn't with the prisoners. Her name is Crucita."

The young man sighed and spoke impatiently, "This woman called herself María, so it wasn't her."

In a whisper, Hugh said, "María de la Cruz Pacheco?"

Lem looked at him. "I don't know. Just 'María' is all I remember."

It was a common name. She could be anyone. "How old do you think she was?"

"Young."

He couldn't ask if she was wearing a brown dress, he simply could not bring himself to say the words. It was too definite, too soon, he did not want the confirmation. But he said, "Do you remember anything particular about her?"

Lem picked up a twig and turned it in his fingers. "I remember perfectly," he said, his voice monotonous and dead.

"Did she have a hat, of any kind?"

"No."

"You're sure?"

"Yeah."

"Was she alone?"

"She had a boy with her. Peter set the grass on fire to smoke out anybody hidin' in it, and this woman had a injured boy with both his legs broke." He twirled the twig between his fingers. "She started calling me to help her move him."

"She spoke English?"

He nodded.

Hugh felt his throat clamp shut and something swell up in his brain. "And did you help her?"

Lem flipped the twig out of his fingers and said with sudden irritation, "She's goddamn dead, all right?"

"Will you tell me where she is?"

Lem's sideburns formed dark shadows in the hollows of his cheeks. "She's two or three miles out on the New Washington road. There's a patch of grass burned down to stubble from the road over to the marsh, and a lone mesquite near where the fire burned, and she's under the mesquite."

"But she isn't burned." He did not ask it like a question.

"No," Lem said. And then he dipped his head and looked sideways at Hugh and said more quietly, "I didn't think he'd kill her. He shot the boy, but I didn't think he'd kill the woman. She was so beautiful you can't imagine."

Hugh shunned the voice and listened to the insects droning in the leaves.

As he walked back through the camp he could not stop his memories, a thousand in a second—the sack of beeswax that she offered him while standing in the little yard of La Bahía chapel, "I am not afraid of bees" . . . her body in the piles of moonlit cotton . . . her face against the trees. He did not know what he believed; he did not know if there was any hope left in his heart at all. A woman, young, who called herself María, "so beautiful you can't imagine," he had said.

He could imagine, perfectly.

Moving in a daze of dread, he passed a fire with three boys sitting around it on mounds of Spanish moss. One was patting out a wad of pasty dough. It was a little fire, burning down to embers with small licks of flame. The boy took the dough in both his hands, twisted it into a rope and twined it round a stick like a snake coiled around a limb, then held the stick above the flames and settled in. Hugh started to move on, but there was something in the boy that made him stop and look again. He was barefoot, wearing pants too long that trailed out on the ground beneath his heels. His shirt was big enough to swallow him. He wore a blue scarf cut from frayed domestic on his head, tied front to back and covering the crown. Shaggy patches like brown, molting fur stuck out beneath the scarf. His face was small and narrow; the eyes were deeply shadowed. A name spoke itself inside Hugh's mind—but firelight was playing tricks on him, glowing red against the boy's face with a waver like the wind.

Two other boys were sitting idly by the fire, one about sixteen years old with a tired countenance and one hand drawn up, crippled, in his lap. The other, of the same age, seemed to be a scrap or remnant of a person.

Hugh's gaze returned and rested on the first boy, the smallest of the three, the name speaking in his mind once more, and then aloud, "Toby? Toby?"

The boy looked up at him, his stick of dough drooping in the flames. "Father?"

Hugh squatted on his heels, studying the boy, uncertain. When the boy leaned slightly toward him, squinting to see better, then he knew for sure. It was Toby's squint, the expression which he always had without his glasses. Hugh felt as if his mind were drifting off. He heard his own voice speaking from another place, the words just coming on their own, "You lost your glasses."

Toby stared at him with eyes sunk out of sight inside his skull. "Yeah. I lost 'em in the river."

Hugh leaned forward into him and took his face in both his hands and ran his palms down Toby's neck and shoulders as if to mold him there beside the fire, as if creating him from air. The feelings were too many, all together. Here was Toby, resurrected from the dead, a skeleton returned to life and sitting by a fire cooking bread. "And Miles—" Hugh said.

Toby's hold was tenuous, confused. He seemed uncertain where to put his hands, whether he should drop the stick of dough and wrap his arms around his father's neck or hold on to the thing already in his grasp. With shaking hands he kept hold of the stick and turned his face back toward the fire where the smoke curled up around the dough. Hugh stared in wonder at the profile he had watched mature from infancy to boyhood, the skin now tight across the bones, the lips chewed into shreds. He could not keep his hands away.

"They shot him," Toby said.

Hugh suffered it again: the loss, confirmed. He had not even known that he had kept a small, abiding hope that Miles had lived, for Miles was not the kind to die. But now the hope just slipped away and left a pocket of pure emptiness where it had been.

Toby said, "I ran away."

Hugh put his hand on Toby's knee, but Toby flinched and made a skittish gesture.

The boy with the crippled hand said, "He's got cactus in his legs. He won't let anybody touch 'em."

Taking hold of one cuff of the baggy trousers, Hugh pulled it carefully above the knee and suffered so much at the sight his heart shuddered and flopped over. "What have I done to you, my son?" he groaned. The leg was swollen twice its normal size, lumpy with red welts that oozed and stank. Thorns were visible beneath the skin. The foot was bare and crusty at the heels. Hugh started working with the buttons of the shirt. "Did you come this far alone?"

Toby held on to his stick but now began to shake all over and answered in an odd, disoriented tone, "The farthest part. Then I found Tad. Did you find Mother?"

He shook his head. "Who is Tad?"

Toby nodded toward the scrappy boy and said whimsically, "That's Tad. You don't remember him?"

Hugh peeled away the shirt, studying the skin, the buds of nipples in the firelight, the rib cage seeming all caved in. Probing with his fingers in the sweaty warmth he found the wound, the scarring drawn so tight that movement was impaired, a kind of webbing of the armpit. Glancing at the boy named Tad, he thought remotely that he did perhaps remember him, one of Fannin's boys, but he had seemed much older then.

The third spoke up. "That ain't his real name—Tad. He forgot his name, we think. He doesn't talk any. General Houston carved him out a little frog, a tadpole, so we call him Tad."

Tad reached inside his trouser pocket for the frog, and held it out to Hugh. Hugh looked at it—a lump of golden wood nestled in a bony palm.

"My name's Terrell Mott," the other said, and raised his twisted hand. "A month ago my horse fell with me on it and my hand is frozen up."

Toby all this time had managed to retain the stick, switching it from one hand to another when Hugh peeled the shirt away, and now as Hugh was buttoning the shirt back on, Toby slid his pants leg down and turned his stick and watched the dough begin to swell. Hugh longed to take him in his arms and cradle him, to lay him down against the ground and get the wicked thorns out of his legs. But Toby did not seem to want his care; he seemed so utterly forsaken, sitting there. "Did you find Mother?" Toby asked again.

"No, son, but we will. They sent me under guard from Goliad. I got here just today." And then the day came rushing back—Crucita underneath the tree with berries in her skirt, the butchery. "Crucita was here with me. And her brother, Adelaido."

"Crucita tried to save my life," Toby said.

It seemed too complicated to assimilate, the fates all tangled up as if they had been twined together in some patchy intermittent way— Crucita gone, and Toby found, the puffy dough twined round and round and growing black with smoke and crusty in the flames. "Did you fight, today?"

Toby shook his head. The bread was burning on the bottom side. "Terrell did," he said. "But me and Tad stayed here by the fire cutting bullet patching." He paused and bit his lower lip and added, "They were doing it for Miles."

Something in the way that Toby spoke those words gave Hugh a glimpse of hope. The boy was changed into a different boy, so far off and secluded, and yet he was the same. He'd chosen not to take part in the killing; he still had Toby's heart, he was still carrying the stones.

Hugh wanted to say it wasn't for Miles they did it, but feared that if he spoke aloud some unknown demon would breathe itself from his throat in a voice he did not know. It was a matter of containment. He could let his voice out like thin trails of fog, but if he opened up his throat just once then he would never stop his soul from emptying into the smoky air.

Toby's bread had burned up to a crisp, and now it caught on fire and he watched it burn, and then the stick caught fire too, and Toby still sat watching as it flamed and started turning into ash. When most of it had burned away he dropped it in the coals.

Hugh spoke the only words that came to mind just then, and spoke them in a whisper, "Where is Coon?"

Toby turned on him a face that had grown old, eyes so deeply shadowed that Hugh could not see the color. "Coon?" he whispered, as if trying to recall. Then his gaze grew dull, and seemed to drift away, and everything grew dim. "I think they shot him."

Toby, Hugh, and Adelaido went together, so battered and fatigued they stumbled, carrying two shovels and a wooden crate down the road through the moonlit battlefield among the wolves skulking in the shadows, among the bodies of the dead and the living who were looting from the dead. They saw a man with a tin bucket pulling teeth to sell for souvenirs—five dollars apiece, he said—another with a shaggy mule, collecting bags of ragged shoes.

They found her lying partly on her side in the long grass underneath the tree. Adelaido went down on his knees. Hugh knelt and touched her face, her hair, and closed her eyes and lifted her up in his arms and carried her off to the woods to bury her.

They dug with shovels and bare hands. Adelaido wept as if he were a child, and smeared his tears away with muddy palms and swore that he would kill the man who killed her.

Hugh worked his shovel hard, and blood ran down his wounded arm. He ripped the bandage off and let the blood run freely, as if to bleed his grief away. He thought of Callum and Métis and life and its futility and said to Adelaido that Crucita would not want him to avenge her death. He said there was no ending to revenge. He said that Callum lost his soul in search of it, and even if he found revenge the soul was gone forever. He said that Callum never would come back. He spoke as an old man speaks when he is dying.

Toby thought of how Crucita used to say "Tobito, Tobito," and to look at him as if she liked him very much. He thought how she had tried to save his life. He felt himself to be an ugly goblin in the spotted shadows of the moon. His father put Crucita in the wooden crate, and Adelaido laid the crippled boy beside her, and they put them in the hole and shoveled on the dirt. Toby watched his own frail hands patting down the dirt, molding it and sculpting it into a mound. He lifted up the palms, and looked at them, and then he could remember and he said aloud, "I strangled him."

Hugh sat back on his heels, and looked in Toby's eyes, then leaned his face up toward the sky and made a sound that was at first a sob and then a cry. Toby watched his father's profile stark against the moon, with wisps of long gray hair, and said to him, to make it clear, "I strangled Coon."

His father took him in his arms and stroked his face and pulled his scarf away, running muddy fingers through his hair. He was gripping Toby's head so hard against his chest that Toby had to breathe out all his air, and draw it in, and his small voice was just a little boy's, crying in a trembling whine that shimmered in the moonlit air, then sucking in such gulps between his anguished sobs that he was choking on his words, "They were coming, they were in the bushes there, and Coon Dog started growling and he wouldn't stop . . . I told him . . . stop, Coon, please . . . Coon . . . Father? Father?"

Hugh held his son and rocked his withered body, sobbing down against the soft and patchy hair.

Adelaido leaned onto the grave and laid his good cheek on the soil, his palms spread out beside his face as if he listened through the dirt, into the grave, to hear the beating of her heart in there.

BURIAL AND RESURRECTION

A U G U S T ,   R A N C H O   D E   L A   R O S A

On the west bank of the river in the early gray light of a summer dawn, Adelaido stripped off his clothes and wrapped them up inside his blanket. He took off his hat—a worn-out straw affair fitting too small on his head—and balancing the wad of clothing on his head with one hand, holding up his hat and boots with the other, he waded naked in the water. The level was down, the current easy, and Adelaido kept his footing all the way across with water swirling to his neck. It was the crossing where the citizens of Goliad had camped, where Adelaido heard the song of Louis Villapando drifting hollow and serene across the misty river on the night he was unhorsed last winter.

On the eastern bank he washed his face, put his clothes back on, tried to smoothe the wrinkles out, and combed his fingers through his hair. He replaced his hat and started up the slope. The refugees had gone away by now but remnants of their many fires lay in scattered heaps of ash among the trees.

As Adelaido left the trees and made his way along the road into the open land, the morning sun rose large and warm ahead of him and cast a rosy light across the chaparral, each blade of wiry grass with its own shadowed likeness stretching prostrate on the pebbled ground, the thorns of prickly pear throwing tiny needled shadows on the green flesh of the plant. A brown snake, not seven inches long, slithered in the rocky soil from one side of the road, across, and birds began to twitter in the brush. A summer day was coming with the sun.

And there before him lay the ruins of Rancho De la Rosa—the Ranch of the Rose—in the rosy morning light. Adelaido grieved and marveled at the sight. The beamed roof of the great *sala* of the house was gone, and the limestone walls were blackened on the inside and crumbled raggedly, though rain had washed the jagged surface stones and they took on a blush of rosy color from the sky. The palisade enclosing all the compound was reduced to charred posts standing here and there, casting their long shadows in the morning air. The row of mud vaqueros' quarters that had been the south side of the palisade was nothing but a pile of blackened rubble with one meager section of the sod roof still intact.

But the place was not abandoned. De la Rosa had his men up early, working on the pen. There were only three of them. They had a pile of new posts lying in a heap, stacked high, and they were rebuilding the pen as it had stood before, 150 varas long by 100 varas wide.

Out past the pen, where the horseshoe track had been, there was a single steer driven by one man, dragging an old-fashioned plow across the land.

Adelaido turned off the road and passed between charred stumps that once had formed the entryway into the compound. He noted that the section of vaqueros' quarters to the right, which had a roof and two walls still intact, was crowded full of camping gear—earthen pots and bedding and a string of dried meat tied from one precarious corner of the sod roof to the other. Two sheep and a skinny goat had got into a sack of corn, and stood nibbling at it with a flock of chickens clucking around their feet. When the goat spied Adelaido he tossed his head and bolted, scattering the fowl, but the sheep just stood there chewing on the corn.

Approaching the vaqueros working on the pen, Adelaido shaded one hand across his brow, beneath the hat, to look at them, and recognized the three who'd stood in judgment on him in the stone room of Portilla's office overlooking La Bahía. They stopped their work and tilted back their colorful sombreros and watched as he approached. The youngest of the three, dressed all in black but for a red sombrero with a rounded crown, raised an arm in greeting and called him by his name. The oldest spoke to him. "Don't you think the hat's a little too small on your head?" he said.

Adelaido smiled. "Better a big head than a small one, Manuel."

"Better a hat that fits," the old vaquero said.

The youngest one observed, "We thought you might be dead."

"I'm still living, with no thanks to you," Adelaido answered with a smile.

"But what happened to your face?"

"It shows the marks of war."

The old man said, "Pacheco, even you can't glorify a face pocked with black powder burn."

He didn't mean to glorify, he saw no glory there at all, and yet he carried his disfigurement with something like a reverence or a duty. When the wound was fresh Hugh Kenner had suggested Adelaido keep a bandage wet with kerosene across the place to draw the powder out, but Adelaido had no interest in his vanity those days. And now, when the intensity of grief had eased, he saw the mark as proof that he'd been touched, and changed. He forced himself to smile. "But this side still retains my charm," he said, and turned to them the good side of his face.

The same vaquero who had taken him before Portilla on that day when he returned to La Bahía from his wanderings, unshaven now and with his hair grown shaggy, offered him a cigarillo from his sweaty pocket. "Which side were you fighting on?" he asked.

Adelaido did not take the cigarillo, his feelings were too strong against the man, for if this man had not insisted on the trial before Portilla, Crucita would still be alive today.

But Adelaido had his own guilt too, and was not seeking revenge. "It's difficult to fight with handcuffs on your wrists," he said.

"Were you in the battle on the San Jacinto?"

"As a prisoner, I was. Where is Don Domingo?"

They nodded toward the field where the man was plowing with the steer. "The *jefe* is planting corn."

The awful sadness washed across his mind. Everything was lost. De la Rosa with his calloused hands so used to rancher's work, was following an old steer and a plow through a field of barren dirt.

"There's no one left to work the fields," the old man, Manuel Sanchez, said.

"Where has everybody gone?"

The old vaquero shrugged, took off his hat to scratch his head, and placed the hat back on again. "To find some work, with pay. The *jefe* fed the refugees for months, and in the end he'd given everything away. Antonio, Miguel, Rafael—they've all gone to work for the Americans. The Americans are buying up the ranches, all around. They came last week—six of them, armed, and threatened Don Domingo in the field. They told him if he didn't sell the land then they would kill his cattle, one by one."

"And what did Don Domingo say?"

"He said to go away. He said he had a field to plow and work to do on the corral."

The youngest of the three smiled jauntily. "Work," he chuckled, "yes, I'd say there's work to do. There's nothing here but two sheep and a goat, and one old steer and one old plow, and four horses living in the rubble of the house."

Adelaido said to him, "And where is mine?"

The young vaquero stopped his laughing then. He stroked his long mustache. "So you've come to get your horse. That's the reason you came back."

Adelaido liked the young vaquero. "I came to get my horse, and see the *jefe*," he answered with a smile.

"I thought that I would keep that horse."

"Not likely," Adelaido said.

"Only if you had been dead."

"Only then, my friend. Have you taken care of him?"

"As if he were my own."

"Where is he, then?"

The young vaquero gestured toward the stone ruins of the house. "I wasn't joking, Donde's living in the *sala*. It's the only pen we have, and Don Domingo said you wouldn't like it if I hobbled him."

Up to now the great ranchero had been so intent on plowing that he hadn't noticed Adelaido talking with the men. But now he glanced in their direction, saw them standing idly in a group instead of working, four instead of three, and drew his steer up to a halt. Adelaido started out to meet him.

When De la Rosa realized it was Adelaido, he broke into a smile so big that Adelaido saw it clearly even from the distance with the low sun glaring in his eyes. He started almost running toward the great ranchero, but checked himself and went on at an even pace with long strides crossing over furrowed dips and swells. When Adelaido reached him, De la Rosa opened his arms and they embraced, then De la Rosa stood with both hands gripping Adelaido's shoulders, and looked into his eyes. He saw the pain. His face grew serious, and Adelaido know what he would ask, and tried to steel his heart.

"Where is she?" the ranchero said.

Adelaido searched so deep into Domingo de la Rosa's Spanish eyes he felt the world had slipped away. He tried to blink away his tears, but De la Rosa touched one finger to the damaged cheek and Adelaido let the tears run free, and stood crying silently.

"*Dios mío*," De la Rosa uttered in a groan, making the sign of the cross upon his heart. "Is she dead?"

"Yes, señor."

The furrowed earth was soft and damp with dew, the sun was growing warm, the air was still. The ox heaved his broad sides out in a sigh and swished his tail.

"Was it merciful?"

"No, not merciful."

"At the hands of the Americans?"

"Yes."

De la Rosa moved his arm out in a slow and gentle gesture toward the land and all that had been lost. "Tell me where you've been."

"I was with Filisola, and Cós, and then with Santa Anna on the day of the battle."

"At San Jacinto?"

"Yes."

"He pardoned you?"

"No. The judgment never came. We arrived just before the battle."

"Crucita was there with you?"

"Yes."

"She was killed in the battle?"

He nodded. "She is dead, because of me."

De la Rosa looked at him, a firm and scrutinizing look with his green eyes, and said, "She is with God."

"Yes, señor." He needed to believe it.

The steer began to chew its cud.

De la Rosa brushed a fly away. "And what about your friend, the doctor, the American?"

"He found his son, the youngest son, at San Jacinto. He'd escaped the executioners at La Bahía and had found his way."

"I remember the boy. He had drawings in his satchel of a river and a cow, with fine detail. The padre told me that his brother is the one who burned this place."

"Yes. His name was Miles." But that seemed centuries ago. "I went with them to find their family," Adelaido said, remembering himself between the father and the son, the three together stumbling eastward like three gutshot animals. They'd found the Kenner family camping on the east side of the Trinity. Hugh Kenner's mother had been drowned, and the others had decided they would go no farther. "They're going back and settling in again," he said.

"Of course," De la Rosa answered. "They have the land. And now they also have a legacy."

But it was not so easy. He had seen the ruin. Hugh Kenner's heart was broken, and Toby . . . Toby was a drifter who might never find his way. Adelaido thought of how the boy had looked when he first saw his mother, how he stood, bewildered, as if he had gone mute. He recalled the woman's silence and her utter solitude on hearing from her husband that their oldest son was dead, and how the girl had held the child— Callum Mackay's abandoned boy—as if she were afraid to put him down and stood so close beside the Englishman that she was in his shadow with a noonday sun. The Englishman was formal and remote in bearing, but caring in his gestures toward them all—the girl especially, attentive of her every move. There was ruin, but there was family, and Adelaido felt both pity and resentment and knew that even for a storyteller like himself there was no way to tell the Kenners' tale with any satisfaction. There was no ending for it, ever.

"So why did Samuel Houston save *El Presidente*'s life, when barbarians were howling for his blood?" the voice was asking. "Was it mercy? Or did he simply need to use him as a pawn."

"It wasn't mercy," Adelaido said.

"Aye, Adelaido. That man—Antonio López de Santa Anna—has cost Mexico her soul and traded Texas for his life. I wish that Houston would have hanged him. If Santa Anna had been killed, Filisola might possibly have listened to Urrea, and stayed to fight another battle instead of dragging all the army back across the Rio Grande like a pack of cur dogs ordered home. I heard that when his captors brought *El Presidente* in he was wearing slippers on his feet and trying to pretend he was a common soldier?"

"It's true, señor. I saw him."

"He disgraces his own blood." A flock of birds passed overhead. The flies were coming with the sun. De la Rosa added, "Santa Anna is a dog himself, with every manner of a dog but loyalty."

"Yes, señor."

De la Rosa said, "And while we're speaking of loyalty, you notice that I don't have many men. I can't afford to pay you much, but if you—"

But Adelaido was shaking his head. "I'm leaving Texas," he said.

"Ahhhh. I see. And where will you be going?"

"First to Goliad, to finish something, and then west."

"And why the west? You could go east."

Adelaido shrugged. "Gold?"

"Ah, gold. My son. You have lost everything but your dreams."

"And I don't have much heart for those."

"It might be that you have a bigger heart for those, now, Adelaido." He paused. "So you came back here only for your horse?"

"For my horse, and also for your blessings."

De la Rosa turned thoughtfully and ran his hand across the old steer's ribs. "You have the slave to thank, for your horse," he said.

"The slave?"

"The one you brought to me, to send south to his freedom. I sent him, but he came back with Urrea. Urrea's army captured Donde from the rebels on the night of the Coleto battle. The slave recognized him and told Urrea he belonged to one of my men—he meant you—and

Urrea sent the horse to me. So your horse has served to pay off several debts: from the slave to you, from Urrea to me, and now from me to you."

"But you don't owe me anything, señor."

"Nothing but my life. Have you forgotten?"

He had not forgotten. But Adelaido's life was now so touched by people whom he loved and who had loved him, he no longer thought in terms of debt.

The great ranchero did. The great ranchero always would. And Adelaido realized in that moment that in this way he had surpassed his teacher, for Adelaido—with his passions and his reckless follies, his schemes and dreams of destiny and all the trouble he'd encountered on the way—Adelaido had a greater heart for love.

"He came through here two days ago," De la Rosa said.

"Who?"

"The slave. In chains with fifteen others. Juan Seguín and some Americans were taking all the slaves back to their owners." He shook his head. "Seguín is going to regret the part he's played, some day, after he's unhorsed by the Americans, and without feet." He let the sentence settle, then nodded toward the road. "I talked to him when he came through. He said the treaty Santa Anna signed agreed that any property the army had which had belonged to settlers would be returned to them. Including slaves."

"But Urrea would not—"

"No, he wouldn't. But the slave wasn't with Urrea when Seguín and the Americans arrived. He was with Filisola. He got the influenza, and Urrea went on south, ahead, leaving him with Filisola to follow after. And when Filisola saw Santa Anna's signature on the treaty, he obliged and turned the slaves in his possession over to Seguín. I talked to him, the slave, briefly, as he passed. He thanked me and he said to thank you, too. He said to tell you, if I saw you, that he'd thought about your story."

"My story?"

De la Rosa shrugged. "It was something about horses."

Adelaido searched his memory, and then recalled the story of the horses who escaped captivity and then were captured once again, and chose to kill themselves instead of to submit a second time. For him, it had been just a story that he told with his dramatic style, but for Joshua it was a choice that he would have to make on every day he lived. "Where will they be taking him?"

"Back. He didn't seem to know exactly where. He said the men who'd claimed to own him had been killed. And if I know the Anglo laws"—he paused and said with emphasis—"the laws we have to live by now, in this new country, Texas—if I know these laws, then he'll belong to their estate and be sold to pay their debts."

If he found gold, Adelaido thought, he would come back and purchase Joshua and give him freedom. If he found gold. . . . But something in him doubted he would find the gold, and doubted, if he did, that he could ever find the slave again. The slave, he felt, was lost to him as everything was lost, the past and everything hauled off in chains.

"It was the cause you fought for, Adelaido," De la Rosa said.

"I wasn't fighting for a cause," Adelaido answered. "I never was. I feel . . ." He stopped, and stared down at the rocky soil that had been turned. "Forgive me, please."

De la Rosa said, "You've always crossed the boundaries, Adelaido. Back and forth, across the boundaries. Why?"

"Ask me anything but why, señor."

"Perhaps because you are more comfortable with living on the edges?"

Adelaido looked out past the great ranchero's shoulder at the deeply furrowed field of light and shadows that ran parallel and never intersected, anywhere. "What future do we have, señor?"

De la Rosa sighed, and when he spoke it was a cautious whisper. "You'll be going west, and taking your soul with you, I believe." It was a blessing of a sort, and Adelaido felt such gratitude he almost went down on his knees. But De la Rosa turned back to the steer and plow and said to Adelaido in a louder voice, and with finality, "You are going off, the slave is going back, and I am staying here." Then he looked at Adelaido one last time.

Adelaido searched the Spanish face with its green eyes and tapered beard and dark skin of an Indian, radiant in morning light and seeming to grow old there in the sun. "You are staying here," he said, "because the blood is strong."

"Go with God, my friend," De la Rosa answered him.

———

Outside the gates of the Presidio, about two hundred paces south and east, beside the old cemetery, there was a new grave. The Anglos had buried their dead. Padre Valdez stood sweating in the midday heat looking at the plot of earth—like a garden never planted, only the soil turned, and then forgotten—and he told Adelaido how two hundred soldiers came from San Jacinto and gathered up the bones out on the prairies, whole skeletons of men, and loaded them in crates and burlap bags and brought them in and buried them. Among these soldiers there were five of Fannin's men who had escaped the massacre—three of them the Irish De la Rosa saved—and these all stood together as official mourners while the guns were fired and the music played. For a while the padre spoke with sadness of the days in early spring he'd spent as prisoner among these men, the battle of Coleto, the night without water, how the dying Anglos, even Protestants, had called for him. He spoke of how he'd tried to change Portilla's mind about the executions, and had failed.

Adelaido told the padre of Crucita's death, and the padre promised he would say a mass for her. Then the two of them together knelt beside the grave, with Donde cropping grass nearby. The padre kissed his cross and said, "Hail Mary, full of grace, the Lord is with Thee. Blessed is thou amongst women and blessed is the fruit of thy womb, Jesus."

"Holy Mary, Mother of God, pray for us sinners now and at the hour of our death," Adelaido whispered.

When the padre went away Adelaido stayed awhile just staring at the plot of earth with his straw hat in his hand. He recalled the faces and the names of men, certain things they'd said or ways they'd treated him. He thought of Miles and Scholar on the windy beach of Matagorda, Miles in his elaborate coat, pushing on ahead in search of glory, Scholar hunting shells, squatting on the sand with his buffalo rug over his shoulder and holding out a shriveled sea horse in his gritty palm. He thought about them crouched beside the fire in the dunes at Paso Caballo, Miles smeared head to toe in reeking fish oil and the trapper dabbed in horse manure, and he had to smile. He had his memories, and when the pain had eased it was still possible that he could string them all together in his stories.

So there has been a burial, he thought, and now, a resurrection, and he tightened up the rope strapped like a girth around his horse's chest, and balanced out the gear, then mounted Donde bareback, for he had no kind of saddle, not even a surcingle of tanned rawhide, and he rode out on the southwest road toward the cemetery for the victims of the cholera, brushing swarms of flies away. He was thankful to be riding now instead of walking; he could not bear to walk that road again, remembering the moonless night, the stars in their disorderly array, Crucita in her men's shoes with her awkward gait and the Lady of Loreto in her arms. He was grateful to the summer sun that hung above the trees and drew his sweat in patches as he rode. He passed the charred jacales and the painted plaster homes, the dog-fight pit, and came upon the cemetery, riding Donde right up to the grave where he had seen Crucita labor with her broken shovel.

There were summer flowers growing on the grave, yellow with a thousand petals each and casting tiny shadows as the afternoon grew late.

He dug it open with his bare hands and a stick, careful not to trespass on his father's resting place.

The Lady was still wrapped up in Crucita's shawl. Tiny roots and clods of dirt clung to rotting fibers in the shawl and Adelaido feared the Lady of Loreto would be rotting too. But when he lifted her and laid her on the prickly summer grass and pulled the shawl away, he saw a miracle. The Lady's face and hands were soiled, but that was all, there were no other marks, not one chip off her painted face to show decay. She was untouched, entirely, her hands still held beneath her face in prayer, the fragile veil still covering her hair. Her small face looked as placid and serene as if no tragedy had taken place at all. Shrouding her again, he tucked her underneath his arm, led Donde over to a stone so he could mount him without hurting her, and rode back northeast to the fort, through the open gates into the old presidio, half in shadow now, to the little churchyard with the stones stained with blood and the willow weeping one frail limb across the wall.

Draping Donde's reins across the picket gate beside the willow limb and hanging his straw hat upon the tallest picket of the gate, he went in through the heavy chapel doors and closed himself inside. Late sun was slanting through the single window high up on the wall, but still it seemed like sudden night inside the chapel with the walls blackened with soot and ashes scattered on the floors. There was the cool and solid smell of stone. There were no benches and no chairs. The stations of the cross were gone. But someone had been praying here, for there were several candles burning on some boards that had been set up as an altar rail. The altarpiece itself was badly damaged with its siding torn away, and in the Virgin's empty niche there was a charcoal drawing of the Lady like a shadow she had left behind—someone trying to replace her image with a likeness, as if she would grow dim and dimmer and then fade away in remnants of the shadows.

He peeled the rotting shawl back from her face and smoothed the veil around her hair. He cradled her inside his arm. The chapel was so quiet he could hear the sizzling of the burning candle wax. Taking the last coins from his trouser pockets, he dropped them in the plate with the jarring ring of metal, and watched them roll, and settle. Then he took a candle, touched it to another that had burned down to a stub, and held the flicker of the light beside the Virgin's face and said, "For Mary of the Cross," in English, hearing his voice echo back in Spanish with the clarity of voices on hard stone, "*Por* María de la Cruz. *Por mi propia crucita.* My own little cross." Lifting the Lady of Loreto from the shawl, he laid the shawl across the railing, rubbed the dirt from her face and hands and stared into her brilliant eyes, then went around the railing to the altar and placed her in her niche.

He could not think of any way to say good-bye. His heart was splitting wide. "Now you will be safe," he said, and touched her face again, and turned away, and left the chapel where he'd learned to pray when he was young, and went out in the sun.

It was sinking down behind the wall. Adelaido put his hat back on. The picket gate was latched, and he unfastened it and then led Donde through and left the gate wide open there behind him. Looking down the slope he saw the tree line of the winding river, and between him and the trees there was the rubble of his home, merging with the rubble of the home next door where Louis Villapando used to sing at night.

But from the far horizon, shone the light.

Adelaido stroked the horse's neck and blew soft breaths into his nose, and underneath the willow tree he mounted him in one swift easy movement, pressing his knees hard into the flesh and bone, feeling the brute power there, a fluid power that could take him anywhere.

There, near the corner where the north and west walls met, he sat a moment staring down the slope at all the ruin and all the long, hot shadows cast among the stones and blackened stumps. Then he spoke to Donde, softly, moved the reins, touched his right knee to the horse's ribs and took the west road with the bright sun blazing in his eyes, glowing radiant upon his face and hands. He followed the dusty road until there was no road, and then he followed the land.

ACKNOWLEDGMENTS

For this book, I owe thanks to many people who shared their time and knowledge.

John Jenkins, now deceased but gratefully remembered, helped me to assimilate the books I needed for my research, often lending volumes from his own collection.

Douglas Taylor and Bernd Schulze told me stories of the Highland Clearances and the Scottish dispossessed who set sail for America. From their tales, I created Callum Mackay. They also introduced me to the Gaelic songs of exile which could be claimed by any of the many displaced peoples in my story.

From a conversation with my friend and colleague Dan Flores in a dark cave in the Texas hill country, I devised the tale of Louie Métis, the Comanches, and the pitted stone. Sitting with flashlights on a floor thick with old guano from bats that long ago had flown away, we talked and I made notes and braided strands into a fable.

Robert Thonhoff and Jack Jackson helped me to envision Spanish ranches in South Texas and to understand *Tejano* ranchers and their strong attachment to the land.

Stephen L. Hardin provided books on military strategies and weaponry and

510

later proofread the draft for technical accuracy. Kevin Young was also open-handed with his knowledge of the war.

María de la Cruz Mendez, Adelaido Mendez, and Eleanor Crook translated documents from Spanish and helped me with Crucita's language—her broken English as it would be spoken with distortions true in phrase and idiom. (I myself claim credit for the labored and "bad" Spanish spoken by my Anglo characters.)

Joel Vasquez explained the game of *pollo enterrado* in such vivid terms I still believe I saw it played.

Luis Cazarez-Rueda always welcomed me to La Bahía, and once allowed me to stay within the gates of the presidio after dark and sit inside the chapel there. The evening was a gift that changed this book.

J. C. Martin was generous with the archives at the San Jacinto monument and museum and also with his knowledge. T. J. Zalar allowed me, with my friends Jeff Long and Steve Harrigan, to climb into the star that tops the monument, from which we had a stunning vantage of the fields.

I owe a heavy debt of gratitude to Rafael Sagalyn of the Sagalyn Literary Agency, and to Lisa DiMona.

I am grateful to Louis Black for his timely suggestions.

To my editor at Doubleday, Jacqueline Kennedy Onassis, I am truly thankful. Her professional attention and personal affirmation sustained my effort; her careful editing improved my book in ways impossible to count.

I feel joyful gratitude to Larry Stone.

I am thankful beyond measure to Marc Lewis for his gentle guidance, his strong support, and his faith in me.

I owe my family more than I can ever say. My parents especially, William H. Crook and Eleanor Butt Crook, were with me at every turn.

We all, myself especially, owe a debt of gratitude to our ancestors of various races and religions who fought on both sides of the Texas rebellion and told of the experience in journals and their memoirs. Their words helped me to resurrect the ghosts of men and women who inhabited the fragile frontier of Texas in such unruly times.

I offer my deepest gratitude to Steve Harrigan and Jeff Long, fine writers and good friends who never failed me in all the many hours I spent groping in the dark from page to page. Their insights were the lights that showed the way.

Colorado River
Bastrop
San Marcos River
Kenner
Burnt Crossing
Mackay Homestead Homestead
Guadalupe River
Gonzales
San Antonio de Béxar
San Antonio River
Coleto Creek
Victo
Rancho de la Rosa
Goliad
Nueces River
Refugio
Copano
San Patricio
Laredo
Carnala Creek
Padre Island
Río Grande River
Mier
miles 0 5 10 20 30 40 50 60
Matamoros